Charles Seymour Robinson

Psalms and Hymns, and Spiritual Songs. A Manual of Worship for the Church of Christ

Charles Seymour Robinson

Psalms and Hymns, and Spiritual Songs. A Manual of Worship for the Church of Christ

Reprint of the original, first published in 1875.

1st Edition 2024 | ISBN: 978-3-38538-423-1

Verlag (Publisher): Outlook Verlag GmbH, Zeilweg 44, 60439 Frankfurt, Deutschland
Vertretungsberechtigt (Authorized to represent): E. Roepke, Zeilweg 44, 60439 Frankfurt, Deutschland
Druck (Print): Books on Demand GmbH, In de Tarpen 42, 22848 Norderstedt, Deutschland

Chants and Occasional Pieces.

PSALMS AND HYMNS,

AND

SPIRITUAL SONGS.

A

MANUAL OF WORSHIP

FOR

THE CHURCH OF CHRIST.

COMPILED AND EDITED BY

CHARLES S. ROBINSON.

A. S. BARNES AND COMPANY,

NEW YORK, CHICAGO, AND NEW ORLEANS.

PREFACE.

THIS Book of Hymns and Tunes has been prepared by a Pastor in charge of a Church. He has undertaken the work with the single aim and hope of encouraging singing by the Congregation, as a part of divine worship. He has not sought to compile a Manual of Hymnology, nor to furnish a collection of pieces of Lyric Poetry. Everything has been bent to the one purpose of actual use.

All the Selections are set to music in sight. But it is not to be understood that each must be sung exactly and invariably to the tune under which it is printed. In most cases a choice is presented; a new or fresher one being matched with one older or more familiar. It may be that mere mechanical reasons have forced the hymn into the place it occupies, when the more appropriate music will be found below, or across on the opposite page. A quiet care in noting the metres will avoid all confusion.

Not all the Tunes are precisely and rigidly adapted to congregational singing. Most of them, however, can be easily learned. It is expected that the people will be led by a competent precentor, or—better still—by a large and trained Choir. And oftentimes skilled and cultivated musicians will desire a slight license of artistic excellence for their own enjoyment and performance on rare occasions; thus quickening their own zest, while instructing others, and elevating the general taste.

MEMORIAL CHURCH;
NEW YORK, *March*, 1875.

TABLE OF CONTENTS.

[Indexes of Texts and First Lines of Stanzas may be obtained on application to the Publishers. They are omitted here in order to lessen the bulk of the Book.]

INDEX OF PSALMS.

7

INDEX OF PSALMS.

9

INDEX OF PSALMS.

10

VERSIONS OF THE PSALMS.

MELODY. C. M.

1. Blest is the man who shuns the place, Where sin-ners love to meet;

Who fears to tread their wick-ed ways, And hates the scof-fer's seat:—

PSALM 1. WATTS.
The righteous and the wicked.

I

Blest is the man who shuns the place,
Where sinners love to meet;
Who fears to tread their wicked ways,
And hates the scoffer's seat:—

2 But in the statutes of the Lord
Has placed his chief delight;
By day he reads or hears the word,
And meditates by night.

3 He, like a plant of generous kind
By living waters set,
Safe from the storms and blasting wind,
Enjoys a peaceful state.

4 Green as the leaf, and ever fair,
Shall his profession shine;
While fruits of holiness appear,
Like clusters on the vine.

5 Not so the impious and unjust:
What vain designs they form!
Their hopes are blown away like dust,
Or chaff before the storm.

6 Sinners in judgment shall not stand
Among the sons of grace,
When Christ, the Judge, at his right hand,
Appoints his saints a place.

PSALM 1. SCOTCH.
The Believer's Advantage.

2

That man hath perfect blessedness
Who walketh not astray
In counsel of ungodly men,
Nor stands in sinners' way,—

2 Nor sitteth in the scorner's chair:
But placeth his delight
Upon God's law, and meditates
On his law day and night.

3 He shall be like a tree that grows
Near planted by a river,
Which in his season yields his fruit,
And his leaf fadeth never:—

4 And all he doth shall prosper well.—
The wicked are not so;
But like they are unto the chaff,
Which wind drives to and fro.

5 In judgment therefore shall not stand
Such as ungodly are:
Nor in the assembly of the just
Shall wicked men appear;—

6 Because the way of godly men
Unto the Lord is known:
Whereas the way of wicked men
Shall quite be overthrown.

JAZER. C. M.

1. Why did the na-tions join to slay The Lord's a-noint-ed Son?

Why did they cast his laws a-way, And tread his gos-pel down?

3

PSALM 2.
Christ exalted.   WATTS.

Why did the nations join to slay
The Lord's anointed Son?
Why did they cast his laws away,
And tread his gospel down?

2 The Lord, who sits above the skies,
Derides their rage below;
He speaks with vengeance in his eyes,
And strikes their spirits through:—

3 "I call him my beloved Son,
And raise him from the dead;
I make my holy hill his throne,
And wide his kingdom spread."

4 Be wise, ye rulers of the earth!
Obey the anointed Lord;
Adore the king of heavenly birth,
And tremble at his word.

5 With humble love address his throne,
For, if he frown, ye die;
Those are secure, and those alone,
Who on his grace rely.

4

PSALM 3.
Doubts and Fears suppressed.   WATTS.

My God! how many are my fears!
How fast my foes increase!
Conspiring my eternal death,
They break my present peace.

2 But thou, my glory and my strength,
Shalt on the tempter tread;
Shalt silence all my threatening guilt,
And raise my drooping head.

3 I cried, and from his holy hill
He bowed a listening ear;
I called my Father and my God,
And he subdued my fear.

4 He shed soft slumbers on mine eyes,
In spite of all my foes;
I woke, and wondered at the grace
That guarded my repose.

5 What though the hosts of death and hell
All armed against me stood?
Terrors no more shall shake my soul;
My refuge is my God.

5

PSALM 4.
Evening Devotion.   WATTS.

Lord! thou wilt hear me when I pray;
I am for ever thine;
I fear before thee all the day,
Nor would I dare to sin.

2 And, while I rest my weary head,
From cares and business free,
'Tis sweet conversing on my bed
With my own heart and thee.

3 I pay this evening-sacrifice;
And, when my work is done,
Great God! my faith, my hope relies
Upon thy grace alone.

4 Thus, with my thoughts composed to peace,
I'll give mine eyes to sleep;
Thy hand in safety keeps my days,
And will my slumbers keep.

WARWICK. C. M.

1. Lord! in the morn-ing thou shalt hear My voice as-cend-ing high;

To thee will I di-rect my pray'r, To thee lift up mine eye;—

6

PSALM 5.   WATTS.
For the Lord's Day Morning.

LORD! in the morning thou shalt hear
My voice ascending high;
To thee will I direct my prayer,
To thee lift up mine eye;—

2 Up to the hills, where Christ has gone
To plead for all his saints,
Presenting, at his Father's throne,
Our songs and our complaints.

3 Thou art a God, before whose sight
The wicked shall not stand;
Sinners shall ne'er be thy delight,
Nor dwell at thy right hand.

4 But to thy house will I resort,
To taste thy mercies there;
I will frequent thy holy court,
And worship in thy fear.

5 Oh, may thy Spirit guide my feet,
In ways of righteousness;
Make every path of duty straight,
And plain before my face.

7

PSALM 6.   ENGLAND.
Divine Help in Affliction.

IN anger, Lord, rebuke me not,
Nor smite my guilty soul;
Let not thy righteous wrath be hot:
Save me and make me whole.

2 My heart is vexed with sore distress;
But thou, O Lord, how long?—
Return in grace and righteousness,
And make thy love my song.

3 Death utters forth no note of praise,
The silent grave no prayer;
Oh, do not now cut short my days,
Nor leave me to despair!

4 Long weary nights of pain and grief
My wasting strength destroy;
Lord, give these weeping eyes relief,
And change my tears to joy.

5 My prayer is heard—the Lord is nigh!
He bids my foes depart;
While shame o'erwhelms them suddenly,
His mercy cheers my heart.

3

PSALM 7.   WATTS.
God's Care of his People.

MY trust is in my heavenly friend,
My hope in thee, my God!
Rise, and my helpless life defend
From those who seek my blood.

2 If I indulge in thoughts unjust,
And wish and seek their woe;
Then let them tread my life to dust,
And lay mine honor low.

3 If there were malice hid in me,—
I know thy piercing eyes,—
I should not dare appeal to thee,
Nor ask my God to rise.

4 Arise, my God! lift up thy hand,
Their pride and power control;
Awake to judgment, and command
Deliverance for my soul.

13

NOEL. C. M.

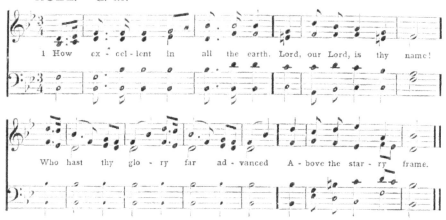

1 How ex - cel - lent in all the earth, Lord, our Lord, is thy name!

Who hast thy glo - ry far ad - vanced A - bove the star - ry frame.

9   **PSALM 8.**   SCOTCH.
God's Condescension.

How excellent in all the earth,
  Lord, our Lord, is thy name!
Who hast thy glory far advanced
  Above the starry frame.

2 When I look up unto the heavens,
  Which thine own fingers framed,
Unto the moon, and to the stars,
  Which were by thee ordained ;—

3 Then say I, What is man, that he
  Remembered is by thee?
Or what the Son of man, that thou
  So kind to him shouldst be?

4 For thou a little lower hast
  Him than the angels made;
With glory and with dignity
  Thou crowned hast his head.

10   **PSALM 8.**   WATTS.
Creation and Redemption.

O Lord our Lord! how wondrous great
  Is thine exalted name!
The glories of thy heavenly state
  Let men and babes proclaim.

2 When I behold thy works on high,
  The moon that rules the night,
And stars that well adorn the sky,
  Those moving worlds of light;—

3 Lord! what is man, or all his race,
  Who dwells so far below,
That thou shouldst visit him with grace,
  And love his nature so?—

4 That thine eternal Son should bear
  To take a mortal form,
Made lower than his angels are,
  To save a dying worm?

5 Yet, while he lived on earth unknown,
  And men would not adore,
Behold obedient nature own
  His Godhead and his power!

6 Let him be crowned with majesty,
  Who bowed his head in death;
And be his honors sounded high,
  By all things that have breath.

11   **PSALM 9.**   WATTS.
Wrath and Mercy.

With my whole heart I'll raise my song,
  Thy wonders I'll proclaim;
Thou sovereign judge of right and wrong
  Wilt put my foes to shame.

2 I'll sing thy majesty and grace;
  My God prepares his throne
To judge the world in righteousness,
  And make his vengeance known.

3 Then shall the Lord a refuge prove
  For all who are oppressed,
To save the people of his love,
  And give the weary rest.

4 Sing praises to the righteous Lord,
  Who dwells on Zion's hill;
Who executes his threatening word,
  And doth his grace fulfill.

12   PSALM 10.   WATTS.
Prayer heard and Saints saved.

WHY doth the Lord stand off so far?
  And why conceal his face,
When great calamities appear,
  And times of deep distress?

2 Lord, shall the wicked still deride
  Thy justice and thy laws?
Shall they advance their heads in pride,
  And slight the righteous cause?

3 Arise, O Lord! lift up thy hand;
  Attend our humble cry;
No enemy shall dare to stand,
  When God ascends on high.

4 Why do the men of malice rage,
  And say, with foolish pride,
"The God of heaven will ne'er engage
  To fight on Zion's side?"

5 But thou for ever art our Lord,
  And mighty is thy hand,
As when the heathen felt thy sword,
  And perished from thy land.

6 Thou wilt prepare our hearts to pray,
  And cause thine ear to hear;
Accept the vows thy children pay,
  And free thy saints from fear.

HADDAM.   H. M.

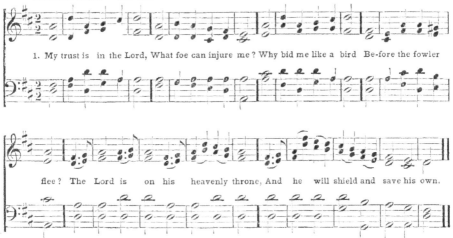

1. My trust is in the Lord, What foe can injure me? Why bid me like a bird Be-fore the fowler flee? The Lord is on his heavenly throne, And he will shield and save his own.

13   PSALM 11.   LYTE.
Trust in God.

MY trust is in the Lord,
  What foe can injure me?
Why bid me like a bird
  Before the fowler flee?
The Lord is on his heavenly throne,
And he will shield and save his own.

2 The wicked may assail,
  The tempter sorely try,
All earth's foundations fail,
  All nature's springs be dry;
Yet God is in his holy shrine,
And I am strong while he is mine.

3 His flock to him is dear,
  He watches them from high;
He sends them trials here
  To form them for the sky;
But safely will he tend and keep
The humblest, feeblest, of his sheep.

4 His foes a season here
  May triumph and prevail;
But ah! the hour is near
  When all their hopes must fail;
While, like the sun, his saints shall rise,
And shine with him above the skies.

15

14

PSALM 12.
A general corruption of manners.   WATTS.

Lord! when iniquities abound,
  And impious men grow bold,
When faith is rarely to be found,
  And love is waxing cold,—

2 Is not thy chariot rolling on?
  Hast thou not given this sign?
May we not rest and live upon
  A promise so divine?

3 "Yes," saith the Lord, "now will I rise
  And make oppressors flee;
I will appear to their surprise,
  And set my servants free."

4 Like silver in the furnace tried,
  Thy word shall still endure;
The men, that in thy truth confide,
  Shall find the promise sure.

MENDEBRAS. 7, 6.

1. How long wilt thou for-get me? Shall it for ev-er be?
  O Lord, how long neglect me, And hide thy face from me? 2. How long my soul take counsel?

Thus sad in heart each day, How long shall foes ex-ult-ing, Subject me to their sway?

15

PSALM 13.
Help in God alone.   SCOTCH.

How long wilt thou forget me?
  Shall it for ever be?
O Lord, how long neglect me,
  And hide thy face from me?

2 How long my soul take counsel?
  Thus sad in heart each day,—
How long shall foes, exulting,
  Subject me to their sway?

3 O Lord, my God, consider,
  And hear my earnest cries;
Lest I in death should slumber,
  Enlighten thou my eyes.

4 Lest foes be heard exclaiming,
  "Against him we prevailed;"
And they that vex my spirit,
  Rejoice when I have failed.

5 But on thy tender mercy
  I ever have relied;
With joy in thy salvation
  My heart shall still confide.

6 And I with voice of singing,
  Will praise the Lord alone,
Because to me his favor
  He hath so largely shown.

16

PSALM 14.
Israel's Return.   LYTE.

Oh, that the Lord's salvation
  Were out of Zion come,
To heal his ancient nation,
  To lead his outcasts home!
How long the holy city
  Shall heathen feet profane?
Return, O Lord, in pity,
  Rebuild her walls again.

2 Let fall thy rod of terror,
  Thy saving grace impart;
Roll back the vail of error,
  Release the fettered heart;
Let Israel, home returning,
  Their lost Messiah see;
Give oil of joy for mourning,
  And bind thy church to thee.

EVAN. C. M.

1. How long wilt thou con-ceal thy face? My God, how long de-lay?

When shall I feel those heav'nly rays That chase my fears a-way?

17　　　PSALM 13.　　　WATTS.
Hope in darkness.

How long wilt thou conceal thy face?
My God, how long delay?
When shall I feel those heavenly rays
That chase my fears away?

2 How long shall my poor laboring soul
Wrestle and toil in vain?
Thy word can all my foes control,
And ease my raging pain.

3 Be thou my sun, and thou my shield,
My soul in safety keep;
Make haste before mine eyes are sealed
In death's eternal sleep.

4 Thou wilt display thy sovereign grace,
Whence all my comforts spring;
I shall employ my lips in praise,
And thy salvation sing.

18　　　PSALM 14.　　　WATTS.
All Men, Sinners.

Fools, in their hearts, believe and say,
That all religion's vain;
There is no God who reigns on high,
Or minds the affairs of men.

2 The Lord, from his celestial throne,
Looked down on things below,
To find the man who sought his grace,
Or did his justice know.

3 By nature, all are gone astray,
Their practice all the same;
There's none that fears his Maker's hand,
There's none that loves his name.

4 Their tongues are used to speak deceit:
Their slanders never cease;
How swift to mischief are their feet!
Nor know the paths of peace.

5 Such seeds of sin—that bitter root—
In every heart are found;
Nor can they bear diviner fruit,
Till grace refine the ground.

19　　　PSALM 15.　　　SCOTCH.
The Citizen of Zion.

Within thy tabernacle, Lord,
Who shall abide with thee?
And in thy high and holy hill
Who shall a dweller be?

2 The man that walketh uprightly,
And worketh righteousness;
And as he thinketh in his heart,
So doth he truth express.

3 Who doth not slander with his tongue,
Nor to his friend doth hurt;
Nor yet against his neighbor doth
Take up an ill report.

4 In whose eyes vile men are despised;
But those that God do fear
He honoreth; and changeth not,
Though to his hurt he swear.

5 His coin puts not to usury,
Nor take reward will he
Against the guiltless. Who doth thus,
Shall never movèd be.

17

FEDERAL STREET.　L. M.

1. Who shall as-cend thy heav'n-ly place, Great God, and dwell be-fore thy face?

The man that minds re-lig-ion now. And hum-bly walks with God be-low.

20　　PSALM 15.　　WATTS.
The Citizen of Zion.

Who shall ascend thy heavenly place,
Great God, and dwell before thy face?
The man that minds religion now,
And humbly walks with God below:

2 Whose hands are pure, whose heart is clean,
Whose lips still speak the thing they mean ;
No slanders dwell upon his tongue;
He hates to do his neighbor wrong.

3 Firm to his word he ever stood,
And always makes his promise good;
Nor dares to change the thing he swears,
Whatever pain or loss he bears.

4 He never deals in bribing gold,
And mourns that justice should be sold:
While others scorn and wrong the poor,
Sweet charity attends his door.

5 He loves his enemies, and prays
For those that curse him to his face;
And doth to all men still the same
That he would hope or wish from them.

6 Yet, when his holiest works are done,
His soul depends on grace alone:
This is the man thy face shall see,
And dwell forever, Lord, with thee.

21　　PSALM 16.　　WATTS.
The Resurrection.

When God is nigh, my faith is strong;
His arm is my almighty prop:
Be glad, my heart—rejoice, my tongue;
My dying flesh shall rest in hope.

2 Though in the dust I lay my head,
Yet, gracious God, thou wilt not leave
My soul forever with the dead,
Nor lose thy children in the grave.

3 My flesh shall thy first call obey,
Shake off the dust and rise on high;
Then shalt thou lead the wondrous way,
Up to thy throne above the sky.

4 There streams of endless pleasure flow,
And full discoveries of thy grace:
Joys we but tasted here below,
Spread heavenly raptures thro' the place.

22　　PSALM 17.　　WATTS.
Prospect of the Believer.

What sinners value I resign;
Lord! 'tis enough that thou art mine;
I shall behold thy blissful face,
And stand complete in righteousness.

2 This life's a dream—an empty show;
But the bright world, to which I go,
Hath joys substantial and sincere;
When shall I wake, and find me there?

3 Oh, glorious hour!—oh, blest abode!
I shall be near, and like my God;
And flesh and sin no more control
The sacred pleasures of the soul.

4 My flesh shall slumber in the ground,
Till the last trumpet's joyful sound;
Then burst the chains, with sweet surprise,
And in my Saviour's image rise!

UXBRIDGE. L. M.

1. Thee will I love, O Lord! my strength, My rock, my tower, my high de - fence;

Thy mighty arm shall be my trust, For I have found sal - va - tion thence.

23   **PSALM 18.**   WATTS.
Deliverance from Despair.

THEE will I love, O Lord! my strength,
    My rock, my tower, my high defence;
Thy mighty arm shall be my trust,
For I have found salvation thence.

2 In my distress, I called my God,
    When I could scarce believe him mine:
He bowed his ear to my complaint;
    Then did his grace appear divine.

3 With speed he flew to my relief,
    As on a cherub's wing he rode;
Awful and bright as lightning shone
    The face of my deliverer God!

4 My song for ever shall record
    That terrible, that joyful hour;
And give the glory to the Lord,
    Due to his mercy and his power.

24   **PSALM 18.**   WATTS.
The Reward of Sincerity.

LORD! thou hast seen my soul sincere,
Hast made thy truth and love appear;
Before mine eyes I set thy laws,
And thou hast owned my righteous cause.

2 What sore temptations broke my rest!
What wars and strugglings in my breast!
But, through thy grace that reigns within,
I guard against my darling sin.

3 The sin that close besets me still,
That works and strives against my will, —
When shall thy Spirit's sovereign power
Destroy it, that it rise no more?

4 With an impartial hand, the Lord
Deals out to mortals their reward:
The kind and faithful souls shall find
A God, as faithful, and as kind.

25   **PSALM 19.**   WATTS.
Nature and Revelation.

THE heavens declare thy glory, Lord!
    In every star thy wisdom shines;
But, when our eyes behold thy word,
    We read thy name in fairer lines.

2 The rolling sun, the changing light,
    And nights and days thy power confess;
But the blest volume thou hast writ
    Reveals thy justice, and thy grace.

3 Sun, moon, and stars convey thy praise,
    Round the whole earth, and never stand;
So, when thy truth began its race,
    It touched and glanced on every land.

4 Nor shall thy spreading gospel rest,
    Till through the world thy truth has run,
Till Christ has all the nations blessed,
    That see the light, or feel the sun.

5 Great Sun of righteousness! arise;
    Bless the dark world with heavenly light;
Thy gospel makes the simple wise,
    Thy laws are pure, thy judgments right.

6 Thy noblest wonders here we view,
    In souls renewed, and sins forgiven:
Lord! cleanse my sins, my soul renew,
    And make thy word my guide to heaven.

19

ST. THOMAS. S. M.

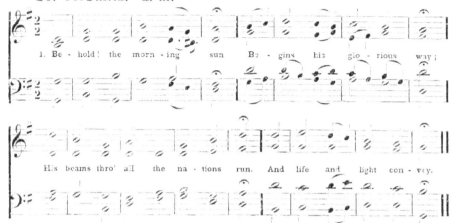

1. Be - hold! the morn - ing sun Be - gins his glo - rious way;

His beams thro' all the na - tions run. And life and light con - vey.

26   PSALM 19.   WATTS.
The Gospel: for the Sabbath.

Behold! the morning sun
  Begins his glorious way;
His beams through all the nations run,
  And life and light convey.

2 But where the gospel comes,
  It spreads diviner light;
It calls dead sinners from their tombs,
  And gives the blind their sight.

3 How perfect is thy word!
  And all thy judgments just!
For ever sure thy promise, Lord!
  And men securely trust.

4 My gracious God! how plain
  Are thy directions given!
Oh, may I never read in vain,
  But find the path to heaven.

27   PSALM 19.   WATTS.
The Books of Nature and Scripture.

Behold! the lofty sky
  Declares its maker, God;
And all his starry works, on high,
  Proclaim his power abroad.

2 The darkness and the light
  Still keep their course the same;
While night to day, and day to night,
  Divinely teach his name.

3 In every different land,
  Their general voice is known;
They show the wonders of his hand,
  And orders of his throne.

4 Ye Christian lands! rejoice;
  Here he reveals his word;
We are not left to nature's voice,
  To bid us know the Lord.

5 His laws are just and pure,
  His truth without deceit;
His promises for ever sure,
  And his rewards are great.

6 While of thy works I sing,
  Thy glory to proclaim,
Accept the praise, my God, my King!
  In my Redeemer's name.

28   PSALM 19.   WATTS.
Prayer and Praise.

I hear thy word with love,
  And I would fain obey;
Send thy good Spirit from above,
  To guide me, lest I stray.

2 Oh, who can ever find
  The errors of his ways?
Yet, with a bold presumptuous mind,
  I would not dare transgress.

3 Warn me of every sin,
  Forgive my secret faults,
And cleanse this guilty soul of mine,
  Whose crimes exceed my thoughts.

4 While, with my heart and tongue,
  I spread thy praise abroad,
Accept the worship and the song,
  My Saviour and my God!

ARCADIA.   C. M.

1. God's law is per-fect, and converts   The   soul   in   sin   that   lies: God's tes-ti-

CODA.

mo - ny is most sure, And makes the sim-ple wise, And makes the sim - ple wise.

29

PSALM 19. SCOTCH.
The Word of God.

God's law is perfect, and converts
  The soul in sin that lies:
God's testimony is most sure,
  And makes the simple wise.

2 The statutes of the Lord are right,
  And do rejoice the heart:
The Lord's command is pure, and doth
  Light to the eyes impart.

3 They more than gold, yea, much fine gold,
  To be desired are:
Than honey, honey from the comb
  That droppeth, sweeter far.

4 Moreover, they thy servant warn
  How he his life should frame:
A great reward provided is
  For them that keep the same.

5 Who can his errors understand?
  Oh, cleanse thou me within
From secret faults! Thy servant keep
  From all presumptuous sin.

30

PSALM 20. WRANGHAM.
Trust in God.

The Lord unto thy prayer attend,
  In trouble's darksome hour:
The name of Jacob's God defend,
  And shield thee by his power.

2 In thy salvation we'll rejoice,
  And triumph in the Lord;
For, when in prayer he hears thy voice,
  He will relief afford.

3 In chariots and on horses some
  For aid and shelter flee;
But in thy name, O Lord! we come,
  And will remember thee.

4 O Lord! to us salvation bring;
  In thee alone we trust;
Hear us, O God, our heavenly King!
  Thou refuge of the just!

31

PSALM 21. WATTS.
National Praise.

Our land, O Lord! with songs of praise
  Shall in thy strength rejoice,
And, blest with thy salvation, raise
  To heaven a cheerful voice.

2 Thy sure defence through nations round
  Hath spread our country's name,
And all her humble efforts crowned
  With freedom and with fame.

3 In deep distress our injured land
  Implored thy power to save;
For life we prayed; thy bounteous hand
  The timely blessing gave.

4 On thee, in want, or woe, or pain,
  Our hearts alone rely;
Our rights thy mercy will maintain,
  And all our wants supply.

5 Thus, Lord, thy wondrous power declare,
  And still exalt thy fame;
While we glad songs of praise prepare
  For thine almighty name.

21

HURLBUT.   C. M. D.

1. My Shepherd will sup-ply my need, Je - ho - vah is his name; In pastures fresh he makes me feed, Be - side the liv - ing stream. He brings my wand'ring spir - it back, When I for - sake his ways; And leads me, for his mer - cy's sake, In paths of truth and grace.

32

PSALM 22.
Christ on the Cross.   WATTS.

"Now, in the hour of deep distress,
My God! support thy Son,
When horrors dark my soul oppress,
Oh, leave me not alone!"

2 Thus did our suffering Saviour pray,
With mighty cries and tears;
God heard him, in that dreadful day,
And chased away his fears.

3 Great was the victory of his death,
His throne's exalted high;
And all the kindreds of the earth
Shall worship,—or shall die.

4 A numerous offspring must arise
From his expiring groans;
They shall be reckoned in his eyes
For daughters and for sons.

5 The meek and humble souls shall see
His table richly spread;
And all that seek the Lord shall be
With joys immortal fed.

6 The isles shall know the righteousness
Of our incarnate God,
And nations yet unborn profess
Salvation in his blood.

33

PSALM 23.
In the Fold.   WATTS.

My Shepherd will supply my need,
Jehovah is his name;
In pastures fresh he makes me feed,
Beside the living stream.

2 He brings my wandering spirit back,
When I forsake his ways;
And leads me, for his mercy's sake,
In paths of truth and grace.

3 When I walk through the shades of death,
Thy presence is my stay;
A word of thy supporting breath
Drives all my fears away.

4 Thy hand, in sight of all my foes,
Doth still my table spread;
My cup with blessings overflows,
Thine oil anoints my head.

5 The sure provisions of my God
Attend me all my days;
Oh, may thy house be mine abode,
And all my works be praise:

6 There would I find a settled rest,
While others go and come,—
No more a stranger, or a guest,
But like a child at home.

SHEPHERD. 11, 10.

The Lord is my Shep-herd, he makes me re-pose Where the pas-tures in beau-ty are grow-ing, He leads me a-far from the world and its woes, Where in peace the still wa-ters are flow-ing.

34 **PSALM 23.** KNOX.
"His rod and his Staff."

THE Lord is my Shepherd, he makes me
  repose
  Where the pastures in beauty are
    growing,
He leads me afar from the world and its
    woes,
  Where in peace the still waters are
    flowing.

2 He strengthens my spirit, he shows me
    the path
  Where the arms of his love shall enfold
    me,
And when I walk through the dark val-
    ley of death,
  His rod and his staff will uphold me!

35 **PSALM 23.** HASTINGS.
See Cant. 1: 7, 8.

OH, tell me, thou Life and Delight of my
    soul,
  Where the flock of thy pasture are
    feeding;
I seek thy protection, I need thy control,
  I would go where my Shepherd is lead-
    ing.

2 Oh, tell me the place where the flock are
    at rest,

Where the noontide will find them re-
    posing;
The tempest now rages, my soul is dis-
    tressed,
  And the pathway of peace I am losing.

3 And why should I stray with the flocks
    of thy foes,
  In the desert where now they are roving;
Where hunger and thirst, where conten-
    tions and woes,
  And fierce conflicts their ruin are
    proving?

4 Ah, when shall my woes and my wander-
    ing cease,
  And the follies that fill me with weeping?
O Shepherd of Israel, restore me that
    peace,
  Thou dost give to the flock thou art
    keeping!

5 A voice from the Shepherd now bids me
    return,
  By the way where the foot-prints are
    lying;
No longer to wander, no longer to mourn:
  And homeward my spirit is flying.

GOSHEN. 11.

1. The Lord is my Shep - herd; no want shall I know; I feed in green
D. S. Re - stores me when

FINE.

D. S.

pas - tures; safe - fold - ed I rest; He lead - eth my soul where the still wa - ters flow,
wand - 'ring, redeems when oppressed.

36

PSALM 23. MONTGOMERY.
"No want shall I know."

The Lord is my Shepherd; no want shall
I know;
I feed in green pastures; safe-folded I rest:
He leadeth my soul where the still waters
flow,
Restores me when wandering, redeems
when oppressed.

2 Through the valley and shadow of death
though I stray,
Since thou art my Guardian, no evil I fear:
Thy rod shall defend me, thy staff be my
stay;
No harm can befall, with my Comforter
near.

3 In the midst of affliction, my table is
spread;
With blessings unmeasured my cup run-
neth o'er;
With perfume and oil thou anointest my
head;—
Oh, what shall I ask of thy providence
more?

4 Let goodness and mercy, my bountiful
God!
Still follow my steps till I meet thee above;
I seek, by the path which my forefathers
trod
Through the land of their sojourn, thy
kingdom of love.

37

PSALM 23. ANON.
"I will be with thee."

Though faint, yet pursuing, we go on our
way;
The Lord is our Leader, his word is our stay:
Though suffering, and sorrow, and trial be
near,
The Lord is our Refuge, and whom can we
fear?

2 He raiseth the fallen, he cheereth the faint;
The weak, and oppressed—he will hear their
complaint;
The way may be weary, and thorny the road,
But how can we falter?—our help is in God!

3 And to his green pastures our footsteps
he leads;
His flock in the desert how kindly he feeds!
The lambs in his bosom he tenderly bears,
And brings back the wanderers all safe
from the snares.

4 Though clouds may surround us, our God
is our light;
Though storms rage around us, our God is
our might;
So, faint, yet pursuing, still onward we come;
The Lord is our Leader, and heaven is our
home!

LEBANON. S. M. D.

1. While my Redeemer's near, My shepherd and my guide, I bid farewell to anxious fear: My
D. S. His gracious hand indulgent leads, And

FINE.   D. S.

wants are all sup-plied. 2. To ev-er fragrant meads, Where rich a-bundance grows,
guards my sweet re-pose.

38 PSALM 23.   STEELE.
Content in Christ.

WHILE my Redeemer's near,
My Shepherd and my guide,
I bid farewell to anxious fear:
My wants are all supplied.

2 To ever fragrant meads,
Where rich abundance grows,
His gracious hand indulgent leads,
And guards my sweet repose.

3 Dear Shepherd, if I stray,
My wandering feet restore;
To thy fair pastures guide my way,
And let me rove no more.

4 Unworthy, as I am,
Of thy protecting care,
Jesus, I plead thy gracious name,
For all my hopes are there.

39 PSALM 23.   WATTS.
The Lord our Shepherd.

THE Lord my Shepherd is,
I shall be well supplied;
Since he is mine, and I am his,
What can I want beside?

2 He leads me to the place
Where heavenly pasture grows,
Where living waters gently pass,
And full salvation flows.

3 If e'er I go astray,
He doth my soul reclaim;
And guide me in his own right way,
For his most holy name.

4 While he affords his aid,
I cannot yield to fear;
Though I should walk through death's
dark shade,
My Shepherd's with me there.

5 In spite of all my foes,
Thou dost my table spread;
My cup with blessings overflows,
And joy exalts my head.

6 The bounties of thy love
Shall crown my future days;
Nor from thy house will I remove,
Nor cease to speak thy praise.

40 PSALM 23.   BONAR.
"He restoreth my soul."

I WAS a wandering sheep,
I did not love the fold,
I did not love my Shepherd's voice,
I would not be controlled.

2 Jesus my Shepherd is,
'Twas he that loved my soul,
'Twas he that washed me in his blood,
'Twas he that made me whole.

3 'Twas he that sought the lost,
That found the wandering sheep,
'Twas he that brought me to the fold,
'Tis he that still doth keep.

4 I was a wandering sheep,
I would not be controlled;
But now I love my Shepherd's voice,
I love, I love the fold!

LA MIRA. C. M.

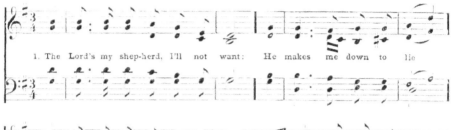

1. The Lord's my shep-herd, I'll not want: He makes me down to lie

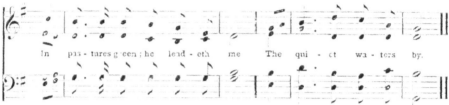

In pas-tures green; he lead-eth me The qui-et wa-ters by.

41
PSALM 23.
The Good Shepherd. SCOTCH.

THE Lord's my shepherd, I'll not want:
He makes me down to lie
In pastures green; he leadeth me
The quiet waters by.

2 My soul he doth restore again;
And me to walk doth make
Within the paths of righteousness,
Ev'n for his own name's sake.

3 Yea, though I walk in death's dark vale,
Yet will I fear no ill;
For thou art with me, and thy rod
And staff me comfort still.

4 My table thou hast furnishèd
In presence of my foes;
My head thou dost with oil anoint,
And my cup overflows.

5 Goodness and mercy, all my life,
Shall surely follow me;
And in God's house for evermore
My dwelling-place shall be.

42
PSALM 23.
The Lord, our Shepherd. TATE-BRADY.

THE Lord himself, the mighty Lord,
Vouchsafes to be my guide;
The shepherd, by whose constant care
My wants are all supplied.

2 In tender-grass he makes me feed,
And gently there repose;
Then leads me to cool shades, and where
Refreshing water flows.

3 I pass the gloomy vale of death,
From fear and danger free;
For there his aiding rod and staff
Defend and comfort me.

4 Since God doth thus his wondrous love
Through all my life extend,
That life to him I will devote,
And in his temple spend.

43
PSALM 24.
The Abode of Saints. WATTS.

THE earth for ever is the Lord's,
With Adam's numerous race;
He raised its arches o'er the floods,
And built it on the seas.

2 But who, among the sons of men,
May visit thine abode?
He that has hands from mischief clean,
Whose heart is right with God.

3 This is the man may rise, and take
The blessings of his grace;
This is the lot of those, that seek
The God of Jacob's face.

4 Now let our souls' immortal powers
To meet the Lord prepare,
Lift up their everlasting doors;
The King of glory's near.

5 The King of glory! who can tell
The wonders of his might?
He rules the nations; but to dwell
With saints is his delight.

ST. GEORGE'S: EDINBURG. C. M. D.

1. Ye gates, lift up your heads on high! Ye doors that last for aye! Be lift-ed up that
3. Ye gates, lift up your heads! ye doors, Doors that do last for aye! Be lift-ed up that

so the King Of glo-ry en-ter may. 2. But who of glory is the King? The ...
so the King Of glo-ry en-ter may. 4. But who is he that is the King? the King, Cf

mighty Lord is this; Ev'n that same Lord, that great in might, And strong in bat-tle is:—
glo-ry? who is this? The Lord of hosts, and none but he, The King of glo-ry is:—

Ev'n that same Lord, that great in might, And strong in bat-tle is. Hal-le-lu-jah,
The Lord of hosts, and none but he, The King of glo-ry is.

Hal-le-lu-jah, Hal-le-lu-jah, Hal-le-lu-jah, Hal-le-lu-jah, A-men, A-men, A-men.

PSALM 24.
"The King of Glory."   SCOTCH.

44

YE gates, lift up your heads on high!
  Ye doors that last for aye!
Be lifted up, that so the King
  Of glory enter may.

2 But who of glory is the King?
  The mighty Lord is this;
Ev'n that same Lord, that great in might,
  And strong in battle is.

3 Ye gates, lift up your heads! ye doors,
  Doors that do last for aye!
Be lifted up, that so the King
  Of glory enter may.

4 But who is he that is the King
  Of glory? who is this?
The Lord of hosts, and none but he,
  The King of glory is.

BENNINGTON. L. M. D.

1. Our Lord is ris - en from the dead, Our Je-sus is gone up on high: The pow'rs of hell are captive led. Dragg'd to the por-tals of the sky. 2. There his triumphant chariot waits, And an-gels chant the sol-emn lay : "Lift up your heads, ye heav'nly gates! Ye ev-erlasting doors, give way."

45   PSALM 24.   C. WESLEY.
Resurrection of Christ.

Our Lord is risen from the dead,
  Our Jesus is gone up on high;
The powers of hell are captive led,
  Dragged to the portals of the sky.
2 There his triumphal chariot waits,
  And angels chant the solemn lay:—
  "Lift up your heads, ye heavenly gates!
  Ye everlasting doors! give way."
3 Loose all your bars of massy light,
  And wide unfold the ethereal scene:
  He claims those mansions as his right;
  Receive the King of glory in.
4 Who is the King of glory—who?
  The Lord who all our foes o'ercame;
  Who sin, and death, and hell o'erthrew;
  And Jesus is the conqueror's name.
5 Lo! his triumphal chariot waits,
  And angels chant the solemn lay:—
  "Lift up your heads, ye heavenly gates!
  Ye everlasting doors! give way."
6 Who is the King of glory—who?
  The Lord of boundless power possessed:
  The King of saints and angels, too,
  God over all, forever blessed.

46   PSALM 24.   WATTS.
The King of glory.

This spacious earth is all the Lord's,
  And men and worms, and beasts and birds;
He raised the building on the seas,
  And gave it for their dwelling-place.
2 But there's a brighter world on high,
  Thy palace, Lord, above the sky;
  Who shall ascend that blest abode,
  And dwell so near his Maker, God?
3 He that abhors and fears to sin,
  Whose heart is pure, whose hands are clean;
  Him shall the Lord, the Saviour, bless,
  And clothe his soul with righteousness.
4 These are the men, the pious race,
  That seek the God of Jacob's face;
  These shall enjoy the blissful sight,
  And dwell in everlasting light.
5 Rejoice, ye shining worlds on high!
  Behold the King of glory nigh,
  Who can this King of glory be?
  The mighty Lord, the Saviour's he!
6 Ye heavenly gates, your leaves display
  To make the Lord, the Saviour, way;
  Laden with spoils from earth and hell,
  The conqueror comes with God to dwell.

LEIGHTON. S. M.

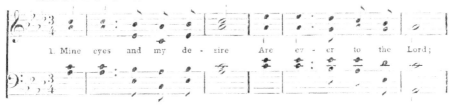

1. Mine eyes and my de-sire Are ev-er to the Lord;

I love to plead his prom-is-es, And rest up-on his word.

47 PSALM 25. WATTS.
Looking to Jesus.

MINE eyes and my desire
Are ever to the Lord;
I love to plead his promises,
And rest upon his word.

2 Lord, turn thee to my soul;
Bring thy salvation near:
When will thy hand release my feet
From sin's destructive snare?

3 When shall the sovereign grace
Of my forgiving God
Restore me from those dangerous ways
My wandering feet have trod?

4 Oh, keep my soul from death,
Nor put my hope to shame!
For I have placed my only trust
In my Redeemer's name.

5 With humble faith I wait
To see thy face again;
Of Israel it shall ne'er be said,
He sought the Lord in vain.

48 PSALM 25. WATTS.
Divine Teaching.

WHERE shall the man be found,
That fears to offend his God,
That loves the gospel's joyful sound,
And trembles at the rod?

2 The Lord shall make him know
The secrets of his heart,
The wonders of his covenant show,
And all his love impart.

3 The dealings of his hand
Are truth and mercy still,
With such as to his covenant stand,
And love to do his will.

4 Their souls shall dwell at ease,
Before their Maker's face;
Their seed shall taste the promises,
In their extensive grace.

49 PSALM 25. SCOTCH.
Prayer for Help.

TO thee I lift my soul;
O Lord, I trust in thee:
My God, let me not be ashamed,
Nor foes exult o'er me.

2 Let none who wait on thee
Be put to shame at all;
But those who causelessly transgress,
On them the shame shall fall.

3 Show me thy ways, O Lord;
Thy paths, oh, teach thou me:
And do thou lead me in thy truth,
Therein my teacher be:—

4 For thou art God that dost
To me salvation send;
And waiting for thee all the day,
Upon thee I attend.

5 Thy tender mercies, Lord,
To mind do thou recall,
And loving-kindnesses, for they
Have been through ages all.

29

ST. MARTINS. C. M.

1. Judge me, O Lord, and try my heart, For thou that heart canst see;

And bid each i - dol thence de - part That dares com - pete with thee.

50   PSALM 26.   LYTE.
Self-examination.

JUDGE me, O Lord, and try my heart,
  For thou that heart canst see;
And bid each idol thence depart
  That dares compete with thee.

2 Though weak and cleaving to the dust,
  My soul adores thee still;
Thy grace and truth are all my trust;
  Oh, mould me to thy will.

3 Thine altar, Lord, I would embrace
  With hands by Christ made clean;
I love thy house, I love the place
  Where thy bright face is seen.

4 Oh, guide me in thy love and fear;
  My soul on thee I cast;
I would not walk with sinners here,
  To share their doom at last.

51   PSALM 27.   WATTS.
The Church, our Delight and Safety.

THE Lord of glory is my light,
  And my salvation too;
God is my strength.—nor will I fear
  What all my foes can do.

2 One privilege my heart desires,—
  Oh, grant me an abode,
Among the churches of thy saints,—
  The temples of my God.

3 There shall I offer my requests,
  And see thy beauty still;
Shall hear thy messages of love,
  And there inquire thy will.

4 When troubles rise, and storms appear,
  There may his children hide;
God has a strong pavilion, where
  He makes my soul abide.

5 Now shall my head be lifted high
  Above my foes around;
And songs of joy and victory
  Within thy temple sound.

52   PSALM 27.   SCOTCH.
Love for Worship.

ONE thing I of the Lord desired,
  And will seek to obtain,
That all days of my life I may
  Within God's house remain;—

2 That I the beauty of the Lord
  Behold may and admire,
And that I in his holy place
  May reverently inquire.

3 For he in his pavilion shall
  Me hide in evil days;
In secret of his tent me hide,
  And on a rock me raise.

4 And now, ev'n at this present time,
  Mine head shall lifted be
Above all those that are my foes,
  And round encompass me.

5 O Lord give ear unto my voice
  When I do cry to thee;
Upon me also mercy have,
  And do thou answer me.

GILEAD. L. M.

1. Blest be the Lord who heard my prayer, The Lord, my shield, my help, my song,

Who saved my soul from sin and fear, And filled with praise my thankful tongue.

53 PSALM 23   DWIGHT.
Divine Assistance acknowledged.

BLEST be the Lord who heard my prayer,
  The Lord, my shield, my help, my song,
Who saved my soul from sin and fear,
  And filled with praise my thankful tongue.

2 In the dark hour of deep distress,
  By foes beset, of death afraid,
My spirit trusted in his grace,
  And sought and found his heavenly aid.

3 O blest Redeemer of mankind!
  Thy shield, thy saving strength, shall be
The shield, the strength of every mind
  That loves thy name, and trusts in thee.

4 Remember, Lord, thy chosen seed;
  Israel defend from guilt and woe;
Thy flock in richest pastures feed,
  And guard their steps from every foe.

5 Zion exalt, her cause maintain,
  With peace and joy her courts surround:
In showers let endless blessings rain,
  And all the world thy praise resound.

54 PSALM 29.   WATTS.
Storm and Thunder.

GIVE to the Lord, ye sons of fame!
  Give to the Lord renown and power;
Ascribe due honors to his name,
  And his eternal might adore.

2 The Lord proclaims his power aloud,
  Over the ocean and the land;
His voice divides the watery cloud,
  And lightnings blaze at his command.

3 He speaks,—and tempest, hail and wind,
  Lay the wide forest bare around;
The fearful hart, and frighted hind,
  Leap at the terror of the sound.

4 To Lebanon he turns his voice,
  And lo! the stately cedars break;
The mountains tremble at the noise,
  The valleys roar, the deserts quake.

5 The Lord sits sovereign on the flood;
  The Thunderer reigns for ever king;
But makes his church his blest abode,
  Where we his awful glories sing.

6 In gentler language there the Lord
  The counsels of his grace imparts;
Amid the raging storm, his word
  Speaks peace and courage to our hearts.

55 PSALM 30.   WATTS.
Recovery from Sickness.

I WILL extol thee, Lord, on high:
  At thy command diseases fly:
Who but a God can speak and save
  From the dark borders of the grave?

2 Sing to the Lord, ye saints, and prove
  How large his grace, how kind his love:
Let all your powers rejoice, and trace
  The wondrous records of his grace.

3 His anger but a moment stays;
  His love is life and length of days:
Though grief and tears the night employ,
  The morning star restores the joy.

31

GORTON. S. M.

1. I will ex - alt thee, Lord, Thou hast ex - alt - ed me:

Since thou hast si - lenced Sa - tan's boast, My boast shall be in thee.

56   PSALM 30.   SPURGEON.
Recovery acknowledged.

1 I WILL exalt thee, Lord,
  Thou hast exalted me;
Since thou hast silenced Satan's boasts,
  My boast shall be in thee.

2 My sins had brought me near
  The grave of black despair;
I looked, but there was none to save,
  Till I looked up in prayer.

3 All through the night, I wept,
  But morning brought relief:
That hand, which broke my bones before,
  Then broke my bonds of grief.

4 My grief to dancing turns,
  For sackcloth joy he gives;
A moment, Lord, thine anger burns,
  But long thy favor lives.

5 Sing with me then, ye saints,
  Who long have known his grace:
With thanks recall the seasons when
  Ye also sought his face.

57   PSALM 31.   LYTE.
Trust in God.

1 My spirit on thy care,
  Blest Saviour, I recline;
Thou wilt not leave me to despair,
  For thou art love divine.

2 In thee I place my trust,
  On thee I calmly rest:
I know thee good, I know thee just,
  And count thy choice the best.

3 Whate'er events betide,
  Thy will they all perform;
Safe in thy breast my head I hide,
  Nor fear the coming storm.

4 Let good or ill befall,
  It must be good for me,—
Secure of having thee in all,
  Of having all in thee.

5 O all ye saints, the Lord
  With eager love pursue;
Who to the just will help afford,
  And give the proud their due.

58   PSALM 32.   WATTS.
Confession of Sin.

1 OH, blesséd souls are they
  Whose sins are covered o'er!
Divinely blest, to whom the Lord
  Imputes their guilt no more.

2 They mourn their follies past,
  And keep their hearts with care;
Their lips and lives, without deceit,
  Shall prove their faith sincere.

3 While I concealed my guilt,
  I felt the festering wound,
Till I confessed my sins to thee,
  And ready pardon found.

4 Let sinners learn to pray,
  Let saints keep near the throne;
Our help in times of deep distress
  Is found in God alone.

32

SWANWICK. C. M.

1. Re - joice, ye right-eous! in the Lord; This work be-longs to you; Sing of his

name his ways his word; How ho - ly, just, and true! How ho - ly, just and true!

59   PSALM 33   WATTS.
Works of Creation and Providence

REJOICE, ye righteous! in the Lord;
  This work belongs to you;
Sing of his name, his ways, his word;
  How holy, just, and true!

2 His mercy, and his righteousness,
  Let heaven and earth proclaim;
His works of nature and of grace
  Reveal his wondrous name.

3 His wisdom and almighty word
  The heavenly arches spread;
And, by the Spirit of the Lord,
  Their shining hosts were made.

4 He scorns the angry nations' rage,
  And breaks their vain designs;
His counsel stands through every age,
  And in full glory shines.

60   PSALM 34.   SCOTCH.
Praise for Protection.

GOD will I bless all times; his praise
  My mouth shall still express.
My soul shall boast in God: the meek
  Shall hear with joyfulness.

2 Oh, let us magnify the Lord,
  Exalt his name with me!
I sought the Lord, and he me heard
  And from all fears set free.

3 The angel of the Lord encamps,
  And he encompasseth
All those who do him truly fear,
  And them delivereth.

4 Oh, taste and see that God is good;
  Who trusts in him is blest.
Fear God, his saints, none that him fear
  Shall be with want oppressed.

5 The lions young may hungry be,
  And they may lack their food;
But they that truly seek the Lord
  Shall not lack any good.

61   PSALM 34.   TATE-BRADY.
Trusting and Praising God.

THROUGH all the changing scenes of life,
  In trouble, and in joy,
The praises of my God shall still
  My heart and tongue employ.

2 Of his deliverance I will boast,
  Till all, who are distressed,
From my example comfort take,
  And charm their griefs to rest.

3 Oh, magnify the Lord with me,
  With me exalt his name!
When in distress to him I called,
  He to my rescue came.

4 The hosts of God encamp around
  The dwellings of the just;
Deliverance he affords to all,
  Who on his succor trust.

5 Oh, make but trial of his love;
  Experience will decide,
How blest are they, and only they,
  Who in his truth confide.

33

ECKHARDTSHEIM. C. M.

1. Oh, plead my cause, my Sav-iour, plead, I trust it all to thee:

O thou who didst for sin-ners bleed, A sin-ner save in me.

62　　　PSALM 35.　　　TYTE.
Trusting God.

Oh, plead my cause, my Saviour, plead.
　I trust it all to thee:
O thou who didst for sinners bleed,
　A sinner save in me.

2 Assure my weak, desponding heart,
　My threatening foes restrain;
Oh, tell me thou my helper art,
　And all their rage is vain.

3 When round thy cross they rushed to kill,
　How was their fury foiled:
Their madness only wrought thy will,
　And on themselves recoiled.

4 The great salvation there achieved
　My hope shall ever be;
My soul has in her Lord believed,
　And he will rescue me.

63　　　PSALM 36.　　　SCOTCH.
God's Perfections.

Thy mercy, Lord, is in the heavens;
　Thy truth doth reach the clouds;
Thy justice is like mountains great;
　Thy judgments deep as floods.

2 Lord, thou preservest man and beast—
　How precious is thy grace!
Therefore, in shadow of thy wings
　Men's sons their trust shall place.

3 They with the fatness of thy house
　Shall be well satisfied;
From rivers of thy pleasures thou
　Wilt drink to them provide.

4 Because of life the fountain pure
　Remains alone with thee;
And in that purest light of thine
　We clearly light shall see.

64　　　PSALM 37.　　　WATTS.
The Safety of the Righteous.

My God! the steps of pious men
　Are ordered by thy will;
Though they should fall, they rise again:
　Thy hand supports them still.

2 The Lord delights to see their ways;
　Their virtue he approves;
He'll ne'er deprive them of his grace,
　Nor leave the men he loves.

3 The heavenly heritage is theirs,
　Their portion and their home;
He feeds them now, and makes them heirs
　Of blessings long to come.

4 The haughty sinner I have seen,
　Not fearing man, nor God;
Like a tall bay-tree, fair and green,
　Spreading his arms abroad.

5 And, lo! he vanished from the ground,
　Destroyed by hands unseen;
Nor root, nor branch, nor leaf, was found,
　Where all that pride had been.

6 But mark the man of righteousness,
　His several steps attend:
True pleasure runs through all his ways,
　And peaceful is his end.

34

ST. AGNES.　C. M.

1. A - mid thy wrath re - mem - ber love,　Re - store thy ser - vant, Lord;

Nor let a Fa - ther's chastening prove　Like an a - ven - ger's sword.

65　　　　PSALM 38.　　　　WATTS.
　　　　Prayer in anguish.

Amid thy wrath remember love,
　Restore thy servant, Lord;
Nor let a Father's chastening prove
　Like an avenger's sword.

2 My sins a heavy load appear,
　　And o'er my head are gone;
　The burden, Lord! I cannot bear,
　　Nor e'er the guilt atone.

3 My thoughts are like a troubled sea,
　　My head still bending down;
　And I go mourning all the day,
　　Beneath my Father's frown.

4 All my desire to thee is known,
　　Thine eye counts every tear;
　And every sigh, and every groan,
　　Is noticed by thine ear.

5 My God, forgive my follies past,
　　And be for ever nigh;
　O Lord of my salvation, haste,
　　Before thy servant die.

66　　　　PSALM 39.　　　　SCOTCH.
　　　　Man's Frailty.

Mine end and measure of my days,
　O Lord, unto me show,
What is the same; that I hereby
　My frailty well may know.

2 Lo, thou hast made my days a span,
　　As nothing are my years;
　Before thy sight, each man at best
　　But vanity appears:—

3 Yea, each man walks in empty show;
　　They vex themselves in vain;
　He heaps up wealth, and knoweth not
　　To whom it shall pertain.

4 And now, O Lord, what wait I for?
　　My hope is fixed on thee.
　Deliver me from all my sins;
　　The fool's scorn make not me.

5 Oh, spare thou me, that I my strength
　　Recover may again,
　Before from hence I do depart,
　　And here no more remain.

67　　　　PSALM 39.　　　　WATTS.
　　　　The Vanity of Man.

Teach me the measure of my days,
　Thou Maker of my frame!
I would survey life's narrow space,
　And learn how frail I am.

2 A span is all that we can boast,—
　　An inch or two of time;
　Man is but vanity and dust,
　　In all his flower and prime.

3 What should I wish, or wait for then,
　　From creatures, earth and dust?
　They make our expectations vain,
　　And disappoint our trust.

4 Now I forbid my carnal hope,
　　My fond desires recall;
　I give my mortal interest up,
　　And make my God my all.

CORINTH. C. M.

1. I wait-ed pa-tient for the Lord,— He bowed to hear my cry;

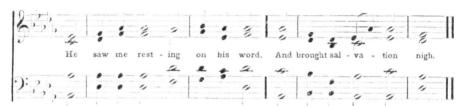

He saw me rest-ing on his word, And brought sal-va-tion nigh.

68

PSALM 40.
Deliverance from deep Distress. WATTS.

1 I WAITED patient for the Lord,—
   He bowed to hear my cry;
   He saw me resting on his word,
   And brought salvation nigh.

2 He raised me from a horrid pit,
   Where, mourning, long I lay;
   And from my bonds released my feet—
   Deep bonds of miry clay.

3 Firm on a rock he made me stand,
   And taught my cheerful tongue,
   To praise the wonders of his hand,
   In a new thankful song.

4 I'll spread his works of grace abroad;
   The saints with joy shall hear;
   And sinners learn to make my God
   Their only hope and fear.

5 How many are thy thoughts of love!
   Thy mercies, Lord! how great!
   We have not words, nor hours enough,
   Their numbers to repeat.

69

PSALM 40.
A new Song. SCOTCH.

1 I WAITED for the Lord my God,
   And patiently did bear;
   At length to me he did incline
   My voice and cry to hear.

2 He took me from a fearful pit,
   And from the miry clay,
   And on a rock he set my feet,
   Establishing my way.

3 He put a new song in my mouth,
   Our God to magnify;
   Many shall see it, and shall fear,
   And on the Lord rely.

4 Oh, blessèd is the man whose trust
   Upon the Lord relies;
   Respecting not the proud, nor such
   As turn aside to lies.

70

PSALM 41.
The Blessedness of Benevolence. BARBAULD.

1 BLEST is the man whose softening heart
   Feels all another's pain;
   To whom the supplicating eye
   Was never raised in vain;—

2 Whose breast expands with generous
       warmth
   A stranger's woes to feel;
   And bleeds in pity o'er the wound
   He wants the power to heal.

3 He spreads his kind, supporting arms,
   To every child of grief;
   His secret bounty largely flows,
   And brings unasked relief.

4 To gentle offices of love
   His feet are never slow;
   He views, through mercy's melting eye,
   A brother in a foe.

5 Peace from the bosom of his God,
   The Saviour's grace shall give;
   And when he kneels before the throne,
   His trembling soul shall live.

GREENPORT. C. M. D.

1. As pants the hart for cooling streams, When heated in the chase, So longs my soul, O God, for thee, And thy re-fresh-ing grace. 2. For thee, my God, the liv-ing God, My thirs-ty soul doth pine; Oh, when shall I be-hold thy face, Thou Ma-jes-ty Di-vine?

'71

PSALM 42.
Desire for God.   TATE-BRADY.

As pants the hart for cooling streams,
  When heated 'n the chase,
So longs my soul, O God, for thee,
  And thy refreshing grace.

2 For thee, my God, the living God,
  My thirsty soul doth pine;
Oh, when shall I behold thy face,
  Thou Majesty Divine?

3 Why restless, why cast down, my soul?
  Trust God, and he'll employ
His aid for thee, and change these sighs
  To thankful hymns of joy.

4 God of my strength, how long shall I,
  Like one forgotten, mourn;
Forlorn, forsaken, and exposed
  To my oppressor's scorn?

5 My heart is pierced, as with a sword,
  While thus my foes upbraid:
"Vain boaster, where is now thy God?
  And where his promised aid!"

6 Why restless, why cast down, my soul?
  Hope still, and thou shalt sing
The praise of him who is thy God,
  Thy health's eternal Spring.

72

PSALM 43.
Cheerful Hope.   SCOTCH.

Against a wicked nation, Lord,
  Plead thou my cause, judge me;
And from unjust and crafty men
  Oh, do thou set me free.

2 O God, my strength, why dost thou me
  Cast off in my distress?
Why go I mourning all the day
  While enemies oppress?

3 Oh, send thy light forth, and thy truth!
  Let them be guides to me,
And bring me to thy holy hill,
  Ev'n where thy dwellings be.

4 Then will I to God's altar go,
  To God my chiefest joy:
Yea, God, my God, thy name to praise
  My harp I will employ.

5 Why art thou then cast down, my soul?
  What should discourage thee?
And why with vexing thoughts art thou
  Disquieted in me?

6 Still trust in God; for him to praise
  Good cause I yet shall have:
He of my countenance is the health,
  My God that doth me save.

37

DEDHAM. C. M.

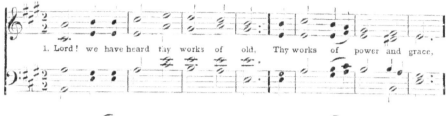

1. Lord! we have heard thy works of old, Thy works of power and grace,

When to our ears our fathers told The won-ders of their days.

73   **PSALM 44.**   WATTS.
Complaint in Declension.

Lord! we have heard thy works of old,
Thy works of power and grace,
When to our ears our fathers told
The wonders of their days:—

2 How thou didst build thy churches here,
And make thy gospel known:
Among them did thine arm appear,
Thy light and glory shone.

3 In God they boasted all the day;
And in a cheerful throng,
Did thousands meet to praise and pray;
And grace was all their song.

4 Redeem us from perpetual shame,
Our Saviour and our God!
We plead the honors of thy name,
The merits of thy blood.

74   **PSALM 45.**   WATTS.
Christ and his glorious Reign.

I'll speak the honors of my King,—
His form divinely fair;
None of the sons of mortal race
May with the Lord compare.

2 Sweet is thy speech, and heavenly grace
Upon thy lips is shed;
Thy God, with blessings infinite,
Hath crowned thy sacred head.

3 Gird on thy sword, victorious Prince!
Ride with majestic sway;
Thy terror shall strike through thy foes,
And make the world obey.

4 Thy throne, O God! for ever stands;
Thy word of grace shall prove
A peaceful sceptre in thy hands,
To rule the saints by love.

5 Justice and truth attend thee still,
But mercy is thy choice;
And God, thy God, thy soul shall fill
With most peculiar joys.

75   **PSALM 45.**   SCOTCH.
The King of kings.

My heart brings forth a goodly thing,
My words that I indite
Concern the King: my tongue's a pen
Of one that swift doth write.

2 Thou fairer art than sons of men:
Into thy lips is store
Of grace infused; God therefore thee
Hath blessed for evermore.

3 For ever and for ever is,
O God, thy throne of might!
The sceptre of thy kingdom is
A sceptre that is right.

4 Behold, the daughter of the King
All glorious is within;
And with embroideries of gold
Her garments wrought have been.

5 She shall be brought with gladness great,
And mirth on every side,
Into the palace of the King,
And there she shall abide.

38

WARD. L. M.

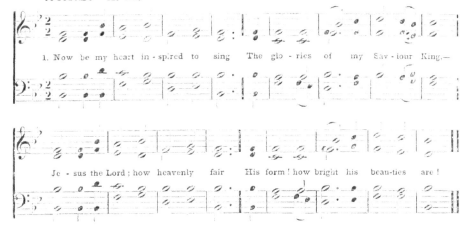

1. Now be my heart in-spired to sing The glo-ries of my Sav-iour King,—

Je-sus the Lord; how heavenly fair His form! how bright his beau-ties are!

76 PSALM 45.   WATTS.
The Glory of Christ.

Now be my heart inspired to sing
The glories of my Saviour King,—
Jesus the Lord; how heavenly fair
His form! how bright his beauties are!

2 O'er all the sons of human race,
He shines with a superior grace:
Love from his lips divinely flows,
And blessings all his state compose.

3 Thy throne, O God, for ever stands;
Grace is the sceptre in thy hands;
Thy laws and works are just and right;
Justice and grace are thy delight.

4 God, thine own God, has richly shed
His oil of gladness on thy head;
And with his sacred spirit blessed
His first-born Son above the rest.

77 PSALM 45.   WATTS.
Christ and his Church.

The King of saints,—how fair his face!
Adorned with majesty and grace,
He comes, with blessings from above,
And wins the nations to his love.

2 At his right hand, our eyes behold
The queen, arrayed in purest gold;
The world admires her heavenly dress,
Her robe of joy and righteousness.

3 Oh, happy hour, when thou shalt rise
To his fair palace in the skies;
And all thy sons, a numerous train,
Each, like a prince, in glory reign.

4 Let endless honors crown his head;
Let every age his praises spread;
While we, with cheerful songs, approve
The condescension of his love.

78 PSALM 46.   WATTS.
The Church Safe.

God is the refuge of his saints,
When storms of sharp distress invade;
Ere we can offer our complaints,
Behold him present with his aid.

2 Let mountains from their seats be hurled
Down to the deep, and buried there,
Convulsions shake the solid world—
Our faith shall never yield to fear.

3 Loud may the troubled ocean roar;
In sacred peace our souls abide;
While every nation, every shore,
Trembles, and dreads the swelling tide.

4 There is a stream whose gentle flow
Supplies the city of our God,
Life, love, and joy, still gliding through,
And watering our divine abode.

5 That sacred stream, thine holy word,
Our grief allays, our fear controls;
Sweet peace thy promises afford,
And give new strength to fainting souls.

6 Zion enjoys her Monarch's love,
Secure against a threatening hour;
Nor can her firm foundation move,
Built on his truth, and armed with power.

DOWNS. C. M.

1. God is our ref - uge and our strength, In straits a pre - sent aid;

There - fore, al - though the earth re - move We will not be a - fraid.

79

PSALM 46. SCOTCH.
The Church Safe.

God is our refuge and our strength,
  In straits a present aid;
Therefore, although the earth remove
  We will not be afraid:—

2 Though hills amidst the seas be cast;
  Though waters roaring make,
And troubled be; yea, though the hills
  By swelling seas do shake.

3 A river is, whose streams do glad
  The city of our God;
The holy place, wherein the Lord
  Most high hath his abode.

4 God in the midst of her doth dwell;
  Nothing shall her remove:
The Lord to her an helper will,
  And that right early, prove.

80

PSALM 47. WATTS.
The Ascension and Reign of Christ.

Oh, for a shout of sacred joy
  To God, the sovereign King;
Let every land their tongues employ,
  And hymns of triumph sing.

2 Jesus, our God, ascends on high;
  His heavenly guards around
Attend him rising through the sky,
  With trumpets' joyful sound.

3 While angels shout and praise their King,
  Let mortals learn their strains;
Let all the earth his honor sing;—
  O'er all the earth he reigns.

40

4 Rehearse his praise with awe profound;
  Let knowledge lead the song;
Nor mock him with a solemn sound
  Upon a thoughtless tongue.

5 In Israel stood his ancient throne:—
  He loved that ancient race;
But now he calls the world his own;
  The heathen taste his grace.

81

PSALM 48. SCOTCH.
The Beauty of the Church.

The Lord is great, and greatly he
  Should be exalted still,
Within the city of our God,
  Upon his holy hill.

2 Mount Zion stands most beautiful,
  The joy of all the land;
The city of the mighty King
  On her north side doth stand.

3 The Lord within her palaces
  Is for a refuge known.
For, lo, the kings that gathered were
  Together, by have gone.

4 Encompass Zion, and go around,
  Her lofty towers tell;
Consider ye her palaces,
  And mark her bulwarks well;—

5 That ye may tell posterity.
  For this God doth abide
Our God for evermore; he will
  Even unto death us guide.

SILVER STREET. S. M.

1. Great is the Lord our God, And let his praise be great;

He makes his church-es his a - bode. His most de - light - ful seat.

82

PSALM 48. WATTS.
The Church, a Bulwark.

GREAT is the Lord our God,
  And let his praise be great;
He makes his churches his abode,
  His most delightful seat.

2 These temples of his grace,
  How beautiful they stand!
The honors of our native place,
  The bulwarks of our land.

3 In Zion God is known
  A refuge in distress;
How bright has his salvation shone
  Through all her palaces!

4 Oft have our fathers told,
  Our eyes have often seen,
How well our God secures the fold
  Where his own sheep have been.

5 In every new distress
  We'll to his house repair,
We'll think upon his wondrous grace,
  And seek deliverance there.

83

PSALM 48. WATTS.
"Beautiful for situation."

FAR as thy name is known,
  The world declares thy praise;
Thy saints, O Lord, before thy throne,
  Their songs of honor raise.

2 With joy thy people stand
  On Zion's chosen hill,
Proclaim the wonders of thy hand,
  And counsels of thy will.

3 Let strangers walk around
  The city where we dwell,
Compass and view thine holy ground,
  And mark the building well—

4 The order of thy house,
  The worship of thy court,
The cheerful songs, the solemn vows;
  And make a fair report.

5 How decent, and how wise!
  How glorious to behold!
Beyond the pomp that charms the eyes,
  And rites adorned with gold.

6 The God we worship now
  Will guide us till we die;
Will be our God, while here below,
  And ours above the sky.

84

PSALM 49. WATTS.
Pride and Death.

WHY doth the rich man grow
  To insolence and pride,
To see his wealth and honors flow
  With every rising tide?

2 Why treat the poor with scorn,
  Made of the self-same clay,
And boast as though his flesh were born
  Of better dust than they?

3 No treasures can procure
  His soul a short reprieve,
Redeem from death one guilty hour,
  Or make his brother live.

BARBY. C. M.

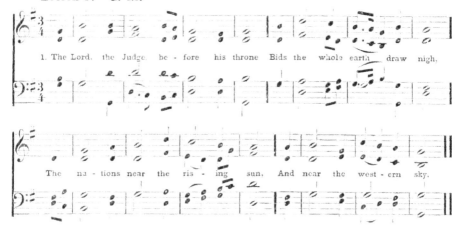

1. The Lord, the Judge, be - fore his throne Bids the whole earth draw nigh,

The na - tions near the ris - ing sun, And near the west - ern sky.

85

PSALM 50. WATTS.
Saints at the Judgment.

The Lord, the Judge, before his throne
  Bids the whole earth draw nigh,
The nations near the rising sun,
  And near the western sky.

2 Throned on a cloud our God shall come,
  Bright flames prepare his way,
Thunder and darkness, fire and storm
  Lead on the dreadful day.

3 Heaven from above his call shall hear,
  Attending angels come,
And earth and hell shall know and fear
  His justice and their doom.

4 "But gather all my saints," he cries,
  "That made their peace with God,
By the Redeemer's sacrifice,
  And sealed it with his blood.

5 Their faith and works, brought forth to light,
  Shall make the world confess,
My sentence of reward is right,
  And heaven adore my grace."

86

PSALM 51. SCOTCH.
Penitence.

In thy great loving-kindness, Lord,
  Be merciful to me;
In thy compassions great blot out
  All my iniquity.

2 Oh, wash me thoroughly from sin;
  From all my guilt me cleanse:
For my transgressions I confess;
  I ever see my sins.

3 All my iniquities blot out,
  My sin hide from thy view.
Create a clean heart, Lord, in me
  A spirit right renew.

4 And from thy gracious presence, Lord,
  Oh, cast me not away;
Thy Holy Spirit utterly
  Take not from me, I pray.

5 The joy which thy salvation brings
  Again to me restore;
With thy free Spirit, oh, do thou
  Uphold me evermore.

87

PSALM 51. WATTS.
Repentance and Faith in Christ.

O God of mercy! hear my call,
  My load of guilt remove;
Break down this separating wall,
  That bars me from thy love.

2 Give me the presence of thy grace;
  Then my rejoicing tongue
Shall speak aloud thy righteousness,
  And make thy praise my song.

3 No blood of goats, nor heifer slain,
  For sin could e'er atone:
The death of Christ shall still remain
  Sufficient and alone.

4 A soul, oppressed with sin's desert,
  My God will ne'er despise;
An humble groan, a broken heart,
  Is our best sacrifice.

DORMAN. L. M.

1. Show pit - y, Lord! O Lord! for - give; Let a re - pent - ing re - bel live;

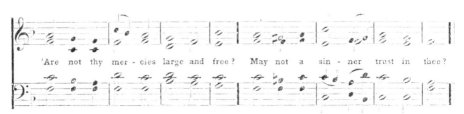

'Are not thy mer - cies large and free? May not a sin - ner trust in thee?

88   PSALM 51   WATTS.
A Penitent pleading for Pardon.

Show pity, Lord! O Lord! forgive;
Let a repenting rebel live;
Are not thy mercies large and free?
May not a sinner trust in thee?

2 Oh, wash my soul from every sin,
And make my guilty conscience clean;
Here on my heart the burden lies,
And past offences pain mine eyes.

3 My lips with shame my sins confess,
Against thy law, against thy grace:
Lord! should thy judgment grow severe,
I am condemned, but thou art clear.

4 Should sudden vengeance seize my breath,
I must pronounce thee just in death;
And, if my soul were sent to hell,
Thy righteous law approves it well.

5 Yet save a trembling sinner, Lord!
Whose hope, still hovering round thy word,
Would light on some sweet promise there,
Some sure support against despair.

89   PSALM 51.   WATTS.
Native and Total Depravity.

Lord! I am vile, conceived in sin,
And born unholy and unclean;
Sprung from the man whose guilty fall
Corrupts the race, and taints us all.

2 Soon as we draw our infant breath,
The seeds of sin grow up for death;
Thy law demands a perfect heart,
But we're defiled in every part.

3 No bleeding bird, nor bleeding beast,
Nor hyssop branch, nor sprinkling priest
Nor running brook, nor flood, nor sea,
Can wash the dismal stain away.

4 Jesus, my God, thy blood alone,
Hath power sufficient to atone;
Thy blood can make me white as snow,
No Jewish types could cleanse me so.

90   PSALM 51.   WATTS.
The backslider penitent and restored.

O thou, that hearest when sinners cry!
Though all my crimes before thee lie,
Behold them not with angry look,
But blot their memory from thy book.

2 A broken heart, my God, my King,
Is all the sacrifice I bring:
The God of grace will ne'er despise
A broken heart for sacrifice.

3 My soul lies humbled in the dust,
And owns thy dreadful sentence just;
Look down, O Lord, with pitying eye,
And save the soul condemned to die.

4 Then will I teach the world thy ways;
Sinners shall learn thy sovereign grace;
I'll lead them to my Saviour's blood,
And they shall praise a pardoning God.

5 Oh, may thy love inspire my tongue!
Salvation shall be all my song;
And all my powers shall join to bless
The Lord, my Strength and Righteousness.

HAVEN. C. M.

1. Why should the might-y make their boast, And heavenly grace de-spise?

In their own arm they put their trust, And fill their mouth with lies.

91
PSALM 52.
The Righteous and the Wicked.   BARLOW.

Why should the mighty make their boast,
  And heavenly grace despise?
In their own arm they put their trust,
  And fill their mouth with lies.

2 Our God in vengeance shall destroy,
  And drive them from his face;
No more shall they his church annoy,
  Nor find on earth a place.

3 But like a cultured olive-grove,
  Dressed in immortal green,
Thy children, blooming in thy love,
  Amid thy courts are seen.

4 On thine eternal grace, O Lord!
  Thy saints shall rest secure,
And all who trust thy holy word,
  Shall find salvation sure.

92
PSALM 53.
The Foes of Zion.   WATTS.

Are all the foes of Zion fools,
  Who thus destroy her saints?
Do they not know her Saviour rules,
  And pities her complaints?

2 In vain the sons of Satan boast
  Of armies in array;
When God on high dismays their host,
  They fall an easy prey.

3 Oh, for a word from Zion's King,
  Her captives to restore!
The joyful saints thy praise shall sing,
  And Israel weep no more.

44

93
PSALM 54.
Victory desired.   ANON.

Behold us, Lord, and let our cry
  Before thy throne ascend;
Cast thou on us a pitying eye,
  And still our lives defend.

2 For impious foes insult us round;
  Oppressive, proud, and vain;
They cast thy temples to the ground,
  And all our rights profane.

3 Yet thy forgiving grace we trust,
  And in thy power rejoice;
Thine arm shall bring our foes to dust,
  Thy praise inspire our voice.

94
PSALM 55.
God, our Refuge.   WATTS.

O God, my refuge! hear my cries,
  Behold my flowing tears;
For earth and hell my hurt devise,
  And triumph in my fears.

2 Oh, were I like a feathered dove,
  Soon would I stretch my wings,
And fly, and make a long remove
  From all these restless things.

3 God shall preserve my soul from fear,
  Or shield me when afraid;
Ten thousand angels must appear
  If he commands their aid.

4 I cast my burdens on the Lord,—
  The Lord sustains them all;
My courage rests upon his word,—
  That saints shall never fall.

WIMBORNE. L. M.

1. God knows the sor-rows of his saints, Their groanings reach his listening ears;

He has a book for their com-plaints. And makes a re-cord of their tears.

95 PSALM 56.   WATTS.
God's care of his people.

God knows the sorrows of his saints,
  Their groanings reach his listening ears;
He has a book for their complaints,
  And makes a record of their tears.

2 When to thy throne I raise my cry,
  The wicked fear thy voice and flee,
So swift is prayer to reach the sky,
  So very near is God to me.

3 In thee, most holy, just, and true,
  I have reposed unfaltering trust;
Nor will I fear what man can do,
  The feeble offspring of the dust.

4 Thy solemn vows are on me, Lord,
  Each day thou shalt receive my praise;
I'll sing, "How faithful is thy word!
  How righteous thou in all thy ways!"

5 Thou hast secured my soul from death;
  My feet from falling, oh, set free,
That heart, and hand, and life, and breath
  May ever be employed for thee.

96 PSALM 57.   WRANGHAM.
Divine Praise.

ETERNAL God, celestial King!
  Exalted be thy glorious name;
Let hosts in heaven thy praises sing,
  And saints on earth thy love proclaim.

2 My heart is fixed on thee, my God!
  I rest my hope on thee alone;
I'll spread thy sacred truths abroad,
  To all mankind thy love make known.

3 Awake, my tongue! awake, my lyre!
  With morning's earliest dawn arise;
Let songs of joy my soul inspire,
  And swell your music to the skies.

4 With those who in thy grace abound,
  To thee I'll raise my thankful voice;
While every land, the earth around,
  Shall hear, and in thy name rejoice.

97 PSALM 57.   WATTS.
Praise for Protection, Grace and Truth.

My God! in whom are all the springs
  Of boundless love and grace unknown,
Hide me beneath thy spreading wings,
  Till the dark cloud be over-blown.

2 Up to the heavens I send my cry,
  The Lord will my desires perform;
He sends his angels from the sky,
  And saves me from the threatening storm.

3 My heart is fixed; my song shall raise
  Immortal honors to thy name;
Awake, my tongue! to sound his praise,—
  My tongue, the glory of my frame.

4 High o'er the earth his mercy reigns,
  And reaches to the utmost sky;
His truth to endless years remains,
  When lower worlds dissolve and die.

5 Be thou exalted, O my God!
  Above the heavens where angels dwell;
Thy power on earth be known abroad,
  And land to land thy wonders tell.

45

FOREST. L. M.

1. Judg-es! who rule the world by laws, Will ye des-pise the righteous cause?

Dare ye condemn the righteous poor, And let rich sin-ners go se-cure?

98
PSALM 58.   WATTS.
Warning to Magistrates.

Judges! who rule the world by laws,
Will ye despise the righteous cause?
Dare ye condemn the righteous poor,
And let rich sinners go secure?

2 Shall gold and greatness bribe your hands
When one oppressed before you stands?
Have ye forgot, or never knew
That God will judge the judges too?

3 Yet ye invade the rights of God:
And send your bold decrees abroad;
High in the heavens his justice reigns,
Yet ye bind conscience in your chains.

4 When once he thunders from the sky,
Your grandeur melts, your titles die;
As empty chaff, when whirlwinds rise,
Your power before the tempest flies.

5 There is a God who rules on high,
A God that hears his children cry;
Thus shall the vengeance of the Lord
Safety and joy to saints afford.

99
PSALM 59.   ALLEN.
"Thou art my Rock."

O thou whose pity reaches those
Whose sorrows meet thy watchful eyes,
Now save me from my wicked foes,
O Lord of hosts, arise, arise!

2 Thou art my rock and my defence;
Thou art a tower unto thy saints;
Thee will I make my confidence,
Thee will I trust, though nature faints.

3 Thy mercies gladly will I sing,
And all thy power and love confess;
For thou hast been, O heavenly King,
My safe resort in each distress.

4 My songs with every morning's light,
O Lord, shall rise up to thy throne;
And all thy saints shall praise thy might,
And thy rich mercy shall make known.

100
PSALM 60.   SPURGEON.
Prayer in Depression.

O God, thou hast cast off thy saints;
Thy face thou dost in anger hide,
And lo, thy church for terror faints,
While breaches all her walls divide!

2 Hard things thou dost upon us lay,
And make us drink most bitter wine;
But still thy banner we display,
And bear aloft thy truth divine.

3 Our courage fails not, though the night
No earthly lamp avails to break,
For thou wilt soon arise in might,
And of our captors captives make.

4 Thy right hand shall thy people aid;
Thy faithful promise makes us strong;
We will Philistia's land invade,
And over Edom chant the song.

5 Through thee we shall most valiant prove,
And tread the foe beneath our feet;
Through thee our faith shall hills remove,
And small as chaff the mountains beat.

DOVER. S. M.

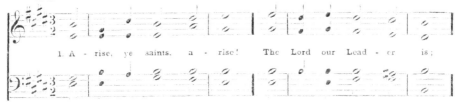

1. A - rise, ye saints, a - rise! The Lord our Lead - er is;

The foe be - fore his ban - ners flies, And vic - to - ry is his.

IOI   PSALM 60.   KELLY.
              The Lord's Banner.

Arise, ye saints, arise!
  The Lord our Leader is;
The foe before his banner flies,
  And victory is his.

2 We follow thee, our Guide,
    Our Saviour, and our King!
  We follow thee, through grace supplied
    From heaven's eternal spring.

4 We soon shall see the day
    When all our toils shall cease;
  When we shall cast our arms away,
    And dwell in endless peace.

4 This hope supports us here;
    It makes our burdens light;
  'T will serve our drooping hearts to cheer,
    Till faith shall end in sight.

5 Till, of the prize possessed,
    We hear of war no more;
  And ever with our Leader rest,
    On yonder peaceful shore.

IO2   PSALM 61.   WATTS.
              Safety in God.

When, overwhelmed with grief,
  My heart within me dies;
Helpless, and far from all relief,
  To heaven I lift mine eyes.

2 Oh, lead me to the rock,
    That's high above my head;
  And make the covert of thy wings
    My shelter and my shade.

3 Within thy presence, Lord!
    For ever I'll abide;
  Thou art the tower of my defence,
    The refuge where I hide.

4 Thou givest me the lot
    Of those that fear thy name;
  If endless life be their reward,
    I shall possess the same.

IO3   PSALM 62.   SCOTCH.
              "My strong Rock is He."

My soul with patience doth
  Depend on God indeed;
My strength and my salvation both
  From him alone proceed.

2 He my salvation is,
    And my strong rock is he;
  He only is my sure defence:
    I shall not movèd be.

3 In God my glory is,
    And my salvation sure;
  In God the rock is of my strength,
    My refuge most secure.

4 God hath it spoken once,
    Yea, this I heard again,
  That power to Almighty God
    Alone doth appertain.

5 Yea, mercy unto thee
    Belongs, O Lord, alone:
  For thou according to his work
    Rewardest every one.

47

LANESBOROUGH. C. M.

1 Ear-ly, my God, with-out de-lay, I haste to seek thy face; My thirst-y spir-it

faints a-way, My thirst-y spir-it faints a-way, With-out thy cheering grace.

PSALM 63.
Morning Worship.   WATTS.

104

EARLY, my God, without delay,
 I haste to seek thy face;
My thirsty spirit faints away,
 Without thy cheering grace.

2 I've seen thy glory and thy power
 Through all thy temple shine;
My God, repeat that heavenly hour,
 That vision so divine.

3 Not life itself, with all its joys,
 Can my best passions move,
Or raise so high my cheerful voice,
 As thy forgiving love.

3 Thus, till my last expiring day,
 I'll bless my God and King;
Thus will I lift my hands to pray,
 And tune my lips to sing.

PSALM 63.
Early Praise.   SCOTCH.

105

LORD, thee, my God, I'll early seek;
 My soul doth thirst for thee;
My flesh longs in a dry, parched land
 Wherein no waters be, ---

2 That I thy power may behold,
 And brightness of thy face,
As I have seen thee heretofore
 Within thy holy place.

3 Since better is thy love than life,
 My lips thee praise shall give,
I in thy name will lift my hands,
 And bless thee while I live:—

4 When I do thee upon my bed
 Remember with delight,
And when on thee I meditate
 In watches of the night.

5 In shadow of thy wings I'll joy,
 For thou mine help hast been,
My soul thee follows hard; and me
 Thy right hand doth sustain.

PSALM 64.
Prayer in Peril.   ANON.

106

HEAR me, O Lord! regard my prayer!
 Foes lurk without, within,
In secret spread the subtle snare
 To lead me into sin.

2 Be thou my shield and hiding-place
 Against their ill design;
Display thy love and covenant grace,
 And show me I am thine.

3 Forgive the sins my heart laments,
 The inward thoughts of wrong;
The listless hours of ease misspent,
 And make thy grace my song.

4 So shall the saints record the hour
 When thou didst bend thine ear,
And manifest thy promised power
 To scatter every fear.

5 In God the righteous shall be glad,
 In him shall put their trust;
While foes shall at their feet be laid
 And humbled in the dust.

HENRY.   C. M.

1. Praise waits in Zi - on, Lord! for thee; There shall our vows be paid;

Thou hast an ear when sin - ners pray; All flesh shall seek thine aid.

107 PSALM 65. WATTS.
Worship of God in his Temple.

PRAISE waits in Zion, Lord! for thee;
  There shall our vows be paid;
Thou hast an ear when sinners pray;
  All flesh shall seek thine aid.

2 O Lord! our guilt and fears prevail,
  But pardoning grace is thine;
And thou wilt grant us power and skill,
  To conquer every sin.

3 Blest are the men, whom thou wilt choose
  To bring them near thy face;
Give them a dwelling in thy house,
  To feast upon thy grace.

4 In answering what thy church requests,
  Thy truth and terror shine;
And works of dreadful righteousness
  Fulfill thy kind design.

5 Thus shall the wondering nations see,
  The Lord is good and just;
The distant isles shall fly to thee,
  And make thy name their trust.

108 PSALM 65. SCOTCH.
Praise in Zion.

PRAISE waits for thee in Zion, Lord,
  To thee vows paid shall be.
O thou, that hearer art of prayer,
  All flesh shall come to thee.

2 The man is blest whom thou dost choose,
  And make approach to thee,
That he within thy courts, O Lord,
  May still a dweller be.

3 We surely shall be satisfied
  With thy abundant grace,
And with the goodness of thy house,
  Ev'n of thy holy place.

4 By fearful works and terrible,
  Thou in thy righteousness,
O God our Saviour, to our prayers
  Thy answer dost express.

5 And so all ends of earth shall place
  Their confidence in thee,
Ev'n those who dwell in distant lands,
  And far off on the sea.

109 PSALM 65. WATTS.
Goodness of God in the Seasons.

T' is by thy strength the mountains stand,
  God of eternal power!
The sea grows calm at thy command,
  And tempests cease to roar.

2 Thy morning light and evening shade
  Successive comforts bring;
Thy plenteous fruits make harvest glad,
  Thy flowers adorn the spring.

3 Seasons and times, and moons and hours,
  Heaven, earth, and air are thine;
When clouds distill in fruitful showers,
  The author is divine.

4 The thirsty ridges drink their fill,
  And ranks of corn appear;
Thy ways abound with blessings still,
  Thy goodness crowns the year.

MERTON. C. M.

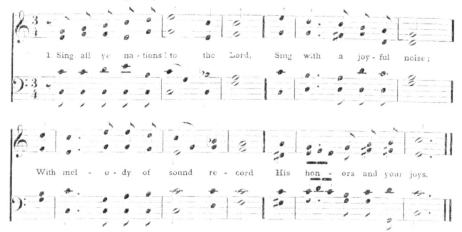

1. Sing all ye na-tions! to the Lord, Sing with a joy-ful noise;

With mel - o - dy of sound re - cord His hon - ors and your joys.

110   **PSALM 66.**   WATTS.
The God of Providence.

Sing, all ye nations! to the Lord,
Sing with a joyful noise;
With melody of sound record
His honors and your joys.

2 Say to the Power that shakes the sky,—
"How terrible art thou!
Sinners before thy presence fly,
Or at thy feet they bow."

3 He made the ebbing channel dry,
While Israel passed the flood;
There did the church begin their joy,
And triumph in their God.

4 Through watery deeps and fiery ways,
We march at thy command,
Led to possess the promised place,
By thine unerring hand.

5 Oh, bless our God, and never cease;
Ye saints! fulfill his praise;
He keeps our life, maintains our peace,
And guides our doubtful ways.

111   **PSALM 66.**   WATTS.
Praise to God for hearing Prayer.

Now shall my solemn vows be paid
To that almighty Power,
Who heard the long requests I made,
In my distressful hour.

2 My lips and cheerful heart prepare
To make his mercies known;
Come, ye who fear my God! and hear
The wonders he has done.

3 When on my head huge sorrows fell,
I sought his heavenly aid;
He saved my sinking soul from hell,
And death's eternal shade.

4 Had sin lain covered in my heart
While prayer employed my tongue,
The Lord had shown me no regard,
Nor I his praises sung.

5 But God—his name be ever blessed—
Hath set my spirit free,
Nor turned from him my poor request,
Nor turned his heart from me.

112   **PSALM 67.**   WATTS.
Enlargement of the Church.

Shine, mighty God, on Zion shine
With beams of heavenly grace;
Reveal thy power through all our coasts,
And show thy smiling face.

2 When shall thy name from shore to shore
Sound all the earth abroad;
And distant nations know and love
Their Saviour and their God?

3 Earth shall obey his high command,
And yield a full increase;
Our God will crown his chosen land
With fruitfulness and peace.

4 God the Redeemer scatters round
His choicest favors here,
While the creation's utmost bound
Shall see, adore, and fear.

50

HAMBURG. L. M.

1. Kingdoms and thrones to God be - long; Crown him, ye na - tions, in your song:

His wondrous names and pow'rs re - hearse; His hon-ors shall en - rich your verse.

113   PSALM 68.   WATTS.
          God's Majesty.

KINGDOMS and thrones to God belong;
Crown him, ye nations, in your song:
His wondrous names and powers rehearse;
His honors shall enrich your verse.

2 He shakes the heavens with loud alarms;
How terrible is God in arms!
In Israel are his mercies known,
Israel is his peculiar throne.

3 Proclaim him king, pronounce him blest;
He's your defence, your joy, your rest;
When terrors rise and nations faint,
God is the strength of every saint.

114   PSALM 68.   WATTS.
          Christ's Ascension.

LORD, when thou didst ascend on high,
Ten thousand angels filled the sky:
Those heavenly guards around thee wait,
Like chariots that attend thy state.

2 Not Sinai's mountain could appear
More glorious when the Lord was there;
While he pronounced his dreadful law,
And struck the chosen tribes with awe.

3 How bright the triumph none can tell,
When the rebellious powers of hell,
That thousand souls had captive made,
Were all in chains, like captives, led.

4 Raised by his Father to the throne,
He sent the promised Spirit down,
With gifts and grace for rebel men,
That God might dwell on earth again.

115   PSALM 69.   WATTS
          Pardon through the Sufferings of Christ.

DEEP in our hearts let us record
The deeper sorrows of our Lord;
Behold the rising billows roll,
To overwhelm his holy soul.

2 Yet, gracious God, thy power and love
Have made the curse a blessing prove;
Those dreadful sufferings of thy Son
Atoned for crimes which we had done.

3 Oh, for his sake our guilt forgive,
And let the mourning sinner live;—
The Lord will hear us in his name,
Nor shall our hope be turned to shame.

116   PSALM 70   DWIGHT.
          Prayer for Christ's Coming.

O THOU whose hand the kingdom sways,
Whom earth, and hell, and heaven obeys;
To help thy chosen sons appear,
And show thy power and glory near.

2 Oh, haste, with every gift inspired,
With glory, truth, and grace attired;
Thou Star of heaven's eternal morn,
Thou Sun whom beams divine adorn!

3 Saints shall be glad before thy face,
And grow in love, and truth, and grace;
Thy church shall blossom in thy sight,
And yield her fruits of pure delight.

4 Oh, hither, then, thy footsteps bend!
Swift as a roe, from hills descend;
Mild as the Sabbath's cheerful ray,
Till life unfolds eternal day.

51

HUMMEL. C. M.

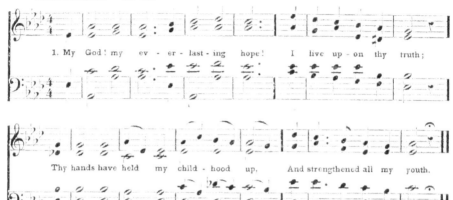

1. My God! my ev-er-last-ing hope! I live up-on thy truth;

Thy hands have held my child-hood up, And strengthened all my youth.

117 PSALM 71. WATTS.
The aged Saint's Reflection and Hope.

My God! my everlasting hope!
  I live upon thy truth;
Thy hands have held my childhood up,
  And strengthened all my youth.

2 Still has my life new wonders seen,
    Repeated every year;
  Behold my days that yet remain,
    I trust them to thy care.

3 Cast me not off when strength declines,
    When hoary hairs arise;
  And round me let thy glories shine,
    Whene'er thy servant dies.

4 Then, in the history of my age,
    When men review my days,
  They'll read thy love in every page,
    In every line—thy praise.

118 PSALM 71. WATTS.
Praise to the Saviour.

My Saviour! my almighty Friend;
  When I begin thy praise,
Where will the growing numbers end,—
  The numbers of thy grace?

2 Thou art my everlasting trust;
    Thy goodness I adore;
  And, since I knew thy graces first,
    I speak thy glories more.

3 My feet shall travel all the length
    Of the celestial road;
  And march, with courage, in thy strength,
    To see my Father God.

4 When I am filled with sore distress
    For some surprising sin,
  I'll plead thy perfect righteousness,
    And mention none but thine.

5 How will my lips rejoice to tell
    The victories of my King!
  My soul, redeemed from sin and hell,
    Shall thy salvation sing.

119 PSALM 72. SCOTCH.
The Church's Increase.

O Lord, thy judgments give the King,
  His Son thy righteousness,
With right he shall thy people judge,
  Thy poor with uprightness.

2 Of corn an handful in the earth
    On tops of mountains high,
  With prosperous fruit shall shake like trees
    On Lebanon that be.

3 His name for ever shall endure;
    Last like the sun it shall:
  Men shall be blessed in him, and blest
    All nations shall him call.

4 Now blesséd be the Lord our God,
    The God of Israel,
  For he alone doth wondrous works,
    In glory that excel.

5 And blesséd be his glorious name
    To all eternity:
  The whole earth let his glory fill,
    Amen, so let it be!

52

WEBB.　7, 6. D.

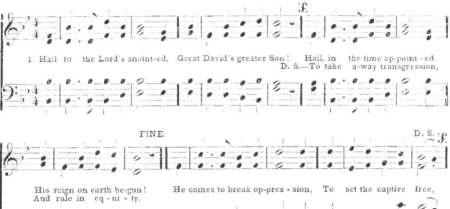

1. Hail to the Lord's anoint-ed, Great David's greater Son!　Hail, in the time ap-point - ed,
D. S.—To take　a-way transgression,

FINE.　　　　　　　　　　　　　　　　　　　　　　　　　　　　D. S.

His reign on earth be-gun!　　He comes to break op-pres - sion, To　set the captive　free,
And rule in　eq - ui - ty.

120　　PSALM 72.　MONTGOMERY.
The Blessings of Christ's Kingdom.

Hail to the Lord's anointed,
　Great David's greater Son!
Hail, in the time appointed,
　His reign on earth begun!
He comes to break oppression,
　To set the captive free,
To take away transgression,
　And rule in equity.

2 He comes, with succor speedy,
　To those who suffer wrong;
To help the poor and needy,
　And bid the weak be strong;
To give them songs for sighing,
　Their darkness turn to light,
Whose souls, condemned and dying,
　Were precious in his sight.

3 He shall come down like showers
　Upon the fruitful earth,
And love, and joy, like flowers,
　Spring in his path to birth:.
Before him, on the mountains,
　Shall peace the herald go,
And righteousness in fountains
　From hill to valley flow.

4 Arabia's desert-ranger
　To him shall bow the knee;
The Ethiopian stranger
　His glory come to see:

With offerings of devotion,
　Ships from the isles shall meet,
To pour the wealth of ocean
　In tribute at his feet.

5 Kings shall fall down before him,
　And gold and incense bring;
All nations shall adore him;
　His praise all people sing;
For he shall have dominion
　O'er river, sea, and shore,
Far as the eagle's pinion
　Or dove's light wing can soar.

6 For him shall prayer unceasing
　And daily vows ascend;
His kingdom still increasing,
　A kingdom without end.
The heavenly dew shall nourish
　A seed in weakness sown,
Whose fruit shall spread and flourish,
　And shake like Lebanon.

7 O'er every foe victorious,
　He on his throne shall rest;
From age to age more glorious,
　All-blessing and all-blessed.
The tide of time shall never
　His covenant remove;
His name shall stand for ever;
　His great, best name of Love!

53

MISSIONARY CHANT. L. M.

1. Je - sus shall reign wher - e'er the sun   Does his suc-cess-ive jour - neys run;

His kingdom stretch from shore to shore,   Till moons shall wax and wane no more.

121   **PSALM 72.**   WATTS.
Christ's Kingdom among the Gentiles.

Jesus shall reign where'er the sun
Does his successive journeys run;
His kingdom stretch from shore to shore,
Till moons shall wax and wane no more.

2 For him shall endless prayer be made,
And endless praises crown his head;
His name, like sweet perfume, shall rise
With every morning-sacrifice.

3 People and realms of every tongue
Dwell on his love, with sweetest song;
And infant voices shall proclaim
Their early blessings on his name.

4 Blessings abound where'er he reigns;
The prisoner leaps to lose his chains;
The weary find eternal rest,
And all the sons of want are blest.

5 Let every creature rise and bring
Peculiar honors to our King;
Angels descend with songs again,
And earth repeat the loud Amen!

122   **PSALM 72.**   WATTS.
The Kingdom of Christ

Great God! whose universal sway
The known and unknown worlds obey,
Now give the kingdom to thy Son;
Extend his power, exalt his throne.

2 As rain on meadows newly mown,
So shall he send his influence down;
His grace, on fainting souls, distills
Like heavenly dew, on thirsty hills.

3 The heathen lands, that lie beneath
The shades of overspreading death,
Revive at his first dawning light;
And deserts blossom at the sight.

4 The saints shall flourish in his days,
Dressed in the robes of joy and praise;
Peace, like a river, from his throne,
Shall flow to nations yet unknown.

123   **PSALM 72**   SCOTCH.
The Church's Growth.

O God, thy judgments give the king,
His royal Son, thy righteousness!
He to thy people right shall bring,
With judgment shall thy poor redress.

2 On hill-tops sown a little corn
Like Lebanon with fruit shall bend;
New life the city shall adorn;
She shall like grass grow and extend.

3 Long as the sun his name shall last,
It shall endure through ages all;
And men shall still in him be blest,
Blest all the nations shall him call.

4 Now blessed be the mighty One,
Jehovah, God of Israel,
For he alone hath wonders done,
And deeds in glory that excel.

5 And blessèd be his glorious name,
Long as the ages shall endure,
O'er all the earth extend his fame:
Amen, amen, for evermore!

54

INVITATION.　C. M.

1. God, my sup - port - er, and my hope, My help for ev - er near,

Thine arm of mer - cy held me up, When sink - ing in des - pair.

124　PSALM 73.　　　　WATTS.
God the Portion of the Soul.

God, my supporter, and my hope,
　My help for ever near,
Thine arm of mercy held me up,
　When sinking in despair.

2 Thy counsels, Lord, shall guide my feet,
　Through this dark wilderness;
Thine hand conduct me near thy seat,
　To dwell before thy face.

3 Were I in heaven, without my God,
　'T would be no joy to me;
And while the earth is my abode,
　I long for none but thee.

4 What if the springs of life were broke,
　And flesh and heart should faint,
Thou art my soul's eternal rock,
　The strength of every saint.

5 Then to draw near to thee, my God,
　Shall be my sweet employ;
My tongue shall sound thy works abroad,
　And tell the world my joy.

125　PSALM 73.　　　　SCOTCH.
Fainting for God.

Oh, whom have I in heavens high
　But thee, O Lord, alone?
And in the earth whom I desire
　Besides thee there is none.

2 My flesh and heart do faint and fail,
　But God my heart sustains;
The strength and portion of my heart
　He evermore remains.

3 But surely it is good for me
　That I draw near to God:
In God I trust, that all thy works
　I may declare abroad.

4 With thy good counsel while I live
　Thou wilt me safely guide;
And into glory afterward
　Receive me to abide.

126　PSALM 74.　　　　WATTS.
The Church in Affliction.

Will God for ever cast us off?
　His wrath for ever smoke
Against the people of his love,—
　His little chosen flock?

2 Think of the tribes, so dearly bought
　With their Redeemer's blood;
Nor let thy Zion be forgot,
　Where once thy glory stood.

3 Oh, come to our relief in haste;
　Aloud our ruin calls;
See, what a wide and fearful waste
　Is made within thy walls.

4 And still, to heighten our distress,
　Thy presence is withdrawn;
Thy wonted signs of power and grace—
　Thy power and grace are gone.

5 No prophet speaks to calm our grief,
　But all in silence mourn;
Nor know the times of our relief,—
　The hour of thy return.

DEVIZES.　C. M.

1. To thee, most high and ho - ly God, To thee our hearts we raise; Thy works de -

clare thy name a - broad, Thy works de - mand our praise, Thy works de-mand our praise.

127　　**PSALM 75.**　　ANON.
Deliverance Acknowledged.

To THEE, most high and holy God,
　To thee our hearts we raise;
Thy works declare thy name abroad,
　Thy works demand our praise.

2 Our fathers once, thy favored sons,
　　Beheld their foes arise;
And sore oppressed by earthly thrones,
　　They sought help from the skies.

3 'Twas then arose, with equal power,
　　Thy vengeance and thy grace,
To scourge invaders from the shore,
　　And save thy chosen race.

4 Now let oppressors sink their pride,
　　Nor lift so high their rod,
But lay their impious thoughts aside,
　　And own the sovereign God.

128　　**PSALM 76.**　　WATTS.
God's Destruction of his ancient Foes.

In Judah, God of old was known;
　His name in Israel great;
In Salem stood his holy throne,
　And Zion was his seat.

2 Among the praises of his saints,
　　His dwelling there he chose;
There he received their just complaints
　　Against their haughty foes.

3 At thy rebuke, O Jacob's God!
　　What haughty monarchs fell;
Who knows the terrors of thy rod?
　　Thy vengeance who can tell?

4 What power can stand before thy sight,
　　When once thy wrath appears?
When heaven shines round with dreadful light,
　　The earth lies still and fears.

5 When God, in his own sovereign ways,
　　Comes down to save the oppressed,
The wrath of man shall work his praise,
　　And he'll restrain the rest.

129　　**PSALM 77.**　　SCOTCH.
The Exodus.

O GOD, most holy is thy way
　In thy divine abode;
Who is so great a god of might
　As our almighty God?

2 Thou art the God of wondrous deeds
　　Performed by thy right hand;
Thou hast declared thy strength among
　　The tribes of every land.

3 The clouds poured out abundant rain,
　　Loud sounds filled all the sky;
Yea, here and there on every side
　　Thy arrows swift did fly.

4 Thy paths were in the waters great,
　　Thy way was in the sea,
Thy footsteps 'mid the deep sea waves
　　Were only known to thee.

5 And like a flock of sheep thou didst
　　Thy people safely guide
By Moses' and by Aaron's hand
　　Through all the desert wide.

56

EWING. 7, 6. D.

1. In time of trib - u - la - tion, Hear, Lord! my fee - ble cries; With humble sup - pli -

ca - tion To thee my spir - it flies: My heart with grief is break - ing; Scarce

can my voice com-plain: Mine eyes, with tears keep wak- ing, Still watch and weep in vain.

PSALM 77. MONTGOMERY.

I30 *Faith prevailing over despondency.*

In time of tribulation,
  Hear, Lord! my feeble cries;
With humble supplication
  To thee my spirit flies:
My heart with grief is breaking;
  Scarce can my voice complain:
Mine eyes, with tears kept waking,
  Still watch and weep in vain.

2 The days of old, in vision,
  Bring vanished bliss to view:
The years of lost fruition
  Their joys in pangs renew:
Remembered songs of gladness,
  Through night's lone silence brought,
Strike notes of deeper sadness,
  And stir desponding thought.

3 Hath God cast off for ever?
  Can time his truth impair?
His tender mercy, never
  Shall I presume to share?
Hath he his loving-kindness
  Shut up in endless wrath?
No: this is mine own blindness,
  That cannot see his path.

4 I call to recollection
  The years of his right hand;
And, strong in his protection,
  Again through faith I stand.
Thy deeds, O Lord, are wonder,
  Holy are all thy ways;
The secret place of thunder
  Shall utter forth thy praise.

5 Thee, with the tribes assembled,
  O God, the billows saw;
They saw thee, and they trembled,
  Turned, and stood still with awe:
The clouds shot hail,—they lightened;
  The earth reeled to and fro;
The fiery pillar brightened
  The gulf of gloom below.

6 Thy way is in great waters:
  Thy footsteps are not known:
Let Adam's sons and daughters
  Confide in thee alone.
Through the wild sea thou leddest
  Thy chosen flock of yore;
Still on the waves thou treadest,
  And thy redeemed pass o'er.

MALVERN. L. M.

1. Great God, how oft did Is - rael prove By turns thine an - ger and thy love!

There in a glass our hearts may see How fic - kle and how false they be.

131   **PSALM 78.**   WATTS.
The old Story of Grace.

GREAT God, how oft did Israel prove
By turns thine anger and thy love!
There in a glass our hearts may see
How fickle and how false they be.

2 The Lord consumed their years in pain,
And made their travels long and vain;
A tedious march through unknown ways,
Wore out their strength, and spent their days.

3 Oft, when they saw their brethren slain,
They mourned, and sought the Lord again;
Called him the Rock of their abode,
Their high Redeemer, and their God.

4 Yet could his sovereign grace forgive
The men who ne'er deserved to live;
His anger oft away he turned,
Or else with gentle flame it burned.

5 He saw their flesh was weak and frail,
He saw temptations still prevail;
The God of Abraham loved them still,
And led them to his holy hill.

132   **PSALM 79.**   BARLOW.
Prayer in Peril.

BEHOLD, O God, what cruel foes,
Thy peaceful heritage invade;
Thy holy temple stands defiled,
In dust thy sacred walls are laid.

2 Deep from the prison's horrid glooms,
Oh, hear the mourning captive sigh,
And let thy sovereign power reprieve
The trembling souls condemned to die.

58

3 Let those who dared insult thy reign,
Return dismayed, with endless shame,
While heathen, who thy grace despise,
Shall from thy justice learn thy name.

4 So shall thy children, freed from death,
Eternal songs of honor raise,
And every future age shall tell
Thy sovereign power and pardoning grace.

133   **PSALM 80.**   WATTS.
Prayer in Declension.

GREAT Shepherd of thine Israel!
Who didst between the cherubs dwell,
And lead the tribes, thy chosen sheep,
Safe through the desert and the deep;—

2 Thy Church is in the desert now;
Shine from on high and guide us through;
Turn us to thee, thy love restore;
We shall be saved, and sigh no more.

3 Hast thou not planted, with thy hand,
A lovely vine in this our land?
Did not thy power defend it round,
And heavenly dews enrich the ground?

4 How did the spreading branches shoot,
And bless the nations with the fruit!
But now, O Lord! look down and see
Thy mourning vine, that lovely tree.

5 Return, almighty God! return,
Nor let thy bleeding vineyard mourn:
Turn us to thee, thy love restore;
We shall be saved, and sigh no more.

MORNINGTON S. M.

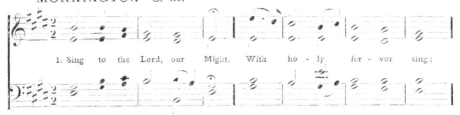

1. Sing to the Lord, our Might, With ho-ly fer-vor sing;

Let hearts and in - stru-ments u - nite To praise our heavenly King.

134   PSALM 81.   *Worship ordained of old.*   LYTE.

Sing to the Lord, our Might,
  With holy fervor sing;
Let hearts and instruments unite
  To praise our heavenly King.

2 This is his holy house;
  And this his festal day,
When he accepts the humblest vows,
  That we sincerely pay.

3 The Sabbath to our sires
  In mercy first was given;
The Church her Sabbaths still requires
  To speed her on to heaven.

4 We still, like them of old,
  Are in the wilderness;
And God is still as near his fold,
  To pity and to bless.

5 Then let us open wide
  Our hearts for him to fill;
And he, that Israel then supplied,
  Will help his Israel still.

135   PSALM 82.   *" The Judge of all the Earth."*   SCOTCH.

Among the men of might,
  The mighty God doth stand:
He stands to order judgment right
  To judges of the land.

2 " How long with wrongful aid,
  The oppressor's cause protect?
How long, by gift and favor swayed,
  The wicked man respect?"

3 They will not understand;
  In darkness on they go:
Quake all the pillars of the land;
  They totter to and fro.

4 O God, assert thy might,
  Pronounce thy just decree;
The heritage of earth by right
  Belongs, O Lord, to thee.

136   PSALM 83.   *" Thy hidden ones."*   WATTS.

And will the God of grace
  Perpetual silence keep?
The God of justice hold his peace,
  And let his vengeance sleep? '

2 Behold what cruel snares
  The men of mischief spread;
The men that hate thy saints and thee,
  Lift up their threatening head.

3 Against thy hidden ones,
  Their counsels they employ;
And malice, with her watchful eye,
  Pursues them to destroy.

4 Awake, almighty God,
  And call thy power to mind;
Make them to bow before thy will,
  And let them pardon find.

5 Then shall the nations know
  Thy glorious, dreadful word;
Jehovah is thy name alone,
  And thou the sovereign Lord.

59

CHURCH. C. M.

1. My soul, how love-ly is the place, To which thy God re-sorts!

'Tis heaven to see his smil-ing face, Though in his earth-ly courts.

137   PSALM 84.   WATTS.
"How lovely is the place."

My soul, how lovely is the place,
  To which thy God resorts!
'Tis heaven to see his smiling face,
  Though in his earthly courts.

2 There the great Monarch of the skies
  His saving power displays;
And light breaks in upon our eyes,
  With kind and quickening rays.

3 With his rich gifts, the heavenly Dove
  Descends and fills the place;
While Christ reveals his wondrous love,
  And sheds abroad his grace.

4 There, mighty God, thy words declare
  The secrets of thy will;
And still we seek thy mercy there,
  And sing thy praises still.

138   PSALM 84.   SCOTCH.
God's House.

How lovely is thy dwelling-place,
  O Lord of hosts, to me!
The tabernacles of thy grace
  How pleasant, Lord they be!

2 My thirsty soul longs veh'mently,
  Yea faints, thy courts to see:
My very heart and flesh cry out,
  O living God, for thee.

3 Lord God of hosts, hear thou my prayer;
  O Jacob's God, give ear:
See, God, our shield; look on the face
  Of thy Anointed dear.

4 For in thy courts one day excels
  A thousand; rather in
My God's house will I keep a door,
  Than dwell in tents of sin.

5 For God the Lord's a sun and shield:
  He'll grace and glory give;
And no good thing will he withhold
  From them that justly live.

6 O thou that art the Lord of hosts!
  That man is truly blest,
Who with unshaken confidence
  On thee alone doth rest.

139   PSALM 84.   MILTON.
Delight in Worship.

How lovely are thy dwellings fair,
  O Lord of hosts! how dear
The pleasant tabernacles are,
  Where thou dost dwell so near!

2 My soul doth long and almost die
  Thy courts, O Lord! to see;
My heart and flesh aloud do cry,
  O living God! for thee.

3 Happy, who in thy house reside,
  Where thee they ever praise;
Happy, whose strength in thee doth bide,
  And in their hearts thy ways.

4 They journey on from strength to strength,
  With joy and gladsome cheer,
Till all before our God at length
  In Zion do appear.

MESSIAH. 7. D.

1. Pleasant are thy courts above, In the land of light and love; Pleasant are thy courts below,

In this land of sin and woe. Oh, my spir-it longs and faints For the converse

of thy saints, For the brightness of thy face, For thy full-ness, God of grace!

140 PSALM 84. LYTE.
"Thine Altars, my God."

PLEASANT are thy courts above,
In the land of light and love;
Pleasant are thy courts below,
In this land of sin and woe.
Oh, my spirit longs and faints
For the converse of thy saints,
For the brightness of thy face,
For thy fullness, God of grace!

2 Happy birds that sing and fly
Round thy altars, O Most High!
Happier souls that find a rest
In their Heavenly Father's breast!
Like the wandering dove that found
No repose on earth around,
They can to their ark repair,
And enjoy it ever there.

3 Happy souls! their praises flow,
Even in this vale of woe;
Waters in the desert rise,
Manna feeds them from the skies:
On they go from strength to strength,
Till they reach thy throne at length;
At thy feet adoring fall,
Who hast led them safe through all.

4 Lord, be mine this prize to win,
Guide me through this world of sin;
Keep me by thy saving grace,
Give me at thy side a place;
Sun and Shield alike thou art,
Guide and guard my erring heart;
Grace and glory flow from thee,
Shed, oh, shed them, Lord, on me.

141 PSALM 84. TURNER.
Delights of public Worship.

LORD of Hosts, how lovely fair,
Ev'n on earth thy temples are;
Here thy waiting people see
Much of heaven, and much of thee.

2 From thy gracious presence flows
Bliss that softens all our woes;
While thy Spirit's holy fire
Warms our hearts with pure desire.

3 Here we supplicate thy throne,
Here thou makest thy glories known;
Here we learn thy righteous ways,
Taste thy love and sing thy praise.

4 Thus with sacred songs of joy,
We our happy lives employ;
Love, and long to love thee more,
Till from earth to heaven we soar.

ZEBULON. H. M.

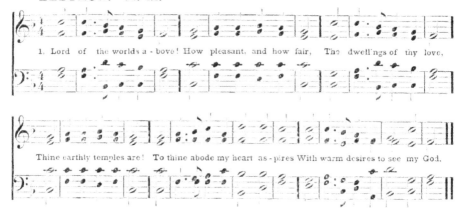

1. Lord of the worlds a - bove! How pleasant, and how fair, The dwell'ngs of thy love,

Thine earthly temples are! To thine abode my heart as - pires With warm desires to see my God.

142 PSALM 84. WATTS.
Divine Worship.

Lord of the worlds above!
　How pleasant, and how fair,
The dwellings of thy love,
　Thine earthly temples are!
To thine abode my heart aspires,
With warm desires to see my God.

2 Oh, happy souls who pray,
　Where God appoints to hear!
Oh, happy men who pay
　Their constant service there!
They praise thee still; and happy they,
Who love the way to Zion's hill.

3 They go from strength to strength,
　Through this dark vale of tears,
Till each arrives at length,
　Till each in heaven appears;
Oh, glorious seat, when God, our King,
Shall thither bring our willing feet!

143 PSALM 84. WATTS.
Joy in God's House.

To spend one sacred day,
　Where God and saints abide,
Affords diviner joy,
　Than thousand days beside;
Where God resorts, I love it more
To keep the door, than shine in courts.

2 God is our sun and shield,
　Our light and our defence;
With gifts his hands are filled,
　We draw our blessings thence;
He shall bestow, on Jacob's race,
Peculiar grace and glory too.

62

3 The Lord his people loves;
　His hand no good withholds
From those his heart approves,
　From pure and pious souls;
Thrice happy he, O God of hosts!
Whose spirit trusts alone in thee.

144 PSALM 84. MONTGOMERY.
Longing for God's House.

How lovely and how fair,
　O Lord of hosts! to me
Thy tabernacles are!
　My flesh cries out for thee;
My heart and soul, with heaven-ward fire,
To thee, the living God, aspire.

2 Lord God of hosts! give ear,
　A gracious answer yield;
O God of Jacob! hear:
　Behold! O God, our shield!
Look on thine own anointed One,
And save through thy beloved Son.

3 Lord! I would rather stand
　A keeper at thy gate,
Than at the king's right hand,
　In tents of worldly state;
One day within thy courts—one day
Is worth a thousand cast away.

4 God is a sun of light,
　Glory and grace to shed;
God is a shield of might,
　To guard the faithful head;
O Lord of hosts! how happy he,—
The man who puts his trust in thee.

ROLLAND. L. M.

1. How pleasant, how di - vine-ly fair, O Lord of hosts! thy dwellings are! With long desire my spir-it faints, To meet th' assemblies of thy saints, To meet th' assemblies of thy saints.

145 PSALM 84. WATTS.
The Pleasures of public Worship.

How pleasant, how divinely fair,
O Lord of hosts! thy dwellings are!
With long desire my spirit faints,
To meet the assemblies of thy saints.

2 My flesh would rest in thine abode,
My panting heart cries out for God;
My God! my King! why should I be
So far from all my joys, and thee?

3 Blest are the saints who sit on high,
Around thy throne of majesty;
Thy brightest glories shine above,
And all their work is praise and love.

4 Blest are the souls, who find a place
Within the temple of thy grace;
There they behold thy gentler rays,
And seek thy face, and learn thy praise.

5 Cheerful they walk with growing strength,
Till all shall meet in heaven at length;
Till all before thy face appear,
And join in nobler worship there.

146 PSALM 84. WATTS.
Divine Worship.

GREAT God! attend, while Zion sings
The joy that from thy presence springs;
To spend one day with thee on earth
Exceeds a thousand days of mirth.

2 Might I enjoy the meanest place
Within thy house, O God of grace!
Not tents of ease, nor thrones of power,
Should tempt my feet to leave thy door.

3 God is our sun, he makes our day;
God is our shield, he guards our way
From all the assaults of hell and sin,
From foes without, and foes within.

4 All needful grace will God bestow,
And crown that grace with glory, too;
He gives us all things, and withholds
No real good from upright souls.

5 O God, our King, whose sovereign sway
The glorious hosts of heaven obey,
Display thy grace, exert thy power,
Till all on earth thy name adore!

147 PSALM 85. WATTS.
Salvation by Christ.

SALVATION is for ever nigh
The souls that fear and trust the Lord;
And grace, descending from on high,
Fresh hopes of glory shall afford.

2 Mercy and truth on earth are met,
Since Christ, the Lord, came down from
By his obedience so complete [heaven;
Justice is pleased, and peace is given.

3 Now truth and honor shall abound,
Religion dwell on earth again,
And heavenly influence bless the ground
In our Redeemer's gentle reign.

4 His righteousness is gone before,
To give us free access to God;
Our wandering feet shall stray no more,
But mark his steps and keep the road

63

AMES. L. M.

1. Thy listening ear, O Lord, in - cline: Hear me, my God, dis-tressed and weak!

Pre-serve my soul, for I am thine; Oh, save me, for thine aid I seek!

148   **PSALM 86.**   MANT.
Prayer in Trouble.

Thy listening ear, O Lord, incline:
  Hear me, my God, distressed and weak!
Preserve my soul, for I am thine;
  Oh, save me, for thine aid I seek!

2 To thee ascend my daily cries:
  Hear, Lord, in mercy hear my voice!
To thee my soul for comfort flies,
  Oh, bid thy servant's soul rejoice.

3 'Tis thine in goodness to abound;
  'Tis thine to pity and forgive;
'Tis thine to heal the bleeding wound,
  And grant the plaintive soul to live.

4 Hear, O Jehovah, when I pray!
  Attend my voice, my suppliant cry!
I call thee in affliction's day,
  For thou wilt listen, thou reply.

5 And thee my heart shall still extol,
  Thy goodness chant, thy praises tell:
For large thy love; and thou my soul
  Hast rescued from the lowest hell.

149   **PSALM 87.**   WATTS.
The Birth-Place of the Saints.

God, in his earthly temple, lays
Foundation for his heavenly praise;
He likes the tents of Jacob well;
But still in Zion loves to dwell.

2 His mercy visits every house,
That pay their night and morning vows,
But makes a more delightful stay,
Where churches meet to praise and pray.

3 What glories were described of old!
What wonders are of Zion told!
Thou city of our God below!
Thy fame shall Tyre and Egypt know.

4 Egypt and Tyre, and Greek and Jew,
Shall there begin their lives anew;
Angels and men shall join to sing
The hill where living waters spring.

5 When God makes up his last account
Of natives in his holy mount,
'Twill be an honor to appear,
As one new-born, or nourished there.

150   **PSALM 88.**   DWIGHT.
The Resurrection.

Shall man, O God of life and light!
  For ever moulder in the grave?
Canst thou forget thy glorious work,
  Thy promise, and thy power to save?

2 Cease, cease, ye vain, desponding fears!
  When Christ, our Lord, from darkness sprang,
Death, the last foe, was captive led,
  And heaven with praise and wonder rang.

3 Faith sees the bright eternal doors
  Unfold to make her children way;
They shall be clothed with endless life,
  And shine in everlasting day.

4 The trump shall sound, the dead shall wake,
  From the cold tomb the slumbers spring;
Thro' heaven, with joy, their myriads rise
  And hail their Saviour and their King!

YORK. C. M.

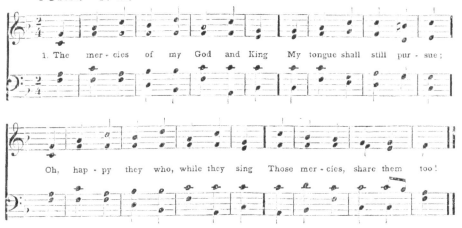

1. The mer-cies of my God and King My tongue shall still pur-sue;

Oh, hap-py they who, while they sing Those mer-cies, share them too!

151 PSALM 89.   LYTE.
God's Mercies.

THE mercies of my God and King
  My tongue shall still pursue:
Oh, happy they who, while they sing
  Those mercies, share them too!

2 As bright and lasting as the sun,
  As lofty as the sky,
From age to age, thy word shall run,
  And chance and change defy.

3 The covenant of the King of kings
  Shall stand for ever sure;
Beneath the shadow of thy wings
  Thy saints repose secure.

4 Thine is the earth, and thine the skies,
  Created at thy will;
The waves at thy command arise,
  At thy command are still.

5 In earth below, in heaven above,
  Who, who is Lord like thee?
Oh, spread the gospel of thy love,
  Till all thy glories see!

152 PSALM 90.   WATTS.
"Our God in ages past."

O GOD, our help in ages past,
  Our hope for years to come,
Our shelter from the stormy blast,
  And our eternal home!

2 Before the hills in order stood,
  Or earth received her frame,
From everlasting thou art God,
  To endless years the same.

3 Time, like an ever-rolling stream,
  Bears all its sons away;
They fly forgotten, as a dream
  Dies at the opening day.

4 Our God, our help in ages past,
  Our hope for years to come,
Be thou our guard while troubles last,
  And our eternal home.

153 PSALM 90.   SCOTCH.
"So number our days."

LORD, thou hast been our dwelling-place
  In generations all.
Before thou ever hadst brought forth
  The mountains great or small;

2 Ere ever thou hadst formed the earth,
  And all the world abroad;
Ev'n thou from everlasting art
  To everlasting God.

3 All our iniquities thou dost
  Before thy presence place;
Our secret sins dost set before
  The brightness of thy face.

4 Who knows the power of thy wrath?
  According to thy fear
So is thy wrath. Lord, teach thou us
  Our end in mind to bear;—

5 And so to count our days, that we
  Our hearts may still apply
To learn thy wisdom and thy truth,
  That we may live thereby.

GERMANY. L. M.

1. Through every age, e-ter-nal God! Thou art our Rest, our safe A-bode;

High was thy throne, ere heaven was made, Or earth thy hum-ble foot-stool laid.

154
PSALM 90.
God's Eternity. WATTS.

THROUGH every age, eternal God!
Thou art our Rest, our safe Abode;
High was thy throne, ere heaven was made,
Or earth thy humble footstool laid.

2 Long hadst thou reigned, ere time began,
Or dust was fashioned into man;
And long thy kingdom shall endure,
When earth and time shall be no more.

3 But man, weak man, is born to die,
Made up of guilt and vanity;
Thy dreadful sentence, Lord! was just,
"Return, ye sinners! to your dust."

4 Death, like an overflowing stream,
Sweeps us away; our life 's a dream;
An empty tale; a morning flower,
Cut down, and withered in an hour.

5 Teach us, O Lord! how frail is man;
And kindly lengthen out our span,
Till a wise care of piety
Fit us to die, and dwell with thee.

155
PSALM 91.
Divine Protection amid Dangers. WATTS.

HE that hath made his refuge God,
Shall find a most secure abode;
Shall walk all day beneath his shade,
And there, at night, shall rest his head.

2 Then will I say,—"My God! thy power
Shall be my fortress and my tower;
I, who am formed of feeble dust,
Make thine almighty arm my trust."

3 Thrice happy man! thy Maker's care
Shall keep thee from the fowler's snare;—
Satan, the fowler, who betrays
Unguarded souls a thousand ways.

4 If burning beams of noon conspire
To dart a pestilential fire;
God is thy life,—his wings are spread,
To shield thee with a healthful shade.

5 If vapors, with malignant breath,
Rise thick and scatter midnight death,
Israel is safe; the poisoned air
Grows pure, if Israel's God be there.

156
PSALM 92.
The church is the garden of God. WATTS.

LORD, 'tis a pleasant thing to stand
In gardens planted by thy hand;
Let me within thy courts be seen,
Like a young cedar fresh and green.

2 There grow thy saints in faith and love,
Blest with thine influence from above;
Not Lebanon, with all its trees,
Yields such a comely sight as these.

3 The plants of grace shall ever live;
Nature decays, but grace must thrive:
Time, that doth all things else impair,
Still makes them flourish strong and fair.

4 Laden with fruits of age, they show,
The Lord is holy, just and true:
None that attend his gates, shall find
A God unfaithful or unkind.

MIGDOL. L. M.

1. Sweet is the work, my God, my King. To praise thy name, give thanks, and sing;

To show thy love by morning light, And talk of all thy truth at night.

157 PSALM 92. WATTS.
Divine Worship.

SWEET is the work, my God, my King,
To praise thy name, give thanks, and sing;
To show thy love by morning light,
And talk of all thy truth at night.

2 Sweet is the day of sacred rest;
No mortal care shall seize my breast;
Oh, may my heart in tune be found,
Like David's harp of solemn sound!

3 My heart shall triumph in my Lord,
And bless his works and bless his word;
Thy works of grace, how bright they shine!
How deep thy counsels! how divine!

4 Lord, I shall share a glorious part,
When grace hath well refined my heart,
And fresh supplies of joy are shed,
Like holy oil to cheer my head.

5 Then shall I see, and hear, and know
All I desired or wished below;
And every power find sweet employ,
In that eternal world of joy.

158 PSALM 93. WATTS.
The eternal and sovereign God.

JEHOVAH reigns; he dwells in light,
Girded with majesty and might;
The world, created by his hands,
Still on its first foundation stands.

2 But, ere this spacious world was made,
Or had its first foundations laid,
Thy throne eternal ages stood,—
Thyself, the ever-living God.

3 Like floods, the angry nations rise,
And aim their rage against the skies:
Vain floods, that aim their rage so high!—
At thy rebuke the billows die.

4 For ever shall thy throne endure,
Thy promise stands for ever sure;
And everlasting holiness
Becomes the dwellings of thy grace.

159 PSALM 94. AUBER.
God's Omniscience.

CAN guilty man, indeed, believe
That he, who made and knows the heart,
Shall not the oppressor's crimes perceive,
Nor take his injured servant's part?

2 Shall he who, with transcendent skill,
Fashioned the eye and formed the ear;
Who modeled nature to his will,
Shall he not see? Shall he not hear?

3 Shall he, who framed the human mind,
And bade its kindling spark to glow,
Who all its varied powers combined,
O mortal, say—shall he not know?

4 Vain hope! his eye at once surveys
Whatever fills creation's space;
He sees our thoughts, and marks our ways,
He knows no bounds of time and place.

5 Surrounded by his saints, the Lord
Shall armed with holy vengeance come;
To each his final lot award,
And seal the sinner's fearful doom.

VALENTIA. C. M.

1. Oh, come, let us, in songs to God, Our cheer-ful voic-es raise,

In joy-ful shouts let us the Rock Of our sal-va-tion praise.

160   **PSALM 95.**   SCOTCH.
"The Rock of our Salvation."

Oh, come, let us, in songs to God,
  Our cheerful voices raise,
In joyful shouts let us the Rock
  Of our salvation praise.

2 Let us before his presence come
  With praise and thankful voice;
Let us sing psalms to him with grace,
  And make a joyful noise.

3 For God, a great God, and great King,
  Above all gods he is.
Depths of the earth are in his hand,
  The strength of hills is his.

4 To him the spacious sea belongs,
  For he the same did make;
The dry land also from his hands
  Its form at first did take.

5 Oh, come, and let us worship him,
  Let us bow down withal,
And on our knees before the Lord
  Our Maker let us fall.

161   **PSALM 96.**   WATTS.
Christ's Coming.

Sing to the Lord, ye distant lands,
  Ye tribes of every tongue;
His new-discovered grace demands
  A new and nobler song.

2 Say to the nations Jesus reigns,
  God's own almighty Son;
His power the sinking world sustains,
  And grace surrounds his throne.

3 Let heaven proclaim the joyful day;
  Joy through the earth be seen;
Let cities shine in bright array,
  And fields in cheerful green.

4 Let an unusual joy surprise
  The islands of the sea;
Ye mountains, sink; ye valleys, rise;
  Prepare the Lord his way.

5 Behold, he comes; he comes to bless
  The nations, as their God.
To show the world his righteousness,
  And send his truth abroad.

162   **PSALM 97.**   WATTS.
The Reign of Christ.

Ye isles and shores of every sea!
  Rejoice—the Saviour reigns;
His word, like fire, prepares his way,
  And mountains melt to plains.

2 Adoring angels, at his birth,
  Make the Redeemer known;
Thus shall he come to judge the earth,
  And angels guard his throne.

3 His foes shall tremble at his sight,
  And hills and seas retire;
His children take their upward flight,
  And leave the world on fire.

4 The seeds of joy and glory, sown
  For saints in darkness here,
Shall rise and spring in worlds unknown,
  And a rich harvest bear.

ANTIOCH. C. M.

1 Joy to the world,--the Lord is come; Let earth re-ceive her King; { Let eve-ry heart } { pre-pare him room, }

And heav'n and nature sing, And heav'n and nature sing,.......... And heav'n and na-ture sing

And heav'n and nature sing, And heav'n and nature sing.

163

PSALM 98.   WATTS.
The joyful Reign of Christ.

Joy to the world,—the Lord is come;
Let earth receive her King;
Let every heart prepare him room,
And heaven and nature sing.

2 Joy to the earth,—the Saviour reigns;
Let men their songs employ;
While fields and floods, rocks, hills, and
Repeat the sounding joy. [plains,

3 No more let sins and sorrows grow,
Nor thorns infest the ground,
He comes to make his blessings flow,
Far as the curse is found.

4 He rules the world with truth and grace,
And makes the nations prove
The glories of his righteousness,
And wonders of his love.

164

PSALM 98.   SCOTCH.
A New Song.

Oh, sing a new song to the Lord,
For wonders he hath done;
His right hand and his holy arm
Him victory hath won.

2 The great salvation wrought by him,
Jehovah hath made known;
His justice in the heathen's sight
He openly hath shown.

3 He mindful of his grace and truth
To Israel's house hath been;
The great salvation of our God
All ends of earth have seen.

4 Let all the earth unto the Lord
Send forth a joyful noise;
Lift up your voice aloud to him,
Sing praises, and rejoice.

5 With harp, with harp, and voice of psalms,
Unto JEHOVAH sing:
With trumpets, cornets, gladly sound
Before the Lord the King.

165

PSALM 99.   WATTS.
The Majesty of Christ.

THE Lord Jehovah reigns alone;
Let all the nations fear;
Let sinners tremble at his throne;
And saints be humble there.

2 Jesus is crowned at his right hand,
Let earth adore its Lord:
Bright cherubs his attendants stand,
And swift fulfill his word.

3 In Zion is his rightful throne,
His honors are divine;
His church shall make his wonders known,
For there his glories shine.

4 How great and holy is his name!
How terrible his praise!
Justice, and truth, and judgment join,
In all his works of grace.

5 Come, let us seek the Lord our God,
And worship at his feet;
His ways are wisdom, power and truth,
And mercy is his seat.

69

OLD HUNDRED. L. M.

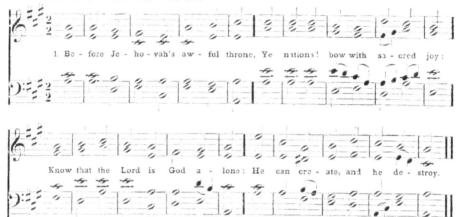

1. Be - fore Je - ho - vah's aw - ful throne, Ye nations! bow with sa - cred joy:

Know that the Lord is God a - lone: He can cre - ate, and he de - stroy.

166   PSALM 100.   WATTS.
The sovereign Jehovah.

BEFORE Jehovah's awful throne,
   Ye nations! bow with sacred joy:
Know that the Lord is God alone:
   He can create, and he destroy.

2 His sovereign power, without our aid,
   Made us of clay, and formed us men:
And when, like wandering sheep, we strayed,
   He brought us to his fold again.

3 We are his people, we his care,—
   Our souls, and all our mortal frame:
What lasting honors shall we rear,
   Almighty Maker! to thy name?

4 We'll crowd thy gates with thankful songs:
   High as the heavens our voices raise;
And earth, with her ten thousand tongues,
   Shall fill thy courts with sounding praise.

5 Wide as the world is thy command,
   Vast as eternity, thy love;
Firm as a rock thy truth must stand,
   When rolling years shall cease to move.

167   PSALM 100.   KETHE.
God's Supremacy.

ALL people that on earth do dwell,
   Sing to the Lord with cheerful voice.
Him serve with mirth, his praise forth tell,
   Come ye before him and rejoice.

2 Know that the Lord is God indeed;
   Without our aid he did us make:
We are his flock, he doth us feed,
   And for his sheep he doth us take.

3 Oh, enter then his gates with praise,
   Approach with joy his courts unto:
Praise, laud, and bless his name always,
   For it is seemly so to do.

4 For why? the Lord our God is good,
   His mercy is for ever sure;
His truth at all times firmly stood,
   And shall from age to age endure.

168   PSALM 101.   WATTS.
The Magistrate's Song.

MERCY and judgment are my song;
   And, since they both to thee belong,
My gracious God! my righteous King!
   To thee my songs and vows I bring.

2 I will not set mine eyes to wrong,
   Reproach shall not to me belong;
The faithful in my sight shall be;
   The true shall dwell in peace with me.

3 Let wisdom all my actions guide,
   And let my God with me reside:
No wicked thing shall dwell with me,
   Which may provoke thy jealousy.

4 Deceivers will I turn away,
   Nor in my house shall liars stay;
The wicked will I thus reward,
   And clear the city of the Lord.

5 O Lord! to thee my praise I bring,
   Of mercy and of judgment sing;
In wisdom will I walk at home.
   When wilt thou to my dwelling come?

OAKSVILLE. C. M.

1. Let Zi - on and her sons re - joice— Be - hold the prom - ised hour!

Her God hath heard her mourn - ing voice, And comes t' ex - alt his power.

169   PSALM 102.   WATTS.
Zion restored.

Let Zion and her sons rejoice—
Behold the promised hour!
Her God hath heard her mourning voice,
  And comes to exalt his power.

2 Her dust and ruins that remain
  Are precious in our eyes;
Those ruins shall be built again,
  And all that dust shall rise.

3 The Lord will raise Jerusalem,
  And stand in glory there;
Nations shall bow before his name,
  And kings attend with fear.

4 He sits a sovereign on his throne,
  With pity in his eyes;
He hears the dying prisoners' groan,
  And sees their sighs arise.

5 He frees the soul condemned to death,
  Nor, when his saints complain,
Shall it be said that praying breath
  Was ever spent in vain.

170   PSALM 102.   SCOTCH.
Christ's Coming.

Thou shall arise, and mercy have
  Upon thy Zion yet;
The time to favor her is come,
  The time that thou hast set.

2 For in her rubbish and her stones
  Thy servants pleasure take;
Yea, they the very dust thereof
  Do favor for her sake.

3 So shall the heathen people fear
  The Lord's most holy name:
And all the kings on earth shall dread
  Thy glory and thy fame.

4 When Zion by the mighty Lord
  Built up again shall be,
In glory then and majesty
  To men appear shall he.

171   PSALM 103.   SCOTCH.
Thanksgiving.

O Thou my soul, bless God the Lord:
  And all that in me is
Be stirred up, his holy name
  To magnify and bless.

2 Bless, O my soul, the Lord thy God!
  And not forgetful be
Of all his gracious benefits
  He hath bestowed on thee.

3 All thine iniquities who doth
  Most graciously forgive:
Who thy diseases all and pains
  Doth heal, and thee relieve.

4 Who doth redeem thy life, that thou
  To death mayst not go down;
Who thee with loving-kindness doth
  And tender mercies crown:—

5 Oh, bless the Lord, all ye his works,
  Wherewith the world is stored
In his dominions everywhere!
  My soul, bless thou the Lord!

BOYLSTON. S. M.

1. Oh, bless the Lord, my soul! Let all with-in me join,

And aid my tongue to bless his name, Whose fa-vors are di - vine.

172   PSALM 103.   WATTS.
Grateful Acknowledgment.

Oh, bless the Lord, my soul!
   Let all within me join,
And aid my tongue to bless his name,
   Whose favors are divine.

2 Oh, bless the Lord, my soul!
   Nor let his mercies lie
Forgotten in unthankfulness,
   And without praises die.

3 'Tis he forgives thy sins;
   'Tis he relieves thy pain;
'Tis he that heals thy sicknesses,
   And makes thee young again.

4 He crowns thy life with love,
   When ransomed from the grave;
He, who redeemed my soul from hell,
   Hath sovereign power to save.

5 He fills the poor with good;
   He gives the sufferers rest:
The Lord hath judgments for the proud,
   And justice for the oppressed.

6 His wondrous works and ways
   He made by Moses known;
But sent the world his truth and grace
   By his beloved Son.

173   PSALM 103.   WATTS.
"God will not always chide."

My soul, repeat his praise,
   Whose mercies are so great;
Whose anger is so slow to rise,
   So ready to abate.

2 God will not always chide;
   And when his strokes are felt,
His strokes are fewer than our crimes,
   And lighter than our guilt.

3 High as the heavens are raised
   Above the ground we tread,
So far the riches of his grace
   Our highest thoughts exceed.

4 His power subdues our sins,
   And his forgiving love,
Far as the east is from the west,
   Doth all our guilt remove.

174   PSALM 103.   WATTS.
The Lord's Pity.

The pity of the Lord,
   To those that fear his name,
Is such as tender parents feel;
   He knows our feeble frame.

2 He knows we are but dust,
   Scattered with every breath:
His anger, like a rising wind,
   Can send us swift to death.

3 Our days are as the grass,
   Or like the morning flower:
If one sharp blast sweep o'er the field
   It withers in an hour.

4 But thy compassions, Lord,
   To endless years endure;
And children's children ever find
   Thy words of promise sure.

WARE. L. M.

1. Bless, O my soul! the liv-ing God. Call home thy thoughts that rove a-broad;

Let all the powers, with-in me, join In work and wor-ship so di-vine.

175 PSALM 103. WATTS.
The Goodness and Mercy of God.

Bless, O my soul! the living God,
Call home thy thoughts that rove abroad:
Let all the powers, within me, join
In work and worship so divine.

2 Bless, O my soul! the God of grace;
His favors claim thy highest praise:
Why should the wonders he hath wrought
Be lost in silence and forgot?

3 'T is he, my soul! who sent his Son
To die for crimes which thou hast done:
He owns the ransom, and forgives
The hourly follies of our lives.

4 Let the whole earth his power confess,
Let the whole earth adore his grace;
The Gentile with the Jew shall join
In work and worship so divine.

176 PSALM 103. WATTS.
The abounding compassion of God.

The Lord, how wondrous are his ways!
How firm his truth, how large his grace!
He takes his mercy for his throne,
And thence he makes his glories known.

2 Not half so high his power hath spread
The starry heavens above our head,
As his rich love exceeds our praise,
Exceeds the highest hopes we raise.

3 Not half so far hath nature placed
The rising morning from the west,
As his forgiving grace removes
The daily guilt of those he loves.

4 How slowly doth his wrath arise!
On swifter wings salvation flies;
And if he lets his anger burn,
How soon his frowns to pity turn!

5 Amid his wrath compassion shines;
His strokes are lighter than our sins;
And while his rod corrects his saints,
His ear indulges their complaints.

177 PSALM 104. WATTS.
God the Creator.

Vast are thy works, almighty Lord,
All nature rests upon thy word;
And the whole race of creatures stand
Waiting their portion from thy hand.

2 But when thy face is hid they mourn,
And, dying, to their dust return;
Both man and beast their souls resign;
Life, breath, and spirit, all are thine.

3 Yet thou canst breathe on dust again,
And fill the world with beasts and men;
A word of thy creating breath
Repairs the wastes of time and death.

4 The earth stands trembling at thy stroke,
And at thy touch the mountains smoke;
Yet humble souls may see thy face,
And tell their wants to sovereign grace.

5 In thee my hopes and wishes meet,
And make my meditations sweet;
Thy praises shall my breath employ,
Till it expire in endless joy.

STERLING. L. M.

1. Give thanks to God, in - voke his name, In loft-y psalms ex - alt his praise; His deeds thro' the whole world pro - claim, And talk of all his works and ways.

178   PSALM 105.   ANON.
"Give thanks to God."

GIVE thanks to God, invoke his name,
In lofty psalms exalt his praise;
His deeds through the whole world proclaim,
And talk of all his works and ways.

2 Ye who have made the Lord your choice,
Recall to mind his works of love;
Recount his wonders, and rejoice
In him who lives and reigns above.

3 Jehovah is our God alone,
His words to endless years endure;
His judgments through the earth are known,
His covenant shall stand secure.

4 For Zion's Lord is true and just,
And he will crown with sure success
The patient souls, who in him trust
And rest upon his faithfulness.

5 Exalt the glory of his name;
His saving strength betimes implore;
Let heart and lip declare his fame—
And seek his presence evermore.

179   PSALM 106.   TATE-BRADY.
God praised for his Goodness and Mercy.

OH, render thanks to God above,
The fountain of eternal love;
Whose mercy firm, through ages past,
Has stood, and shall for ever last.

2 Who can his mighty deeds express,
Not only vast, but numberless?
What mortal eloquence can raise
His tribute of immortal praise?

74

3 Extend to me that favor, Lord!
Thou to thy chosen dost afford;
When thou returnest to set them free,
Let thy salvation visit me.

4 Oh, render thanks to God above,
The fountain of eternal love;
Whose mercy firm, through ages past,
Has stood, and shall for ever last.

180   PSALM 107.   WATTS.
Israel led to Canaan, and Christians to Heaven.

GIVE thanks to God—he reigns above;
Kind are his thoughts, his name is love;
His mercy ages past have known,
And ages long to come shall own.

2 Let the redeemèd of the Lord
The wonders of his grace record;
Israel, the nation whom he chose,
And rescued from their mighty foes.

3 So when our first release we gain
From sin's own yoke, and Satan's chain,
We have this desert world to pass,—
A dangerous and a tiresome place.

4 He feeds and clothes us all the way,
He guides our footsteps, lest we stray;
He guards us with a powerful hand,
And brings us to the heavenly land.

5 Oh, let us, then, with joy record
The truth and goodness of the Lord;
How great his works—how kind his ways!
Let every tongue pronounce his praise.

ST. GEORGE. 7. D.

1. Thank and praise Jehovah's name; For his mercies, firm and sure, From eterni-ty the same, To eternity endure. 2. Let the ransomed thus rejoice, Gathered out of every land, As the people of his choice, Pluck'd from the destroyer's hand.

181
PSALM 107. MONTGOMERY.
Prayer for Divine Guidance.

Thank and praise Jehovah's name;
  For his mercies firm and sure,
From eternity the same,
  To eternity endure.

2 Let the ransomed thus rejoice,
  Gathered out of every land,
As the people of his choice,
  Plucked from the destroyer's hand.

3 In the wilderness astray,
  Hither, thither, while they roam,
Hungry, fainting by the way,
  Far from refuge, shelter, home,—

4 Then unto the Lord they cry;
  He inclines a gracious ear,
Sends deliverance from on high,
  Rescues them from all their fear.

5 To a pleasant land he brings,
  Where the vine and olive grow,
Where from flowery hills the springs
  Through luxuriant valleys flow.

6 Oh, that men would praise the Lord
  For his goodness to their race;
For the wonders of his word,
  And the riches of his grace.

182
PSALM 107. MONTGOMERY.
The Dangers of the Ocean.

They who toil upon the deep,
  And, in vessels light and frail,
O'er the mighty waters sweep,
  With the billow and the gale,
Mark what wonders God performs,—
  When he speaks, and, unconfined,
Rush to battle all his storms,
  In the chariots of the wind.

2 Up to heaven their bark is whirled,
  On the mountain of the wave;
Down as suddenly 'tis hurled
  To the abysses of the grave;
To and fro they reel—they roll,
  As intoxicate with wine;
Terrors paralyze their soul,
  Helm they quit, and hope resign.

3 Then unto the Lord they cry;
  He inclines a gracious ear,
Sends deliverance from on high,
  Rescues them from all their fear:
Oh, that men would praise the Lord,
  For his goodness to their race;
For the wonders of his word,
  And the riches of his grace.

THORNTON.   C. M. D.

FINE.

D. C.

1. A - wake, my soul, to sound his praise, A - wake my harp to sing;
Join all my pow'rs the song to raise, And morn-ing in - cense bring.
D. C.—Glad songs of praise will I pre-pare, And there his name re - sound

2. A - mong the peo - ple of his care, And thro' the na - tions round,

183   PSALM 108.   BARLOW.
A morning Song.

Awake, my soul, to sound his praise,
Awake my harp to sing;
Join all my powers the song to raise,
And morning incense bring.

2 Among the people of his care,
And through the nations round,
Glad songs of praise will I prepare,
And there his name resound.

3 Be thou exalted, O my God,
Above the starry train;
Diffuse thy heavenly grace abroad,
And teach the world thy reign.

4 So shall thy chosen sons rejoice,
And throng thy courts above;
While sinners hear thy pardoning voice,
And taste redeeming love.

184   PSALM 109.   WATTS.
The Example of Christ.

God of my mercy and my praise!
Thy glory is my song;
Though sinners speak against thy grace
With a blaspheming tongue.

2 When, in the form of mortal man,
Thy Son on earth was found,
With cruel slanders, false and vain,
They compassed him around.

3 Their miseries his compassion move,
Their peace he still pursued;
They render hatred for his love
And evil for his good.

4 Their malice raged without a cause;
Yet, with his dying breath,
He prayed for murderers on his cross,
And blessed his foes in death.

5 Lord! shall thy bright example shine
In vain before my eyes?
Give me a soul a-kin to thine,
To love mine enemies.

6 The Lord shall on my side engage,
And, in my Saviour's name,
I shall defeat their pride and rage,
Who slander and condemn.

185   PSALM 110.   WATTS.
Christ's Kingdom and Priesthood.

Jesus, our Lord! ascend thy throne,
And near thy Father sit:
In Zion shall thy power be known,
And make thy foes submit.

2 What wonders shall thy gospel do!
Thy converts shall surpass
The numerous drops of morning dew,
And own thy sovereign grace.

3 God hath pronounced a firm decree,
Nor changes what he swore;—
"Eternal shall thy priesthood be,
When Aaron is no more."

4 Jesus, our priest, for ever lives,
To plead for us above:
Jesus, our king, for ever gives
The blessings of his love.

186

PSALM 111.
"Great is the Lord." WATTS.

GREAT is the Lord; his works of might
Demand our noblest songs;
Let his assembled saints unite
Their harmony of tongues.

2 Great is the mercy of the Lord,
He gives his children food;
And, ever mindful of his word,
He makes his promise good.

3 His Son, the great Redeemer, came
To seal his covenant sure;
Holy and reverend is his name,
His ways are just and pure.

4 They that would grow divinely wise,
Must with his fear begin;
Our fairest proof of knowledge lies
In hating every sin.

187

PSALM 112.
Liberality rewarded. WATTS.

HAPPY is he who fears the Lord,
And follows his commands;
Who lends the poor without reward,
Or gives with liberal hands.

2 As pity dwells within his breast,
To all the sons of need,
So God shall answer his request,
With blessings on his seed.

3 In times of danger and distress,
Some beams of light shall shine,
To show the world his righteousness,
And give him peace divine.

4 His works of piety and love
Remain before the Lord;
Honor on earth, and joys above,
Shall be his sure reward.

HEROLD. 7.

1. Hal - le - lu - jah! raise, oh, raise To our God the song of praise:
All his ser - vants join to sing God our Sav - iour and our King.

188

PSALM 113.
Hallelujah. CONDER.

HALLELUJAH! raise, oh, raise
To our God the song of praise:
All his servants join to sing
God our Saviour and our King.

2 Blessèd be for evermore
That dread name which we adore:
Round the world his praise be sung,
Through all lands, in every tongue.

3 O'er all nations God alone,
Higher than the heavens his throne;
Who is like to God most high,
Infinite in majesty?

4 Yet to view the heavens he bends;
Yea, to earth he condescends;
Passing by the rich and great,
For the low and desolate.

5 He can raise the poor to stand
With the princes of the land;
Wealth upon the needy shower:
Set the meanest high in power.

6 He the broken spirit cheers;
Turns to joy the mourner's tears;
Such the wonders of his ways;
Praise his name—for ever praise.

77

TRURO. L. M.

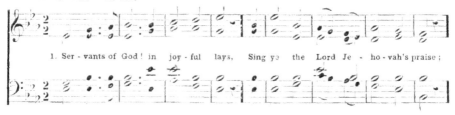

1. Ser - vants of God! in joy - ful lays, Sing ye the Lord Je - ho - vah's praise;

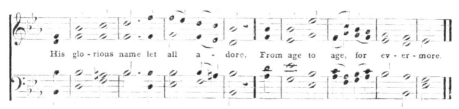

His glo - rious name let all a - dore, From age to age, for ev - er - more.

189 **PSALM 113.** MONTGOMERY.
Praise for God's Condescension.

SERVANTS of God! in joyful lays,
Sing ye the Lord Jehovah's praise;
His glorious name let all adore,
From age to age, for evermore.

2 Blest be that name, supremely blest,
From the sun's rising to its rest:
Above the heavens his power is known;
Through all the earth his goodness shown.

3 Who is like God?—so great, so high,
He bows himself to view the sky;
And yet, with condescending grace,
Looks down upon the human race.

4 He hears the uncomplaining moan,
Of those who sit and weep alone;
He lifts the mourner from the dust,
And saves the poor in him who trust.

5 Servants of God! in joyful lays,
Sing ye the Lord Jehovah's praise;
His saving name let all adore,
From age to age, for evermore.

190 **PSALM 114.** WATTS.
Miracles attending Israel's Journey.

WHEN Israel, freed from Pharaoh's hand,
Left the proud tyrant and his land,
The tribes, with cheerful homage, own
Their King,—and Judah was his throne.

2 Across the deep their journey lay;
The deep divides to make them way:
Jordan beheld their march, and fled,
With backward current, to his head.

3 What power could make the deep divide—
Make Jordan backward roll his tide?
Why did ye leap, ye little hills?
And whence the fright that Sinai feels?

4 Let every mountain, every flood
Retire and know the approaching God,
The King of Israel: see him here;
Tremble, thou earth; adore and fear.

5 He thunders, and all nature mourns,
The rock to standing pools he turns;
Flints spring with fountains at his word,
And fires and seas confess the Lord.

191 **PSALM 115.** WATTS.
The true God; our hope and trust.

NOT to ourselves, who are but dust,
Not to ourselves is glory due;
Eternal God! thou only just,
Thou only gracious, wise and true!

2 The God we serve maintains his throne,
Above the clouds, beyond the skies;
Through all the earth his will is done;
He knows our groans, he hears our cries.

3 O Israel! make the Lord thy hope,
Thy help, thy refuge, and thy rest;
The Lord shall build thy ruins up,
And bless the people and the priest.

4 The dead no more can speak thy praise,
They dwell in silence in the grave;
But we shall live to sing thy grace,
And tell the world thy power to save.

LUCERNE.   C. M. D.

1. { What shall I ren-der to my God, For all his kind-ness shown?)
   { My feet shall vis-it thine a-bode, My songs ad-dress thy throne.)
D. C.—There shall my zeal per-form the vows, My soul in an-guish made.

2. A - mong the saints that fill thine house, My of-fering shall be paid;

---

192   PSALM 116.   WATTS.
         Personal Consecration.

WHAT shall I render to my God,
  For all his kindness shown?
My feet shall visit thine abode,
  My songs address thy throne.

2 Among the saints that fill thine house,
  My offering shall be paid;
There shall my zeal perform the vows,
  My soul in anguish made.

3 How much is mercy thy delight,
  Thou ever blessèd God!
How dear thy servants in thy sight!
  How precious is their blood!

4 How happy all thy servants are!
  How great thy grace to me!
My life, which thou hast made thy care,
  Lord, I devote to thee.

---

193   PSALM 116.   SCOTCH.
         "Return unto thy rest."

God merciful and righteous is,
  Yea, gracious is our Lord.
God saves the meek; I was brought low,
  He did me help afford.

2 O thou my soul! do thou return
  Unto thy quiet rest;
For largely, lo, the Lord to thee
  His bounty hath expressed.

3 For my distressèd soul from death
  Delivered was by thee;
Thou didst my mourning eyes from tears,
  My feet from falling, free.

---

4 I'd of salvation take the cup,
  On God's name will I call;
I'll pay my vows now to the Lord
  Before his people all.

194   PSALM 117.   WATTS.
         Praise to God from all Nations.

O ALL ye nations! praise the Lord,
  Each with a different tongue;
In every language learn his word,
  And let his name be sung.

2 His mercy reigns through every land,—
  Proclaim his grace abroad;
For ever firm his truth shall stand,—
  Praise ye the faithful God.

195   PSALM 118.   WATTS.
         Christ, the Foundation of his Church.

BEHOLD the sure foundation-stone,
  Which God, in Zion lays
To build our heavenly hopes upon,
  And his eternal praise.

2 Chosen of God, to sinners dear;
  And saints adore his name:
They trust their whole salvation here,
  Nor shall they suffer shame.

3 The foolish builders, scribe and priest,
  Reject it with disdain;
Yet on this rock the church shall rest,
  And envy rage in vain.

4 What though the gates of hell withstood?
  Yet must the building rise:
'Tis thine own work, almighty God!
  And wondrous in our eyes.

79

MARLOW. C. M.

1. This is the day the Lord hath made; He calls the hours his own;

Let heaven re - joice, let earth be glad, And praise sur-round the throne.

196   PSALM 118.   WATTS.
The Lord's Day.

This is the day the Lord hath made;
  He calls the hours his own;
Let heaven rejoice, let earth be glad,
  And praise surround the throne.

2 To-day he rose, and left the dead,
  And Satan's empire fell;
To-day the saints his triumph spread,
  And all his wonders tell.

3 Hosanna to the anointed King,
  To David's holy Son;
Help us, O Lord; descend, and bring
  Salvation from thy throne.

4 Blest be the Lord, who comes to men
  With messages of grace;
Who comes, in God his Father's name,
  To save our sinful race.

5 Hosanna in the highest strains
  The church on earth can raise;
The highest heavens, in which he reigns,
  Shall give him nobler praise.

197   PSALM 119.   SCOTCH.
The Blessing of Obedience.

BLESSED are they that undefiled
  And straight are in the way;
Who in the Lord's most holy law
  Do walk, and do not stray.

2 Blessed are they who to observe
  His statutes are inclined;
And who do seek the living God
  With their whole heart and mind.

3 Such in his ways do walk, and they
  Do no iniquity.
Thou hast commanded us to keep
  Thy precepts carefully.

4 Oh, that thy statutes to observe
  Thou wouldst my ways direct!
Then shall I not be shamed when I
  Thy precepts all respect.

5 Then, with integrity of heart,
  Thee will I praise and bless,
When I the judgments all have learned
  Of thy pure righteousness.

198   PSALM 119.   WATTS.
Sincerity and Obedience.

Thou art my portion, O my God!
  Soon as I know thy way,
My heart makes haste to obey thy word,
  And suffers no delay.

2 I choose the path of heavenly truth,
  And glory in my choice;
Not all the riches of the earth
  Could make me so rejoice.

3 The testimonies of thy grace
  I set before mine eyes;
Thence I derive my daily strength,
  And there my comfort lies.

4 Now I am thine,—for ever thine;—
  Oh, save thy servant, Lord!
Thou art my shield, my hiding-place,
  My hope is in thy word.

ELIZABETHTOWN. C. M.

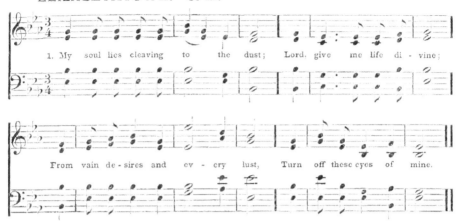

1. My soul lies cleaving to the dust; Lord, give me life di-vine;

From vain de-sires and ev-ery lust, Turn off these eyes of mine.

199 PSALM 119. WATTS.
The Word quickens.

My soul lies cleaving to the dust;
  Lord, give me life divine;
From vain desires and every lust,
  Turn off these eyes of mine.

2 I need the influence of thy grace
  To speed me in thy way,
Lest I should loiter in my race
  Or turn my feet astray.

3 Are not thy mercies sovereign still,
  And thou a faithful God?
Wilt thou not grant me warmer zeal
  To run the heavenly road?

4 Does not my heart thy precepts love,
  And long to see thy face?
And yet how slow my spirits move
  Without enlivening grace!

5 Then shall I love thy gospel more,
  And ne'er forget thy word,
When I have felt its quickening power
  To draw me near the Lord.

200 PSALM 119. WATTS.
The Holy Law.

Oh how I love thy holy law!
  'Tis daily my delight;
And thence my meditations draw
  Divine advice by night.

2 How doth thy word my heart engage!
  How well employ my tongue!
And in my tiresome pilgrimage
  Yields me a heavenly song.

3 Am I a stranger, or at home,
  'Tis my perpetual feast:
Not honey dropping from the comb,
  So much allures the taste.

4 No treasures so enrich the mind,
  Nor shall thy word be sold
For loads of silver well-refined,
  Nor heaps of choicest gold.

5 When nature sinks, and spirits droop,
  Thy promises of grace
Are pillars to support my hope,
  And there I write thy praise.

201 PSALM 119. WATTS.
Comfort from the Bible.

Lord! I have made thy word my choice,
  My lasting heritage;
There shall my noblest powers rejoice,
  My warmest thoughts engage.

2 I'll read the histories of thy love,
  And keep thy laws in sight,
While through the promises I rove,
  With ever-fresh delight.

3 'Tis a broad land of wealth unknown,
  Where springs of life arise,
Seeds of immortal bliss are sown,
  And hidden glory lies:—

4 The best relief that mourners have;
  It makes our sorrows blest:—
Our fairest hope beyond the grave,
  And our eternal rest.

KNOX. C. M.

1. How precious is the book di - vine, By in - spi - ra - tion given!

Bright as a lamp its doctrines shine, To guide our souls to heaven.

202 PSALM 119. FAWCETT.
The Book of books.

How precious is the book divine,
By inspiration given!
Bright as a lamp its doctrines shine,
To guide our souls to heaven.

2 O'er all the strait and narrow way
Its radiant beams are cast;
A light whose never weary ray
Grows brightest at the last.

3 It sweetly cheers our drooping hearts,
In this dark vale of tears;
Life, light, and joy it still imparts,
And quells our rising fears.

4 This lamp, through all the tedious night
Of life, shall guide our way,
Till we behold the clearer light
Of an eternal day.

203 PSALM 119. WATTS.
Keeping God's Statutes.

Oh, that the Lord would guide my ways
To keep his statutes still!
Oh, that my God would grant me grace
To know and do his will.

2 Oh, send thy Spirit down, to write
Thy law upon my heart;
Nor let my tongue indulge deceit,
Or act the liar's part.

3 From vanity turn off my eyes;
Let no corrupt design,
Nor covetous desires, arise
Within this soul of mine.

4 Order my footsteps by thy word,
And make my heart sincere;
Let sin have no dominion, Lord!
But keep my conscience clear.

5 Make me to walk in thy commands—
'Tis a delightful road;
Nor let my head, or heart, or hands,
Offend against my God.

204 PSALM 119. SCOTCH.
Youthful Piety.

By what means shall a young man learn
His way to purify?
If he according to thy word
Thereto attentive be.

2 Unfeignedly thee have I sought
With all my soul and heart:
Oh, let me not from the right path
Of thy commands depart.

3 Thy word I in my heart have hid,
That I offend not thee.
O Lord, thou ever blessèd art,
Thy statutes teach thou me.

4 The judgments of thy mouth each one
My lips declarèd have:
More joy thy testimonies' way
Than riches all me gave.

5 Upon thy statutes my delight
Shall constantly be set:
And, by thy grace, I never will
Thy holy word forget.

82

IOLA.   C. M.

1 How shall the young se-cure their hearts, And guard their lives from sin?

Thy word the choicest rules imparts To keep the conscience clean, To keep the conscience clean.

205 **PSALM 119.** WATTS.
Instruction from the Scriptures.

How shall the young secure their hearts,
  And guard their lives from sin?
Thy word the choicest rules imparts
  To keep the conscience clean.

2 When once it enters to the mind,
  It spreads such light abroad;
The meanest souls instruction find,
  And raise their thoughts to God.

3 'Tis like the sun, a heavenly light,
  That guides us all the day;
And, through the dangers of the night,
  A lamp to lead our way.

4 Thy precepts make me truly wise;
  I hate the sinner's road;
I hate my own vain thoughts that rise,
  But love thy law, my God!

5 Thy word is everlasting truth;
  How pure is every page!
That holy book shall guide our youth,
  And well support our age.

206 **PSALM 120.** WATTS.
Complaint of Strife.

Thou God of love, thou ever-blest!
  Pity my suffering state;
When wilt thou set my soul at rest,
  From lips that love deceit?

2 Oh, might I fly to change my place,
  How would I choose to dwell
In some wide lonesome wilderness,
  And leave these gates of hell!

3 Peace is the blessing that I seek;
  How lovely are its charms!
I am for peace,—but when I speak,
  They all declare for arms.

4 Should burning arrows smite them through,
  Strict justice would approve;
But I would rather spare my foe,
  And melt his heart with love.

207 **PSALM 121.** WATTS.
Constant Preservation.

To heaven I lift my waiting eyes:
  There all my hopes are laid:
The Lord that built the earth and skies
  Is my perpetual aid.

2 Their steadfast feet shall never fall
  Whom he designs to keep;
His ear attends the softest call,
  His eyes can never sleep.

3 Israel, rejoice, and rest secure;
  Thy keeper is the Lord:
His wakeful eyes employ his power
  For thine eternal guard.

4 No scorching sun, nor sickly moon,
  Shall have his leave to smite;
He shields thy head from burning noon,
  From blasting damps at night.

5 He guards thy soul, he keeps thy breath
  Where thickest dangers come;
Go and return, secure from death,
  Till God commands thee home.

83

MEAR.   C. M.

1. I to the hills will lift mine eyes, From whence doth come mine aid.

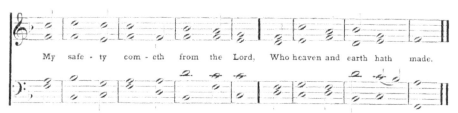

My safe - ty com - eth from the Lord, Who heaven and earth hath made.

208   PSALM 121.   SCOTCH.
Looking to God.

I to the hills will lift mine eyes,
  From whence doth come mine aid.
My safety cometh from the Lord,
  Who heaven and earth hath made.

2 Thy foot he'll not let slide, nor will
  He slumber that thee keeps.
Behold, he that keeps Israel,
  He slumbers not, nor sleeps.

3 The Lord shall keep thy soul; he shall
  Preserve thee from all ill.
Henceforth thy going out and in
  God keep for ever will.

209   PSALM 122.   WATTS.
Going to Church.

How did my heart rejoice to hear
  My friends devoutly say,—
"In Zion let us all appear,
  And keep the solemn day."

2 I love her gates, I love the road;
  The church, adorned with grace,
Stands like a palace built for God,
  To show his milder face.

3 Up to her courts, with joys unknown,
  The holy tribes repair;
The Son of David holds his throne,
  And sits in judgment there.

4 He hears our praises and complaints;
  And, while his awful voice
Divides the sinners from the saints,
  We tremble and rejoice.

84

5 Peace be within this sacred place,
  And joy a constant guest!
With holy gifts and heavenly grace,
  Be her attendants blest!

6 My soul shall pray for Zion still,
  While life or breath remains;
There my best friends, my kindred, dwell,
  There God, my Saviour, reigns.

210   PSALM 122.   LYTE.
Sabbath Service.

With joy we hail the sacred day
  Which God hath called his own;
With joy the summons we obey
  To worship at his throne.

2 Thy chosen temple, Lord, how fair!
  Where willing votaries throng
To breathe the humble, fervent prayer,
  And pour the choral song.

3 Spirit of grace! oh, deign to dwell
  Within thy church below;
Make her in holiness excel,
  With pure devotion glow.

4 Let peace within her walls be found;
  Let all her sons unite,
To spread with grateful zeal around
  Her clear and shining light.

5 Great God, we hail the sacred day
  Which thou hast called thine own;
With joy the summons we obey
  To worship at thy throne.

DALSTON. S. P. M.

1. How pleas'd and blest was I, To hear the people cry,—"Come, let us seek our God to-day!"

Yes, with a cheerful zeal, We haste to Zi-on's hill, And there our vows and hon-ors pay.

211
PSALM 122.
Going to Church.
WATTS.

How pleased and blessed was I,
To hear the people cry,—
"Come, let us seek our God to-day!"
Yes, with a cheerful zeal,
We haste to Zion's hill,
And there our vows and honors pay.

2 Zion! thrice happy place,
Adorned with wondrous grace,
And walls of strength embrace thee [round:
In thee our tribes appear
To pray, and praise, and hear
The sacred gospel's joyful sound.

3 May peace attend thy gate,
And joy within thee wait,
To bless the soul of every guest:
The man who seeks thy peace,
And wishes thine increase—
A thousand blessings on him rest!

4 My tongue repeats her vows:—
"Peace to this sacred house!"
For here my friends and kindred dwell:
And, since my glorious God
Makes thee his blest abode,
My soul shall ever love thee well.

212
PSALM 123.
Pleading with Submission.
WATTS.

O THOU, whose grace and justice reign,
Enthroned above the skies,
To thee our hearts would tell their pain,
To thee we lift our eyes.

2 As servants watch their master's hand,
And fear the angry stroke;
Or maids before their mistress stand,
And wait a peaceful look;—

3 So, for our sins we justly feel
Thy discipline, O God!
Yet wait the gracious moment still,
Till thou remove thy rod.

4 Our foes insult us, but our hope
In thy compassion lies;
This thought shall bear our spirits up,—
That God will not despise.

213
PSALM 124.
Victory from God.
ANON.

HAD not the God of truth and love,
When hosts against us rose,
Displayed his vengeance from above,
And crushed the conquering foes;—

2 Their armies like a raging flood,
Had swept the guardless land,
Destroyed on earth his blest abode,
And 'whelmed our feeble band.

3 And now our souls shall bless the Lord,
Who broke the deadly snare;
Who saved us from the murdering sword,
And made our lives his care.

4 Our help is in Jehovah's name,
Who formed the heavens above;
He that supports their wondrous frame,
Can guard his church by love.

85

GERHARDT. 7, 6. D.

1. He that in God con - fid - eth, Like Zi - on Mount shall be, Which ev - er - more a -

bid - eth Un - moved e - ter - nal - ly. 2. As mountains, which de - fend her, Je -

ru - sa - lem surround, His saints se - cure to ren - der, God com - passeth a - round.

214 PSALM 125. SCOTCH.
"Mountains round about Jerusalem."

HE that in God confideth,
  Like Zion Mount shall be,
Which evermore abideth
  Unmoved eternally.
2 As mountains, which defend her,
  Jerusalem surround,
His saints secure to render,
  God compasseth around.

3 The sinner's rod shall never
  On just men's lot abide,
Lest upright men should ever
  To sin be turned aside.
4 Thy goodness, Lord, our Saviour,
  To all the good impart;
And ever show thy favor
  To men of upright heart.

5 But those whose choice is rather
  In crooked ways to go;
With sinners God shall gather;
  On Israel peace bestow.
6 Great God of earth and heaven!
  To thee our songs we raise;
To thee be glory given
  And everlasting praise!

215 PSALM 126. SCOTCH.
"The Lord hath done great things."

WHEN God arose, the nation
  From bondage to redeem,
The joy of our salvation
  Came to us like a dream.
Our hearts with triumph bounded,
  Our lips ran o'er with praise,
The heathen stood confounded
  At God's mysterious ways.

2 They said, The Lord hath wonders
  Wrought for his captives sad;
The Lord hath done great wonders,
  And therefore we are glad.
Lord, all the remnant weary
  Bring back to Zion still,
As brooks in south lands dreary
  Their thirsty channels fill.

3 Full many cast in sadness
  Their seed on parching soil,
Who yet shall reap in gladness
  The harvest of their toil.
He who in tears departed
  With precious seed at morn,
Shall homeward fare light-hearted
  With sheaves of golden corn.

STOCKWELL. 8, 7.

1. He that go-eth forth with weep-ing, Bearing pre-cious seed in love,

Nev-er tir-ing, nev-er sleep-ing, Find-eth mer-cy from a-bove.

216 PSALM 126. HASTINGS.
Sowing in Tears.

HE that goeth forth with weeping,
Bearing precious seed in love,
Never tiring, never sleeping,
Findeth mercy from above.

2 Soft descend the dews of heaven,
Bright the rays celestial shine;
Precious fruits will thus be given,
Through an influence all divine.

3 Sow thy seed, be never weary,
Let no fears thy soul annoy;
Be the prospect ne'er so dreary,
Thou shalt reap the fruits of joy.

4 Lo, the scene of verdure brightening!
See the rising grain appear;
Look again! the fields are whitening,
For the harvest time is near.

217 PSALM 127. AUBER.
Success from God.

VAIN were all our toil and labor,
Did not God that labor bless;
Vain, without his grace and favor,
Every talent we possess.

2 Vainer still the hope of heaven,
That on human strength relies;
But to him shall help be given,
Who in humble faith applies.

3 Seek we, then, the Lord's Anointed;
He shall grant us peace and rest:
Ne'er was suppliant disappointed,
Who through Christ his prayer addressed.

218 PSALM 123. SCOTCH.
A Godly Fear.

BLEST the man who fears Jehovah,
Walking ever in his ways;
Thou shalt eat of thy hands' labor,
And be happy all thy days.

2 Lo, on him that fears Jehovah,
Shall this blessedness attend;
Thus Jehovah out of Zion
Shall to thee his blessings send.

3 Thou shalt see Jerusalem prosper,
Long as thou on earth shalt dwell;
Thou shalt see thy children's children,
And the peace of Israel.

219 PSALM 129. ANON.
Conflict and Growth.

Many a day the church grows weary,
Worn like Israel of old,
With the strokes of deep affliction,
And with many a pain untold.

2 Yet her constant step is onward;
Precious seed is ever sown
In the furrows foes are ploughing—
Plenteous harvests ever grown.

3 For the Lord our God is faithful;
And the disciplines he sends
Are our enemies' worst allies,
And the church's choicest friends.

4 As the grass upon the housetops,
Wither hopes from wicked hands—
As the sheaves bound in his bosom
Are the blessings he commands.

87

SERENITY. C. M.

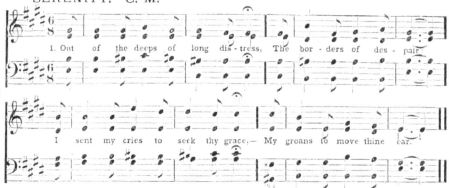

1. Out of the deeps of long dis-tress, The bor-ders of des-pair,
I sent my cries to seek thy grace,— My groans to move thine ear.

220   **PSALM 130.**   WATTS.
Trust in a pardoning God.

Out of the deeps of long distress,
  The borders of despair,
I sent my cries to seek thy grace,—
  My groans to move thine ear.

2 Great God! should thy severer eye,
  And thine impartial hand,
Mark and revenge iniquity,
  No mortal flesh could stand.

3 But there are pardons with my God,
  For crimes of high degree;
Thy Son has bought them with his blood,
  To draw us near to thee.

4 I wait for thy salvation, Lord!
  With strong desires I wait;
My soul, invited by thy word,
  Stands watching at thy gate.

GUIDE. 7, 6l.   END.

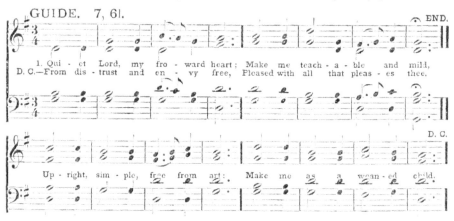

1. Qui-et Lord, my fro-ward heart; Make me teach-a-ble and mild,
D. C.—From dis-trust and en-vy free, Pleased with all that pleas-es thee.

Up-right, sim-ple, free from art: Make me as a wean-ed child.

221   **PSALM 131.**   NEWTON.
The Child-like Heart.

Quiet, Lord, my froward heart;
  Make me teachable and mild,
Upright, simple, free from art:
  Make me as a weanèd child,
From distrust and envy free,
  Pleased with all that pleases thee.

2 What thou shalt to-day provide,
  Let me as a child receive;

What to-morrow may betide,
  Calmly to thy wisdom leave:
'Tis enough that thou wilt care;
  Why should I the burden bear?

3 As a little child relies
  On a care beyond his own,
Knows he's neither strong nor wise,
  Fears to stir a step alone;
Let me thus with thee abide,
  As my Father, Guard, and Guide.

ARLINGTON. C. M.

1. A - rise, O King of grace! a - rise, And en - ter to thy rest;

Lo! the church waits, with long - ing eyes, Thus to be owned and blest.

222 PSALM 132. WATTS.
Prayer for the Reign of Christ.

Arise, O King of grace! arise,
　And enter to thy rest;
Lo! thy church waits, with longing eyes,
　Thus to be owned and blest.

2 Enter, with all thy glorious train,—
　Thy Spirit and thy word;
All that the ark did once contain
　Could no such grace afford.

3 Here, mighty God! accept our vows;
　Here let thy praise be spread:
Bless the provisions of thy house,
　And fill thy poor with bread.

4 Here let the Son of David reign,
　Let God's Anointed shine;
Justice and truth his court maintain,
　With love and power divine.

5 Here let him hold a lasting throne;
　And, as his kingdom grows,
Fresh honors shall adorn his crown,
　And shame confound his foes.

223 PSALM 133. SCOTCH.
Christian Fellowship.

Behold, how good a thing it is,
　And how becoming well,
Together such as brethren are
　In unity to dwell!

2 Like precious ointment on the head,
　That down the beard did flow,
Ev'n Aaron's beard, and to the skirts
　Did of his garments go.

3 As Hermon's dew, the dew that doth
　On Zion hills descend;
For there the blessing God commands,
　Life that shall never end.

224 PSALM 133. LYTE.
Excellence of Christian Unanimity.

Spirit of peace! celestial Dove!
　How excellent thy praise!
No richer gift than Christian love
　Thy gracious power displays.

2 Sweet as the dew on herb and flower,
　That silently distils,
At evening's soft and balmy hour,
　On Zion's fruitful hills:—

3 So, with mild influence from above,
　Shall promised grace descend,
Till universal peace and love
　O'er all the earth extend.

225 PSALM 134. WATTS.
Constant Devotion.

Bless ye the Lord with solemn rite,—
　In hymns extol his name;
Ye who, within his house, by night,
　Watch round the altar's flame.

2 Lift up your hands amid the place,
　Where burns the sacred sign,
And pray, that thus Jehovah's face
　O'er all the earth may shine.

3 From Zion, from his holy hill,
　The Lord, our Maker, send
The perfect knowledge of his will,—
　Salvation without end.

89

HURSLEY. L. M.

1. Praise ye the Lord; ex- alt his name, While in his earth-ly courts ye wait,

Ye saints, that to his house be - long, Or stand at - tend - ing at his gate.

226　　PSALM 125.　　WATTS.
The church, God's house and care.

PRAISE ye the Lord; exalt his name,
　While in his earthly courts ye wait,
Ye saints, that to his house belong,
　Or stand attending at his gate.

2 Praise ye the Lord, the Lord is good,
　To praise his name is sweet employ:
Israel he chose of old, and still
　His church is his peculiar joy.

3 The Lord himself will judge his saints;
　He treats his servants as his friends:
And when he hears their sore complaints,
　Repents the sorrows that he sends.

4 Through every age the Lord declares
　His name, and breaks the oppressor's rod:
He gives his suffering servants rest,
　And will be known the almighty God.

5 Bless ye the Lord who taste his love,
　People and priests exalt his name;
Among his saints he ever dwells;
　His church is his Jerusalem.

227　　PSALM 136.　　WATTS.
Thanks for Creation and Redemption.

GIVE to our God immortal praise;—
　Mercy and truth are all his ways;
Wonders of grace to God belong;—
　Repeat his mercies in your song.

2 He built the earth, he spread the sky,
　And fixed the starry lights on high:
Wonders of grace to God belong;—
　Repeat his mercies in your song.

3 He fills the sun with morning light,
　He bids the moon direct the night:
His mercies ever shall endure,
　When suns and moons shall shine no more.

4 He sent his Son, with power to save
　From guilt, and darkness, and the grave:
Wonders of grace to God belong;—
　Repeat his mercies in your song.

5 Through this vain world he guides our feet,
　And leads us to his heavenly seat:
His mercies ever shall endure,
　When this vain world shall be no more.

228　　PSALM 137.　　TATE-BRADY.
The Desolations of Zion lamented.

WHEN we, our wearied limbs to rest,
　Sat down by proud Euphrates' stream,
We wept, with doleful thoughts oppressed,
　And Zion was our mournful theme.

2 Our harps, that when with joy we sung,
　Were wont their tuneful parts to bear,
With silent strings, neglected hung,
　On willow-trees that withered there.

3 How shall we tune our voice to sing,
　Or touch our harps with skillful hands?
Shall hymns of joy, to God our King,
　Be sung by slaves in foreign lands?

4 O Salem, our once-happy seat!
　When I of thee forgetful prove,
Let then my trembling hand forget
　The tuneful strings with art to move.

STATE STREET. S. M.

1. I love thy king-dom, Lord, The house of thine a-bode,

The church, our blest Re-deem-er saved With his own pre-cious blood.

229

PSALM 137.
Love to the Church. DWIGHT.

I love thy kingdom, Lord,
The house of thine abode,
The church, our blest Redeemer saved
With his own precious blood.

2 I love thy church, O God!
Her walls before thee stand,
Dear as the apple of thine eye,
And graven on thy hand.

3 For her my tears shall fall,
For her my prayers ascend;
To her my cares and toils be given,
Till toils and cares shall end.

4 Beyond my highest joy
I prize her heavenly ways;
Her sweet communion, solemn vows,
Her hymns of love and praise.

5 Sure as thy truth shall last,
To Zion shall be given
The brightest glories earth can yield,
And brighter bliss of heaven.

230

PSALM 137.
Away from home. LYTE.

Far from my heavenly home,
Far from my Father's breast,
Fainting, I cry, " Blest Spirit, come,
And speed me to my rest."

2 Upon the willows long
My harp has silent hung;
How should I sing a cheerful song,
Till thou inspire my tongue?

3 My spirit homeward turns,
And fain would thither flee;
My heart, O Zion, droops and yearns,
When I remember thee.

4 God of my life, be near;
On thee my hopes I cast;
Oh, guide me through the desert here,
And bring me home at last!

SHIRLAND. S. M.

1. I love thy king-dom, Lord, The house of thine a-bode,

The church, our blest Re-deem-er saved With his own pre-cious blood.

ALL SAINTS. L. M.

1. With all my powers of heart and tongue I'll praise my Ma-ker in my song:

An-gels shall hear the notes I raise, Ap-prove the song, and join the praise.

231 PSALM 138. WATTS.
Restoring Grace.

With all my powers of heart and tongue
I'll praise my Maker in my song:
Angels shall hear the notes I raise,
Approve the song, and join the praise.

2 I'll sing thy truth and mercy, Lord;
I'll sing the wonders of thy word;
Not all the works and names below,
So much thy power and glory show.

3 To God I cried when troubles rose;
He heard me and subdued my foes;
He did my rising fears control,
And strength diffused through all my soul.

4 Amidst a thousand snares I stand,
Upheld and guarded by thy hand;
Thy words my fainting soul revive,
And keep my dying faith alive.

5 Grace will complete what grace begins,
To save from sorrows and from sins;
The work that wisdom undertakes,
Eternal mercy ne'er forsakes.

232 PSALM 139 WATTS.
God's Omniscience.

Lord! thou hast searched and seen me thro';
Thine eye commands, with piercing view,
My rising and my resting hours,
My heart and flesh, with all their powers.

2 My thoughts, before they are my own,
Are to my God distinctly known;
He knows the words I mean to speak,
Ere from my opening lips they break.

3 Within thy circling power I stand;
On every side I find thy hand;
Awake, asleep, at home, abroad,
I am surrounded still with God.

4 Amazing knowledge, vast and great!
What large extent! what lofty height!
My soul, with all the powers I boast,
Is in the boundless prospect lost.

5 Oh, may these thoughts possess my breast,
Where'er I rove, where'er I rest;
Nor let my weaker passions dare
Consent to sin, for God is there.

233 PSALM 140. LYTE.
Conflict necessary.

The Christian, like his Lord of old,
Must look for foes and trials here:
Yet may the weakest saint be bold,
With such a friend as Jesus near.

2 The lion's roar need not alarm,
O Lord, the feeblest of thy sheep;
The serpent's venom cannot harm,
While thou art nigh to watch and keep.

3 Before, when dangers round me spread,
I cried to thee, Almighty Friend;
Thou coveredst my defenceless head;
And shall I not on thee depend?

4 O refuge of the poor and weak!
Regard thy suffering people's cry;
Humble the proud, uphold the meek,
And bring us safe to thee on high.

ILLINOIS. L. M.

1. Lord, let my prayer like in - cense rise: And when I lift my hands to thee,

As in the evening sac - ri - fice, Look down from heaven, well pleased, on me.

234   **PSALM 141.**   MONTGOMERY.
Christian Watchfulness and Reproof.

Lord, let my prayer like incense rise:
  And when I lift my hands to thee,
As in the evening sacrifice,   [on me.
  Look down from heaven, well pleased,

2 Set thou a watch to keep my tongue,
  Let not my heart to sin incline;
Save me from men who practise wrong:
  Let me not share their mirth and wine.

3 But let the righteous, when I stray,
  Smite me in love: his strokes are kind:
His mild reproofs, like oil, allay
  The wounds they make, and heal the mind.

4 But oh, redeem me from the snares
  With which the world surrounds my feet,
Its riches, vanities, and cares,
  Its love, its hatred, and deceit.

235   **PSALM 142.**   MANT.
God, our Hope.

Behold me unprotected stand,
No friendly guardian at my hand;
No place of flight, no refuge near,
And none to whom my soul is dear.

2 But, Lord, to thee I pour my vow,
My hope, my place of refuge thou:
And whilst the light of life I see,
I still my portion find in thee.

3 Come loose my prison-bands, set free
My soul, that I may sing to thee:
Then shall the righteous round me press,
And join thy bounteous love to bless.

236   **PSALM 143.**   MONTGOMERY.
Mental Afflictions and Trials.

Hear me, O Lord! in my distress,
Hear me, in truth and righteousness;
For, at thy bar of judgment tried,
None living can be justified.

2 Oh, let me not thus hopeless lie,
Like one condemned at morn to die:
But, with the morning, may I see,
Thy loving-kindness visit me.

3 Teach me thy will, subdue my own;
Thou art my God, and thou alone;
By thy good Spirit, guide me still,
Safe from all foes to Zion's hill.

4 Release my soul from trouble, Lord!
Quicken and keep me by thy word;
May all its promises be mine;
Be thou my portion,—I am thine.

237   **PSALM 144.**   ANON.
The Prospered City.

Happy the city, where their sons
  Like pillars round a palace set,
And daughters, bright as polished stones,
  Give strength and beauty to the state.

2 Happy the land in culture dressed,
  Whose flocks and corn have large increase;
Where men securely work or rest,
  Nor sons of plunder break their peace.

3 Happy the nation thus endowed;
  But more divinely blest are those
On whom the all-sufficient God,
  Himself, with all his grace bestows.

238   PSALM 145.   WATTS.
The greatness of God.

My God, my King, thy various praise
Shall fill the remnant of my days:
Thy grace employ my humble tongue
Till death and glory raise the song.

2 The wings of every hour shall bear
Some thankful tribute to thine ear;
And every setting sun shall see
New works of duty done for thee.

3 Thy works with sovereign glory shine,
And speak thy majesty divine:

Let Zion in her courts proclaim
The sound and honor of thy name.

4 Let distant times and nations raise
The long succession of thy praise;
And unborn ages make my song
Thy joy and labor of their tongue.

5 But who can speak thy wondrous deeds?
Thy greatness all our thoughts exceeds:
Vast and unsearchable thy ways;
Vast and immortal be thy praise.

NEWCOURT. L. P. M.

1. I'll praise my Mak - er with my breath, And, when my voice is lost in death,

Praise shall em - ploy my no - bler pow'rs; My days of praise shall ne'er be past,

While life, and thought, and be - ing last, Or im - mor - tal - i - ty en - dures.

239   PSALM 146.   WATTS.
God's Goodness and Mercy.

I'LL praise my Maker with my breath,
And, when my voice is lost in death,
  Praise shall employ my nobler powers:
My days of praise shall ne'er be past,
While life, and thought, and being last,
  Or immortality endures.

2 Happy the man, whose hopes rely
On Israel's God;—he made the sky,
  And earth, and seas, with all their train:
His truth for ever stands secure;
He saves the oppressed, he feeds the poor:
  And none shall find his promise vain.

3 He loves his saints—he knows them well,
But turns the wicked down to hell:
  Thy God, O Zion! ever reigns;
Let every tongue, let every age,
In this exalted work engage:
  Praise him in everlasting strains.

4 I'll praise him while he lends me breath,
And, when my voice is lost in death,
  Praise shall employ my nobler powers:
My days of praise shall ne'er be past,
While life, and thought, and being last,
  Or immortality endures.

ROCKINGHAM. L. M.

1. Praise ye the Lord: my heart shall join In work so pleasant, so di-vine;

Now while the flesh is mine a-bode, And when my soul as-cends to God.

240   PSALM 146.   WATTS.
Perpetual Praise.

PRAISE ye the Lord: my heart shall join
In work so pleasant, so divine;
Now while the flesh is mine abode
And when my soul ascends to God.

2 Praise shall employ my noblest powers,
While immortality endures;
My days of praise shall ne'er be past,
While life, and thought, and being last.

3 Happy the man whose hopes rely
On Israel's God: he made the sky,
And earth, and seas, with all their train:
And none shall find his promise vain.

4 His truth for ever stands secure;
He saves the oppressed, he feeds the poor;
He helps the stranger in distress,
The widow and the fatherless.

5 He loves his saints, he knows them well,
But turns the wicked down to hell;
Thy God, O Zion, ever reigns;
Praise him in everlasting strains.

241   PSALM 147.   WATTS.
Praise for divine Grace.

PRAISE ye the Lord!—'tis good to raise
Our hearts and voices in his praise;
His nature and his works invite
To make this duty our delight.

2 The Lord builds up Jerusalem,
And gathers nations to his name!
His mercy melts the stubborn soul!
And makes the broken spirit whole.

3 He formed the stars—those heavenly flames,
He counts their numbers, calls their names:
His wisdom's vast, and knows no bound,—
A deep, where all our thoughts are drowned.

4 Great is our Lord, and great his might,
And all his glories infinite:
He crowns the meek, rewards the just,
And treads the wicked to the dust.

5 But saints are lovely in his sight;
He views his children with delight;
He sees their hope, he knows their fear,
And looks, and loves his image there.

242   PSALM 148.   WATTS.
Hallelujah to Jehovah.

LOUD hallelujahs to the Lord,   [dwell!
From distant worlds where creatures
Let heaven begin the solemn word,
And sound it dreadful down to hell.

2 Wide as his vast dominion lies,
Make the Creator's name be known;
Loud as his thunder, shout his praise,
And sound it lofty as his throne.

3 Jehovah—'tis a glorious word!
Oh, may it dwell on every tongue!
But saints who best have known the Lord,
Are bound to raise the noblest song.

4 Speak of the wonders of that love
Which Gabriel plays on every chord:
From all below and all above,
Loud hallelujahs to the Lord!

95

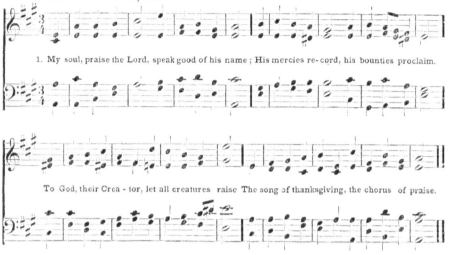

HANOVER. 10, 11.

1. My soul, praise the Lord, speak good of his name ; His mercies re-cord, his bounties proclaim.

To God, their Crea - tor, let all creatures raise The song of thanksgiving, the chorus of praise.

243   PSALM 148.   PARK.
Universal Praise.

My soul, praise the Lord, speak good of
  his name ;
His mercies record, his bounties proclaim.
To God, their Creator, let all creatures
  raise
The song of thanksgiving, the chorus of
  praise.

2 Though hidden from sight, God sits on
  his throne,
Yet here by his works their Creator is
  known:
The world shines a mirror its Maker to
  show,
And heaven views its image reflected below.

3 By knowledge supreme, by wisdom divine,
God governs the earth with gracious design.
O'er beast, bird, and insect his providence
  reigns,
Whose will first created, whose love still
  sustains.

4 And man, his last work, with reason endued,
Though fallen through sin, by grace is
  renewed:
To God, his Redeemer, let man ever raise
The song of thanksgiving, the chorus of
  praise.

244   PSALM 149.   SCOTCH.
"Praise ye the Lord."

On, praise ye the Lord! prepare your
  glad voice,
New songs with his saints assembled
  to sing;
Before his Creator let Israel rejoice,
And children of Zion be glad in their
  King.

2 And let them his name extol in the dance,
With timbrel and harp his praises express;
Jehovah takes pleasure his saints to advance,
And with his salvation the humble to
  bless.

3 Aloud let his saints in glory rejoice,
And rest undismayed, with songs in the
  night;
The praise of Jehovah their lips shall
  employ;
A sword in their right hand, two-edged
  for the fight.

4 The heathen to judge, their pride to con-
  sume;
To fetter their kings, their princes to
  bind;
To execute on them the long-decreed doom;
Such honor for ever the holy shall find.

ST. CASSIMER. 8, 7, D. or 7, D.

1. { Praise the Lord; ye heavens, a - dore him! Praise him, an - gels in the height! }
   { Sun and moon re - joice be - fore him; Praise him, all ye stars of light! }

2. Praise the Lord.—for he hath spo - ken; Worlds his might - y voice o - beyed;

Laws, which nev - er can be bro - ken, For their guid - ance he hath made.

245　　PSALM 149.　　KEMPTHORNE.
　　　　Praise to God.

PRAISE the Lord; ye heavens, adore him!
　Praise him, angels in the height!
Sun and moon! rejoice before him;
　Praise him, all ye stars of light!
2 Praise the Lord,—for he hath spoken;
　Worlds his mighty voice obeyed;
Laws, which never can be broken,
　For their guidance he hath made.
3 Praise the Lord,—for he is glorious;
　Never shall his promise fail;
God hath made his saints victorious,
　Sin and death shall not prevail.
4 Praise the God of our salvation;
　Hosts on high! his power proclaim;
Heaven and earth, and all creation!
　Praise and magnify his name.

246　　PSALM 150.　　WRANGHAM.
　　　　Exhortation to praise.

PRAISE the Lord—his power confess;
Praise him in his holiness;
Praise him, as the theme inspires;
Praise him, as his fame requires.
2 Let the trumpet's lofty sound
Spread its loudest notes around;
Let the harp unite, in praise,
With the sacred minstrel's lays.

3 Let the organ join to bless
　God—the Lord of righteousness;
Tune your voice to spread the fame
Of the great Jehovah's name.
4 All who dwell beneath his light!
In his praise, your hearts unite;
While the stream of song is poured,—
Praise and magnify the Lord.

247　　PSALM 150.　　LYTE.
　　　　General Praise.

PRAISE the Lord, his glories show,
Saints within his courts below,
Angels round his throne above,
All that see and share his love.
2 Earth to heaven, and heaven to earth,
Tell his wonders, sing his worth;
Age to age, and shore to shore,
Praise him, praise him, evermore!
3 Praise the Lord, his mercies trace;
Praise his providence and grace,
All that he for man hath done,
All he sends us through his Son.
4 Strings and voices, hands and hearts,
In the concert bear your parts;
All that breathe, your Lord adore,
Praise him, praise him, evermore!

ONIDO. 7, D.

1. God e-ter-nal, Lord of all! Low-ly at thy feet we fall: All the world doth worship thee;

We a-mid the throng would be. 2. All the ho-ly an-gels cry, Hail, thrice-ho-ly,

God most high! Lord of all the heavenly pow'rs, Be the same loud anthem ours.

---

248 *" Te Deum."* MILLARD.

God eternal, Lord of all!
Lowly at thy feet we fall:
All the world doth worship thee;
We amidst the throng would be.

2 All the holy angels cry,
Hail, thrice-holy, God most high!
Lord of all the heavenly powers,
Be the same loud anthem ours.

3 Glorified apostles raise,
Night and day, continual praise;
Hast thou not a mission too
For thy children here to do?

4 With the prophets' goodly line
We in mystic bond combine;
For thou hast to babe revealed
Things that to the wise were sealed.

5 Martyrs, in a noble host,
Of thy cross are heard to boast;
Since so bright the crown they wear,
We with them thy cross would bear.

6 All thy church, in heaven and earth,
Jesus! hail thy spotless birth;—
Seated on the judgment-throne,
Number us among thine own!

249 *" Gloria in Excelsis."* C. WESLEY.

Glory be to God on high,—
God, whose glory fills the sky;
Peace on earth to man forgiven,—
Man, the well-beloved of heaven.

2 Sovereign Father, Heavenly King!
Thee we now presume to sing;
Glad thine attributes confess,
Glorious all, and numberless.

3 Hail, by all thy works adored!
Hail, the everlasting Lord!
Thee with thankful hearts we prove,—
God of power, and God of love!

4 Christ our Lord and God we own,—
Christ the Father's only Son;
Lamb of God, for sinners slain,
Saviour of offending man.

5 Jesus! in thy name we pray,
Take, oh, take our sins away!
Powerful Advocate with God!
Justify us by thy blood.

6 Hear, for thou, O Christ! alone,
Art with thy great Father one;
One the Holy Ghost with thee;—
One supreme eternal Three.

Hymns and Spiritual Songs.

SABBATH. 7, 6l, or D.

1. Safe - ly through an-oth-er week, God has brought us on our way ; Let us now a blessing

seek, Wait-ing in his courts to - day: Day of all the week the best, Emblem

of e - ter-nal rest, Day of all the week the best, Emblem of e - ter - nal rest.

250 *"The Sabbath a Delight."* NEWTON.

Safely through another week,
  God has brought us on our way;
Let us now a blessing seek,
  Waiting in his courts to-day:
Day of all the week the best,
Emblem of eternal rest.

2 While we seek supplies of grace,
  Through the dear Redeemer's name,
Show thy reconciling face—
  Take away our sin and shame;
From our worldly cares set free,—
May we rest this day in thee.

3 Here we come thy name to praise;
  Let us feel thy presence near;
May thy glory meet our eyes,
  While we in thy house appear:
Here afford us, Lord, a taste
Of our everlasting rest.

4 May the gospel's joyful sound
  Wake our minds to raptures new;

Let thy victories abound,—
Unrepenting souls subdue:
Thus let all our Sabbaths prove,
Till we rest in thee above.

251 *"Prayer with Thanks."* ANON.

Heavenly Father, sovereign Lord,
Be thy glorious name adored!
Lord! thy mercies never fail;
Hail, celestial goodness, hail!

2 Though unworthy, Lord, thine ear,
Deign our humble songs to hear;
Purer praise we hope to bring,
When around thy throne we sing.

3 While on earth ordained to stay,
Guide our footsteps in thy way,
Till we come to dwell with thee,
Till we all thy glory see.

4 Then, with angel-harps again,
We will wake a nobler strain;
There, in joyful songs of praise,
Our triumphant voices raise.

ANVERN. L. M.

1. Thine earthly Sabbaths, Lord, we love, But there's a no-bler rest a-bove; To that our

long-ing souls a-spire, With cheerful hope and strong desire, With cheerful hope and strong desire.

252   *"A nobler Rest above."*   DODDRIDGE.

Thine earthly Sabbaths, Lord, we love,
But there's a nobler rest above;
To that our longing souls aspire,
With cheerful hope and strong desire.

2 No more fatigue, no more distress,
Nor sin nor death shall reach the place;
No groans shall mingle with the songs
That warble from immortal tongues.

3 No rude alarms of raging foes,
No cares to break the long repose,
No midnight shade, no clouded sun,
But sacred, high, eternal noon.

4 O long-expected day, begin!
Dawn on these realms of woe and sin;
Fain would we leave this weary road,
And sleep in death to rest with God.

253   *Sabbath Morning.*   HUTTON.

My opening eyes with rapture see
The dawn of thy returning day;
My thoughts, O God, ascend to thee,
While thus my early vows I pay.

2 Oh, bid this trifling world retire,
And drive each carnal thought away;
Nor let me feel one vain desire—
One sinful thought through all the day.

3 Then, to thy courts when I repair,
My soul shall rise on joyful wing,
The wonders of thy love declare,
And join the strains which angels sing.
100

254   *Ephesians, 3:19.*   WATTS.

Come, gracious Lord, descend and dwell,
By faith and love, in every breast;
Then shall we know, and taste, and feel
The joys that cannot be expressed.

2 Come, fill our hearts with inward strength,
Make our enlargéd souls possess,
And learn the height, and breadth, and length
Of thine eternal love and grace.

3 Now to the God whose power can do
More than our thoughts and wishes know,
Be everlasting honors done,
By all the church, through Christ his Son.

255   *"Sabbath is begun."*   STENNETT.

Another six days' work is done,
Another Sabbath is begun;
Return, my soul! enjoy thy rest,
Improve the day thy God hath blessed.

2 Oh, that our tho'ts and thanks may rise,
As grateful incense to the skies;
And draw from heaven that sweet repose,
Which none, but he that feels it, knows.

3 This heavenly calm, within the breast,
Is the dear pledge of glorious rest,
Which for the church of God remains—
The end of cares, the end of pains.

4 In holy duties, let the day,
In holy pleasures, pass away;
How sweet a Sabbath thus to spend,
In hope of one that ne'er shall end.

LOWRY. L. M.

1. A-wake, my soul, and with the sun The dai - ly stage of du - ty run;

Shake off dull sloth, and joy - ful rise To pay thy morn - ing sac - ri - fice.

256   *Morning Song.*   KEN.

AWAKE, my soul, and with the sun
Thy daily stage of duty run;
Shake off dull sloth, and joyful rise
To pay thy morning sacrifice.

2 Awake, lift up thyself, my heart,
And with the angels bear thy part,
Who all night long unwearied sing
High praises to the eternal King.

3 Glory to thee, who safe hast kept,
And hast refreshed me when I slept;
Grant, Lord, when I from death shall wake,
I may of endless life partake.

4 Lord, I my vows to thee renew:
Scatter my sins as morning dew;
Guard my first springs of thought and will,
And with thyself my spirit fill.

5 Direct, control, suggest, this day,
All I design, or do, or say;
That all my powers, with all their might,
In thy sole glory may unite.

257   *Psalm* 118.   WATTS.

Lo! what a glorious corner-stone
The Jewish builders did refuse!
But God hath built his church thereon,
In spite of envy and the Jews.

2 Great God, the work is all divine,
The joy and wonder of our eyes;
This is the day that proves it thine,
The day that saw our Saviour rise.

3 Sinners rejoice, and saints be glad;
Hosanna, let his name be blest;
A thousand honors on his head,
With peace, and light, and glory rest!

4 In God's own name he comes to bring
Salvation to our dying race;
Let the whole church address their King,
With hearts of joy, and songs of praise.

258   *Psalm* 65.   LYTE.

PRAISE, Lord, for thee in Zion waits;
Prayer shall besiege thy temple gates;
All flesh shall to thy throne repair,
And find, through Christ, salvation there.

2 How blest thy saints! how safely led!
How surely kept! how richly fed!
Saviour of all in earth and sea,
How happy they who rest in thee!

3 Thy hand sets fast the mighty hills,
Thy voice the troubled ocean stills!
Evening and morning hymn thy praise,
And earth thy bounty wide displays.

4 The year is with thy goodness crowned;
Thy clouds drop wealth the world around;
Through thee the deserts laugh and sing,
And nature smiles and owns her king.

5 Lord, on our souls thy Spirit pour;
The moral waste within restore;
Oh, let thy love our spring-tide be,
And make us all bear fruit to thee.

PETERBORO'. C. M.

1. Once more, my soul, the ris - ing day   Sa - lutes thy wak - ing eyes;

Once more, my voice, thy trib - ute pay   To him   that rules the skies.

259   *"The rising day."*   WATTS.

ONCE more, my soul, the rising day
  Salutes thy waking eyes;
Once more, my voice, thy tribute pay
  To him that rules the skies.

2 Night unto night his name repeats,
  The day renews the sound,
Wide as the heaven on which he sits,
  To turn the seasons round.

3 'Tis he supports my mortal frame;
  My tongue shall speak his praise;
My sins would rouse his wrath to flame,
  And yet his wrath delays.

4 Great God, let all my hours be thine,
  While I enjoy the light;
Then shall my sun in smiles decline,
  And bring a pleasant night.

260   *Retirement.*   COWPER.

FAR from the world, O Lord, I flee,
  From strife and tumult far;
From scenes where Satan wages still
  His most successful war.

2 The calm retreat, the silent shade,
  With prayer and praise agree;
And seem by thy sweet bounty made
  For those who follow thee.

3 There, if thy Spirit touch the soul,
  And grace her mean abode,
Oh, with what peace, and joy, and love,
  Does she commune with God!

4 There, like the nightingale, she pours
  Her solitary lays;
Nor asks a witness of her song,
  Nor thirsts for human praise.

5 Author and guardian of my life,
  Sweet source of light divine,
And—all harmonious names in one—
  My Saviour, thou art mine!

6 The thanks I owe thee, and the love,—
  A boundless, endless store—
Shall echo through the realms above,
  When time shall be no more.

261   *"Light, in thy light"*   C. WESLEY.

ETERNAL Sun of righteousness,
  Display thy beams divine,
And cause the glory of thy face
  Upon my heart to shine.

2 Light, in thy light, oh, may I see,
  Thy grace and mercy prove,
Revived, and cheered, and blest by thee
  The God of pardoning love.

3 Lift up thy countenance serene,
  And let thy happy child
Behold, without a cloud between,
  The Father reconciled.

4 On me thy promised peace bestow,
  The peace by Jesus given;—
The joys of holiness below,
  And then the joys of heaven.

HYMN. C. M.

1. Come, thou De-sire of all thy saints! Our hum-ble strains at-tend,

While with our prais-es and com-plaints, Low at thy feet we bend.

262   *"Come, Lord!"*   STEELE.

Come, thou Desire of all thy saints!
  Our humble strains attend,
While with our praises and complaints,
  Low at thy feet we bend.

2 How should our songs, like those above,
  With warm devotion rise!
How should our souls, on wings of love,
  Mount upward to the skies!

3 Come, Lord! thy love alone can raise
  In us the heavenly flame;
Then shall our lips resound thy praise,
  Our hearts adore thy name.

4 Dear Saviour, let thy glory shine,
  And fill thy dwellings here,
Till life, and love, and joy divine
  A heaven on earth appear.

5 Then shall our hearts enraptured say,
  Come, great Redeemer! come,
And bring the bright, the glorious day,
  That calls thy children home.

263   *Praise to Christ.*   STEELE.

Come, ye that love the Saviour's name,
  And joy to make it known;
The Sovereign of your hearts proclaim,
  And bow before his throne.

2 Behold your King, your Saviour, crowned
  With glories all divine;
And tell the wondering nations round,
  How bright those glories shine.

3 When in his earthly courts we view
  The beauties of our King,
We long to love as angels do,
  And with their voice to sing.

4 Oh, for the day, the glorious day!
  When heaven and earth shall raise
With all their powers, the raptured lay,
  To celebrate thy praise.

264   *A heart of Prayer.*   NEWTON.

Again our earthly cares we leave,
  And to thy courts repair;
Again with joyful feet we come,
  To meet our Saviour here.

2 Great Shepherd of thy people, hear!
  Thy presence now display;
We bow within thy house of prayer;
  Oh, give us hearts to pray!

3 The clouds which vail thee from our sight,
  In pity, Lord, remove;
Dispose our minds to hear aright
  The message of thy love.

4 The feeling heart, the melting eye,
  The humble mind, bestow;
And shine upon us from on high,
  To make our graces grow.

5 Show us some token of thy love,
  Our fainting hopes to raise;
And pour thy blessing from above,
  To aid our feeble praise.

ST. THOMAS. S. M.

1. Come, we who love the Lord, And let our joys be known;

Join in a song of sweet ac - cord, And thus sur - round the throne.

265   *"Any Merry? Sing Psalms."*   WATTS.

COME, we who love the Lord,
  And let our joys be known;
Join in a song of sweet accord,
  And thus surround the throne.

2 Let those refuse to sing
  Who never knew our God;
But children of the heavenly King
  May speak their joys abroad.

3 The men of grace have found
  Glory begun below;
Celestial fruits on earthly ground
  From faith and hope may grow.

4 The hill of Zion yields
  A thousand sacred sweets
Before we reach the heavenly fields,
  Or walk the golden streets.

5 Then let our songs abound,
  And every tear be dry;
We're marching thro' Immanuel's ground
  To fairer worlds on high.

266   *Psalm 92.*   AUBER.

SWEET is the work, O Lord,
  Thy glorious name to sing;
To praise and pray—to hear thy word,
  And grateful offerings bring.

2 Sweet—at the dawning light,
  Thy boundless love to tell;
And when approach the shades of night,
  Still on the theme to dwell.
104

3 Sweet—on this day of rest,
  To join in heart and voice,
With those who love and serve thee best,
  And in thy name rejoice.

4 To songs of praise and joy
  Be every Sabbath given,
That such may be our blest employ
  Eternally in heaven.

267   *"Moses and the Lamb."*   HAMMOND.

AWAKE, and sing the song
  Of Moses and the Lamb;
Wake, every heart and every tongue
  To praise the Saviour's name.

2 Sing of his dying love;
  Sing of his rising power;
Sing, how he intercedes above
  For those whose sins he bore.

3 Ye pilgrims! on the road
  To Zion's city, sing!
Rejoice ye in the Lamb of God,—
  In Christ, the eternal King.

4 Soon shall we hear him say,—
  "Ye blessèd children! come;"
Soon will he call us hence away,
  And take his wanderers home.

5 There shall each raptured tongue
  His endless praise proclaim;
And sweeter voices tune the song
  Of Moses and the Lamb.

LISBON. S. M.

1. How charming is the place Where my Re - deem - er, God,

Un - vails the beau - ty of his face, And sheds his love a - broad!

268   *Social Worship.*   STENNETT.

How charming is the place
    Where my Redeemer, God,
Unvails the beauty of his face,
    And sheds his love abroad!

2 Not the fair palaces,
    To which the great resort,
Are once to be compared with this,
    Where Jesus holds his court.

3 Here, on the mercy-seat,
    With radiant glory crowned,
Our joyful eyes behold him sit
    And smile on all around.

4 Give me, O Lord, a place
    Within thy blest abode,
Among the children of thy grace,
    The servants of my God.

269   *Psalm 63.*   WATTS.

My God! permit my tongue
    This joy, to call thee mine;
And let my early cries prevail
    To taste thy love divine.

2 My thirsty fainting soul
    Thy mercy doth implore;
Not travelers, in desert lands,
    Can pant for water more.

3 For life, without thy love,
    No relish can afford;
No joy can be compared to this,—
    To serve and please the Lord.

4 In wakeful hours at night,
    I call my God to mind;
I think how wise thy counsels are,
    And all thy dealings kind.

5 Since thou hast been my help,
    To thee my spirit flies;
And, on thy watchful providence,
    My cheerful hope relies.

6 The shadow of thy wings
    My soul in safety keeps;
I follow where my Father leads,
    And he supports my steps.

270   *Psalm 84.*   WATTS.

WELCOME, sweet day of rest,
    That saw the Lord arise!
Welcome to this reviving breast,
    And these rejoicing eyes!

2 The King himself comes near,
    And feasts his saints to-day;
Here may we sit, and see him here,
    And love, and praise, and pray.

3 One day, amid the place
    Where my dear Lord hath been,
Is sweeter than ten thousand days
    Within the tents of sin.

4 My willing soul would stay
    In such a frame as this,
And sit and sing herself away
    To everlasting bliss.

MENDEBRAS.   7, 6. D.

1. { O day of rest and gladness, O day of joy and light, }
   { O balm of care and sadness, Most beau-ti-ful, most bright; } On thee, the high and lowly,

Bend-ing be-fore the throne, Sing, Ho-ly, Ho-ly, Ho-ly, To the Great Three in One.

271   *The Day of Rest.*   WORDSWORTH.

O DAY of rest and gladness,
   O day of joy and light,
O balm of care and sadness,
   Most beautiful, most bright;
On thee, the high and lowly,
   Bending before the throne,
Sing, Holy, Holy, Holy,
   To the Great Three in One.

2 To-day on weary nations
   The heavenly manna falls;
To holy convocations
   The silver trumpet calls,
Where gospel light is glowing
   With pure and radiant beams,
And living water flowing
   With soul-refreshing streams.

3 New graces ever gaining
   From this our day of rest,
We reach the rest remaining
   To spirits of the blest.
To Holy Ghost be praises,
   To Father and to Son;
The Church her voice upraises
   To thee, blest Three in One.

272   *Desire for Heaven.*   DAVIS.

FROM every earthly pleasure,
   From every transient joy,
From every mortal treasure,
   That soon will fade and die;—
No longer these desiring,
   Upward our wishes tend,
To nobler bliss aspiring,
   And joys that never end.

106

2 From every piercing sorrow,
   That heaves our breast to-day,
Or threatens us to-morrow,
   Hope turns our eyes away;
On wings of faith ascending,
   We see the land of light,
And feel our sorrows ending,
   In infinite delight.

3 'Tis true we are but strangers
   And pilgrims here below,
And countless snares and dangers
   Surround the path we go:
Though painful and distressing,
   Yet there's a rest above;
And onward still we're pressing,
   To reach that land of love.

273   *"Thine holy day."*   RAY PALMER.

THINE holy day's returning,
   Our hearts exult to see;
And with devotion burning,
   Ascend, O God, to thee!
To-day with purest pleasure,
   Our thoughts from earth withdraw;
We search for heavenly treasure,
   We learn thy holy law.

2 We join to sing thy praises,
   Lord of the Sabbath day;
Each voice in gladness raises
   Its loudest, sweetest lay!
Thy richest mercies sharing,
   Inspire us with thy love,
By grace our souls preparing
   For nobler praise above.

LISCHER. H. M.

1. { Welcome, de-light-ful morn, Thou day of sa-cred rest; }
{ I hail thy kind re-turn;—Lord, make these moments blest: } From the low train Of mor-tal toys,

I soar to reach Im-mor-tal joys; I soar to reach Im-mor-tal joys.

I soar to reach Im-mor-tal joys.

274   *Welcome Worship.*   HAYWARD.

WELCOME, delightful morn,
    Thou day of sacred rest;
I hail thy kind return;—
    Lord, make these moments blest:

| From the low train | I soar to reach |
| Of mortal toys, | Immortal joys. |

2 Now may the King descend
    And fill his throne of grace;
Thy sceptre, Lord, extend,
    While saints address thy face:

| Let sinners feel | And learn to know |
| Thy quickening word. | And fear the Lord. |

3 Descend, celestial Dove,
    With all thy quickening powers;
Disclose a Saviour's love,
    And bless the sacred hours:

| Then shall my soul | Nor Sabbaths be |
| New life obtain, | Enjoyed in vain. |

275   *Sabbath Morning.*   COTTERILL.

AWAKE, ye saints, awake!
    And hail this sacred day;
In loftiest songs of praise
    Your joyful homage pay!
Come bless the day that God hath blest,
The type of heaven's eternal rest.

2 On this auspicious morn
    The Lord of life arose;
He burst the bars of death,
    And vanquished all our foes;
And now he pleads our cause above,
And reaps the fruits of all his love.

3 All hail, triumphant Lord!
    Heaven with hosannas rings,
And earth in humbler strains
    Thy praise responsive sings:
Worthy the Lamb that once was slain,
Through endless years to live and reign.

276   *Psalm 43.*   DWIGHT.

Now, to thy sacred house,
    With joy I turn my feet,
Where saints, with morning-vows,
    In full assembly meet:
Thy power divine shall there be shown,
And from thy throne thy mercy shine.

2 Oh, send thy light abroad;
    Thy truth, with heavenly ray,
Shall lead my soul to God,
    And guide my doubtful way;
I'll hear thy word with faith sincere,
And learn to fear and praise the Lord.

3 Here reach thy bounteous hand,
    And all my sorrows heal,
Here health and strength divine,
    Oh, make my bosom feel;
Like balmy dew, shall Jesus' voice
My heart rejoice, my strength renew.

4 Now in thy holy hill,
    Before thine altar, Lord!
My harp and song shall sound
    The glories of thy word:
Henceforth, to thee, O God of grace!
A hymn of praise, my life shall be.

ADMAH. L. M. 6l.

1. Great God! this sa - cred day of thine De - mands the soul's col - lect - ed pow'rs;

With joy we now to thee re - sign These sol - emn, con - se - crat - ed hours:

Oh, may our souls, a - dor - ing, own The grace that calls us to thy throne.

277 *The Sacred Day.* STEELE.

GREAT God! this sacred day of thine
 Demands the soul's collected powers;
With joy we now to thee resign
 These solemn, consecrated hours:
Oh, may our souls, adoring, own
The grace that calls us to thy throne.

2 Hence, ye vain cares and trifles, fly!
 Where God resides appear no more;
Omniscient God, thy piercing eye
 Can every secret thought explore;
Oh, may thy grace our hearts refine,
And fix our thoughts on things divine.

3 Thy Spirit's powerful aid impart;
 Oh, may thy word, with life divine,
Engage the ear and warm the heart,
 Then shall the day indeed be thine:
Then shall our souls, adoring, own
The grace which calls us to thy throne.

278 *Psalm 19.* MONTGOMERY.

THY glory, Lord, the heavens declare;
 The firmament displays thy skill;
The changing clouds, the viewless air,
 Tempest and calm thy words fulfill;
Day unto day doth utter speech,
And night to night thy knowledge teach.

2 Though voice nor sound inform the ear,
 Well known the language of their song,
When one by one the stars appear,
 Led by the silent moon along,
Till round the earth, from all the sky,
Thy beauty beams on every eye.

3 While these transporting visions shine,
 Along the path of Providence,
Glory eternal, joy divine,
 Thy word reveals, transcending sense;
My soul thy goodness longs to see,
Thy love to man, thy love to me.

279 *Quiet in Service.* HEBER.

FORTH from the dark and stormy sky,
Lord, to thine altar's shade we fly;
Forth from the world, its hope and fear,
Father, we seek thy shelter here;
Weary and weak thy grace we pray;
Turn not, O Lord, thy guests away.

2 Long have we roamed in want and pain,
Long have we sought thy rest in vain;
Wildered in doubt, in darkness lost,
Long have our souls been tempest-tossed;
Low at thy feet our sins we lay;
Turn not, O Lord, thy guests away.

YOAKLEY. L. M. 6l.

1. { When streaming from the east - ern skies, The morn-ing light sa-lutes mine eyes, }
{ O Sun of right - eousness di - vine, On me with beams of mer - cy shine! }

Oh, chase the clouds of guilt a - way, And turn my dark-ness in - to day.

280　　　*Constant Devotion.*　　GRANT.

WHEN, streaming from the eastern skies,
The morning light salutes mine eyes,
O Sun of righteousness divine,
On me with beams of mercy shine!
Oh, chase the clouds of guilt away,
And turn my darkness into day.

2 And when to heaven's all-glorious King
My morning sacrifice I bring,
And, mourning o'er my guilt and shame,
Ask mercy in my Saviour's name;
Then, Jesus, cleanse me with thy blood,
And be my Advocate with God.

3 When each day's scenes and labors close,
And wearied nature seeks repose,
With pardoning mercy richly blest,
Guard me, my Saviour, while I rest;
And, as each morning sun shall rise,
Oh, lead me onward to the skies!

281　　*Thirsting for God.—Ps. 42.*　　BOWDLER.

As, panting in the sultry beam,
The hart desires the cooling stream,
So to thy presence, Lord, I flee,
So longs my soul, O God, for thee;
Athirst to taste thy living grace,
And see thy glory face to face.

2 But rising griefs distress my soul,
And tears on tears successive roll;
For many an evil voice is near
To chide my woe and mock my fear;
And silent memory weeps alone
O'er hours of peace and gladness flown.

3 Ah, why, by passing clouds oppressed,
Should vexing thoughts distract thy breast?
Turn, turn to him, in every pain,
Whom suppliants never sought in vain;
Thy strength, in joy's ecstatic day,
Thy hope, when joy has passed away.

282　　*The Good Shepherd.—Ps. 23.*　　ADDISON.

THE Lord my pasture shall prepare,
And feed me with a shepherd's care;
His presence shall my wants supply,
And guard me with a watchful eye;
My noonday walks he shall attend,
And all my midnight hours defend.

2 When in the sultry glebe I faint,
Or on the thirsty mountain pant,
To fertile vales, and dewy meads,
My weary, wandering steps he leads;
Where peaceful rivers, soft and slow,
Amid the verdant landscape flow.

3 Though in the paths of death I tread,
With gloomy horrors overspread,
My steadfast heart shall fear no ill,
For thou, O Lord, art with me still;
Thy friendly rod shall give me aid,
And guide me through the dreadful shade.

4 Though in a bare and rugged way,
Through devious, lonely wilds I stray,
Thy presence shall my pains beguile:
The barren wilderness shall smile,
With sudden greens and herbage crowned;
And streams shall murmur all around.

109

HENDON. 7.

1. Lord, we come be-fore thee now, At thy feet we humbly bow; Oh, do not our

suit dis-dain! Shall we seek thee, Lord, in vain? Shall we seek thee, Lord, in vain?

283   *Seeking God's Face.*   HAMMOND.

Lord, we come before thee now,
At thy feet we humbly bow;
Oh, do not our suit disdain!
Shall we seek thee, Lord, in vain?

2 Lord, on thee our souls depend,
In compassion now descend;
Fill our hearts with thy rich grace,
Tune our lips to sing thy praise.

3 In thine own appointed way,
Now we seek thee; here we stay;
Lord, we know not how to go,
Till a blessing thou bestow.

4 Comfort those who weep and mourn;
Let the time of joy return;
Those that are cast down lift up;
Make them strong in faith and hope.

5 Grant that all may seek and find
Thee a God supremely kind;
Heal the sick; the captive free;
Let us all rejoice in thee.

284   *Psalm 23.*   MERRICK.

To thy pastures fair and large,
Heavenly Shepherd, lead thy charge,
And my couch, with tenderest care,
'Mid the springing grass prepare.

2 When I faint with summer's heat,
Thou shalt guide my weary feet
To the streams that, still and slow,
Through the verdant meadows flow.

3 Safe the dreary vale I tread,
By the shades of death o'erspread,
With thy rod and staff supplied,
This my guard—and that my guide.

4 Constant to my latest end,
Thou my footsteps shalt attend;
And shalt bid thy hallowed dome
Yield me an eternal home.

285   *Going to Church.*   MONTGOMERY.

To thy temple we repair—
Lord, we love to worship there,
When within the vail we meet
Thee upon the mercy-seat.

2 While thy glorious name is sung,
Tune our lips—unloose our tongue;
Then our joyful souls shall bless
Thee, the Lord our Righteousness.

3 While to thee our prayers ascend,
Let thine ear in love attend;
Hear us, for thy Spirit pleads—
Hear, for Jesus intercedes.

4 While thy word is heard with awe,
While we tremble at thy law,
Let thy gospel's wondrous love
Every doubt and fear remove.

5 From thy house when we return,
Let our hearts within us burn;
That at evening we may say—
'We have walked with God to-day.'

110

SEYMOUR. 7.

1. Soft - ly fades the twi - light ray Of the ho - ly Sab - bath day;

Gent - ly as life's set - ting sun, When the Christian's course is run.

286   *Sabbath Evening.*   S. F. SMITH.

SOFTLY fades the twilight ray
Of the holy Sabbath day;
Gently as life's setting sun,
When the Christian's course is run.

2 Night her solemn mantle spreads
O'er the earth as daylight fades;
All things tell of calm repose,
At the holy Sabbath's close.

3 Peace is on the word abroad;
'Tis the holy peace of God—
Symbol of the peace within
When the spirit rests from sin.

4 Still the Spirit lingers near,
Where the evening worshiper
Seeks communion with the skies,
Pressing onward to the prize.

5 Saviour! may our Sabbaths be
Days of joy and peace in thee,
Till in heaven our souls repose,
Where the Sabbath ne'er shall close.

287   *" The True Light."*   C. WESLEY.

LIGHT of life, seraphic fire,
Love divine, thyself impart;
Every fainting soul inspire;
Enter every drooping heart;—

2 Every mournful sinner cheer;
Scatter all our guilty gloom;
Father! in thy grace appear,
To thy human temples come.

3 Come, in this accepted hour,
Bring thy heavenly kingdom in;
Fill us with thy glorious power,
Set us free from all our sin.

4 Nothing more can we require,
We will covet nothing less;
Be thou all our heart's desire,
All our joy, and all our peace.

288   *Christian Fellowship.*   BURDER.

SWEET the time, exceeding sweet,
When the saints together meet,
When the Saviour is the theme,
When they joy to sing of him!

2 Sing we then eternal love,
Such as did the Father move;
He beheld the world undone,—
Loved the world, and gave his Son.

3 Sing the Son's amazing love;
How he left the realms above,
Took our nature and our place,
Lived and died to save our race.

4 Sing we, too, the Spirit's love;
With our wretched hearts he strove,
Took the things of Christ, and showed
How to reach his blest abode.

5 Sweet the place, exceeding sweet,
Where the saints in glory meet;
Where the Saviour's still the theme,
Where they see and sing of him.

111

HALLE. 7, 6l.

Christ, whose glo - ry fills the skies, Christ, the true, the on - ly light,
Sun of Right - eous - ness, a - rise, Tri - umph o'er the shades of night;

Day - spring from on high, be near, Day - star in my heart ap - pear.

289   *Sun of Righteousness.*   C. WESLEY.

Christ, whose glory fills the skies,
  Christ, the true, the only light,
Sun of Righteousness, arise,
  Triumph o'er the shades of night;
Day-spring from on high, be near,
Day-star in my heart appear.

2 Dark and cheerless is the morn,
  If thy light is hid from me;
Joyless is the day's return,
  Till thy mercy's beams I see;
Till they inward light impart,
Warmth and gladness to my heart.

3 Visit, then, this soul of mine;
  Pierce the gloom of sin and grief;
Fill me, radiant Sun divine!
  Scatter all my unbelief;
More and more thyself display,
Shining to the perfect day.

290   *The First Rest.*   J. A. ELLIOTT.

Hail, thou bright and sacred morn,
  Risen with gladness in thy beams!
Light, which not of earth is born,
  From thy dawn in glory streams;
Airs of heaven are breathed around,
And each place is holy ground.

Great Creator! who this day
  From thy perfect work didst rest;
By the souls that own thy sway
  Hallowed be its hours and blest;
Cares of earth aside be thrown,
This day given to heaven alone!

291   *Psalm 42.*   MONTGOMERY.

As the hart, with eager looks,
Panteth for the water-brooks,
So my soul, athirst for thee,
Pants the living God to see;
When, oh, when, with filial fear,
Lord, shall I to thee draw near?

2 Why art thou cast down, my soul?
God, thy God, shall make thee whole;
Why art thou disquieted?
God shall lift thy fallen head,
And his countenance benign
Be the saving health of thine.

292   *Evening Worship.*   HASTINGS.

Now, from labor and from care,
  Evening shades have set me free;
In the work of praise and prayer,
  Lord! I would converse with thee:
Oh, behold me from above,
Fill me with a Saviour's love.

2 Sin and sorrow, guilt and woe,
  Wither all my earthly joys;
Naught can charm me here below,
  But my Saviour's melting voice;
Lord! forgive—thy grace restore,
Make me thine for evermore.

4 For the blessings of this day,
  For the mercies of this hour,
For the gospel's cheering ray,
  For the Spirit's quickening power,—
Grateful notes to thee I raise;
Oh, accept my song of praise.

SOLNEY. 8, 7.

1. Lord of hosts, thy tents how love-ly! Liv-ing God, thy courts to see

My soul longeth, e - ven fainteth— Heart and flesh cry out for thee.

293　　*Psalm 84.*　　J. T. DUFFIELD.

Lord of hosts, thy tents how lovely!
　Living God, thy courts to see
My soul longeth, even fainteth—
　Heart and flesh cry for thee.

2 Lord of hosts, my supplication
　Hear—O God of Jacob's race—
God, our shield and our salvation—
　Look on thine Anointed's face.

3 One day in thy courts is better
　Than a thousand—yea, therein
I had rather be doorkeeper
　Than to dwell in tents of sin.

4 Sun and shield art thou, bestowing
　Grace and glory on the just—
No good thing from them withholding;
　Blest are all who in thee trust.

294　　*Joyous Praise.*　　FAWCETT.

Praise to thee, thou great Creator!
　Praise to thee from every tongue;
Join, my soul, with every creature,
　Join the universal song.

2 Father! source of all compassion!
　Pure, unbounded grace is thine:
Hail the God of our salvation,
　Praise him for his love divine!

3 For ten thousand blessings given,
　For the hope of future joy,
Sound his praise thro' earth and heaven,
　Sound Jehovah's praise on high!

4 Praise to God, the great Creator,
　Father, Son, and Holy Ghost;
Praise him, every living creature,
　Earth and heaven's united host.

5 Joyfully on earth adore him,
　Till in heaven our song we raise;
Then enraptured fall before him,
　Lost in wonder, love, and praise!

295　　*Psalm 135.*　　J. T. DUFFIELD.

Praise the Lord, oh, praise Jehovah,
　Sing ye praises to his name;
Ye who serve him, Hallelujah
　To the Lord of hosts proclaim.

2 Ye who stand within his temple,
　Praise his name—Jehovah laud;
Ye who in his courts assemble,
　Praise the Lord of hosts, our God.

3 Praise him, he is good and gracious,
　He is merciful and true;
Shout aloud Jehovah's praises,
　It is comely so to do.

4 Praise him, for in his good pleasure,
　He in Zion loves to dwell;
Praise him, his peculiar treasure
　Is the seed of Israel.

5 Ye who fear him, oh, draw near him!
　Ye his saints, with one accord
Come before him and adore him:
　Hallelujah, praise the Lord!

113

SWEET HOUR. L. M. D.

1 Sweet hour of prayer! sweet hour of prayer! That calls me from a world of care,
D. C. And oft es-caped the tempt-er's snare By thy re-turn, sweet hour of prayer!

And bids me at my Fa-ther's throne Make all my wants and wish-es known:
And oft es-caped the tempter's snare By thy re-turn, sweet hour of prayer!

In sea-sons of dis-tress and grief, My soul has oft-en found re-lief:

296   *"Sweet Hour."*   WALFORD.

Sweet hour of prayer! sweet hour of prayer!
That calls me from a world of care,
And bids me, at my Father's throne,
Make all my wants and wishes known:
In seasons of distress and grief,
My soul has often found relief,
And oft escaped the tempter's snare,
By thy return, sweet hour of prayer!

2 Sweet hour of prayer! sweet hour of prayer!
Thy wings shall my petition bear,
To him, whose truth and faithfulness
Engage the waiting soul to bless:
And, since he bids me seek his face,
Believe his word, and trust his grace,
I'll cast on him my every care,
And wait for thee, sweet hour of prayer!

297   *Prayer anywhere.*   COWPER.

Jesus, where'er thy people meet,
There they behold thy mercy-seat;
Where'er they seek thee thou art found,
And every place is hallowed ground.

2 For thou, within no walls confined,
Inhabitest the humble mind;
Such ever bring thee where they come,
And going, take thee to their home.

3 Great Shepherd of thy chosen few,
Thy former mercies here renew;
Here to our waiting hearts proclaim
The sweetness of thy saving name.

4 Here may we prove the power of prayer,
To strengthen faith and sweeten care,
To teach our faint desires to rise,
And bring all heaven before our eyes.

298   *Hour of Prayer.*   RAFFLES.

Blest hour! when mortal man retires
To hold communion with his God,
To send to heaven his warm desires,
And listen to the sacred word.

2 Blest hour! when earthly cares resign
Their empire o'er his anxious breast,
While all around the calm divine
Proclaims the holy day of rest.

3 Blest hour! when God himself draws nigh,
Well pleased his people's voice to hear,
To hush the penitential sigh,
And wipe away the mourner's tear.

4 Blest hour! for where the Lord resorts—
Foretastes of future bliss are given;
And mortals find his earthly courts
The house of God, the gate of Heaven!

114

OBERLIN. L. M.

1. Where high the heavenly tem - ple stands, The house of God not made with hands,

A great High Priest our na - ture wears,—The Guardian of man-kind ap - pears.

299 *" Our infirmities."* BRUCE.

WHERE high the heavenly temple stands,
The house of God not made with hands,
A great High Priest our nature wears,—
The Guardian of mankind appears.

2 Though now ascended up on high,
He bends on earth a brother's eye;
Partaker of the human name,
He knows the frailty of our frame.

3 Our Fellow-sufferer yet retains
A fellow feeling of our pains;
And still remembers, in the skies,
His tears, his agonies, and cries.

4 In every pang that rends the heart,
The Man of Sorrows had a part;
He sympathizes with our grief,
And to the sufferer sends relief.

5 With boldness, therefore, at the throne,
Let us make all our sorrows known;
And ask the aid of heavenly power,
To help us in the evil hour.

300 *Prayers hindered.* COWPER.

WHAT various hindrances we meet
In coming to a mercy-seat!
Yet who that knows the worth of prayer
But wishes to be often there?

2 Pray'r makes the darken'd clouds withdraw;
Prayer climbs the ladder Jacob saw,
Gives exercise to faith and love,
Brings every blessing from above.

3 Restraining prayer, we cease to fight;
Prayer makes the Christian's armor bright;
And Satan trembles when he sees
The weakest saint upon his knees.

4 Have you no words? ah! think again;
Words flow apace when you complain,
And fill a fellow-creature's ear
With the sad tale of all your care.

5 Were half the breath thus vainly spent
To heaven in supplication sent,
Our cheerful song would oftener be,
"Hear what the Lord hath done for me!"

301 *" Ask what thou wilt."* NEWTON.

AND dost thou say, "Ask what thou wilt?"
Lord, I would seize the golden hour:
I pray to be released from guilt,
And freed from sin and Satan's power.

2 More of thy presence, Lord, impart;
More of thine image let me bear:
Erect thy throne within my heart,
And reign without a rival there.

3 Give me to read my pardon sealed,
And from thy joy to draw my strength:
Oh, be thy boundless love revealed
In all its height and breadth and length.

4 Grant these requests—I ask no more,
But to thy care the rest resign:
Sick, or in health, or rich, or poor,
All shall be well, if thou art mine.

115

RETREAT. L. M.

1. From ev - ery storm-y wind that blows, From ev - ery swell-ing tide of woes,

There is a calm, a sure re - treat; 'Tis found beneath the mer - cy seat.

302   *The Mercy-seat.*   STOWELL.

From every stormy wind that blows,
From every swelling tide of woes,
There is a calm, a sure retreat;
'Tis found beneath the mercy-seat.

2 There is a place where Jesus sheds
The oil of gladness on our heads,—
A place than all besides more sweet;
It is the blood-bought mercy-seat.

3 There is a scene where spirits blend,
Where friend holds fellowship with friend:
Though sundered far, by faith they meet
Around one common mercy-seat.

4 There, there, on eagle wings we soar,
And sense and sin molest no more,
And heaven comes down our souls to greet,
And glory crowns the mercy-seat.

5 Oh, let my hand forget her skill,
My tongue be silent, cold, and still,
This throbbing heart forget to beat,
If I forget the mercy-seat.

303   *"The Tranquil Hour."*   RAY PALMER.

Thou, Saviour, from thy throne on high,
Enrobed with light and girt with power,
Dost note the thought, the prayer, the sigh,
Of hearts that love the tranquil hour.

2 Now to our souls, withdrawn awhile
From earth's rude noise, thy face reveal:
And as we worship, kindly smile,
And for thine own our spirits seal.

3 To thee we bring each grief and care,
To thee we fly while tempests lower;
Thou wilt the weary burdens bear
Of hearts that love the tranquil hour.

304   *"The Gate of Heaven."*   KELLY.

How sweet to leave the world awhile,
And seek the presence of our Lord!
Dear Saviour! on thy people smile,
And come, according to thy word.

2 From busy scenes we now retreat,
That we may here converse with thee:
Ah, Lord! behold us at thy feet;
Let this the "gate of heaven" be.

3 "Chief of ten thousand!" now appear,
That we by faith may see thy face:
Oh, speak, that we thy voice may hear
And let thy presence fill this place.

305   *"Two or Three."*   STENNETT.

Where two or three, with sweet accord,
Obedient to their sovereign Lord,
Meet to recount his acts of grace,
And offer solemn prayer and praise;—

2 There will the gracious Saviour be,
To bless the little company;
There, to unvail his smiling face,
And bid his glories fill the place.

3 We meet at thy command, O Lord!
Relying on thy faithful word;
Now send the Spirit from above,
And fill our hearts with heavenly love.

BYEFIELD. C. M.

1. Prayer is the soul's sin - cere de - sire, Ut - tered or un - ex - pressed;

The mo - tion of a hid - den fire That trem - bles in the breast.

306　　　*What Prayer is.*　　　MONTGOMERY.

PRAYER is the soul's sincere desire,
　Uttered or unexpressed;
The motion of a hidden fire
　That trembles in the breast.

2 Prayer is the burden of a sigh,
　The falling of a tear,
The upward glancing of an eye,
　When none but God is near.

3 Prayer is the simplest form of speech
　That infant lips can try;
Prayer the sublimest strains that reach
　The Majesty on high.

4 Prayer is the Christian's vital breath,
　The Christian's native air:
His watchword at the gates of death—
　He enters heaven with prayer.

5 Prayer is the contrite sinner's voice,
　Returning from his ways;
While angels in their songs rejoice,
　And cry—"Behold he prays!"

6 O thou, by whom we come to God—
　The Life, the Truth, the Way;·
The path of prayer thyself hast trod;
　Lord! teach us how to pray.

307　　　*"Watch and Pray."*　　　HASTINGS.

THE Saviour bids thee watch and pray
　Through life's momentous hour;
And grants the Spirit's quickening ray
　To those who seek his power.

2 The Saviour bids thee watch and pray,
　Maintain a warrior's strife;
O Christian! hear his voice to-day:
　Obedience is thy life.

3 The Saviour bids thee watch and pray,
　For soon the hour will come
That calls thee from the earth away
　To thy eternal home.

4 The Saviour bids thee watch and pray,
　Oh, hearken to his voice,
And follow where he leads the way,
　To heaven's eternal joys!

308　　　*Comfort in Prayer.*　　　BEDDOME.

PRAYER is the breath of God in man,
　Returning whence it came;
Love is the sacred fire within,
　And prayer the rising flame.

2 It gives the burdened spirit ease,
　And soothes the troubled breast;
Yields comfort to the mourning soul,
　And to the weary rest.

3 When God inclines the heart to pray,
　He hath an ear to hear;
To him there's music in a sigh,
　And beauty in a tear.

4 The humble suppliant cannot fail
　To have his wants supplied,
Since he for sinners intercedes,
　Who once for sinners died.

SOUTHPORT.   C. M.

1. Hail, tranquil hour of clos-ing day! Be - gone, dis-turb - ing care!

And look, my soul, from earth a - way, To him who hear - eth prayer.

309 *Evening Prayer.* BACON.

Hail, tranquil hour of closing day!
Begone, disturbing care!
And look, my soul, from earth away,
To him who heareth prayer.

2 How sweet the tear of penitence,
Before his throne of grace,
While, to the contrite spirit's sense,
He shows his smiling face.

3 How sweet, thro' long remembered years,
His mercies to recall;
And, pressed with wants, and griefs, and fears,
To trust his love for all.

4 How sweet to look, in thoughtful hope,
Beyond this fading sky,
And hear him call his children up
To his fair home on high.

5 Calmly the day forsakes our heaven
To dawn beyond the west;
So let my soul, in life's last even,
Retire to glorious rest.

310 *" Two or Three."* HASTINGS.

Wherever two or three may meet,
To worship in thy name,
Bending beneath thy mercy-seat,
This promise they may claim:—

2 Jesus in love will condescend
To bless the hallowed place;
The Saviour will himself attend,
And show his smiling face.

118

3 How bright the assurance! gracious Lord,
Fountain of peace and love,
Fulfill to us thy precious word,
Thy loving-kindness prove.

4 Now to our God—the Father, Son,
And Holy Spirit, sing!
With praise to God, the Three in One,
Let all creation ring.

311 *Evening Devotion.* H. K. WHITE.

O Lord, another day is flown;
And we, a lowly band,
Are met once more before thy throne,
To bless thy fostering hand.

2 And wilt thou bend a listening ear
To praises low as ours?
Thou wilt! for thou dost love to hear
The song which meekness pours.

3 Thy heavenly grace to each impart;
All evil far remove;
And shed abroad in every heart
Thy everlasting love.

4 Thus chastened, cleansed, entirely thine,
A flock by Jesus led,
The Sun of holiness shall shine
In glory on our head.

5 And thou wilt turn our wandering feet,
And thou wilt bless our way;
Till worlds shall fade, and faith shall greet
The dawn of lasting day.

WOODSTOCK. C. M.

1. I love to steal a - while a - way From ev - ery cum - bering care,

And spend the hours of set - ting day In hum - ble grate - ful prayer.

312 *Prayer in Retirement.* BROWN.

I LOVE to steal awhile away
  From every cumbering care,
And spend the hours of setting day
  In humble, grateful prayer.

2 I love in solitude to shed
  The penitential tear,
And all his promises to plead,
  Where none but God can hear.

3 I love to think on mercies past,
  And future good implore,
And all my cares and sorrows cast
  On him whom I adore.

4 I love by faith to take a view
  Of brighter scenes in heaven;
The prospect doth my strength renew,
  While here by tempests driven.

5 Thus, when life's toilsome day is o'er,
  May its departing ray
Be calm as this impressive hour,
  And lead to endless day.

313 *Prayer a Power.* WALLACE.

THERE is an eye that never sleeps
  Beneath the wing of night;
There is an ear that never shuts,
  When sink the beams of light.

2 There is an arm that never tires,
  When human strength gives way;
There is a love that never fails,
  When earthly loves decay.

3 That eye is fixed on seraph throngs;
  That arm upholds the sky;
That ear is filled with angel songs;
  That love is throned on high.

4 But there's a power which man can wield
  When mortal aid is vain,
That eye, that arm, that love to reach,
  That listening ear to gain.

5 That power is prayer, which soars on high,
  Through Jesus, to the throne;
And moves the hand which moves the world,
  To bring salvation down!

314 *" A safe Retreat."* STEELE.

DEAR Father, to thy mercy-seat
  My soul for shelter flies:
'Tis here I find a safe retreat
  When storms and tempests rise.

2 My cheerful hope can never die,
  If thou, my God, art near;
Thy grace can raise my comforts high,
  And banish every fear.

3 My great Protector, and my Lord!
  Thy constant aid impart;
Oh, let thy kind, thy gracious word
  Sustain my trembling heart.

4 Oh, never let my soul remove
  From this divine retreat;
Still let me trust thy power and love,
  And dwell beneath thy feet.

SHIRLAND. S. M.

1. Our heaven-ly Fa - ther calls, And Christ in - vites us near;

With both, our friend-ship shall be sweet, And our com - mun - ion dear.

315　　　"Christ invites us."　　DODDRIDGE.

Our heavenly Father calls,
　And Christ invites us near;
With both our friendship shall be sweet,
　And our communion dear.

2 God pities all our griefs:
　He pardons every day;
Almighty to protect our souls,
　And wise to guide our way.

3 How large his bounties are!
　What various stores of good,
Diffused from our Redeemer's hand,
　And purchased with his blood!

4 Jesus, our living Head,
　We bless thy faithful care;
Our Advocate before the throne,
　And our Forerunner there.

5 Here fix, my roving heart!
　Here wait, my warmest love!
Till the communion be complete,
　In nobler scenes above.

316　　　Morning Prayer.　　SPURGEON.

Sweetly the holy hymn
　Breaks on the morning air;
Before the world with smoke is dim,
　We meet to offer prayer.

2 While flowers are wet with dews,
　Dew of our souls descend:
Ere yet the sun the day renews,
　O Lord, thy Spirit send.

120

3 Upon the battle field,
　Before the fight begins,
We seek, O Lord, thy sheltering shield,
　To guard us from our sins.

4 On the lone mountain side,
　Before the morning's light,
The Man of Sorrows wept and cried,
　And rose refreshed with might.

5 Oh, hear us, then, for we
　Are very weak and frail,
We make the Saviour's name our plea,
　And surely must prevail.

317　　　"Never Faint."　　NEWTON.

Jesus, who knows full well
　The heart of every saint,
Invites us all, our grief to tell,
　To pray and never faint.

2 He bows his gracious ear,—
　We never plead in vain;
Then let us wait till he appear,
　And pray, and pray again.

3 Jesus, the Lord, will hear
　His chosen when they cry;
Yes, though he may a while forbear,
　He'll help them from on high.

4 Then let us earnest cry,
　And never faint in prayer;
He sees, he hears, and, from on high,
　Will make our cause his care,

STATE STREET. S. M.

1. How sweet the melt - ing lay Which breaks up - on the ear,

When at the hour of ris - ing day Christ-ians u - nite in prayer.

318   *Morning Prayer.*   MRS. BROWN.

How sweet the melting lay
Which breaks upon the ear,
When at the hour of rising day
Christians unite in prayer.

2 The breezes waft their cries
Up to Jehovah's throne;
He listens to their humble sighs,
And sends his blessings down.

3 So Jesus rose to pray
Before the morning light—
Once on the chilling mount did stay,
And wrestle all the night.

4 So Jesus still doth pray
Before the morning bright,
On heavenly mountains far away,
While we toil here in night.

5 Leave, Lord, thy vigil there,
Descend upon life's wave;
Come to the bark through midnight air,
The storm shall cease to rave.

319   *"The Throne of Grace."*   NEWTON.

Behold the throne of grace!
The promise calls me near;
There Jesus shows a smiling face,
And waits to answer prayer.

2 That rich atoning blood,
Which sprinkled round I see,
Provides for those who come to God
An all-prevailing plea.

3 My soul! ask what thou wilt;
Thou canst not be too bold:
Since his own blood for thee he spilt,
What else can he withhold?

4 Thine image, Lord, bestow,
Thy presence and thy love;
I ask to serve thee here below,
And reign with thee above.

5 Teach me to live by faith;
Conform my will to thine;
Let me victorious be in death,
And then in glory shine.

320   *"Thy Holy Spirit."*   ANON.

Lord, bid thy light arise
On all thy people here,
And when we raise our longing eyes
Oh, may we find thee near!

2 Thy Holy Spirit send,
To quicken every soul;
And hearts the most rebellious bend
To thy divine control.

3 Let all that own thy name
Thy sacred image bear;
And light in every heart the flame
Of watchfulness and prayer.

4 Since in thy love we see
Our only sure relief,
Oh, raise our earthly minds to thee,
And help our unbelief.

121

HORTON. 7.

1. Come, my soul, thy suit pre-pare, Je - sus loves to an - swer prayer;

He him-self has bid thee pray, Therefore will not say thee nay.

321   *"Thy suit prepare."*   NEWTON.

Come, my soul, thy suit prepare,
Jesus loves to answer prayer;
He himself has bid thee pray,
Therefore will not say thee nay.

2 With my burden I begin:—
Lord! remove this load of sin;
Let thy blood, for sinners spilt,
Set my conscience free from guilt.

3 Lord! I come to thee for rest,
Take possession of my breast;
There, thy sovereign right maintain,
And, without a rival, reign.

4 While I am a pilgrim here,
Let thy love my spirit cheer;
Be my Guide, my Guard, my Friend,
Lead me to my journey's end.

5 Show me what I have to do,
Every hour my strength renew;
Let me live a life of faith,
Let me die thy people's death.

322   *An urgent Case.*   NEWTON.

Lord! I cannot let thee go,
Till a blessing thou bestow;
Do not turn away thy face,
Mine's an urgent, pressing case.

2 Once a sinner, near despair,
Sought thy mercy-seat by prayer;
Mercy heard and set him free—
Lord! that mercy came to me.

122

3 Many days have passed since then,
Many changes I have seen;
Yet have been upheld till now;
Who could hold me up but thou?

4 Thou hast helped in every need—
This emboldens me to plead;
After so much mercy past,
Canst thou let me sink at last?

5 No—I must maintain my hold;
'Tis thy goodness makes me bold;
I can no denial take,
Since I plead for Jesus' sake.

323   *God Everywhere.*   ANON.

They who seek the throne of grace
Find that throne in every place;
If we live a life of prayer,
God is present everywhere.

2 In our sickness and our health,
In our want, or in our wealth,
If we look to God in prayer,
God is present everywhere.

3 When our earthly comforts fail,
When the foes of life prevail,
'Tis the time for earnest prayer;
God is present everywhere.

4 Then, my soul, in every strait,
To thy Father come, and wait;
He will answer every prayer:
God is present everywhere.

HAMLIN. 7, D.

1. Let us with a joy-ful mind Praise the Lord, for he is kind, For his mer-cies

shall en-dure, Ev-er faith-ful, ev-er sure. Let us sound his name a-broad, For of

gods he is the God Who by wisdom did cre-ate Heaven's expanse and all its state ;—

324 *"Ever Faithful."* MILTON.

Let us with a joyful mind
Praise the Lord, for he is kind,
For his mercies shall endure,
Ever faithful, ever sure.
Let us sound his name abroad,
For of gods he is the God
Who by wisdom did create
Heaven's expanse and all its state;—

2 Did the solid earth ordain
How to rise above the main;
Who, by his commanding might,
Filled the new-made world with light:
Caused the golden-tressèd sun
All the day his course to run;
And the moon to shine by night,
'Mid her spangled sisters bright.

3 All his creatures God doth feed,
His full hand supplies their need;
Let us, therefore, warble forth
His high majesty and worth.
He his mansion hath on high,
'Bove the reach of mortal eye;
And his mercies shall endure,
Ever faithful, ever sure.

325 *Sabbath Praise.—Ps. 92.* SANDYS.

Thou who art enthroned above,
Thou by whom we live and move!
Oh, how sweet, with joyful tongue,
To resound thy praise in song!
When the morning paints the skies,
When the sparkling stars arise,
All thy favors to rehearse,
And give thanks in grateful verse.

2 Sweet the day of sacred rest,
When devotion fills the breast,
When we dwell within thy house,
Hear thy word, and pay our vows;
Notes to heaven's high mansions raise
Fill its courts with joyful praise;
With repeated hymns proclaim
Great Jehovah's awful name.

3 From thy works our joys arise,
O thou only good and wise!
Who thy wonders can declare?
How profound thy counsels are!
Warm our hearts with sacred fire;
Grateful fervors still inspire;
All our powers, with all their might,
Ever in thy praise unite.

123

OLD HUNDRED. L. M.

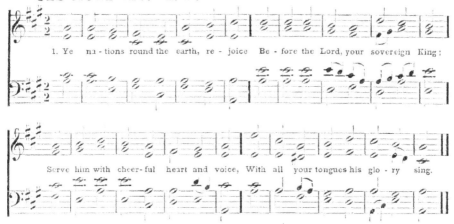

1. Ye na-tions round the earth, re - joice Be - fore the Lord, your sovereign King;

Serve him with cheer-ful heart and voice, With all your tongues his glo - ry sing.

326　　　*Psalm 100.*　　　WATTS.

YE nations round the earth, rejoice
　Before the Lord, your sovereign King:
Serve him with cheerful heart and voice,
　With all your tongues his glory sing.

2 The Lord is God—'t is he alone
　Doth life and breath and being give:
We are his work—and not our own,
　The sheep that on his pastures live.

3 Enter his gates with songs of joy,
　With praises to his courts repair;
And make it your divine employ,
　To pay your thanks and honors there.

4 The Lord is good—the Lord is kind;
　Great is his grace—his mercy sure;
And all the race of man shall find
　His truth from age to age endure.

327　　　*Psalm 39.*　　　WATTS.

JEHOVAH reigns; his throne is high;
　His robes are light and majesty;
His glory shines with beams so bright,
　No mortal can sustain the sight.

2 His terrors keep the world in awe;
　His justice guards his holy law;
Yet love reveals a smiling face,
　And truth and promise seal the grace.

3 Through all his works his wisdom shines,
　And baffles Satan's deep designs;
His power is sovereign to fulfil
　The noblest counsels of his will.

124

4 And will this glorious Lord descend
　To be my Father and my Friend?
Then let my songs with angels' join,
　Heaven is secure, if God be mine.

328　　　*Psalm 117.*　　　WATTS.

FROM all that dwell below the skies,
　Let the Creator's praise arise:
Let the Redeemer's name be sung,
　Through every land, by every tongue.

2 Eternal are thy mercies, Lord!
　Eternal truth attends thy word:
Thy praise shall sound from shore to shore,
　Till suns shall rise and set no more.

329　　　*God's Glory.*　　　BLACKLOCK.

COME, O my soul! in sacred lays
　Attempt thy great Creator's praise:
But, oh, what tongue can speak his fame?
　What mortal verse can reach the theme?

2 Enthroned amid the radiant spheres,
　He glory like a garment wears;
To form a robe of light divine,
　Ten thousand suns around him shine.

3 In all our Maker's grand designs,
　Almighty power with wisdom shines;
His works, thro' all this wondrous frame,
　Declare the glory of his name.

4 Raised on devotion's lofty wing,
　Do thou, my soul, his glories sing;
And let his praise employ thy tongue,
　Till listening worlds shall join the song!

WARE. L. M.

1. Now to the Lord a no-ble song! A-wake, my soul! a-wake, my tongue!

Ho-san-na to th'e-ter-nal name, And all his boundless love pro-claim.

330   *"A noble Song."*   WATTS.

Now to the Lord a noble song!
Awake, my soul! awake, my tongue!
Hosanna to the eternal name,
And all his boundless love proclaim.

2 See where it shines in Jesus' face,—
The brightest image of his grace!
God, in the person of his Son,
Hath all his mightiest works outdone.

3 Grace!—'tis a sweet, a charming theme:
My thoughts rejoice at Jesus' name:
Ye angels! dwell upon the sound:
Ye heavens! reflect it to the ground.

4 Oh, may I reach that happy place,
Where he unvails his lovely face,
Where all his beauties you behold,
And sing his name to harps of gold.

331   *Psalm 36.*   WATTS.

High in the heavens, eternal God!
    Thy goodness in full glory shines;
Thy truth shall break through every cloud
    That vails and darkens thy designs.

2 For ever firm thy justice stands,
    As mountains their foundations keep:
Wise are the wonders of thy hands;
    Thy judgments are a mighty deep.

3 My God, how excellent thy grace!
    Whence all our hope and comfort
The sons of Adam, in distress, [springs;
    Fly to the shadow of thy wings.

4 From the provisions of thy house
    We shall be fed with sweet repast;
There, mercy like a river flows,
    And brings salvation to our taste.

5 Life, like a fountain rich and free,
    Springs from the presence of my Lord;
And in thy light our souls shall see
    The glories promised in thy word.

332   *"Te Deum."*   ANON.

Lord God of Hosts, by all adored!
Thy name we praise with one accord;
The earth and heavens are full of thee,
Thy light, thy love, thy majesty.

2 Lord hallelujahs to thy name
Angels and seraphim proclaim;
Eternal praise to thee is given
By all the powers and thrones in heaven.

3 The apostles join the glorious throng,
The prophets aid to swell the song,
The noble and triumphant host
Of martyrs make of thee their boast.

4 The holy church in every place
Throughout the world exalts thy praise;
Both heaven and earth do worship thee,
Thou Father of eternity!

5 From day to day, O Lord, do we
Highly exalt and honor thee;
Thy name we worship and adore,
World without end for evermore.

OAKSVILLE. C. M.

1. Sing we the song of those who stand A - round th' e - ter - nal throne,

Of ev - ery kin - dred, clime, and land, A mul - ti - tude un - known.

333   *"Worthy the Lamb."*   MONTGOMERY.

SING we the song of those who stand
  Around the eternal throne,
Of every kindred, clime, and land,
  A multitude unknown.

2 Life's poor distinctions vanish here;
  To-day the young, the old,
Our Saviour and his flock appear
  One Shepherd and one fold.

3 Toil, trial, sufferings still await
  On earth the pilgrims' throng;
Yet learn we in our low estate
  The Church Triumphant's song.

4 "Worthy the Lamb for sinners slain,—"
  Cry the redeemed above,
"Blessing and honor to obtain,
  And everlasting love!"

5 "Worthy the Lamb" on earth we sing,
  "Who died our souls to save!
Henceforth, O Death! where is thy sting?
  Thy victory, O Grave!"

334   *Psalm* 148.   WATTS.

PRAISE ye the Lord, immortal choir!
  In heavenly heights above,
With harp, and voice, and soul of fire,
  Burning with perfect love.

2 Shine to his glory, worlds of light!
  Ye million suns of space;
Ye moons and glistening stars of night,
  Running your mystic race.

3 Shout to Jehovah, surging main!
  In deep eternal roar;
Let wave to wave resound the strain,
  And shore reply to shore.

4 Storm, lightning, thunder, hail, and snow,
  Wild winds that keep his word,
With the old mountains far below,
  Unite to bless the Lord.

5 And round the wide world let it roll,
  Whilst man shall lead it on;
Join, every ransomed human soul,
  In glorious unison.

335   *Rejoicing in God.*   HIGGINBOTHAM.

COME, shout aloud the Father's grace,
  And sing the Saviour's love;
Soon shall we join the glorious theme,
  In loftier strains above.

2 God, the eternal, mighty God,
  To dearer names descends;
Calls us his treasure and his joy,
  His children and his friends.

3 My Father, God! and may these lips
  Pronounce a name so dear?
Not thus could heaven's sweet harmony
  Delight my listening ear.

4 Thanks to my God for every gift
  His bounteous hands bestow;
And thanks eternal for that love
  Whence all those comforts flow.

SILVER STREET. S. M.

1. Come, sound his praise a - broad, And hymns of glo - ry sing:

Je - ho - vah is the sove - reign God, The u - - ni - ver - sal King.

WATTS.

336   *Psalm* 95.

Come, sound his praise abroad,
  And hymns of glory sing:
Jehovah is the sovereign God,
  The universal King.

2 He formed the deeps unknown;
  He gave the seas their bound;
The watery worlds are all his own,
  And all the solid ground.

3 Come, worship at his throne,
  Come, bow before the Lord:
We are his work, and not our own,
  He formed us by his word.

4 To-day attend his voice,
  Nor dare provoke his rod;
Come, like the people of his choice,
  And own our gracious God.

WATTS.

337   *Psalm* 118.

See, what a living stone
  The builders did refuse:
Yet God hath built his church thereon,
  In spite of envious Jews.

2 The scribe and angry priest
  Reject thine only Son;
Yet on this rock shall Zion rest,
  As the chief corner-stone.

3 The work, O Lord! is thine,
  And wondrous in our eyes;
This day declares it all divine;
  This day did Jesus rise.

4 This is the glorious day,
  That our Redeemer made:
Let us rejoice, and sing, and pray;
  Let all the church be glad.

5 Hosanna to the King
  Of David's royal blood;
Bless him, ye saints!—he comes to bring
  Salvation from your God.

MONTGOMERY.

338   *Call to Praise.*

Stand up, and bless the Lord,
  Ye people of his choice;
Stand up and bless the Lord your God,
  With heart and soul and voice.

2 Though high above all praise,
  Above all blessing high,
Who would not fear his holy name,
  And laud, and magnify?

3 Oh, for the living flame
  From his own altar brought,
To touch our lips, our souls inspire,
  And wing to heaven our thought!

4 God is our strength and song,
  And his salvation ours:
Then be his love in Christ proclaimed,
  With all our ransomed powers.

5 Stand up and bless the Lord;
  The Lord your God adore;
Stand up, and bless his glorious name,
  Henceforth, for evermore.

LYONS. 5, 6.

1. Oh, worship the King, All-glorious a - bove; Oh, gratefully sing His pow'r and his love;

Our shield and defender, The Ancient of Days, Pa-vilioned in splendor, And girded with praise.

339   *God's Perfections.*   GRANT.

Oh, worship the King,
  All-glorious above;
And gratefully sing
  His power and his love;
Our shield and defender,
  The Ancient of Days,
Pavilioned in splendor,
  And girded with praise.

2 Oh, tell of his might,
  Oh, sing of his grace,
Whose robe is the light,
  Whose canopy, space;
Whose chariots of wrath
  The deep thunder-clouds form;
And dark is his path
  On the wings of the storm.

3 Thy bountiful care
  What tongue can recite?
It breathes in the air,
  It shines in the light,
It streams from the hills,
  It descends to the plain,
And sweetly distils
  In the dew and the rain.

4 Frail children of dust,
  And feeble as frail,
In thee do we trust,
  Nor find thee to fail;
Thy mercies how tender,
  How firm to the end,
Our Maker, Defender,
  Redeemer, and Friend!

340   *" Salvation to God."*   C. WESLEY.

Ye servants of God,
  Your Master proclaim,
And publish abroad
  His wonderful name:
The name, all victorious,
  Of Jesus extol;
His kingdom is glorious,
  And rules over all.

2 God ruleth on high,
  Almighty to save;
And still he is nigh;
  His presence we have:
The great congregation
  His triumph shall sing,
Ascribing salvation
  To Jesus, our King.

3 "Salvation to God,
  Who sits on the throne,"
Let all cry aloud,
  And honor the Son:
Our Saviour's high praises
  The angels proclaim,—
Fall down on their faces,
  And worship the Lamb.

4 Then let us adore,
  And give him his right—
All glory and power,
  And wisdom and might;
All honor and blessing,
  With angels above,
And thanks never ceasing,
  And infinite love!

LEONI. P. M.

1. The God of Abraham praise, Who reigns enthroned a - bove, Ancient of ev - er -
last - ing days, And God of love! Je - ho - vah! great I Am! By
earth and heaven con-fest; I bow and bless the sa - cred name, For ev - er blest!

341   *"The God of Abraham."*   OLIVERS.

THE God of Abraham praise,
  Who reigns enthroned above,
Ancient of everlasting days,
  And God of love!
Jehovah! great I Am!
  By earth and heaven confessed;
I bow and bless the sacred name,
  For ever blest!

2 The God of Abraham praise!
  At whose supreme command
From earth I rise, and seek the joys
  At his right hand:
I all on earth forsake,
  Its wisdom, fame, and power,
And him my only portion make,
  My shield and tower.

3 The God of Abraham praise!
  Whose all-sufficient grace
Shall guide me all my happy days
  In all my ways:
He calls a worm his friend!
  He calls himself my God!
And he shall save me to the end
  Through Jesus' blood!

342   *"The Great I Am."*   OLIVERS.

GOD by himself hath sworn,
  I on his oath depend;
I shall, on eagles' wings upborne,
  To heaven ascend;
I shall behold his face,
  I shall his power adore,
And sing the wonders of his grace
  For evermore!

2 The God who reigns on high
  The great archangels sing;
And, "Holy, holy, holy," cry,
  Almighty King!
Who was and is the same,
  And evermore shall be;
Jehovah, Father, great I Am,
  We worship thee.

3 The whole triumphant host
  Give thanks to God on high;
"Hail! Father, Son, and Holy Ghost!"
  They ever cry:
Hail! Abraham's God, and mine!
  I join the heavenly lays;
All might and majesty are thine,
  And endless praise!

HEBRON. L. M.

1. Thus far the Lord has led me on; Thus far his pow'r pro-longs my days;

And ev-ery even-ing shall make known Some fresh me-mo-rial of his grace.

343   *Helped Hitherto.*   WATTS.

Thus far the Lord has led me on;
  Thus far his power prolongs my days;
And every evening shall make known
  Some fresh memorial of his grace.

2 Much of my time has run to waste,
  And I, perhaps, am near my home;
But he forgives my follies past,
  And gives me strength for days to come.

3 I lay my body down to sleep;
  Peace is the pillow for my head;
While well-appointed angels keep
  Their watchful stations round my bed.

4 Thus when the night of death shall come,
  My flesh shall rest beneath the ground,
And wait thy voice to break my tomb,
  With sweet salvation in the sound.

344   *Evening Song.*   STEELE.

Great God! to thee my evening song
  With humble gratitude I raise;
Oh, let thy mercy tune my tongue,
  And fill my heart with lively praise.

2 My days unclouded as they pass,
  And every gentle, rolling hour,
Are monuments of wondrous grace,
  And witness to thy love and power.

3 And yet this thoughtless, wretched heart,
  Too oft regardless of thy love,
Ungrateful, can from thee depart,
  And, fond of trifles, vainly rove.

4 Seal my forgiveness in the blood
  Of Jesus; his dear name alone
I plead for pardon, gracious God!
  And kind acceptance at thy throne.

345   *Dismissal.*   HART.

Dismiss us with thy blessing, Lord!
  Help us to feed upon thy word;
All that has been amiss, forgive,
  And let thy truth within us live.

2 Though we are guilty, thou art good;
  Wash all our works in Jesus' blood;
Give every burdened soul release,
  And bid us all depart in peace.

346   *Service ended.*   ANON.

Ere to the world again we go,
  Its pleasures, cares, and idle show,
Thy grace, once more, O God, we crave,
  From folly and from sin to save.

2 May the great truths we here have heard,
  The lessons of thy holy word—
Dwell in our inmost bosoms deep,
  And all our souls from error keep.

Oh, may the influence of this day
  Long as our memory with us stay,
And as a constant guardian prove,
  To guide us to our home above.

3 To God the Father, God the Son,
  And God the Spirit, three in one,
Be honor, praise, and glory given,
  By all on earth, and all in heaven.

EVENING HYMN. L. M.

1. Glo - ry to thee, my God, this night, For all the blessings of the light;

Keep me, oh, keep me, King of kings! Be - neath thine own al - migh - ty wings.

347   *Evening Hymn.*   KEN.

GLORY to thee, my God, this night,
For all the blessings of the light;
Keep me, oh, keep me, King of kings!
Beneath thine own almighty wings.

2 Forgive me, Lord, for thy dear Son,
The ill which I this day have done;
That with the world, myself, and thee,
I, ere I sleep, at peace may be.

3 Teach me to live, that I may dread
The grave as little as my bed:
Teach me to die, that so I may
Rise glorious at the judgment-day.

4 Oh, let my soul on thee repose,
And may sweet sleep mine eyelids close!
Sleep, which shall me more vigorous make,
To serve my God when I awake.

5 Be thou my guardian, while I sleep
Thy watchful station near me keep;
My heart with love celestial fill,
And guard me from the approach of ill.

6 Lord, let my soul for ever share,
The bliss of thy paternal care:
'Tis heaven on earth, 'tis heaven above,
To see thy face, and sing thy love!

348   *"The Peace of God."*   NEWTON.

THE peace which God alone reveals,
And by his word of grace imparts,
Which only the believer feels,
Direct, and keep, and cheer our hearts!

2 And may the holy Three in One,
The Father, Word, and Comforter,
Pour an abundant blessing down
On every soul assembled here!

3 Praise God, from whom all blessings flow;
Praise him, all creatures here below;
Praise him above, ye heavenly host!
Praise Father, Son, and Holy Ghost.

349   *The Close of the Sabbath.*   EDMESTON.

ANOTHER day has passed along,
And we are nearer to the tomb,—
Nearer to join the heavenly song,
Or hear the last eternal doom.

2 Sweet is the light of Sabbath-eve,
And soft the sunbeams lingering there;
For these blest hours, the world I leave,
Wafted on wings of faith and prayer.

3 The time, how lovely and how still;
Peace shines and smiles on all below,—
The plain, the stream, the wood, the hill,—
All fair with evening's setting glow.

4 Season of rest! the tranquil soul
Feels the sweet calm, and melts to love,—
And while these sacred moments roll,
Faith sees a smiling heaven above.

5 Nor will our days of toil be long,
Our pilgrimage will soon be trod;
And we shall join the ceaseless song,—
The endless Sabbath of our God.

EVENTIDE. 10.

1. A - bide with me! Fast falls the e-ven-tide, The darkness deepens—Lord, with me a - bide;

5th Verse.

When oth-er helpers fail, and comforts flee, Help of the helpless, oh, abide with me! A-men.

350   *"Abide with me."*   LYTE.

ABIDE with me! Fast falls the eventide,
The darkness deepens—Lord, with me
   abide!
When other helpers fail, and comforts flee,
Help of the helpless, oh, abide with me!

2 Swift to its close ebbs out life's little day;
Earth's joys grow dim, its glories pass
   away;
Change and decay in all around I see;
O thou, who changest not, abide with me!

3 I need thy presence every passing hour,
What but thy grace can foil the tempter's
   power?
Who, like thyself, my guide and stay
   can be?
Through cloud and sunshine, oh, abide
   with me!

4 Not a brief glance I long, a passing word;
But as thou dwell'st with thy disciples,
   Lord,
Familiar, condescending, patient, free,
Come, not to sojourn, but abide, with me!

5 Hold thou thy cross before my closing eyes;
Shine through the gloom, and point me
   to the skies;
Heaven's morning breaks, and earth's
   vain shadows flee!
In life, in death, O Lord, abide with me!

351   *Parting Hymn.*   ELLERTON.

SAVIOUR, again to thy dear name we raise
With one accord our parting hymn of
   praise;
We rise to bless thee ere our worship
   cease,
And, now departing, wait thy word of
   peace.

2 Grant us thy peace upon our homeward
   way;
With thee began, with thee shall end the
   day;
Guard thou the lips from sin, the hearts
   from shame,
That in this house have called upon thy
   name.

3 Grant us thy peace, Lord, through the
   coming night,
Turn thou for us its darkness into light;
From harm and danger keep thy children free,
For dark and light are both alike to
   thee.

4 Grant us thy peace throughout our earth-
   ly life,
Our balm in sorrow, and our stay in strife;
Then, when thy voice shall bid our con-
   flict cease,
Call us, O Lord, to thine eternal peace.

HOLLEY. 7.

1. Soft - ly now the light of day Fades up - on my sight a - way;

Free from care, from la - bor free, Lord, I would com-mune with thee.

352   *Evening Song.*   DOANE.

SOFTLY now the light of day
Fades upon my sight away;
Free from care, from labor free,
Lord, I would commune with thee.

2 Thou, whose all-pervading eye
Naught escapes without, within,
Pardon each infirmity,
Open fault, and secret sin.

3 Soon, for me, the light of day
Shall for ever pass away;
Then, from sin and sorrow free,
Take me, Lord, to dwell with thee.

4 Thou who, sinless, yet hast known
All of man's infirmity;
Then from thine eternal throne,
Jesus, look with pitying eye.

353   *Closing Hymn.*   NEWTON.

FOR a season called to part,
Let us now ourselves commend
To the gracious eye and heart
Of our ever present Friend.

2 Jesus! hear our humble prayer,
Tender Shepherd of thy sheep!
Let thy mercy and thy care
All our souls in safety keep.

3 Then if thou thy help afford,
Joyful songs to thee shall rise,
And our souls shall praise the Lord,
Who regards our humble cries.

354   *Hymn at Parting.*   ANON.

THOU, from whom we never part,
Thou, whose love is everywhere,
Thou, who seest every heart,
Listen to our evening prayer.

2 Father, fill our hearts with love,
Love unfailing, full and free;
Love that no alarm can move,
Love that ever rests on thee.

3 Heavenly Father! through the night
Keep us safe from every ill;
Cheerful as the morning light,
May we wake to do thy will.

355   *The mercies of a day.*   MONTGOMERY.

FOR the mercies of the day,
For this rest upon our way,
Thanks to thee alone be given,
Lord of earth and King of heaven!

2 Cold our services have been,
Mingled every prayer with sin:
But thou canst and wilt forgive;
By thy grace alone we live.

3 While this thorny path we tread,
May thy love our footsteps lead;
When our journey here is past,
May we rest with thee at last.

4 Let these earthly Sabbaths prove
Foretastes of our joys above;
While their steps thy children bend
To the rest which knows no end.

133

VESPER. S. M.

1. The day is past and gone, The even-ing shades ap-pear; Oh, may we all re-mem-ber well The night of death draws near.

356　　*Evening hymn.*　　LELAND.

THE day is past and gone,
　The evening shades appear;
Oh, may we all remember well
　The night of death draws near.

2 We lay our garments by,
　Upon our beds to rest;
So death will soon disrobe us all
　Of what we here possessed.

3 Lord, keep us safe this night,
　Secure from all our fears;
May angels guard us while we sleep,
　Till morning light appears.

4 And when we early rise,
　And view the unwearied sun,
May we set out to win the prize,
　And after glory run.

5 And when our days are past,
　And we from time remove,
Oh, may we in thy bosom rest,
　The bosom of thy love.

357　　*Sabbath over.*　　STEELE.

THE day of praise is done;
　The evening shadows fall;
Yet pass not from us with the sun,
　True Light that lightenest all!

2 Around thy throne on high,
　Where night can never be,
The white-robed harpers of the sky
　Bring ceaseless hymns to thee.

3 Too faint our anthems here;
　Too soon of praise we tire;
But oh, the strains how full and clear
　Of that eternal choir!

4 Yet, Lord! to thy dear will
　If thou attune the heart,
We in thine angels' music still
　May bear our lower part.

5 Shine thou within us, then,
　A day that knows no end,
Till songs of angels and of men
　In perfect praise shall blend.

358　　*"Closing hour."*　　E. T. FITCH.

LORD, at this closing hour,
　Establish every heart
Upon thy word of truth and power,
　To keep us when we part.

2 Peace to our brethren give;
　Fill all our hearts with love;
In faith and patience may we live,
　And seek our rest above.

3 Through changes, bright or drear,
　We would thy will pursue;
And toil to spread thy kingdom here,
　Till we its glory view.

4 To God, the only wise,
　In every age adored,
Let glory from the church arise
　Through Jesus Christ our Lord!

BRADEN. S. M.

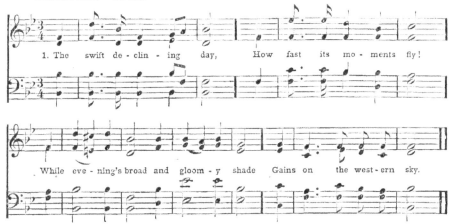

1. The swift de - clin - ing day, How fast its mo - ments fly!

While eve - ning's broad and gloom - y shade Gains on the west - ern sky.

359   *"Do it with thy might."*   DODDRIDGE.

The swift declining day,
  How fast its moments fly!
While evening's broad and gloomy shade
  Gains on the western sky.

2 Ye mortals, mark its pace,
  And use the hours of light;
And know, its Maker can command
  At once eternal night.

3 Give glory to the Lord,
  Who rules the whirling sphere;
Submissive at his footstool bow,
  And seek salvation there.

4 Then shall new lustre break
  Through death's impending gloom,
And lead you to unchanging light,
  In your celestial home.

360   *Doxology.*   WATTS.

To God the only wise,
  Who keeps us by his word,
Be glory now and evermore,
  Through Jesus Christ our Lord.

2 Hosanna to the Word,
  Who from the Father came;
Ascribe salvation to the Lord,
  And ever bless his name.

3 The grace of Christ our Lord,
  The Father's boundless love,
The Spirit's blest communion, too,
  Be with us from above.

361   *"Abide with us."*   NEALE.

The day, O Lord, is spent;
  Abide with us, and rest;
Our hearts' desires are fully bent
  On making thee our guest.

2 We have not reached that land,
  That happy land, as yet,
Where holy angels round thee stand,
  Whose sun can never set.

3 Our sun is sinking now,
  Our day is almost o'er;
O Sun of Righteousness, do thou
  Shine on us evermore!

362   *Parting Hymn.*   HART.

Once more, before we part,
  Oh, bless the Saviour's name;
Let every tongue and every heart
  Adore and praise the same.

2 Lord, in thy grace we came,
  That blessing still impart;
We met in Jesus' sacred name,
  In Jesus' name we part.

3 Still on thy holy word
  Help us to feed, and grow,
Still to go on to know the Lord,
  And practise what we know.

4 Now, Lord, before we part,
  Help us to bless thy name:
Let every tongue and every heart
  Adore and praise the same.

135

GREENVILLE.   8, 7, D, or 8, 7, 4.

1 { May the grace of Christ our Sav-iour, And the Fa-ther's boundless love, }
{ With the Ho-ly Spir-it's fa-vor, Rest up-on us from a-bove. }
D. C.—And pos-sess in sweet com-mun-ion, Joys which earth can-not af-ford.

2. Thus may we a-bide In un-ion, With each oth-er and the Lord;

363   *Benediction.*   NEWTON.

MAY the grace of Christ our Saviour,
  And the Father's boundless love,
With the Holy Spirit's favor,
  Rest upon us from above!
2 Thus may we abide in union
  With each other and the Lord;
And possess, in sweet communion,
  Joys which earth can not afford.

364   *"An Evening Blessing."*   EDMESTON.

SAVIOUR, breathe an evening blessing,
  Ere repose our spirits seal;
Sin and want we come confessing;
  Thou canst save, and thou canst heal.
2 Though destruction walk around us,
  Though the arrow near us fly,
Angel guards from thee surround us;
  We are safe if thou art nigh.
3 Though the night be dark and dreary,
  Darkness cannot hide from thee;
Thou art he who, never weary,
  Watcheth where thy people be.
4 Should swift death this night o'ertake us,
  And our couch become our tomb,
May the morn in heaven awake us,
  Clad in light and deathless bloom.

365   *The Pilgrim.*   HASTINGS.

GENTLY, Lord, oh, gently lead us,
  Through this lonely vale of tears;
Through the changes thou'st decreed us,
  Till our last great change appears.

126

When temptation's darts assail us,
  When in devious paths we stray,
Let thy goodness never fail us,
  Lead us in thy perfect way.
2 In the hour of pain and anguish,
  In the hour when death draws near,
Suffer not our hearts to languish,
  Suffer not our souls to fear.
And when mortal life is ended,
  Bid us in thine arms to rest,
Till by angel bands attended,
  We awake among the blest.

366   *Close of Worship.*   SHIRLEY.

LORD, dismiss us with thy blessing,
  Fill our hearts with joy and peace;
Let us each, thy love possessing,
  Triumph in redeeming grace;
    Oh, refresh us,
Traveling through this wilderness.

2 Thanks we give, and adoration,
  For thy gospel's joyful sound,
May the fruits of thy salvation
  In our hearts and lives abound;
    May thy presence
With us evermore be found.

3 So, whene'er the signal's given,
  Us from earth to call away;
Borne on angels' wings to heaven,
  Glad to leave our cumbrous clay,
    May we, ready,
Rise and reign in endless day.

OLIPHANT. 8, 7, 4.

Guide me, O thou great Je-ho-vah, Pil-grim through this bar-ren land;
I am weak, but thou art might-y;

Hold me with thy powerful hand: Bread of hea-ven! Bread of hea-ven!

Feed me till I want no more, Feed me till I want no more.

367 *" Guide Me."* WILLIAMS.

Guide me, O thou great Jehovah,
   Pilgrim through this barren land;
I am weak, but thou art mighty;
   Hold me with thy powerful hand:
      Bread of heaven!
      Feed me till I want no more.

2 Open thou the crystal fountain,
   Whence the healing streams do flow;
Let the fiery, cloudy pillar
   Lead me all my journey through:
      Strong Deliverer!
      Be thou still my strength and shield.

3 When I tread the verge of Jordan,
   Bid my anxious fears subside;
Death of death! and hell's Destruction!
   Land me safe on Canaan's side:
      Songs of praises
      I will ever give to thee.

368 *" Saviour, Keep us."* KELLY.

God of our salvation! hear us;
   Bless, oh, bless us, ere we go;
When we join the world, be near us,
   Lest we cold and careless grow.
      Saviour! keep us;
      Keep us safe from every foe.

2 As our steps are drawing nearer
   To our everlasting home,
May our view of heaven grow clearer,
   Hope more bright of joys to come;
      And, when dying,
      May thy presence cheer the gloom.

369 *" Guard us, guide us."* EDMESTON.

Lead us, heavenly Father, lead us
   O'er the world's tempestuous sea;
Guard us, guide us, keep us, feed us,
   For we have no help but thee;
Yet possessing every blessing,
   If our God our Father be.

2 Saviour, breathe forgiveness o'er us,
   All our weakness thou dost know;
Thou didst tread this earth before us,
   Thou didst feel its keenest woe;
Lone and dreary, faint and weary,
   Through the desert thou didst go.

3 Spirit of our God, descending,
   Fill our hearts with heavenly joy;
Love with every passion blending,
   Pleasure that can never cloy:
Thus provided, pardoned, guided,
   Nothing can our peace destroy.

ONE MORE DAY.   P. M.

1. One more day's work for Jesus, One less of life for me! But heav'n is nearer, And Christ is dearer   Than yes-ter-day, to me; His love and light Fill all my soul to-night. One more day's work for Je - sus, One more day's work for Jesus, One more day's work for Jesus, One less of life for me.

370   *"One More Day."*   ANON.

One more day's work for Jesus,
One less of life for me!
But heaven is nearer, And Christ is dearer
Than yesterday, to me;
His love and light
Fill all my soul to-night.—Cho.

2 One more day's work for Jesus;
How sweet the work has been,
To tell the story, To show the glory,
Where Christ's flock enter in!
How it did shine
In this poor heart of mine!—Cho.

3 One more day's work for Jesus—
Oh, yes, a weary day;
But heaven shines clearer And rest comes nearer,
At each step of the way;
And Christ in all—
Before his face I fall.—Cho.

4 Oh, blesséd work for Jesus!
Oh, rest at Jesus' feet!
There toil seems pleasure, My wants are treasure,
And pain for him is sweet.
Lord, if I may,
I'll serve another day!—Cho.

GLORIA PATRI.   (HY. 371)

Glo - ry be to the Fa - ther, and to the Son, and to the Ho - ly Ghost; As it was in the be-gin-ning, is now, and ev - er shall be, world without end, A - men. A - men.

ST. MATTHIAS. L. M. 6l.

1. Sweet Saviour, bless us ere we go: Thy word in - to our minds in - still;

And make our lukewarm hearts to glow With low - ly love and fer - vent will.

REFRAIN.

Through life's long day and death's dark night, O gen - tle Je - sus be our light.

372   *"The day is gone."*   FABER.

SWEET Saviour, bless us ere we go:
Thy word into our minds instill;
And make our lukewarm hearts to glow
With lowly love and fervent will.—REF.

2 The day is gone, its hours have run,
And thou hast taken count of all,
The scanty triumphs grace hath won,
The broken vow, the frequent fall.—REF.

3 Do more than pardon; give us joy,
Sweet fear, and sober liberty,

And simple hearts without alloy
That only long to be like thee.—REF.

4 Labor is sweet, for thou hast toiled;
And care is light, for thou hast cared;
Ah! never let our works be soiled
With strife, or by deceit ensnared.—REF.

5 For all we love, the poor, the sad,
The sinful, unto thee we call;
Oh, let thy mercy make us glad:
Thou art our Jesus, and our All.—REF.

THE LORD'S PRAYER.

373   *Matt.* 6 : 9—13.

1 Our Father, who art in heaven, | hallowed | be thy | name ; || thy kingdom come,
thy will be done on | earth, as it | is in | heaven ;

2 Give us this | day our | daily | bread ; || and forgive us our trespasses, as we for-
give | them that | trespass a- | gainst us.

3 And lead us not into temptation, but de-| liver | us from | evil ; || for thine is the
kingdom, and the power, and the | glory, for- | ever. A- | men.   139

NIGHTFALL. 11. 5.

1. Now God be with us, for the night is clos-ing, The light and dark-ness are of his dis-pos-ing; And 'neath his sha-dow here to rest we yield us, For he will shield us.

374   *Evening Song.*   WINKWORTH, Tr.

Now God be with us, for the night is
    closing,
The light and darkness are of his disposing;
And 'neath his shadow here to rest we
    yield us;
    For he will shield us.

2 Let evil thoughts and spirits flee before us:
Till morning cometh, watch, O Father!
    o'er us;
In soul and body thou from harm defend us,
    Thine angels send us.

3 Let pious thoughts be ours when sleep
    o'ertakes us;
Our earliest thoughts be thine when morn-
    ing wakes us;
All sick and mourners, we to thee com-
    mend them,
    Do thou befriend them.

4 We have no refuge, none on earth to
    aid us,
But thee, O Father! who thine own hast
    made us;
Keep us in life; forgive our sins; deliver
    Us now and ever.

5 Praise be to thee through Jesus our salva-
    tion,
God, three in one, the Ruler of creation,
High throned, o'er all thine eye of mercy
    casting,
    Lord everlasting!

375   *Evening Confession.*   BOWRING.

From the recesses of a lowly spirit,
Our humble prayer ascends; O Father!
    hear it,
Upsoaring on the wings of awe and meek-
    ness;
    Forgive its weakness!

2 We see thy hand; it leads us, it supports us!
We hear thy voice; it counsels and it
    courts us:
And then we turn away; and still thy
    kindness
    Forgives our blindness.

3 Oh, how long-suffering, Lord! but thou
    delightest
To win with love the wandering; thou in-
    vitest,
By smiles of mercy, not by frowns or terrors,
    Man from his errors.

4 Father and Saviour! plant within each
    bosom
The seeds of holiness, and bid them blossom
In fragrance and in beauty bright and vernal,
    And spring eternal.

5 Then place them in thine everlasting gar-
    dens,
Where angels walk, and seraphs are the
    wardens;
Where every flower escaped through
    death's dark portal,
    Becomes immortal.

LAST BEAM. P. M.

1. Fad - ing, still fad-ing, the last beam is shining; Fa-ther in heav-en, the day is de-clining;

Safe-ty and innocence fly with the light, Temptation and danger walk forth with the night : From the

fall of the shade till the morning bells chime, Shield me from dan-ger, save me from crime.

REFRAIN.   2nd Verse.

Father, have mercy, Father, have mercy, Father, have mercy thro' Jesus Christ our Lord, Amen.

376

" The Last Beam."   ANON.

FADING, still fading, the last beam is shining,
Father in heaven, the day is declining;
Safety and innocence fly with the light,
Temptation and danger walk forth with the night:
From the fall of the shade till the morning bells chime,
Shield me from danger, save me from crime!—REF.

2 Father in heaven, oh, hear when we call!
Hear, for Christ's sake, who is Saviour of all;
Feeble and fainting, we trust in thy might;
In doubting and darkness, thy love be our light;
Let us sleep on thy breast while the night taper burns,
Wake in thy arms when morning returns.—REF.

ILLA.   L. M.

1. God, in the gos-pel   of   his   Son, Makes his e - ter - nal coun-sels known,

Where love in all   its   glo - ry   shines, And truth is drawn in   fair - est   lines.

377   *Christ in the Gospel.*   BEDDOME.

God, in the gospel of his Son,
Makes his eternal counsels known,
Where love in all its glory shines,
And truth is drawn in fairest lines.

2 Here, sinners of an humble frame
May taste his grace, and learn his name:
May read, in characters of blood,
The wisdom, power, and grace of God.

3 Here, faith reveals, to mortal eyes,
A brighter world beyond the skies;
Here, shines the light which guides our way
From earth to realms of endless day.

4 Oh, grant us grace, almighty Lord!
To read and mark thy holy word,
Its truths with meekness to receive,
And by its holy precepts live.

378   *A written Revelation.*   WATTS.

Let everlasting glories crown
  Thy head, my Saviour, and my Lord!
Thy hands have brought salvation down
  And writ the blessings in thy word.

2 In vain the trembling conscience seeks
  Some solid ground to rest upon;
With long despair the spirit breaks,
  Till we apply to Christ alone.

3 How well thy blessèd truths agree!
  How wise and holy thy commands!
Thy promises—how firm they be!
  How firm our hope and comfort stands!

142

379   *Inspiration.*   WATTS.

'Twas by an order from the Lord
The ancient prophets spoke his word;
His Spirit did their tongues inspire,
And warmed their hearts with heavenly fire.

2 The works and wonders which they wrought
Confirmed the messages they brought:
The prophet's pen succeeds his breath,
To save the holy words from death.

3 Great God, mine eyes with pleasure look
On the dear volume of thy book;
There my Redeemer's face I see,
And read his name who died for me.

380   *Psalm 19.*   GRANT.

The starry firmament on high,
And all the glories of the sky,
Yet shine not to thy praise, O Lord,
So brightly as thy written word.

2 The hopes that holy word supplies,
Its truths divine and precepts wise,
In each a heavenly beam I see,
And every beam conducts to thee.

3 Almighty Lord, the sun shall fail,
The moon forget her nightly tale,
And deepest silence hush on high
The radiant chorus of the sky:—

4 But fixed for everlasting years,
Unmoved, amid the wreck of spheres,
Thy word shall shine in cloudless day,
When heaven and earth have passed away.

WILLINGTON. L. M.

1. Now let my soul, e - ter - nal King, To thee its grate - ful trib - ute bring;

My knee with hum - ble hom - age bow, My tongue per - form its sol - emn vow.

381 HEGINBOTHAM.
Nature and the Word.

Now let my soul, eternal King,
To thee its grateful tribute bring;
My knee with humble homage bow,
My tongue perform its solemn vow.

2 All nature sings thy boundless love,
In worlds below, and worlds above;
But in thy blessèd word I trace
Diviner wonders of thy grace.

3 Here what delightful truths I read!
Here I behold the Saviour bleed;
His name salutes my listening ear,
Revives my heart and checks my fear.

4 Here Jesus bids my sorrows cease,
And gives my laboring conscience peace;
Here lifts my grateful passions high,
And points to mansions in the sky.

5 For love like this, oh, let my song,
Through endless years, thy praise prolong;
Let distant climes thy name adore,
Till time and nature are no more.

382 KELLY.
"A little Book Open."

I LOVE the sacred Book of God!
No other can its place supply;
It points me to his own abode;
It gives me wings, and bids me fly.

2 Sweet Book! in thee my eyes discern
The very image of my Lord;
From thine instructive page I learn
The joys his presence will afford.

3 In thee I read my title clear
To mansions that will ne'er decay;—
Dear Lord, oh, when wilt thou appear,
And bear thy prisoner away?

4 While I am here, these leaves supply
His place, and tell me of his love;
I read with faith's discerning eye,
And gain a glimpse of joys above.

5 I know in them the Spirit breathes
To animate his people here;
Oh, may these truths prove life to all,
Till in his presence we appear!

383 BOWRING.
Progress of Truth.

UPON the Gospel's sacred page
The gathered beams of ages shine;
And, as it hastens, every age
But makes its brightness more divine.

2 On mightier wing, in loftier flight,
From year to year does knowledge soar;
And, as it soars, the Gospel light
Becomes effulgent more and more.

3 More glorious still, as centuries roll,
New regions blest, new powers unfurled,
Expanding with the expanding soul,
Its radiance shall o'erflow the world,—

4 Flow to restore, but not destroy;
As when the cloudless lamp of day
Pours out its floods of light and joy,
And sweeps the lingering mist away.

BEMERTON. C. M.

1. Thou love-ly source of true de-light, Whom I un-seen a - dore!

Un - vail thy beau - ties to my sight, That I may love thee more.

384 *Love to Christ desired.* STEELE.

Thou lovely source of true delight,
  Whom I unseen adore!
Unvail thy beauties to my sight,
  That I may love thee more.

2 Thy glory o'er creation shines;—
  But in thy sacred word,
I read, in fairer, brighter lines,
  My bleeding, dying Lord.

3 'Tis here, whene'er my comforts droop,
  And sin and sorrow rise,
Thy love, with cheering beams of hope,
  My fainting heart supplies.

4 But ah! too soon the pleasing scene
  Is clouded o'er with pain;
My gloomy fears rise dark between,
  And I again complain.

5 Jesus, my Lord, my life, my light!
  Oh, come with blissful ray;
Break radiant through the shades of night,
  And chase my fears away.

6 Then shall my soul with rapture trace
  The wonders of thy love:
But the full glories of thy face
  Are only known above.

385 *Unfaithfulness lamented.* WATTS.

Long have I sat beneath the sound
  Of thy salvation, Lord!
But still how weak my faith is found,
  And knowledge of thy word!

2 Oft I frequent thy holy place,
  And hear almost in vain;
How small a portion of thy grace
  My memory can retain!

3 How cold and feeble is my love!
  How negligent my fear!
How low my hope of joys above!
  How few affections there!

4 Great God! thy sovereign power impart,
  To give thy word success:
Write thy salvation in my heart,
  And make me learn thy grace.

5 Show my forgetful feet the way
  That leads to joys on high:
There knowledge grows without decay,
  And love shall never die.

386 *A blessed Gospel—Ps 89.* WATTS.

Blest are the souls that hear and know
  The gospel's joyous sound;
Peace shall attend the path they go,
  And light their steps surround.

2 Their joy shall bear their spirits up,
  Through their Redeemer's name;
His righteousness exalts their hope,
  Nor Satan dares condemn.

3 The Lord, our glory and defence,
  Strength and salvation gives;
Israel! thy King for ever reigns,
  Thy God for ever lives.

CHIMES. C. M.

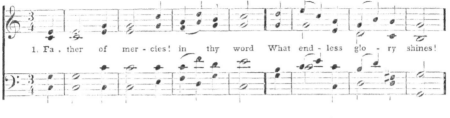

1. Fa - ther of mer - cies! in thy word What end - less glo - ry shines!

For ev - er be thy name a - dored, For these ce - les - tial lines.

387 *The Bible suited to our Wants.* STEELE.

FATHER of mercies! in thy word
What endless glory shines!
For ever be thy name adored,
For these celestial lines.

2 Here, the fair tree of knowledge grows,
And yields a free repast;
Sublimer sweets than nature knows
Invite the longing taste.

3 Here, the Redeemer's welcome voice
Spreads heavenly peace around;
And life, and everlasting joys
Attend the blissful sound.

4 Oh, may these heavenly pages be
My ever dear delight;
And still new beauties may I see,
And still increasing light.

5 Divine instructor, gracious Lord!
Be thou for ever near;
Teach me to love thy sacred word,
And view my Saviour there.

388 *The Word Decisive.* WATTS.

LADEN with guilt, and full of fears,
I fly to thee, my Lord,
And not a glimpse of hope appears,
But in thy written word.

2 This is the field where hidden lies,
The pearl of price unknown;
That merchant is divinely wise,
Who makes the pearl his own.

3 This is the judge that ends the strife,
Where wit and reason fail;
My guide to everlasting life,
Through all this gloomy vale.

4 Oh, may thy counsels, mighty God!
My roving feet command;
Nor I forsake the happy road,
That leads to thy right hand.

389 *Psalm 119.* COWPER.

THE Spirit breathes upon the word,
And brings the truth to sight;
Precepts and promises afford
A sanctifying light.

2 A glory gilds the sacred page,
Majestic, like the sun;
It gives a light to every age;—
It gives, but borrows none.

3 The hand, that gave it, still supplies
The gracious light and heat;
Its truths upon the nations rise,—
They rise, but never set.

4 Let everlasting thanks be thine,
For such a bright display,
As makes a world of darkness shine
With beams of heavenly day.

5 My soul rejoices to pursue
The steps of him I love,
Till glory breaks upon my view,
In brighter worlds above.

145

CHENIES. 7, 6, D.

1. O Word of God in-car-nate, O Wis-dom from on high, O Truth unchanged, un-changing, O Light of our dark sky! We praise thee for the ra-diance That from the hallowed page, A lantern to our footsteps, Shines on from age to age.

390   *Thanks for the Bible.*   HOW.

O WORD of God incarnate,
  O Wisdom from on high,
O Truth unchanged, unchanging,
  O Light of our dark sky!
We praise thee for the radiance
  That from the hallowed page,
A lantern to our footsteps,
  Shines on from age to age.

2 The Church from her dear Master
  Received the gift divine,
And still that light she lifteth
  O'er all the earth to shine.
It is the golden casket
  Where gems of truth are stored
It is the heaven-drawn picture
  Of Christ the living Word.

3 Oh, make thy Church, dear Saviour,
  A lamp of burnished gold,
To bear before the nations
  Thy true light as of old;
Oh, teach thy wandering pilgrims
  By this their path to trace,
Till, clouds and darkness ended,
  They see thee face to face.

391   *Psalm* 19.   CONDER.

THE heavens declare his glory,
  Their Maker's skill the skies:
Each day repeats the story,
  And night to night replies.
Their silent proclamation
  Throughout the earth is heard;
The record of creation,
  The page of nature's word.

2 So pure, so soul-restoring,
  Is truth's diviner ray;
A brighter radiance pouring
  Than all the pomp of day:
The wanderer surely guiding,
  It makes the simple wise;
And, evermore abiding,
  Unfailing joy supplies.

3 Thy word is richer treasure
  Than lurks within the mine;
And daintiest fare less pleasure
  Yields than this food divine.
How wise each kind monition!
  Led by thy counsels, Lord,
How safe the saints' condition,
  How great is their reward!

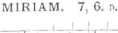

392   *Everlasting. —Ps. 90.*   BICKERSTETH.

O God, the Rock of Ages,
  Who evermore hast been,
What time the tempest rages,
  Our dwelling-place serene:
Before thy first creations,
  O Lord, the same as now,
To endless generations
  The Everlasting thou!

2 Our years are like the shadows
  On sunny hills that lie,
Or grasses in the meadows
  That blossom but to die:
A sleep, a dream, a story,
  By strangers quickly told,
An unremaining glory
  Of things that soon are old.

3 O thou who canst not slumber,
  Whose light grows never pale,
Teach us aright to number
  Our years before they fail.
On us thy mercy lighten,
  On us thy goodness rest,
And let thy Spirit brighten
  The hearts thyself hast blessed!

393   *Omnipresent.*   DUTCH HY.

On mountains and in valleys,
  Where'er we go is God;
The cottage and the palace,
  Alike are his abode.

With watchful eye abiding
  Upon us with delight;
Our souls, in him confiding,
  He keeps both day and night.

2 Above me and beside me,
  My God is ever near,
To watch, protect, and guide me,
  Whatever ills appear.
Though other friends may fail me,
  In sorrows dark abode,
Though death itself assail me,
  I'm ever safe with God.

394   *Sovereign Love.*   CONDER.

'Tis not that I did choose thee,
  For, Lord! that could not be;
This heart would still refuse thee;
  But thou hast chosen me;—
Hast, from the sin that stained me,
  Washed me and set me free,
And to this end ordained me,
  That I should live to thee.

2 'Twas sovereign mercy called me,
  And taught my opening mind;
The world had else enthralled me,
  To heavenly glories blind.
My heart owns none above thee;
  For thy rich grace I thirst;
This knowing,—if I love thee,
  Thou must have loved me first.

JUDGMENT. L. M.

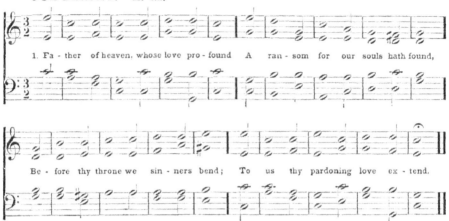

1. Fa - ther of heaven, whose love pro - found A ran - som for our souls hath found,

Be - fore thy throne we sin - ners bend; To us thy pardoning love ex - tend.

COOPER.

395   *The Trinity.*

FATHER of heaven, whose love profound
A ransom for our souls hath found,
Before thy throne we sinners bend;
To us thy pardoning love extend.

2 Almighty Son—incarnate Word—
Our Prophet, Priest, Redeemer, Lord !
Before thy throne we sinners bend;
To us thy saving grace extend.

3 Eternal Spirit! by whose breath
The soul is raised from sin and death,—
Before thy throne we sinners bend;
To us thy quickening power extend.

4 Jehovah!—Father, Spirit, Son!—
Mysterious Godhead!—Three in One!
Before thy throne we sinners bend;
Grace, pardon, life to us extend.

ANON.

396   *Unsearchableness.—Job 11: 7.*

WITH deepest reverence at thy throne,
Jehovah, peerless and unknown!
Our feeble spirits strive, in vain,
A glimpse of thee, great God! to gain.

2 Who, by the closest search, can find
The eternal, uncreated mind?
Nor-men, nor angels can explore
Thy heights of love, thy depths of power.

3 That power we trace on every side;
Oh, may thy wisdom be our guide!
And while we live, and when we die,
May thine almighty love be nigh.
118

ANON.

397   *Long-Suffering—Luke 13: 6.*

GOD of my life, to thee belong
The grateful heart, the joyful song;
Touched by thy love, each tuneful chord
Resounds the goodness of the Lord

2 Yet why, dear Lord, this tender care? :
Why doth thy hand so kindly rear
A useless cumberer of the ground,
On which so little fruit is found?

3 Still let the barren fig-tree stand
Upheld and fostered by thy hand;
And let its fruit and verdure be
A grateful tribute, Lord, to thee.

FLDDOME.

398   *Mystery—Ps. 46: 10.*

WAIT, O my soul! thy Maker's will;
Tumultuous passions, all be still!
Nor let a murmuring thought arise;
His ways are just, his counsels wise.

2 He in the thickest darkness dwells,
Performs his work, the cause conceals;
But, though his methods are unknown,
Judgment and truth support his throne.

3 In heaven, and earth, and air, and seas,
He executes his firm decrees;
And by his saints it stands confessed,
That what he does is ever best.

4 Wait, then, my soul! submissive wait,
Prostrate before his awful seat;
And, 'mid the terrors of his rod,
Trust in a wise and gracious God.

LOUVAN. L. M.

1. Lord of all be - ing; throned a - far, Thy glo - ry flames from sun and star;

Cen - tre and soul of eve - ry sphere, Yet to each lov - ing heart how near!

399   *Omnipresence.*   HOLMES.

Lord of all being; throned afar,
Thy glory flames from sun and star;
Centre and soul of every sphere,
Yet to each loving heart how near!

2 Sun of our life, thy quickening ray
Sheds on our path the glow of day;
Star of our hope, thy softened light
Cheers the long watches of the night.

3 Our midnight is thy smile withdrawn;
Our noontide is thy gracious dawn;
Our rainbow arch thy mercy's sign;
All, save the clouds of sin, are thine!

4 Lord of all life, below, above,
Whose light is truth, whose warmth is love,
Before thy ever-blazing throne
We ask no lustre of our own.

5 Grant us thy truth to make us free,
And kindling hearts that burn for thee,
Till all thy living altars claim
One holy light, one heavenly flame!

400   *Mysteries of Providence.*   STEELE.

Lord, how mysterious are thy ways!
How blind are we, how mean our praise!
Thy steps no mortal eyes explore;
'Tis ours to wonder and adore.

2 Great God! I do not ask to see
What in futurity shall be;
Let light and bliss attend my days,
And then my future hours be praise.

3 Are darkness and distress my share?
Give me to trust thy guardian care;
Enough for me, if love divine
At length through every cloud shall shine.

4 Yet this my soul desires to know,
Be this my only wish below;
That Christ is mine!—this great request,
Grant, bounteous God, and I am blest.

401   *Sovereignty.*   PALMER.

Lord, my weak thought in vain would climb
To search the starry vault profound;
In vain would wing her flight sublime,
To find creation's outmost bound.

2 But weaker yet that thought must prove
To search thy great eternal plan,—
Thy sovereign counsels, born of love
Long ages ere the world began.

3 When my dim reason would demand
Why that, or this, thou dost ordain,
By some vast deep I seem to stand,
Whose secrets I must ask in vain.

4 When doubts disturb my troubled breast,
And all is dark as night to me,
Here, as on solid rock, I rest;
That so it seemeth good to thee.

5 Be this my joy, that evermore
Thou rulest all things at thy will;
Thy sovereign wisdom I adore,
And calmly, sweetly, trust thee still.

149

REPENTANCE. L. M.

1. May not the sovereign Lord on high Dispense his fa - vors as he will,

Choose some to life, while oth - ers die, And yet be just and gra - cious still?

402   *Sovereignty.—Rom. 9 : 20.*   WATTS.

May not the sovereign Lord on high
  Dispense his favors as he will,
Choose some to life, while others die,
  And yet be just and gracious still?

2 What if he means to show his grace,
  And his electing love employs
To mark out some of mortal race,
  And form them fit for heavenly joys?

3 Shall man reply against the Lord,
  And call his Maker's ways unjust,
The thunder of whose dreadful word
  Can crush a thousand worlds to dust!

4 But, O my soul! if truth so bright
  Should dazzle and confound thy sight,
Yet still his written will obey,
  And wait the great decisive day.

403   *Unsearchableness.*   E. SCOTT.

What finite power, with ceaseless toil,
  Can fathom the eternal Mind?
Or who the almighty Three in One
  By searching, to perfection find?

2 Angels and men in vain may raise,
  Harmonious, their adoring songs;
The laboring thought sinks down, opprest,
  And praises die upon their tongues.

3 Yet would I lift my trembling voice
  A portion of his ways to sing;
And mingling with his meanest works,
  My humble, grateful tribute bring.

150

404   *Goodness.—Ps. 34 : 8.*   DODDRIDGE.

Triumphant Lord, thy goodness reigns
  Through all the wide celestial plains;
And its full streams unceasing flow
  Down to the abodes of men below.

2 Through nature's work its glories shine;
  The cares of providence are thine;
And grace erects our ruined frame
  A fairer temple to thy name.

3 Oh, give to every human heart
  To taste, and feel how good thou art;
With grateful love and reverent fear,
  To know how blest thy children are.

405   *Faithfulness.*   WATTS.

Praise, everlasting praise, be paid
  To him that earth's foundation laid;
Praise to the God whose strong decrees
  Sway the creation as he please.

2 Praise to the goodness of the Lord,
  Who rules his people by his word;
And there, as strong as his decrees,
  He sets his kindest promises.

3 Oh, for a strong, a lasting faith
  To credit what the Almighty saith!
To embrace the message of his Son,
  And call the joys of heaven our own!

4 Then, should the earth's old pillars shake,
  And all the wheels of nature break,
Our steady souls should fear no more
  Than solid rocks when billows roar.

CEPHAS.   L. M. ᴅ.

1. { The spacious fir-ma-ment on high, With all the blue e-thereal sky, }
   { And spangled heavens, a shining frame, [*Omit*............................] } Their great O-

rig-i-nal pro-claim; Th' unwearied sun, from day to day, Does his Crea-tor's power display;

And pub-lish-es to eve-ry land The work of an al-might-y hand.

406   *In Nature—Ps.* **19.**   ADDISON.

Tʜᴇ spacious firmament on high,
With all the blue ethereal sky,
And spangled heavens, a shining frame,
Their great Original proclaim:
The unwearied sun, from day to day,
Does his Creator's power display;
And publishes to every land
The work of an almighty hand.

2 Soon as the evening shades prevail,
The moon takes up the wondrous tale;
And nightly, to the listening earth,
Repeats the story of her birth;
While all the stars that round her burn,
And all the planets in their turn,
Confirm the tidings as they roll,
And spread the truth from pole to pole.

3 What though in solemn silence, all
Move round the dark terrestrial ball,—
What though no real voice nor sound
Amid their radiant orbs be found,—
In reason's ear they all rejoice,
And utter forth a glorious voice,
For ever singing as they shine,—
"The hand that made us is divine."

407   *In the Seasons.*   DODDRIDGE.

Eᴛᴇʀɴᴀʟ Source of every joy,
Well may thy praise our lips employ,
While in thy temple we appear,
To hail thee, Sovereign of the year!

2 Wide as the wheels of nature roll,
Thy hand supports and guides the whole,
The sun is taught by thee to rise,
And darkness when to vail the skies.

3 The flowery spring at thy command,
Perfumes the air, adorns the land;
The summer rays with vigor shine,
To raise the corn, to cheer the vine.

4 Thy hand, in autumn, richly pours,
Through all our coasts, redundant stores:
And winters, softened by thy care,
No more the face of horror wear.

5 Seasons and months, and weeks and days,
Demand successive songs of praise;
And be the grateful homage paid,
With morning light and evening shade.

6 Here in thy house let incense rise,
And circling Sabbaths bless our eyes,
Till to those lofty heights we soar,
Where days and years revolve no more.

BRATTLE STREET. C. M. D.

While thee I seek pro-tect-ing Power! Be my vain wish-es stilled; And may this con-se-crat-ed hour [Omit .... With

bet-ter hopes be filled! Thy love the power of thought bestowed; To thee my thoughts would

soar: Thy mer-cy o'er my life has flowed; That mer-cy I a-dore.

408   *Providence.*   MISS WILLIAMS.

WHILE thee I seek, protecting Power!
  Be my vain wishes stilled;
And may this consecrated hour
  With better hopes be filled!
Thy love the power of thought bestowed;
  To thee my thoughts would soar:
Thy mercy o'er my life has flowed;
  That mercy I adore.

2 In each event of life, how clear
  Thy ruling hand I see!
Each blessing to my soul more dear
  Because conferred by thee.
In every joy that crowns my days,
  In every pain I bear,
My heart shall find delight in praise
  Or seek relief in prayer.

3 When gladness wings my favored hour,
  Thy love my thoughts shall fill;
Resigned, when storms of sorrow lower,
  My soul shall meet thy will.

152

My lifted eye, without a tear,
  The gathering storm shall see;
My steadfast heart shall know no fear;
  That heart will rest on thee.

409   *Psalm* 107.   ADDISON.

How are thy servants blessed, O Lord!
  How sure is their defence!
Eternal Wisdom is their guide,
  Their help, Omnipotence.

2 When by the dreadful tempest borne
  High on the broken wave,
They know thou art not slow to hear,
  Nor impotent to save.

3 The storm is laid, the winds retire,
  Obedient to thy will;
The sea, that roars at thy command,
  At thy command is still.

4 In midst of dangers, fears, and deaths,
  Thy goodness we'll adore;
We'll praise thee for thy mercies past,
  And humbly hope for more.

GENEVA. C. M.

1. When all thy mer-cies, O my God! My ris-ing soul sur-veys,

Transport - ed with the view, I'm lost In won-der, love, and praise.

410   *Continued help.*   ADDISON.

WHEN all thy mercies, O my God!
  My rising soul surveys,
Transported with the view, I'm lost
  In wonder, love, and praise.

2 Unnumbered comforts, to my soul,
  Thy tender care bestowed,
Before my infant heart conceived
  From whom those comforts flowed.

3 When, in the slippery paths of youth,
  With heedless steps, I ran,
Thine arm, unseen, conveyed me safe,
  And led me up to man.

4 Ten thousand thousand precious gifts
  My daily thanks employ;
Nor is the least a cheerful heart,
  That tastes those gifts with joy.

5 Through every period of my life,
  Thy goodness I'll pursue;
And after death, in distant worlds,
  The glorious theme renew.

6 Through all eternity, to thee
  A joyful song I'll raise:
For, oh, eternity's too short
  To utter all thy praise!

411   *In the Winds.*   DODDRIDGE.

GREAT Ruler of all nature's frame!
  We own thy power divine;
We hear thy breath in every storm,
  For all the winds are thine.

2 Wide as they sweep their sounding way
  They work thy sovereign will;
And, awed by thy majestic voice,
  Confusion shall be still.

3 Thy mercy tempers every blast
  To them that seek thy face,
And mingles with the tempest's roar
  The whispers of thy grace.

4 Those gentle whispers let me hear,
  Till all the tumult cease;
And gales of Paradise shall lull
  My weary soul to peace.

412   *Lord of All.*   H. K. WHITE.

THE Lord our God is Lord of all;
  His station who can find?
I hear him in the waterfall!
  I hear him in the wind.

2 If in the gloom of night I shroud,
  His face I cannot fly;
I see him in the evening cloud,
  And in the morning sky.

3 He smiles, we live! he frowns, we die!
  We hang upon his word;
He rears his mighty arm on high,
  We fall before his sword.

4 He bids his gales the fields deform;
  Then, when his thunders cease,
He paints his rainbow on the storm,
  And lulls the winds to peace.

ST ANN'S.　C. M.

1. The Lord, our God, is full of might, The winds o - bey his will;

He speaks,—and, in his heaven-ly height, The roll - ing sun stands still.

413　　　*Almighty Power.*　　H. K. WHITE.

The Lord, our God, is full of might,
　The winds obey his will;
He speaks,—and, in his heavenly height,
　The rolling sun stands still.

2 Rebel, ye waves, and o'er the land
　With threatening aspect roar;
The Lord uplifts his awful hand,
　And chains you to the shore.

3 Howl, winds of night, your force combine;
　Without his high behest,
Ye shall not, in the mountain pine,
　Disturb the sparrow's nest.

4 His voice sublime is heard afar,
　In distant peals it dies;
He yokes the whirlwind to his car,
　And sweeps the howling skies.

5 Ye nations, bend—in reverence bend;
　Ye monarchs, wait his nod,
And bid the choral song ascend
　To celebrate your God.

414　　*Omnipotence.—Isa.* 12 : 4.　　WATTS.

The Lord, how fearful is his name!
　How wide is his command!
Nature, with all her moving frame,
　Rests on his mighty hand.

2 Immortal glory forms his throne,
　And light his awful robe;
While with a smile, or with a frown,
　He manages the globe.

3 A word of his almighty breath
　Can swell or sink the seas;
Build the vast empires of the earth,
　Or break them as he please.

4 On angels, with unvailed face
　His glory beams above;
On men, he looks with softest grace,
　And takes his title, Love.

415　　　*Providence.*　　WATTS.

Keep silence, all created things!
　And wait your Maker's nod;
My soul stands trembling, while she sings
　The honors of her God.

2 Life, death, and hell, and worlds unknown,
　Hang on his firm decree;
He sits on no precarious throne,
　Nor borrows leave to be.

3 His providence unfolds the book,
　And makes his counsels shine;
Each opening leaf, and every stroke,
　Fulfills some deep design.

4 My God! I would not long to see
　My fate, with curious eyes—
What gloomy lines are writ for me,
　Or what bright scenes may rise.

5 In thy fair book of life and grace,
　Oh, may I find my name
Recorded in some humble place,
　Beneath my Lord, the Lamb.

NOEL. C. M.

1. Fa - ther! how wide thy glo - ry shines! How high thy won-ders rise!

Known through the earth by thou - sand signs, By thousand through the skies.

416   *Nature and Grace.*   WATTS.

FATHER! how wide thy glory shines!
  How high thy wonders rise!
Known thro' the earth by thousand signs,
  By thousand through the skies.

2 Those mighty orbs proclaim thy power,
  Their motions speak thy skill;
And on the wings of every hour,
  We read thy patience still.

3 But, when we view thy strange design
  To save rebellious worms,
Where vengeance and compassion join
  In their divinest forms,—

4 Here the whole Deity is known;
  Nor dares a creature guess,
Which of the glories brightest shone,
  The justice, or the grace.

5 Now the full glories of the Lamb
  Adorn the heavenly plains;
Bright seraphs learn Immanuel's name,
  And try their choicest strains.

6 Oh, may I bear some humble part,
  In that immortal song;
Wonder and joy shall tune my heart,
  And love-command my tongue.

417   *In Nature.*   STEELE.

LORD, when my raptured thought surveys
  Creation's beauties o'er,
All nature joins to teach thy praise,
  And bid my soul adore.

2 Where'er I turn my gazing eyes,
  Thy radiant footsteps shine;
Ten thousand pleasing wonders rise,
  And speak their source divine.

3 On me thy providence has shone
  With gentle smiling rays;
Oh, let my lips and life make known
  Thy goodness and thy praise.

4 All-bounteous Lord, thy grace impart!
  Oh, teach me to improve
Thy gifts with humble, grateful heart,
  And crown them with thy love.

418   *Goodness.—Ps.* 145.   WATTS.

SWEET is the memory of thy grace,
  My God, my heavenly King;
Let age to age thy righteousness
  In sounds of glory sing.

2 God reigns on high; but ne'er confines
  His goodness to the skies:
Through the whole earth his bounty shines
  And every want supplies.

3 With longing eyes thy creatures wait
  On thee for daily food;
Thy liberal hand provides their meat,
  And fills their mouth with good.

4 How kind are thy compassions, Lord!
  How slow thine anger moves!
But soon he sends his pardoning word
  To cheer the souls he loves.

DUNDEE. C. M.

1. Great God! how in-fi-nite art thou! What worthless worms are we!

Let the whole race of creatures bow, And pay their praise to thee.

419   *Eternity.—Ps.* **90: 1.**   WATTS.

Great God! how infinite art thou!
  What worthless worms are we!
Let the whole race of creatures bow,
  And pay their praise to thee.

2 Thy throne eternal ages stood,
  Ere seas or stars were made:
Thou art the ever-living God,
  Were all the nations dead.

3 Eternity, with all its years,
  Stands present in thy view;
To thee there's nothing old appears—
  Great God! there's nothing new.

4 Our lives through various scenes are drawn,
  And vexed with trifling cares;
While thine eternal thought moves on
  Thine undisturbed affairs.

5 Great God! how infinite art thou!
  What worthless worms are we!
Let the whole race of creatures bow,
  And pay their praise to thee.

420   *" Te Deum."*   PATRICK.

O God! we praise thee, and confess
  That thou the only Lord
And everlasting Father art,
  By all the earth adored.

2 To thee, all angels cry aloud;
  To thee the powers on high,
Both cherubim and seraphim,
  Continually do cry:—

3 O holy, holy, holy Lord,
  Whom heavenly hosts obey,
The world is with the glory filled
  Of thy majestic sway!

4 The apostles' glorious company,
  And prophets crowned with light,
With all the martyrs' noble host,
  Thy constant praise recite.

5 The holy church throughout the world,
  O Lord, confesses thee,
That thou the eternal Father art,
  Of boundless majesty.

421   *Omniscience.—Ps.* **139.**   WATTS.

Lord! where shall guilty souls retire,
  Forgotten and unknown?
In hell they meet thy dreadful fire—
  In heaven thy glorious throne.

2 If, winged with beams of morning light,
  I fly beyond the west,
Thy hand, which must support my flight,
  Would soon betray my rest.

3 If, o'er my sins, I think to draw
  The curtains of the night,
Those flaming eyes, that guard thy law,
  Would turn the shades to light.

4 The beams of noon, the midnight hour,
  Are both alike to thee:
Oh, may I ne'er provoke that power,
  From which I cannot flee.

MORAVIAN. C. M. D.

1. { The Lord de-scend-ed from a-bove, And bowed the heavens most high; }
   { And un-der-neath his feet he cast The dark-ness of the sky. }
   D. C.—on the wings of might-y winds Came fly-ing all a-broad.

2. On cher-ub and on cher-u-bim, Full roy-al-ly he rode; And

422 Majesty.—Psalm 18.   STERNHOLD.

THE Lord descended from above,
  And bowed the heavens most high;
And underneath his feet he cast
  The darkness of the sky.

2 On cherub and on cherubim,
    Full royally he rode;
  And on the wings of mighty winds
    Came flying all abroad.

3 He sat serene upon the floods,
    Their fury to restrain;
  And he, as sovereign Lord and King,
    For evermore shall reign.

4 The Lord will give his people strength,
    Whereby they shall increase;
  And he will bless his chosen flock
    With everlasting peace.

423 In the Seasons.—Psalm 147.   WATTS.

WITH songs and honors sounding loud,
  Address the Lord on high;
Over the heavens he spreads his cloud,
  And waters vail the sky.
He sends his showers of blessings down,
  To cheer the plains below;
He makes the grass the mountains crown,
  And corn in valleys grow.

2 His steady counsels change the face
    Of the declining year;
  He bids the sun cut short his race,
    And wintry days appear.

His hoary frost, his fleecy snow,
  Descend and clothe the ground;
The liquid streams forbear to flow,
  In icy fetters bound.

3 He sends his word and melts the snow,
    The fields no longer mourn;
  He calls the warmer gales to blow,
    And bids the spring return.
  The changing wind, the flying cloud,
    Obey his mighty word:
  With songs and honors sounding loud,
    Praise ye the sovereign Lord.

424 Incarnation.   STEELE.

AWAKE, awake the sacred song
  To our incarnate Lord!
Let every heart and every tongue
  Adore the eternal Word.

2 That awful Word, that sovereign Power,
    By whom the worlds were made—
  Oh, happy morn! illustrious hour!—
    Was once in flesh arrayed!

3 Then shone almighty power and love,
    In all their glorious forms,
  When Jesus left his throne above,
    To dwell with sinful worms.

4 Adoring angels tuned their songs
    To hail the joyful day;
  With rapture then let mortal tongues
    Their grateful worship pay.

DOWNS. C. M.

1 Come, ye that know and fear the Lord, And raise your thoughts a - bove:

Let ev - ery heart and voice ac - cord, To sing that "God is love."

425   *Love.—1 John 4 : 8.*   BURDER.

Come, ye that know and fear the Lord,
  And raise your thoughts above:
Let every heart and voice accord,
  To sing that "God is love."

2 This precious truth his word declares,
  And all his mercies prove;
Jesus, the gift of gifts, appears,
  To show that "God is love."

3 Behold his patience, bearing long
  With those who from him rove;
Till mighty grace their hearts subdues,
  To teach them—"God is love."

4 Oh, may we all, while here below,
  This best of blessings prove;
Till warmer hearts, in brighter worlds,
  Proclaim that "God is love."

426   *In Nature.*   KEBLE.

There is a book that all may read,
  Which heavenly truth imparts,
And all the lore its scholars need,
  Pure eyes and Christian hearts.

2 The works of God above, below,
  Within us and around,
Are pages in that book, to show
  How God himself is found.

3 The glorious sky, embracing all,
  Is like the Maker's love,
Wherewith encompassed, great and small,
  In peace and order move.

The dew of heaven is like thy grace,
  It steals in silence down;
But where it lights, the favored place
  By richest fruits is known.

5 Thou, who hast given me eyes to see,
  And love this sight so fair,
Give me a heart to find out thee,
  And read thee everywhere.

427   *Omnipresence.—Ps. 139.*   WATTS.

In all my vast concerns with thee,
  In vain my soul would try,
To shun thy presence, Lord! or flee
  The notice of thine eye.

2 Thine all-surrounding sight surveys
  My rising and my rest,
My public walks, my private ways,
  And secrets of my breast.

3 My thoughts lie open to the Lord,
  Before they're formed within;
And, ere my lips pronounce the word,
  He knows the sense I mean.

4 Oh, wondrous knowledge, deep and high,
  Where can a creature hide?
Within thy circling arms I lie,
  Enclosed on every side.

5 So let thy grace surround me still,
  And like a bulwark prove,
To guard my soul from every ill,
  Secured by sovereign love.

VARINA. C. M. D.

1 ⎰ Je - ho-vah God! thy gracious power On every hand we see; ⎱
  ⎱ Oh, may the blessings of each hour Lead all our thoughts to thee. ⎰ 2. Thy power is in the ocean deeps,

And reaches to the skies; Thine eye of mer - cy nev-er sleeps, Thy goodness never dies.

428 *Omniscience.—Ps.* **139.** THOMPSON.

JEHOVAH God! thy gracious power
  On every hand we see;
Oh, may the blessings of each hour
  Lead all our thoughts to thee.

2 Thy power is in the ocean deeps,
  And reaches to the skies;
Thine eye of mercy never sleeps,
  Thy goodness never dies.

3 From morn till noon, till latest eve,
  The hand of God we see;
And all the blessings we receive,
  Ceaseless proceed from thee.

4 In all the varying scenes of time,
  On thee our hopes depend;
In every age, in every clime,
  Our Father and our Friend.

429 *Perfections.—Ps.* **77 : 11-14.** WATTS.

I SING the almighty power of God,
  That made the mountains rise,
That spread the flowing seas abroad,
  And built the lofty skies.

2 I sing the wisdom that ordained
  The sun to rule the day;
The moon shines full at his command,
  And all the stars obey.

3 I sing the goodness of the Lord,
  That filled the earth with food;
He formed the creatures with his word,
  And then pronounced them good.

4 Lord! how thy wonders are displayed
  Where'er I turn mine eye;
If I survey the ground I tread,
  Or gaze upon the sky!

5 There's not a plant or flower below
  But makes thy glories known;
And clouds arise, and tempests blow,
  By order from thy throne.

6 Creatures that borrow life from thee
  Are subject to thy care;
There's not a place where we can flee,
  But God is present there.

430 *Mystery.—1 Cor.* **13 : 12.** FAWCETT.

THY way, O Lord, is in the sea;
  Thy paths I cannot trace,
Nor comprehend the mystery
  Of thine unbounded grace.

2 As, through a glass, I dimly see
  The wonders of thy love;
How little do I know of thee,
  Or of the joys above!

3 'Tis but in part I know thy will;
  I bless thee for the sight:
When will thy love the rest reveal,
  In glory's clearer light?

4 With rapture shall I then survey
  Thy providence and grace;
And spend an everlasting day
  In wonder, love, and praise.

MANOAH.   C. M.

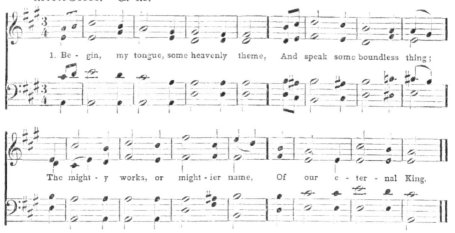

1. Be-gin, my tongue, some heavenly theme, And speak some boundless thing;

The might-y works, or might-ier name, Of our e-ter-nal King.

431   *Faithfulness.—Psalm 36 : 5.*   WATTS.

BEGIN, my tongue, some heavenly theme,
  And speak some boundless thing;
The mighty works, or mightier name,
  Of our eternal King.

2 Tell of his wondrous faithfulness,
  And sound his power abroad;
Sing the sweet promise of his grace,
  And the performing God.

3 His very word of grace is strong,
  As that which built the skies;
The voice that rolls the stars along,
  Speaks all the promises.

4 Oh, might I hear thy heavenly tongue
  But whisper, " Thou art mine!"
Those gentle words should raise my song
  To notes almost divine.

432   *Providence.*   COWPER.

GOD moves in a mysterious way
  His wonders to perform;
He plants his footsteps in the sea,
  And rides upon the storm.

2 Deep in unfathomable mines
  Of never-failing skill,
He treasures up his bright designs,
  And works his sovereign will.

3 Ye fearful saints, fresh courage take!
  The clouds ye so much dread,
Are big with mercy, and will break
  In blessings on your head.

4 Judge not the Lord by feeble sense,
  But trust him for his grace;
Behind a frowning providence
  He hides a smiling face.

5 His purposes will ripen fast,
  Unfolding every hour;
The bud may have a bitter taste,
  But sweet will be the flower.

6 Blind unbelief is sure to err,
  And scan his work in vain;
God is his own interpreter,
  And he will make it plain.

433   *Holiness.—Psalm 111 : 9.*   NEEDHAM.

HOLY and reverend is the name
  Of our eternal King,
Thrice holy Lord! the angels cry;
  Thrice holy! let us sing.

2 The deepest reverence of the mind,
  Pay, O my soul! to God;
Lift with thy hands a holy heart
  To his sublime abode.

3 With sacred awe pronounce his name,
  Whom words nor thoughts can reach;
A broken heart shall please him more
  Than the best forms of speech.

4 Thou holy God! preserve our souls
  From all pollution free;
The pure in heart are thy delight,
  And they thy face shall see.

ABRIDGE. C. M.

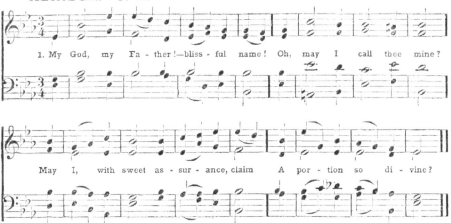

1. My God, my Fa-ther!—bliss-ful name! Oh, may I call thee mine?

May I, with sweet as-sur-ance, claim A por-tion so di-vine?

434 *Our Father.—Psalm 31.* STEELE.

My God, my Father!—blissful name!
Oh, may I call thee mine?
May I, with sweet assurance, claim
A portion so divine?

2 This only can my fears control,
And bid my sorrows fly:
What harm can ever reach my soul,
Beneath my Father's eye?

3 Whate'er thy providence denies,
I calmly would resign;
For thou art just, and good, and wise;
Oh, bend my will to thine.

4 Whate'er thy sacred will ordains,
Oh, give me strength to bear;
And let me know my Father reigns,
And trust his tender care.

5 If pain and sickness rend this frame,
And life almost depart,
Is not thy mercy still the same,
To cheer my drooping heart?

6 My God, my Father! be thy name
My solace and my stay;
Oh, wilt thou seal my humble claim,
And drive my fears away?

435 *The Trinity.* WATTS.

FATHER of glory! to thy name
Immortal praise we give,
Who dost an act of grace proclaim,
And bid us rebels live.

2 Immortal honor to the Son
Who makes thine anger cease;
Our lives he ransomed with his own,
And died to make our peace.

3 To thine almighty Spirit be
Immortal glory given,
Whose influence brings us near to thee,
And trains us up for heaven.

4 Let men with their united voice
Adore the eternal God;
And spread his honors and their joys
Through nations far abroad.

436 *In the Universe.* WATTS.

ETERNAL Wisdom! thee we praise,
Thee the creation sings;
With thy loved name, rocks, hills, and seas,
And heaven's high palace rings.

2 How wide thy hand hath spread the sky!
How glorious to behold!
Tinged with a blue of heavenly dye,
And starred with sparkling gold.

3 Infinite strength and equal skill,
Shine through the worlds abroad,
Our souls with vast amazement fill,
And speak the builder, God.

4 But still the wonders of thy grace
Our softer passions move;
Pity divine in Jesus' face
We see, adore, and love.

161

FABEN. 8, 7. D.

1. Lord, thy glo - ry fills the heaven; Earth is with its fullness stored; Un-to thee be glo-ry giv - en, Ho-ly, ho - ly, ho-ly Lord! Heaven is still with anthems ringing; Earth takes up the an-gels' cry, Ho-ly ho - ly, ho-ly, sing-ing, Lord of hosts, thou Lord most high.

437　　*Holiness.—Rev.* 4 : 8.　　MANT.

Lord, thy glory fills the heaven;
　Earth is with its fullness stored;
Unto thee be glory given,
　Holy, holy, holy Lord!
Heaven is still with anthems ringing;
　Earth takes up the angels' cry,
Holy, holy, holy, singing,
　Lord of hosts, thou Lord most high.

2 Ever thus in God's high praises,
　Brethren, let our tongues unite,
While our thoughts his greatness raises,
　And our love his gifts excite:
With his seraph train before him,
　With his holy church below,
Thus unite we to adore him,
　Bid we thus our anthem flow.

3 Lord, thy glory fills the heaven;
　Earth is with its fullness stored;
Unto thee be glory given,
　Holy, holy, holy Lord!
Thus thy glorious name confessing,
　We adopt the angels' cry,
Holy, holy, holy, blessing
　Thee, the Lord our God most high!

438　　*Grace.*　　KEY.

Lord, with glowing heart I'd praise thee
　For the bliss thy love bestows;
For the pardoning grace that saves me,
　And the peace that from it flows:
Help, O God, my weak endeavor;
　This dull soul to rapture raise;
Thou must light the flame, or never
　Can my love be warmed to praise.

2 Praise, my soul, the God that sought thee,
　Wretched wanderer, far astray;
Found thee lost, and kindly brought thee
　From the paths of death away;
Praise, with love's devoutest feeling,
　Him who saw thy guilt-born fear,
And, the light of hope revealing,
　Bade the blood-stained cross appear.

3 Lord, this bosom's ardent feeling
　Vainly would my lips express:
Low before thy footstool kneeling,
　Deign thy suppliant's prayer to bless;
Let thy grace, my soul's chief treasure,
　Love's pure flame within me raise;
And, since words can never measure,
　Let my life show forth thy praise.

VESPER HYMN. 8, 7. D.

1. { God is love; his mercy brightens All the path in which we rove; }
{ Bliss he wakes and woe he lightens; God is wisdom, God is love. } 2. Chance and change are busy
ev - er; Man decays, and ages move; But his mercy waneth never; God is wisdom, God is love.

439   *Wisdom and Love.*   BOWRING.

GOD is love; his mercy brightens
  All the path in which we rove;
Bliss he wakes and woe he lightens;
  God is wisdom, God is love.

2 Chance and change are busy ever;
  Man decays, and ages move;
But his mercy waneth never;
  God is wisdom, God is love.

3 Ev'n the hour that darkest seemeth,
  Will his changeless goodness prove;
From the gloom his brightness streameth,
  God is wisdom, God is love.

4 He with earthly cares entwineth
  Hope and comfort from above:
Everywhere his glory shineth;
  God is wisdom, God is love.

440   *Divine Love.*   MASSIE. *Tr.*

SEE, oh, see what love the Father
  Hath bestowed upon our race!
How he bends, with sweet compassion,
  Over us his beaming face!
See how he his best and dearest,
  For the very worst, hath given,—
His own Son for us poor sinners;
  See, oh, see the love of heaven!

2 See, oh, see, what love the Saviour,
  Also, hath on us bestowed!
How he bled for us and suffered,
  How he bore the heavy load!

On the cross and in the garden,
  Oh, how sore was his distress!
Is not this a love, that passeth
  Aught that tongue can e'er express?

3 See, oh, see, what love is shown us,
  Also, by the Holy Ghost!
How he strives with us, poor sinners,
  Even when we sin the most,
Teaching, comforting, correcting,
  Where he sees it needful is!
Oh, what heart would not be thankful
  For a threefold love like this?

441   *Perfections.—Ps.* 145.   MANT.

GOD, my King, thy might confessing,
  Ever will I bless thy name;
Day by day thy throne addressing,
  Still will I thy praise proclaim.

2 Nor shall fail from memory's treasure,
  Works by love and mercy wrought—
Works of love surpassing measure,
  Works of mercy passing thought.

3 Full of kindness and compassion,
  Slow of anger, vast in love,
God is good to all creation;
  All his works his goodness prove.

4 All thy works, O Lord, shall bless thee,
  Thee shall all thy saints adore;
King supreme shall they confess thee,
  And proclaim thy sovereign power.

ITALIAN HYMN. 6, 4.

1. Come, thou al - might - y King, Help us thy name to sing, Help us to praise:

Father! all-glo - ri - ous, O'er all vic-to - ri - ous, Come, and reign over us, Ancient of Days.

442　　*"One in Three."*　　MADAN.

Come, thou almighty King,
Help us thy name to sing,
　Help us to praise:
Father! all-glorious,
O'er all victorious,
Come, and reign over us,
　Ancient of Days!

2 Come, thou incarnate Word,
Gird on thy mighty sword;
　Our prayer attend;
Come, and thy people bless,
And give thy word success:
Spirit of holiness!
　On us descend.

3 Come, holy Comforter!
Thy sacred witness bear,
　In this glad hour:
Thou, who almighty art,
Now rule in every heart,
And ne'er from us depart,
　Spirit of power!

4 To the great One in Three,
The highest praises be,
　Hence evermore!
His sovereign majesty
May we in glory see,
And to eternity
　Love and adore.

443　　*Psalm 150.*　　GOODE.

Praise ye Jehovah's name;
Praise through his courts proclaim;
　Rise and adore;
High o'er the heavens above,
Sound his great acts of love,
While his rich grace we prove,
　Vast as his power.

2 Now let the trumpet raise
Sounds of triumphant praise,
　Wide as his fame;
There let the harp be found;
Organs, with solemn sound,
Roll your deep notes around,
　Filled with his name.

3 While his high praise you sing,
Shake every sounding string;
　Sweet the accord!
He vital breath bestows;
Let every breath that flows,
His noble fame disclose;
　Praise ye the Lord.

4 To God, the Father, Son,
And Spirit, Three in One,
　All praise be given!
Crown him in every song;
To him your hearts belong
Let all his praise prolong
　On earth, in heaven!

EIN' FESTE BURG. P. M.

1. { A mighty fortress is our God, A bulwark never fail-ing: }
{ Our Helper he, a-mid the flood Of mortal ills pre-vail-ing. } For still our ancient foe Doth

seek to work his woe; His craft and power are great, And armed with cruel hate, On earth is not his equal.

444 HEDGE. *Tr.*
"A Mighty Fortress."

A MIGHTY fortress is our God,
　A bulwark never failing :
Our Helper he, amid the flood
　Of mortal ills prevailing.
For still our ancient foe
Doth seek to work his woe;
His craft and power are great,
And armed with cruel hate,
　On earth is not his equal.

2 Did we in our own strength confide,
　Our striving would be losing;
Were not the right man on our side,
　The man of God's own choosing.
Dost ask who that may be?
Christ Jesus, it is he;
Lord Sabaoth is his name,
From age to age the same,
　And he must win the battle.

3 And though this world, with devils filled,
　Should threaten to undo us;
We will not fear, for God hath willed
　His truth to triumph through us.
The Prince of darkness grim,—
We tremble not for him;
His rage we can endure,
For lo! his doom is sure,—
　One little word shall fell him!

4 That word above all earthly powers—
　No thanks to them—abideth;
The Spirit and the gifts are ours
　Through him who with us sideth.
Let goods and kindred go,
This mortal life also:
The body they may kill:
God's truth abideth still,
　His kingdom is for ever.

445 BAKER.
The Only True God.

REJOICE to-day with one accord,
　Sing out with exultation;
Rejoice and praise our mighty Lord,
　Whose arm hath brought salvation;
His works of love proclaim
The greatness of his name;
For he is God alone,
Who hath his mercy shown;
　Let all his saints adore him.

2 When in distress to him we cried,
　He heard our sad complaining;
Oh, trust in him, whate'er betide,
　His love is all sustaining;
Triumphant songs of praise
To him our hearts shall raise;
Now every voice shall say,
"Oh, praise our God alway;"
　Let all his saints adore him.

NUN DANKET. P. M.

1. Now thank we all our God, With heart, and hands, and voices,
Who wondrous things hath done, In whom his world re-joic - es; Who from our mother's arms

Hath blest us on our way With countless gifts of love, And still is ours to - day.

446 *Bounteous Care.* WINKWORTH. *Tr.*

Now thank we all our God,
  With heart, and hands, and voices,
Who wondrous things hath done,
  In whom his world rejoices;
Who from our mother's arms
  Hath blessed us on our way
With countless gifts of love,
  And still is ours to-day.

2 Oh, may this bounteous God
  Through all our life be near us,
With ever joyful hearts
  And blessèd peace to cheer us;
And keep us in his grace,
  And guide us when perplexed,
And free us from all ills
  In this world and the next.

447 *Eternity.* LAURENTI.

O thou essential Word,
  Who wast from everlasting
With God, for thou wast God;
  On thee our burden casting,
O Saviour of our race,
  Welcome indeed thou art,
Redeemer, Fount of Grace,
  To this my longing heart.

2 Come, self-existent Word,
  And speak thou in my spirit;
The soul where thou art heard,
  Doth endless peace inherit.

Thou Light that lightenest all,
  Abide through faith in me,
Nor let me from thee fall,
  Nor seek a guide but thee.

448 *Beneficence.* PIERSON.

To thee, O God, we raise
  Our voice in choral singing;
We come with prayer and praise,
  Our hearts' oblations bringing;
Thou art our fathers' God,
  And ever shalt be ours;
Our lips and lives shall laud
  Thy name, with all our powers.

2 Thy goodness, like the dew
  On Hermon's hill descending,
Is every morning new,
  And tells of love unending.
We bless thy tender care
  That led our wayward feet,
Past every fatal snare,
  To streams and pastures sweet.

3 We bless thy Son, who bore
  The cross, for sinners dying;
Thy Spirit we adore,
  The precious blood applying.
Let work and worship send
  Their incense unto thee;
Till song and service blend,
  Beside the crystal sea.

BLUMENTHAL. 7. D.

1. Holy Father, hear my cry;
Holy Saviour, bend thine ear;
Holy Spirit, come thou nigh:
Father, Saviour, Spirit, hear!

2. Father, save me from my sin;
Saviour, I thy mercy crave;
Gracious Spirit, make me clean:
Father, Son, and Spirit, save!

449   *The Trinity.*   BONAR.

HOLY Father, hear my cry;
  Holy Saviour, bend thine ear;
Holy Spirit, come thou nigh:
  Father, Saviour, Spirit, hear!
2 Father, save me from my sin;
  Saviour, I thy mercy crave;
Gracious Spirit, make me clean:
  Father, Son, and Spirit, save!
3 Father, let me taste thy love;
  Saviour, fill my soul with peace;
Spirit, come my heart to move:
  Father, Son, and Spirit, bless!
4 Father, Son, and Spirit—thou
    One Jehovah, shed abroad
  All thy grace within me now;
    Be my Father and my God!

450   *"Holy, holy, holy."*   MONTGOMERY.

HOLY, holy, holy Lord
  God of Hosts! when heaven and earth,
Out of darkness, at thy word
  Issued into glorious birth,
All thy works before thee stood,
And thine eye beheld them good,
While they sung with sweet accord,
Holy, holy, holy Lord!
2 Holy, holy, holy! thee,
  One Jehovah evermore,
Father, Son, and Spirit! we,
  Dust and ashes, would adore:

Lightly by the world esteemed,
From that world by thee redeemed,
Sing we here with glad accord,
Holy, holy, holy Lord!
3 Holy, holy, holy! all
  Heaven's triumphant choir shall sing,
While the ransomed nations fall
  At the footstool of their King:
Then shall saints and seraphim,
Harps and voices, swell one hymn,
Blending in sublime accord,
Holy, holy, holy Lord!

451   *The Divine Presence.*   GRANT.

LORD of earth! thy forming hand
Well this beauteous frame hath planned;
Woods that wave, and hills that tower,
Ocean rolling in his power:
Yet, amid this scene so fair,
Should I cease thy smile to share,
What were all its joys to me?
Whom have I on earth but thee?

2 Lord of heaven! beyond our sight
Shines a world of purer light;
There in love's unclouded reign
Parted hands shall meet again:
Oh, that world is passing fair!
Yet, if thou wert absent there,
What were all its joys to me?
Whom have I in heaven but thee?

CULLODEN. H. M.

1. We give im-mor-tal praise For God the Father's love, For all our comforts here, And

bet-ter hopes a-bove: He sent his own e - ter - nal Son To die for sins that we had done.

452   *The Trinity.*   WATTS.

WE give immortal praise
For God the Father's love,
For all our comforts here,
  And better hopes above:
He sent his own eternal Son
To die for sins that we had done.

2 To God the Son belongs
Immortal glory too,
Who bought us with his blood
  From everlasting woe:
And now he lives and now he reigns,
And sees the fruit of all his pains.

3 To God the Spirit's name
Immortal worship give,
Whose new-creating power
  Makes the dead sinner live:
His work completes the great design,
And fills the soul with joy divine.

4 Almighty God! to thee
Be endless honor done,
The undivided Three,
  The great and glorious One:
Where reason fails, with all her powers,
There faith prevails and love adores.

453   *Psalm* 148.   WATTS.

Ye tribes of Adam, join
With heaven, and earth, and seas,
And offer notes divine
  To your Creator's praise:
Ye holy throng | In worlds of light,
Of angels bright, | Begin the song.
168

2 The shining worlds above
In glorious order stand;
Or in swift courses move,
  By his supreme command:
He spake the word, | From nothing came,
And all their frame | To praise the Lord!

3 Let all the nations fear
The God that rules above;
He brings his people near,
  And makes them taste his love:
While earth and sky | His saints shall raise
Attempt his praise, | His honors high.

454   *Our Friend.—Ps.* 97.   WATTS.

THE Lord Jehovah reigns;
His throne is built on high;
The garments he assumes
  Are light and majesty:
His glories shine with beams so bright,
No mortal eye can bear the sight.

2 Through all his ancient works,
Surprising wisdom shines;
Confounds the powers of hell,
  And breaks their cursed designs:
Strong is his arm—and shall fulfill
His great decrees—his sovereign will.

3 And can this mighty King
Of glory condescend,—
And will he write his name,—
  "My Father and my Friend?"
I love his name,—I love his word;
Join, all my powers! and praise the Lord.

SUTHERLAND. H. M.

455 *The Trinity.* WATTS.

To him that chose us first,
　Before the world began;
To him that bore the curse
　To save rebellious man;
To him that formed | Is endless praise
Our hearts anew, | And glory due.

2 The Father's love shall run
　Through our immortal songs;
We bring to God the Son
　Hosannas on our tongues;
Our lips address | With equal praise
The Spirit's name | And zeal the same

3 Let every saint above,
　And angel round the throne,
For ever bless and love
　The sacred Three in One;
Thusheavenshallraise | Whenearthandtime
His honors high, | Grow old and die.

456 *Love.—Eph. 2 : 17.* YOUNG.

Oh, for a shout of joy,
　Worthy the theme we sing;
To this divine employ
　Our hearts and voices bring;
Sound, sound, through all the earth abroad,
The love, the eternal love of God.

2 Unnumbered myriads stand,
　Of seraphs bright and fair,
Or bow at thy right hand,

And pay their homage there;
But strive in vain with loudest chord,
To sound thy wondrous love, O Lord.

3 Yet sinners saved by grace,
　In songs of lower key,
In every age and place,
　Have sung thy mystery,—
Have told in strains of sweet accord,
Thy love, thy sovereign love, O Lord.

457 *Protection.—Ps. 121.* WATTS.

Upward I lift mine eyes,
　From God is all my aid;
The God who built the skies,
　And earth and nature made:
God is the tower | His grace is nigh
To which I fly; | In every hour.

2 My feet shall never slide,
　Nor fall in fatal snares,
Since God, my guard and guide,
　Defends me from my fears:
Those wakeful eyes | Shall Israel keep
That never sleep, | When dangers rise.

3 No burning heats by day,
　Nor blasts of evening air,
Shall take my health away,
　If God be with me there:
Thou art my sun, | To guard my head
And thou my shade, | By night or noon.

THANKSGIVING. 11, 8.

1. Be joy-ful in God, all ye lands of the earth ; Oh, serve him with gladness and fear ; Exult in his

presence with music and mirth ; With love and devotion draw near. 2. For Je-ho-vah is God, and Je -

ho-vah a - lone, Cre - a - tor and Rul-er o'er all, ... And we are his peo-ple, his

sceptre we own ; His sheep, and we follow his call ; we follow his call, we follow his call.

458   *"Jehovah alone."—Ps.* **100.**   MONTGOMERY.

Be joyful in God, all ye lands of the earth:
Oh, serve him with gladness and fear;
Exult in his presence with music and mirth;
With love and devotion draw near.

2 For Jehovah is God, and Jehovah alone,
Creator and Ruler o'er all;
And we are his people, his sceptre we own;
His sheep, and we follow his call.

3 Oh, enter his gates with thanksgiving and
song;
Your vows in his temple proclaim;
His praise with melodious accordance prolong,
And bless his adorable name.

4 For good is the Lord, inexpressibly good,
And we are the work of his hand;
His mercy and truth from eternity stood,
And shall to eternity stand.

NICÆA. P. M.

1. Ho - ly, ho - ly, ho - ly, Lord God Al - might - y! Ear - ly in the
morn - ing our song shall rise to thee; Ho - ly, ho - ly, ho - ly,
mer - ci - ful and might - y, God in three per - sons, bless-ed Trin - i - ty.

HEBER.

459 *The Trinity.*

Holy, holy, holy, Lord God Almighty!
Early in the morning our song shall rise
to thee;
Holy, holy, holy, merciful and mighty,
God in three persons, blessed Trinity!

2 Holy, holy, holy! all the saints adore thee,
Casting down their golden crowns
around the glassy sea;
Cherubim and seraphim falling down be-
fore thee, [shalt be.
Which wert and art and evermore

3 Holy, holy, holy! though the darkness
hide thee,
Though the eye of sinful man thy glory
may not see; [thee,
Only thou art holy; there is none beside
Perfect in power, in love and purity.

4 Holy, holy, holy! Lord God Almighty!
All thy works shall praise thy name, in
earth and sky and sea;
Holy, holy, holy! merciful and mighty;
God in three persons, blessed Trinity!

---

460 *The Great Jehovah.—Ps. 48.* MONTGOMERY.

Oh, great is Jehovah, and great be his
praise,
In the city of God he is King;
Proclaim ye his triumphs in jubilant lays;
On the mount of his holiness sing.

2 The joy of the earth, from her beautiful
Is Zion's impregnable hill; [height,
The Lord in her temple still taketh delight,
God reigns in her palaces still.

3 Go, walk about Zion, and measure the
length,
Her walks and her bulwarks, mark well;
Contemplate her palaces, glorious in
strength,
Her towers and her pinnacles tell.

4 Then say to your children—"Our refuge
is tried,
This God is our God to the end;
His people for ever his counsels shall guide,
His arm shall for ever defend."

171

HERALD ANGELS. 7. D.

1. Hark! the her-ald an-gels sing "Glo-ry to the new-born King; Peace on earth, and

mer-cy mild, God and sin-ners re-con-ciled!" Joy-ful, all ye na-tions, rise,

Join the tri-umph of the skies; With th'angel-ic host proclaim, Christ is born in

Beth-le-hem! With th'an-gel-ic host proclaim, Christ is born in Beth-le-hem!

461 *The Nativity.* C. WESLEY.

Hark! the herald angels sing
"Glory to the new-born King;
Peace on earth, and mercy mild,
God and sinners reconciled!"
Joyful, all ye nations, rise,
Join the triumph of the skies;
With the angelic host proclaim,
Christ is born in Bethlehem!

2 Christ, by highest heaven adored;
Christ, the everlasting Lord;
Late in time behold him come,
Offspring of the Virgin's womb:
Vailed in flesh the Godhead see;
Hail the incarnate Deity,
Pleased as man with men to dwell;
Jesus, our Immanuel!

3 Hail! the heaven-born Prince of peace!
Hail! the Sun of Righteousness!
Light and life to all he brings,
Risen with healing in his wings.
Mild he lays his glory by,
Born that man no more may die:
Born to raise the sons of earth,
Born to give them second birth.

172

462   *"Songs of Praise."*   MONTGOMERY.

Songs of praise the angels sang,
Heaven with hallelujahs rang,
When Jehovah's work begun,
When he spake, and it was done.

2 Songs of praise awoke the morn,
When the Prince of Peace was born;
Songs of praise arose, when he
Captive led captivity.

3 Heaven and earth must pass away—
Songs of praise shall crown that day;
God will make new heavens and earth—
Songs of praise shall hail their birth.

4 And shall man alone be dumb,
Till that glorious kingdom come?
No; the Church delights to raise
Psalms and hymns and songs of praise.

5 Saints below, with heart and voice,
Still in songs of praise rejoice;
Learning here, by faith and love,
Songs of praise to sing above.

6 Borne upon their latest breath
Songs of praise shall conquer death;
Then, amid eternal joy,
Songs of praise their powers employ.

463   *"The Christ of God."*   DONAR.

He has come! the Christ of God
Left for us his glad abode;
Stooping from his throne of bliss,
To this darksome wilderness.

2 He has come! the Prince of Peace;
Come to bid our sorrows cease;
Come to scatter with his light
All the shadows of our night.

3 He the mighty King has come!
Making this poor earth his home;
Come to bear our sin's sad load;
Son of David, Son of God.

4 He has come, whose name of grace
Speaks deliverance to our race;
Left for us his glad abode;
Son of Mary, Son of God!

5 Unto us a child is born!
Ne'er has earth beheld a morn,
Among all the morns of time,
Half so glorious in its prime.

6 Unto us a Son is given!
He has come from God's own heaven,
Bringing with him from above
Holy peace and holy love.

464   *Immanuel.*   ANON.

God with us! oh, glorious name!
Let it shine in endless fame;
God and man in Christ unite;
Oh, mysterious depth and height!

2 God with us! the eternal Son
Took our soul, our flesh, and bone;
Now, ye saints, his grace admire,
Swell the song with holy fire.

3 God with us! but tainted not
With the first transgressor's blot;
Yet did he our sins sustain,
Bear the guilt, the curse, the pain.

4 God with us! oh, wondrous grace!
Let us see him face to face;
That we may Immanuel sing,
As we ought, our God and King!

465   *Advent Morning.*   MONTGOMERY.

Bright and joyful is the morn;
For to us a Child is born;
From the highest realms of heaven
Unto us a Son is given.

2 On his shoulders he shall bear
Power and majesty—and wear
On his vesture, and his thigh,
Names most awful, names most high.

3 Wonderful in counsel he;
The incarnate Deity,
Sires of Ages ne'er to cease;
King of kings, and Prince of Peace.

4 Come and worship at his feet,
Yield to Christ the homage meet;
From his manger to his throne,
Homage due to God alone.

466   *The Angels' Song.*   GERMAN.

Hail the night, all hail the morn,
When the Prince of Peace was born!
When, amid the wakeful fold,
Tidings good the angels told.

2 Now our solemn chant we raise
Duly to the Saviour's praise;
Now with carol hymns we bless
Christ the Lord, our Righteousness.

3 While resounds the joyful cry,
"Glory be to God on high,
Peace on earth, good-will to men!"
Gladly we respond, "Amen!"

4 Thus we greet this holy day,
Pouring forth our festive lay;
Thus we tell, with saintly mirth,
Of Immanuel's wondrous birth.   173

SOLID ROCK. L. M. D.

1. When, mar - shaled on the night - ly plain, The glitter-ing host be -
   One star a - lone. of all the train, Can fix the sin - ner's

stud the sky, } { Hark! hark! to God the cho - rus breaks From
wandering eye. } { But one a - lone the Sav - iour speaks,— It

eve - ry host, from eve - ry gem; } It is the Star of Beth - le - hem.
is the Star of Beth - le - hem; }

467   *"The Star of Bethlehem."*   H. K. WHITE.

WHEN, marshaled on the nightly plain,
  The glittering host bestud the sky,
One star alone, of all the train,
  Can fix the sinner's wandering eye.
Hark! hark! to God the chorus breaks
  From every host, from every gem;
But one alone the Saviour speaks,—
  It is the Star of Bethlehem.

2 Once on the raging seas I rode,
  The storm was loud, the night was dark,
The ocean yawned, and rudely blowed
  The wind that tossed my foundering bark.
Deep horror then my vitals froze;
  Death-struck, I ceased the tide to stem:
When suddenly a star arose,
  It was the Star of Bethlehem!

3 It was my guide, my light, my all;
  It bade my dark forebodings cease,
And through the storm and danger's thrall
  It led me to the port of peace.
Now safely moored, my perils o'er,
  I'll sing, first in night's diadem,
For ever and for evermore,
  The Star, the Star of Bethlehem!

468   *The Angels' Song.*   CAMPBELL.

WHEN Jordan hushed his waters still,
  And silence slept on Zion's hill;
When Salem's shepherds thro' the night
  Watched o'er their flocks by starry light;
2 Hark! from the midnight hills around,
  A voice of more than mortal sound
In distant hallelujahs stole,
  Wild murmuring o'er the raptured soul.

3 On wheels of light, on wings of flame,
  The glorious hosts of Zion came;
High heaven with songs of triumph rung,
  While thus they struck their harps and sung:
4 "O Zion, lift thy raptured eye;
  The long-expected hour is nigh;
The joys of nature rise again,
  The Prince of Salem comes to reign.

5 "He comes to cheer the trembling heart,
  Bids Satan and his host depart;
Again the Daystar gilds the gloom,
  Again the bowers of Eden bloom."
6 O Zion! lift thy raptured eye;
  The long-expected hour is nigh;
The joys of nature rise again:
  The Prince of Salem comes to reign.

HARMONY GROVE. L. M.

1. Wake, O my soul, and hail the morn, For un-to us a Sav-iour's born;

See, how the an-gels wing their way, To ush-er in the glo-rious day!

469   *Jesus' Birth.*   ANON.

WAKE, O my soul, and hail the morn,
  For unto us a Saviour's born;
See, how the angels wing their way,
  To usher in the glorious day!

2 Hark! what sweet music, what a song,
  Sounds from the bright, celestial throng!
Sweet song, whose melting sounds impart
  Joy to each raptured, listening heart.

3 Come, join the angels in the sky,
  Glory to God, who reigns on high;
Let peace and love on earth abound,
  While time revolves and years roll round.

470   *"The Word was God."*   WATTS.

BEFORE the heavens were spread abroad,
  From everlasting was the Word;
With God he was, the Word was God!
  And must divinely be adored.

2 By his own power were all things made;
  By him supported, all things stand;
He is the whole creation's head,
  And angels fly at his command.

3 Ere sin was born, or Satan fell,
  He led the host of morning stars:
His generation who can tell,
  Or count the number of his years?

4 But lo, he leaves those heavenly forms:
  The Word descends and dwells in clay,
That he may converse hold with worms,
  . Dressed in such feeble flesh as they.

5 Mortals with joy behold his face,
  The eternal Father's only Son:
How full of truth, how full of grace,
  When in his eyes the Godhead shone!

6 Archangels leave their high abode,
  To learn new mysteries here, and tell
The love of our descending God,
  The glories of Immanuel.

471   *"A Little Child."*   LUTHER.

ALL praise to thee, eternal Lord,
  Clothed in a garb of flesh and blood;
Choosing a manger for thy throne,
  While worlds on worlds are thine alone!

2 Once did the skies before thee bow;
  A virgin's arms contain thee now;
Angels, who did in thee rejoice,
  Now listen for thine infant voice.

3 A little child, thou art our guest,
  That weary ones in thee may rest;
Forlorn and lowly is thy birth,
  That we may rise to heaven from earth.

4 Thou comest in the darksome night
  To make us children of the light;
To make us, in the realms divine,
  Like thine own angels round thee shine.

5 All this for us thy love hath done;
  By this to thee our love is won;
For this we tune our cheerful lays,
  And shout our thanks in ceaseless praise.

NEWBOLD. C. M.

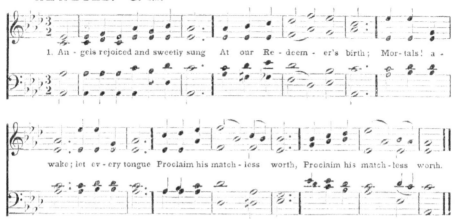

1. An - gels rejoiced and sweetly sung   At our Re - deem - er's birth;   Mor - tals! a -
wake; let ev - ery tongue Proclaim his match - less worth, Proclaim his match - less worth.

472   *The Angels' Song.*   HURN.

ANGELS rejoiced and sweetly sung
At our Redeemer's birth;
Mortals! awake; let every tongue
Proclaim his matchless worth.

2 Glory to God, who dwells on high,
And sent his only Son
To take a servant's form, and die,
For evils we had done!

3 Good-will to men; ye fallen race!
Arise, and shout for joy;
He comes, with rich abounding grace,
To save, and not destroy.

4 Lord! send the gracious tidings forth,
And fill the world with light,
That Jew and Gentile, through the earth,
May know thy saving might.

473   *"The Saviour Comes."*   DODDRIDGE.

HARK, the glad sound! the Saviour comes,
The Saviour promised long;
Let every heart prepare a throne,
And every voice a song.

2 He comes, the prisoner to release,
In Satan's bondage held;
The gates of brass before him burst,
The iron fetters yield.

3 He comes, from thickest films of vice
To clear the mental ray,
And, on the eyes long closed in night,
To pour celestial day.

4 He comes, the broken heart to bind,
The bleeding soul to cure,
And, with the treasures of his grace,
Enrich the humble poor.

5 Our glad hosannas, Prince of Peace,
Thy welcome shall proclaim,
And heaven's eternal arches ring
With thy belovéd name.

474   *"Glory to God."*   E. H. SEARS.

CALM on the listening ear of night,
Come heaven's melodious strains,
Where wild Judea stretches far
Her silver-mantled plains.

2 Celestial choirs, from courts above,
Shed sacred glories there,
And angels, with their sparkling lyres,
Make music on the air.

3 The answering hills of Palestine
Send back the glad reply;
And greet, from all their holy heights,
The day-spring from on high.

4 O'er the blue depths of Galilee
There comes a holier calm,
And Sharon waves, in solemn praise,
Her silent groves of palm.

5 "Glory to God!" the sounding skies
Loud with their anthems ring—
"Peace to the earth, good-will to men,
From heaven's eternal King!"

CHRISTMAS. C. M.

1. While shepherds watched their flocks by night, All seat-ed on the ground; The an-gel of the Lord came down, And glo-ry shone a-round, And glo-ry shone a-round.

TATE-BRADY.

475 *Luke 2.*

WHILE shepherds watched their flocks by
All seated on the ground; [night,
The angel of the Lord came down,
And glory shone around.

2 "Fear not," said he,—for mighty dread
Had seized their troubled mind,—
"Glad tidings of great joy I bring,
To you and all mankind.

3 "To you in David's town this day,
Is born of David's line,
The Saviour, who is Christ, the Lord,
And this shall be the sign;—

4 "The heavenly babe you there shall find
To human view displayed,
All meanly wrapped in swathing bands,
And in a manger laid."

5 Thus spake the seraph— and forthwith
Appeared a shining throng
Of angels, praising God, who thus
Addressed their joyful song:—

6 "All glory be to God on high,
And to the earth be peace;
Good-will henceforth from heaven to men
Begin, and never cease!"

ZERAH. C. M.

1. To us a Child of hope is born; To us a Son is given; Him shall the tribes of earth o-bey, Him all the hosts of heaven; Him shall the tribes of earth obey, Him all the hosts of heaven.

BRUCE.

476 *Isaiah 9:6.*

2 His name shall be the Prince of Peace,
For evermore adored,
The Wonderful, the Counselor,
The great and mighty Lord!

3 His power increasing still shall spread,
His reign no end shall know:
Justice shall guard his throne above,
And peace abound below.

FOLSOM. 11, 10.

1. Brightest and best of the sons of the morning! Dawn on our darkness, and lend us thine aid;

Star of the East, the ho-ri-zon a-dorning, Guide where our in-fant Re-deem-er is laid.

477　　　　"Star of the East."　　HEBER.

Brightest and best of the sons of the
　morning!
　Dawn on our darkness and lend us thine
　　aid;
Star of the East, the horizon adorning,
　Guide where our infant Redeemer is laid.

2 Cold on his cradle the dew-drops are
　shining;
　Low lies his head with the beasts of the
　　stall:
Angels adore him, in slumber reclining,
　Maker, and Monarch, and Saviour of all!

3 Say shall we yield him, in costly devotion,
　Odors of Edom, and offerings divine?
Gems of the mountain, and pearls of the
　ocean,
　Myrrh from the forest, or gold from the
　　mine?

4 Vainly we offer each ample oblation,
　Vainly with gold would his favors secure:
Richer, by far, is the heart's adoration;
　Dearer to God are the prayers of the poor.

5 Brightest and best of the sons of the
　morning!
　Dawn on our darkness and lend us thine
　　aid;
Star of the East, the horizon adorning,
　Guide where our infant Redeemer is laid.

478　　　　"Daughter of Zion."　　ANON.

[Sound the loud timbrel o'er Egypt's dark sea,
Jehovah hath triumphed, his people are free.]
Daughter of Zion! awake from thy sadness:
　Awake, for thy foes shall oppress thee
　　no more;
Bright o'er thy hills dawns the day-star of
　gladness;
　Arise! for the night of thy sorrow is o'er.

2 Strong were thy foes, but the arm that
　subdued them,
　And scattered their legions, was mightier
　　far;
They fled, like the chaff, from the scourge
　that pursued them;
　For vain were their steeds and their
　　chariots of war!

3 Daughter of Zion! the Power that hath
　saved thee,
　Extolled with the harp and the timbrel
　　should be:
Shout! for the foe is destroyed that en-
　slaved thee,
　Th' oppressor is vanquished, and Zion is
　　free!

AVISON. 11, 10.

Shout the glad tidings, exult-ing-ly sing; .... Je-rusalem triumphs, Messiah is King. 1. Zion, the

marvelous story be tell-ing, The Son of the Highest, how lowly his birth; The brightest archangel in

Repeat 1st Chorus.   Chorus after Last Verse.

glo-ry ex-cell-ing, He stoops to redeem thee, he reigns up-on earth.   Shout the glad tidings, ex-

ult-ing-ly sing; .... Je-ru-salem triumphs, Messiah is King, Messiah is King, Messiah is King.

479   *"Messiah is King."*   MUHLENBERG.

Cho.—Shout the glad tidings, exultingly sing;
  Jerusalem triumphs, Messiah is King.
Zion, the marvelous story, be telling,
  The Son of the Highest, how lowly his
    birth;
The brightest archangel in glory excelling,
  He stoops to redeem thee, he reigns
    upon earth.
    Cho.—Shout the glad tidings, etc.

    Cho.—Shout the glad tidings, etc.
2 Tell how he cometh; from nation to nation,
  The heart-cheering news let the earth
    echo round;

How free to the faithful he offers salvation!
  How his people with joy everlasting
    are crowned!
    Cho.—Shout the glad tidings, etc.

    Cho.—Shout the glad tidings, etc.
3 Mortals, your homage be gratefully bring-
    ing,
  And sweet let the gladsome hosanna a-
    rise;
Ye angels, the full hallelujah be singing;
  One chorus resound through the earth
    and the skies.
    Cho.—Shout the glad tidings, etc.

HARK. P. M.

1. Hark! hark, my soul; an - gel - ic songs are swell - ing O'er earth's green fields and
   How sweet the truth those bless-ed strains are [Omit ....
   o - cean's wave-beat shore: } tell - ing Of that new life when sin shall be no more.

CHORUS.

An - gels of Je - sus, An - gels of light, Sing-ing to welcome the pilgrims of the night.

480 *" The Heavenly Host."* FABER.

2 Onward we go, for still we hear them singing,
"Come, weary souls, for Jesus bids you
come:" [ringing,
And, through the dark its echoes sweetly
The music of the gospel leads us home.
Cho.

3 Far, far away, like bells at evening pealing,
The voice of Jesus sounds o'er land
and sea,

And laden souls by thousands meekly
stealing,
Kind Shepherd, turn their weary steps
to thee.—Cho.

4 Angels, sing on! your faithful watches
keeping; [above;
Sing us sweet fragments of the songs
Till morning's joy shall end the night of
weeping,
And life's long shadows break in cloudless love.—Cho. [Amen.]

ANGELS' SONG. P. M.

1. Hark! hark, my soul; angelic songs are swelling O'er earth's green fields and ocean's wave-beat shore.

How sweet the truth those blessed strains are telling Of that new life when sin shall be no more.

REGENT SQUARE. 8, 7.

1. Hark! what mean those holy voices, Sweetly warbling in the skies? Sure, th' angelic host re-joic-es,—

Loudest hal-le-lu-jahs rise, Sure, th' angelic host re-joic-es,—Loudest hal-le-lu-jahs rise.

481 *" Those Holy Voices."* CAWOOD.

Hark! what mean those holy voices,
  Sweetly warbling in the skies?
Sure, the angelic host rejoices—
  Loudest hallelujahs rise.

2 Listen to the wondrous story,
  Which they chant in hymns of joy;—
"Glory in the highest, glory;
  Glory be to God most high!

3 "Peace on earth, good-will from heaven,
  Reaching far as man is found;
Souls redeemed, and sins forgiven;—
  Loud our golden harps shall sound.

4 "Christ is born, the great Anointed;
  Heaven and earth his glory sing:
Glad, receive whom God appointed,
  For your Prophet, Priest, and King.

5 "Hasten, mortals! to adore him;
  Learn his name, and taste his joy;
Till in heaven you sing before him,—
  Glory be to God most high!"

6 Let us learn the wondrous story
  Of our great Redeemer's birth,
Spread the brightness of his glory,
  Till it cover all the earth.

ANGELS' SONG. (CONTINUED.)

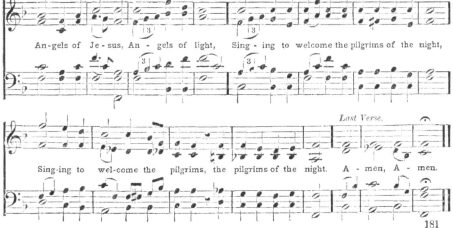

CHORUS.

An-gels of Je-sus, An-gels of light, Sing-ing to welcome the pilgrims of the night,

Sing-ing to wel-come the pilgrims, the pilgrims of the night. A-men, A-men.

Last Verse.

ATHENS. C. M. D.

1. It came up-on the midnight clear, That glorious song of old, From angels bend'ng near the earth
D. S.—The earth in solemn stillness lay,

FINE.　　　D. S.

To touch their harps of gold; " Peace to the earth, good-will to man, From heaven's all-gracious King ;"
To hear the an-gels sing.

482　　*The Angels' Song.*　　SEARS.

It came upon the midnight clear,
　That glorious song of old,
From angels bending near the earth
　To touch their harps of gold;
" Peace to the earth, good-will to man,
　From heaven's all-gracious King:"
The earth in solemn stillness lay,
　To hear the angels sing.

2 Still through the cloven skies they come,
　With peaceful wings unfurled;
And still celestial music floats
　O'er all the weary world;
Above its sad and lowly plains
　They bend on heavenly wing,
And ever o'er its Babel sounds,
　The blessèd angels sing.

3 O ye, beneath life's crushing load,
　Whose forms are bending low,
Who toil along the climbing way,
　With painful steps and slow;—
Look up! for glad and golden hours
　Come swiftly on the wing;
Oh, rest beside the weary road,
　And hear the angels sing!

4 For lo! the days are hastening on,
　By prophet-bards foretold,
When with the ever-circling years
　Comes round the age of gold!

When peace shall over all the earth
　Its final splendors fling;
And the whole world send back the song
　Which now the angels sing!

483　　*Jesus' Words.*　　BONAR.

I HEARD the voice of Jesus say,—
　" Come unto me and rest;
Lay down, thou weary one, lay down
　Thy head upon my breast!"
I came to Jesus as I was,
　Weary, and worn, and sad,
I found in him a resting-place,
　And he hath made me glad.

2 I heard the voice of Jesus say,—
　" Behold, I freely give
The living water; thirsty one,
　Stoop down, and drink, and live!"
I came to Jesus, and I drank
　Of that life-giving stream;
My thirst was quenched, my soul revived,
　And now I live in him.

3 I heard the voice of Jesus say,—
　" I am this dark world's light;
Look unto me, thy morn shall rise
　And all thy day be bright!"
I looked to Jesus, and I found
　In him my Star, my Sun;
And in that light of life I'll walk,
　Till all my journey's done.

ORTONVILLE. C. M.

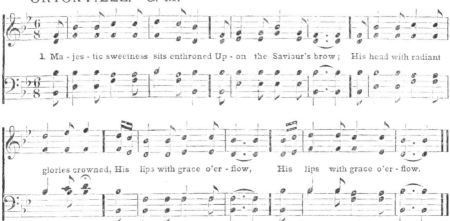

1. Ma - jes - tic sweetness sits enthroned Up - on the Saviour's brow; His head with radiant

glories crowned, His lips with grace o'er - flow, His lips with grace o'er - flow.

484   *"Altogether Lovely."*   STENNETT.

Majestic sweetness sits enthroned
  Upon the Saviour's brow;
His head with radiant glories crowned,
  His lips with grace o'erflow.

2 No mortal can with him compare,
  Among the sons of men;
Fairer is he than all the fair
  That fill the heavenly train.

3 He saw me plunged in deep distress,
  He flew to my relief;
For me he bore the shameful cross,
  And carried all my grief.

4 To him I owe my life and breath,
  And all the joys I have;
He makes me triumph over death,
  He saves me from the grave.

5 To heaven, the place of his abode,
  He brings my weary feet;
Shows me the glories of my God,
  And makes my joy complete.

6 Since from his bounty I receive
  Such proofs of love divine,
Had I a thousand hearts to give,
  Lord! they should all be thine.

485   *The Name, "Jesus."*   STEELE.

The Saviour! oh, what endless charms
  Dwell in the blissful sound!
Its influence every fear disarms,
  And spreads sweet comfort round.

2 The almighty Former of the skies
  Stooped to our vile abode;
While angels viewed with wondering eyes
  And hailed the incarnate God.

3 Oh, the rich depths of love divine!
  Of bliss a boundless store!
Dear Saviour, let me call thee mine;
  I cannot wish for more.

4 On thee alone my hope relies,
  Beneath thy cross I fall;
My Lord, my Life, my Sacrifice,
  My Saviour, and my All!

486   *Bethlehem not Sinai.*   FABER.

Oh, see how Jesus trusts himself
  Unto our childish love!
As though by his free ways with us
  Our earnestness to prove.

2 His sacred name a common word
  On earth he loves to hear;
There is no majesty in him
  Which love may not come near.

3 The light of love is round his feet,
  His paths are never dim;
And he comes nigh to us when we
  Dare not come nigh to him.

4 Let us be simple with him then,
  Not backward, stiff, nor cold,
As though our Bethlehem could be
  What Sinai was of old.

TRENT. C. M.

1. Be - hold, where, in   a   mor - tal form,   Ap - pears each grace di - vine!

The vir - tues, all in Je - sus met, With mild - est   ra - diance shine.

487   *"Our Pattern."*   ENFIELD.

BEHOLD, where, in a mortal form,
    Appears each grace divine!
The virtues, all in Jesus met,
    With mildest radiance shine.

2 To spread the rays of heavenly light,
    To give the mourner joy,
To preach glad tidings to the poor,
    Was his divine employ.

3 'Mid keen reproach and cruel scorn,
    He meek and patient stood;
His foes, ungrateful, sought his life,
    Who labored for their good.

4 In the last hour of deep distress,
    Before his Father's throne,
With soul resigned he bowed and said,—
    "Thy will, not mine, be done!"

5 Be Christ our pattern, and our guide,
    His image may we bear;
Oh, may we tread his holy steps,—
    His joy and glory share.

488   *"The wine-press alone."*   BONAR.

A PILGRIM through this lonely world,
    The blessèd Saviour passed;
A mourner all his life was he,
    A dying Lamb at last.

2 That tender heart that felt for all,
    For all its life-blood gave;
It found on earth no resting-place,
    Save only in the grave.

3 Such was our Lord; and shall we fear
    The cross, with all its scorn?
Or love a faithless evil world,
    That wreathed his brow with thorn?

4 No! facing all its frowns or smiles,
    Like him, obedient still,
We homeward press through storm or calm,
    To Zion's blessèd hill.

489   1 *Peter* 2: 21-23.   DENNY.

WHAT grace, O Lord, and beauty shone
    Around thy steps below;
What patient love was seen in all
    Thy life and death of woe.

2 For, ever on thy burdened heart
    A weight of sorrow hung;
Yet no ungentle, murmuring word
    Escaped thy silent tongue.

3 Thy foes might hate, despise, revile,
    Thy friends unfaithful prove;
Unwearied in forgiveness still,
    Thy heart could only love.

4 Oh, give us hearts to love like thee!
    Like thee, O Lord, to grieve
Far more for others' sins than all
    The wrongs that we receive.

5 One with thyself, may every eye,
    In us, thy brethren, see
The gentleness and grace that spring
    From union, Lord! with thee.

HELENA. C. M.

1. Je - sus! thy love shall we for - get, And nev - er bring to mind

The grace that paid our hope - less debt, And bade us par - don find?

490   *"Shall we Forget?"*   MITCHELL.

JESUS! thy love shall we forget,
  And never bring to mind
The grace that paid our hopeless debt,
  And bade us pardon find?

2 Shall we thy life of grief forget,
  Thy fasting and thy prayer;
Thy locks with mountain vapors wet,
  To save us from despair?

3 Gethsemane can we forget—
  Thy struggling agony;
When night lay dark on Olivet,
  And none to watch with thee?

4 Our sorrows and our sins were laid
  On thee, alone on thee;
Thy precious blood our ransom paid—
  Thine all the glory be!

5 Life's brightest joys we may forget—
  Our kindred cease to love;
But he who paid our hopeless debt,
  Our constancy shall prove.

491   *" Forgive, as we Forgive."*   GURNEY.

LORD, as to thy dear cross we flee,
  And pray to be forgiven,
So let thy life our pattern be,
  And form our souls for heaven.

2 Help us, through good report and ill,
  Our daily cross to bear;
Like thee, to do our Father's will,
  Our brother's griefs to share.

3 Let grace our selfishness expel,
  Our earthliness refine;
And kindness in our bosoms dwell
  As free and true as thine.

4 If joy shall at thy bidding fly,
  And grief's dark day come on,
We, in our turn, would meekly cry,
  "Father, thy will be done!"

5 Kept peaceful in the midst of strife,
  Forgiving and forgiven,
Oh, may we lead the pilgrim's life,
  And follow thee to heaven!

492   *John 14 : 6.*   DOANE.

THOU art the Way: to thee alone
  From sin and death we flee;
And he who would the Father seek,
  Must seek him, Lord, by thee.

2 Thou art the Truth: thy word alone
  True wisdom can impart;
Thou only canst instruct the mind,
  And purify the heart.

3 Thou art the Life: the rending tomb
  Proclaims thy conquering arm;
And those who put their trust in thee
  Nor death nor hell shall harm.

4 Thou art the Way, the Truth, the Life:
  Grant us to know that Way;
That Truth to keep, that Life to win,
  Which leads to endless day.

ROCKINGHAM L. M.

1. My dear Re-deem-er, and my Lord, I read my du-ty in thy word;

But in thy life the law ap-pears, Drawn out in liv-ing char-ac-ters.

493   *"Be thou my pattern."*   WATTS.

My dear Redeemer, and my Lord,
I read my duty in thy word;
But in thy life the law appears,
Drawn out in living characters.

2 Such was thy truth, and such thy zeal,
Such deference to thy Father's will,
Such love, and meekness so divine,
I would transcribe and make them mine.

3 Cold mountains and the midnight air
Witnessed the fervor of thy prayer;
The desert thy temptations knew,
Thy conflict and thy victory too.

4 Be thou my pattern; make me bear
More of thy gracious image here;
Then God, the Judge, shall own my name
Among the followers of the Lamb.

494   *"Make us like thee."—Rom.* **12:2.**   STEELE.

Make us, by thy transforming grace,
Dear Saviour, daily more like thee!
Thy fair example may we trace,
To teach us what we ought to be!

2 To do thy heavenly Father's will
Was thy employment and delight;
Humility and holy zeal
Shone through thy life divinely bright.

3 But ah! how blind! how weak we are!
How frail! how apt to turn aside!
Lord, we depend upon thy care,
And ask thy Spirit for our guide.

495   *"To save sinners."*   WATTS.

Not to condemn the sons of men,
Did Christ, the Son of God, appear;
No weapons in his hands are seen,
No flaming sword, nor thunder there.

2 Such was the pity of our God,
He loved the race of man so well,
He sent his Son to bear our load
Of sins, and save our souls from hell.

3 Sinners, believe the Saviour's word;
Trust in his mighty name, and live:
A thousand joys his lips afford,
His hands a thousand blessings give.

496   *Our Companion.*   WATTS.

My God! permit me not to be
A stranger to myself and thee;
Amidst a thousand thoughts I rove,
Forgetful of my highest love.

2 Why should my passions mix with earth,
And thus debase my heavenly birth?
Why should I cleave to things below,
And let my God, my Saviour, go?

3 Call me away from flesh and sense;
One sovereign word can draw me thence;
I would obey the voice divine,
And all inferior joys resign.

4 Be earth, with all her scenes, withdrawn,
Let noise and vanity be gone;
In secret silence of the mind,
My heaven, and there my God, I find.

CRAWFORD. L. M.

1. How sweetly flowed the gospel sound From lips of gentleness and grace, When listening thousands

gathered round, And joy and glad-ness filled the place! And joy and gladness filled the place!

497 *" Common people heard gladly."* BOWRING.

How sweetly flowed the gospel sound
 From lips of gentleness and grace,
When listening thousands gathered round,
 And joy and gladness filled the place!

2 From heaven he came, of heaven he spoke,
 To heaven he led his followers' way;
Dark clouds of gloomy night he broke,
 Unvailing an immortal day.

3 "Come, wanderers, to my Father's home,
 Come, all ye weary ones, and rest:"
Yes, sacred Teacher, we will come,
 Obey thee, love thee, and be blest!

4 Decay then, tenements of dust;
 Pillars of earthly pride, decay:
A nobler mansion waits the just,
 And Jesus has prepared the way.

498 *"Holy, harmless, undefiled."* COXE.

How beauteous were the marks divine,
That in thy meekness used to shine,
That lit thy lonely pathway, trod
In wondrous love, O Son of God!

2 Oh, who like thee, so calm, so bright,
So pure, so made to live in light?
Oh, who like thee did ever go
So patient through a world of woe?

3 Oh, who like thee so humbly bore
The scorn, the scoffs of men, before?
So meek, forgiving, godlike, high,
So glorious in humility?

4 Even death, which sets the prisoner free,
Was pang, and scoff, and scorn to thee;
Yet love through all thy torture glowed,
And mercy with thy life-blood flowed.

5 Oh, in thy light be mine to go,
Illuming all my way of woe!
And give me ever on the road
To trace thy footsteps, Son of God.

499 *" And He healed them."* MONTGOMERY.

WHEN, like a stranger on our sphere,
The lowly Jesus wandered here,
Where'er he went, affliction fled,
And sickness reared her fainting head.

2 The eye that rolled in irksome night,
Beheld his face,—for God is light;
The opening ear, the loosened tongue,
His precepts heard, his praises sung.

3 With bounding steps the halt and lame,
To hail their great Deliverer came;
O'er the cold grave he bowed his head,
He spake the word, and raised the dead.

4 Despairing madness, dark and wild,
In his inspiring presence smiled;
The storm of horror ceased to roll,
And reason lightened through the soul.

5 Through paths of loving-kindness led,
Where Jesus triumphed we would tread;
To all, with willing hands dispense
The gifts of our benevolence.

OLIVE'S BROW. L. M.

1. 'Tis midnight; and on Olive's brow The star is dimmed that late-ly shone:

'Tis midnight; in the gar-den, now, The suffering Sav-iour prays a-lone.

500　　　*Gethsemane.*　　　TAPPAN.

'T is midnight; and on Olive's brow
　The star is dimmed that lately shone:
'Tis midnight; in the garden, now,
　The suffering Saviour prays alone.

2 'Tis midnight; and from all removed,
　The Saviour wrestles lone with fears;
Ev'n that disciple whom he loved
　Heeds not his master's grief and tears.

3 'Tis midnight; and for others' guilt
　The Man of Sorrows weeps in blood;
Yet he that hath in anguish knelt
　Is not forsaken by his God.

4 'Tis midnight; and from ether-plains
　Is borne the song that angels know;
Unheard by mortals are the strains
　That sweetly soothe the Saviour's woe.

501　　　*"'T is finished!"*　　　STENNETT.

"'Tis finished!"—so the Saviour cried,
And meekly bowed his head and died:
"'Tis finished!"—yes, the race is run,
The battle fought, the victory won.

2 'Tis finished!—all that heaven foretold
By prophets in the days of old;
And truths are opened to our view
That kings and prophets never knew.

3 'Tis finished!—Son of God, thy power
Hath triumphed in this awful hour;
And yet our eyes with sorrow see
That life to us was death to thee.

4 'Tis finished!—let the joyful sound
Be heard through all the nations round:
'Tis finished!—let the triumph rise,
And swell the chorus of the skies.

SOLITUDE. L. M.

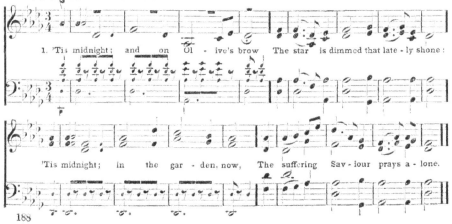

1. 'Tis midnight; and on Ol-ive's brow The star is dimmed that late-ly shone:

'Tis midnight; in the gar-den, now, The suffering Sav-iour prays a-lone.

HEBER. (HASLAM.) L. M.

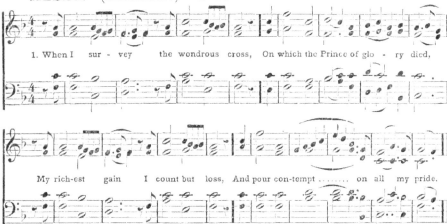

1. When I sur-vey the wondrous cross, On which the Prince of glo-ry died,
My rich-est gain I count but loss, And pour con-tempt .... on all my pride.

502 *Glorying in the Cross.* WATTS.

WHEN I survey the wondrous cross,
  On which the Prince of glory died,
My richest gain I count but loss,
  And pour contempt on all my pride.

2 Forbid it, Lord! that I should boast,
  Save in the death of Christ, my God;
All the vain things that charm me most
  I sacrifice them to his blood.

3 See, from his head, his hands, his feet,
  Sorrow and love flow mingled down;
Did e'er such love and sorrow meet,
  Or thorns compose so rich a crown?

4 His dying crimson, like a robe,
  Spreads o'er his body on the tree;
Then I am dead to all the globe,
  And all the globe is dead to me.

5 Were the whole realm of nature mine,
  That were a present far too small;
Love so amazing, so divine,
  Demands my soul, my life, my all.

503 *"Eloi, Eloi!"* CUNNINGHAM.

FROM Calvary a cry was heard—
  A bitter and heart-rending cry;
My Saviour! every mournful word
  Bespoke thy soul's deep agony.

2 A horror of great darkness fell
  On thee, thou spotless, holy One!
And all the eager hosts of hell
  Conspired to tempt God's only Son.

3 The scourge, the thorns, the deep disgrace—
  These thou couldst bear, nor once repine;
But when Jehovah vailed his face,
  Unutterable pangs were thine.

4 Let the dumb world its silence break;
  Let pealing anthems rend the sky;
Awake, my sluggish soul, awake!
  He died, that we might never die.

504 *Wounded for us.* BONAR.

JESUS, whom angel hosts adore,
  Became a man of griefs for me;
In love, though rich, becoming poor,
  That I through him enriched might be.

2 Though Lord of all, above, below,
  He went to Olivet for me:
There drank my cup of wrath and woe,
  When bleeding in Gethsemane.

3 The ever-blessed Son of God
  Went up to Calvary for me;
There paid my debt, there bore my load,
  In his own body on the tree.

4 Jesus, whose dwelling is the skies,
  Went down into the grave for me;
There overcame my enemies,
  There won the glorious victory.

5 'T is finished all: the vail is rent,
  The welcome sure, the access free:—
Now then, we leave our banishment,
  O Father, to return to thee!

AVON. C. M.

1. A - las! and did my Sav - iour bleed, And did my Sove - reign die?

Would he de - vote that sa - cred head For such a worm as I?

505   *"There was Darkness."*   WATTS.

ALAS! and did my Saviour bleed,
    And did my Sovereign die?
Would he devote that sacred head
    For such a worm as I?

2 Was it for crimes that I had done
    He groaned upon the tree?
Amazing pity! grace unknown!
    And love beyond degree!

3 Well might the sun in darkness hide,
    And shut his glories in,
When Christ, the great Creator, died
    For man, the creature's sin.

4 Thus might I hide my blushing face
    While his dear cross appears;
Dissolve my heart in thankfulness,
    And melt my eyes to tears.

5 But drops of grief can ne'er repay
    The debt of love I owe;
Here, Lord, I give myself away,
    'Tis all that I can do.

506   *Matthew* 27: 50-53.   WESLEY.

BEHOLD the Saviour of mankind,
    Nailed to the shameful tree!
How vast the love that him inclined
    To bleed and die for me!

2 Hark! how he groans, while nature shakes,
    And earth's strong pillars bend!
The temple's vail asunder breaks,
    The solid marbles rend.

3 'Tis finished! now the ransom's paid,
    "Receive my soul!" he cries:
See—how he bows his sacred head!
    He bows his head and dies!

4 But soon he'll break death's iron chain,
    And in full glory shine;
O Lamb of God! was ever pain—
    Was ever love like thine!

507   *"Crucified the Flesh."*—Gal. **5: 24.**   WATTS.

OH, if my soul were formed for woe,
    How would I vent my sighs!
Repentance should like rivers flow
    From both my streaming eyes.

2 'Twas for my sins my dearest Lord
    Hung on the cursed tree,
And groaned away a dying life
    For thee, my soul! for thee.

3 Oh, how I hate these lusts of mine
    That crucified my Lord;
Those sins that pierced and nailed his flesh
    Fast to the fatal wood!

4 Yes, my Redeemer—they shall die;
    My heart has so decreed;
Nor will I spare the guilty things
    That made my Saviour bleed.

5 While with a melting, broken heart,
    My murdered Lord I view,
I'll raise revenge against my sins,
    And slay the murderers too.

MANOAH. C. M.

1. In e - vil long I took de - light, Un - awed by shame or fear,

Till a new ob - ject struck my sight, And stopped my wild ca - reer.

508   *"The Mystery of Grace."*   NEWTON.

In evil long I took delight,
  Unawed by shame or fear,
Till a new object struck my sight,
  And stopped my wild career.

2 I saw One hanging on a tree,
  In agony and blood,
Who fixed his languid eyes on me,
  As near his cross I stood.

3 Sure never, till my latest breath,
  Can I forget that look;
It seemed to charge me with his death,
  Though not a word he spoke.

4 My conscience felt and owned the guilt;
  And plunged me in despair;
I saw my sins his blood had spilt,
  And helped to nail him there.

5 A second look he gave, which said,
  "I freely all forgive;
This blood is for thy ransom paid;
  I die, that thou mayst live."

6 Thus, while his death my sin displays
  In all its blackest hue,
Such is the mystery of grace,
  It seals my pardon too.

509   *"O Christ of God."*   PALMER.

O Jesus! sweet the tears I shed,
  While at thy cross I kneel,
Gaze on thy wounded, fainting head,
  And all thy sorrows feel.

2 My heart dissolves to see thee bleed,
  This heart so hard before;
I hear thee for the guilty plead,
  And grief o'erflows the more.

3 O Christ of God! O spotless Lamb!
  By love my soul is drawn;
Henceforth for ever thine I am;
  Here life and peace are born.

4 In patient hope the cross I'll bear,
  Thine arm shall be my stay;
And thou, enthroned, my soul shalt spare
  On thy great judgment-day.

510   *"He remembers Calvary."*   WATTS.

How condescending and how kind
  Was God's eternal Son!
Our misery reached his heavenly mind,
  And pity brought him down.

2 He sunk beneath our heavy woes,
  To raise us to his throne;
There's ne'er a gift his hand bestows,
  But cost his heart a groan.

3 This was compassion, like a God,
  That when the Saviour knew
The price of pardon was his blood,
  His pity ne'er withdrew.

4 Now, though he reigns exalted high,
  His love is still as great;
Well he remembers Calvary,
  Nor let his saints forget.

PASSION CHORALE. 7, 6. D.

1. { O sa - cred Head, now wound - ed, With grief and shame weighed down, }
{ Now scorn - ful - ly sur - round - ed With thorns, thine on - ly crown; }

O sa - cred Head, what glo - ry, What bliss, till now was thine!

Yet, though des - pised and go - ry, I joy to call thee mine.

511 *"Mine was the transgression."* GERHARDT.

O SACRED Head, now wounded,
  With grief and shame weighed down,
Now scornfully surrounded
  With thorns, thine only crown;
O sacred Head, what glory,
  What bliss, till now was thine!
Yet, though despised and gory,
  I joy to call thee mine.

2 What thou, my Lord, hast suffered
  Was all for sinners' gain:
Mine, mine was the transgression,
  But thine the deadly pain:
Lo, here I fall, my Saviour!
  'Tis I deserve thy place;
Look on me with thy favor,
  Vouchsafe to me thy grace.

3 The joy can ne'er be spoken,
  Above all joys beside,
When in thy body broken
  I thus with safety hide:
My Lord of life, desiring
  Thy glory now to see,
Beside thy cross expiring,
  I'd breathe my soul to thee.

4 What language shall I borrow,
  To praise thee, heavenly Friend:
For this, thy dying sorrow,
  Thy pity without end?
Lord, make me thine for ever,
  Nor let me faithless prove:
Oh, let me never, never,
  Abuse such dying love.

5 Forbid that I should leave thee;
  O Jesus, leave not me!
By faith I would receive thee;
  Thy blood can make me free!
When strength and comfort languish,
  And I must hence depart,
Release me then from anguish,
  By thine own wounded heart.

6 Be near when I am dying,
  Oh, show thy cross to me!
And for my succor flying,
  Come, Lord, and set me free!
These eyes, new faith receiving,
  From Jesus shall not move;
For he who dies believing,
  Dies safely—through thy love.

PATNAH. 7, 6. D.

1. { O Je-sus, we a-dore thee, Up-on the cross, our King: / We bow our hearts before thee; Thy gracious Name we sing: { That Name hath brought salvation,

That Name, in life our stay; Our peace, our con-so-la-tion When life shall fade a-way.

512 *Jesus on the Cross.* J. WESLEY.

O JESUS, we adore thee,
　Upon the cross, our King:
We bow our hearts before thee;
　Thy gracious Name we sing:
That Name hath brought salvation,
　That Name, in life our stay;
Our peace, our consolation
　When life shall fade away.

2 Yet doth the world disdain thee,
　Still pressing by thy cross:
Lord, may our hearts retain thee;
　All else we count but loss.
The grief thy soul endured,
　Who can that grief declare?
Thy pains have thus assured
　That thou thy foes will spare.

3 Ah, Lord, our sins arraigned thee,
　And nailed thee to the tree:
Our pride, O Lord, disdained thee;
　Yet deign our hope to be.
O glorious King, we bless thee,
　No longer pass thee by;
O Jesus, we confess thee
　Our Lord enthroned on high.

4 Thy wounds, thy grief beholding,
　With thee, O Lord, we grieve;
Thee in our hearts enfolding,
　Our hearts thy wounds receive:

Lord, grant to us remission;
　Life through thy death restore;
Yea, grant us the fruition
　Of life for evermore.

513 *"Lamb of God."* DECK.

O LAMB of God! still keep me
　Near to thy wounded side;
'Tis only there in safety
　And peace I can abide!
What foes and snares surround me!
　What doubts and fears within!
The grace that sought and found me,
　Alone can keep me clean.

2 'Tis only in thee hiding,
　I feel my life secure—
Only in thee abiding,
　The conflict can endure:
Thine arm the victory gaineth
　O'er every hateful foe;
Thy love my heart sustaineth
　In all its care and woe.

3 Soon shall my eyes behold thee,
　With rapture, face to face;
One half hath not been told me
　Of all thy power and grace:
Thy beauty, Lord, and glory,
　The wonders of thy love,
Shall be the endless story
　Of all thy saints above.

HASTINGS.   C. L. M.

1. How calm and beautiful the morn, That gilds the sacred tomb, Where Christ the crucified was borne,

And vailed in midnight gloom! Oh, weep no more the Saviour slain, The Lord is risen, he lives again.

514
Gethsemane.   HEMANS.

HE knelt, the Saviour knelt and prayed,
   When but his Father's eye
Looked through the lonely garden's shade,
   On that dread agony;
The Lord of all above, beneath,
Was bowed with sorrow unto death.

2 The sun set in a fearful hour,
   The skies might well grow dim,
When this mortality had power
   So to o'ershadow him!
That he who gave man's breath, might know
The very depths of human woe.

3 He knew them all; the doubt the strife,
   The faint, perplexing dread,
The mists that hang o'er parting life,
   All darkened round his head;
And the Deliverer knelt to pray;
Yet passed it not, that cup, away.

4 It passed not, though the stormy wave
   Had sunk beneath his tread;
It passed not, though to him the grave
   Had yielded up its dead.
But there was sent him from on high,
A gift of strength for man to die.

5 And was his mortal hour beset
   With anguish and dismay?
How may we meet our conflict yet,
   In the dark, narrow way?
How but through him, that path who trod?
Save or we perish, Son of God!

515
"The Lord is risen."   HASTINGS.

How calm and beautiful the morn,
   That gilds the sacred tomb,
Where Christ the crucified was borne,
   And vailed in midnight gloom!
Oh, weep no more the Saviour slain,
The Lord is risen, he lives again.

2 Ye mourning saints, dry every tear
   For your departed Lord,
"Behold the place, he is not here!"
   The tomb is all unbarred:
The gates of death were closed in vain,
The Lord is risen, he lives again.

3 Now cheerful to the house of prayer,
   Your early footsteps bend;
The Saviour will himself be there,
   Your Advocate and Friend:
Once by the law, your hopes were slain,
But now in Christ, ye live again.

4 How tranquil now the rising day!
   'Tis Jesus still appears,
A risen Lord, to chase away
   Your unbelieving fears:
Oh, weep no more your comforts slain,
The Lord is risen, he lives again.

5 And when the shades of evening fall,
   When life's last hour draws nigh,
If Jesus shines upon the soul,
   How blissful then to die!
Since he hath risen that once was slain,
Ye die in Christ to live again.

HERMAS. 7, 6. D.

1. All glo - ry, laud, and hon - or To thee, Redeem - er, King! To whom the lips of

chil - dren Made sweet ho - san - nas ring. 2. Thou art the King of Is - rael, Thou,

David's roy - al Son, Who in the Lord's name com - est, The King and Blessed One.

516 NEALE. *Tr.*

ALL glory, laud, and honor
    To thee, Redeemer, King!
To whom the lips of children
    Made sweet hosannas ring.
2 Thou art the King of Israel,
    Thou, David's royal Son,
Who in the Lord's name comest,
    The King and Blessèd One.

3 The company of angels
    Are praising thee on high,
And mortal men, and all things
    Created, make reply.
4 The people of the Hebrews
    With palms before thee went;
Our praise, and prayer, and anthems,
    Before thee we present.

5 To thee, before thy passion,
    They sang their hymns of praise;
To thee, now high exalted,
    Our melody we raise.
6 Thou didst accept their praises,
    Accept the prayers we bring,
Who in all good delightest,
    Thou good and gracious King!

517 *"Wisdom crieth without."* COWPER.

ERE God had built the mountains,
    Or raised the fruitful hills;
Before he filled the fountains
    That feed the running rills;
In ME, from everlasting,
    The wonderful I AM
Found pleasures never wasting;
    And Wisdom is my name.

2 When, like a tent to dwell in,
    He spread the skies abroad,
And swathed about the swelling
    Of ocean's mighty flood,
He wrought by weight and measure;
    And I was with him then:
Myself the Father's pleasure,
    And mine, the sons of men.

3 Thus Wisdom's words discover
    Thy glory and thy grace,
Thou everlasting lover
    Of our unworthy race:
Thy gracious eye surveyed us,
    Ere stars were seen above;
In wisdom thou hast made us,
    And died for us in love.

EASTER HYMN. 7.

1. Christ, the Lord, is risen to - day, Al - le - lu - ia. Sons of men, and an - gels,

say; Al - le - lu - ia. Raise your joys and triumphs high! Al - le - la -

ia. Sing, ye heavens! and earth, re - ply! Al - le - lu - ia.

518

"The Lord is risen."   C. WESLEY.

Christ, the Lord, is risen to-day,
Sons of men, and angels, say;
Raise your joys and triumphs high!
Sing, ye heavens! and earth, reply!

2 Love's redeeming work is done,
Fought the fight, the battle won;
Lo, our Sun's eclipse is o'er,
Lo, he sets in blood no more.

3 Vain the stone, the watch, the seal!
Christ hath burst the gates of hell;
Death in vain forbids his rise;
Christ hath opened Paradise.

4 Lives again our glorious King;
"Where, O Death, is now thy sting?"
Once he died our souls to save;
"Where's thy victory, boasting Grave?"

5 Soar we now where Christ has led,
Following our exalted Head;
Made like him, like him we rise;
Ours the cross, the grave, the skies!

519

"Again, I say, rejoice."   KELLY.

Joyful be the hours to-day;
Joyful let the seasons be;
Let us sing, for well we may:
Jesus! we will sing of thee.

2 Should thy people silent be,
Then the very stones would sing:
What a debt we owe to thee,
Thee our Saviour, thee our King!

3 Joyful are we now to own,
Rapture thrills us as we trace
All the deeds thy love hath done,
All the riches of thy grace.

4 'T is thy grace alone can save;
Every blessing comes from thee—
All we have, and hope to have,
All we are, and hope to be.

5 Thine the Name to sinners dear!
Thine the Name all names before!
Blessèd here and everywhere;
Blessèd now and evermore!

MOZART. 7.

1. Christ the Lord, is ris'n to-day, Our tri-umphant ho-ly-day: He endured the cross and grave, Sinners to re-deem and save, Sin-ners to re-deem and save.

520   *The Resurrection.*   ANON.

CHRIST, the Lord, is risen to-day,
Our triumphant holy-day:
He endured the cross and grave,
Sinners to redeem and save.

2 Lo! he rises, mighty King!
Where, O Death! is now thy sting?
Lo! he claims his native sky!
Grave! where is thy victory?

3 Sinners, see your ransom paid,
Peace with God for ever made:
With your risen Saviour rise;
Claim with him the purchased skies.

4 Christ, the Lord, is risen to-day,
Our triumphant holy-day;
Loud the song of victory raise;
Shout the great Redeemer's praise.

521   *"Hail the Day!"*   MADAN.

HAIL the day that sees him rise,
Glorious, to his native skies!
Christ, awhile to mortals given,
Enters now the gates of heaven.

2 There the glorious triumph waits;
Lift your heads, eternal gates!
Christ hath vanquished death and sin;
Take the King of glory in.

3 See, the heaven its Lord receives!
Yet he loves the earth he leaves:
Though returning to his throne,
Still he calls mankind his own.

4 Still for us he intercedes,
His prevailing death he pleads;
Near himself prepares our place,
Great Forerunner of our race.

5 What, though parted from our sight,
Far above yon starry height;
Thither our affections rise,
Following him beyond the skies.

522   *"Hallelujah!"*   WINKWORTH. *Tr.*

CHRIST the Lord is risen again;
Christ hath broken every chain;
Hark! angelic voices cry,
Singing evermore on high,
Hallelujah! Praise the Lord!

2 He who bore all pain and loss,
Comfortless, upon the cross,
Lives in glory now on high,
Pleads for us, and hears our cry:
Hallelujah! Praise the Lord!

3 He who slumbered in the grave
Is exalted now to save;
Now through Christendom it rings
That the Lamb is King of kings:
Hallelujah! Praise the Lord!

5 Now he bids us tell abroad
How the lost may be restored,
How the penitent forgiven,
How we, too, may enter heaven:
Hallelujah! Praise the Lord!

197

ROTHWELL.   L. M.

1. He lives! the great Redeem-er lives! What joy the blest as-sur-ance gives! And now, be-

fore his Fa-ther, God, Pleads the full mer-it of his blood, Pleads the full mer - it of his blood.

523   *"We have an Advocate."*   STEELE.

He lives! the great Redeemer lives!
What joy the blest assurance gives!
And now, before his Father, God,
Pleads the full merit of his blood.

2 Repeated crimes awake our fears,
And justice armed with frowns appears;
But in the Saviour's lovely face
Sweet mercy smiles, and all is peace.

3 In every dark, distressful hour,
When sin and Satan join their power,
Let this dear hope repel the dart,
That Jesus bears us on his heart.

4 Great Advocate, almighty Friend!
On him our humble hopes depend;
Our cause can never, never fail,
For Jesus pleads, and must prevail.

524   2 *Timothy* 1: 9, 10.   WATTS.

Now to the power of God supreme
Be everlasting honors given;
He saves from hell,—we bless his name,—
He guides our wandering feet to heaven.

2 Not for our duties or deserts,
But of his own abounding grace,
He works salvation in our hearts,
And forms a people for his praise.

3 'Twas his own purpose that began
To rescue rebels doomed to die:
He gave us grace in Christ, his Son,
Before he spread the starry sky.

158

4 Jesus, the Lord, appears at last,
And makes his Father's counsel known;
Declares the great transaction past,
And brings immortal blessings down.

5 He dies; and in that dreadful night
Doth all the powers of hell destroy;
Rising he brings our heaven to light,
And takes possession of the joy.

525   *" Weep not."—Luke* 24: 46.   WATTS.

He dies!—the friend of sinners dies;
Lo! Salem's daughters weep around;
A solemn darkness vails the skies;
A sudden trembling shakes the ground.

2 Here's love and grief beyond degree:
The Lord of glory dies for men;
But lo! what sudden joys we see,
Jesus, the dead, revives again.

3 The rising God forsakes the tomb;
Up to his Father's court he flies;
Cherubic legions guard him home,
And shout him welcome to the skies.

4 Break off your tears, ye saints, and tell
How high our great Deliverer reigns;
Sing how he spoiled the hosts of hell,
And led the tyrant Death in chains.

5 Say—live for ever, glorious King,
Born to redeem, and strong to save!
Where now, O Death, where is thy sting?
And where thy victory, boasting Grave?

BLOOMFIELD CHANT. L. M.

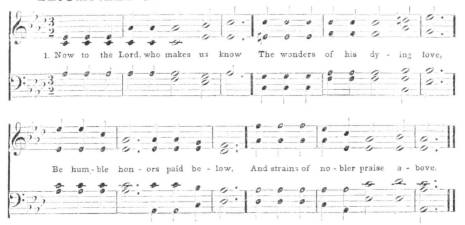

1. Now to the Lord, who makes us know The wonders of his dy - ing love,

Be hum - ble hon - ors paid be - low, And strains of no - bler praise a - bove.

526 *Revelation* 1: 5-7. WATTS.

Now to the Lord, who makes us know
The wonders of his dying love,
Be humble honors paid below,
And strains of nobler praise above.

2 'Twas he who cleansed our foulest sins,
And washed us in his precious blood;
'Tis he who makes us priests and kings,
And brings us rebels near to God.

3 To Jesus, our atoning Priest,
To Jesus, our eternal King,
Be everlasting power confessed!
Let every tongue his glory sing.

4 Behold! on flying clouds he comes,
And every eye shall see him move;
Though with our sins we pierced him once,
He now displays his pardoning love.

5 The unbelieving world shall wail,
While we rejoice to see the day;
Come, Lord! nor let thy promise fail,
Nor let thy chariot long delay.

527 *"Worthy the Lamb."* MONTGOMERY.

Come, let us sing the song of songs, —
The saints in heaven began the strain—
The homage which to Christ belongs:
"Worthy the Lamb, for he was slain!"

2 Slain to redeem us by his blood,
To cleanse from every sinful stain,
And make us kings and priests to God—
"Worthy the Lamb, for he was slain!"

3 To him who suffered on the tree,
Our souls, at his soul's price, to gain,
Blessing, and praise, and glory be:
"Worthy the Lamb, for he was slain!"

4 To him, enthroned by filial right,
All power in heaven and earth proclaim,
Honor, and majesty, and might:
"Worthy the Lamb, for he was slain!"

5 Long as we live, and when we die,
And while in heaven with him we reign:
This song, our song of songs shall be:
"Worthy the Lamb, for he was slain!"

528 *Christ is God.* WATTS.

Bright King of Glory, dreadful God!
Our spirits bow before thy feet:
To thee we lift an humble thought,
And worship at thine awful seat.

2 A thousand seraphs strong and bright
Stand round the glorious Deity;
But who, among those sons of light,
Pretends comparison with thee?

3 Yet there is One of human frame,
Jesus, arrayed in flesh and blood,
Thinks it no robbery to claim
A full equality with God.

4 Then let the name of Christ our King
With equal honors be adored;
His praise let every angel sing
And all the nations own the Lord.

199

CYPRUS. L. M.

1. What e-qual honors shall we bring To thee, O Lord our God, the Lamb, When all the

notes that angels sing, Are far in-fe-rior to thy name? Are far in-fe-rior to thy name?

529   *"Worthy the Lamb."*   WATTS.

WHAT equal honors shall we bring
  To thee, O Lord our God, the Lamb,
When all the notes that angels sing,
  Are far inferior to thy name?

2 Worthy is he that once was slain, [died,
  The Prince of Peace that groaned and
Worthy to rise and live, and reign,
  At his almighty Father's side.

3 Honor immortal must be paid
  Instead of scandal and of scorn;
While glory shines around his head,
  And a bright crown without a thorn.

4 Blessings for ever on the Lamb,
  Who bore the curse for wretched men:
Let angels sound his sacred name,
  And every creature say, Amen!

530   *"O Christ, our King."*   PALMER. *Tr.*

O CHRIST! our King, Creator, Lord!
Saviour of all who trust thy word!
To them who seek thee ever near,
Now to our praises bend thine ear.

2 In thy dear cross a grace is found,—
  It flows from every streaming wound,—
Whose power our inbred sin controls,
Breaks the firm bond, and frees our souls.

3 Thou didst create the stars of night;
  Yet thou hast vailed in flesh thy light,
Hast deigned a mortal form to wear,
A mortal's painful lot to bear.

200

4 When thou didst hang upon the tree,
  The quaking earth acknowledged thee;
When thou didst there yield up thy breath,
The world grew dark as shades of death.

5 Now in the Father's glory high,
  Great Conqueror! never more to die,
Us by thy mighty power defend,
And reign through ages without end.

531   Universal Praise to Christ.   PALMER. *Tr.*

O CHRIST, the Lord of heaven! to thee,
  Clothed with all majesty divine,
Eternal power and glory be!
  Eternal praise, of right, is thine.

2 Reign, Prince of life! that once thy brow
  Didst yield to wear the wounding thorn;
Reign, throned beside the Father now,
  Adored the Son of God first-born.

3 From angel hosts that round thee stand,
  With forms more pure than spotless snow,
From the bright burning seraph band,
  Let praise in lofty numbers flow.

4 To thee, the Lamb, our mortal songs,
  Born of deep fervent love, shall rise;
All honor to thy name belongs,
  Our lips would sound it to the skies.

5 "Jesus!"—all earth shall speak the word;
  "Jesus!"—all heaven resound it still!
Immanuel, Saviour, Conqueror, Lord!
  Thy praise the universe shall fill.

DUANE STREET. L. M. D.

1. Jesus, my All, to heaven is gone, He whom I fix my hopes upon; His track I'll see. and I'll pursue
D. S.—The King's high way of holiness,

FINE. D. S.

The narrow way till him I view. The way the holy prophets went, The road that leads from banishment,
I'll go, for all the paths are peace.

532   *"He was parted from them."*   CENNICK.

Jesus, my All, to heaven is gone,
He whom I fix my hopes upon;
His track I see, and I'll pursue
The narrow way till him I view.
The way the holy prophets went,
The road that leads from banishment,
The King's highway of holiness,
I'll go for all the paths are peace.

2 This is the way I long had sought,
And mourned because I found it not;
My grief, my burden, long had been
Because I could not cease from sin.
The more I strove against its power,
I sinned and stumbled but the more;
Till late I heard my Saviour say,
"Come hither, soul, I am the Way!"

3 Lo! glad I come; and thou, dear Lamb,
Shalt take me to thee as I am:
Nothing but sin I thee can give;
Yet help me, and thy praise I'll live:
I'll tell to all poor sinners round
What a dear Saviour I have found;
I'll point to thy redeeming blood,
And say, " Behold the way to God!"

533   *Matthew* 21: 16.   ANON.

What are those soul-reviving strains
Which echo thus from Salem's plains?
What anthems loud, and louder still,
Sweetly resound from Zion's hill?

2 Lo, 'tis an infant chorus sings
Hosanna to the King of kings:
The Saviour comes, and babes proclaim
Salvation sent in Jesus' name.

3 Nor these alone their voice shall raise,
For we will join this song of praise;
Still Israel's children forward press,
To hail the Lord their Righteousness.

4 Proclaim hosannas, loud and clear;
See David's Son and Lord appear:
Glory and praise on earth be given;
Hosanna in the highest heaven.

534   *Christ, the supreme God.*   KELLY.

Around the Saviour's lofty throne,
Ten thousand times ten thousand sing;
They worship him as God alone,
And crown him—everlasting King.

2 Approach, ye saints! this God is yours;
'Tis Jesus, fills the throne above:
Ye cannot fail, while God endures;
Ye cannot want, while God is love.

3 Jesus, thou everlasting King!
To thee the praise of heaven belongs;
Yet, smile on us who fain would bring
The tribute of our humbler songs.

4 Though sin defile our worship here,
We hope ere long thy face to view,
In heaven with angels to appear,
And praise thy name as angels do.

201

CORONATION. C. M.

1. All hail the power of Jesus' name! Let angels prostrate fall; Bring forth the royal di-a-dem, And

crown him Lord of all; Bring forth the royal di-a-dem, And crown him Lord of all.

PERRONET.

535 *Philippians* 2: 10, 11.

ALL hail the power of Jesus' name!
  Let angels prostrate fall;
Bring forth the royal diadem,
  And crown him Lord of all.

2 Crown him, ye martyrs of our God,
  Who from his altar call;
Extol the stem of Jesse's rod,
  And crown him Lord of all.

3 Ye chosen seed of Israel's race,
  Ye ransomed from the fall;
Hail him, who saves you by his grace,
  And crown him Lord of all.

4 Sinners, whose love can ne'er forget
  The wormwood and the gall,
Go, spread your trophies at his feet,
  And crown him Lord of all.

5 Let every kindred, every tribe,
  On this terrestrial ball,
To him all majesty ascribe,
  And crown him Lord of all.

6 Oh, that with yonder sacred throng,
  We at his feet may fall!
We'll join the everlasting song,
  And crown him Lord of all.

MILES' LANE. C. M.

1. All hail the power of Je-sus' name! Let an-gels pros-trate fall; Bring forth the

roy-al di-a-dem, And crown him, crown him, crown him, crown him Lord of all.

AZMON. (DENFIELD.) C. M.

1. Come, let us join our cheer-ful songs With an-gels round the throne;

Ten thousand thou-sand are their tongues, But all their joys are one.

536   *"Worthy the Lamb!"*   WATTS.

Come, let us join our cheerful songs
  With angels round the throne;
Ten thousand thousand are their tongues,
  But all their joys are one.

2 "Worthy the Lamb that died," they cry,
  "To be exalted thus!"
"Worthy the Lamb!" our lips reply,
  "For he was slain for us."

3 Jesus is worthy to receive
  Honor and power divine;
And blessings, more than we can give,
  Be, Lord, for ever thine!

4 Let all that dwell above the sky,
  And air, and earth, and seas,
Conspire to lift thy glories high,
  And speak thine endless praise.

5 The whole creation join in one,
  To bless the sacred name
Of him who sits upon the throne,
  And to adore the Lamb!

537   *"Crowned with glory and honor."*   KELLY.

The head that once was crowned with
  Is crowned with glory now;   [thorns,
A royal diadem adorns
  The mighty Victor's brow.

2 The highest place that heaven affords,
  Is his by sovereign right;
The King of kings, and Lord of lords,
  He reigns in glory bright;—

3 The joy of all who dwell above,
  The joy of all below,
To whom he manifests his love,
  And grants his name to know.

4 To them the cross with all its shame,
  With all its grace, is given;
Their name—an everlasting name,
  Their joy—the joy of heaven.

5 To them the cross is life and health,
  Though shame and death to him;
His people's hope, his people's wealth,
  Their everlasting theme.

538   *"The third, the appointed Day."*   WATTS.

Blest morning! whose young dawning rays
  Beheld our rising God;
That saw him triumph o'er the dust,
  And leave his dark abode.

2 In the cold prison of a tomb
  The great Redeemer lay,
Till the revolving skies had brought
  The third, the appointed day.

3 Hell and the grave combined their force
  To hold our Lord, in vain;
The sleeping conqueror arose,
  And burst their feeble chain.

4 To thy great name, almighty Lord,
  These sacred hours we pay,
And loud hosannas shall proclaim
  The triumph of the day.

BRADFORD. C. M.

1. I know that my Re-deem-er lives, And ev - er prays for me:

A to - ken of his love he gives, A pledge of lib - er - ty.

539   *Job* 19: 25.   C. WESLEY.

I KNOW that my Redeemer lives,
  And ever prays for me:
A token of his love he gives,
  A pledge of liberty.

2 I find him lifting up my head;
  He brings salvation near:
His presence makes me free indeed,
  And he will soon appear.

3 He wills that I should holy be;
  What can withstand his will?
The counsel of his grace in me,
  He surely shall fulfill.

4 Jesus, I hang upon thy word:
  I steadfastly believe
Thou wilt return, and claim me, Lord,
  And to thyself receive.

540   *"The Lord of Glory."*   NEWTON.

HE, who on earth as man was known,
  And bore our sins and pains,
Now, seated on the eternal throne,
  The Lord of glory reigns.

2 His hands the wheels of nature guide
  With an unerring skill;
And countless worlds, extended wide,
  Obey his sovereign will.

3 While harps unnumbered sound his praise
  In yonder world above,
His saints on earth admire his ways,
  And glory in his love.

4 When troubles, like a burning sun,
  Beat heavy on their head;
To this almighty rock they run,
  And find a pleasing shade.

5 How glorious he—how happy they,
  In such a glorious friend!
Whose love secures them all the way,
  And crowns them at the end.

541   *Hebrews* 4: 14-16.   PIRKIE.

COME, let us join our songs of praise
  To our ascended Priest;
He entered heaven with all our names
  Engraven on his breast.

2 Below he washed our guilt away,
  By his atoning blood;
Now he appears before the throne,
  And pleads our cause with God.

3 Clothed with our nature still, he knows
  The weakness of our frame,
And how to shield us from the foes
  Whom he himself o'ercame.

4 Nor time, nor distance, e'er shall quench
  The fervor of his love;
For us he died in kindness here,
  For us he lives above.

5 Oh, may we ne'er forget his grace,
  Nor blush to bear his name;
Still may our hearts hold fast his faith—
  Our lips his praise proclaim.

CINCINNATI. C. M.

1. The gold-en gates are lift-ed up, The doors are o - - pened wide,

The King of glo - ry is gone in Un - to his Fa - - ther's side.

542 *Return of Christ to heaven.* ANON.

The golden gates are lifted up,
The doors are opened wide,
The King of glory is gone in
Unto his Father's side.

2 Thou art gone up before us, Lord,
To make for us a place,
That we may be where now thou art,
And look upon God's face.

3 And ever on thine earthly path
A gleam of glory lies;
A light still breaks behind the cloud
That vailed thee from our eyes.

4 Lift up our hearts, lift up our minds,
Let thy dear grace be given,
That while we tarry here below,
Our treasure be in heaven!

5 That where thou art, at God's right hand,
Our hope, our love may be;
Dwell thou in us, that we may dwell
For evermore in thee!

543 *"Not to condemn, but Save."* WATTS.

Come, happy souls, approach your God
With new, melodious songs;
Come, render to almighty grace
The tribute of your tongues.

2 So strange, so boundless was the love
That pitied dying men,
The Father sent his equal Son
To give them life again.

3 Thy hands, dear Jesus, were not armed
With an avenging rod;
No hard commission to perform
The vengeance of a God.

4 But all was merciful and mild,
And wrath forsook the throne,
When Christ on the kind errand came,
And brought salvation down.

5 See, dearest Lord, our willing souls
Accept thine offered grace;
We bless the great Redeemer's love,
And give the Father praise.

544 *Isaiah 49:16.* DODDRIDGE.

Now let our cheerful eyes survey
Our great High Priest above,
And celebrate his constant care,
And sympathetic love.

2 Though raised to a superior throne,
Where angels bow around,
And high o'er all the shining train,
With matchless honors crowned;—

3 The names of all his saints he bears
Engraven on his heart;
Nor shall a name once treasured there
E'er from his care depart.

4 So, gracious Saviour! on my breast,
May thy dear name be worn,
A sacred ornament and guard,
To endless ages borne.

BENJAMIN. S. M. D.

1 "The Lord is ris'n in - deed!" And are the tidings true? Yes, they beheld the Sav - iour

bleed, And saw him liv-ing too. 2. "The Lord is ris'n in - deed!" Then justice asks no more ;

Who stood, Who stood op - posed be - fore.

Mer - cy and truth are now agreed, Who stood opposed be - fore, Who stood opposed be - fore.

545 *The Resurrection Morning.* KELLY.

"The Lord is risen indeed!"
And are the tidings true?
Yes, they beheld the Saviour bleed,
And saw him living too.

2 "The Lord is risen indeed!"
Then justice asks no more;
Mercy and truth are now agreed,
Who stood opposed before.

3 "The Lord is risen indeed!"
Then is his work performed;
The mighty Captive now is freed,
And death, our foe, disarmed.

4 "The Lord is risen indeed!"
He lives to die no more;
He lives, the sinner's cause to plead,
Whose curse and shame he bore.

5 "The Lord is risen indeed!"
Attending angels! hear;
Up to the courts of heaven, with speed
The joyful tidings bear.

6 Then wake your golden lyres,
And strike each cheerful chord;
Join, all ye bright, celestial choirs!
To sing our risen Lord.

546 Acts 1: 11. EMMA TOKE.

Thou art gone up on high
To mansions in the skies,
And round thy throne unceasingly
The songs of praise arise.

2 But we are lingering here
With sin and care oppressed:
Lord! send thy promised Comforter,
And lead us to thy rest!

3 Thou art gone up on high:
But thou didst first come down,
Through earth's most bitter misery
To pass unto thy crown.

4 And girt with griefs and fears
Our onward course must be;
But only let that path of tears
Lead us at last to thee!

5 Thou art gone up on high:
But thou shalt come again
With all the bright ones of the sky
Attendant in thy train.

6 Oh, by thy saving power
So make us live and die,
That we may stand in that dread hour.
At thy right hand on high!

DIADEMATA. S. M. D.

1. Crown him with ma - ny crowns, The Lamb up - on his throne; Hark! how the heavenly
an - them drowns All mu - sic but its own! A - wake, my soul, and sing
Of him who died for thee; And hail him as thy matchless King Through all eter - ni - ty.

BRIDGES.

547   *"On his head, many crowns."*

Crown him with many crowns,
  The Lamb upon his throne;
Hark! how the heavenly anthem drowns
  All music but its own!
Awake, my soul, and sing
  Of him who died for thee;
And hail him as thy matchless King
  Through all eternity.

2 Crown him the Lord of love!
    Behold his hands and side,—
  Those wounds, yet visible above,
    In beauty glorified:
  No angel in the sky
    Can fully bear that sight,
  But downward bends his wondering eye
    At mysteries so bright.

3 Crown him the Lord of heaven!
    One with the Father known,—
  And the blest Spirit through him given
    From yonder Triune throne!
  All hail, Redeemer, hail!
    For thou hast died for me:
  Thy praise and glory shall not fail
    Throughout eternity.

TURNER.

548   *"Hail, Prince of Life!"*

Beyond the starry skies,
  Far as the eternal hills,
There in the boundless world of light
  Our great Redeemer dwells.

2 Around him angels fair
    In countless armies shine;
  And ever, in exalted lays,
    They offer songs divine.

3 "Hail, Prince of life!" they cry,
    "Whose unexampled love,
  Moved thee to quit these glorious realms
    And royalties above."

4 And when he stooped to earth,
    And suffered rude disdain,
  They cast their honors at his feet,
    And waited in his train.

5 They saw him on the cross,
    While darkness vailed the skies,
  And when he burst the gates of death,
    They saw the conqueror rise.

6 They thronged his chariot wheels,
    And bore him to his throne;
  Then swept their golden harps and sung,—
    "The glorious work is done."

207

HARWELL. 8, 7. D.

1. { Hark! ten thousand harps and voices Sound the note of praise above; }
   { Jesus reigns, and heaven rejoices; Jesus reigns, the God of love: } See, he sits on yonder throne;
   See, he sits

Jesus rules the world alone. Hal-le - lu-jah, Hal-le - lu-jah, Hal-le - lu - jah. A - men.
Je - sus rules the world a-lone.

549 *"King of Glory."* KELLY.

HARK! ten thousand harps and voices
　Sound the note of praise above;
Jesus reigns, and heaven rejoices;
　Jesus reigns, the God of love:
See, he sits on yonder throne;
　Jesus rules the world alone.

2 King of glory! reign for ever—
　Thine an everlasting crown;
Nothing, from thy love, shall sever
　Those whom thou hast made thine own;—
Happy objects of thy grace,
　Destined to behold thy face.

3 Saviour! hasten thine appearing;
　Bring, oh, bring the glorious day,
When the awful summons hearing,
　Heaven and earth shall pass away;—
Then, with golden harps, we'll sing,—
　"Glory, glory to our King!"

550 *The glorious Conqueror.* WORDSWORTH.

SEE, the Conqueror mounts in triumph!
　See the King in royal state,
Riding on the clouds, his chariot,
　To his heavenly palace gate!
Hark! the choirs of angel voices
　Joyful hallelujahs sing,
And the portals high are lifted
　To receive their heavenly King.

2 Who is this that comes in glory,
　With the trump of jubilee?

Lord of battles, God of armies,
　He has gained the victory;
He, who on the cross did suffer,
　He, who from the grave arose,
He has vanquished sin and Satan,
　He by death has spoiled his foes.

3 Thou hast raised our human nature,
　On the clouds to God's right hand;
There we sit in heavenly places,
　There with thee in glory stand;
Jesus reigns, adored by angels;
　Man with God is on the throne;
Mighty Lord! in thine ascension,
　We by faith behold our own.

4 Lift us up from earth to heaven,
　Give us wings of faith and love,
Gales of holy aspirations,
　Wafting us to realms above;
That, with hearts and minds uplifted,
　We with Christ our Lord may dwell,
Where he sits enthroned in glory,
　In the heavenly citadel.

5 So at last, when he appeareth,
　We from out our graves may spring,
With our youth renewed like eagles',
　Flocking round our heavenly King,
Caught up on the clouds of heaven,
　And may meet him in the air,
Rise to realms where he is reigning,
　And may reign for ever there.

AUTUMN. 8, 7. D.

1. Mighty God! while angels bless thee, May a mortal lisp thy name? Lord of men, as well as angels!
D.S. Sounded through the wide creation,

Thou art every creature's theme : Lord of ev - ery land and nation! Ancient of   e - ternal days!
Be thy just and aw-ful praise.

551 R. ROBINSON.
" The Brightness of his Glory."

Mighty God! while angels bless thee,
   May a mortal lisp thy name?
Lord of men, as well as angels!
   Thou art every creature's theme:
Lord of every land and nation!
   Ancient of eternal days!
Sounded through the wide creation,
   Be thy just and awful praise.

2 For the grandeur of thy nature,—
   Grand, beyond a seraph's thought;
For the wonders of creation,
   Works with skill and kindness wrought:
For thy providence, that governs
   Through thine empire's wide domain,
Wings an angel, guides a sparrow;
   Blessèd be thy gentle reign.

3 For thy rich, thy free redemption,
   Bright, though vailed in darkness long,
Thought is poor, and poor expression;
   Who can sing that wondrous song?
Brightness of the Father's glory!
   Shall thy praise unuttered lie?
Break, my tongue! such guilty silence,
   Sing the Lord who came to die:—

4 From the highest throne of glory,
   To the cross of deepest woe,
Came to ransom guilty captives!—
   Flow, my praise, for ever flow:

Re-ascend, immortal Saviour!
   Leave thy footstool, take thy throne;
Thence return and reign for ever;—
   Be the kingdom all thine own!

552 GOODE.
Matthew 21: 9.

Crown his head with endless blessing,
   Who, in God the Father's name,
With compassions never ceasing,
   Comes salvation to proclaim.
Hail, ye saints, who know his favor,
   Who within his gates are found;
Hail, ye saints, the exalted Saviour,
   Let his courts with praise resound.

2 Lo, Jehovah, we adore thee;
   Thee our Saviour! thee our God!
From his throne his beams of glory
   Shine through all the world abroad.
In his word his light arises,
   Brightest beams of truth and grace;
Bind, oh, bind your sacrifices,
   In his courts your offerings place.

3 Jesus, thee our Saviour hailing,
   Thee our God in praise we own;
Highest honors, never failing,
   Rise eternal round thy throne;
Now, ye saints, his power confessing,
   In your grateful strains adore;
For his mercy, never ceasing,
   Flows, and flows for evermore.

MILLINGTON.   8, 7, 7. or 7, 6 l.

1. { Jesus comes, his conflict over,—Comes to claim his great reward; /
   { Angels round the Victor hover, Crowding to behold their Lord;   } Haste, ye saints! your tribute bring,

Crown him, ev-er-lasting King, Haste, ye saints! your tribute bring. Crown him, ever-last-ing King.

---

553   *Christ's return to heaven.*   KELLY.

JESUS comes, his conflict over,—
    Comes to claim his great reward;
Angels round the Victor hover,
    Crowding to behold their Lord;
Haste, ye saints! your tribute bring,
Crown him, everlasting King.

3 Yonder throne for him erected,
    Now becomes the Victor's seat;
Lo, the Man on earth rejected!
    Angels worship at his feet:
Haste, ye saints! your tribute bring,
Crown him, everlasting King.

3 Day and night they cry before him,—
    "Holy, holy, holy Lord!"
All the powers of heaven adore him,
    All obey his sovereign word;
Haste, ye saints! your tribute bring,
Crown him, everlasting King.

554   *"The King of Glory waits."*   KELLY.

GLORY, glory to our King!
    Crowns unfading wreathe his head;
Jesus is the name we sing,—
    Jesus, risen from the dead;
Jesus, Conqueror o'er the grave;
Jesus, mighty now to save.

2 Jesus is gone up on high:
    Angels come to meet their King;
Shouts triumphant rend the sky,
    While the Victor's praise they sing:
"Open now, ye heavenly gates!
'Tis the King of glory waits."

3 Now behold him high enthroned,
    Glory beaming from his face,
By adoring angels owned,
    God of holiness and grace!
Oh, for hearts and tongues to sing—
"Glory, glory to our King!"

555   *Isaiah* **63 : 1.**   KELLY.

WHO is this that comes from Edom,
    All his raiment stained with blood;
To the slave proclaiming freedom;
    Bringing and bestowing good:
Glorious in the garb he wears,
Glorious in the spoils he bears?

2 'Tis the Saviour, now victorious,
    Traveling onward in his might;
'Tis the Saviour, oh how glorious
    To his people is the sight!
Jesus now is strong to save;
Mighty to redeem the slave.

3 Why that blood his raiment staining?
    'Tis the blood of many slain;
Of his foes there's none remaining,
    None the contest to maintain:
Fallen they, no more to rise,
All their glory prostrate lies.

4 Mighty Victor, reign for ever;
    Wear the crown so dearly won;
Never shall thy people, never
    Cease to sing what thou hast done;
Thou hast fought thy people's foes;
Thou hast healed thy people's woes.

SEGUR. 8, 7, 4.

1. Look, ye saints, the sight is glorious; See the Man of sor-rows now

From the fight re-turned vic-to-rious! Ev-ery knee to him shall bow:

Crown him! crown him! Crown him! crown him! Crowns be-come the Victor's brow.

---

556 *"The sight is glorious."* KELLY.

Look, ye saints, the sight is glorious;
  See the Man of sorrows now
From the fight returned victorious!
  Every knee to him shall bow:
    Crown him! crown him!
  Crowns become the Victor's brow.

2 Crown the Saviour, angels, crown him!
  Rich the trophies Jesus brings;
In the seat of power enthrone him,
  While the vault of heaven rings:
    Crown him! crown him!
  Crown the Saviour King of kings!

3 Sinners in derision crowned him,
  Mocking thus the Saviour's claim;
Saints and angels, crowd around him,
  Own his title, praise his name!
    Crown him! crown him!
  Spread abroad the Victor's fame.

4 Hark, those bursts of acclamation!
  Hark, those loud, triumphant chords!
Jesus takes the highest station;
  Oh, what joy the sight affords!
    Crown him! crown him!
  King of kings and Lord of lords!

---

557 *"It is finished."* EVANS.

Hark! the voice of love and mercy
  Sounds aloud from Calvary;
See! it rends the rocks asunder,
  Shakes the earth, and vails the sky:
    "It is finished!"
  Hear the dying Saviour cry.

2 "It is finished!" Oh, what pleasure
  Do these charming words afford!
Heavenly blessings, without measure,
  Flow to us from Christ, the Lord:
    "It is finished!"
  Saints, the dying words record.

3 Finished all the types and shadows
  Of the ceremonial law;
Finished all that God had promised;
  Death and hell no more shall awe.
    "It is finished!"
  Saints, from hence your comfort draw.

4 Tune your harps anew, ye seraphs;
  Join to sing the pleasing theme:
All on earth and all in heaven,
  Join to praise Immanuel's name:
    Hallelujah!
  Glory to the bleeding Lamb!

BROOKLYN. H. M.

1. Come, ev - ery pi - ous heart, That loves the Sav-iour's name, Your no - blest powers exert, ... To cel - e - brate his fame; Tell all a - bove, and all be - low,
The debt of love to him you owe, The debt of love to him you owe.

558　*"The Debt of Love."*　STENNETT.

COME, every pious heart,
　That loves the Saviour's name,
Your noblest powers exert
　To celebrate his fame;
Tell all above, and all below,
The debt of love to him you owe.

2 He left his starry crown,
　And laid his robes aside,
On wings of love came down,
　And wept, and bled, and died;
What he endured, oh, who can tell,
To save our souls from death and hell?

3 From the dark grave he rose,
　The mansions of the dead,
And thence his mighty foes
　In glorious triumph led;
Up through the sky the Conqueror rode,
And reigns on high, the Saviour God.

4 Jesus, we ne'er can pay
　The debt we owe thy love;
Yet tell us how we may
　Our gratitude approve;
Our hearts, our all to thee we give;
The gift, though small, thou wilt receive.

559　*"Rejoice the Lord is King!"*　C. WESLEY.

REJOICE! the Lord is King;
　Your Lord and King adore:
Mortals, give thanks and sing,
　And triumph evermore!
Lift up your hearts, lift up your voice;
Rejoice!—again I say, rejoice!

2 Jesus, the Saviour, reigns,
　The God of truth and love;
When he had purged our stains,
　He took his seat above:
Lift up your hearts, lift up your voice;
Rejoice!—again I say, rejoice!

3 His kingdom can not fail;
　He rules o'er earth and heaven;
The keys of death and hell
　Are to our Jesus given:
Lift up your hearts, lift up your voice;
Rejoice!—again I say, rejoice!

4 Rejoice in glorious hope:
　Jesus, the Judge, shall come,
And take his servants up
　To their eternal home:
We soon shall hear the archangel's voice;
The trump of God shall sound, Rejoice!

DORT. 6, 4.

1. Rise, glorious Conqueror, rise; In - to thy na - tive skies,—Assume thy right: And where in
many a fold The clouds are backward rolled—Pass through those gates of gold, And reign in light!

560 *"Lion of Judah."* BRIDGES.

RISE, glorious Conqueror, rise;
Into thy native skies,—
  Assume thy right:
And where in many a fold
The clouds are backward rolled—
Pass through those gates of gold,
  And reign in light!

2 Victor o'er death and hell!
Cherubic legions swell
  Thy radiant train:
Praises all heaven inspire;
Each angel sweeps his lyre,
And waves his wings of fire,—
  Thou Lamb once slain!

3 Enter, incarnate God!—
No feet but thine, have trod
  The serpent down;
Blow the full trumpets, blow!
Wider yon portals throw!
Saviour triumphant—go,
  And take thy crown!

4 Lion of Judah—Hail!
And let thy name prevail
  From age to age;
Lord of the rolling years;—
Claim for thine own the spheres,
For thou hast bought with tears
  Thy heritage!

5 And then was heard afar
Star answering to star—
  "Lo! these have come,
Followers of him who gave

His life their lives to save;
  And now their palms they wave,
  Brought safely home."

561 *"Worthy the Lamb."* ALLEN.

GLORY to God on high!
Let heaven and earth reply,
  "Praise ye his name!"
His love and grace adore,
Who all our sorrows bore;
Sing loud for evermore,
  "Worthy the Lamb!"

2 While they around the throne
Cheerfully join in one,
  Praising his name,—
Ye who have felt his blood
Sealing your peace with God,
Sound his dear name abroad,
  "Worthy the Lamb!"

3 Join, all ye ransomed race,
Our Lord and God to bless;
  Praise ye his name!
In him we will rejoice,
And make a joyful noise,
Shouting with heart and voice,
  "Worthy the Lamb!"

4 Soon must we change our place,
Yet will we never cease
  Praising his name;
To him our songs we bring;
Hail him our gracious King;
And, through all ages sing,
  "Worthy the Lamb!"

213

WIMBORNE. L. M.

1. E-ter-nal Spir-it, we con-fess And sing the won-ders of thy grace;

Thy power conveys our bless-ings down From God the Fa-ther and the Son.

562   *"Inward Teachings."*   WATTS.

ETERNAL Spirit, we confess
And sing the wonders of thy grace:
Thy power conveys our blessings down
From God the Father and the Son.

2 Enlightened by thy heavenly ray,
Our shades and darkness turn to-day;
Thine inward teachings make us know
Our danger and our refuge too.

3 Thy power and glory work within,
And break the chains of reigning sin;
All our imperious lusts subdue,
And form our wretched hearts anew.

563   *"Veni Creator!"*   CASWALL.

COME, O Creator Spirit blest!
And in our souls take up thy rest;
Come, with thy grace and heavenly aid,
To fill the hearts which thou hast made.

2 Great Comforter! to thee we cry;
O highest gift of God most high!
O fount of life! O fire of love!
Send sweet anointing from above!

3 Kindle our senses from above,
And make our hearts o'erflow with love;
With patience firm, and virtue high,
The weakness of our flesh supply.

4 Far from us drive the foe we dread,
And grant us thy true peace instead;
So shall we not, with thee for guide,
Turn from the path of life aside.

214

564   *"Loose the Seals."*   BEDDOME.

COME, blessèd Spirit! source of light!
Whose power and grace are unconfined,
Dispel the gloomy shades of night—
The thicker darkness of the mind.

2 To mine illumined eyes, display
The glorious truth thy word reveals;
Cause me to run the heavenly way,
Thy book unfold, and loose the seals.

3 Thine inward teachings make me know
The mysteries of redeeming love,
The vanity of things below,
And excellence of things above.

4 While through this dubious maze I stray,
Spread, like the sun, thy beams abroad,
To show the dangers of the way,
And guide my feeble steps to God.

565   *A new heart.*   DODDRIDGE.

COME, sacred Spirit, from above,
And fill the coldest heart with love:
Oh, turn to flesh the flinty stone,
And let thy sovereign power be known.

2 Speak thou, and from the haughtiest eyes
Shall floods of contrite sorrow rise;
While all their glowing souls are borne
To seek that grace which now they scorn.

3 Oh, let a holy flock await
In crowds around thy temple-gate!
Each pressing on with zeal to be
A living sacrifice to thee.

QUIETUDE. L. M.

1. Come, Ho-ly Spir - it! calm my mind, And fit me to ap-proach my God;

Re-move each vain, each world-ly thought, And lead me to thy blest a - bode.

566   *" Calm my mind."*   BURDER.

Come, Holy Spirit! calm my mind,
And fit me to approach my God;
Remove each vain, each worldly thought,
And lead me to thy blest abode.

2 Hast thou imparted to my soul
A living spark of holy fire?
Oh, kindle now the sacred flame;
Make me to burn with pure desire.

3 A brighter faith and hope impart,
And let me now my Saviour see;
Oh, soothe and cheer my burdened heart,
And bid my spirit rest in thee.

567   *" Creator, Spirit."*   DRYDEN.

Creator Spirit, by whose aid
The world's foundations first were laid,
Come, visit every waiting mind;
Come, pour thy joys on human-kind.

2 Thrice holy Fount, thrice holy Fire,
Our hearts with heavenly love inspire;
Come, and thy sacred unction bring
To sanctify us, while we sing.

3 O Source of uncreated light,
The Father's promised Paraclete,—
From sin and sorrow set us free,
And make us temples worthy thee!

4 Make us eternal truths receive,
And practise all that we believe;
Give us thyself, that we may see
The Father and the Son, by thee.

568   *" Led by the Spirit."*   BROWNE.

Come, gracious Spirit, heavenly Dove,
With light and comfort from above:
Be thou our guardian, thou our guide!
O'er every thought and step preside.

2 To us the light of truth display,
And make us know and choose thy way;
Plant holy fear in every heart,
That we from God may ne'er depart.

3 Lead us to holiness—the road
That we must take to dwell with God;
Lead us to Christ, the living way,
Nor let us from his precepts stray.

4 Lead us to God, our final rest,
To be with him for ever blest;
Lead us to heaven, its bliss to share—
Fullness of joy for ever there!

569   *Pentecost.*   ANON.

Blest day! when our ascended Lord
Fulfilled his own prophetic word;
Sent down his Spirit, to inspire
His saints, baptized with holy fire.

2 While by his power these signs were wrought,
While divers tongues his wisdom taught,
His love one only subject gave—
That Jesus died the world to save!

3 Sure peace with God!—the joyful sound
Pours wide its sacred influence round;
Relenting foes his grace receive,
And humbled myriads hear and live!

215

ZEPHYR. L. M.

1. Sure the blest Com - fort - er is nigh, 'Tis he sus - tains my faint - ing heart;

Else would my hopes for - ev - er die, And ev - ery cheer - ing ray de - part.

570   *The Comforter.*   STEELE.

Sure the blest Comforter is night,
   'Tis he sustains my fainting heart;
Else would my hopes for ever die,
   And every cheering ray depart.

2 Whene'er, to call the Saviour mine,
   With ardent wish my heart aspires,—
Can it be less than power divine,
   That animates these strong desires?

3 And, when my cheerful hope can say,—
   I love my God and taste his grace,—
Lord! is it not thy blissful ray,
   That brings this dawn of sacred peace?

4 Let thy good Spirit in my heart
   For ever dwell, O God of love!
And light and heavenly peace impart,—
   Sweet earnest of the joys above.

571   *"Take not thy Spirit from me."*   C. WESLEY.

Stay, thou insulted Spirit, stay!
   Though I have done thee such despite,
Cast not a sinner quite away,
   Nor take thine everlasting flight.

2 Though I have most unfaithful been
   Of all who e'er thy grace received;
Ten thousand times thy goodness seen,
   Ten thousand times thy goodness grieved;

3 Yet, oh, the chief of sinners spare,
   In honor of my great High Priest!
Nor, in thy righteous anger, swear
   I shall not see thy people's rest.

572   *"He shall come down like rain."*   RIPPON.

As when in silence vernal showers
Descend and cheer the fainting flowers,
   So, in the secrecy of love,
   Falls the sweet influence from above.

2 That heavenly influence let me find
In holy silence of the mind,
   While every grace maintains its bloom,
   Diffusing wide its rich perfume.

3 Nor let these blessings be confined
To me, but poured on all mankind,
   Till earth's wild wastes in verdure rise,
   And a young Eden bless our eyes.

573   *Prayer for the Spirit.*   MONTGOMERY.

O Spirit of the living God,
In all thy plentitude of grace,
   Where'er the foot of man hath trod,
   Descend on our apostate race.

2 Give tongues of fire and hearts of love,
To preach the reconciling word;
   Give power and unction from above,
   Where'er the joyful sound is heard.

3 Be darkness, at thy coming, light;
Confusion, order, in thy path;
   Souls without strength inspire with might;
   Bid mercy triumph over wrath.

4 Baptize the nations! far and nigh
The triumphs of the cross record;
   The name of Jesus glorify,
   Till every people call him Lord.

NEW HAVEN. 6, 4.

1. Come, Ho-ly Ghost! in love, Shed on us, from a-bove, Thine own bright ray: Di-vinely

good thou art; Thy sa-cred gifts im-part, To gladden each sad heart; Oh, come to-day!

574 *"Oh, come to-day."* PALMER. *Tr.*

Come, Holy Ghost! in love,
Shed on us, from above,
  Thine own bright ray:
Divinely good thou art;
Thy sacred gifts impart,
To gladden each sad heart;
  Oh, come to-day!

2 Come, tenderest Friend, and best,
Our most delightful Guest!
  With soothing power;
Rest, which the weary know;
Shade, 'mid the noontide glow;
Peace, when deep griefs o'erflow;
  Cheer us, this hour!

3 Come, Light serene! and still
Our inmost bosoms fill;
  Dwell in each breast:
We know no dawn but thine;
Send forth thy beams divine,
On our dark souls to shine,
  And make us blest.

4 Exalt our low desires;
Extinguish passion's fires;
  Heal every wound;
Our stubborn spirits bend;
Our icy coldness end;
Our devious steps attend,
  While heavenward bound.

5 Come, all the faithful bless;
Let all, who Christ confess,
  His praise employ;
Give virtue's rich reward;

Victorious death accord,
And, with our glorious Lord,
  Eternal joy!

575 *"Let there be light!"* MARRIOTT.

Thou! whose almighty word
Chaos and darkness heard,
  And took their flight,
Hear us, we humbly pray,
And, where the gospel's day
Sheds not its glorious ray,
  "Let there be light!"

2 Thou! who didst come to bring,
On thy redeeming wing,
  Healing and sight,
Health to the sick in mind,
Sight to the inly blind,—
Oh, now to all mankind
  "Let there be light!"

3 Spirit of truth and love,
Life-giving holy Dove!
  Speed forth thy flight:
Move o'er the waters' face,
Bearing the lamp of grace,
And, in earth's darkest place,
  "Let there be light!"

4 Blessèd and holy Three,
All-glorious Trinity,—
  Wisdom, Love, Might!
Boundless as ocean's tide
Rolling in fullest pride,
Through the world, far and wide,—
  "Let there be light!"

217

STEPHENS. C. M.

1. Come, Ho - ly Spir - it, heaven-ly Dove! With all thy quickening powers,

Kin - dle a flame of sa - cred love In these cold hearts of ours.

576   *Invocation.*   WATTS.

Come, Holy Spirit, heavenly Dove!
  With all thy quickening powers,
Kindle a flame of sacred love
  In these cold hearts of ours.

2 Look! how we grovel here below,
  Fond of these trifling toys!
Our souls can neither fly nor go
  To reach eternal joys.

3 In vain we tune our formal songs;
  In vain we strive to rise;
Hosannas languish on our tongues,
  And our devotion dies.

4 Dear Lord, and shall we ever live
  At this poor, dying rate—
Our love so faint, so cold to thee,
  And thine to us so great?

5 Come, Holy Spirit, heavenly Dove!
  With all thy quickening powers;
Come shed abroad a Saviour's love,
  And that shall kindle ours.

577   *Fruits of the Spirit.*   ANON.

Our blest Redeemer, ere he breathed
  His tender, last farewell,
A Guide, a Comforter bequeathed,
  With us on earth to dwell.

2 He came in tongues of living flame,
  To teach, convince, subdue;
All-powerful as the wind he came,
  And all as viewless, too.

3 He came, sweet influence to impart,
  A gracious, willing Guest,
While he can find one humble heart
  Wherein to fix his rest.

4 And every virtue we possess,
  And every virtue won,
And every thought of holiness
  Is his and his alone.

5 Spirit of purity and grace!
  Our weakness pitying see;
Oh, make our hearts thy dwelling-place,
  Purer and worthier thee!

578   *"The Gift of God."*   TATE.

Come, Holy Ghost, Creator, come,
  Inspire these souls of thine;
Till every heart which thou hast made
  Be filled with grace divine.

2 Thou art the Comforter, the gift
  Of God, and fire of love;
The everlasting spring of joy,
  And unction from above.

3 Enlighten our dark souls, till they
  Thy sacred love embrace;
Assist our minds, by nature frail,
  With thy celestial grace.

4 Teach us the Father to confess,
  And Son, from death revived,
And thee, with both, O Holy Ghost,
  Who art from both derived.

CHESTER. C. M.

1. O Ho-ly Ghost, the Com-fort-er, How is thy love de-spised, While the heart longs for sym-pa-thy And friends are i-dol-ized, And friends are i-dol-ized.

579   *The love of the Spirit.*   ANON.

O Holy Ghost, the Comforter
  How is thy love despised,
While the heart longs for sympathy
  And friends are idolized.

2 O Spirit of the living God,
  Brooding with dove-like wings
Over the helpless and the weak
  Among created things!

3 Where should our feebleness find strength,
  Our helplessness a stay,
Didst thou not bring us hope and help,
  And comfort, day by day?

4 Great are thy consolations, Lord,
  And mighty is thy power,
In sickness and in solitude,
  In sorrow's darkest hour.

5 Oh, if the souls that now despise
  And grieve thee, heavenly Dove,
Would seek thee, and would welcome thee,
  How would they prize thy love!

580   *Pentecost.*   KEBLE.

When God, of old, came down from heaven,
  In power and wrath he came;
Before his feet the clouds were riven,
  Half darkness and half flame.

2 But when he came the second time,
  He came in power and love;
Softer than gales at morning prime,
  Hovered his holy Dove.

3 The fires that rushed on Sinai down
  In sudden torrents dread,
Now gently light a glorious crown
  On every sainted head.

4 Like arrows went those lightnings forth,
  Winged with the sinner's doom;
But these, like tongues, o'er all the earth
  Proclaiming life to come.

581   *1 John 5: 6-10.*   GERMAN.

Glory to God the Father be,
  Glory to God the Son,
Glory to God the Holy Ghost—
  Glory to God alone!

2 My soul doth magnify the Lord,
  My spirit doth rejoice
In God, my Saviour and my God;
  I hear his joyful voice.

3 I need not go abroad for joy,
  Who have a feast at home;
My sighs are turnéd into songs,
  The Comforter is come!

4 Down from on high the blesséd Dove
  Is come into my breast,
To witness God's eternal love;
  This is my heavenly feast.

5 Glory to God the Father be,
  Glory to God the Son,
Glory to God the Holy Ghost—
  Glory to God alone!

BOARDMAN. C. M.

1. Why should the chil-dren of a King Go mourn-ing all their days?

Great Com-fort-er, de-scend, and bring Some to-kens of thy grace.

582   *Comfortable Assurance.*   WATTS.

Why should the children of a King
Go mourning all their days?
Great Comforter, descend, and bring
Some token of thy grace.

2 Dost thou not dwell in all the saints,
And seal the heirs of heaven?
When wilt thou banish my complaints,
And show my sins forgiven?

3 Assure my conscience of her part
In the Redeemer's blood;
And bear thy witness with my heart,
That I am born of God.

4 Thou art the earnest of his love,
The pledge of joys to come;
And thy soft wings, celestial Dove,
Will safe convey me home.

583   *The Indweller.*   C. WESLEY.

Come, Holy Ghost! our hearts inspire,
Let us thine influence prove;
Source of the old prophetic fire!
Fountain of life and love!

2 Water with heavenly dew thy word,
In this appointed hour;
Attend it with thy presence, Lord,
And bid it come with power.

3 Open the hearts of them that hear,
To make the Saviour room;
Now let us find redemption near;
Let faith by hearing come.

220

584   *"He shall testify of me."*   ANON.

Spirit of truth, oh, let me know
The love of Christ to me;
Its conquering, quickening power bestow,
To set me wholly free.

2 I long to know its depth and height,
To scan its breadth and length;
Drink in its ocean of delight,
And triumph in its strength.

3 It is thine office to reveal
My Saviour's wonderous love;
Oh, deepen on my heart thy seal,
And bless me from above.

585   *The Abiding Presence.*   COTTERILL.

Eternal Spirit, God of truth,
Our contrite hearts inspire;
Revive the flame of heavenly love,
And feed the pure desire.

2 'Tis thine to soothe the sorrowing mind,
With guilt and fear oppressed;
'Tis thine to bid the dying live,
And give the weary rest.

3 Subdue the power of every sin,
Whate'er that sin may be,
That we, with humble, holy heart,
May worship only thee.

4 Then with our spirits witness bear
That we are sons of God,
Redeemed from sin, from death and hell,
Through Christ's atoning blood.

ROMBERG. C. M.

1. Our Ho - ly Fa - ther and our God! We come be - fore thy face,

To bless thee for that gift di - vine, The Spir - it of thy grace.

586   *"Abba, Father."*   ANON.

OUR Holy Father and our God!
  We come before thy face,
To bless thee for that gift divine,
  The Spirit of thy grace.

2 Precious the promise, now fulfilled
  Through Jesus set on high;
The spirit of adoption ours,
  We, Abba, Father, cry.

3 By him our faith, and hope, and love
  Are kept alive and grow;
Through Jesus' blood he gives the heart
  A perfect peace to know.

4 The souls, in his communion blest,
  Pant for the things above;
As seeks the hart for water-brooks,
  So we the springs of love.

5 Blest Comforter of all thy saints,
  Who love the heavenly way,
We, by thy might, would run the race,
  Till we have won the day.

587   *The Indweller.*   REED.

SPIRIT Divine! attend our prayer,
  And make our hearts thy home;
Descend with all thy gracious power:
  Come, Holy Spirit, come!

2 Come as the light: to us reveal
  Our sinfulness and woe;
And lead us in those paths of life
  Where all the righteous go.

3 Come as the fire, and purge our hearts,
  Like sacrificial flame:
Let our whole soul an offering be
  To our Redeemer's name.

4 Come as the wind, with rushing sound,
  With Pentecostal grace;
And make the great salvation known
  Wide as the human race.

5 Spirit Divine, attend our prayer,
  And make our hearts thy home;
Descend with all thy gracious power:
  Come, Holy Spirit, come!

588   *"Thy Spirit in our heart."*   HAWEIS.

ENTHRONED on high, almighty Lord!
  The Holy Ghost send down;
Fulfill in us thy faithful word,
  And all thy mercies crown.

2 Though on our heads no tongues of fire
  Their wondrous powers impart,
Grant, Saviour, what we more desire,
  Thy Spirit in our heart.

3 Spirit of life, and light, and love,
  Thy heavenly influence give;
Quicken our souls, our guilt remove,
  That we in Christ may live.

4 To our benighted minds reveal
  The glories of his grace,
And bring us where no clouds conceal
  The brightness of his face.

OLNEY. S. M.

1. 'Tis God the Spir-it leads In paths be-fore un-known;

The work to be per-formed is ours, The strength is all his own.

589   *"Philippians 2: 12, 13.*   ANON.

'Tis God the Spirit leads
   In paths before unknown;
The work to be performed is ours,
   The strength is all his own.

2 Supported by his grace,
   We still pursue our way;
And hope at last to reach the prize,
   Secure in endless day.

3 'Tis he that works to will,
   'Tis he that works to do;
His is the power by which we act,
   His be the glory too.

590   *The Comforter here.*   ANON.

The Comforter has come,
   We feel his presence here,
Our hearts would now no longer roam,
   But bow in filial fear.

2 This tenderness of love,
   This hush of solemn power,—
'Tis heaven descending from above,
   To fill this favored hour.

3 Earth's darkness all has fled,
   Heaven's light serenely shines,
And every heart, divinely led,
   To holy thought inclines.

4 No more let sin deceive,
   Nor earthly cares betray,
Oh, let us never, never grieve
   The Comforter away!

591   *"The earnest in our hearts."*   ANON.

Come, Spirit, source of light,
   Thy grace is unconfined;
Dispel the gloomy shades of night,
   The darkness of the mind.

2 Now to our eyes display
   The truth thy words reveal;
Cause us to run the heavenly way,
   Delighting in thy will.

3 Thy teachings make us know
   The mysteries of thy love,
The vanity of things below,
   The joy of things above.

4 While through this maze we stray,
   Oh, spread thy beams abroad;
Disclose the dangers of the way,
   And guide our steps to God.

592   *Invocation.*   BEDDOME.

Come, Holy Spirit, come,
   With energy divine;
And on this poor benighted soul;
   With beams of mercy shine.

2 Oh, melt this frozen heart:
   This stubborn will subdue;
Each evil passion overcome,
   And form me all anew.

3 Mine will the profit be,
   But thine shall be the praise;
And unto thee I will devote
   The remnant of my days.

HAYDN. S. M.

1. Come, Ho - ly Spir - it, come! Let thy bright beams a - rise:

Dis - pel the sor - row from our minds, The dark - ness from our eyes.

593 *Invocation.* HART.

Come, Holy Spirit, come!
 Let thy bright beams arise;
Dispel the sorrow from our minds,
 The darkness from our eyes.

2 Convince us of our sin;
 Then lead to Jesus' blood,
And to our wondering view reveal
 The mercies of our God.

3 Revive our drooping faith,
 Our doubts and fears remove,
And kindle in our breasts the flame
 Of never-dying love.

4 'Tis thine to cleanse the heart,
 To sanctify the soul,
To pour fresh life in every part,
 And new-create the whole.

5 Come, Holy Spirit, come;
 Our minds from bondage free;
Then shall we know, and praise, and love,
 The Father, Son, and thee.

594 *Pentecost.* MONTGOMERY.

Lord God, the Holy Ghost!
 In this accepted hour,
As on the day of Pentecost
 Descend in all thy power!

2 We meet with one accord
 In our appointed place,
And wait the promise of our Lord,
 The Spirit of all grace.

3 Like mighty rushing wind
 Upon the waves beneath,
Move with one impulse every mind,
 One soul, one feeling breathe.

4 The young, the old inspire
 With wisdom from above;
And give us hearts and tongues of fire
 To pray, and praise, and love.

5 Spirit of truth, be thou
 In life and death our guide!
O Spirit of adoption, now
 May we be sanctified.

595 *" Comforter Divine."* SIGOURNEY.

Blest Comforter divine!
 Let rays of heavenly love
Amid our gloom and darkness shine,
 And guide our souls above.

2 Turn us, with gentle voice,
 From every sinful way,
And bid the mourning saint rejoice,
 Though earthly joys decay.

3 By thine inspiring breath
 Make every cloud of care,
And ev'n the gloomy vale of death,
 A smile of glory wear.

4 Oh, fill thou every heart
 With love to all our race;
Great Comforter, to us impart
 These blessings of thy grace.

223

FULTON. 7.

1. Gra - cious Spir - it, Love di - vine! Let thy light with - in me shine;

All my guilt - y fears re - move, Fill me with thy heaven-ly love.

596   *"Love Divine."*   STOCKER.

GRACIOUS Spirit, Love divine!
Let thy light within me shine;
All my guilty fears remove,
Fill me with thy heavenly love.

2 Speak thy pardoning grace to me,
Set the burdened sinner free;
Lead me to the Lamb of God,
Wash me in his precious blood.

3 Life and peace to me impart,
Seal salvation on my heart;
Breathe thyself into my breast,—
Earnest of immortal rest.

4 Let me never from thee stray,
Keep me in the narrow way;
Fill my soul with joy divine,
Keep me, Lord! for ever thine.

597   *"Lord of Light."*   LYRA CATH.

HOLY Spirit! Lord of Light!
From thy clear celestial height,
Come, thou Light of all that live!
Thy pure beaming radiance give!

2 Come, thou Father of the poor!
Come with treasures which endure;
Thou, of all consolers best,
Visiting the troubled breast.

3 Thou in toil art comfort sweet;
Pleasant coolness in the heat;
Solace in the midst of woe;
Dost refreshing peace bestow.

4 Light immortal! light divine!
Visit thou these hearts of thine;
If thou take thy grace away,
Nothing pure in man will stay.

5 Heal our wounds—our strength renew;
On our dryness pour thy dew;
Wash the stains of guilt away;
Guide the steps that go astray.

6 Give us comfort when we die;
Give us life with thee on high;
In thy sevenfold gifts descend;
Give us joys which never end.

598   *Luke* **11: 13.**   REED.

HOLY Ghost! with light divine,
Shine upon this heart of mine;
Chase the shades of night away,
Turn my darkness into day.

2 Holy Ghost! with power divine,
Cleanse this guilty heart of mine;
Long hath sin, without control,
Held dominion o'er my soul.

3 Holy Ghost! with joy divine,
Cheer this saddened heart of mine;
Bid my many woes depart,
Heal my wounded, bleeding heart.

4 Holy Spirit! all-divine,
Dwell within this heart of mine;
Cast down every idol-throne,
Reign supreme—and reign alone.

MERCY. 7.

1. Ho - ly Spir - it! gen - tly come, Raise us from our fall - en state;
Fix thy ev - er - last - ing home In the hearts thou didst cre - ate.

599   *John* 16: 13.   HAMMOND.

Holy Spirit! gently come,
  Raise us from our fallen state;
Fix thy everlasting home
  In the hearts thou didst create.

2 Now thy quickening influence bring,
  On our spirits sweetly move;
Open every mouth to sing
  Jesus' everlasting love.

3 Take the things of Christ, and show
  What our Lord for us hath done;
May we God the Father know
  Through his well-beloved Son.

600   *"Work in all."*   ANON.

Holy Ghost, thou Source of light!
  We invoke thy kindling ray:
Dawn upon our spirits' night,
  Turn our darkness into day.

2 To the anxious soul impart
  Hope, all other hopes above;
Stir the dull and hardened heart
  With a longing and a love.

3 Give the struggling, peace for strife;
  Give the doubting, light for gloom;
Speed the living into life,
  Warn the dying of their doom.

4 Work in all, in all renew,
  Day by day, the life divine;
All our wills to thee subdue,
  All our hearts to thee incline.

601   *"Our hearts inspire."*   ANON.

Come, divine and peaceful Guest,
  Enter each devoted breast;
Holy Ghost, our hearts inspire,
  Kindle there the Gospel fire.

2 Bid our sin and sorrow cease;
  Fill us with thy heavenly peace;
Joy divine we then shall prove,
  Light of truth—and fire of love.

602   *Invocation.*   BATHURST.

Holy Spirit, from on high,
  Bend on us a pitying eye;
Animate the drooping heart,
  Bid the power of sin depart.

2 Light up every dark recess
  Of our heart's ungodliness;
Show us every devious way,
  Where our steps have gone astray.

3 Teach us with repentant grief
  Humbly to implore relief,
Then the Saviour's blood reveal,
  All our deep disease to heal.

4 Other groundwork should we lay,
  Sweep those empty hopes away;
Make us feel that Christ alone
  Can for human guilt atone.

5 May we daily grow in grace,
  And pursue the heavenly race,
Trained in wisdom, led by love,
  Till we reach our rest above.

WELLS. L. M.

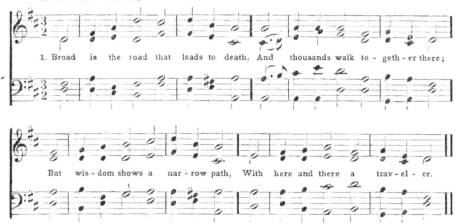

1. Broad is the road that leads to death, And thousands walk to - geth - er there;

But wis - dom shows a nar - row path, With here and there a trav - el - er.

603   *Luke* 9:23.   WATTS.

Broad is the road that leads to death,
  And thousands walk together there;
But wisdom shows a narrow path,
  With here and there a traveler.

2 "Deny thyself and take thy cross,"—
  Is the Redeemer's great command:
Nature must count her gold but dross,
  If she would gain this heavenly land.

3 The fearful soul that tires and faints,
  And walks the ways of God no more,
Is but esteemed almost a saint,
  And makes his own destruction sure.

4 Lord! let not all my hopes be vain:
  Create my heart entirely new:
Which hypocrites could ne'er attain,
  Which false apostates never knew.

604   *"One thing needful."*   MEDLEY.

Jesus, engrave it on my heart,
That thou the one thing needful art;
I could from all things parted be,
But never, never, Lord, from thee.

2 Needful is thy most precious blood,
To reconcile my soul to God;
Needful is thy indulgent care;
Needful thy all-prevailing prayer.

3 Needful thy presence, dearest Lord,
True peace and comfort to afford;
Needful thy promise, to impart
Fresh life and vigor to my heart.

226

4 Needful art thou, my guide, my stay,
Through all life's dark and weary way;
Nor less in death thou'lt needful be,
To bring my spirit home to thee.

5 Then needful still, my God, my King,
Thy name eternally I'll sing!
Glory and praise be ever his, —
The one thing needful Jesus is!

605   *Job* 4:17-21.   WATTS.

Shall the vile race of flesh and blood
Contend with their Creator, God?
Shall mortal worms presume to be
More holy, wise, or just, than he?

2 Behold! he puts his trust in none
Of all the spirits round his throne;
Their natures, when compared with his,
Are neither holy, just, nor wise.

3 But how much meaner things are they
Who spring from dust, and dwell in clay·
Touched by the finger of thy wrath,
We faint and vanish like a moth.

4 From night to day, from day to night,
We die by thousands in thy sight;
Buried in dust whole nations lie,
Like a forgotten vanity.

5 Almighty Power, to thee we bow;
How frail are we! how glorious thou!
No more the sons of earth shall dare
With an eternal God compare.

GANGES. C. P. M.

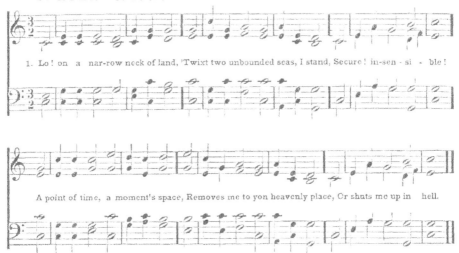

1. Lo! on a nar-row neck of land, 'Twixt two unbounded seas, I stand, Secure! in-sen - si - ble!

A point of time, a moment's space, Removes me to yon heavenly place, Or shuts me up in hell.

606   *"In jeopardy every hour."*   C. WESLEY.

Lo! on a narrow neck of land,
'Twixt two unbounded seas, I stand,
  Secure! insensible!
A point of time, a moment's space,
Removes me to yon heavenly place,
  Or shuts me up in hell.

2 O God! my inmost soul convert,
And deeply on my thoughtful heart
  Eternal things impress:
Give me to feel their solemn weight,
And save me ere it be too late;
  Wake me to righteousness.

3 Before me place, in dread array,
The pomp of that tremendous day,
  When thou with clouds shalt come
To judge the nations at thy bar;
And tell me, Lord! shall I be there
  To meet a joyful doom!

4 Be this my one great business here,—
With holy trembling, holy fear,
  To make my calling sure!
Thine utmost counsel to fulfil,
And suffer all thy righteous will,
  And to the end endure!

5 Then Saviour, then my soul receive,
Then bid me in thy presence live,
  And reign with thee above;

Where faith is sweetly lost in sight,
And hope, in full, supreme delight,
  And everlasting love.

607   *"Must be born again."*   OCCOM.

AWAKED by Sinai's awful sound,
My soul in bonds of guilt I found,
  And knew not where to go;
One solemn truth increased my pain,
"The sinner must be born again,"
  Or sink to endless woe.

2 I heard the law its thunders roll,
While guilt lay heavy on my soul—
  A vast oppressive load;
All creature-aid I saw was vain;
"The sinner must be born again,"
  Or drink the wrath of God.

3 The saints I heard with rapture tell—
How Jesus conquered death and hell
  To bring salvation near;
Yet still I found this truth remain—
"The sinner must be born again,"
  Or sink in deep despair.

4 But while I thus in anguish lay,
The bleeding Saviour passed that way,
  My bondage to remove;
The sinner, once by justice slain,
Now by his grace is born again,
  And sings redeeming love.

HUMMEL. C. M.

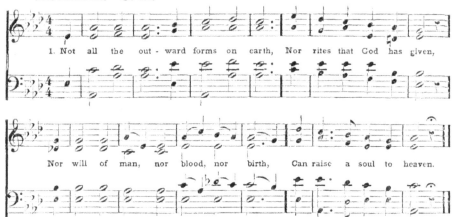

1. Not all the out-ward forms on earth, Nor rites that God has given,

Nor will of man, nor blood, nor birth, Can raise a soul to heaven.

608   *John 1:12, 13.*   WATTS.

Nor all the outward forms on earth,
  Nor rites that God has given,
Nor will of man, nor blood, nor birth,
  Can raise a soul to heaven.

2 The sovereign will of God alone
  Creates us heirs of grace;
Born in the image of his Son,
  A new, peculiar race.

3 The Spirit, like some heavenly wind,
  Breathes on the sons of flesh,
New-models all the carnal mind,
  And forms the man afresh.

4 Our quickened souls awake and rise
  From the long sleep of death;
On heavenly things we fix our eyes,
  And praise employs our breath.

609   *"All become guilty."*   WATTS.

Vain are the hopes, the sons of men
  On their own works have built;
Their hearts, by nature, all unclean,
  And all their actions, guilt.

2 Let Jew and Gentile stop their mouths,
  Without a murmuring word;
And the whole race of Adam stand
  Guilty before the Lord.

3 Jesus! how glorious is thy grace;—
  When in thy name we trust,
Our faith receives a righteousness,
  That makes the sinner just.

610   *Matthew 7:14.*   WATTS.

Strait is the way, the door is strait,
  That leads to joys on high;
'T is but a few that find the gate
  While crowds mistake and die.

2 Belovéd self must be denied,
  The mind and will renewed,
Passion suppressed, and patience tried,
  And vain desires subdued.

3 Lord! can a feeble, helpless worm,
  Fulfill a task so hard!
Thy grace must all my work perform,
  And give the free reward.

611   *"Prisoners out of the Pit."*   WATTS.

How sad our state by nature is!
  Our sin—how deep it stains!
And Satan holds our captive minds
  Fast in his slavish chains.

2 But there's a voice of sovereign grace,
  Sounds from the sacred word:
"Ho! ye despairing sinners, come,
  And trust a pardoning Lord."

3 My soul obeys the almighty call,
  And runs to this relief;
I would believe thy promise, Lord:
  Oh, help my unbelief!

4 A guilty, weak, and helpless worm,
  On thy kind arms I fall;
Be thou my Strength and Righteousness,
  My Saviour and my All.

MONSON. C. M.

STEELE.

1. How help - less guilt - y na - ture lies, Un - con - scious of its load!

The heart, unchanged, can nev - er rise To hap - pi - ness and God.

612   *Perfectly helpless.*

How helpless guilty nature lies,
Unconscious of its load!
The heart, unchanged, can never rise
To happiness and God.

2 Can aught, beneath a power divine,
The stubborn will subdue?
'Tis thine, almighty Spirit! thine,
To form the heart anew.

3 'Tis thine, the passions to recall,
And upward bid them rise;
To make the scales of error fall,
From reason's darkened eyes;—

4 To chase the shades of death away,
And bid the sinner live;
A beam of heaven, a vital ray,
'Tis thine alone to give.

5 Oh, change these wretched hearts of ours,
And give them life divine;
Then shall our passions and our powers,
Almighty Lord, be thine.

613   *No life by law.*   WATTS.

In vain we seek for peace with God
By methods of our own:
Nothing, O Saviour! but thy blood
Can bring us near the throne.

2 The threatenings of the broken law
Impress the soul with dread:
If God his sword of vengeance draw,
It strikes the spirit dead.

3 But thine illustrious sacrifice
Hath answered these demands;
And peace and pardon from the skies
Are offered by thy hands.

4 'Tis by thy death we live, O Lord!
'Tis on thy cross we rest:
For ever be thy love adored,
Thy name for ever blessed.

614   *Romans 7: 7-13.*   WATTS.

Lord, how secure my conscience was,
And felt no inward dread!
I was alive without the law,
And thought my sins were dead.

2 My hopes of heaven were firm and bright;
But since the precept came
With a convincing power and light,
I find how vile I am.

3 My guilt appeared but small before,
Till terribly I saw
How perfect, holy, just, and pure,
Is thine eternal law.

4 Then felt my soul the heavy load;
My sins revived again:
I had provoked a dreadful God,
And all my hopes were slain.

5 My God, I cry with every breath
For some kind power to save,
To break the yoke of sin and death,
And thus redeem the slave.

IOWA. (KENTUCKY) S. M.

1. A charge to keep I have, A God to glo - ri - fy,

A nev - er - dy - ing soul to save, And fit it for the sky.

615　"I say unto all, Watch."　C. WESLEY.

A CHARGE to keep I have,
　A God to glorify,
A never-dying soul to save,
　And fit it for the sky.

2 To serve the present age,
　My calling to fulfill;
Oh, may it all my powers engage
　To do my Master's will.

3 Arm me with jealous care,
　As in thy sight to live;
And oh, thy servant, Lord, prepare
　A strict account to give.

4 Help me to watch and pray,
　And on thyself rely,
Assured, if I my trust betray,
　I shall for ever die.

616　"Thy work alone."　BONAR.

Not what these hands have done
　Can save this guilty soul:
Not what this toiling flesh has borne
　Can make my spirit whole.

2 Not what I feel or do
　Can give me peace with God;
Not all my prayers, and sighs, and tears,
　Can bear my awful load.

3 Thy work alone, O Christ,
　Can ease this weight of sin;
Thy blood alone, O Lamb of God,
　Can give me peace within.

617　Psalm 15.　ANON.

CAN sinners hope for heaven,
　Who love this world so well!
Or dream of future happiness,
　While on the road to hell?

2 Shall they hosannas sing,
　With an unhallowed tongue?
Shall palms adorn the guilty hand
　Which does its neighbor wrong?

3 Thy grace, O God, alone,
　Good hope can e'er afford!
The pardoned and the pure shall see
　The glory of the Lord.

618　Necessity of Atonement.　WATTS.

LIKE sheep we went astray,
　And broke the fold of God,—
Each wandering in a different way,
　But all the downward road.

2 How dreadful was the hour,
　When God our wanderings laid,
And did at once his vengeance pour,
　Upon the Shepherd's head!

3 How glorious was the grace,
　When Christ sustained the stroke!
His life and blood the Shepherd pays,
　A ransom for the flock.

4 But God shall raise his head,
　O'er all the sons of men,
And make him see a numerous seed,
　To recompense his pain.

SHAWMUT. S. M.

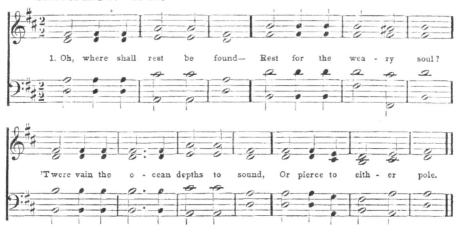

1. Oh, where shall rest be found— Rest for the wea - ry soul?

'T were vain the o - cean depths to sound, Or pierce to eith - er pole.

619 *Deuteronomy* **30 : 19.** MONTGOMERY.

Oh, where shall rest be found—
Rest for the weary soul?
'T were vain the ocean depths to sound,
Or pierce to either pole.

2 The world can never give
The bliss for which we sigh:
'Tis not the whole of life to live,
Nor all of death to die.

3 Beyond this vale of tears
There is a life above,
Unmeasured by the flight of years;
And all that life is love.

4 There is a death whose pang
Outlasts the fleeting breath:
Oh, what eternal horrors hang
Around the second death!

5 Lord God of truth and grace!
Teach us that death to shun;
Lest we be banished from thy face,
And evermore undone.

620 *2 Corinthians* **5 : 21.** WATTS.

How heavy is the night
That hangs upon our eyes,
Till Christ with his reviving light
Over our souls arise!

2 Our guilty spirits dread
To meet the wrath of heaven;
But, in his righteousness arrayed,
We see our sins forgiven.

3 Unholy and impure
Are all our thoughts and ways:
His hand infected nature cure
With sanctifying grace.

4 Lord, we adore thy ways
To bring us near to God,
Thy sovereign power, thy healing grace,
And thine atoning blood.

621 *The atonement.* WATTS.

Not all the blood of beasts
On Jewish altars slain,
Could give the guilty conscience peace,
Or wash away the stain.

2 But Christ the heavenly Lamb
Takes all our sins away,
A sacrifice of nobler name
And richer blood than they.

3 My faith would lay her hand
On that dear head of thine,
While like a penitent I stand,
And there confess my sin.

4 My soul looks back to see
The burdens thou didst bear,
When hanging on the cursèd tree,
And hopes her guilt was there.

5 Believing, we rejoice
To see the curse remove;
We bless the Lamb with cheerful voice,
And sing his dying love.

231

COWPER. C. M.

1. There is a fount-ain filled with blood, Drawn from Im-man-uel's veins, And sinners, plunged beneath that flood, Lose all their guil-ty stains; Lose all their guil-ty stains.

622   *Zechariah* 13:1.   COWPER.

THERE is a fountain filled with blood,
  Drawn from Immanuel's veins;
And sinners, plunged beneath that flood,
  Lose all their guilty stains.

2 The dying thief rejoiced to see
  That fountain in his day;
And there may I, though vile as he,
  Wash all my sins away.

3 Dear dying Lamb, thy precious blood
  Shall never lose its power,
Till all the ransomed church of God
  Be saved, to sin no more.

4 E'er since, by faith, I saw the stream
  Thy flowing wounds supply,

Redeeming love has been my theme,
  And shall be, till I die.

5 Then in a nobler, sweeter song,
  I'll sing thy power to save,
When this poor lisping, stammering tongue
  Lies silent in the grave.

6 Lord, I believe thou hast prepared,
  Unworthy though I be,
For me a blood-bought, free reward,
  A golden harp for me.

7 'Tis strung, and tuned for endless years,
  And formed by power divine,
To sound in God the Father's ears
  No other name but thine.

FOUNTAIN. C. M.

1. There is a fountain filled with blood, Drawn from Immanuel's veins, And sinners, plunged beneath [that flood,

FINE.   *D. S.*

Lose all their guil-ty stains, Lose all their guil-ty stains, Lose all their guil-ty stains.

ARLINGTON. C. M.

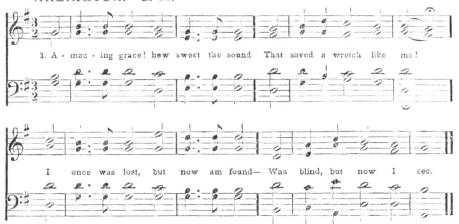

1. A - maz - ing grace! how sweet the sound That saved a wretch like me!

I once was lost, but now am found— Was blind, but now I see.

623   *"Amazing Grace."*   NEWTON.

AMAZING grace! how sweet the sound
  That saved a wretch like me!
I once was lost, but now am found—
  Was blind, but now I see.

2 'Twas grace that taught my heart to fear,
  And grace my fears relieved;
How precious did that grace appear,
  The hour I first believed!

3 Through many dangers, toils, and snares,
  I have already come;
'Tis grace hath brought me safe thus far,
  And grace will lead me home.

4 Yea—when this flesh and heart shall fail,
  And mortal life shall cease,
I shall possess, within the vail,
  A life of joy and peace.

5 The earth shall soon dissolve like snow,
  The sun forbear to shine;
But God, who called me here below,
  Will be for ever mine.

624   *God Reconciled.*   WATTS

COME, let us lift our joyful eyes,
  Up to the courts above,
And smile to see our Father there,
  Upon a throne of love.

2 Now we may bow before his feet,
  And venture near the Lord:
No fiery cherub guards his seat,
  Nor double flaming sword.

3 The peaceful gates of heavenly bliss
  Are opened by the Son;
High let us raise our notes of praise,
  And reach the almighty throne.

4 To thee ten thousand thanks we bring,
  Great Advocate on high,
And glory to the eternal King,
  Who lays his anger by.

625   *"Oh, amazing Love!"*   WATTS.

PLUNGED in a gulf of dark despair,
  We wretched sinners lay,
Without one cheerful beam of hope,
  Or spark of glimmering day.

2 With pitying eyes the Prince of grace
  Beheld our helpless grief;
He saw, and—oh, amazing love!—
  He ran to our relief.

3 Down from the shining seats above,
  With joyful haste he fled,
Entered the grave in mortal flesh,
  And dwelt among the dead.

4 Oh, for this love let rocks and hills
  Their lasting silence break;
And all harmonious human tongues
  The Saviour's praises speak.

5 Angels! assist our mighty joys;
  Strike all your harps of gold;
But, when you raise your highest notes,
  His love can ne'er be told.

ATHENS. C. M. D.

1. A-wake, my heart, arise, my tongue, Prepare a tuneful voice; In God, the life of all my joys,
D. S.—Up - on a poor, pollut-ed worm,

FINE.

A - loud will I re - joice. 2. 'Tis he adorned my nak-ed soul, And made sal-va-tion mine;
He makes his graces shine.

D. S.

626   *The Saviour's Robe.*   WATTS.

Awake, my heart, arise, my tongue,
  Prepare a tuneful voice;
In God, the life of all my joys,
  Aloud will I rejoice.

2 'Tis he adorned my naked soul,
  And made salvation mine;
Upon a poor, polluted worm,
  He makes his graces shine.

3 And lest the shadow of a spot
  Should on my soul be found,
He took the robe the Saviour wrought,
  And cast it all around.

4 How far the heavenly robe excels
  What earthly princes wear!
These ornaments how bright they shine!
  How white the garments are!

5 The Spirit wrought my faith and love,
  And hope and every grace;
But Jesus spent his life to work
  The robe of righteousness.

6 Strangely, my soul, art thou arrayed,
  By the great sacred Three;
In sweetest harmony of praise,
  Let all thy powers agree.

627   *"Good-will and Peace."*   MEDLEY.

Mortals, awake, with angels join
  And chant the solemn lay;
Joy, love, and gratitude combine
  To hail the auspicious day.

2 In heaven the rapturous song began,
  And sweet seraphic fire
Through all the shining legions ran,
  And strung and tuned the lyre.

3 Swift through the vast expanse it flew,
  And loud the echo rolled;
The theme, the song, the joy, was new,
  'Twas more than heaven could hold.

4 Down through the portals of the sky
  The impetuous torrent ran;
And angels flew, with eager joy,
  To bear the news to man.

5 Hark! the cherubic armies shout,
  And glory leads the song;   [out
" Good-will and peace" are heard through-
  The harmonious angel-throng.

6 With joy the chorus we'll repeat,—
  "Glory to God on high!
Good-will and peace are now complete;
  Jesus was born to die!"

234

GLASGOW. C. M.

1. Great God, when I ap-proach thy throne, And all thy glo-ry see;

This is my stay, and this a-lone, That Je-sus died for me.

628 *"Jesus died for me."* ANON.

GREAT God, when I approach thy throne,
　And all thy glory see;
This is my stay, and this alone,
　That Jesus died for me.

2 How can a soul condemned to die,
　Escape the just decree?
Helpless, and full of sin am I,
　But Jesus died for me.

3 Burdened with sin's oppressive chain,
　Oh, how can I get free?
No peace can all my efforts gain,
　But Jesus died for me.

4 And Lord, when I behold thy face,
　This must be all my plea;
Save me by thy almighty grace,
　For Jesus died for me.

629 *"Salvation!"—Ps.* **58: 10.** WATTS.

SALVATION!—oh, the joyful sound!
　'Tis pleasure to our ears;
A sovereign balm for every wound,
　A cordial for our fears.

2 Buried in sorrow and in sin,
　At hell's dark door we lay;—
But we arise by grace divine,
　To see a heavenly day.

3 Salvation!—let the echo fly
　The spacious earth around;
While all the armies of the sky
　Conspire to raise the sound.

630 *Luke* **15: 7.** NEEDHAM.

OH, how divine, how sweet the joy,
　When but one sinner turns,
And, with an humble, broken heart,
　His sins and errors mourns.

2 Pleased with the news, the saints below
　In songs their tongues employ;
Beyond the skies the tidings go,
　And heaven is filled with joy.

3 Nor angels can their joys contain,
　But kindle with new fire;—
"The sinner lost is found," they sing,
　And strike the sounding lyre.

631 *God's compassion.* STEELE.

JESUS,—and didst thou leave the sky,
　To bear our griefs and woes?
And didst thou bleed, and groan and die,
　For thy rebellious foes?

2 Well might the heavens with wonder view
　A love so strange as thine!
No thought of angels ever knew
　Compassion so divine!

3 Is there a heart that will not bend
　To thy divine control?
Descend, O sovereign love, descend,
　And melt that stubborn soul.

4 Oh, may our willing hearts confess
　Thy sweet, thy gentle sway;
Glad captives of thy matchless grace,
　Thy righteous rule obey

LENOX. H. M.

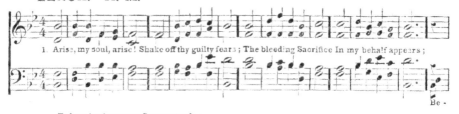

1. Arise, my soul, arise! Shake off thy guilty fears; The bleeding Sacrifice In my behalf appears;

Be -

Before the throne my Surety stands:

Before the throne my Surety stands: My name is written on his hands.

fore the throne my Surety stands: Before the throne my Surety stands: My name is written on his hands.

632   *Our Surety.*   C. WESLEY.

Arise, my soul, arise!
   Shake off thy guilty fears;
The bleeding Sacrifice
   In my behalf appears;
Before the throne my Surety stands:
My name is written on his hands.

2 He ever lives above,
   For me so intercede,
His all-redeeming love,
   His precious blood to plead;
His blood atoned for all our race,
And sprinkles now the throne of grace.

3 My God is reconciled;
   His pardoning voice I hear;
He owns me for his child;
   I can no longer fear;
With confidence I now draw nigh,
And Father, Abba, Father, cry.

633   *The year of Jubilee.*   C. WESLEY.

Blow ye the trumpet, blow;
   The gladly solemn sound
Let all the nations know,
   To earth's remotest bound;
The year of Jubilee is come:
Return, ye ransomed sinners, home.

2 Extol the Lamb of God,
   The all-atoning Lamb;
Redemption in his blood
   Throughout the world proclaim.
          The year, etc.

3 Ye who have sold for naught
   Your heritage above,
Come, take it back unbought,
   The gift of Jesus' love. The, etc.

4 The gospel trumpet hear,
   The news of heavenly grace,
And saved from earth appear
   Before your Saviour's face. The, etc.

634   *"It is finished."*   KELLY.

The atoning work is done,
   The Victim's blood is shed,
And Jesus now is gone
   His people's cause to plead;
He stands in heaven, their great High Priest,
He bears their names upon his breast.

2 He sprinkles with his blood
   The mercy-seat above;
For justice had withstood
   The purposes of love;
But justice now withstands no more,
And mercy yields her boundless store.

3 No temple made with hands,
   His place of service is;
In heaven itself he stands,
   A heavenly priesthood his:
In him the shadows of the law
Are all fulfilled, and now withdraw.

4 And though a while he be
   Hid from the eyes of men,
His people look to see
   Their great High Priest again;
In brightest glory he will come,
And take his waiting people home.

SCOTLAND. 12.

1. The voice of free grace cries, Escape to the mountain, For Adam's lost race Christ hath

opened a fountain; { For sin and uncleanness, and ev - ery trans - gression, His
{ Halle - lu - jah to the Lamb, who hath purchased our pardon, We'll

blood flows most freely in streams of salvation, His blood flows most freely in streams of salvation. }
praise him again, when we pass over Jordan! We'll praise him again, when we pass over Jordan! }

635 *"Escape for thy life."* BURDSALL.

THE voice of free grace cries, Escape to
 the mountain,
For Adam's lost race Christ hath opened
 a fountain;
For sin and uncleanness, and every trans-
 gression,
His blood flows most freely in streams
 of salvation.
Hallelujah to the Lamb, who hath purchas-
 ed our pardon,
We'll praise him again, when we pass over
 Jordan!

2 Ye souls that are wounded! oh, flee to
 the Saviour!
He calls you in mercy, 'tis infinite favor:
Your sins are increasing, escape to the
 mountain—
His blood can remove them, it flows from
 the fountain.
 Hallelujah to the Lamb, etc.

3 O Jesus! ride onward, triumphantly
 glorious!
O'er sin, death, and hell, thou art more
 than victorious:
Thy name is the theme of the great congregation,
While angels and men raise the shout of
 salvation.
 Hallelujah to the Lamb, etc.

4 With joy shall we stand, when escaped
 to the shore;
With harps in our hands, we'll praise
 him the more!
We'll range the sweet plains on the
 banks of the river,
And sing of salvation for ever and ever!
Hallelujah to the Lamb, who hath purchas-
 ed our pardon,
We'll praise him again, when we pass over
 Jordan!

LOVING-KINDNESS. L. M.

1. Awake, my soul, to joyful lays, And sing the great Redeemer's praise; He justly claims a song from me:

His loving-kindness, oh, how free! Loving-kindness, loving kindness, His loving-kindness, oh, how free!

636 *"Loving-kindness."—Ps.* 26: **7.** MEDLEY.

Awake, my soul, to joyful lays,
And sing the great Redeemer's praise;
He justly claims a song from me:
His loving-kindness, oh, how free!

2 He saw me ruined in the fall,
Yet loved me, notwithstanding all;
He saved me from my lost estate:
His loving-kindness, oh, how great!

3 Though numerous hosts of mighty foes,
Though earth and hell my way oppose,
He safely leads my soul along:
His loving-kindness, oh, how strong!

4 When trouble, like a gloomy cloud,
Has gathered thick and thundered loud,
He near my soul has always stood:
His loving-kindness, oh, how good!

5 Soon shall I pass the gloomy vale;
Soon all my mortal powers must fail:
Oh, may my last expiring breath
His loving-kindness sing in death!

6 Then let me mount and soar away
To the bright world of endless day;
And sing, with rapture and surprise,
His loving-kindness in the skies!

HIDING PLACE. L. M.

1. Hail, sovereign love, that formed the plan To save rebellious, ruined man! Hail, matchless, free, e-

ter - nal grace, That gave my soul a hid - ing-place, That gave my soul a hid - ing-place.

JESUS PAID IT ALL. P. M.

1. Nothing, eith-er great or small, Remains for me to do; Je-sus died, and paid it all, Yes all the debt I owe.

CHORUS.

Je-sus paid it all,........ Je-sus paid it, paid it all.

All the debt I owe, Je-sus died and paid it all, Yes, all the debt I owe.

637 *"It is Finished!"* PROCTER. *alt.*

NOTHING, either great or small,
　Remains for me to do;
Jesus died, and paid it all,
　Yes, all the debt I owe!—CHO.

2 When he from his lofty throne,
　Stooped down to do and die,
Everything was fully done;
　"'Tis finished!" was his cry.—CHO.

3 Weary not, O toiling one,
　Whate'er thy conflict be,

Work for him with cheerful heart,
　Who suffered all for thee.—CHO.

4 Clinging to the Saviour's cross,
　Look up by simple faith,
Praise him for the pardoning love
　That saves from endless death.—CHO.

5 Bring a willing sacrifice—
　Thy soul to Jesus' feet;
Stand in him, in him alone,
　All glorious and complete.—CHO.

638 *A hiding-place.—Ps.* **32:7.** BREWER.

HAIL, sovereign love, that formed the plan
To save rebellious, ruined man!
Hail, matchless, free, eternal grace,
That gave my soul a hiding-place.

2 Against the God that rules the sky
I fought, with weapons lifted high;
I madly ran the sinful race,
Regardless of a hiding-place.

3 Yet when God's justice rose in view,
To Sinai's burning mount I flew;

Keen were the pangs of my distress—
The mountain was no hiding-place.

4 But a celestial voice I heard,
A bleeding Saviour then appeared;
Led by the Spirit of his grace,
I found in him a hiding-place.

5 On him the weight of vengeance fell,
That else had sunk a world to hell;
Then, O my soul, for ever praise
Thy Saviour God, thy hiding-place!

ALL TO CHRIST I OWE.

1. I hear the Saviour say, Thy strength indeed is small; Child of weakness, watch and pray,

CHORUS.

Find in me thine all in all. Je - sus paid it all, All to him I owe;

Sin had left a crim - son stain; He washed it white as snow.

639   *"Jesus paid it all."*   HALL.

I hear the Saviour say,
  Thy strength indeed is small;
Child of weakness, watch and pray,
  Find in me thine all in all.
Cho.—Jesus paid it all,
    All to him I owe;
  Sin had left a crimson stain;
    He washed it white as snow.

2 Lord, now indeed I find
  Thy faith, and thine alone,
Can change the leper's spots,
  And melt the heart of stone.—Cho.

3 For nothing good have I
  Whereby thy grace to claim—
I'll wash my garment white
  In the blood of Calvary's Lamb.—Cho.

4 When from my dying bed
  My ransomed soul shall rise,
Then "Jesus paid it all"
  Shall rend the vaulted skies.—Cho.

5 And when before the throne
  I stand in him complete,
I'll lay my trophies down,
  All down at Jesus' feet.—Cho.

SPANISH HYMN. 7. 6l.

1. From the cross uplifted high,Where the Saviour deigns to die, { What melodious sounds we hear, }
D.C."Love's redeeming work is done—Come and welcome, sinner, come! } Bursting on the ravished ear!—}

I AM COMING. P. M.

1. I hear thy welcome voice, That calls me, Lord, to thee; For cleansing in thy precious blood, That flowed on Cal - va - ry.

CHORUS.

I am com - ing, Lord! Com - ing now to thee! Wash me, cleanse me, in the blood That flowed on Cal - va - ry!

HARTSOUGH.

640 *"Thy face will I seek."*

I HEAR thy welcome voice,
　That calls me, Lord, to thee;
For cleansing in thy precious blood,
　That flowed on Calvary.

2 Though coming weak and vile,
　Thou dost my strength assure;
Thou dost my vileness fully cleanse,
　Till spotless all, and pure.

3 'Tis Jesus calls me on
　To perfect faith and love,

To perfect hope, and peace, and trust,
　For earth and heaven above.

4 And he the witness gives
　To loyal hearts and free,
That every promise is fulfilled,
　If faith but brings the plea.

5 All hail! atoning blood!
　All hail! redeeming grace!
All hail! the gift of Christ, our Lord,
　Our Strength and Righteousness.

HAWEIS.

641 *"Come and welcome."*

FROM the cross uplifted high,
Where the Saviour deigns to die,
What melodious sounds we hear,
Bursting on the ravished ear!—
"Love's redeeming work is done—
Come and welcome, sinner, come!

2 "Sprinkled now with blood the throne—
Why beneath thy burdens groan?
On my piercéd body laid,
Justice owns the ransom paid—
Bow the knee, and kiss the Son—
Come and welcome, sinner, come!

4 "Spread for thee, the festal board
See with richest bounty stored;
To thy Father's bosom pressed,
Thou shalt be a child confessed,
Never from his house to roam;
Come and welcome, sinner, come!

4 "Soon the days of life shall end—
Lo, I come—your Saviour, Friend!
Safe your spirit to convey
To the realms of endless day,
Up to my eternal home—
Come and welcome, sinner, come!"

OLD, OLD STORY. 7, 6. D.

1. Tell me the old, old sto - ry Of unseen things a - bove, Of Je-sus and his glo - ry,

Of Je - sus and his love. Tell me the sto - ry sim - ply, As to a lit - tle child,

For I am weak and wea - ry, And helpless and de - filed.

CHORUS.

Tell me the old, old sto - ry,

Tell me the old, old sto - ry, Tell me the old, old sto - ry, Of Je-sus and his love.

642 *"The old, old Story."—John* **3: 16.** ANON.

TELL me the old, old story
Of unseen things above,
Of Jesus and his glory,
Of Jesus and his love.
Tell me the story simply,
As to a little child,
For I am weak and weary,
And helpless and defiled.—CHO.

2 Tell me the story slowly,
That I may take it in—
That wonderful Redemption
God's remedy for sin!
Tell me the story often,
For I forget so soon!
The "early dew" of morning
Has passed away at noon!—CHO.

3 Tell me the story softly,
With earnest tones, and grave;
Remember! I'm the sinner
Whom Jesus came to save.
Tell me that story always,
If you would really be,
In any time of trouble,
A comforter to me.—CHO.

4 Tell me the same old story,
When you have cause to fear
That this world's empty glory
Is costing me too dear.
Yes, and when that world's glory
Is drawing on my soul,
Tell me the old, old story:
"Christ Jesus makes thee whole."—CHO.

TELL THE STORY. 7, 6. D.

1. I love to tell the sto-ry, Of unseen things above, Of Jesus and his glory, Of Jesus and his love.

I love to tell the story, Because I know 'tis true; It satisfies my longings, As nothing else can do.

CHORUS.

I love to tell the story, 'Twill be my theme in glory, To tell the old, old story Of Jesus and his love.

643   *The Story of the Cross.*   MISS HANKEY.

I LOVE to tell the story,
　Of unseen things above,
Of Jesus and his glory,
　Of Jesus and his love.
I love to tell the story,
　Because I know 'tis true;
It satisfies my longings,
　As nothing else can do.—Cho.

2 I love to tell the story:
　'Tis pleasant to repeat
What seems, each time I tell it,
　More wonderfully sweet.
I love to tell the story:
　For some have never heard
The message of salvation,
　From God's own holy word.—Cho.

3 I love to tell the story;
　For those who know it best
Seem hungering and thirsting
　To hear it like the rest.
And when, in scenes of glory,
　I'll sing the NEW, NEW SONG,
'Twill be—the OLD, OLD STORY
　That I have loved so long.—Cho.

644   *"The Cross of Jesus."*   ANON.

I SAW the cross of Jesus,
　When burdened with my sin;
I sought the cross of Jesus,
　To give me peace within;
I brought my soul to Jesus,
　He cleansed it in his blood;
And in the cross of Jesus
　I found my peace with God.
Cho.—No righteousness, no merit,
　No beauty can I plead;
Yet in the cross I glory,
　My title there I read.

2 Sweet is the cross of Jesus!
　There let my weary heart
Still rest in peace unshaken,
　Till with him, ne'er to part;
And then in strains of glory
　I'll sing his wondrous power,
Where sin can never enter,
　And death is known no more.
Cho.—I love the cross of Jesus,
　It tells me what I am;
A vile and guilty creature,
　Saved only through the Lamb.

BERA. L. M.

1. Why will ye waste on tri - fling cares That life which God's com-pas - sion spares?

While, in the va - rious range of thought, The one thing need - ful is for - got?

645 "One thing needful." DODDRIDGE.

Why will ye waste on trifling cares
That life which God's compassion spares?
While, in the various range of thought,
The one thing needful is forgot?

2 Shall God invite you from above?
Shall Jesus urge his dying love?
Shall troubled conscience give you pain?
And all these pleas unite in vain?

3 Not so your eyes will always view
Those objects which you now pursue:
Not so will heaven and hell appear,
When death's decisive hour is near.

4 Almighty God! thy grace impart;
Fix deep conviction on each heart;
Nor let us waste on trifling cares
That life which thy compassion spares.

646 Psalm 88. DWIGHT.

While life prolongs its precious light,
Mercy is found, and peace is given;
But soon, ah! soon, approaching night
Shall blot out every hope of heaven.

2 While God invites, how blest the day!
How sweet the gospel's charming sound!
Come, sinners, haste, oh, haste away,
While yet a pardoning God is found.

3 Soon, borne on time's most rapid wing,
Shall death command you to the grave,
Before his bar your spirits bring,
And none be found to hear or save.

244

4 In that lone land of deep despair
No Sabbath's heavenly light shall rise;
No God regard your bitter prayer,
Nor Saviour call you to the skies.

5 Now God invites—how blest the day!
How sweet the gospel's charming sound!
Come, sinners, haste, oh, haste away,
While yet a pardoning God is found.

647 "Not always strive." HYDE.

Say, sinner! hath a voice within
Oft whispered to thy secret soul,
Urged thee to leave the ways of sin,
And yield thy heart to God's control?

2 Sinner! it was a heavenly voice,—
It was the Spirit's gracious call;
It bade thee make the better choice,
And haste to seek in Christ thine all.

3 Spurn not the call to life and light;
Regard, in time, the warning kind;
That call thou mayst not always slight,
And yet the gate of mercy find.

4 God's Spirit will not always strive
With hardened, self-destroying man;
Ye who persist his love to grieve,
May never hear his voice again.

5 Sinner! perhaps, this very day,
Thy last accepted time may be:
Oh, shouldst thou grieve him now away,
Then hope may never beam on thee.

DESIRE. L. M.

1. Come, wea-ry souls with sins distressed, Come, and ac-cept the prom-ised rest;

The Sav-iour's gra-cious call o-bey, And cast your gloom-y fears a-way.

648   *"Come, weary souls!"*   STEELE.

Come, weary souls! with sin distressed,
Come, and accept the promised rest;
The Saviour's gracious call obey,
And cast your gloomy fears away.

2 Here mercy's boundless ocean flows,
To cleanse your guilt and heal your woes;
Pardon and life, and endless peace,—
How rich the gift, how free the grace!

3 Lord! we accept, with thankful heart,
The hope thy gracious words impart;
We come, with trembling; yet rejoice,
And bless the kind inviting voice.

4 Dear Saviour! let thy powerful love
Confirm our faith,—our fears remove;
Oh, sweetly reign in every breast,
And guide us to eternal rest.

649   *"God calling yet!"*   BORTHWICK. *Tr.*

God calling yet! shall I not hear?
Earth's pleasures shall I still hold dear?
Shall life's swift passing years all fly,
And still my soul in slumbers lie?

2 God calling yet! shall I not rise?
Can I his loving voice despise,
And basely his kind care repay?
He calls me still; can I delay?

3 God calling yet! and shall he knock,
And I my heart the closer lock?
He still is waiting to receive,
And shall I dare his Spirit grieve?

4 God calling yet! and shall I give
No heed, but still in bondage live?
I wait, but he does not forsake;
He calls me still; my heart, awake!

5 God calling yet! I cannot stay;
My heart I yield without delay;
Vain world, farewell! from thee I part;
The voice of God hath reached my heart.

650   *"A Stranger at the door."*   GRIGG.

Behold a Stranger at the door!
He gently knocks, has knocked before,
Has waited long, is waiting still;
You treat no other friend so ill.

2 Oh, lovely attitude! he stands
With melting heart and laden hands;
Oh, matchless kindness! and he shows
This matchless kindness to his foes.

3 But will he prove a friend indeed?
He will, the very friend you need—
The Friend of sinners; yes, 'tis he,
With garments dyed on Calvary.

4 Rise, touched with gratitude divine,
Turn out his enemy and thine,
That soul-destroying monster sin,
And let the heavenly Stranger in.

5 Admit him ere his anger burn,
His feet, departed, ne'er return;
Admit him, or the hour's at hand
When at his door denied you'll stand.

BALERMA. C. M.

1. Come, trembling sin - ner, in whose breast A thou - sand thoughts re - volve;

Come, with your guilt and fear oppressed, And make this last re - solve:—

651   *Esther* 4: 16.   JONES.

Come, trembling sinner, in whose breast
  A thousand thoughts revolve;
Come, with your guilt and fear oppressed,
  And make this last resolve:—

2 "I'll go to Jesus, though my sins
  Like mountains round me close;
I know his courts, I'll enter in,
  Whatever may oppose.

3 "Prostrate I'll lie before his throne,
  And there my guilt confess;
I'll tell him I'm a wretch undone,
  Without his sovereign grace.

4 "Perhaps he will admit my plea,
  Perhaps will hear my prayer;
But if I perish, I will pray,
  And perish only there.

5 "I can but perish if I go;
  I am resolved to try;
For if I stay away, I know
  I must for ever die."

652   *"The Saviour calls."*   STEELE.

The Saviour calls;—let every ear
  Attend the heavenly sound;
Ye doubting souls! dismiss your fear,
  Hope smiles reviving round.

2 For every thirsty, longing heart,
  Here streams of bounty flow,
And life, and health, and bliss impart,
  To banish mortal woe.

3 Ye sinners! come; 'tis mercy's voice:
  The gracious call obey;
Mercy invites to heavenly joys,—
  And can you yet delay?

4 Dear Saviour! draw reluctant hearts;
  To thee let sinners fly,
And take the bliss thy love imparts,
  And drink and never die.

653   *The Gospel call.*   WATTS.

Let every mortal ear attend,
  And every heart rejoice;
The trumpet of the gospel sounds,
  With an inviting voice.

2 Ho! all ye hungry, starving souls!
  That feed upon the wind,
And vainly strive, with earthly toys,
  To fill an empty mind;—

3 Eternal wisdom has prepared
  A soul-reviving feast,
And bids your longing appetites,
  The rich provision taste.

4 Ho! ye that pant for living streams,
  And pine away and die!
Here you may quench your raging thirst,
  With springs that never dry.

5 The happy gates of gospel grace
  Stand open night and day;
Lord! we are come to seek supplies,
  And drive our wants away.

RETURN. C. M.

1. Re - turn, O wan - derer, to thy home, Thy Fa - ther calls for thee:

No long - er now an ex - ile roam In guilt and mis - e - ry. Re - turn, re - turn!

654   *The Prodigal Son.*   HASTINGS.

Return, O wanderer, to thy home,
   Thy Father calls for thee:
No longer now an exile roam
   In guilt and misery.

2 Return, O wanderer, to thy home,
   Thy Saviour calls for thee:
"The Spirit and the Bride say, Come;"
   Oh, now for refuge flee!

3 Return, O wanderer, to thy home,
   'Tis madness to delay:
There are no pardons in the tomb;
   And brief is mercy's day!

655   *Come sincerely.*   ANON.

O sinner, bring not tears alone,
   Or outward form of prayer,
But let it in thy heart be known
   That penitence is there.

2 To smite the breast, the clothes to rend,
   God asketh not of thee;
Thy secret soul he bids thee bend
   In true humility.

3 Oh, let us, then, with heartfelt grief,
   Draw near unto our God,
And pray to him to grant relief,
   And stay the lifted rod.

4 O righteous Judge! if thou wilt deign
   To grant us what we need,
We pray for time to turn again,
   And grace to turn indeed.

656   *Isaiah 55:7.*   COLLYER.

Return, O Wanderer, now return,
   And seek thy Father's face!
Those new desires, which in thee burn,
   Were kindled by his grace.

2 Return, O wanderer, now return!
   He hears thy humble sigh;
He sees thy softened spirit mourn,
   When no one else is nigh.

3 Return, O wanderer, now return!
   Thy Saviour bids thee live:
Go to his bleeding feet, and learn
   How freely he'll forgive.

4 Return, O wanderer, now return,
   And wipe the falling tear!
Thy Father calls—no longer mourn:
   His love invites thee near.

657   *Amazing Grace.*   MEDLEY.

Oh, what amazing words of grace
   Are in the gospel found,
Suited to every sinner's case
   Who hears the joyful sound!

2 Come, then, with all your wants and wounds
   Your every burden bring;
Here love, unchanging love, abounds,—
   A deep celestial spring.

3 This spring with living water flows,
   And heavenly joy imparts;
Come, thirsty souls! your wants disclose
   And drink, with thankful hearts.

DETROIT. S. M.

1. Did Christ o'er sin - ners weep, And shall our cheeks be dry?

Let floods of pen - i - ten - tial grief Burst forth from ev - ery eye.

658   *Luke 19 : 41.*   BEDDOME.

Did Christ o'er sinners weep,
  And shall our cheeks be dry?
Let floods of penitential grief
  Burst forth from every eye.

2 The Son of God in tears
  Angels with wonder see;
Be thou astonished, O my soul!
  He shed those tears for thee.

3 He wept that we might weep;
  Each sin demands a tear:
In heaven alone no sin is found,
  And there's no weeping there.

659   *"The Spirit and the Bride."*   ONDERDONK.

The Spirit, in our hearts,
  Is whispering, "Sinner, come;"
The bride, the Church of Christ, proclaims,
  To all his children, "Come!"

2 Let him that heareth say
  To all about him, "Come!"
Let him that thirsts for righteousness
  To Christ, the fountain, come!

3 Yes, whosoever will,
  Oh, let him freely come,
And freely drink the stream of life;
  'Tis Jesus bids him come.

4 Lo! Jesus, who invites,
  Declares, "I quickly come;"
Lord, even so; we wait thine hour;
  O blest Redeemer, come!

248

660   *The accepted time.*   DOBELL.

Now is the accepted time,
  Now is the day of grace;
O sinners! come, without delay,
  And seek the Saviour's face.

2 Now is the accepted time,
  The Saviour calls to-day;
To-morrow it may be too late;—
  Then why should you delay?

3 Now is the accepted time,
  The gospel bids you come;
And every promise in his word
  Declares there yet is room.

4 Lord, draw reluctant souls,
  And feast them with thy love;
Then will the angels spread their wings,
  And bear the news above.

661   *Expostulation.*   HYDE.

And canst thou, sinner! slight
  The call of love divine?
Shall God, with tenderness invite,
  And gain no thought of thine?

2 Wilt thou not cease to grieve
  The Spirit from thy breast,
Till he thy wretched soul shall leave
  With all thy sins oppressed?

3 To-day, a pardoning God
  Will hear the suppliant pray,
To-day, a Saviour's cleansing blood
  Will wash thy guilt away.

NONE BUT JESUS. P. M.

1. Weeping will not save me—Though my face were bathed in tears, That could not al - lay my fears,

CHORUS.

Could not wash the sins of years, Weeping will not save me. Jesus wept and died for me;

Je - sus suffered on the tree: Jesus waits to make me free; He a - lone can save me.

LOWRY.

662
"No other name."

WEEPING will not save me—
Though my face were bathed in tears,
That could not allay my fears,
Could not wash the sins of years,
   Weeping will not save me.—CHO.

2 Working will not save me—
Purest deeds that I can do,
Honest thought and feelings too,
Cannot form my soul anew,
   Working will not save me.—CHO.

3 Waiting will not save me—
Helpless, guilty, lost, I lie;
In my ear is mercy's cry;
If I wait I can but die—
   Waiting will not save me.—CHO.

4 Faith in Christ will save me—
Let me trust thy weeping Son;
Trust the work that he has done;
To his arms, Lord, help me run—
   Faith in Christ will save me.—CHO.

TO-DAY. P. M.

1. To - day the Saviour calls! Ye wanderers, come; Oh, ye benighted souls, Why longer roam?

HASTINGS.

663
Heb. **3: 15.**

TO-DAY the Saviour calls!
   Ye wanderers, come;
Oh, ye benighted souls,
   Why longer roam?

2 To-day the Saviour calls;
   Oh, hear him now!
Within these sacred walls
   To Jesus bow.

3 To-day the Saviour calls;
   For refuge fly;
The storm of justice falls,
   And death is nigh.

4 The Spirit calls to-day:
   Yield to his power;
Oh, grieve him not away!
   'Tis mercy's hour.

COME, YE DISCONSOLATE.   11, 10.

Choir.

1. Come, ye dis-con-so-late, where'er ye lan-guish; Come to the mercy-seat, fer-vently kneel;

Congregation.

Here bring your wounded hearts, here tell your anguish, Earth has no sorrow that heaven cannot heal.

664   *"Here speaks the Comforter"*   MOORE.

COME, ye disconsolate, where'er ye languish:
    Come to the mercy-seat, fervently kneel;
Here bring your wounded hearts, here tell
        your anguish;
    Earth has no sorrow that heaven can-
        not heal.

2 Joy of the comfortless, light of the stray-
        ing,
    Hope of the penitent, fadeless and pure;

Here speaks the Comforter, tenderly say-
        ing—
    Earth has no sorrow that heaven can-
        not cure.

3 Here see the Bread of Life; see waters
        flowing
    Forth from the throne of God, pure
        from above;
Come to the feast of love—come, ever
        knowing   [remove.
    Earth has no sorrow but heaven can

AVA.   P. M.

FINE.   D. C.

1. { Child of sin and sor - row! Filled with dis - may, }
   { Wait not for to - mor -row, Yield thee to - day: } Heaven bids thee come While yet there's room.
D.C. Child of sin and sor - row! Hear and o - bey.

665   *" Children of wrath."*   HASTINGS.

2 Child of sin and sorrow,
    Why wilt thou die?
Come while thou canst borrow
    Help from on high:
        Grieve not that love
        Which from above,
    Child of sin and sorrow,
        Would bring thee nigh.

3 Child of sin and sorrow,
    Thy moments glide,
Like the flitting arrow,
    Or the rushing tide;
        Ere time is o'er,
        Heaven's grace implore;
    Child of sin and sorrow,
        In Christ confide.

EXPOSTULATION. 11.

1. Oh, turn ye, oh, turn ye, for why will ye die, When God in great mercy is com-ing so nigh?

Now Je - sus in-vites you, the Spir - it says, Come, And an-gels are wait-ing to welcome you home.

666　　*"Why will ye die!"*　　ANON.

Oh, turn ye, oh, turn ye, for why will ye die,
　When God in great mercy is coming so nigh?
Now Jesus invites you, the Spirit says,
　Come,
　And angels are waiting to welcome you
　　home.

2 And now Christ is ready your souls to
　　receive,
　Oh, how can you question, if you will
　　believe.
　If sin is your burden, why will you not
　　come?
　'Tis you he bids welcome; he bids you
　　come home.

667　　*"I made haste."*—Ps. 119:60.　HASTINGS.

Delay not, delay not, O sinner, draw near,
　The waters of life are now flowing for
　　thee;
　No price is demanded, the Saviour is here;
　Redemption is purchased, salvation is
　　free.

2 Delay not, delay not, why longer abuse
　The love and compassion of Jesus thy
　　God?
　A fountain is open, how canst thou refuse
　To wash and be cleansed in his par-
　　doning blood?

3 Delay not, delay not, O sinner, to come,
　For Mercy still lingers and calls thee
　　to-day:

Her voice is not heard in the vale of the
　　tomb;
　Her message unheeded will soon pass
　　away.

4 Delay not, delay not, the Spirit of grace
　Long grieved and resisted may take his
　　sad flight,
　And leave thee in darkness to finish thy
　　race,
　To sink in the gloom of eternity's night.

5 Delay not, delay not, the hour is at hand,
　The earth shall dissolve, and the heav-
　　ens shall fade,
　The dead, small and great, in the judgment
　　shall stand;
　What power then, O sinner, will lend
　　thee its aid!

668　　*"Acquaint thyself."*—Job 22:21.　KNOX.

Acquaint thyself quickly, O sinner, with
　　God,
　And joy, like the sunshine, shall beam
　　on thy road;
　And peace, like the dewdrop, shall fall
　　on thy head,
　And sleep, like an angel, shall visit thy bed.

2 Acquaint thyself quickly, O sinner, with
　　God,
　And he shall be with thee when fears are
　　abroad;
　Thy Safeguard in danger that threatens
　　thy path;
　Thy Joy in the valley and shadow of death.

251

MARTYN. 7. D.

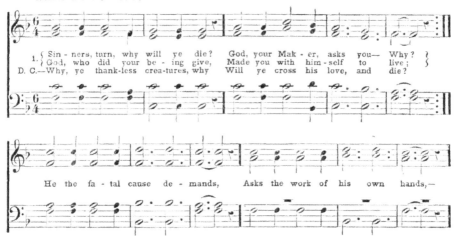

1. { Sin - ners, turn, why will ye die? God, your Mak - er, asks you— Why? }
   { God, who did your be - ing give, Made you with him - self to live; }
D. C.— Why, ye thank-less crea-tures, why Will ye cross his love, and die?

He the fa - tal cause de - mands, Asks the work of his own hands,—

669 *Ezekiel* 33 : 11. C. WESLEY.

Sinners, turn, why will ye die?
God, your Maker, asks you—Why?
God, who did your being give,
Made you with himself to live;
He the fatal cause demands,
Asks the work of his own hands,—
Why, ye thankless creatures, why
Will ye cross his love, and die?

2 Sinners, turn, why will ye die?
God, your Saviour, asks you—Why?
He who did your souls retrieve,
Died himself, that ye might live.
Will ye let him die in vain?
Crucify your Lord again?
Why, ye ransomed sinners, why
Will ye slight his grace, and die?

3 Sinners, turn, why will ye die?
God, the Spirit, asks you—Why?
He, who all your lives hath strove,
Urged you to embrace his love:
Will ye not his grace receive?
Will ye still refuse to live?
O ye dying sinners! why,
Why will ye for ever die?

670 *Christ's free call.* BARBAULD.

Come, said Jesus' sacred voice,
Come, and make my paths your choice;
I will guide you to your home;
Weary pilgrim, hither come.

2 Thou who, homeless and forlorn,
Long hast borne the proud world's scorn;
Long hast roamed the barren waste,
Weary wanderer, hither haste.

3 Ye, who, tossed on beds of pain,
Seek for ease, but seek in vain!
Ye, by fiercer anguish torn,
In remorse for guilt who mourn!

4 Hither come, for here is found
Balm that flows for every wound,
Peace that ever shall endure,
Rest eternal, sacred, sure.

671 *"To-morrow."*—*Jas.* 4 : 13. T. SCOTT.

Hasten, sinner! to be wise,
Stay not for the morrow's sun;
Wisdom, if thou still despise,
Harder is it to be won.

2 Hasten mercy to implore,
Stay not for the morrow's sun,
Lest thy season should be o'er,
Ere this evening's stage be run.

3 Hasten, sinner! to return,
Stay not for the morrow's sun,
Lest thy lamp should cease to burn,
Ere salvation's work is done.

4 Hasten, sinner! to be blest,
Stay not for the morrow's sun,
Lest perdition thee arrest,
Ere the morning is begun.

AN OPEN DOOR. P. M.

1. The mistakes of my life are many, The sins of my heart are more, And I scarce can see for weeping; But I knock at the o-pen door.

CHORUS.

I know I am weak and sin-ful, It comes to me more and more; But when the dear Saviour shall bid me come in, I'll enter that open door.

---

672   *The Door Open.*   ANON.

The mistakes of my life are many,
The sins of my heart are more,
And I scarce can see for weeping;
But I knock at the open door.
Cho.—I know I am weak and sinful,
   It comes to me more and more;
   But when the dear Saviour shall bid
      me come in,
   I'll enter that open door.

2 I am lowest of those who love him,
   I am weakest of those who pray:

But I come, as he has bidden,
   And he will not say me nay.—Cho.

3 My mistakes his free grace will cover,
   My sins he will wash away,
And the feet that shrink and falter,
   Shall walk thro' the gate of day.—Cho.

4 The mistakes of my life are many,
   And my spirit is sick with sin,
And I scarce can see for weeping,—
   But the Saviour will let me in.—Cho.

---

673   *"It is finished."*   TOPLADY.

Surely Christ thy grief has borne;
Weeping soul, no longer mourn:
View him bleeding on the tree,
Pouring out his life for thee.

2 Weary sinner, keep thine eyes
On the atoning sacrifice:
There the incarnate Deity,
Numbered with transgressors, see.

3 Cast thy guilty soul on him,
Find him mighty to redeem;
At his feet thy burden lay,
Look thy doubts and cares away.

4 Lord, thine arm must be revealed,
Ere I can by faith be healed;
Since I scarce can look to thee,
Cast a gracious eye on me.

LIFE.   8, 7, 7, or 8, 7, 4.

1. Come to Calvary's holy mountain, Sinners, ruined by the fall! Here a pure and healing fountain Flows to [you, to

me, to all,— In a full per-pet-ual tide, Opened when our Saviour died, Opened when our Saviour died.

MONTGOMERY.

674   *A Fountain Opened.*

2 Come, in sorrow and contrition,
   Wounded, impotent, and blind!
Here the guilty, free remission,
   Here the troubled, peace may find;
Health this fountain will restore,
He that drinks shall thirst no more.

3 He that drinks shall live for ever;
   'Tis a soul-renewing flood:
God is faithful; God will never
   Break his covenant in blood,
Signed when our Redeemer died,
Sealed when he was glorified.

HART.

675   "*Ho, every one.*"—*Isa.* 55:1.

Come, ye sinners, poor and wretched,
   Weak and wounded, sick and sore,

Jesus ready stands to save you,
   Full of pity, love and power.
He is able,
   He is willing, doubt no more.

2 Ho, ye needy; come, and welcome;
   God's free bounty glorify!
True belief and true repentance,
   Every grace that brings us nigh,
Without money,
   Come to Jesus Christ, and buy.

3 Let not conscience make you linger,
   Nor of fitness fondly dream;
All the fitness he requireth
   Is to feel your need of him;
This he gives you;
   'Tis the Spirit's rising beam.

GRACE.   8, 7, 4.

1. Come, ye sinners, poor and wretched, Weak and wounded, sick and sore, Je-sus ready stands to save you,
D. S. He is a-ble, he is a-ble,

FINE. Full of pi-ty, love and power. He is a-ble, he is a-ble, He is willing, doubt no more.
He is willing, doubt no more.

D. S.

AURELIA. 7, 6. D.

1. O Je-sus, thou art stand-ing Out-side the fast-closed door, In low-ly patience wait - ing To pass the threshold o'er: We bear the name of Christians, His name and sign we bear: Oh, shame, thrice shame up-on us! To keep him standing there.

676   *Jesus at the door.*   HOW.

O JESUS, thou art standing
  Outside the fast-closed door,
In lowly patience waiting
  To pass the threshold o'er:
We bear the name of Christians,
  His name and sign we bear:
Oh, shame, thrice shame upon us!
  To keep him standing there.

2 O Jesus, thou art knocking:
  And lo! that hand is scarred,
And thorns thy brow encircle,
  And tears thy face have marred:
Oh, love that passeth knowledge,
  So patiently to wait!
Oh, sin that hath no equal,
  So fast to bar the gate!

3 O Jesus, thou art pleading
  In accents meek and low,
"I died for you, my children,
  And will ye treat me so?"
O Lord, with shame and sorrow
  We open now the door:
Dear Saviour, enter, enter,
  And leave us nevermore!

677   *John* 6 : 68.   RAY PALMER.

WE stand in deep repentance,
  Before thy throne of love;
O God of grace, forgive us;
  The stain of guilt remove;
Behold us while with weeping
  We lift our eyes to thee;
And all our sins subduing,
  Our Father, set us free!

2 Oh, shouldst thou from us fallen
  Withhold thy grace to guide,
For ever we should wander,
  From thee, and peace, aside;
But thou to spirits contrite
  Dost light and life impart,
That man may learn to serve thee
  With thankful, joyous heart.

3 Our souls—on thee we cast them,
  Our only refuge thou!
Thy cheering words revive us,
  When pressed with grief we bow:
Thou bearest the trusting spirit
  Upon thy loving breast,
And givest all thy ransomed
  A sweet, unending rest.

WOODWORTH. L. M.

1. Just as I am, with-out one plea, But that thy blood was shed for me,

And that thou bid'st me come to thee, O Lamb of God, I come! I come!

678   *John* 1:29.   C. ELLIOTT.

Just as I am, without one plea,
But that thy blood was shed for me,
And that thou bid'st me come to thee,
O Lamb of God, I come! I come!

2 Just as I am, and waiting not
To rid my soul of one dark blot,
To thee whose blood can cleanse each spot,
O Lamb of God, I come! I come!

3 Just as I am, though tossed about
With many a conflict, many a doubt,
Fightings within, and fears without,
O Lamb of God, I come! I come!

4 Just as I am—poor, wretched, blind;
Sight, riches, healing of the mind,
Yea, all I need, in thee to find,
O Lamb of God, I come! I come!

5 Just as I am—thou wilt receive,
Wilt welcome, pardon, cleanse, relieve;
Because thy promise I believe,
O Lamb of God, I come! I come!

6 Just as I am—thy love unknown
Hath broken every barrier down;
Now, to be thine, yea, thine alone,
O Lamb of God, I come! I come!

679   "*Come to Me.*"—*Matt.* 11:28.   C. ELLIOTT.

With tearful eyes I look around;
Life seems a dark and stormy sea;
Yet, 'mid the gloom, I hear a sound,
A heavenly whisper, "Come to me!"

2 It tells me of a place of rest;
It tells me where my soul may flee:
Oh, to the weary, faint, oppressed,
How sweet the bidding, "Come to me!"

3 "Come, for all else must fail and die!
Earth is no resting-place for thee;
To heaven direct thy weeping eye,
I am thy portion; Come to me!"

4 O voice of mercy! voice of love!
In conflict, grief, and agony,
Support me, cheer me from above!
And gently whisper, "Come to me!"

680   "*I come.*"—*Ps.* 31:5.   ANON.

God of my life! thy boundless grace
Chose, pardoned, and adopted me;
My rest, my home, my dwelling-place;
Father! I come, I come to thee.

2 Jesus, my hope, my rock, my shield!
Whose precious blood was shed for me,
Into thy hands my soul I yield;
Saviour! I come, I come to thee.

3 Spirit of glory and of God!
Long hast thou deigned my guide to be;
Now be thy comfort sweet bestowed;
My God! I come, I come to thee.

4 I come to join that countless host
Who praise thy name unceasingly;
Blest Father, Son, and Holy Ghost!
My God! I come, I come to thee.

WARNER. L. M.

1. With bro - ken heart and con - trite sigh, A trembling sin - ner, Lord, I cry:

Thy pardoning grace is rich and free: O God, be mer - ci - ful to me!

681 "*Be merciful.*"—*Luke* 18: 13. C. ELVEN.

WITH broken heart and contrite sigh,
A trembling sinner, Lord, I cry:
Thy pardoning grace is rich and free:
O God, be merciful to me!

2 I smite upon my troubled breast,
With deep and conscious guilt oppressed;
Christ and his cross my only plea:
O God, be merciful to me!

3 Far off I stand with tearful eyes,
Nor dare uplift them to the skies;
But thou dost all my anguish see:
O God, be merciful to me!

4 Nor alms, nor deeds that I have done,
Can for a single sin atone;
To Calvary alone I flee:
O God, be merciful to me!

5 And when redeemed from sin and hell,
With all the ransomed throng I dwell,
My raptured song shall ever be,
God hath been merciful to me!

682 *Psalm* 130. WATTS.

FROM deep distress and troubled thoughts,
To thee, my God, I raise my cries;
If thou severely mark our faults,
No flesh can stand before thine eyes.

2 But thou hast built thy throne of grace,
Free to dispense thy pardons there;
That sinners may approach thy face,
And hope and love, as well as fear.

3 As the benighted pilgrims wait,
And long and wish for breaking day,
So waits my soul before thy gate:
When will my God his face display?

4 My trust is fixed upon thy word,
Nor shall I trust thy word in vain;
Let mourning souls address the Lord,
And find relief from all their pain.

5 Great is his love, and large his grace,
Through the redemption of his Son;
He turns our feet from sinful ways,
And pardons what our hands have done.

683 *Micah* 6: 6-8. C. WESLEY.

WHEREWITH, O God, shall I draw near,
And bow myself before thy face?
How, in thy purer eyes, appear?
What shall I bring to gain thy grace?

2 Can gifts avert the wrath of God?
Can these wash out my guilty stain?
Rivers of oil, and seas of blood,
Alas! they all must flow in vain.

3 Ev'n though my life henceforth be thine,
Present for past can ne'er atone:
Though I to thee the whole resign,
I only give thee back thine own.

4 Guilty I stand before thy face;
On me I feel thy wrath abide;
'Tis just the sentence should take place:
'Tis just,—but oh, thy Son hath died!

257

BLAKE. L. M.

1. Thou on - ly Sovereign of my heart, My Ref - uge, my al - might - y Friend—

And can my soul from thee de - part, On whom a - lone my hopes de-pend!

684   *"To whom shall we go?"*   STEELE.

Thou only Sovereign of my heart,
  My Refuge, my almighty Friend—
And can my soul from thee depart,
  On whom alone my hopes depend!

2 Whither, ah! whither shall I go,
  A wretched wanderer from my Lord?
Can this dark world of sin and woe
  One glimpse of happiness afford?

3 Eternal life thy words impart;
  On these my fainting spirit lives;
Here sweeter comforts cheer my heart,
  Than all the round of nature gives.

4 Thy name my inmost powers adore;
  Thou art my life, my joy, my care;
Depart from thee—'tis death, 'tis more;
  'Tis endless ruin, deep despair!

5 Low at thy feet my soul would lie;
  Here safety dwells, and peace divine;
Still let me live beneath thine eye,
  For life, eternal life, is thine.

635   1 *John* 5:4.   WATTS.

I send the joys of earth away;
  Away, ye tempters of the mind,
False as the smooth, deceitful sea,
  And empty as the whistling wind.

2 Your streams were floating me along,
  Down to the gulf of dark despair;
And while I listened to your song,
  Your streams had ev'n conveyed me there.

3 Lord, I adore thy matchless grace,
  Which warned me of that dark abyss,
Which drew me from those treacherous seas,
  And bade me seek superior bliss.

4 Now to the shining realms above,
  I stretch my hands and glance my eyes;
Oh, for the pinions of a dove,
  To bear me to the upper skies!

5 There, from the bosom of our God,
  Oceans of endless pleasure roll;
There would I fix my last abode,
  And drown the sorrows of my soul.

686   *"Thou hast died."*—*John* 15:5.   C. WESLEY.

Jesus, the sinner's Friend, to thee
Lost and undone, for aid I flee;
Weary of earth, myself, and sin,
Open thine arms and take me in.

2 Pity and save my ruined soul;
'Tis thou alone canst make me whole;
Dark, till in me thine image shine,
And lost I am, till thou art mine.

3 At last I own it cannot be
That I should fit myself for thee:
Here, then, to thee I all resign;
Thine is the work, and only thine.

4 What can I say thy grace to move?
Lord, I am sin,—but thou art love:
I give up every plea beside,
Lord, I am lost,—but thou hast died!

ERNAN. L. M.

1. No more, my God! I boast no more, Of all the du - ties I have done;

I quit the hopes I held be - fore, To trust the mer - its of thy Son.

687 *Philippians* 3: 7-10. WATTS.

No more, my God! I boast no more,
　Of all the duties I have done;
I quit the hopes I held before,
　To trust the merits of thy Son.

2 Now, for the love I bear his name,
　What was my gain, I count my loss;
My former pride I call my shame,
　And nail my glory to his cross.

3 Yes,—and I must, and will esteem
　All things but loss for Jesus' sake;
Oh, may my soul be found in him,
　And of his righteousness partake.

4 The best obedience of my hands
　Dares not appear before thy throne;
But faith can answer thy demands,
　By pleading what my Lord has done.

688 1 *Peter* 1: 12. HILLHOUSE.

Trembling before thine awful throne,
　O Lord! in dust my sins I own:
Justice and mercy for my life
　Contend!—oh, smile and heal the strife!

2 The Saviour smiles! upon my soul
　New tides of hope tumultuous roll—
His voice proclaims my pardon found—
　Seraphic transport wings the sound.

3 Earth has a joy unknown in heaven,
　The new-born peace of sin forgiven!
Tears of such pure and deep delight,
　Ye angels! never dimmed your sight.

4 Ye saw of old, on chaos rise
The beauteous pillars of the skies:
Ye know where morn exulting springs,
And evening folds her drooping wings.

5 Bright heralds of the eternal Will,
Abroad his errands ye fulfill;
Or, throned in floods of beamy day,
Symphonious, in his presence play.

6 But I amid your choirs shall shine,
And all your knowledge will be mine:
Ye on your harps must lean to hear
A secret chord that mine will bear.

689 *"Look unto me!"—Isaiah* 45: 22. MEDLEY.

See a poor sinner, dearest Lord,
Whose soul, encouraged by thy word,
At mercy's footstool would remain,
And then would look,—and look again.

2 Ah! bring a wretched wanderer home,
Now to thy footstool let me come,
And tell thee all my grief and pain,
And wait and look,—and look again!

3 Take courage, then, my trembling soul;
One look from Christ will make thee whole:
Trust thou in him, 'tis not in vain,
But wait and look,—and look again!

4 Ere long that happy day will come,
When I shall reach my blissful home;
And when to glory I attain,
Oh, then I'll look and look again!

AVON. C. M.

1. O thou, whose ten - der mer - cy hears Con - tri - tion's hum - ble sigh;

Whose hand in - dul - gent wipes the tears From sor - row's weep - ing eye;—

690   *"Return."—Hosea* 14:1.   STEELE.

O THOU, whose tender mercy hears
  Contrition's humble sigh;
Whose hand indulgent wipes the tears
  From sorrow's weeping eye;—

2 See, Lord, before thy throne of grace,
  A wretched wanderer mourn:
Hast thou not bid me seek thy face?
  Hast thou not said—"Return?"

3 And shall my guilty fears prevail
  To drive me from thy feet?
Oh, let not this dear refuge fail,
  This only safe retreat!

4 Oh, shine on this benighted heart,
  With beams of mercy shine!
And let thy healing voice impart
  The sense of joy divine.

691   *"Weary, heavy-laden."*   NEWTON.

APPROACH, my soul! the mercy-seat,
  Where Jesus answers prayer;
There humbly fall before his feet,
  For none can perish there.

2 Thy promise is my only plea,
  With this I venture nigh:
Thou callest burdened souls to thee,
  And such, O Lord! am I.

3 Bowed down beneath a load of sin,
  By Satan sorely pressed;
By wars without, and fears within,
  I come to thee for rest.

4 Be thou my shield and hiding-place,
  That, sheltered near thy side,
I may my fierce accuser face,
  And tell him—thou hast died.

5 Oh, wondrous Love—to bleed and die,
  To bear the cross and shame,
That guilty sinners, such as I,
  Might plead thy gracious name!

692   *"His great love."—Eph.* 2:4.   BROWNE.

LORD! at thy feet we sinners lie,
  And knock at mercy's door:
With heavy heart and downcast eye,
  Thy favor we implore.

2 On us the vast extent display
  Of thy forgiving love;
Take all our heinous guilt away;
  This heavy load remove.

3 'Tis mercy—mercy we implore;
  We would thy pity move:
Thy grace is an exhaustless store,
  And thou thyself art love.

4 Oh, for thine own, for Jesus' sake,
  Our numerous sins forgive!
Thy grace our rocky hearts can break:
  Heal us, and bid us live.

5 Thus melt us all, thus make us bend,
  And thy dominion own;
Nor let a rival more pretend
  To repossess thy throne.

CHESTERFIELD. C. M.

1. Oh, that I knew the se - cret place, Where I might find my God!
I'd spread my wants be - fore his face, And pour my woes a - broad.

693 *Job 23: 3, 4.* WATTS.

OH, that I knew the sacred place,
  Where I might find my God!
I'd spread my wants before his face,
  And pour my woes abroad.

2 I'd tell him how my sins arise,
  What sorrows I sustain;
How grace decays, and comfort dies,
  And leaves my heart in pain.

3 He knows what arguments I'd take
  To wrestle with my God:
I'd plead for his own mercy's sake—
  I'd plead my Saviour's blood.

4 My God will pity my complaints;
  And drive my foes away;
He knows the meaning of his saints
  When they in sorrow pray.

5 Arise, my soul! from deep distress,
  And banish every fear;
He calls thee to his throne of grace,
  To spread thy sorrow there.

694 *Deep Penitence.* STENNETT.

PROSTRATE, dear Jesus! at thy feet,
  A guilty rebel lies;
And upwards, to thy mercy-seat,
  Presumes to lift his eyes.

2 Let not thy justice frown me hence;
  Oh, stay the vengeful storm;
Forbid it, that Omnipotence
  Should crush a feeble worm.

3 If tears of sorrow could suffice
  To pay the debt I owe,
Tears should, from both my weeping eyes,
  In ceaseless currents flow.

4 But no such sacrifice I plead
  To expiate my guilt;
No tears, but those which thou hast shed,—
  No blood, but thou hast spilt.

5 Think of thy sorrows, dearest Lord!
  And all my sins forgive;
Then justice will approve the word,
  That bids the sinner live.

695 *" Trembleth at my word."* C. WESLEY.

OH, for that tenderness of heart,
  That bows before the Lord;
That owns how just and good thou art,
  And trembles at thy word.

2 Oh, for those humble, contrite tears,
  Which from repentance flow;
That sense of guilt which, trembling, fears
  The long-suspended blow!

3 Saviour! to me, in pity give,
  For sin, the deep distress;
The pledge thou wilt, at last, receive,
  And bid me die in peace.

4 Oh, fill my soul with faith and love,
  And strength to do thy will;
Raise my desires and hopes above,—
  Thyself to me reveal.

261

EVEN ME. P. M.

696 *"Rain on mown Grass."* CODNER.

Lord, I hear of showers of blessing
Thou art scattering full and free;
Showers the thirsty soul refreshing;
Let some droppings fall on me!—REF.

2 Pass me not, O gracious Father!
Lost and sinful though I be;
Thou might'st curse me, but the rather
Let thy mercy light on me.—REF.

3 Have I long in sin been sleeping?
Long been slighting, grieving thee!
Has the world my heart been keeping,
Oh, forgive and rescue me!—REF.

4 Pass me not, O mighty Spirit!
Thou canst make the blind to see;
Testify of Jesus' merit,
Speak the word of peace to me.—REF.

PASS ME NOT. 8, 5.

697 *"A blessing for me also."* CROSBY.

Pass me not, O gentle Saviour,
Hear my humble cry;
While on others thou art smiling,
Do not pass me by.—CHO.

2 Let me at a throne of mercy
Find a sweet relief;

Kneeling there in deep contrition,
Help my unbelief.—CHO.

3 Trusting only in thy merit,
Would I seek thy face;
Heal my wounded, broken spirit,
Save me by thy grace.—CHO.

I NEED THEE. P. M.

1. I need thee ev - ery hour, Most gra - cious Lord; No ten-der voice like thine

REFRAIN.

Can peace af - ford, I need thee, oh, I need thee; Ev - ery hour I

need thee; Oh, bless me now, my Sav - iour! I come to thee.

---

698 *"I need thee."* MRS. HAWKS.

I NEED thee every hour,
  Most gracious Lord;
No tender voice like thine
  Can peace afford.
REF.—I need thee, oh, I need thee;
    Every hour I need thee;
  Oh, bless me now, my Saviour!
    I come to thee.

2 I need thee every hour;
  Stay thou near by;
Temptations lose their power
  When thou art nigh.—REF.

3 I need thee every hour,
  In joy or pain;
Come quickly and abide
  Or life is vain.—REF.

4 I need thee every hour;
  Teach me thy will;
And thy rich promises
  In me fulfill.—REF.

5 I need thee every hour,
  Most Holy One;
Oh, make me thine indeed,
  Thou blesséd Son.—REF.

699 *"Jesus hath died."* BONAR.

No, not despairingly
  Come I to thee;
No, not distrustingly
  Bend I the knee;
Sin hath gone over me,
Yet is this still my plea,
Yet is this still my plea,
  Jesus hath died.

2 Lord! I confess to thee
  Sadly my sin;
All I am tell I thee,
  All I have been;
Purge thou my sin away,
Wash thou my soul this day;
Wash thou my soul this day;
  Lord! make me clean.

3 Faithful and just art thou,
  Forgiving all;
Loving and kind art thou
  When poor ones call;
Lord! let the cleansing blood,
Blood of the Lamb of God,
Blood of the Lamb of God,
  Pass o'er my soul!

PENITENCE.   7, 6, 8.

1. Je-sus, let thy pitying eye   Call back a wandering sheep; False to thee, like Pe-ter, I
D. S. Turn, and look up-on me, Lord

FINE.

Would fain like Pe-ter weep!   Let me   be   by grace restored, On me   be all long-suffering shown,
And break my heart of stone.

700   *"My heart of stone."*   C. WESLEY.

2 Saviour, Prince, enthroned above,
  Repentance to impart,
Give me, through thy dying love,
  The humble, contrite heart:
Give what I have long implored,
  A portion of thy grief unknown;
Turn, and look upon me, Lord!
  And break my heart of stone.

701   *"Jesus Only."*   C. WESLEY.

Vain, delusive world, adieu,
  With all of creature good!
Only Jesus I pursue,
  Who bought me with his blood:
All thy pleasures I forego;
  I trample on thy wealth and pride;
Only Jesus will I know,
  And Jesus crucified.

2 Other knowledge I disdain;
  'Tis all but vanity:
Christ, the Lamb of God, was slain,—
  He tasted death for me.
Me to save from endless woe,
  The sin-atoning Victim died:
Only Jesus will I know,
  And Jesus, crucified.

NEAR THE CROSS.   7, 6.

1. Jesus, keep me near the Cross, There a precious fountain. Free to all a healing stream, Flows from Calvary's [mountain.

CHORUS.

In the Cross, In the Cross Be my glo-ry ever, Till my raptured soul shall find Rest beyond the river.

702   *"Near the Cross."*   CROSBY.

2 Near the Cross, a trembling soul,
  Love and mercy found me;
There the bright and morning star
264   Sheds its beams around me.—Cho.

3 Near the Cross! oh, Lamb of God,
  Bring its scenes before me;
Help me walk from day to day,
  With its shadow o'er me.—Cho.

HYMN OF JOY. 8, 7. D.

1. Take me, O my Father, take me! Take me, save me, through thy Son; That which thou wouldst have me, make me, Let thy will in me be done. Long from thee my foot-steps straying, Thorny proved the way I trod; Weary come I now, and praying—Take me to thy love, my God!

703   *"Father, take me!"*   RAY PALMER.

Take me, O my Father, take me!
  Take me, save me, through thy Son;
That which thou wouldst have me, make me,
  Let thy will in me be done.
Long from thee my footsteps straying,
  Thorny proved the way I trod;
Weary come I now, and praying—
  Take me to thy love, my God!

2 Fruitless years with grief recalling,
  Humbly I confess my sin;
At thy feet, O Father, falling,
  To thy household take me in.
Freely now to thee I proffer
  This relenting heart of mine;
Freely life and soul I offer—
  Gift unworthy love like thine.

3 Once the world's Redeemer dying,
  Bare our sins upon the tree;
On that sacrifice relying,
  Now I look in hope to thee;
Father, take me! all forgiving
  Fold me to thy loving breast;
In thy love for ever living,
  I must be for ever blest!

704   *"The Lord pitieth.—Ps.* **103:13.**   TURNER.

Jesus! full of all compassion,
  Hear thy humble suppliant's cry,
Let me know thy great salvation;
  See, I languish, faint and die;
Guilty, but with heart relenting,
  Overwhelmed with helpless grief,
Prostrate at thy feet repenting,
  Send, oh send me quick relief!

2 Whither should a wretch be flying
  But to him who comfort gives?
Whither from the dread of dying
  But to him who ever lives?
While I view thee, wounded, grieving,
  Breathless on the cursèd tree,
Fain I'd feel my heart believing
  Thou didst suffer thus for me.

3 With thy righteousness and Spirit
  I am more than angels blessed;
Heir with thee, all things inherit,
  Peace and joy and endless rest:
Saved! the deed shall spread new glory
  Through the shining realms above;
Angels sing the pleasing story,
  All enraptured with thy love.

NUREMBURG. 7. 6l.

Once I thought my moun-tain strong, Firm-ly fixed no more to move;
Then my Sav-iour was my song, Then my soul was filled with love;

Those were hap-py, gold-en days, Sweet-ly spent in prayer and praise.

705   *Backsliding confessed.*   NEWTON.

ONCE I thought my mountain strong,
  Firmly fixed no more to move;
Then my Saviour was my song,
  Then my soul was filled with love;
Those were happy, golden days,
Sweetly spent in prayer and praise.

2 Little then myself I knew,
    Little thought of Satan's power;
  Now I feel my sins anew;
    Now I feel the stormy hour!
  Sin has put my joys to flight;
  Sin has turned my day to night.

3 Saviour, shine and cheer my soul,
    Bid my dying hopes revive;
  Make my wounded spirit whole,
    Far away the tempter drive;
  Speak the word and set me free,
  Let me live alone to thee.

706   *Psalm 31.*   LYTE.

LORD! I look for all to thee;
Thou hast been a rock to me:
Still thy wonted aid afford:
Still be near, my shield, my sword!
I my soul commit to thee,
Lord! thy blood has ransomed me.

2 Faint and sinking on my road,
  Still I cling to thee, my God!
  Bending 'neath a weight of woes,
  Harassed by a thousand foes,
  Hope still chides my rising fears;
  Joys still mingle with my tears.

266

3 On thy word I take my stand:
  All my times are in thy hand:
  Make thy face upon me shine;
  Take me 'neath thy wings divine;
  Lord! thy grace is all my trust;
  Save, oh, save thy trembling dust.

4 Oh, what mercies still attend
  Those who make the Lord their friend!
  Sweetly, safely shall they 'bide
  'Neath his eye, and at his side:
  Lord! may this my station be:
  Seek it, all ye saints! with me.

707   *Psalm 123.*   BOWDLER.

LORD, before thy throne we bend;
Now to thee our prayers ascend:
Servants to our Master true,
Lo! we yield thee homage due:
Children, to thy throne we fly,
Abba, Father, hear our cry!

2 Low before thee, Lord! we bow,
  We are weak—but mighty thou:
  Sore distressed, yet suppliant still,
  Here we wait thy holy will;
  Bound to earth, and rooted here,
  Till our Saviour God appear.

3 Leave us not beneath the power
  Of temptation's darkest hour:
  Swift to seal their captives' doom,
  See our foes exulting come!
  Jesus, Saviour! yet be nigh,
  Lord of life and victory.

THARAU. 7. 6l.

1. {Wea - ry, Lord, of strug-gling here   With this cons-tant doubt and fear, }
   {Bur - dened by the pains I bear,   And the tri - als I must share— }

Help me, Lord, a - gain to flee   To the rest that's found in thee.

708   *"Weary, Lord."*   RANDOLPH.

WEARY, Lord, of struggling here
With this constant doubt and fear,
Burdened by the pains I bear,
And the trials I must share—
· Help me, Lord, again to flee
To the rest that's found in thee.

2 Weakened by the wayward will
Which controls, yet cheats me still;
Seeking something undefined
With an earnest, darkened mind—
Help me, Lord, again to flee
To the light that breaks from thee.

3 Fettered by this earthly scope
In the reach and aim of hope,
Fixing thought in narrow bound
Where no living truth is found—
Help me, Lord, again to flee
To the hope that's fixed in thee.

4 Fettered, burdened, wearied, weak,
Lord, once more thy grace I seek;
Turn, oh, turn me not away,
Help me, Lord, to watch and pray—
That I never more may flee
From the rest that's found in thee.

709   *"Hearer of prayer."*   CONDER.

O THOU God who hearest prayer
Every hour and everywhere!
For his sake, whose blood I plead,
Hear me in my hour of need: ·
Only hide not now thy face,
God of all-sufficient grace!

2 Hear and save me, gracious Lord!
For my trust is in thy word;
Wash me from the stain of sin,
That thy peace may rule within:
May I know myself thy child,
Ransomed, pardoned, reconciled.

710   *"The Lamb of God."*   RAY PALMER.

JESUS, Lamb of God, for me
Thou, the Lord of life, didst die;
Whither—whither, but to thee,
Can a trembling sinner fly!
Death's dark waters o'er me roll,
Save, oh, save my sinking soul!

2 Never bowed a martyr's head
Weighed with equal sorrow down;
Never blood so rich was shed,
Never king wore such a crown;
To thy cross and sacrifice
Faith now lifts her tearful eyes.

3 All my soul, by love subdued,
Melts in deep contrition there;
By thy mighty grace renewed,
New-born hope forbids despair:
Lord! thou canst my guilt forgive,
Thou hast bid me look and live.

4 While with broken heart I kneel,
Sinks the inward storm to rest;
Life—immortal life—I feel
Kindled in my throbbing breast;
Thine—for ever thine—I am!
Glory to thee, bleeding Lamb!

COOLING. C. M.

1. Sweet was the time when first I felt The Sav - iour's pardoning blood

Ap - plied to cleanse my soul from guilt, And bring me home to God.

711   *"Where is the blessedness?"*   NEWTON.

SWEET was the time when first I felt
The Saviour's pardoning blood
Applied to cleanse my soul from guilt,
And bring me home to God.

2 Soon as the morn the light revealed,
His praises tuned my tongue;
And, when the evening shade prevailed,
His love was all my song.

3 In prayer, my soul drew near the Lord,
And saw his glory shine;
And when I read his holy word,
I called each promise mine.

4 Now, when the evening shade prevails,
My soul in darkness mourns;
And when the morn the light reveals,
No light to me returns.

5 Rise, Saviour! help me to prevail,
And make my soul thy care;
I know thy mercy cannot fail,
Let me that mercy share.

712   *"Never was a heart so base."*   STENNETT.

WITH tears of anguish I lament,
Here, at thy feet, my God,
My passion, pride, and discontent,
And vile ingratitude.

2 Sure, never was a heart so base,
So false as mine has been;
So faithless to its promises,
So prone to every sin.

268

3 Reason, I hear, her counsels weigh,
And all her words approve;
But still I find it hard to obey,
And harder yet to love.

4 How long, dear Saviour, shall I feel
These struggles in my breast?
When wilt thou bow my stubborn will,
And give my conscience rest?

5 Break, sovereign grace, oh, break the charm,
And set the captive free;
Reveal, almighty God, thine arm,
And haste to rescue me.

713   *"Nearer to thee."*   CLEVELAND.

OH, could I find, from day to day
A nearness to my God,
Then would my hours glide sweet away
While leaning on his word.

2 Lord, I desire with thee to live
Anew from day to day,
In joys the world can never give,
Nor ever take away.

3 Blest Jesus, come and rule my heart,
And make me wholly thine,
That I may never more depart,
Nor grieve thy love divine.

4 Thus, till my last, expiring breath,
Thy goodness I'll adore;
And when my frame dissolves in death,
My soul shall love thee more.

HERMON. C. M.

1. Oh, for a clos-er walk with God, A calm and heaven - ly frame,—
A light to shine up - on the road That leads me to the Lamb!

714   *The closer walk.*   COWPER.

Oh, for a closer walk with God,
  A calm and heavenly frame,—
A light to shine upon the road
  That leads me to the Lamb!

2 Where is the blessedness I knew
  When first I saw the Lord?
Where is the soul-refreshing view
  Of Jesus and his word?

3 What peaceful hours I once enjoyed!
  How sweet their memory still!
But they have left an aching void
  The world can never fill.

4 Return, O holy Dove, return,
  Sweet messenger of rest!
I hate the sins that made thee mourn,
  And drove thee from my breast.

5 The dearest idol I have known,
  Whate'er that idol be,
Help me to tear it from thy throne,
  And worship only thee.

6 So shall my walk be close with God,
  Calm and serene my frame;
So purer light shall mark the road
  That leads me to the Lamb.

715   *"This wretched heart!"*   STEELE.

How oft, alas! this wretched heart
  Has wandered from the Lord!
How oft my roving thoughts depart,
  Forgetful of his word!

2 Yet sovereign mercy calls—"Return!"
  Dear Lord, and may I come?
My vile ingratitude I mourn:
  Oh, take the wanderer home!

3 And canst thou,—wilt thou yet forgive,
  And bid my crimes remove?
And shall a pardoned rebel live,
  To speak thy wondrous love?

4 Almighty grace, thy healing power,
  How glorious, how divine!
That can to life and bliss restore
  A heart so vile as mine.

5 Thy pardoning love, so free, so sweet,
  Dear Saviour, I adore;
Oh, keep me at thy sacred feet,
  And let me rove no more!

716   *"Search me, O God."*   MORRIS.

SEARCHER of hearts! from mine erase
  All thoughts that should not be,
And in its deep recesses trace
  My gratitude to thee!

2 Hearer of prayer! oh, guide aright
  Each word and deed of mine;
Life's battle teach me how to fight,
  And be the victory thine.

3 Father, and Son, and Holy Ghost!
  Thou glorious Three in One!
Thou knowest best what I need most,
  And let thy will be done.

CADDO. C. M.

1. O thou, from whom all good - ness flows, I lift my soul to thee;

In all my sor - rows, con - flicts, woes, O Lord, re - mem - ber me!

717   *"Remember me."—Luke* **23: 42.**   HAWEIS.

O THOU, from whom all goodness flows,
  I lift my soul to thee;
In all my sorrows, conflicts, woes,
  O Lord, remember me?

2 When on my aching, burdened heart
  My sins lie heavily,
Thy pardon grant, new peace impart;
  Thus, Lord, remember me!

3 When trials sore obstruct my way,
  And ills I cannot flee,
Oh, let my strength be as my day—
  Dear Lord, remember me!

4 When in the solemn hour of death
  I wait thy just decree;
Be this the prayer of my last breath:
  Now, Lord, remember me!

718   *"What hourly dangers!"*   STEELE.

ALAS! what hourly dangers rise!
  What snares beset my way!
To heaven, oh, let me lift mine eyes,
  And hourly watch and pray.

2 How oft my mournful thoughts complain,
  And melt in flowing tears!
My weak resistance, ah, how vain!
  How strong my foes and fears!

3 O gracious God! in whom I live,
  My feeble efforts aid;
Help me to watch, and pray, and strive,
  Though trembling and afraid.

4 Increase my faith, increase my hope,
  When foes and fears prevail;
And bear my fainting spirit up,
  Or soon my strength will fail.

5 Oh, keep me in thy heavenly way,
  And bid the tempter flee!
And let me never, never stray
  From happiness and thee.

719   *Long-suffering.—Rom.* **2: 4.**   STEELE.

DEAR Saviour, when my thoughts recall
  The wonders of thy grace,
Low at thy feet ashamed, I fall,
  And hide this wretched face.

2 Shall love like thine be thus repaid?
  Ah, vile, ungrateful heart!
By earth's low cares so oft betrayed,
  From Jesus to depart.

3 But he for his own mercy's sake,
  My wandering soul restores;
He bids the mourning heart partake
  The pardon it implores.

4 Oh, while I breathe to thee, my Lord,
  The deep repentant sigh,
Confirm the kind, forgiving word,
  With pity in thine eye.

5 Then shall the mourner at thy feet
  Rejoice to seek thy face;
And grateful, own how kind, how sweet,
  Thy condescending grace.

EXHORTATION. C. M.

1. Oh, for a heart to praise my God, A heart from sin set free; A heart that's sprinkled with the blood So free-ly shed for me! A heart that's sprinkled with the blood So free-ly shed for me! A heart that's sprinkled with the blood So free-ly shed for me! A heart that's sprinkled with the blood

C. WESLEY.

720 *"A clean heart."—Ps. 51: 10.*

Oh, for a heart to praise my God,
    A heart from sin set free;
A heart that's sprinkled with the blood
    So freely shed for me!

2 A heart resigned, submissive, meek,
    My dear Redeemer's throne;
Where only Christ is heard to speak,
    Where Jesus reigns alone!

3 Oh, for a lowly, contrite heart,
    Believing, true, and clean!
Which neither life nor death can part
    From him that dwells within.

4 A heart in every thought renewed,
    And filled with love divine;
Perfect, and right, and pure, and good;
    An image, Lord! of thine.

5 Thy nature, gracious Lord! impart;
    Come quickly from above;
Write thy new name upon my heart,—
    Thy new, best name of Love.

C. WESLEY.

721 *Thanks for victory.*

Oh, for a thousand tongues to sing
    My dear Redeemer's praise!
The glories of my God and King,
    The triumphs of his grace!

2 My gracious Master and my God!
    Assist me to proclaim,
To spread, through all the earth abroad,
    The honors of thy name.

3 Jesus—the name that calms my fears,
    That bids my sorrows cease;
'Tis music to my ravished ears;
    'Tis life, and health, and peace.

4 He breaks the power of reigning sin,
    He sets the prisoner free;
His blood can make the foulest clean;
    His blood availed for me.

5 Let us obey, we then shall know,
    Shall feel our sins forgiven;
Anticipate our heaven below,
    And own, that love is heaven.

271

ALETTA. 7.

1. Depth of mer - cy!—can there be Mer - cy still re - served for me?

Can my God his wrath for - bear? Me, the chief of sin - ners, spare?

722   *"My repentings are kindled."*   C. WESLEY.

Depth of mercy!—can there be
Mercy still reserved for me?
Can my God his wrath forbear?
Me, the chief of sinners, spare?

2 I have long withstood his grace;
Long provoked him to his face;
Would not hearken to his calls;
Grieved him by a thousand falls.

3 Kindled his relentings are;
Me he now delights to spare;
Cries, How shall I give thee up?—
Let the lifted thunder drop.

4 There for me the Saviour stands;
Shows his wounds and spreads his hands!
God is love! I know, I feel;
Jesus weeps, and loves me still.

723   *" God of mercy."*   J. TAYLOR.

God of mercy! God of grace!
   Hear our sad, repentant song;
Sorrow dwells on every face,
   Penitence on every tongue.

2 Foolish fears and fond desires,
   Vain regrets for things as vain;
Lips too seldom taught to praise,
   Oft to murmur and complain;—

3 These, and every secret fault,
   Filled with grief and shame we own;
Humbled at thy feet we lie,
   Seeking pardon from thy throne.

272

724   *"In wrath, remember mercy."*   RAFFLES.

Sovereign Ruler, Lord of all!
Prostrate at thy feet I fall!
Hear, oh, hear my earnest cry,
Frown not, lest I faint and die.

2 Justly might thy righteous dart
Pierce this bleeding, broken heart;
Justly might thy angry breath
Blast me in eternal death.

3 But with thee there's mercy found,
Balm to heal my every wound:
Soothe, oh, soothe the troubled breast,
Give the weary wanderer rest.

725   *" My dying soul."*   HASTINGS.

Jesus, save my dying soul;
Make the broken spirit whole:
Humble in the dust I lie:
Saviour, leave me not to die.

2 Jesus, full of every grace,
Now reveal thy smiling face;
Grant the joy of sin forgiven,
Foretaste of the bliss of heaven.

3 All my guilt to thee is known;
Thou art righteous, thou alone:
All my help is from thy cross,
All beside I count but loss.

4 Lord, in thee I now believe;
Wilt thou, wilt thou not forgive?
Helpless at thy feet I lie;
Saviour, leave me not to die.

TRUSTING. 7.

I am com-ing to the cross; I am poor and weak and blind;
CHO.—I am trust-ing, Lord, in thee, Dear Lamb of Cal-va-ry;

I am count-ing all but dross; I shall full sal-va-tion find.
Hum-bly at thy cross I bow; Save me, Je-sus, save me now.

726   *"Cleanseth from all sin."*   MCDONALD;

I AM coming to the cross;
  I am poor and weak and blind;
I am counting all but dross;
  I shall full salvation find.—CHO.

2 Long my heart has sighed for thee;
  Long has evil dwelt within;
Jesus sweetly speaks to me,
  I will cleanse you from all sin.—CHO.

3 Here I give my all to thee,—
  Friends and time and earthly store;
Soul and body thine to be—
  Wholly thine for evermore.—CHO.

4 In the promises I trust;
  Now I feel the blood applied;
I am prostrate in the dust;
  I with Christ am crucified.—CHO.

727   *"Come unto Me."*   NEWTON.

DOES the Gospel word proclaim
  Rest for those that weary be?
Then, my soul, advance thy claim—
  Sure that promise speaks to thee!

2 Burdened with a load of sin,
  Harrassed with tormenting doubt,
Hourly conflicts from within,
  Hourly crosses from without;—

3 All my little strength is gone,
  Sink I must without supply;
Sure upon the earth is none
  Can more weary be than I.

4 In the ark the weary dove
  Found a welcome resting-place;
Thus my spirit longs to prove
  Rest in Christ, the Ark of grace.

5 Tempest-tossed I long have been,
  And the flood increases fast;
Open, Lord, and take me in,
  Till the storm be overpast!

728   *"Lovest thou Me?"*   NEWTON.

'TIS a point I long to know,
  Oft it causes anxious thought;
Do I love the Lord, or no?
  Am I his, or am I not?

2 Could my heart so hard remain,
  Prayer a task and burden prove,
Every trifle give me pain,
  If I knew a Saviour's love?

3 Yet I mourn my stubborn will,
  Find my sin a grief and thrall;
Should I grieve for what I feel,
  If I did not love at all?

4 Could I joy with saints to meet,
  Choose the ways I once abhorred,
Find at times the promise sweet,
  If I did not love the Lord?

5 Lord, decide the doubtful case,
  Thou who art thy people's Sun;
Shine upon thy work of grace,
  If it be indeed begun.

REFUGE. 7. D.

C. WESLEY.

729   *"Thy billows are gone over me."*

Jesus! lover of my soul,
  Let me to thy bosom fly
While the billows near me roll,
  While the tempest still is high;
Hide me, O my Saviour! hide,
  Till the storm of life is past;
Safe into the haven guide;
  Oh, receive my soul at last!

2 Other refuge have I none;
  Hangs my helpless soul on thee;
Leave, ah! leave me not alone,
  Still support and comfort me.
All my trust on thee is stayed;
  All my help from thee I bring;
Cover my defenceless head
  With the shadow of thy wing.

3 Thou, O Christ! art all I want;
  More than all in thee I find;
Raise the fallen, cheer the faint,
  Heal the sick, and lead the blind.
Just and holy is thy name,
  I am all unrighteousness;
Vile and full of sin I am,
  Thou art full of truth and grace.

4 Plenteous grace with thee is found,—
  Grace to pardon all my sin;
Let the healing streams abound,
  Make and keep me pure within;
Thou of life the fountain art,
  Freely let me take of thee;
Spring thou up within my heart,
  Rise to all eternity.

MARTYN. 7. D.

HOLLINGSIDE. 7. D.

1. Je-sus, mer-ci-ful and mild, Lead me as a helpless child: On no oth-er arm but thine

Would my wea-ry soul re-cline; Thou art read-y to for-give, Thou canst bid the

sin-ner live— Guide the wanderer, day by day, In the straight and nar-row way.

730   *"Lead me."—Ps.* 31: 3.   HASTINGS.

JESUS, merciful and mild,
Lead me as a helpless child:
On no other arm but thine
Would my weary soul recline;
Thou art ready to forgive,
Thou canst bid the sinner live—
Guide the wanderer, day by day,
In the strait and narrow way.

2 Thou canst fit me by thy grace
For the heavenly dwelling-place;
All thy promises are sure,
Ever shall thy love endure;
Then what more could I desire,
How to greater bliss aspire?
All I need, in thee I see,
Thou art all in all to me.

3 Jesus, Saviour all divine,
Hast thou made me truly thine?
Hast thou bought me by thy blood?
Reconciled my heart to God?
Hearken to my tender prayer,
Let me thine own image bear;
Let me love thee more and more,
Till I reach heaven's blissful shore.

731   *" Jesus, visit me!"*   DUNN. *Tr.*

JESUS, Jesus! visit me;
How my soul longs after thee!
When, my best, my dearest Friend!
Shall our separation end?
Lord! my longings never cease;
Without thee I find no peace;
'T is my constant cry to thee,—
Jesus, Jesus! visit me.

2 Mean the joys of earth appear,
All below is dark and drear;
Naught but thy belovéd voice
Can my wretched heart rejoice.
Thou alone, my gracious Lord!
Art my shield and great reward;
All my hope, my Saviour thou,—
To thy sovereign will I bow.

3 Come, inhabit then my heart;
Purge its sin, and heal its smart;
See, I ever cry to thee,—
Jesus, Jesus! visit me.
Patiently I wait the day;
For this gift alone I pray,
That, when death shall visit me,
Thou my Light and Life wilt be.

275

BENEVENTO. 7. D.

1. Saviour, when in dust, to thee Low we bow th' ador-ing knee; When, repentant, to the skies
D. S. Bending from thy throne on high,

FINE.

Scarce we lift our weeping eyes: Oh, by all thy pains and woe, Suffered once for man be-low,
Hear our solemn Lit - a - ny!

732   *The Ancient Litany.*   GRANT.

SAVIOUR, when in dust, to thee
Low we bow the adoring knee;
When, repentant, to the skies
Scarce we lift our weeping eyes;
Oh, by all thy pains and woe
Suffered once for man below,
Bending from thy throne on high,
Hear our solemn Litany!

2 By thy helpless infant years,
By thy life of want and tears,
By thy days of sore distress
In the savage wilderness;
By the dread mysterious hour
Of the insulting tempter's power,
Turn, oh, turn a favoring eye;
Hear our solemn Litany!

3 By thine hour of dire despair;
By thine agony of prayer;
By the cross, the nail, the thorn,
Piercing spear, and torturing scorn;
By the gloom that vailed the skies
O'er the dreadful sacrifice;
Listen to our humble cry,
Hear our solemn Litany!

4 By thy deep expiring groan;
By the sad sepulchral stone;
By the vault, whose dark abode
Held in vain the rising God;

Oh, from earth to heaven restored,
Mighty re-ascending Lord!
Listen, listen to the cry
Of our solemn Litany!

733   *" Without, fightings ; within, fears."*   BONAR.

OH, this soul, how dark and blind!
Oh, this foolish, earthly mind!
Oh, this froward, selfish will,
Which refuses to be still!
Oh, these ever-roaming eyes,
Upward that refuse to rise!
Oh, these wayward feet of mine,
Found in every path but thine!

2 Oh, this stubborn, prayerless knee,
Hands so seldom clasped to thee,
Longings of the soul, that go
Like the wild wind, to and fro!
To and fro, without an aim,
Turning idly whence they came,
Bringing in no joy, no bliss,
Only adding weariness!

3 Giver of the heavenly peace!
Bid, oh, bid these tumults cease;
Minister thy holy balm;
Fill me with thy Spirit's calm:
Thou, the Life, the Truth, the Way,
Leave me not in sin to stay;
Bearer of the sinner's guilt,
Lead me, lead me, as thou wilt.

MESSIAH. 7. D.

1. Brethren, while we sojourn here, Fight we must, but should not fear ; Foes we have, but we've a Friend,

One that loves us to the end : Forward, then, with cour - age go ; Long we shall not

dwell be - low ; Soon the joy - ful news will come, "Child, your Father calls—come home !"

ANON.

FRANCKE.

734   *"Child, your Father calls."*

BRETHREN, while we sojourn here,
Fight we must, but should not fear;
Foes we have, but we've a Friend,
One that loves us to the end:
Forward, then, with courage go;
Long we shall not dwell below;
Soon the joyful news will come,
"Child, your Father calls—come home!"

2 In the way a thousand snares
Lie, to take us unawares;
Satan, with malicious art,
Watches each unguarded part:
But, from Satan's malice free,
Saints shall soon victorious be;
Soon the joyful news will come,
"Child, your Father calls—come home!"

3 But of all the foes we meet,
None so oft mislead our feet,
None betray us into sin
Like the foes that dwell within;
Yet let nothing spoil our peace,
Christ shall also conquer these;
Soon the joyful news will come,
"Child, your Father calls—come home!"

735   *"Thou art my rock."*

LORD, thou art my rock of strength,
And my home is in thine arms;
Thou wilt send me help at length,
And I feel no wild alarms:
Sin nor death can pierce the shield
Thy defence has o'er me thrown,
Up to thee myself I yield,
And my sorrows are thine own.

2 When my trials tarry long
Unto thee I look and wait;
Knowing none, though keen and strong,
Can my trust in thee abate;
And this faith I long have nursed,
Comes alone, O God, from thee;
Thou my heart didst open first,
Thou didst set this hope in me.

3 Let thy mercy's wings be spread
O'er me, keep me close to thee;
In the peace thy love doth shed,
Let me dwell eternally!
Be my all: in all I do,
Let me only seek thy will;
Let my heart to thee be true
And thus peaceful, calm, and still.

277

MISSIONARY CHANT. L. M.

1. Stand up, my soul, shake off thy fears, And gird the gos-pel ar-mor on;
March to the gates of end-less joy, Where Je-sus, thy great Captain's gone.

736   *Ephesians* **6 : 14.**   WATTS.

Stand up, my soul, shake off thy fears,
  And gird the gospel armor on;
March to the gates of endless joy,
  Where Jesus, thy great Captain's gone.

2 Hell and thy sins resist thy course;
  But hell and sin are vanquished foes;
Thy Saviour nailed them to the cross,
  And sung the triumph when he rose.

3 Then let my soul march boldly on,—
  Press forward to the heavenly gate;
There peace and joy eternal reign,
  And glittering robes for conquerors wait.

4 There shall I wear a starry crown,
  And triumph in almighty grace,
While all the armies of the skies
  Join in my glorious Leader's praise.

737   *Isaiah* **40 : 28-31.**   WATTS.

Awake, our souls! away, our fears!
  Let every trembling thought be gone;
Awake, and run the heavenly race,
  And put a cheerful courage on!

2 True, 'tis a strait and thorny road,
  And mortal spirits tire and faint;
But they forget the mighty God,
  Who feeds the strength of every saint—

3 The mighty God, whose matchless power
  Is ever new and ever young,
And firm endures, while endless years
  Their everlasting circles run.

4 From thee, the overflowing spring,
  Our souls shall drink a fresh supply;
While such as trust their native strength
  Shall melt away, and droop, and die.

5 Swift as an eagle cuts the air,
  We'll mount aloft to thine abode;
On wings of love our souls shall fly,
  Nor tire amid the heavenly road!

738   *"The whole armor."*   BARBAULD.

Awake, my soul! lift up thine eyes;
See where thy foes against thee rise,
In long array, a numerous host;
Awake, my soul! or thou art lost.

2 See where rebellious passions rage,
And fierce desires and lusts engage;
The meanest foe of all the train
Has thousands and ten thousands slain.

3 Thou treadest on enchanted ground;
Perils and snares beset thee round;
Beware of all, guard every part—
But most the traitor in thy heart.

4 The terror and the charm repel,
The powers of earth, and powers of hell;
The Man of Calvary triumphed here:
Why should his faithful followers fear?

5 Come then, my soul! now learn to wield
The weight of thine immortal shield;
Put on the armor, from above,
Of heavenly truth, and heavenly love.

PARK STREET. L. M.

1. Fountain of grace, rich, full and free, What need I, that is not in thee: Full par-don,

strength to meet the day, And peace which none can take away, And peace which none can take away.

739   *"All fullness."—Col.* 1: 19.   ANON.

FOUNTAIN of grace, rich, full, and free,
What need I, that is not in thee:
Full pardon, strength to meet the day,
And peace which none can take away.

2 Doth sickness fill my heart with fear,
'Tis sweet to know that thou art near;
Am I with dread of justice tried,
'Tis sweet to know that Christ hath died.

3 In life, thy promises of aid
Forbid my heart to be afraid;
In death, peace gently vails the eyes,—
Christ rose, and I shall surely rise.

740   *"Jesus is for ever mine."*   STEELE.

WHEN sins and fears, prevailing rise,
And fainting hope almost expires,
To thee, O Lord, I lift my eyes;
To thee I breathe my soul's desires.

2 Art thou not mine, my living Lord?
And can my hope, my comfort die?
'Tis fixed on thine almighty word—
That word which built the earth and sky.

3 If my immortal Saviour lives,
Then my immortal life is sure;
His word a firm foundation gives;
Here may I build and rest secure.

4 Here, O my soul, thy trust repose;
If Jesus is for ever mine,
Not death itself—that last of foes—
Shall break a union so divine.

741   *"Complete in Him."—Col.* 4: 12.   MRS. HINSDALE.

MY soul complete in Jesus stands!
It fears no more the law's demands;
The smile of God is sweet within,
Where all before was guilt and sin.

2 My soul at rest in Jesus lives;
Accepts the peace his pardon gives;
Receives the grace his death secured,
And pleads the anguish he endured.

3 My soul its every foe defies,
And cries—'Tis God that justifies!
Who charges God's elect with sin?
Shall Christ, who died their peace to win?

4 A song of praise my soul shall sing,
To our eternal, glorious King!
Shall worship humbly at his feet,
In whom alone it stands complete.

742   *2 Corinthians* 12: 19.   WATTS.

LET me but hear my Saviour say,
"Strength shall be equal to thy day;"
Then I rejoice in deep distress,
Leaning on all-sufficient grace.

I can do all things—or can bear
All suffering, if my Lord be there;
Sweet pleasures mingle with the pains,
While he my sinking head sustains.

3 I glory in infirmity,
That Christ's own power may rest on me;
When I am weak, then am I strong;
Grace is my shield, and Christ my song.

CHRISTMAS.　C. M.

1. A - wake, my soul, stretch ev - ery nerve, And press with vig - or on ; A heavenly

race de-mands thy zeal, And an im - mor - tal crown, And an im - mor - tal crown.

743　　*The Race.—Phil.* **3 : 14.**　DODDRIDGE.

Awake, my soul, stretch every nerve,
　And press with vigor on;
A heavenly race demands thy zeal,
　And an immortal crown.

2　A cloud of witnesses around
　　Hold thee in full survey;
　Forget the steps already trod,
　　And onward urge thy way.

3　'Tis God's all-animating voice,
　　That calls thee from on high;
　'Tis his own hand presents the prize
　　To thine aspiring eye.

4　Blest Saviour, introduced by thee,
　　Have I my race begun;
　And, crowned with victory, at thy feet
　　I'll lay my honors down.

744　　*The Warfare.—2 Tim.* **2 : 3.**　WATTS.

Am I a soldier of the cross,
　A follower of the Lamb?
And shall I fear to own his cause,
　Or blush to speak his name?

2　Must I be carried to the skies
　　On flowery beds of ease?
　While others fought to win the prize,
　　And sailed through bloody seas?

3　Are there no foes for me to face?
　　Must I not stem the flood?
　Is this vile world a friend to grace,
　　To help me on to God?

280

4　Sure I must fight, if I would reign;
　　Increase my courage, Lord!
　I'll bear the toil, endure the pain,
　　Supported by thy word.

5　Thy saints, in all this glorious war,
　　Shall conquer, though they die;
　They view the triumph from afar,
　　And seize it with their eye.

6　When that illustrious day shall rise,
　　And all thy armies shine
　In robes of victory through the skies,
　　The glory shall be thine.

745　　*"I'm not ashamed."*　WATTS.

I'm not ashamed to own my Lord,
　Or to defend his cause;
Maintain the honor of his word,
　The glory of his cross.

2　Jesus, my God!—I know his name-
　　His name is all my trust;
　Nor will he put my soul to shame,
　　Nor let my hope be lost.

3　Firm as his throne his promise stands,
　　And he can well secure
　What I've committed to his hands,
　　Till the decisive hour.

4　Then will he own my worthless name
　　Before his Father's face,
　And in the new Jerusalem
　　Appoint my soul a place.

MAITLAND. C. M.

1. Must Je - sus bear the cross a - lone, And all the world go free?

No, there's a cross for ev - ery one, And there's a cross for me.

746   *" Take up his cross daily."*   ALLEN.

Must Jesus bear the cross alone,
  And all the world go free?
No, there's a cross for every one,
  And there's a cross for me.

2 This consecrated cross I'll bear,
  Till death shall set me free,
And then go home my crown to wear,
  For there's a crown for me.

3 Upon the crystal pavement, down
  At Jesus' piercéd feet,
Joyful, I'll cast my golden crown,
  And his dear name repeat.

4 And palms shall wave, and harps shall ring,
  Beneath heaven's arches high;
The Lord that lives, the ransomed sing,
  That lives no more to die.

5 Oh, precious cross! oh, glorious crown!
  Oh, resurrection day!
Ye angels, from the stars come down,
  And bear my soul away.

747   *Psalm* 125.   WATTS.

Unshaken as the sacred hill,
  And fixed as mountains be,
Firm as a rock the soul shall rest,
  That leans, O Lord! on thee.

2 Not walls, nor hills, could guard so well
  Old Salem's happy ground,
As those eternal arms of love,
  That every saint surround.

3 The rod of wickedness shall ne'er
  Against the just prevail,
Lest innocence should find a snare,
  And tempted virtue fail.

4 Do good, O Lord! do good to those,
  Who cleave to thee in heart,
Who on thy truth alone repose,
  Nor from thy law depart.

5 Deal gently, Lord, with souls sincere,
  And lead them safely on
To the bright gates of paradise,
  Where Christ their Lord is gone.

748   *Isaiah* 35 : 8-10.   DODDRIDGE.

Sing, all ye ransomed of the Lord,
  Your great Deliverer sing:
Ye pilgrims, now for Zion bound,
  Be joyful in your King.

2 His hand divine shall lead you on,
  Through all the blissful road;
Till to the sacred mount you rise,
  And see your gracious God.

3 Bright garlands of immortal joy
  Shall bloom on every head;
While sorrow, sighing, and distress,
  Like shadows, all are fled.

4 March on in your Redeemer's strength;
  Pursue his footsteps still;
And let the prospect cheer your eye
  While laboring up the hill.

CAMBRIDGE. C. M.

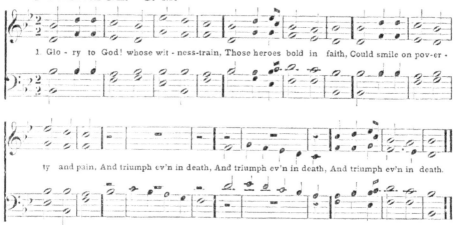

1. Glo - ry to God! whose wit - ness-train, Those heroes bold in faith, Could smile on pov-er -

ty and pain, And triumph ev'n in death, And triumph ev'n in death, And triumph ev'n in death.

749   *Martyr-faith.—Heb.* **11: 13.**   MORAVIAN.

GLORY to God! whose witness-train,
    Those heroes bold in faith,
Could smile on poverty and pain,
    And triumph ev'n in death.

2 Oh, may that faith our hearts sustain,
    Wherein they fearless stood,
When, in the power of cruel men,
    They poured their willing blood.

3 God whom we serve, our God, can save,
    Can damp the scorching flame,
Can build an ark, can smooth the wave,
    For such as love his name.

4 Lord! if thine arm support us still
    With its eternal strength,
We shall o'ercome the mightiest ill,
    And conquerors prove at length.

750   *Psalm* 91.   SCOTCH.

HE that doth in the secret place
    Of the Most High reside,
Under the shade of him that is
    Almighty shall abide.

2 I of the Lord my God will say,
    He is my refuge still,
He is my fortress, and my God,
    And in him trust I will.

3 Thou shalt not need to be afraid
    For terrors of the night;
Nor for the arrow that doth fly
    By day, while it is light;—

4 Nor for the pestilence, that walks
    In darkness secretly;
Nor for destruction, that doth waste
    At noon-day openly.

5 A thousand at thy side shall fall,
    On thy right hand shall lie
Ten thousand dead; yet unto thee
    It shall not once come nigh.

6 Only thou with thine eyes shall look,
    And a beholder be;
And thou therein the just reward
    Of wicked men shall see.

751   *" The elders."—Heb.* **11: 13.**   NEEDHAM.

RISE, O my soul, pursue the path
    By ancient worthies trod;
Aspiring, view those holy men
    Who lived and walked with God.

2 Though dead, they speak in reason's ear,
    And in example live;
Their faith, and hope, and mighty deeds
    Still fresh instruction give.

3 'Twas through the Lamb's most precious
    They conquered every foe;   [blood
And to his power and matchless grace
    Their crowns of life they owe.

4 Lord, may I ever keep in view
    The patterns thou hast given,
And ne'er forsake the blessèd road
    That led them safe to heaven.

WIRTH. C. M.

1. In time of fear, when trou-ble's near, I look to thine a - bode;

Though help-ers fail, and foes pre - vail,........ I'll put my trust in God.

752 *"What time I am afraid."* HASTINGS.

In time of fear, when trouble's near,
  I look to thine abode;
Though helpers fail, and foes prevail,
  I'll put my trust in God.

2 And what is life, 'mid toil and strife?
  What terror has the grave?
Thine arm of power, in peril's hour,
  The trembling soul will save.

3 In darkest skies, though storms arise,
  I will not be dismayed:
O God of light, and boundless might,
  My soul on thee is stayed!

753 *"I shall be with him."* BAXTER.

Lord, it belongs not to my care
  Whether I die or live;
To love and serve thee is my share,
  And this thy grace must give.

2 If life be long, I will be glad
  That I may long obey;
If short, yet why should I be sad
  To soar to endless day?

3 Christ leads me through no darker rooms
  Than he went through before;
No one into his kingdom comes,
  But through his opened door.

4 Come, Lord, when grace has made me meet,
  Thy blessèd face to see;
For if thy work on earth be sweet,
  What will thy glory be!

5 Then shall I end my sad complaints,
  And weary, sinful days,
And join with all triumphant saints
  Who sing Jehovah's praise.

6 My knowledge of that life is small;
  The eye of faith is dim;
But 'tis enough that Christ knows all,
  And I shall be with him.

754 *"If God be for us."—Rom.* 8: 31. FABER.

God's glory is a wondrous thing,
  Most strange in all its ways,
And, of all things on earth, least like
  What men agree to praise.

2 Oh, blest is he to whom is given
  The instinct that can tell
That God is on the field, when he
  Is most invisible!

3 And blest is he who can divine
  Where real right doth lie,
And dares to take the side that seems
  Wrong to man's blindfold eye!

4 Oh, learn to scorn the praise of men!
  Oh, learn to lose with God!
For Jesus won the world through shame,
  And beckons thee his road.

5 And right is right, since God is God;
  And right the day must win;
To doubt would be disloyalty,
  To falter would be sin!

283

OLMUTZ. S. M.

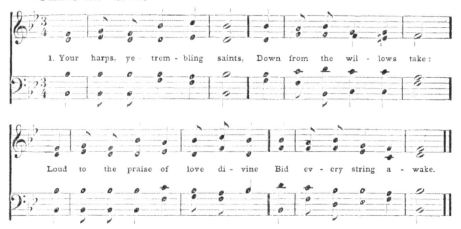

1. Your harps, ye trem-bling saints, Down from the wil-lows take:

Loud to the praise of love di-vine Bid ev-'ry string a - wake.

755   *Our Salvation near.—Rom.* **13:11.**   TOPLADY.

Your harps, ye trembling saints,
  Down from the willows take:
Loud to the praise of love divine
  Bid every string awake.

2 Though in a foreign land,
  We are not far from home;
And nearer to our house above
  We every moment come.

3 His grace will to the end
  Stronger and brighter shine;
Nor present things, nor things to come,
  Shall quench the spark divine.

4 When we in darkness walk,
  Nor feel the heavenly flame,
Then is the time to trust our God,
  And rest upon his name.

5 Soon shall our doubts and fears
  Subside at his control;
His loving-kindness shall break through
  The midnight of the soul.

6 Blest is the man, O Lord,
  Who stays himself on thee;
Who waits for thy salvation, Lord,
  Shall thy salvation see.

756   *"Be of good courage."—Ps* **27:14.**   GERHARDT.

Give to the winds thy fears;
  Hope, and be undismayed;
God hears thy sighs and counts thy tears;
  God shall lift up thy head
284

2 Through waves, and clouds, and storms,
  He gently clears thy way;
Wait thou his time; so shall this night
  Soon end in joyous day.

3 Far, far above thy thought
  His counsel shall appear,
When fully he the work hath wrought,
  That caused thy needless fear.

4 What though thou rulest not!
  Yet heaven, and earth, and hell
Proclaim, God sitteth on the throne,
  And ruleth all things well.

757   *"In wrath, a moment."—Isa.* **54:8.**   GALLAGHER.

The sun himself shall fade,
  The starry worlds shall fall;
Yet through a vast eternity,
  Shall God be all in all.

2 Though now his ways are dark,
  Concealed from mortal sight,
His counsels are divinely wise,
  And all his judgments right.

3 In God my trust shall stand,
  While waves of sorrow roll;
In life or death his name shall be
  The refuge of my soul.

4 Cease, cease my tears to flow,
  Cease, cease my heart to moan;
Betide what may to me, I'll say,
  His holy will be done!

OWEN. S. M.

Sing rapidly.

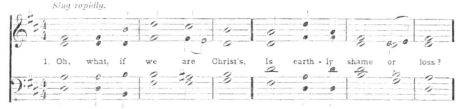

1. Oh, what, if we are Christ's, Is earth-ly shame or loss?

Bright shall the crown of glo-ry be, When we have borne the cross.

758   *"Hold that fast which thou hast."*   BAKER.

Oh, what, if we are Christ's,
  Is earthly shame or loss?
Bright shall the crown of glory be,
  When we have borne the cross.

2 Keen was the trial once,
  Bitter the cup of woe,
When martyred saints, baptized in blood,
  Christ's sufferings shared below.

3 Bright is their glory now,
  Boundless their joy above,
Where, on the bosom of their God,
  They rest in perfect love.

4 Lord, may that grace be ours!
  Like them in faith to bear
All that of sorrow, grief, or pain,
  May be our portion here!

5 Enough, if thou at last
  The word of blessing give,
And let us rest beneath thy feet,
  Where saints and angels live!

759   *"I can do all things."—Phil.* **4:13.**   ANON.

O Saviour, who didst come
  By water and by blood;
Confessed on earth, adored in heaven,
  Eternal Son of God!

2 Jesus, our life and hope,
  To endless years the same;
We plead thy gracious promises,
  And rest upon thy name.

3 By faith in thee we live,
  By faith in thee we stand,
By thee we vanquish sin and death,
  And gain the heavenly land.

4 O Lord, increase our faith;
  Our fearful spirits calm;
Sustain us through this mortal strife,
  Then give the victor's palm!

760   *"I have peace."*   BONAR.

I hear the words of love,
  I gaze upon the blood,
I see the mighty sacrifice,
  And I have peace with God.

2 'Tis everlasting peace,
  Sure as Jehovah's name;
'Tis stable as his steadfast throne,
  For evermore the same.

3 The clouds may go and come,
  And storms may sweep my sky;
This blood-sealed friendship changes not,
  The cross is ever nigh.

4 I change—he changes not;
  The Christ can never die;
His love, not mine, the resting-place;
  His truth, not mine, the tie.

5 My love is ofttimes low,
  My joy still ebbs and flows;
But peace with him remains the same,
  No change Jehovah knows.

LABAN. S. M.

1. My soul, be on thy guard, Ten thou-sand foes a-rise;

And hosts of sin are press-ing hard To draw thee from the skies.

761   *"Watch."—Matt.* 26:41.   HEATH.

My soul, be on thy guard,
Ten thousand foes arise;
And hosts of sin are pressing hard
To draw thee from the skies.

2 Oh, watch, and fight, and pray!
The battle ne'er give o'er;
Renew it boldly every day,
And help divine implore.

3 Ne'er think the victory won,
Nor lay thine armor down;
Thine arduous work will not be done,
Till thou obtain thy crown.

4 Fight on, my soul, till death
Shall bring thee to thy God!
He'll take thee at thy parting breath,
Up to his blest abode.

762   *The Warfare—Eph.* 6:14.   C. WESLEY.

SOLDIERS of Christ, arise,
And put your armor on,
Strong in the strength which God supplies
Through his eternal Son.

2 Strong in the Lord of hosts
And in his mighty power,
Who in the strength of Jesus trusts
Is more than conqueror.

3 Stand then in his great might,
With all his strength endued,
And take, to arm you for the fight,
The panoply of God.

4 That, having all things done,
And all your conflicts past,
You may o'ercome through Christ alone,
And stand entire at last.

5 From strength to strength go on;
Wrestle, and fight, and pray;
Tread all the powers of darkness down,
And win the well-fought day.

6 Still let the Spirit cry
In all his soldiers, come!
Till Christ the Lord descend from high,
And take the conquerors home.

763   *Watchfulness.—Luke* 12:37.   DODDRIDGE.

YE servants of the Lord!
Each in his office wait,
Observant of his heavenly word,
And watchful at his gate.

2 Let all your lamps be bright,
And trim the golden flame;
Gird up your loins as in his sight,
For awful is his name.

3 Watch,—'tis your Lord's command;
And while we speak he's near;
Mark the first signal of his hand,
And ready all appear.

4 Oh, happy servant he,
In such a posture found!
He shall his Lord with rapture see,
And be with honor crowned.

LATHROP. S. M.

1. How gen - tle God's com - mands! How kind his pre - cepts are!

Come, cast your bur - dens on the Lord, And trust his cons - tant care.

764 *"He careth."—1 Pet. 5:7.* DODDRIDGE.

How gentle God's commands!
  How kind his precepts are!
Come, cast your burdens on the Lord,
  And trust his constant care.

2 Beneath his watchful eye
  His saints securely dwell;
That hand which bears creation up
  Shall guard his children well.

3 Why should this anxious load
  Press down your weary mind?
Haste to your heavenly Father's throne,
  And sweet refreshment find.

4 His goodness stands approved,
  Unchanged from day to day:
I'll drop my burden at his feet,
  And bear a song away.

765 *"Jehovah Jireh."—Gen. 22:14.* SWAIN.

I stand on Zion's mount,
  And view my starry crown;
No power on earth my hope can shake,
  Nor hell can thrust me down.

2 The lofty hills and towers,
  That lift their heads on high,
Shall all be leveled low in dust—
  Their very names shall die.

3 The vaulted heavens shall fall,
  Built by Jehovah's hands;
But firmer than the heavens, the Rock
  Of my salvation stands!

766 *"Goeth forth with weeping."* BURGESS.

The harvest dawn is near,
  The year delays not long;
And he who sows with many a tear,
  Shall reap with many a song.

2 Sad to his toil he goes,
  His seed with weeping leaves;
But he shall come, at twilight's close,
  And bring his golden sheaves.

767 *On the way to heaven.* ANON.

The people of the Lord
  Are on their way to heaven;
There they obtain their great reward;
  The prize will there be given.

2 'Tis conflict here below;
  'Tis triumph there, and peace:
On earth we wrestle with the foe;
  In heaven our conflicts cease.

3 'Tis gloom and darkness here;
  'Tis light and joy above;
There all is pure, and all is clear;
  There all is peace and love.

4 There rest shall follow toil,
  And ease succeed to care:
The victors there divide the spoil;
  They sing and triumph there.

5 Then let us joyful sing;
  The conflict is not long:
We hope in heaven to praise our King
  In one eternal song.

CASKEY. 7, 6. D.

1. Sometimes a light sur - pris - es The Christian while he sings; It is the Lord. who ris - es

D. S. A season of clear shin - ing,

FINE.

With heal-ing in his wings; When comforts are de - clin - ing, He grants the soul a - gain

To cheer it af - ter rain.

D. S.

768   *Matthew* **6 : 25 34.**   COWPER.

SOMETIMES a light surprises
  The Christian while he sings;
It is the Lord, who rises
  With healing in his wings:
When comforts are declining,
  He grants the soul again
A season of clear shining,
  To cheer it after rain.

2 In holy contemplation,
  We sweetly then pursue
The theme of God's salvation,
  And find it ever new:
Set free from present sorrow,
  We cheerfully can say,
Let the unknown to-morrow
  Bring with it what it may.

3 It can bring with it nothing,
  But he will bear us through;
Who gives the lilies clothing,
  Will clothe his people too:
Beneath the spreading heavens,
  No creature but is fed;
And he who feeds the ravens,
  Will give his children bread.

4 Though vine nor fig-tree neither,
  Their wonted fruit should bear,
Though all the fields should wither,
  Nor flocks nor herds be there;

Yet God the same abiding,
  His praise shall tune my voice,
For while in him confiding,
  I cannot but rejoice.

769   *"Thou wilt keep him in perfect peace."* WARING.

IN heavenly love abiding,
  No change my heart shall fear,
And safe is such confiding,
  For nothing changes here:
The storm may roar without me,
  My heart may low be laid,
But God is round about me,
  And can I be dismayed?

2 Wherever he may guide me,
  No want shall turn me back;
My Shepherd is beside me,
  And nothing can I lack:
His wisdom ever waketh,
  His sight is never dim;
He knows the way he taketh,
  And I will walk with him.

3 Green pastures are before me,
  Which yet I have not seen;
Bright skies will soon be o'er me,
  Where darkest clouds have been:
My hope I cannot measure;
  My path to life is free;
My Saviour has my treasure,
  And he will walk with me.

YARMOUTH. 7, 6. D.

1. Stand up!—stand up for Je - sus! Ye soldiers of the cross; Lift high the roy- al ban - ner, It must not suffer loss; From vict'ry un - to vic - t'ry His army shall he lead, Till every foe is vanquished, Till every foe is vanquished, Till every foe is vanquished, And Christ is Lord in - deed.

770   *"Having done all, stand."*   DUFFIELD.

Stand up!—stand up for Jesus!
Ye soldiers of the cross;
Lift high his royal banner,
It must not suffer loss:
From victory unto victory
His army shall he lead,
Till every foe is vanquished,
And Christ is Lord indeed.

2 Stand up!—stand up for Jesus!
The trumpet call obey;
Forth to the mighty conflict,
In this his glorious day:
"Ye that are men, now serve him,"
Against unnumbered foes;
Your courage rise with danger,
And strength to strength oppose.

3 Stand up!—stand up for Jesus!
Stand in his strength alone;
The arm of flesh will fail you—
Ye dare not trust your own:
Put on the gospel armor,
And, watching unto prayer,
Where duty calls, or danger,
Be never wanting there.

4 Stand up!—stand up for Jesus!
The strife will not be long;
This day the noise of battle,
The next the victor's song:
To him that overcometh,
A crown of life shall be;
He with the King of Glory
Shall reign eternally!

771   *Psalm 27.*   MONTGOMERY.

God is my strong salvation;
What foe have I to fear?
In darkness and temptation,
My Light, my Help is near:
Though hosts encamp around me,
Firm in the fight I stand;
What terror can confound me,
With God at my right hand?

2 Place on the Lord reliance;
My soul, with courage wait;
His truth be thine affiance,
When faint and desolate:
His might thy heart shall strengthen,
His love thy joy increase;
Mercy thy day shall lengthen;
The Lord will give thee peace!

289

PLEYEL'S HYMN. 7.

1. Children of the heavenly King, As ye jour-ney, sweet-ly sing;

Sing your Sav-iour's wor-thy praise, Glorious in his works and ways.

772 *Isaiah 35: 8-10.* CENNICK.

CHILDREN of the heavenly King,
As ye journey, sweetly sing;
Sing your Saviour's worthy praise,
Glorious in his works and ways.

2 Ye are traveling home to God
In the way the fathers trod;
They are happy now and ye
Soon their happiness shall see.

3 Shout, ye little flock, and blest!
You on Jesus' throne shall rest;
There your seat is now prepared;
There your kingdom and reward.

4 Fear not, brethren; joyful stand
On the borders of your land;
Jesus Christ, your Father's Son,
Bids you undismayed go on.

5 Lord, submissive make us go,
Gladly leaving all below;
Only thou our Leader be,
And we still will follow thee.

773 *Sin canceled by love.* MADAN.

Now begin the heavenly theme,
Sing aloud in Jesus' name;
Ye, who his salvation prove,
Triumph in redeeming love.

2 Ye, who see the Father's grace
Beaming in the Saviour's face,
As to Canaan on ye move,
Praise, and bless redeeming love.

290

3 Mourning souls! dry up your tears;
Banish all your sinful fears;
See your guilt and curse remove,—
Canceled by redeeming love.

4 When his Spirit leads us home,
When we to his glory come,
We shall all the fullness prove
Of the Lord's redeeming love.

774 *"Ye shall have tribulation."* ANON.

FAINT not, Christian! though the road,
Leading to thy blest abode,
Darksome be, and dangerous too,
Christ thy Guide will bring thee through.

2 Faint not, Christian! though in rage
Satan would thy soul engage,
Gird on faith's anointed shield,—
Bear it to the battle-field.

3 Faint not, Christian! though the world
Has its hostile flag unfurled;
Hold the cross of Jesus fast,
Thou shalt overcome at last.

4 Faint not, Christian! Jesus near
Soon in glory will appear;
And his love will then bestow
Power to conquer every foe.

5 Faint not, Christian! look on high;
See the harpers in the sky:
Patient, wait, and thou wilt join—
Chant with them of love divine.

THEODORA. 7.

1. Ev - er - last - ing arms of love Are be - neath, a - round, a - bove;

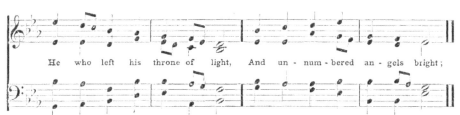

He who left his throne of light, And un - num - bered an - gels bright;

775   *"The everlasting arms."*   ANON.

EVERLASTING arms of love
Are beneath, around, above;
He who left his throne of light,
And unnumbered angels bright;—

2 He who on the accursèd tree
Gave his precious life for me;
He it is that bears me on,
His the arm I lean upon.

3 All things hasten to decay,
Earth and sea will pass away;
Soon will yonder circling sun
Cease his blazing course to run.

4 Scenes will vary, friends grow strange,
But the Changeless cannot change:
Gladly will I journey on,
With his arm to lean upon.

776   *"The good fight."*   H. K. WHITE.

MUCH in sorrow, oft in woe,
Onward, Christians, onward go;
Fight the fight; and, worn with strife,
Steep with tears the bread of life.

2 Onward, Christians, onward go;
Join the war, and face the foe;
Faint not: much doth yet remain;
Dreary is the long campaign.

3 Shrink not, Christians—will ye yield?
Will ye quit the battle-field?
Fight till all the conflict's o'er,
Nor your foes shall rally more.

4 Let your drooping hearts be glad;
March, in heavenly armor clad;
Fight, nor think the battle long;
Victory soon shall tune your song.

5 Let not sorrow dim your eye;
Soon shall every tear be dry;
Let not woe your course impede;
Great your strength, if great your need.

6 Onward, then; to battle move;
More than conquerors ye shall prove;
Though opposed by many a foe,
Christian soldiers! onward go.

777   *Deuteronomy* 33: 25.   LLOYD.

WAIT, my soul, upon the Lord,
To his gracious promise flee,
Laying hold upon his word,
"As thy days thy strength shall be."

2 If the sorrows of thy case
Seem peculiar still to thee,
God has promised needful grace,
"As thy days thy strength shall be."

3 Days of trial, days of grief,
In succession thou mayst see;
This is still thy sweet relief,
"As thy days thy strength shall be."

4 Rock of Ages, I'm secure,
With thy promise full and free;
Faithful, positive, and sure—
"As thy days thy strength shall be."

291

LATTER DAY. 8, 7. D.

1. We are liv - ing, we are dwelling, In a grand and aw - ful time, In an age on

a - ges telling, To be liv - ing is sublime. Hark! the waking up of na - tions, Gog and

Magog to the fray. Hark! what soundeth? is cre - a - tion Groaning for its lat - ter day?

778   *The Latter day.*   COXE.

WE are living, we are dwelling,
  In a grand and awful time,
In an age on ages telling,
  To be living is sublime.
Hark! the waking up of nations,
  Gog and Magog to the fray.
Hark! what soundeth? is creation
  Groaning for its latter day?

2 Will ye play, then, will ye dally,
    With your music and your wine?
  Up! it is Jehovah's rally!
    God's own arm hath need of thine.
  Hark! the onset! will you fold your
    Faith-clad arms in lazy lock?
  Up, oh, up, thou drowsy soldier;
    Worlds are charging to the shock.

3 Worlds are charging—heaven beholding.
    Thou hast but an hour to fight;
  Now the blazoned cross unfolding,
    On—right onward, for the right!
  On! let all the soul within you
    For the truth's sake go abroad!
  Strike! let every nerve and sinew
    Tell on ages—tell for God!

292

779   *The Divine Protection.—Ps.* 91.   MONTGOMERY.

CALL Jehovah thy salvation,
  Rest beneath the Almighty's shade;
In his secret habitation,
  Dwell, and never be dismayed:
There no tumult can alarm thee,
  Thou shalt dread no hidden snare;
Guile nor violence can harm thee,
  In eternal safeguard there.

2 From the sword, at noonday wasting,
    From the noisome pestilence.
  In the depth of midnight, blasting,
    God shall be thy sure defence:
  Fear not thou the deadly quiver,
    When a thousand feel the blow;
  Mercy shall thy soul deliver,
    Though ten thousand be laid low.

3 Since, with pure and firm affection,
    Thou on God has set thy love,
  With the wings of his protection,
    He will shield thee from above;
  Thou shalt call on him in trouble,
    He will hearken, he will save;
  Here, for grief, reward thee double,
    Crown with life beyond the grave.

ELLESDIE. 8, 7. D.

1. Je - sus, I my cross have tak - en, All to leave, and fol - low thee;

Nak - ed, poor, de - spised, for - sak - en, Thou, from hence, my all shalt be!
D. S.—Yet how rich is my con - di - tion, God and heaven are still my own!

Per - ish, ev - ery fond am - bi - tion, All I've sought, or hoped, or known,

780　Luke 9: 23.　LYTE.

Jesus, I my cross have taken,
　All to leave, and follow thee;
Naked, poor, despised, forsaken,
　Thou, from hence, my all shalt be!
Perish, every fond ambition,
　All I've sought, or hoped, or known,
Yet how rich is my condition,
　God and heaven are still my own!

2 Let the world despise and leave me,
　They have left my Saviour, too;
Human hearts and looks deceive me—
　Thou art not, like them, untrue;
Oh, while thou dost smile upon me,
　God of wisdom, love, and might,
Foes may hate, and friends disown me,
　Show thy face, and all is bright.

3 Man may trouble and distress me,
　'Twill but drive me to thy breast,
Life with trials hard may press me,
　Heaven will bring me sweeter rest!
Oh, 'tis not in grief to harm me,
　While thy love is left to me;
Oh, 'twere not in joy to charm me,
　Were that joy unmixed with thee.

4 Go then, earthly fame and treasure!
　Come disaster, scorn, and pain!
In thy service pain is pleasure,
　With thy favor, loss is gain.
I have called thee Abba, Father!
　I have stayed my heart on thee!
Storms may howl, and clouds may gather,
　All must work for good to me.

5 Soul, then know thy full salvation,
　Rise o'er sin, and fear, and care;
Joy to find in every station
　Something still to do or bear.
Think what Spirit dwells within thee;
　Think what Father's smiles are thine;
Think that Jesus died to win thee;
　Child of heaven, canst thou repine?

6 Haste thee on from grace to glory,
　Armed by faith, and winged by prayer!
Heaven's eternal day's before thee,
　God's own hand shall guide thee there:
Soon shall close thy earthly mission,
　Soon shall pass thy pilgrim days,
Hope shall change to glad fruition,
　Faith to sight, and prayer to praise.

ST. ALBAN. 6, 5. D.

1. Brightly gleams our banner, Pointing to the sky, Waving wanderers onward To their home on high.

Journeying o'er the desert, Gladly thus we pray, And with hearts united Take our heavenward way.

REFRAIN.

Brightly gleams our banner, Pointing to the sky, Waving wanderers onward To their home on high.

781
"Jehovah Nissi."   POTTER.

BRIGHTLY gleams our banner,
  Pointing to the sky,
Waving wanderers onward
  To their home on high.
Journeying o'er the desert,
  Gladly thus we pray,
And with hearts united
  Take our heavenward way.—REF.

2 Jesus, Lord and Master,
  At thy sacred feet,
Here with hearts rejoicing
  See thy children meet;
Often have we left thee,
  Often gone astray,
Keep us, mighty Saviour,
  In the narrow way.—REF.

3 All our days direct us
  In the way we go,
Lead us on victorious
  Over every foe:
Bid thine angels shield us
  When the storm-clouds lower,
Pardon thou and save us
  In the last dread hour.—REF.

294

782
"Listen, Saviour."   THWING.

SAVIOUR, blessèd Saviour,
  Listen whilst we sing,
Hearts and voices raising
  Praises to our King.
All we have we offer,
  All we hope to be,
Body, soul, and spirit,
  All we yield to thee.
REF.—Saviour, blessèd Saviour, etc.

2 Nearer, ever nearer,
  Christ, we draw to thee,
Deep in adoration
  Bending low the knee:
Thou for our redemption
  Cam'st on earth to die;
Thou, that we might follow,
  Hast gone up on high.—REF.

3 Great and ever greater
  Are thy mercies here,
True and everlasting
  Are the glories there,
Where no pain, or sorrow,
  Toil, or care, is known,
Where the angel-legions
  Circle round thy throne—REF.

ST. GERTRUDE. 6, 5. D.

1. Onward, Christian sol - diers, Marching as to war, With the cross of Je - sus Go-ing on be - fore.

Christ the roy-al Mas - ter Leads against the foe ; Forward in - to bat - tle, See, his banners go.

CHORUS.

Onward, Christian soldiers, Marching as to war, With the cross of Je - sus Go-ing on be - fore.

war. With the cross of Je - sus

783

"Fight the good fight." GOULD.

ONWARD, Christian soldiers,
Marching as to war,
With the cross of Jesus
Going on before.
Christ the royal Master
Leads against the foe;
Forward into battle,
See, his banners go.
Onward, Christian soldiers,
Marching as to war,
With the cross of Jesus
Going on before.

2 At the sign of triumph
Satan's host doth flee;
On, then, Christian soldiers,
On to victory.
Hell's foundations quiver
At the shout of praise;
Brothers, lift your voices,
Loud your anthems raise.—CHO.

3 Like a mighty army
Moves the Church of God;
Brothers, we are treading
Where the saints have trod;

We are not divided,
All one body we,
One in hope and doctrine,
One in charity.—CHO.

4 Crowns and thrones may perish,
Kingdoms rise and wane,
But the Church of Jesus
Constant will remain;
Gates of hell can never
'Gainst that Church prevail;
We have Christ's own promise,
And that cannot fail.—CHO.

5 Onward, then, ye people,
Join our happy throng,
Blend with ours your voices
In the triumph-song;
Glory, laud, and honor,
Unto Christ the King;
This through countless age,
Men and angels sing.
Onward, Christian soldiers,
Marching as to war,
With the cross of Jesus
Going on before.

WILLOWBY. C. P. M.

1. Come on, my partners in distress, My comrades through the wilderness, Who still your bodies feel:

Awhile forget your griefs and fears, And look beyond this vale of tears, To that celestial hill.

---

784 *"Bliss-inspiring hope."* C. WESLEY.

Come on, my partners in distress,
My comrades through the wilderness,
 Who still your bodies feel:
Awhile forget your griefs and fears,
And look beyond this vale of tears,
 To that celestial hill.

2 Beyond the bounds of time and space,
Look forward to that heavenly place,
 The saints' secure abode;
On faith's strong eagle pinions rise,
And force your passage to the skies,
 And scale the mount of God.

3 Who suffer with our Master here,
We shall before his face appear,
 And by his side sit down;
To patient faith the prize is sure;
And all that to the end endure
 The cross, shall wear the crown.

4 Thrice blessèd, bliss-inspiring hope!
It lifts the fainting spirits up;
 It brings to life the dead:
Our conflicts here shall soon be past,
And you and I ascend at last,
 Triumphant with our Head.

---

785 *"Casting all care on God."* ANSTICE.

O Lord! how happy should we be,
If we could cast our care on thee,
 If we from self could rest;
And feel, at heart, that One above,
In perfect wisdom, perfect love,
 Is working for the best!

2 How far from this our daily life,
Ever disturbed by anxious strife,
 By sudden, wild alarms!
Oh, could we but relinquish all
Our earthly props, and simply fall
 On thine almighty arms!—

3 Could we but kneel, and cast our load,
Ev'n while we pray, upon our God,
 Then rise, with lightened cheer,
Sure that the Father, who is nigh
To still the famished raven's cry,
 Will hear, in that we fear!

4 Lord! make these faithless hearts of ours
Such lessons learn from birds and flowers;
 Make them from self to cease,
Leave all things to a Father's will,
And taste, before him lying still,
 Ev'n in affliction, peace.

BREMEN. C. P. M.

1. Fear not, O lit - tle flock, the foe Who mad - ly seeks your o - ver-throw, Dread not his rage and power; What though your courage sometimes faints, His seeming triumph o'er God's saints Lasts but a little hour.

786 *"Fear not, little flock."* WINKWORTH. *Tr.*

FEAR not, O little flock, the foe
Who madly seeks your overthrow;
  Dread not his rage and power;
What tho' your courage sometimes faints,
His seeming triumph o'er God's saints
  Lasts but a little hour.

2 Be of good cheer; your cause belongs
To him who can avenge your wrongs;
  Leave it to him, our Lord!
Though hidden yet from all our eyes,
He sees the Gideon that shall rise
  To save us, and his word.

3 As true as God's own word is true,
Not earth nor hell with all their crew
  Against us shall prevail;
A jest and by-word are they grown;
God is with us, we are his own,
  Our victory cannot fail!

4 Amen, Lord Jesus, grant our prayer!
Great Captain, now thine arm make bare,
  Fight for us once again!
So shall thy saints and martyrs raise
A mighty chorus to thy praise,
  World without end: Amen!

787 *"Our cross was light."* DENNY.

CHILDREN of light! arise and shine;
Your birth, your hopes, are all divine,
  Your home is in the skies:
Oh, then, for heavenly glory born,
Look down on all, with holy scorn,
  That earthly spirits prize.

2 O blessèd Lord! we yet shall reign,
Redeemed from sorrow, sin, and pain,
  And walk with thee in white:
We suffer now; but, oh, at last
We'll bless thee, Lord! for all the past,
  And own our cross was light.

788 *"Complete in him."—Col.* 2: 10. ANON.

COME join, ye saints, with heart and voice,
Alone in Jesus to rejoice,
  And worship at his feet;
Come, take his praises on your tongues,
And raise to him your thankful songs,
  "In him ye are complete!"

2 In him, who all our praise excels,
The fullness of the Godhead dwells,
  And all perfections meet:
The head of all celestial powers,
Divinely theirs, divinely ours;
  "In him ye are complete!"

3 Still onward urge your heavenly way,
Dependent on him day by day,
  His presence still entreat:
His precious name for ever bless,
Your glory, strength and righteousness,
  "In him ye are complete!"

4 Nor fear to pass the vale of death;
In his dear arms resign your breath,
  He'll make the passage sweet:
The gloom and fears of death shall flee,
And your departing souls shall see
  "In him ye are complete!"

297

PORTUGUESE HYMN. 11.

1. How firm a foun-da-tion, ye saints of the Lord! Is laid for your faith in his ex-cel-lent word; What more can he say, than to you he hath said,— To you, who for ref-uge to Je-sus have fled? To you, who for ref-uge to Je-sus have fled?

789   *"The foundation standeth sure."*   KIRKHAM.

How firm a foundation, ye saints of the
    Lord!
Is laid for your faith in his excellent word!
What more can he say, than to you he
    hath said,—
To you, who for refuge to Jesus have fled?

2 "Fear not, I am with thee, oh, be not
    dismayed,
For I am thy God, I will still give thee aid;
I'll strengthen thee, help thee, and cause
    thee to stand,
Upheld by my gracious, omnipotent hand.

3 "When through the deep waters I call
    thee to go,
The rivers of sorrow shall not overflow;
For I will be with thee thy trials to bless,
And sanctify to thee thy deepest distress.

4 "When through fiery trials thy pathway
    shall lie,
My grace, all sufficient, shall be thy supply,
The flame shall not hurt thee; I only
    design
Thy dross to consume, and thy gold to refine.

5 "Ev'n down to old age all my people shall
    prove
My sovereign, eternal, unchangeable love;
And then, when gray hairs shall their
    temples adorn,
Like lambs they shall still in my bosom be
    borne.

6 "The soul that on Jesus hath leaned for
    repose,
I will not—I will not desert to his foes;
That soul—though all hell should en-
    deavor to shake,
I'll never—no never—no never forsake!"

LYONS. 5, 6. D.

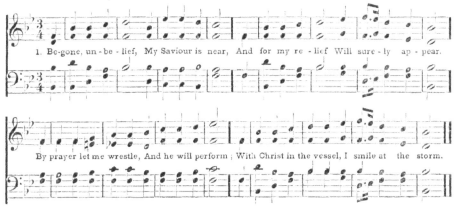

1. Be-gone, un-be-lief, My Saviour is near, And for my re-lief Will sure-ly ap-pear.

By prayer let me wrestle, And he will perform ; With Christ in the vessel, I smile at the storm.

790   *"Begone, unbelief."*   NEWTON.

BEGONE, unbelief,
  My Saviour is near,
And for my relief
  Will surely appear.
By prayer let me wrestle,
  And he will perform;
With Christ in the vessel,
  I smile at the storm.

2 Though dark be my way,
  Since he is my guide,
'Tis mine to obey;
  'T is his to provide;
Though cisterns be broken,
  And creatures all fail,
The word he hath spoken
  Shall surely prevail.

3 His love in time past
  Forbids me to think
He'll leave me at last
  In trouble to sink:
Each sweet Ebenezer
  I have in review—
Confirms his good pleasure
  To help me quite through.

4 Since all that I meet
  Shall work for my good,
The bitter is sweet,
  The medicine is food;
Though painful at present,
  'T will cease before long,
And then, oh, how pleasant
  The conqueror's song!

791   *"The Lord will provide."*   NEWTON.

THOUGH troubles assail,
  And dangers affright,
Though friends should all fail,
  And foes all unite:
Yet one thing secures us,
  Whatever betide,
The Scripture assures us
  The Lord will provide.

2 The birds without barn
  Or storehouse are fed,
From them let us learn
  To trust for our bread:
His saints, what is fitting,
  Shall ne'er be denied,
So long as 't is written,
  The Lord will provide.

3 We may, like the ships,
  By tempests be tossed
On perilous deeps,
  But cannot be lost:
Though Satan enrages
  The wind and the tide,
The promise engages
  The Lord will provide.

4 His call we obey,
  Like Abra'm of old,
Not knowing our way,
  But faith makes us bold:
For though we are strangers,
  We have a good guide,
And trust, in all dangers,
  The Lord will provide.

BADEN. L. M.

1. Oh, that I could for ev - er dwell, De - light - ed at the Sav - iour's feet;

Be - hold the form I love so well, And all his ten - der words re - peat!

792   *"At the Saviour's feet."*   REED.

Oh, that I could for ever dwell,
Delighted at the Saviour's feet;
Behold the form I love so well,
And all his tender words repeat!

2 The world shut out from all my soul,
And heaven brought in with all its bliss,—
Oh, is their aught, from pole to pole,
One moment to compare with this?

3 This is the hidden life I prize—
A life of penitential love;
When most my follies I despise,
And raise my highest thoughts above:

4 When all I am I clearly see,
And freely own, with deepest shame;
When the Redeemer's love to me
Kindles within a deathless flame.

5 Thus would I live till nature fail,
And all my former sins forsake;
Then rise to God within the vail,
And of eternal joys partake.

793   *The Saviour's Presence.*   WATTS.

Far from my thoughts, vain world, begone!
Let my religious hours alone:
Fain would mine eyes my Saviour see:
I wait a visit, Lord, from thee.

2 My heart grows warm with holy fire,
And kindles with a pure desire:
Come, my dear Jesus! from above,
And feed my soul with heavenly love.

300

3 Blest Saviour! what delicious fare,
How sweet thine entertainments are!
Never did angels taste, above,
Redeeming grace and dying love.

4 Hail, great Immanuel, all-divine!
In thee thy Father's glories shine:
Thou brightest, sweetest, fairest One
That eyes have seen, or angels known!

794   *"Immanuel"*   RAY PALMER.

Oh, sweetly breathe the lyres above,
When angels touch the quivering string,
And wake, to chant Immanuel's love,
Such strains as angel-lips can sing!

2 And sweet, on earth, the choral swell,
From mortal tongues, of gladsome lays;
When pardoned souls their raptures tell,
And, grateful, hymn Immanuel's praise.

3 Jesus, thy name our souls adore;
We own the bond that makes us thine;
And carnal joys, that charmed before,
For thy dear sake we now resign.

4 Our hearts, by dying love subdued,
Accept thine offered grace to-day;
Beneath the cross, with blood bedewed,
We bow, and give ourselves away.

5 In thee we trust,—on thee rely;
Though we are feeble, thou art strong;
Oh, keep us till our spirits fly
To join the bright, immortal throng!

HURSLEY. L. M.

1. Sun of my soul! thou Sav-iour dear, It is not night if thou be near:

Oh, may no earth-born cloud a-rise To hide thee from thy ser-vant's eyes!

795   *Evening Song.*   KEBLE.

Sun of my soul! thou Saviour dear,
It is not night if thou be near:
Oh, may no earth-born cloud arise
To hide thee from thy servant's eyes!

2 When soft the dews of kindly sleep
My wearied eyelids gently steep,
Be my last thought,—how sweet to rest
For ever on my Saviour's breast!

3 Abide with me from morn till eve,
For without thee I cannot live;
Abide with me when night is nigh,
For without thee I dare not die.

4 Be near to bless me when I wake,
Ere through the world my way I take;
Abide with me till in thy love
I lose myself in heaven above.

796   *" To babes revealed."*   ANON.

Light of the soul! O Saviour blest!
Soon as thy presence fills the breast,
Darkness and guilt are put to flight,
And all is sweetness and delight.

2 Son of the Father! Lord most high!
How glad is he who feels thee nigh!
Come in thy hidden majesty;
Fill us with love, fill us with thee.

3 Jesus is from the proud concealed,
But evermore to babes revealed;
Through him, unto the Father be
Glory and praise eternally!

797   *Immanuel.*   WATTS.

Go, worship at Immanuel's feet;
See in his face what wonders meet;
Earth is too narrow to express
His worth, his glory, or his grace.

2 Nor earth, nor seas, nor sun, nor stars,
Nor heaven, his full resemblance bears:
His beauties we can never trace,
Till we behold him face to face.

3 Oh, let me climb those higher skies,
Where storms and darkness never rise:
There he displays his power abroad,
And shines, and reigns, the incarnate God.

798   *An ancient morning Psalm.*   RAY PALMER. *Tr.*

O Christ! with each returning morn
Thine image to our heart be borne;
And may we ever clearly see
Our God and Saviour, Lord, in thee!

2 All hallowed be our walk this day;
May meekness form our early ray,
And faithful love our noontide light,
And hope our sunset, calm and bright.

3 May grace each idle thought control,
And sanctify our wayward soul;
May guile depart, and malice cease,
And all within be joy and peace.

4 Our daily course, O Jesus, bless;
Make plain the way of holiness:
From sudden falls our feet defend,
And cheer at last our journey's end.

DWIGHT. L. M.

1. O Love Di-vine! that stooped to share   Our sharpest pang, our bit-terest tear,

On thee we cast each earth-born care,   We smile at pain while Thou art near.

799   *"Thou art near, O Lord."—Ps. 119:151.*   HOLMES.

O Love Divine! that stooped to share
  Our sharpest pang, our bitterest tear,
On thee we cast each earth-born care,
  We smile at pain while thou art near.

2 Though long the weary way we tread,
  And sorrow crown each lingering year,
No path we shun, no darkness dread,
  Our hearts still whispering, thou art near.

3 When drooping pleasure turns to grief,
  And trembling faith is changed to fear,
The murmuring wind, the quivering leaf,
  Shall softly tell us thou art near.

4 On thee we fling our burdening woe,
  O Love Divine, for ever dear;
Content to suffer while we know,
  Living or dying, thou art near!

800   *John 17: 24.*   C. ELLIOTT.

Let me be with thee where thou art,
  My Saviour, my eternal Rest;
Then only will this longing heart
  Be fully and for ever blest.

2 Let me be with thee where thou art,
  Thine unvailed glory to behold;
Then only will this wandering heart
  Cease to be false to thee and cold.

3 Let me be with thee where thou art,
  Where none can die, where none remove;
There neither death nor life will part
  Me from thy presence and thy love.

801   *"Give me thine heart."*   STEELE.

Jesus demands this heart of mine,
  Demands my love, my joy, my care;
But ah! how dead to things divine,
  How cold my best affections are!

2 'Tis sin, alas! with dreadful power,
  Divides my Saviour from my sight;
Oh, for one happy, cloudless hour
  Of sacred freedom, sweet delight!

3 Come, gracious Lord! thy love can raise
  My captive powers from sin and death,
And fill my heart and life with praise,
  And tune my last expiring breath.

802   *"I am the living bread."*   RAY PALMER.

Away from earth my spirit turns,
  Away from every transient good;
With strong desire my bosom burns,
  To feast on heaven's immortal food.

2 Thou, Saviour, art the living bread;
  Thou wilt my every want supply:
By thee sustained, and cheered, and led,
  I'll press through dangers to the sky.

3 What though temptations oft distress,
  And sin assails and breaks my peace;
Thou wilt uphold, and save, and bless,
  And bid the storms of passion cease.

4 Then let me take thy gracious hand,
  And walk beside thee onward still;
Till my glad feet shall safely stand,
  For ever firm on Zion's hill.

MY LIFE FLOWS ON. P. M.

1. My life flows on in endless song; A-bove Earth's la-men-ta-tion, I catch the sweet, tho'
far-off hymn That hails a new cre-a-tion; Through all the tu-mult and the strife, I
hear the mu-sic ringing; It finds an e-cho in my soul— How can I keep from singing?

803 *"How can I keep from singing?"* LOWRY.

My life flows on in endless song;
  Above earth's lamentation,
I catch the sweet, though far-off hymn
  That hails a new creation;
Through all the tumult and the strife,
  I hear the music ringing;
It finds an echo in my soul—
  How can I keep from singing?

2 What though my joys and comforts die?
  The Lord my Saviour liveth;
What though the darkness gather round?
  Songs in the night he giveth;
No storm can shake my inmost calm,
  While to that refuge clinging;
Since Christ is Lord of heaven and earth,
  How can I keep from singing?

3 I lift my eyes; the cloud grows thin;
  I see the blue above it;
And day by day this pathway smooths,
  Since first I learned to love it;
The peace of Christ makes fresh my heart,
  A fountain ever springing;
All things are mine since I am his—
  How can I keep from singing?

804 *"Closer than a brother."* ANON.

I've found a friend; oh, such a friend!
  He loved me ere I knew him;
He drew me with the cords of love,
  And thus he bound me to him.
And round my heart still closely twine
  Those ties which naught can sever,
For I am his, and he is mine,
  For ever and for ever.

2 I've found a friend; oh, such a friend!
  He bled, he died to save me;
And not alone the gift of life,
  But his own self he gave me.
Naught that I have my own I call,
  I hold it for the Giver:
My heart, my strength, my life, my all,
  Are his, and his for ever.

3 I've found a friend; oh, such a friend!
  All power to him is given,
To guard me on my onward course,
  And bring me safe to heaven.
The eternal glories gleam afar,
  To nerve my faint endeavor:
So now to watch, to work, to war,
  And then to rest for ever!

GEER. C. M.

1. To our Redeem-er's glo-rious name, A-wake the sa-cred song!

Oh, may his love— im-mor-tal flame— Tune ev-ery heart and tongue!

805   *"The Saviour died for me."*   STEELE.

To our Redeemer's glorious name,
  Awake the sacred song!
Oh, may his love—immortal flame—
  Tune every heart and tongue!

2 His love, what mortal thought can reach?
  What mortal tongue display?
Imagination's utmost stretch,
  In wonder, dies away.

3 Dear Lord! while we adoring pay
  Our humble thanks to thee,
May every heart with rapture say,—
  "The Saviour died for me!"

4 Oh, may the sweet, the blissful theme,
  Fill every heart and tongue,
Till strangers love thy charming name,
  And join the sacred song.

806   *Christ above all.*   NEWTON.

Let worldly minds the world pursue—
  It has no charms for me;
Once I admired its trifles too,
  But grace hath set me free.

2 Its joys can now no longer please,
  Nor ev'n content afford:
Far from my heart be joys like these,
  For I have seen the Lord.

3 As by the light of opening day
  The stars are all concealed,
So earthly pleasures fade away
  When Jesus is revealed.

4 Creatures no more divide my choice—
  I bid them all depart;
His name, his love, his gracious voice,
  Have fixed my roving heart.

5 And may I hope that thou wilt own
  A worthless worm like me?
Dear Lord! I would be thine alone,
  And wholly live to thee.

807   *"He is precious."*—1 Pet. 2 : 7.   HEGINBOTHAM.

Blest Jesus! when my soaring thoughts
  O'er all thy graces rove,
How is my soul in transport lost,—
  In wonder, joy, and love!

2 Not softest strains can charm my ears,
  Like thy beloved name;
Nor aught beneath the skies inspire
  My heart with equal flame.

3 Where'er I look, my wondering eyes
  Unnumbered blessings see;
But what is life, with all its bliss,
  If once compared with thee?

4 Hast thou a rival in my breast?
  Search, Lord, for thou canst tell
If aught can raise my passions thus,
  Or please my soul so well.

5 No; thou art precious to my heart,
  My portion and my joy:
For ever let thy boundless grace
  My sweetest thoughts employ.

SOUTHPORT. C. M.

1. O Lord! I would de-light in thee, And on thy care de-pend;

To thee in ev-ery trou-ble flee, My best, my on-ly Friend.

808 *"Whom have I but thee?"* RYLAND.

O Lord! I would delight in thee,
  And on thy care depend;
To thee in every trouble flee,
  My best, my only Friend.

2 When all created streams are dried,
  Thy fullness is the same;
May I with this be satisfied,
  And glory in thy name!

3 No good in creatures can be found,
  But may be found in thee;
I must have all things, and abound,
  While God is God to me.

4 O Lord! I cast my care on thee;
  I triumph and adore;
Henceforth my great concern shall be
  To love and please thee more.

809 *"Strength, Fortress, Refuge."—Jer. 16:19.* STEELE.

Dear Refuge of my weary soul,
  On thee, when sorrows rise,
On thee, when waves of trouble roll,
  My fainting hope relies.

2 To thee I tell each rising grief,
  For thou alone canst heal;
Thy word can bring a sweet relief
  For every pain I feel.

3 But oh, when gloomy doubts prevail,
  I fear to call thee mine;
The springs of comfort seem to fail,
  And all my hopes decline.

4 Yet, gracious God, where shall I flee?
  Thou art my only trust:
And still my soul would cleave to thee,
  Though prostrate in the dust.

5 Thy mercy-seat is open still,
  Here let my soul retreat,
With humble hope attend thy will,
  And wait beneath thy feet.

810 *"Whom unseen, we love."* RAY PALMER.

Jesus, these eyes have never seen
  That radiant form of thine!
The vail of sense hangs dark between
  Thy blessèd face and mine!

2 I see thee not, I hear thee not,
  Yet art thou oft with me;
And earth hath ne'er so dear a spot,
  As where I meet with thee.

3 Like some bright dream that comes un-
  When slumbers o'er me roll, [sought,
Thine image ever fills my thought,
  And charms my ravished soul.

4 Yet though I have not seen, and still
  Must rest in faith alone;
I love thee, dearest Lord!—and will,
  Unseen, but not unknown.

5 When death these mortal eyes shall seal,
  And still this throbbing heart,
The rending vail shall thee reveal,
  All glorious as thou art!

305

PENIEL. C. M.

1, My God! the spring of all my joys, The life of my de- lights,

The glo - ry of my bright - est days, And com - fort of my nights!

811 *"Altogether Lovely."—Cant.* 2: 16. WATTS.

My God! the spring of all my joys,
The life of my delights,
The glory of my brightest days,
And comfort of my nights!

2 In darkest shades if he appear,
My dawning is begun:
He is my soul's sweet morning star,
And he my rising sun.

3 The opening heavens around me shine
With beams of sacred bliss,
While Jesus shows his heart is mine,
And whispers, I am his!

4 My soul would leave this heavy clay,
At that transporting word;
Run up with joy the shining way,
To embrace my dearest Lord!

5 Fearless of hell and ghastly death,
I'd break through every foe;
The wings of love and arms of faith
Should bear me conqueror through.

812 1 *Cor.* 1: 22-24. WATTS.

Dearest of all the names above,
My Jesus and my God,
Who can resist thy heavenly love,
Or trifle with thy blood?

2 'Tis by the merits of thy death
Thy Father smiles again;
'Tis by thine interceding breath
The Spirit dwells with men.

3 Till God in human flesh I see,
My thoughts no comfort find;
The holy, just, and sacred Three
Are terrors to my mind.

4 But if Immanuel's face appear,
My hope, my joy, begin;
His name forbids my slavish fear;
His grace removes my sin.

5 While Jews on their own law rely,
And Greeks of wisdom boast,
I love the incarnate Mystery,
And there I fix my trust.

813 *"To live is Christ."* NEWTON.

Jesus, who on his glorious throne
Rules heaven, and earth, and sea,
Is pleased to claim me for his own
And give himself to me.

2 His person fixes all my love,
His blood removes my fear;
And while he pleads for me above,
His arm preserves me here.

3 His word of promise is my food,
His Spirit is my guide;
Thus daily is my strength renewed,
And all my wants supplied.

4 For him I count as gain each loss,
Disgrace for him renown;
Well may I glory in my cross,
While he prepares my crown.

HEBER.   C. M.

1. How sweet the name of Je - sus sounds In a be - liev - er's ear!

It soothes his sor - rows, heals his wounds, And drives a - way his fear.

814   *"He is precious."—1 Pet. 2:7.*   NEWTON.

How sweet the name of Jesus sounds
  In a believer's ear!
It soothes his sorrows, heals his wounds,
  And drives away his fear.

2 It makes the wounded spirit whole,
  And calms the troubled breast;
'Tis manna to the hungry soul,
  And to the weary, rest.

3 Jesus! my Shepherd, Guardian, Friend,
  My Prophet, Priest, and King;
My Lord, my Life, my Way, my End,
  Accept the praise I bring.

4 Weak is the effort of my heart,
  And cold my warmest thought;
But when I see thee as thou art,
  I'll praise thee as I ought.

5 Till then I would thy love proclaim,
  With every fleeting breath;
And may the music of thy name,
  Refresh my soul in death.

815   *"His name Jesus."—Matt. 1:21.*   DODDRIDGE.

Jesus! I love thy charming name,
  'Tis music to mine ear;
Fain would I sound it out so loud,
  That earth and heaven should hear.

2 Yes!—thou art precious to my soul,
  My transport and my trust;
Jewels, to thee, are gaudy toys,
  And gold is sordid dust.

3 All my capacious powers can wish,
  In thee doth richly meet;
Not to mine eyes is light so dear,
  Nor friendship half so sweet.

4 Thy grace still dwells upon my heart,
  And sheds its fragrance there;—
The noblest balm of all its wounds,
  The cordial of its care.

816   *"Jesus only."—Matt. 17:8.*   BERNARD.

Jesus, the very thought of thee,
  With sweetness fills my breast:
But sweeter far thy face to see
  And in thy presence rest.

2 Nor voice can sing, nor heart can frame,
  Nor can the memory find
A sweeter sound than thy blest name,
  O Saviour of mankind!

3 O Hope of every contrite heart
  O Joy of all the meek!
To those who fall, how kind thou art!
  How good to those who seek!

4 But what to those who find? Ah! this,
  Nor tongue nor pen can show;
The love of Jesus, what it is,
  None but his loved ones know.

5 Jesus, our only joy be thou,
  As thou our prize wilt be;
Jesus, be thou our glory now,
  And through eternity.

STILLINGFLEET. S. M.

1 Not with our mor - tal eyes Have we be - held the Lord;

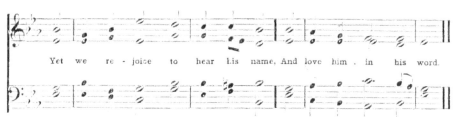

Yet we re - joice to hear his name, And love him . in his word.

817   *"Unseen, we love."*   WATTS.

Not with our mortal eyes
Have we beheld the Lord;
Yet we rejoice to hear his name;
And love him in his word.

2 On earth we want the sight
Of our Redeemer's face;
Yet, Lord, our inmost thoughts delight
To dwell upon thy grace.

3 And when we taste thy love,
Our joys divinely grow
Unspeakable, like those above,
And heaven begins below.

818   *"Jesus, my strength."*   C. WESLEY.

Jesus, my strength, my hope,
On thee I cast my care,
With humble confidence look up,
And know thou hear'st my prayer.

2 Give me on thee to wait,
Till I can all things do;
On thee, almighty to create,
Almighty to renew.

3 I want a sober mind,
A self-renouncing will,
That tramples down, and casts behind
The lures of pleasing ill;—

4 A soul inured to pain,
To hardship, grief and loss,
Bold to take up, firm to sustain
The consecrated cross;—

5 I want a godly fear,
A quick-discerning eye,
That looks to thee when sin is near,
And sees the tempter fly;—

6 A spirit still prepared,
And armed with jealous care,
For ever standing on its guard,
And watching unto prayer.

819   *"The Master is come."*   GILL.

Dear Lord and Master mine!
Thy happy servant see;
My Conqueror! with what joy divine
Thy captive clings to thee!

2 I would not walk alone,
But still with thee, my God,
At every step my blindness own,
And ask of thee the road.

3 The weakness I enjoy
That casts me on thy breast:
The conflicts that thy strength employ
Make me divinely blest.

4 Dear Lord and Master mine!
Still keep thy servant true;
My Guardian and my Guide divine!
Bring, bring thy pilgrim through.

5 My Conqueror and my King!
Still keep me in thy train;
And with thee thy glad captive bring
When thou return'st to reign.

GREENWOOD. S. M.

1. Since Je - sus is my friend, And I to him be - long,
It matters not what foes in - tend, How - ev - er fierce and strong.

820 "*Jesus is my Friend.*" GERHARDT.

SINCE Jesus is my friend,
  And I to him belong,
It matters not what foes intend,
  However fierce and strong.

2 He whispers in my breast
  Sweet words of holy cheer,
How they who seek in God their rest
  Shall ever find him near;—

3 How God hath built above
  A city fair and new,
Where eye and heart shall see and prove
  What faith has counted true.

4 My heart for gladness springs;
  It cannot more be sad;
For very joy it smiles and sings,—
  Sees naught but sunshine glad.

5 The sun that lights mine eyes
  Is Christ, the Lord I love;
I sing for joy of that which lies
  Stored up for me above.

821 "*Whom have I but thee?*" WATTS.

MY God, my Life, my Love,
  To thee, to thee I call;
I cannot live, if thou remove,
  For thou art all in all.

2 To thee, and thee alone,
  The angels owe their bliss:
They sit around thy gracious throne,
  And dwell where Jesus is.

3 Not all the harps above
  Can make a heavenly place,
If God his residence remove,
  Or but conceal his face.

4 Nor earth, nor all the sky,
  Can one delight afford—
No, not a drop of real joy
  Without thy presence, Lord.

5 Thou art the sea of love,
  Where all my pleasures roll;
The circle where my passions move,
  And centre of my soul.

822 "*To live is Christ.*" ANON.

FOR me to live is Christ,
  To die is endless gain,
For him I gladly bear the cross,
  And welcome grief and pain.

2 Faithful may I endure,
  And hear my Saviour say,
Thrice welcome home, beloved child,
  Inherit endless day!

3 A pilgrimage my lot,
  My home is in the skies,
I nightly pitch my tent below,
  And daily higher rise.

4 My journey soon will end,
  My scrip and staff laid down;
Oh, tempt me not with earthly toys,
  I go to wear a crown.

WILMOT. 8, 7.

1. One there is, a - bove all oth - ers, Well de - serves the name of Friend;

His is love be - yond a broth - er's, Cost - ly, free, and knows no end.

823 *" Closer than a brother."* NEWTON.

One there is, above all others,
  Well deserves the name of Friend;
His is love beyond a brother's,
  Costly, free, and knows no end.

2 Which of all our friends, to save us,
  Could or would have shed his blood?
But our Jesus died to have us
  Reconciled in him to God.

3 When he lived on earth abased,
  Friend of sinners was his name;
Now above all glory raised,
  He rejoices in the same.

4 Oh, for grace our hearts to soften,
  Teach us, Lord, at length, to love;
We, alas! forget too often
  What a friend we have above.

824 *" Jesus only."—Matt.* 17 : 8. NASON.

Jesus only, when the morning
  Beams upon the path I tread;
Jesus only, when the darkness
  Gathers round my weary head.

2 Jesus only, when the billows
  Cold and sullen o'er me roll;
Jesus only, when the trumpet
  Rends the tomb and wakes the soul.

3 Jesus only, when, adoring,
  Saints their crowns before him bring;
Jesus only, I will, joyous,
  Through eternal ages sing.

825 *None but Jesus.* MRS. COUSIN.

None but Christ: his merit hides me,
  He was faultless—I am fair;
None but Christ, his wisdom guides me,
  He was out-cast—I'm his care.

2 None but Christ: his Spirit seals me,
  Gives me freedom, with control;
None but Christ, his bruising heals me,
  And his sorrow soothes my soul.

3 None but Christ: his life sustains me,
  Strength and song to me he is;
None but Christ, his love constrains me,
  He is mine and I am his.

826 *" With you always."—Matt.* 28 : 20. NEVIN.

Always with us, always with us—
  Words of cheer and words of love;
Thus the risen Saviour whispers,
  From his dwelling-place above.

2 With us when we toil in sadness,
  Sowing much and reaping none;
Telling us that in the future
  Golden harvests shall be won.

3 With us when the storm is sweeping
  O'er our pathway dark and drear;
Waking hope within our bosoms,
  Stilling every anxious fear.

4 With us in the lonely valley,
  When we cross the chilling stream;
Lighting up the steps to glory
  With salvation's radiant beam.

310

BAYLEY. 8, 7. D.

1. Love di-vine, all love ex-cell-ing, Joy of heaven, to earth come down!

Fix in us thy hum-ble dwell-ing, All thy faith-ful mer-cies crown:
D. S.—Vis-it us with thy sal-va-tion, En-ter ev-er-y trem-bling heart.

Je-sus! thou art all com-pas-sion, Pure, un-bound-ed love thou art;

827   *"Finish thy new creation."*   C. WESLEY.

LOVE divine, all love excelling,—
  Joy of heaven, to earth come down!
Fix in us thy humble dwelling,
  All thy faithful mercies crown:
Jesus! thou art all compassion,
  Pure, unbounded love thou art;
Visit us with thy salvation,
  Enter every trembling heart.

2 Breathe, oh, breathe thy loving Spirit
  Into every troubled breast!
Let us all in thee inherit,
  Let us find thy promised rest:
Come, almighty to deliver,
  Let us all thy life receive!
Speedily return, and never,
  Never more thy temples leave!

3 Finish then thy new creation,
  Pure, unspotted may we be:
Let us see our whole salvation
  Perfectly secured by thee!
Changed from glory into glory,
  Till in heaven we take our place;
Till we cast our crowns before thee,
  Lost in wonder, love, and praise.

828   *Seamen.—Mark* **4**: 38.   ANON.

TOSSED upon life's raging billow,
  Sweet it is, O Lord! to know
Thou didst press a sailor's pillow,
  And canst feel a sailor's woe;
Never slumbering, never sleeping,
  Though the night be dark and drear,
Thou the faithful watch art keeping;
  "All, all's well," thy constant cheer.

2 And though loud the wind is howling,
  Fierce though flash the lightnings red,
Darkly though the storm-cloud's scowling
  O'er the sailor's anxious head;—
Thou canst calm the raging ocean,
  All its noise and tumult still,
Hush the tempest's wild commotion,
  At the bidding of thy will.

3 Thus my heart the hope will cherish,
  While to thee I lift mine eye,
Thou wilt save me ere I perish,
  Thou wilt hear the sailor's cry:
And though mast and sail be riven,
  Soon life's voyage will be o'er,
Safely moored in heaven's wide haven,
  Storm and tempest vex no more.

MADISON. 8. D.

1. Ye angels! who stand round the throne, And view my Immanuel's face,—In rapturous songs make him known, Oh, tune your soft harps to his praise: He formed you the spirits you are, So hap - py, so no - ble, so good; When oth - ers sank down in despair, Confirmed by his pow - er, ye stood.

829   *Philippians* 1: 23.   DE FLEURY.

Ye angels! who stand round the throne,
  And view my Immanuel's face,—
In rapturous songs make him known,
  Oh, tune your soft harps to his praise:
He formed you the spirits you are,
  So happy, so noble, so good;
When others sank down in despair,
  Confirmed by his power, ye stood.

2 Ye saints! who stand nearer than they,
  And cast your bright crowns at his feet,
His grace and his glory display,
  And all his rich mercy repeat;
He snatched you from hell and the grave,
  He ransomed from death and despair:
For you he was mighty to save,
  Almighty to bring you safe there.

3 Oh, when will the period appear
  When I shall unite in your song?
I'm weary of lingering here,
  And I to your Saviour belong!
I want—oh, I want to be there,
  To sorrow and sin bid adieu—
Your joy and your friendship to share—
  To wonder, and worship with you!

312

830   *" Whom unseen we love."*   COWPER.

My Saviour, whom absent I love,
  Whom, not having seen, I adore,
Whose name is exalted above
  All glory, dominion, and power,—
Dissolve thou those bands that detain
  My soul from her portion in thee;
Ah, strike off this adamant chain,
  And make me eternally free!

2 When that happy era begins,
  When arrayed in thy glories I shine,
Nor grieve any more, by my sins,
  The bosom on which I recline,
Oh, then shall the vail be removed,
  And round me thy brightness be poured!
I shall meet him, whom absent I loved,
  I shall see, whom unseen I adored.

3 And then, nevermore shall the fears,
  The trials, temptations, and woes,
Which darken this valley of tears,
  Intrude on my blissful repose:
To Jesus, the crown of my hope,
  My soul is in haste to be gone;
Oh, bear me, ye cherubim, up,
  And waft me away to his throne!

DE FLEURY. 8. D.

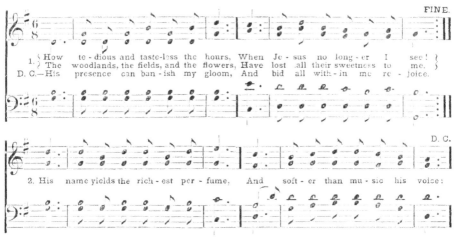

1. How te-dious and taste-less the hours, When Je-sus no long-er I see!
The woodlands, the fields, and the flowers, Have lost all their sweetness to me.
D. C.—His presence can ban-ish my gloom, And bid all with-in me re-joice.

2. His name yields the rich-est per-fume, And soft-er than mu-sic his voice:

831 *"Whom have I but thee?"* NEWTON.

How tedious and tasteless the hours,
When Jesus no longer I see!
The woodlands, the fields, and the flowers,
Have lost all their sweetness to me.

2 His name yields the richest perfume,
And softer than music his voice;
His presence can banish my gloom,
And bid all within me rejoice.

3 Dear Lord! if indeed I am thine,
And thou art my light and my song;
Say, why do I languish and pine,
And why are my winters so long?

4 Oh, drive these dark clouds from the sky,
Thy soul-cheering presence restore;
Or bid me soar upward on high,
Where winters and storms are no more.

832 *"Ministering Spirits."—Heb. 1:14.* TOPLADY.

INSPIRER and hearer of prayer,
Thou Shepherd and Guardian of thine,
My all to thy covenant care
I sleeping or waking resign.

2 If thou art my shield and my sun,
The night is no darkness to me;
And, fast as my moments roll on,
They bring me but nearer to thee.

3 Thy ministering spirits descend
To watch while thy saints are asleep;
By day and by night they attend,
The heirs of salvation to keep.

4 Bright seraphs, despatched from the throne,
Repair to their stations assigned;
And angels elect are sent down,
To guard the redeemed of mankind.

5 Their worship no interval knows;
Their fervor is still on the wing;
And, while they protect my repose,
They chant to the praise of my King.

6 I, too, at the season ordained,
Their chorus for ever shall join,
And love and adore, without end,
Their faithful Creator and mine.

833 *"Altogether lovely."—Rev. 1:5, 6.* FRANCIS.

My gracious Redeemer I love,
His praises aloud I'll proclaim:
And join with the armies above,
To shout his adorable name.

2 To gaze on his glories divine
Shall be my eternal employ;
To see them incessantly shine,
My boundless, ineffable joy.

3 He freely redeemed with his blood,
My soul from the confines of hell,
To live on the smiles of my God,
And in his sweet presence to dwell:—

4 To shine with the angels in light,
With saints and with seraphs to sing,
To view, with eternal delight,
My Jesus, my Saviour, my King!

313

ST. JUDE. 7, 6. D.

1. I need thee, precious Je - sus, For I am ver - y poor; A stranger and a
pil - grim, I have no earth-ly store: I need the love of Je - sus To
cheer me on my way, To guide my doubting footsteps, To be my strength and stay.

834　　"I need thee!"　　WHITFIELD.

I NEED thee, precious Jesus
　For I am very poor;
A stranger and a pilgrim,
　I have no earthly store:
I need the love of Jesus
　To cheer me on my way,
To guide my doubting footsteps,
　To be my strength and stay.

2 I need thee, precious Jesus,
　I need a friend like thee,
A friend to soothe and pity,
　A friend to care for me:
I need the heart of Jesus
　To feel each anxious care,
To tell my every trial,
　And all my sorrows share.

3 I need thee, precious Jesus,
　I need thee, day by day,
To fill me with thy fullness,
　To lead me on my way;
I need thy Holy Spirit
　To teach me what I am,
To show me more of Jesus,
　And point me to the Lamb.

4 I need thee, precious Jesus,
　And hope to see thee soon
Encircled with the rainbow,
　And seated on thy throne;
There, with thy blood-bought children,
　My joy shall ever be
To sing thy praises, Jesus,
　To gaze, my Lord, on thee.

835　　"Without Me, nothing."　　MASSIE. Tr.

I KNOW no life divided,
　O Lord of life! from thee;
In thee is life provided
　For all mankind, for me;
I know no death, O Jesus!
　Because I live in thee;
Thy death it is which frees us
　From death eternally.

2 I fear no tribulation,
　Since, whatsoe'er it be,
It makes no separation
　Between my Lord and me;
If thou, my God and Teacher!
　Vouchsafe to be my own,
Though poor, I shall be richer
　Than monarch on his throne.

HODNET. 7, 6. D.

1. { I lay my sins on Je - sus, The spotless Lamb of God; }
   { He bears them all, and frees us.............................} From the ac - curs-ed load;

{ I bring my guilt to Je - sus, To wash my crimson stains }
{ White in his blood most precious,..............................} Till not a stain remains.

836 *"He hath borne our griefs."—Isa.* 53: 4. BONAR.

I LAY my sins on Jesus,
The spotless Lamb of God;
He bears them all, and frees us
From the accursèd load;
I bring my guilt to Jesus,
To wash my crimson stains
White in his blood most precious,
Till not a stain remains.

2 I lay my wants on Jesus;
All fullness dwells in him;
He healeth my diseases,
He doth my soul redeem:
I lay my griefs on Jesus,
My burdens and my cares;
He from them all releases,
He all my sorrows shares.

3 I rest my soul on Jesus,
This weary soul of mine;
His right hand me embraces,
I on his breast recline:
I love the name of Jesus,
Immanuel, Christ, the Lord;
Like fragrance on the breezes,
His name abroad is poured.

4 I long to be like Jesus,
Meek, loving, lowly, mild;
I long to be like Jesus,
The Father's holy child:

I long to be with Jesus
Amid the heavenly throng,
To sing with saints his praises,
And learn the angels' song.

837 *" God, our Saviour."—Jude* 25. HAWEIS.

To thee, my God and Saviour!
My heart exulting sings,
Rejoicing in thy favor,
Almighty King of kings!
I'll celebrate thy glory,
With all thy saints above,
And tell the joyful story
Of thy redeeming love.

2 Soon as the morn, with roses
Bedecks the dewy east,
And when the sun reposes
Upon the ocean's breast,
My voice, in supplication,
Well-pleased the Lord shall hear:
Oh, grant me thy salvation,
And to my soul draw near.

3 By thee, through life supported,
I'll pass the dangerous road,
With heavenly hosts escorted,
Up to thy bright abode;
Then cast my crown before thee,
And, all my conflicts o'er,
Unceasingly adore thee:—
What could an angel more?

MAGILL. 11.

1. Come, Je-sus, Redeemer, a-bide thou with me; Come, gladden my spirit, that waiteth for thee;

Thy smile every shadow shall chase from my heart, And soothe every sorrow though keen be the smart.

838   *"I will come to you."*   RAY PALMER.

COME, Jesus, Redeemer, abide thou with
   me;
Come, gladden my spirit that waiteth for
   thee;
Thy smile every shadow shall chase from
   my heart,
And soothe every sorrow though keen be
   the smart.

2 Without thee but weakness, with thee I
   am strong;
By day thou shalt lead me, by night be
   my song,
Though dangers surround me, I still every
   fear,
Since thou, the Most Mighty, my Helper,
   art near.

3 Thy love, oh, how faithful! so tender, so
   pure!
Thy promise, faith's anchor, how steadfast
   and sure!
That love, like sweet sunshine, my cold
   heart can warm,
That promise make steady my soul in the
   storm.

4 Breathe, breathe on my spirit, oft ruffled,
   thy peace;
From restless, vain wishes, bid thou my
   heart cease;
In thee all its longings henceforward shall
   end,
Till, glad, to thy presence my soul shall
   ascend.

5 Oh, then, blessèd Jesus, who once for me
   died,
Made clean in the fountain that gushed
   from thy side,
I shall see thy full glory, thy face shall
   behold,
And praise thee with raptures for ever
   untold!

839   *"Distresses for Christ's sake."*   C. FRY.

FOR what shall I praise thee, my God and
   my King,
For what blessings the tribute of gratitude
   bring?
Shall I praise thee for pleasure, for health,
   or for ease,
For the sunshine of youth, for the garden
   of peace?

2 For this I should praise; but if only for
   this,
I should leave half untold the donation
   of bliss!
I thank thee for sickness, for sorrow, and
   care,
For the thorns I have gathered, the anguish I bear;—

3 For nights of anxiety, watching, and tears,
A present of pain, a prospective of fears;
I praise thee, I bless thee, my Lord and
   my God,
For the good and the evil thy hand hath
   bestowed!

ROBINSON. 11.

1. I once was a stranger to grace and to God; I knew not my danger, and felt not my load;

Though friends spoke in rapture of Christ on the tree, Jehovah, my Saviour, seemed nothing to me.

840 *Love and assurance.— Jer. 23: 5.* MC'CHEYNE.

I once was a stranger to grace and to God;
I knew not my danger, and felt not my
   load;
Though friends spoke in rapture of Christ
   on the tree,
Jehovah, my Saviour, seemed nothing to
   me.

2 When free grace awoke me by light from
   on high,
Then legal fears shook me: I trembled to
   die:
No refuge, no safety, in self could I see:
Jehovah, thou only my Saviour must be!

3 My terrors all vanished before his sweet
   name;
My guilty fears banished, with boldness
   I came
To drink at the fountain, so copious and
   free:
Jehovah, my Saviour, is all things to me.

4 Jehovah, the Lord, is my treasure and
   boast;
Jehovah, my Saviour, I ne'er can be lost;
In thee I shall conquer, by flood and by
   field,
Jehovah my anchor, Jehovah my shield!

841 *"Looking unto Jesus."—Heb. 12: 2.* ANON.

O eyes that are weary, and hearts that
   are sore!
Look off unto Jesus, now sorrow no more!
The light of his countenance shineth so
   bright,
That here, as in heaven, there need be no
   night.

2 While looking to Jesus, my heart cannot
   fear;
I tremble no more when I see Jesus near;
I know that his presence my safeguard
   will be,
For, "Why are you troubled?" he saith
   unto me.

3 Still looking to Jesus, oh, may I be found,
When Jordan's dark waters encompass
   me round:
They bear me away in his presence to be:
I see him still nearer whom always I see.

4 Then, then shall I know the full beauty
   and grace
Of Jesus, my Lord, when I stand face to
   face;
Shall know how his love went before me
   each day,
And wonder that ever my eyes turned
   away.

317

LYTE. 6, 4.

1. Je - sus, thy name I love, All oth - er names above, Je - sus, my Lord! Oh, thou art

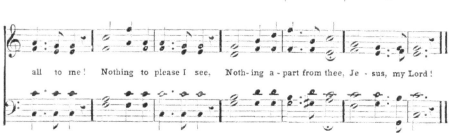

all to me! Nothing to please I see, Noth - ing a - part from thee, Je - sus, my Lord!

842

"Jesus, my Lord?"   DECK.

Jesus, thy name I love,
All other names above,
    Jesus, my Lord!
Oh, thou art all to me!
Nothing to please I see,
Nothing apart from thee,
    Jesus, my Lord!

2 Thou, blessèd Son of God,
Hast bought me with thy blood,
    Jesus, my Lord!
Oh, how great is thy love,
All other loves above,
Love that I daily prove,
    Jesus, my Lord!

3 When unto thee I flee,
Thou wilt my refuge be,
    Jesus, my Lord!
What need I now to fear?
What earthly grief or care,
Since thou art ever near?
    Jesus, my Lord!

4 Soon thou wilt come again!
I shall be happy then,
    Jesus, my Lord!
Then thine own face I'll see,
Then I shall like thee be,
Then evermore with thee,
    Jesus, my Lord!

843

A faithful friend.—Ps. 37:25.   H. HOPE.

Now I have found a Friend
Whose love shall never end;
    Jesus is mine.
Though earthly joys decrease,
Though human friendships cease,
Now I have lasting peace;
    Jesus is mine.

2 Though I grow poor and old,
He will my faith uphold;
    Jesus is mine.
He shall my wants supply;
His precious blood is nigh,
Naught can my hope destroy;
    Jesus is mine.

3 When earth shall pass away,
In the great judgment day,
    Jesus is mine.
Oh, what a glorious thing
Then to behold my King,
On tuneful harps to sing,
    Jesus is mine.

4 Father! thy name I bless;
Thine was the sovereign grace;
    Praise shall be thine;
Spirit of holiness!
Sealing the Father's grace,
Thou mad'st my soul embrace
    Jesus as mine.

OLIVET. 6, 4.

1. My faith looks up to thee, Thou Lamb of Cal-va-ry, Saviour di-vine! Now hear me

while I pray, Take all my guilt a-way, Oh, let me from this day Be whol-ly thine!

844   *"Look unto Me."—Isa.* 45:22.   RAY PALMER.

My faith looks up to thee,
Thou Lamb of Calvary,
   Saviour divine!
Now hear me while I pray,
Take all my guilt away,
Oh, let me from this day
   Be wholly thine!

2 May thy rich grace impart
Strength to my fainting heart;
   My zeal inspire;
As thou hast died for me,
Oh, may my love to thee
Pure, warm, and changeless be,
   A living fire.

3 While life's dark maze I tread,
And griefs around me spread,
   Be thou my guide;
Bid darkness turn to day,
Wipe sorrow's tears away,
Nor let me ever stray
   From thee aside.

4 When ends life's transient dream,
When death's cold, sullen stream
   Shall o'er me roll,
Blest Saviour! then, in love,
Fear and distrust remove;
Oh, bear me safe above,
   A ransomed soul!

845   *"Jesus only."—Heb.* 12: 2.   HASTINGS.

Saviour, I look to thee,
Be not thou far from me,
   'Mid storms that lower:
On me thy care bestow,
Thy loving-kindness show,
Thine arms around me throw
   This trying hour.

2 Saviour, I look to thee,
Feeble as infancy,
   Gird up my heart:
Author of life and light,
Thou hast an arm of might,
Thine is the sovereign right,
   Thy strength impart.

3 Saviour, I look to thee,
Let me thy fullness see,
   Save me from fear;
While at thy cross I kneel,
All my backslidings heal,
And a free pardon seal,
   My soul to cheer.

4 Saviour, I look to thee,
Thine shall the glory be,
   Hearer of prayer:
Thou art my only aid,
On thee my soul is stayed,
Naught can my heart invade,
   While thou art near.

BETHANY. 6, 4.

1. Nearer, my God, to thee, Nearer to thee! Ev'n tho' it be a cross That raiseth me!

Still all my song shall be, Nearer, my God, to thee, Nearer, my God, to thee, Near-er to thee.

846

Genesis 28: 10-22.   S. F. ADAMS.

NEARER, my God, to thee,
   Nearer to thee!
Ev'n though it be a cross
   That raiseth me!
Still all my song shall be,
Nearer, my God, to thee,
   Nearer to thee!

2 Though like the wanderer,
   The sun gone down,
Darkness be over me,
   My rest a stone,
Yet in my dreams I'd be
Nearer, my God, to thee,
   Nearer to thee!

3 There let the way appear,
   Steps unto heaven;
All that thou sendest me,
   In mercy given;
Angels to beckon me
Nearer, my God, to thee,
   Nearer to thee!

4 Then, with my waking thoughts
   Bright with thy praise,
Out of my stony griefs
   Bethel I'll raise;
So by my woes to be
Nearer, my God, to thee,
   Nearer to thee!

5 Or if, on joyful wing
   Cleaving the sky,
Sun, moon and stars forgot,

Upward I fly,
Still all my song shall be,
Nearer, my God, to thee,
   Nearer to thee!

847

"Lovest thou me?"—John 21: 17.   MRS. PRENTISS.

MORE love to thee, O Christ!
   More love to thee!
Hear thou the prayer I make,
   On bended knee;
This is my earnest plea,—
More love, O Christ! to thee,
   More love to thee!

2 Once earthly joy I craved,
   Sought peace and rest;
Now thee alone I seek,
   Give what is best:
This all my prayer shall be,—
More love, O Christ, to thee,
   More love to thee!

3 Let sorrow do its work,
   Send grief and pain;
Sweet are thy messengers,
   Sweet their refrain,
When they can sing with me,—
More love, O Christ, to thee,
   More love to thee!

4 Then shall my latest breath
   Whisper thy praise;
This be the parting cry
   My heart shall raise,—
This still its prayer shall be,—
More love, O Christ! to thee,
   More love to thee!

SOMETHING FOR JESUS. 6, 4.

1. Saviour! I fol-low on, Guided by thee, See-ing not yet the hand That lead-eth me;

Hushed be my heart and still, Fear I no fur-ther ill, On-ly to meet thy will My will shall be.

848 *"A way they knew not."—Isa.* 42:16. C. S. ROBINSON.

SAVIOUR! I follow on,
　Guided by thee,
Seeing not yet the hand
　That leadeth me;
Hushed be my heart and still,
Fear I no further ill,
Only to meet thy will
　My will shall be.

2 Riven the rock for me
　Thirst to relieve,
Manna from heaven falls
　Fresh every eve;
Never a want severe
Causeth my eye a tear,
But thou dost whisper near,
　"Only believe!"

3 Often to Marah's brink
　Have I been brought;
Shrinking the cup to drink,
　Help I have sought;
And with the prayer's ascent,
Jesus the branch hath rent,
Quickly relief hath sent,
　Sweetening the draught.

4 Saviour! I long to walk
　Closer with thee;
Led by thy guiding hand,
　Ever to be;
Constantly near thy side,
Quickened and purified,
Living for him who died
　Freely for me!

849 *"Jesus is mine."—Cant.* 2:16. MRS. BONAR.

FADE, fade, each earthly joy;
　Jesus is mine!
Break, every tender tie;
　Jesus is mine:
Dark is the wilderness;
Earth has no resting-place;
Jesus alone can bless;
　Jesus is mine.

2 Tempt not my soul away;
　Jesus is mine:
Here would I ever stay;
　Jesus is mine:
Perishing things of clay
Born but for one brief day,
Pass from my heart away,
　Jesus is mine.

3 Farewell, ye dreams of night,
　Jesus is mine:
Lost in this dawning bright,
　Jesus is mine:
All that my soul has tried,
Left but a dismal void;
Jesus has satisfied;
　Jesus is mine.

4 Farewell, mortality;
　Jesus is mine:
Welcome, eternity;
　Jesus is mine:
Welcome, O loved and blest!
Welcome, sweet scenes of rest;
Welcome, my Saviour's breast;
　Jesus is mine!

ARIEL.   C. P. M.

1. Oh, could I speak the match-less worth, Oh, could I sound the glories forth,

Which in my Saviour shine! I'd soar, and touch the heavenly strings, And vie with Gabriel

while he sings   In   notes al - most di - vine,   In notes al - most   di - vine.

850   *"He is precious."*—1 Pet. 2: 7.   MEDLEY.

Oh, could I speak the matchless worth,
Oh, could I sound the glories forth,
    Which in my Saviour shine!
I'd soar, and touch the heavenly strings,
And vie with Gabriel while he sings
    In notes almost divine.

2 I'd sing the precious blood he spilt,
My ransom from the dreadful guilt,
    Of sin and wrath divine!
I'd sing his glorious righteousness,
In which all-perfect heavenly dress
    My soul shall ever shine.

3 I'd sing the characters he bears,
And all the forms of love he wears,
    Exalted on his throne:
In loftiest songs of sweetest praise,
I would to everlasting days
    Make all his glories known.

4 Well—the delightful day will come,
When my dear Lord will bring me home,
    And I shall see his face:

Then with my Saviour, Brother, Friend,
A blest eternity I'll spend,
    Triumphant in his grace.

851   *The Incarnation.*—Matt. 1: 21.   ROSCOE.

Oh, let your mingling voices rise
In grateful rapture to the skies,
    And hail a Saviour's birth;
Let songs of joy the day proclaim,
When Jesus all-triumphant came
    To bless the sons of earth.

2 He came to bid the weary rest;
To heal the sinner's wounded breast;
    To bind the broken heart;
To spread the light of truth around;
And to the world's remotest bound,
    The heavenly gift impart.

3 He came our trembling souls to save,
From sin, from sorrow, and the grave,
    And chase our fears away;
Victorious over death and time,
To lead us to a happier clime,
    Where reigns eternal day.

SPANISH HYMN. 7. 6l.

1. Shepherd! with thy tenderest love, Guide me to thy fold a - bove; Let me hear thy gentle voice:

More and more in thee re-joice; From thy fullness grace receive, Ev - er in thy Spir-it live.

852   *Psalm 23.*   ANON.

SHEPHERD! with thy tenderest love,
Guide me to thy fold above;
Let me hear thy gentle voice;
More and more in thee rejoice;
From thy fullness grace receive,
Ever in thy Spirit live.

2 Filled by thee my cup o'erflows,
For thy love no limit knows:
Guardian angels, ever nigh,
Lead and draw my soul on high;
Constant to my latest end,
Thou my footsteps wilt attend.

3 Jesus, with thy presence blest,
Death is life, and labor rest;
Guide me while I draw my breath,
Guard me through the gate of death,
And at last, oh, let me stand,
With the sheep at thy right hand.

853   *"Only thee."—Phil.* **3: 8.**   DUFFIELD.

BLESSED Saviour! thee I love,
All my other joys above;
All my hopes in thee abide,
Thou my hope, and naught beside:
Ever let my glory be,
Only, only, only thee.

2 Once again beside the cross,
All my gain I count but loss;
Earthly pleasures fade away,—
Clouds they are that hide my day:
Hence, vain shadows! let me see
Jesus crucified for me.

3 Blessèd Saviour, thine am I,
Thine to live, and thine to die;
Height or depth, or earthly power,
Ne'er shall hide my Saviour more:
Ever shall my glory be
Only, only, only thee!

854   *"How much I owe."*   MC CHEYNE.

CHOSEN not for good in me,
Waked from coming wrath to flee,
Hidden in the Saviour's side,
By the Spirit sanctified—
Teach me, Lord, on earth to show,
By my love, how much I owe.

2 Oft I walk beneath the cloud,
Dark as midnight's gloomy shroud:
But, when fear is at the height,
Jesus comes, and all is light;
Blessèd Jesus! bid me show
Doubting saints how much I owe.

3 Oft the nights of sorrow reign—
Weeping, sickness, sighing, pain;
But a night thine anger burns—
Morning comes, and joy returns:
God of comforts! bid me show
To thy poor how much I owe.

4 When in flowery paths I tread,
Oft by sin I'm captive led;
Oft I fall, but still arise—
Jesus comes—the tempter flies:
Blessed Jesus! bid me show
Weary sinners all I owe.

FULTON. 7.

1. Sav - iour! teach me, day by day, Love's sweet les - son to o - bey;

Sweet - er les - son can - not be, Lov - ing him who first loved me.

855   *"He first loved us."—John* **4: 19.**   ANON.

SAVIOUR! teach me, day by day,
Love's sweet lesson to obey;
Sweeter lesson cannot be,
Loving him who first loved me.

2 With a childlike heart of love,
At thy bidding may I move;
Prompt to serve and follow thee,
Loving him who first loved me.

3 Teach me all thy steps to trace,
Strong to follow in thy grace;
Learning how to love from thee,
Loving him who first loved me.

4 Love in loving finds employ—
In obedience all her joy;
Ever new that joy will be,
Loving him who first loved me.

5 Thus may I rejoice to show
That I feel the love I owe;
Singing, till thy face I see,
Of his love who first loved me.

856   *Psalm* **131.**   C. WESLEY.

LORD, if thou thy grace impart,
Poor in spirit, meek in heart,
I shall as my Master be,—
Rooted in humility!

2 Simple, teachable and mild,
Changed into a little child;
Pleased with all the Lord provides,
Weaned from all the world besides.

324

3 Father, fix my soul on thee;
Every evil let me flee;
Nothing want, beneath, above,
Happy in thy precious love.

4 Oh, that all may seek and find
Every good in Jesus joined!
Him let Israel still adore,
Trust him, praise him evermore.

857   *"I am what I am."*   KELLY.

BLESSED fountain, full of grace!
Grace for sinners, grace for me,
To this source alone I trace
What I am and hope to be.

2 What I am, as one redeemed,
Saved and rescued by the Lord;
Hating what I once esteemed,
Loving what I once abhorred.

3 What I hope to be ere long,
When I take my place above;
When I join the heavenly throng;
When I see the God of love.

4 Then I hope like him to be,
Who redeemed his saints from sin,
Whom I now obscurely see,
Through a vail that stands between.

5 Blessèd fountain, full of grace!
Grace for sinners, grace for me;
To this source alone I trace
What I am, and hope to be.

KARL. 7.

1. Earth has noth-ing sweet or fair, Love-ly forms or beau-ties rare,

But be - fore my eyes they bring Christ, of beau - ty Source and Spring.

858   *"Altogether Lovely."—Cant.* **5:16.**   SCHEFFLER.

Earth has nothing sweet or fair,
Lovely forms or beauties rare,
But before my eyes they bring
Christ, of beauty Source and Spring.

2 When the morning paints the skies,
When the golden sunbeams rise,
Then my Saviour's form I find
Brightly imaged on my mind.

3 When the star-beams pierce the night,
Oft I think on Jesus' light,
Think how bright that light will be,
Shining through eternity.

4 Come, Lord Jesus! and dispel
This dark cloud in which I dwell,
And to me the power impart
To behold thee as thou art.

859   *"Immanuel."—Isa.* **7:14.**   NEWTON.

Sweeter sounds than music knows
Charm me in Immanuel's name;
All her hopes my spirit owes
To his birth, and cross, and shame.

2 When he came, the angels sung,
"Glory be to God on high:"
Lord, unloose my stammering tongue;
Who should louder sing than I?

3 Did the Lord a man become,
That he might the law fulfill,
Bleed and suffer in my room,—
And canst thou, my tongue, be still?

4 No; I must my praises bring,
Though they worthless are, and weak;
For, should I refuse to sing,
Sure the very stones would speak.

5 O my Saviour! Shield and Sun,
Shepherd, Brother, Lord, and Friend—
Every precious name in one!
I will love thee without end.

860   *"To live is Christ."—Phil.* **1: 21.**   WARDLAW.

Christ, of all my hopes the Ground,
Christ, the Spring of all my joy,
Still in thee let me be found,
Still for thee my powers employ.

2 Fountain of o'erflowing grace!
Freely from thy fullness give;
Till I close my earthly race,
Be it "Christ for me to live!"

3 Firmly trusting in thy blood,
Nothing shall my heart confound;
Safely I shall pass the flood,
Safely reach Immanuel's ground.

4 When I touch the blessèd shore,
Back the closing waves shall roll!
Death's dark stream shall nevermore
Part from thee my ravished soul.

5 Thus,—oh, thus an entrance give
To the land of cloudless sky;
Having known it "Christ to live,"
Let me know it "gain to die."

BROWNELL. L. M. 6l.

1. Je - sus, thy boundless love to me No thought can reach, no tongue de - clare;

Oh, knit my thankful heart to thee, And reign with - out a ri - val there:

Thine whol - ly, thine a - lone, I am: Be thou a - lone my con - stant flame.

861   *"Thy boundless love."*   J. WESLEY. *Tr.*

JESUS, thy boundless love to me
  No tho't can reach, no tongue declare:
Oh, knit my thankful heart to thee,
  And reign without a rival there:
Thine wholly, thine alone, I am;
Be thou alone my constant flame.

2 Oh, grant that nothing in my soul
  May dwell, but thy pure love alone:
Oh, may thy love possess me whole,—
  My joy, my treasure, and my crown;
Strange flames far from my heart remove;
My every act, word, thought, be love.

3 O Love! how cheering is thy ray!
  All pain before thy presence flies;
Care, anguish, sorrow, melt away,
  Where'er thy healing beams arise:
O Jesus! nothing may I see,
Nothing desire, or seek but thee!

4 In suffering be thy love my peace;
  In weakness be thy love my power;
And when the storms of life shall cease,
  Jesus, in that important hour,
In death as life be thou my guide,
And save me, who for me hast died.

326

862   *"My Strength, my Tower."*   J. WESLEY. *Tr.*

THEE will I love, my Strength, my Tower!
  Thee will I love, my Joy, my Crown;
Thee will I love, with all my power,
  In all thy works, and thee alone:
Thee will I love, till the pure fire
Fill my whole soul with chaste desire.

2 I thank thee, uncreated Sun!
  That thy bright beams on me have shined;
I thank thee, who hast overthrown
  My foes, and healed my wounded mind:
I thank thee, whose enlivening voice
Bids my freed heart in thee rejoice.

3 Uphold me in the doubtful race,
  Nor suffer me again to stray;
Strengthen my feet, with steady pace
  Still to press forward in thy way;
That all my powers, with all their might,
In thy sole glory may unite.

4 Thee will I love, my Joy, my Crown!
  Thee will I love, my Lord, my God!
Thee will I love, beneath thy frown
  Or smile, thy sceptre or thy rod.
What though my heart and flesh decay?
Thee shall I love in endless day.

ST. PETERSBURGH. L. M. 6l.

1. { Je - sus, thou source of calm re - pose, All full - ness dwells in thee di - vine; }
{ Our strength, to quell the proud-est foes; Our light, in deep - est gloom to shine; }

Thou art our fort-ress, strength and tower, Our trust and por - tion, ev - er - more.

863   *"All fullness."—Col.* **1: 19.**   C. WESLEY.

JESUS, thou source of calm repose,
  All fullness dwells in thee divine;
Our strength, to quell the proudest foes;
  Our light, in deepest gloom to shine;
Thou art our fortress, strength and tower,
Our trust and portion, evermore.

2 Jesus, our Comforter thou art;
  Our rest in toil, our ease in pain;
The balm to heal each broken heart,
  In storms our peace, in loss our gain;
Our joy, beneath the worldling's frown;
In shame, our glory and our crown;—

3 In want, our plentiful supply;
  In weakness, our almighty power;
In bonds, our perfect liberty;
  Our refuge in temptation's hour;
Our comfort, amidst grief and thrall;
Our life in death; our all in all.

864   *"Just such as I."—Heb.* **2: 14-18.**   EDMESTON.

As oft with worn and weary feet,
  We tread earth's rugged valley o'er,
The thought, how comforting and sweet,
  Christ trod this very path before!
Our wants and weaknesses he knows,
From life's first dawning till its close.

2 If Satan tempt our hearts to stray,
  And whisper evil things within,

So did he in the desert way,
  Assail our Lord with thoughts of sin:
When worn, and in a feeble hour,
The tempter came with all his power.

3 Just such as I, this earth he trod,
  With every human ill but sin;
And, though indeed the very God,
  As I am now, so he has been;
My God, my Saviour! look on me
With pity, love, and sympathy.

865   *The Solid Rock.*   E. MOTE.

My hope is built on nothing less
Than Jesus' blood and righteousness;
I dare not trust the sweetest frame,
But wholly lean on Jesus' name:
  On Christ, the solid rock, I stand;
  All other ground is sinking sand.

2 When darkness seems to vail his face,
I rest on his unchanging grace;
In every high and stormy gale,
My anchor holds within the vail:
  On Christ, the solid rock, I stand;
  All other ground is sinking sand.

3 His oath, his covenant, and blood,
Support me in the whelming flood:
When all around my soul gives way,
He then is all my hope and stay:
  On Christ, the solid rock, I stand;
  All other ground is sinking sand.

GRATITUDE. L. M.

1. My God, how end-less is thy love! Thy gifts are ev-ery eve-ning new;

And morn-ing mer-cies from a-bove, Gent-ly dis-till like ear-ly dew.

866   *Gratitude.—Lam* 3: 23.   WATTS.

My God, how endless is thy love!
  Thy gifts are every evening new;
And morning mercies from above,
  Gently distill like early dew.

2 Thou spread'st the curtains of the night,
  Great guardian of my sleeping hours;
Thy sovereign word restores the light,
  And quickens all my drowsy powers.

3 I yield my powers to thy command;
  To thee I consecrate my days;
Perpetual blessings from thine hand
  Demand perpetual songs of praise.

867   *Faith.—Ps.* 23: 4.   NEWTON.

By faith in Christ I walk with God,
  With heaven, my journey's end, in view;
Supported by his staff and rod,
  My road is safe and pleasant too.

2 Tho' snares and dangers throng my path,
  And earth and hell my course withstand,
I triumph over all by faith,
  Guarded by his almighty hand.

3 The wilderness affords no food,
  But God for my support prepares,
Provides me every needful good,
  And frees my soul from wants and cares.

4 With him sweet converse I maintain;
  Great as he is, I dare be free;
I tell him all my grief and pain,
  And he reveals his love to me.

868   *Contentment.—Phil.* 4: 11.   GUION.

O Lord, how full of sweet content
Our years of pilgrimage are spent!
Where'er we dwell, we dwell with thee,
In heaven, in earth, or on the sea.

2 To us remains nor place nor time;
Our country is in every clime:
We can be calm and free from care
On any shore, since God is there.

3 While place we seek, or place we shun,
The soul finds happiness in none;
But with our God to guide our way,
'Tis equal joy to go or stay.

4 Could we be cast where thou art not,
That were indeed a dreadful lot;
But regions none remote we call,
Secure of finding God in all.

869   *Meekness.—Matt.* 5: 5.   J. SCOTT.

Happy the meek whose gentle breast,
  Clear as the summer's evening ray,
Calm as the regions of the blest,
  Enjoys on earth celestial day.

2 His heart no broken friendships sting,
  No storms his peaceful tent invade;
He rests beneath the Almighty's wing,
  Hostile to none, of none afraid.

3 Spirit of grace, all meek and mild!
  Inspire our breasts, our souls possess:
Repel each passion rude and wild,
  And bless us as we aim to bless.

DUKE STREET. L. M.

1. 'Tis by the faith of joys to come, We walk through deserts dark as night;

Till we ar-rive at heaven, our home, Faith is our guide, and faith our light.

870 *Faith.—Heb. 11: 8.* WATTS.

'Tis by the faith of joys to come
  We walk through deserts dark as night;
Till we arrive at heaven, our home,
  Faith is our guide, and faith our light.

2 The want of sight she well supplies;
  She makes the pearly gates appear;
Far into distant worlds she pries,
  And brings eternal glories near.

3 Cheerful we tread the desert through,
  While faith inspires a heavenly ray;
Though lions roar, and tempests blow,
  And rocks and dangers fill the way.

871 *Self-denial.—Luke 9: 23.* KEBLE.

If on our daily course our mind
Be set, to hallow all we find,
New treasures still, of countless price,
God will provide for sacrifice.

2 Old friends, old scenes, will lovelier be,
As more of heaven in each we see;
Some softening gleam of love and prayer
Shall dawn on every cross and care.

3 The trivial round, the common task,
Will furnish all we ought to ask;—
Room to deny ourselves, a road
To bring us daily nearer God.

4 Only, O Lord, in thy dear love,
Fit us for perfect rest above;
And help us this and every day,
To live more nearly as we pray.

872 *Love.—1 Cor. 13: 1.* WATTS.

Had I the tongues of Greeks and Jews,
And nobler speech than angels use,
If love be absent, I am found
Like tinkling brass, an empty sound.

2 Were I inspired to preach and tell
All that is done in heaven and hell—
Or could my faith the world remove,
Still I am nothing without love.

3 Should I distribute all my store
To feed the hungry, clothe the poor;
Or give my body to the flame,
To gain a martyr's glorious name:

4 If love to God and love to men
Be absent, all my hopes are vain;
Nor tongues, nor gifts, nor fiery zeal,
The work of love can e'er fulfill.

873 *Consistency.—Titus 2: 10-13.* WATTS.

So let our lips and lives express
The holy gospel we profess;
So let our works and virtues shine,
To prove the doctrine all divine.

2 Thus shall we best proclaim abroad
The honors of our Saviour God;
When his salvation reigns within,
And grace subdues the power of sin.

3 Religion bears our spirits up,
While we expect that blessèd hope,—
The bright appearance of the Lord:
And faith stands leaning on his word.

NAOMI. C. M.

1. Fa - ther! whate'er of earth - ly bliss Thy sovereign will de - nies,

Ac - cept - ed at thy throne of grace, Let this pe - ti - tion rise :—

874   *Humble Devotion.*   STEELE.

FATHER! whate'er of earthly bliss
  Thy sovereign will denies,
Accepted at thy throne of grace,
  Let this petition rise:—

2 "Give me a calm, a thankful heart,
  From every murmur free;
The blessings of thy grace impart,
  And make me live to thee.

3 "Let the sweet hope that thou art mine
  My life and death attend;
Thy presence through my journey shine,
  And crown my journey's end."

875   *Calmness.—Isa. 26:3.*   BONAR.

CALM me, my God, and keep me calm;
  Let thine outstretched wing
Be like the shade of Elim's palm,
  Beside her desert spring.

2 Yes, keep me calm, though loud and rude
  The sounds my ear that greet,—
Calm in the closet's solitude,
  Calm in the bustling street,—

3 Calm in the hour of buoyant health,
  Calm in the hour of pain,
Calm in my poverty or wealth,
  Calm in my loss or gain,—

4 Calm in the sufferance of wrong,
  Like him who bore my shame,
Calm 'mid the threatening, taunting throng,
  Who hate thy holy name.

5 Calm me, my God, and keep me calm,
  Soft resting on thy breast;
Soothe me with holy hymn and psalm,
  And bid my spirit rest.

876   *Humility.—Isa. 57:15.*   ANON.

THY home is with the humble, Lord!
  The simple are the best;
Thy lodging is in child-like hearts;
  Thou makest there thy rest.

2 Dear Comforter! eternal Love!
  If thou wilt stay with me,
Of lowly thoughts and simple ways,
  I'll build a house for thee.

3 Who made this breathing heart of mine
  But thou, my heavenly Guest?
Let no one have it, then, but thee,
  And let it be thy rest!

877   *Docility.—Ps. 131.*   WATTS.

Is there ambition in my heart?
  Search, gracious God, and see;
Or do I act a haughty part?
  Lord, I appeal to thee.

2 I charge my thoughts, be humble still,
  And all my carriage mild;
Content, my Father, with thy will,
  And quiet as a child.

3 The patient soul, the lowly mind,
  Shall have a large reward;
Let saints in sorrow lie resigned,
  And trust a faithful Lord.

MOUNT AUBURN. C. M.

1. Lord, I be-lieve; thy power I own; Thy word I would o-bey;

I wan-der com-fort-less and lone, When from thy truth I stray.

878   *Faith.—Mark 9: 24.*   WREFORD.

Lord, I believe; thy power I own;
Thy word I would obey;
I wander comfortless and lone,
When from thy truth I stray.

2 Lord, I believe; but gloomy fears,
Sometimes bedim my sight;
I look to thee with prayers and tears,
And cry for strength and light.

3 Lord, I believe; but oft, I know,
My faith is cold and weak:
My weakness strengthen, and bestow
The confidence I seek.

4 Yes! I believe; and only thou
Canst give my soul relief:
Lord, to thy truth my spirit bow;
"Help thou mine unbelief!"

879   *Growth in grace.—Gal. 5: 22.*   NETTLETON.

Come, Holy Ghost, my soul inspire—
This one great gift impart—
What most I need—and most desire,
An humble, holy heart.

2 Bear witness I am born again,
My many sins forgiven:
Nor let a gloomy doubt remain
To cloud my hope of heaven.

3 More of myself grant I may know,
From sin's deceit be free,
In all the Christian graces grow,
And live alone to thee.

880   *Charitableness.*   FLETCHER.

Think gently of the erring one!
And let us not forget,
However darkly stained by sin,
He is our brother yet.

2 Heir of the same inheritance,
Child of the self-same God;
He hath but stumbled in the path,
We have in weakness trod.

3 Forget not thou hast often sinned,
And sinful yet must be:
Deal gently with the erring one,
As God has dealt with thee.

881   *Love.—1 Cor. 13: 13.*   WATTS.

Happy the heart where graces reign,
Where love inspires the breast:
Love is the brightest of the train,
And strengthens all the rest.

2 Knowledge—alas! 'tis all in vain,
And all in vain our fear;
Our stubborn sins will fight and reign,
If love be absent there.

3 This is the grace that lives and sings,
When faith and hope shall cease;
'Tis this shall strike our joyful strings,
In the sweet realms of bliss.

4 Before we quite forsake our clay,
Or leave this dark abode,
The wings of love bear us away,
To see our smiling God.

REMSEN. C. M.

1. Fa - ther of mer - cies! send thy grace, All power - ful from a - bove,

To form in our o - be - dient souls, The im - age of thy love.

882   *Brotherly Kindness.*   DODDRIDGE.

FATHER of mercies! send thy grace,
  All powerful from above,
To form in our obedient souls,
  The image of thy love.

2 Oh, may our sympathizing breasts
  The generous pleasure know,
Kindly to share in others' joy,
  And weep for others' woe!

3 When the most helpless sons of grief
  In low distress are laid,
Soft be our hearts their pains to feel,
  And swift our hands to aid.

4 So Jesus looked on dying men,
  When throned above the skies;
And mid the embraces of his God,
  He felt compassion rise.

5 On wings of love the Saviour flew,
  To raise us from the ground,
And made the richest of his blood
  A balm for every wound.

883   *Meekness.—Luke* 1 : 53.   GILL.

LORD! when I all things would possess,
  I crave but to be thine;
Oh, lowly is the loftiness
  Of these desires divine.

2 Each gift but helps my soul to learn
  How boundless is thy store;
I go from strength to strength, and yearn
  For thee, my Helper, more.

3 How can my soul divinely soar,
  How keep the shining way,
And not more tremblingly adore,
  And not more humbly pray!

4 The more I triumph in thy gifts,
  The more I wait on thee;
The grace that mightily uplifts
  Most sweetly humbleth me.

5 The heaven where I would stand complete
  My lowly love shall see,
And stronger grow the yearning sweet,
  My holy One! for thee.

884   *Minute Fidelity.—Eccl.* 11 : 6.   ANON.

SCORN not the slightest word or deed,
  Nor deem it void of power;
There's fruit in each wind-wafted seed,
  That waits its natal hour.

2 A whispered word may touch the heart,
  And call it back to life;
A look of love bid sin depart,
  And still unholy strife.

3 No act falls fruitless; none can tell
  How vast its power may be,
Nor what results infolded dwell
  Within it silently.

4 Work on, despair not, bring thy mite,
  Nor care how small it be;
God is with all that serve the right,
  The holy, true, and free.

VALENTIA. C. M.

1. Oh, gift of gifts! oh, grace of faith! My God! how can it be That thou, who hast dis - cern - ing love, Shouldst give that gift to me?

885 *Faith.—Eph. 2: 8.* FABER.

Oh, gift of gifts! oh, grace of faith!
My God! how can it be
That thou, who hast discerning love,
Shouldst give that gift to me?

2 How many hearts thou mightst have had
More innocent than mine!
How many souls more worthy far
Of that sweet touch of thine!

3 Ah, grace! into unlikeliest hearts
It is thy boast to come,
The glory of thy light to find
In darkest spots a home.

4 The crowd of cares, the weightiest cross,
Seem trifles less than light—
Earth looks so little and so low
When faith shines full and bright.

5 Oh, happy, happy that I am!
If thou canst be, O Faith,
The treasure that thou art in life,
What wilt thou be in death!

886 *Godly Sincerity.—Eph. 5 . 8.* BARTON.

Walk in the light! so shalt thou know
That fellowship of love,
His Spirit only can bestow,
Who reigns in light above.

2 Walk in the light! and thou shalt find
Thy heart made truly his,
Who dwells in cloudless light enshrined,
In whom no darkness is.

3 Walk in the light! and ev'n the tomb
No fearful shade shall wear;
Glory shall chase away its gloom,
For Christ hath conquered there.

4 Walk in the light! and thou shalt see
Thy path, though thorny, bright,
For God by grace shall dwell in thee,
And God himself is light.

887 *Faith.—2 Cor. 5: 7.* WATTS.

Faith adds new charms to earthly bliss,
And saves me from its snares;
Its aid, in every duty, brings,
And softens all my cares.

2 The wounded conscience knows its power
The healing balm to give;
That balm the saddest heart can cheer,
And make the dying live.

3 Wide it unvails celestial worlds,
Where deathless pleasures reign;
And bids me seek my portion there,
Nor bids me seek in vain.

4 It shows the precious promise sealed
With the Redeemer's blood;
And helps my feeble hope to rest
Upon a faithful God.

5 There—there unshaken would I rest,
Till this frail body dies;
And then, on faith's triumphant wings,
To endless glory rise.

HUNTINGTON. S. M.

1. Re - joice in God al - way; When earth looks heaven - ly bright,

When joy makes glad the live-long day, And peace shuts in the night.

888   *Joy.—Phil. 4: 4.*   MOULTRIE.

REJOICE in God alway;
  When earth looks heavenly bright,
When joy makes glad the livelong day,
  And peace shuts in the night.

2 Rejoice when care and woe
  The fainting soul oppress;
When tears at wakeful midnight flow,
  And morn brings heaviness.

3 Rejoice in hope and fear;
  Rejoice in life and death;
Rejoice when threatening storms are near,
  And comfort languisheth.

4 When should not they rejoice,
  Whom Christ his brethren calls;
Who hear and know his guiding voice,
  When on their hearts it falls?

5 So, though our path is steep,
  And many a tempest lowers,
Shall his own peace our spirits keep,
  And Christ's dear love be ours.

889   *Grateful Confidence.*   BONAR.

I BLESS the Christ of God,
  I rest on love divine,
And with unfaltering lip and heart,
  I call the Saviour mine.

2 His cross dispels each doubt;
  I bury in his tomb
Each thought of unbelief and fear,
  Each lingering shade of gloom.

3 I praise the God of peace;
  I trust his truth and might;
He calls me his, I call him mine,
  My God, my joy, my light.

4 In him is only good,
  In me is only ill;
My ill but draws his goodness forth,
  And me he loveth still.

5 'Tis he who saveth me,
  And freely pardon gives:
I love because he loveth me;
  I live because he lives.

6 My life with him is hid,
  My death has passed away,
My clouds have melted into light,
  My midnight into day.

890   *Purity.—Matt. 5: 8.*   KEBLE.

BLEST are the pure in heart,
  For they shall see their God;
The secret of the Lord is theirs;
  Their soul is Christ's abode.

2 He to the lowly soul
  Doth still himself impart,
And for his dwelling, and his throne,
  Chooseth the pure in heart.

3 Lord! we thy presence seek;
  May ours this blessing be;
Oh, give the pure and lowly heart,—
  A temple meet for thee.

ROSEFIELD. 7. 6l.

1. { Bles - sed are the sons of God, They are bought with Je - sus' blood; }
{ They are ran - somed from the grave; Life e - ter - nal they shall have: }

With them numbered may we be, Here, and in e - ter - ni - ty.

891   *Brotherly love.*   HUMPHREYS.

BLESSED are the sons of God,
They are bought with Jesus' blood;
They are ransomed from the grave;
Life eternal they shall have:
With them numbered may we be,
Here, and in eternity.

2 They are justified by grace,
They enjoy the Saviour's peace;
All their sins are washed away;
They shall stand in God's great day:
With them numbered may we be,
Here, and in eternity.

3 They are lights upon the earth,
Children of a heavenly birth,—
One with God, with Jesus one:
Glory is in them begun:
With them numbered may we be,
Here, and in eternity.

892   *Charity.—1 Cor.* **13: 1.**   LANGE.

THOUGH I speak with angel tongues
  Bravest words of strength and fire,
They are but as idle songs,
  If no love my heart inspire;
All the eloquence shall pass
As the noise of sounding brass.

2 Though I lavish all I have
  On the poor in charity,

Though I shrink not from the grave,
  Or unmoved the stake can see,—
Till by love the work be crowned,
All shall profitless be found.

3 Come, thou Spirit of pure love,
  Who didst forth from God proceed,
Never from my heart remove;
  Let me all thy impulse heed;
Let my heart henceforward be
Moved, controlled, inspired by thee.

893   *Spirituality.—Rom.* **8: 15.**   C. WESLEY.

ABBA, Father, hear thy child,
Late in Jesus reconciled;
Hear, and all the graces shower,
All the joy, and peace, and power;
All my Saviour asks above,
All the life and heaven of love.

2 Heavenly Father, Life divine,
Change my nature into thine:
Move and spread throughout my soul,
Renovate and fill the whole;
Lord, I will not let thee go
Till the blessing thou bestow.

3 Holy Ghost, no more delay;
Come, and in thy temple stay:
Now, thine inward witness bear,
Strong, and permanent, and clear:
Spring of life, thyself impart;
Rise eternal in my heart.

SPOHR. L. M.

1. Not all the no-bles of the earth, Who boast the hon-ors of their birth,

So high a dig-ni-ty can claim, As those who bear the Chris-tian name.

894   *Adoption.*   STENNETT.

Not all the nobles of the earth,
Who boast the honors of their birth,
So high a dignity can claim,
As those who bear the Christian name.

2 To them the privilege is given
To be the sons and heirs of heaven;
Sons of the God who reigns on high,
And heirs of joy beyond the sky.

3 His will he makes them early know,
And teaches their young feet to go;
Whispers instruction to their minds,
And on their hearts his precepts binds.

4 Their daily wants his hands supply,
Their steps he guards with watchful eye;
Leads them from earth to heaven above,
And crowns them with eternal love.

895   *Pardoned Sin.*   HEGINBOTHAM.

Sweet peace of conscience, heavenly guest,
Come, fix thy mansion in my breast;
Dispel my doubts, my fears control,
And heal the anguish of my soul.

2 Come, smiling hope, and joy sincere,
Come, make your constant dwelling here;
Still let your presence cheer my heart,
Nor sin compel you to depart.

3 O God of hope and peace divine!
Make thou these secret pleasures mine;
Forgive my sins, my fears remove,
And fill my heart with joy and love.

896   *Grace.—Luke* 10:20.   DODDRIDGE.

No more, ye wise! your wisdom boast;
No more, ye strong! your valor trust;
No more, ye rich! survey your store,
Elate with heaps of shining ore.

2 Glory, ye saints, in this alone,—
That God, your God, to you is known;
That you have owned his sovereign sway,
That you have felt his cheering ray.

3 All else, which we our treasure call,
May in one fatal moment fall;
But what their happiness can move,
Whom God, the blessed, deigns to love!

897   *Completeness.—Col.* 2:10.   WOLFE.

Complete in thee! no work of mine
May take, dear Lord, the place of thine;
Thy blood has pardon bought for me,
And I am now complete in thee.

2 Complete in thee—no more shall sin,
Thy grace has conquered, reign within;
Thy voice will bid the tempter flee,
And I shall stand complete in thee.

3 Complete in thee—each want supplied,
And no good thing to me denied,
Since thou my portion, Lord, wilt be,
I ask no more—complete in thee.

4 Dear Saviour! when, before thy bar
All tribes and tongues assembled are,
Among thy chosen may I be
At thy right hand—complete in thee.

WARRINGTON. L. M.

1. Lord, how se-cure and blest are they Who feel the joys of par-doned sin!

Should storms of wrath shake earth and sea, Their minds have heaven and peace with-in.

898   *Security and Rest.*   WATTS.

Lord, how secure and blest are they
  Who feel the joys of pardoned sin!
Should storms of wrath shake earth and sea
  Their minds have heaven and peace
    within.

2 The day glides swiftly o'er their heads,
  Made up of innocence and love;
And soft and silent as the shades,
  Their nightly minutes gently move.

3 Quick as their thoughts their joys come on,
  But fly not half so swift away:
Their souls are ever bright as noon,
  And calm as summer evenings be.

4 How oft they look to heavenly hills,
  Where streams of living pleasures flow;
And longing hopes and cheerful smiles
  Sit undisturbed upon their brow!

5 They scorn to seek earth's golden toys,
  But spend the day, and share the night
In numbering o'er the richer joys
  That heaven prepares for their delight.

899   *Perseverance.—Rom. 8: 33.*   WATTS.

Who shall the Lord's elect condemn?
  'Tis God who justifies their souls;
And mercy, like a mighty stream,
  O'er all their sins divinely rolls.

2 Who shall adjudge the saints to hell?
  'Tis Christ who suffered in their stead;
And their salvation to fulfill,
  Behold him rising from the dead!

3 He lives! he lives! and sits above,
  For ever interceding there:
Who shall divide us from his love,
  Or what shall tempt us to despair?

4 Shall persecution, or distress,
  Famine, or sword, or nakedness?
He who hath loved us bears us through,
  And makes us more than conquerors too!

5 Not all that men on earth can do,
  Nor powers on high, nor powers below,
Shall cause his mercy to remove,
  Or wean our hearts from Christ, our love.

900   *Remembrance.—Ps. 112: 6.*   LOWRING.

Earth's transitory things decay;
Its pomps, its pleasures, pass away;
But the sweet memory of the good
Survives in the vicissitude.

2 As, 'mid the ever-rolling sea,
The eternal isles established be,
'Gainst which the surges of the main
Fret, dash, and break themselves in vain;—

3 As, in the heavens, the urns divine
Of golden light for ever shine;
Tho' clouds may darken, storms may rage,
They still shine on from age to age;—

4 So, through the ocean tide of years,
The memory of the just appears;
So, through the tempest and the gloom,
The good man's virtues light the tomb.

BROWN. C. M.

1. When I can read my ti - tle clear To man - sions in the skies,

I bid fare-well to ev - ery fear, And wipe my weep-ing eyes.

901   *Assurance.*—2 *Pet.* 1:10.   WATTS.

WHEN I can read my title clear
  To mansions in the skies,
I bid farewell to every fear,
  And wipe my weeping eyes.

2 Should earth against my soul engage,
  And fiery darts be hurled,
Then I can smile at Satan's rage,
  And face a frowning world.

3 Let cares like a wild deluge come,
  And storms of sorrow fall;
May I but safely reach my home,
  My God, my heaven, my all!—

4 There shall I bathe my weary soul
  In seas of heavenly rest;
And not a wave of trouble roll
  Across my peaceful breast.

902   *Liberty.*—*John* 8: 36.   C. WESLEY.

If thou impart thyself to me,
  No other good I need!
If thou, the Son, shalt make me free,
  I shall be free indeed.

2 I cannot rest till in thy blood
  I full redemption have;
But thou, through whom I come to God,
  Canst to the utmost save.

3 I, too, with thee, shall walk in white;
  With all thy saints shall prove
What is the length and breadth and height
  And depth of perfect love.

903   *Perseverance.*—*Phil.* 1: 6.   WATTS.

FIRM as the earth thy gospel stands,
  My Lord, my hope, my trust;
If I am found in Jesus' hands,
  My soul can ne'er be lost.

2 His honor is engaged to save
  The meanest of his sheep;
All, whom his heavenly Father gave,
  His hands securely keep.

3 Nor death nor hell shall e'er remove
  His favorites from his breast;
In the dear bosom of his love
  They must for ever rest.

904   *"Saints' Inventory."*—1 *Cor.* 3: 21-23.   BEDDOME.

IF God is mine, then present things
  And things to come are mine;
Yea, Christ, his word, and Spirit too,
  And glory all divine.

2 If he is mine, then from his love
  He every trouble sends;
All things are working for my good,
  And bliss his rod attends.

3 If he is mine, let friends forsake,
  Let wealth and honor flee;
Sure he who giveth me himself
  Is more than these to me.

4 Oh, tell me, Lord, that thou art mine;
  What can I wish beside?
My soul shall at the fountain live,
  When all the streams are dried.

338

ST. ASAPH. C. M. D.

1. Thou art my hid-ing-place, O Lord! In thee I put my trust; En-couraged by thy ho-ly word, A fee-ble child of dust: I have no ar-gu-ment be-side, I urge no oth-er plea; And 'tis enough my Saviour died, My Saviour died for me!......

RAFFLES.

905 *Hiding-place.—Ps.* **32: 7.**

Thou art my hiding-place, O Lord!
    In thee I put my trust;
Encouraged by thy holy word,
    A feeble child of dust:
I have no argument beside,
    I urge no other plea;
And 'tis enough my Saviour died,
    My Saviour died for me!

2 When storms of fierce temptation beat,
    And furious foes assail,
My refuge is the mercy-seat,
    My hope within the vail:
From strife of tongues, and bitter words,
    My spirit flies to thee;
Joy to my heart the thought affords,
    My Saviour died for me!

3 And when thine awful voice commands
    This body to decay,
And life, in its last lingering sands,
    Is ebbing fast away;—
Then, though it be in accents weak,
    My voice shall call on thee,
And ask for strength in death to speak,
    "My Saviour died for me."

DECK.

906 *Union to Christ.*

Lord Jesus, are we one with thee?
    Oh, height! oh, depth of love!
With thee we died upon the tree,
    In thee we live above.

2 Such was thy grace, that for our sake
    Thou didst from heaven come down,
Thou didst of flesh and blood partake,
    In all our sorrows one.

3 Our sins, our guilt, in love divine,
    Confessed and borne by thee;
The gall, the curse, the wrath were thine,
    To set thy members free.

4 Ascended now, in glory bright,
    Still one with us thou art;
Nor life, nor death, nor depth, nor height,
    Thy saints and thee can part.

5 Oh, teach us, Lord, to know and own
    This wondrous mystery,
That thou with us art truly one,
    And we are one with thee!

6 Soon, soon shall come that glorious day,
    When, seated on thy throne,
Thou shalt to wondering worlds display,
    That thou with us art one.

COOLING. C. M.

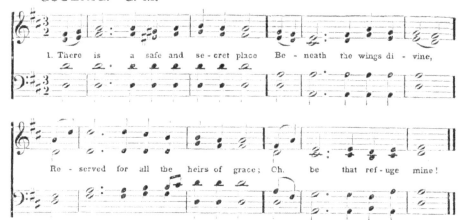

1. There is a safe and se-cret place Be-neath the wings di - vine,

Re-served for all the heirs of grace; Oh, be that ref-uge mine!

907   *Security.—Ps. 91:1.*   LYTE.

THERE is a safe and secret place
  Beneath the wings divine,
Reserved for all the heirs of grace,
  Oh, be that refuge mine!

2 The least and feeblest there may bide,
  Uninjured and unawed;
While thousands fall on every side,
  He rests secure in God.

3 He feeds in pastures large and fair,
  Of love and truth divine;
O child of God, O glory's heir!
  How rich a lot is thine!

4 A hand almighty to defend,
  An ear for every call,
An honored life, a peaceful end,
  And heaven to crown it all!

908   *Reconciliation.—2 Cor. 5:19.*   GERMAN.

Father, thy thoughts are peace towards me,
  Safe am I in thy hands;
Could I but firmly build on thee,
  For sure thy counsel stands!

2 Though mountains crumble into dust,
  Thy covenant standeth fast;
Who follows thee in pious trust,
  Shall reach the goal at last.

3 Though strange and winding seems the way
  While yet on earth I dwell;
In heaven my heart shall gladly say,
  Thou, God, dost all things well!

909   *Adoption.—Rom. 8:15.*   DODDRIDGE.

My Father, God! how sweet the sound!
  How tender and how dear!
Not all the melody of heaven
  Could so delight the ear.

2 Come, sacred Spirit, seal the name
  On my expanding heart;
And show, that in Jehovah's grace
  I share a filial part.

3 Cheered by a signal so divine,
  Unwavering I believe;
My spirit Abba, Father! cries,
  Nor can the sign deceive.

910   *The Covenant.*   DODDRIDGE.

My God, the covenant of thy love
  Abides for ever sure;
And in its matchless grace I feel
  My happiness secure.

2 Since thou, the everlasting God,
  My Father art become,
Jesus my Guardian and my Friend,
  And heaven my final home;—

3 I welcome all thy sovereign will,
  For all that will is love;
And when I know not what thou dost,
  I wait the light above.

4 Thy covenant in the darkest gloom
  Shall heavenly rays impart,
And when my eyelids close in death,
  Sustain my fainting heart.

ARMENIA. C. M.

1. Do not I love thee, O my Lord? Be-hold my heart, and see;

And turn the dear-est i-dol out That dares to ri-val thee.

---

911 *Loving and Beloved.* DODDRIDGE.

Do not I love thee, O my Lord?
  Behold my heart, and see;
And turn the dearest idol out
  That dares to rival thee.

2 Is not thy name melodious still
  To mine attentive ear?
Doth not each pulse with pleasure bound,
  My Saviour's voice to hear?

3 Hast thou a lamb in all thy flock
  I would disdain to feed?
Hast thou a foe, before whose face
  I fear thy cause to plead?

4 Would not my heart pour forth its blood
  In honor of thy name?
And challenge the cold hand of death
  To damp the immortal flame?

5 Thou knowest that I love thee, Lord;
  But oh, I long to soar
Far from the sphere of mortal joys,
  And learn to love thee more.

912 *God's Peace.—Phil.* 4: 7. ANON.

We bless thee for thy peace, O God!
  Deep as the soundless sea,
Which falls like sunshine on the road
  Of those who trust in thee.

2 We ask not, Father, for repose
  Which comes from outward rest,
If we may have through all life's woes
  Thy peace within our breast;—

3 That peace which suffers and is strong,
  Trusts where it cannot see,
Deems not the trial way too long,
  But leaves the end with thee;—

4 That peace which flows serene and deep—
  A river in the soul,
Whose banks a living verdure keep:
  God's sunshine o'er the whole!

5 Such, Father, give our hearts such peace,
  Whate'er the outward be,
Till all life's discipline shall cease,
  And we go home to thee.

913 *"The Secret."—Ps.* 25: 14. WESLEY.

Speak to me, Lord, thyself reveal,
  While here on earth I rove;
Speak to my heart, and let me feel
  The kindling of thy love.

2 With thee conversing, I forget
  All time and toil and care;
Labor is rest, and pain is sweet,
  If thou, my God, art here.

3 Thou callest me to seek thy face;
  Thy face, O God, I seek,—
Attend the whispers of thy grace,
  And hear thee inly speak.

4 Let this my every hour employ,
  Till I thy glory see,
Enter into my Master's joy,
  And find my heaven in thee.

THATCHER. S. M.

1. Thou ver-y pre-sent Aid In suf-fering and dis-tress,

The mind which still on thee is stayed, Is kept in per-fect peace.

914   *Peace.—Isa. 26 : 2.*   C. WESLEY.

Thou very present Aid
  In suffering and distress,
The mind which still on thee is stayed,
  Is kept in perfect peace.

2 The soul by faith reclined
  On the Redeemer's breast,
'Mid raging storms, exults to find
  An everlasting rest.

3 Sorrow and fear are gone,
  Whene'er thy face appears;
It stills the sighing orphan's moan,
  And dries the widow's tears.

4 It hallows every cross;
  It sweetly comforts me;
Makes me forget my every loss,
  And find my all in thee.

5 Jesus, to whom I fly,
  Doth all my wishes fill;
What though created streams are dry?
  I have the fountain still.

6 Stripped of each earthly friend,
  I find them all in one,
And peace and joy which never end,
  And heaven, in Christ, begun.

915   *The faithful love of God.*   ANON.

In every trying hour
  My soul to Jesus flies;
I trust in his almighty power,
  When swelling billows rise.

2 His comforts bear me up;
  I trust a faithful God;
The sure foundation of my hope
  Is in my Saviour's blood.

3 Loud hallelujahs sing
  To our Redeemer's name;
In joy or sorrow—life or death—
  His love is still the same.

916   *Adoption.—1 John 3 : 1-3.*   WATTS.

Behold what wondrous grace
  The Father has bestowed
On sinners of a mortal race,
  To call them sons of God!

2 Nor doth it yet appear
  How great we must be made;
But when we see our Saviour there,
  We shall be like our Head.

3 A hope so much divine
  May trials well endure,
May purge our souls from sense and sin,
  As Christ the Lord is pure.

4 If in my Father's love
  I share a filial part,
Send down thy Spirit, like a dove,
  To rest upon my heart.

5 We would no longer lie
  Like slaves beneath the throne;
Our faith shall Abba, Father! cry,
  And thou the kindred own.

LUTHER. S. M.

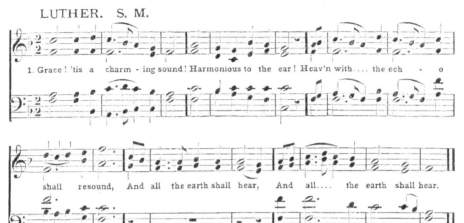

1. Grace! 'tis a charm - ing sound! Harmonious to the ear! Heav'n with.... the ech - o

shall resound, And all the earth shall hear, And all.... the earth shall hear.

917 *Grace.—Eph.* 2: 8. DODDRIDGE.

Grace! 'tis a charming sound!
　　Harmonious to the ear!
Heaven with the echo shall resound,
　　And all the earth shall hear.

2 Grace first contrived a way
　　To save rebellious man;
And all the steps that grace display,
　　Which drew the wondrous plan.

3 Grace led my roving feet
　　To tread the heavenly road;
And new supplies each hour I meet
　　While pressing on to God.

4 Grace all the work shall crown,
　　Through everlasting days;
It lays in heaven the topmost stone,
　　And well deserves the praise.

918 *Confidence.—Ps.* 37: 3-7. GERHARDT.

Here I can firmly rest;
　　I dare to boast of this,
That God, the highest and the best,
　　My Friend and Father is.

2 Naught have I of my own,
　　Naught in the life I lead;
What Christ hath given, that alone
　　I dare in faith to plead.

3 I rest upon the ground
　　Of Jesus and his blood;
It is through him that I have found
　　My soul's eternal good.

4 At cost of all I have,
　　At cost of life and limb,
I cling to God who yet shall save;—
　　I will not turn from him.

5 His Spirit in me dwells,
　　O'er all my mind he reigns;
My care and sadness he dispels,
　　And soothes away my pains.

6 He prospers day by day
　　His work within my heart,
Till I have strength and faith to say,
　　Thou, God, my Father art!

919 *Kept of God.—Isa.* 3: 10. KENT.

What cheering words are these;
　　Their sweetness who can tell?
In time and to eternal days,
　　"'Tis with the righteous well!"

2 Well when they see his face,
　　Or sink amidst the flood;
Well in affliction's thorny maze,
　　Or on the mount with God.

3 'Tis well when joys arise,
　　'Tis well when sorrows flow,
'Tis well when darkness vails the skies,
　　And strong temptations grow.

4 'Tis well when Jesus calls,—
　　"From earth and sin arise,
To join the hosts of ransomed souls,
　　Made to salvation wise!"

AND CAN IT BE? L. M. 6l.

And can it be that I should gain An interest in the Saviour's blood?
Died he for me, who caused his pain? For me, who him to death pur - sued?

A - maz - ing love! how can it be, That thou, my Lord, shouldst die for me?

A - maz - ing love! how can it be, That thou, my Lord, shouldst die for me?

C. WESLEY.

920   *"No condemnation."—Rom.* 8: 1.

AND can it be that I should gain
  An interest in the Saviour's blood?
Died he for me, who caused his pain?
  For me, who him to death pursued?
Amazing love! how can it be,
That thou, my Lord, shouldst die for me?

2 'Tis myst'ry all,—the Immortal dies!
  Who can explore his strange design?
In vain the first-born seraph tries
  To sound the depths of love divine;
'Tis mercy all! let earth adore:
Let angel minds inquire no more.

3 He left his Father's throne above;
  (So free, so infinite his grace!)
Emptied himself of all but love,
  And bled for Adam's helpless race;
'Tis mercy all, immense and free,
For, O my God, it found out me!

4 Long my imprisoned spirit lay,
  Fast bound in sin and nature's night:
Thine eye diffused a quickening ray;
  I woke; the dungeon flamed with light;
My chains fell off, my heart was free,—
I rose, went forth, and followed thee.

5 No condemnation now I dread,—
  Jesus, with all in him, is mine;
Alive in him, my living Head,
  And clothed in righteous-ness divine,
Bold I approach the eternal throne,
And claim the crown, thro' Christ my own.

WITHINGTON.

921   *"For me."—Phil.* 2: 5-8.

O SAVIOUR of a world undone!
Whose dying sorrows blot the sun,
Whose painful groans and bowing head
Could rend the vail and wake the dead,
Say, from that execrated tree
Descends the ruddy tide for me?

2 For me did he who reigns above,
The object of paternal love,
Consent a servant's form to bear
That I a kingly crown might wear?
Is his deep loss my boundless gain,
And comes my victory from his pain?

3 Oh, let me own the deep decree
That wounded him and rescued me!
His death, his cross, his funeral sleep,
Instruct repentance how to weep;
He poured for me the vital flood;
My tears shall mingle with his blood.

VALLEY OF BLESSING. P. M.

1. I have en-tered the val-ley of blessing so sweet, And Je-sus a-bides with me there;

And his Spir-it and blood make my cleansing complete, And his per-fect love casteth out fear.

CHORUS.

Oh, come to this val-ley of blessing so sweet, Where Je-sus will full-ness be-stow—

And be-lieve, and receive, and confess him,...... That all his sal-va-tion may know.

MRS. WITTEMEYER.

922 *Ezekiel* **34 : 26.**

I have entered the valley of blessing so sweet,
    And Jesus abides with me there;
And his Spirit and blood make my cleansing
      complete,
And his perfect love casteth out fear.—Cho.

2 There is peace in the valley of blessing so
      sweet,
    And plenty the land doth impart;
There is rest for the weary-worn traveler's
      feet,
    And joy for the sorrowing heart.—Cho.

3 There is love in the valley of blessing so
      sweet,
    Such as none but the blood-washed may
      feel;
When heaven comes down, redeemed spir-
      its to greet,
And Christ sets his covenant seal.—Cho.

SWAIN.

923 *Communion with Christ.*

O thou, in whose presence my soul takes
    On whom in affliction I call, [delight,
My comfort by day, and my song in the
    My hope, my salvation, my all! [night,
Where dost thou, at noon-tide, resort with
      thy sheep,
To feed them in pastures of love?
Say, why in the valley of death should I
    Or alone in this wilderness rove? [weep,

2 Oh, why should I wander an alien from
    Or cry in the desert for bread? [thee,
Thy foes will rejoice when my sorrows they
      see,
    And smile at the tears I have shed.
Dear Shepherd! I hear, and will follow thy
      call;
    I know the sweet sound of thy voice;
Restore and defend me, for thou art my all,
    And in thee I will ever rejoice.

345

WELTON. L. M.

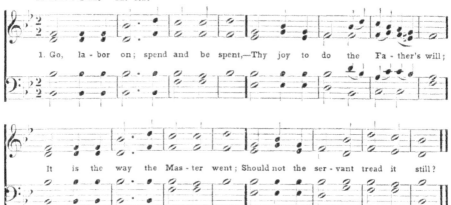

1. Go, la-bor on; spend and be spent,—Thy joy to do the Fa-ther's will;
It is the way the Mas-ter went; Should not the ser-vant tread it still?

924　　　*Zeal.—John* 12: 43.　　　BONAR.

Go, labor on; spend and be spent,—
　Thy joy to do the Father's will;
It is the way the Master went;
　Should not the servant tread it still?

2 Go, labor on; 'tis not for naught;
　Thine earthly loss is heavenly gain;
Men heed thee, love thee, praise thee not:
　The Master praises,—what are men?

3 Go, labor on; enough, while here,
　If he shall praise thee, if he deign
Thy willing heart to mark and cheer:
　No toil for him shall be in vain.

4 Toil on, and in thy toil rejoice;
　For toil comes rest, for exile home;
Soon shalt thou hear the Bridegroom's
　　voice,
　The midnight peal: "Behold, I come!"

925　　　*The Poor.—Luke* 6: 20.　　　ANON.

Thou God of hope, to thee we bow!
　Thou art our Refuge in distress;
The Husband of the widow thou,
　The Father of the fatherless.

2 The poor are thy peculiar care;
　To them thy promises are sure:
Thy gifts the poor in spirit share;
　Oh, may we always thus be poor!

3 May we thy law of love fulfill,
　To bear each other's burdens here,
Endure and do thy righteous will,
　And walk in all thy faith and fear.

346

926　　　*Faith and Works.*　　　DRUMMOND.

One cup of healing oil and wine,
　One offering laid on mercy's shrine,
Is thrice more grateful, Lord, to thee,
　Than lifted eye or bended knee.

2 In true and inward faith we trace
　The source of every outward grace;
Within the pious heart it plays,
　A living fount of joy and praise.

3 Kind deeds of peace and love betray
　Where'er the stream has found its way;
But, where these spring not rich and fair,
　The stream has never wandered there.

927　　　*Liberality.—Prov.* 11: 24.　　　GIBBONS.

When Jesus dwelt in mortal clay,
　What were his works from day to day,
But miracles of power and grace,
　That spread salvation through our race?

2 Teach us, O Lord, to keep in view
　Thy pattern, and thy steps pursue;
Let alms bestowed, let kindness done,
　Be witnessed by each rolling sun.

3 That man may last, but never lives,
　Who much receives, but nothing gives;
Whom none can love, whom none can
　　thank,
　Creation's blot, creation's blank!

4 But he who marks, from day to day,
　In generous acts his radiant way,
Treads the same path his Saviour trod,
　The path to glory and to God.

DARLEY. L. M.

1. Go, la-bor on, while it is day; The world's dark night is hastening on: Speed, speed thy work,—cast sloth a - way! It is not thus that souls are won. It is not thus that souls are won.

928   *Zeal.—John 9: 4.*   BONAR.

Go, labor on, while it is day;
  The world's dark night is hastening on;
Speed, speed thy work,—cast sloth away!
  It is not thus that souls are won.

2 Men die in darkness at your side,
  Without a hope to cheer the tomb:
Take up the torch and wave it wide—
  The torch that lights time's thickest
    gloom.

3 Toil on,—faint not; keep watch and pray!
  Be wise the erring soul to win;
Go forth into the world's highway;
  Compel the wanderer to come in.

4 Go, labor on; your hands are weak;
  Your knees are faint, your soul cast down;
Yet falter not; the prize you seek
  Is near,—a kingdom and a crown!

929   *Forgiveness.—Matt. 6: 12.*   RIPPON.

Oh, what stupendous mercy shines
  Around the majesty of heaven?
Rebels he deigns to call his sons—
  Their souls renewed, their sins forgiven.

2 Go, imitate the grace divine—
  The grace that blazes like a sun;
Hold forth your fair, though feeble light,
  Through all your lives let mercy run.

3 When all is done, renounce your deeds,
  Renounce self-righteousness with scorn:
Thus will you glorify your God,
  And thus the Christian name adorn.

930   *The Poor.—Mark 14: 7.*   WOODMAN.

God guard the poor! we may not see
  The deepest sorrows of the soul;
These are laid open, Lord, to thee,
  And subject to thy wise control.

2 Make us thy messengers to shed,
  Within the home of want and woe,
The blessings of thy bounty, spread
  So freely on thy world below.

3 Let us go forth, with joyful hand,
  To strengthen, comfort, and relieve;
Then in thy presence may we stand,
  And hope thy blessing to receive.

931   *Consecration.*   MONTGOMERY.

Jesus! our best belovéd Friend,
  On thy redeeming name we call;
Jesus! in love to us descend,
  Pardon and sanctify us all.

2 Our souls and bodies we resign,
  To fear and follow thy commands;
Oh, take our hearts, our hearts are thine,
  Accept the service of our hands.

3 Firm, faithful, watching unto prayer,
  Our Master's voice will we obey,
Toil in the vineyard here, and bear
  The heat and burden of the day.

4 Yet, Lord, for us a resting-place,
  In heaven, at thy right hand, prepare;
And till we see thee face to face,
  Be all our conversation there.

WATCHMAN. S. M.

1. Make haste, O man, to live, For thou so soon must die;

Time hur - ries past thee like the breeze; How swift its moments fly!

932　　*Energy.—2 Pet. 3: 11, 12.*　　ANON.

Make haste, O man, to live,
　For thou so soon must die;
Time hurries past thee like the breeze;
　How swift its moments fly!

2 To breathe, and wake, and sleep,
　To smile, to sigh, to grieve,
To move in idleness through earth—
　This, this is not to live.

3 Make haste, O man, to do
　Whatever must be done;
Thou hast no time to lose in sloth,
　Thy day will soon be gone.

4 Up, then, with speed, and work;
　Fling ease and self away—
This is no time for thee to sleep—
　Up, watch, and work, and pray!

933　　*"Beside all waters sow".*　　MONTGOMERY.

Sow in the morn thy seed,
　At eve hold not thy hand;
To doubt and fear give thou no heed;
　Broad-cast it o'er the land.

2 Beside all waters sow,
　The highway furrows stock,
Drop it where thorns and thistles grow,
　Scatter it on the rock.

3 And duly shall appear
　In verdure, beauty, strength,
The tender blade, the stalk, the ear,
　And the full corn at length.

4 Thou canst not toil in vain;
　Cold, heat, the moist and dry,
Shall foster and mature the grain
　For garners in the sky.

5 Then, when the glorious end,
　The day of God shall come,
The angel-reapers shall descend,
　And heaven sing, "Harvest home!"

934　　*Reform.*　　ANON.

Mourn for the thousands slain,
　The youthful and the strong;
Mourn for the wine-cup's fearful reign,
　And the deluded throng.

2 Mourn for the tarnished gem,
　For reason's light divine,
Quenched from the soul's bright diadem,
　Where God hath bid it shine.

3 Mourn for the ruined soul,—
　Eternal life and light
Lost by the fiery, maddening bowl,
　And turned to helpless night.

4 Mourn for the lost,—but call,
　Call to the strong, the free;
Rouse them to shun that dreadful fall,
　And to the refuge flee.

5 Mourn for the lost,—but pray,
　Pray to our God above,
To break the fell destroyer's sway,
　And show his saving love.

LEIGHTON. S. M.

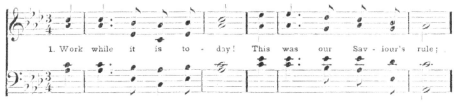

1. Work while it is to - day! This was our Sav - iour's rule;

With do - cile minds let us o - bey, As learn - ers in his school.

935   *Expedition.—John 9:4.*   MONTGOMERY.

WORK while it is to-day!
  This was our Saviour's rule;
With docile minds let us obey,
  As learners in his school.

2 Lord Christ, we humbly ask
  Of thee the power and will,
With fear and meekness, every task
  Of duty to fulfill.

3 At home, by word and deed,
  Adorn redeeming grace;
And sow abroad the precious seed
  Of truth in every place.

4 That thus the wilderness
  May blossom like the rose,
And trees spring up of righteousness,
  Where'er life's river flows.

5 For thee our all to spend,
  Still may we watch and pray,
And persevering to the end,
  Work while it is to-day.

936   *Contribution.—1 Cor. 4:7.*   HOW.

WE give thee but thine own,
  Whate'er the gift may be:
All that we have is thine alone,
  A trust, O Lord, from thee.

2 May we thy bounties thus
  As stewards true receive,
And gladly, as thou blessest us,
  To thee our first-fruits give.

3 To comfort and to bless,
  To find a balm for woe,
To tend the lone and fatherless
  Is angel's work below.

4 The captive to release,
  To God the lost to bring,
To teach the way of life and peace,
  It is a Christ-like thing.

5 And we believe thy word,
  Though dim our faith may be;
Whate'er for thine we do, O Lord,
  We do it unto thee.

937   *Active Effort.—Eccl. 9:10.*   SIGOURNEY.

LABORERS of Christ, arise,
  And gird you for the toil!
The dew of promise from the skies
  Already cheers the soil.

2 Go where the sick recline,
  Where mourning hearts deplore;
And where the sons of sorrow pine,
  Dispense your hallowed store.

3 Be faith, which looks above,
  With prayer, your constant guest;
And wrap the Saviour's changeless love
  A mantle round your breast.

4 So shall you share the wealth
  That earth may ne'er despoil,
And the blest gospel's saving health
  Repay your arduous toil.

ST. SYLVESTER. 8, 7.

1. Cast thy bread up-on the wa-ters,   Think-ing not 'tis thrown a - way;

God himself saith, thou shalt gath - er   It a - gain some fu - ture day.

938   *Benevolent Efforts.—Eccl.* **11: 1.**   ANON.

Cast thy bread upon the waters,
  Thinking not 'tis thrown away;
God himself saith, thou shalt gather
  It again some future day.

2 Cast thy bread upon the waters;
  Wildly though the billows roll,
They but aid thee as thou toilest
  Truth to spread from pole to pole.

3 As the seed, by billows floated,
  To some distant island lone,
So to human souls benighted,
  That thou flingest may be borne.

4 Cast thy bread upon the waters;
  Why wilt thou still doubting stand?
Bounteous shall God send the harvest,
  If thou sow'st with liberal hand.

5 Give them freely of thy substance—
  O'er this cause the Lord doth reign;
Cast thy bread, and toil with patience,
  Thou shalt labor not in vain.

939   *"Not your own."*—**1 Cor. 6: 20.**   MRS. ALDERSON.

Lord of glory! thou hast bought us,
  With thy life-blood as the price,
Never grudging, for the lost ones,
  That tremendous sacrifice;—

2 And, with that, hast freely given
  Blessings, countless as the sand,
To the unthankful and the evil,
  With thine own unsparing hand.

3 Grant us hearts, dear Lord! to yield thee
  Gladly, freely, of thine own;
With the sunshine of thy goodness,
  Melt our thankless hearts of stone;—

4 Till our cold and selfish natures,
  Warmed by thee, at length believe,
That more happy, and more blessèd,
  'Tis to give than to receive.

5 Wondrous honor hast thou given
  To our humblest charity,
In thine own mysterious sentence,—
  "Ye have done it unto me!"

6 Give us faith, to trust thee boldly,
  Hope, to stay our souls on thee;
But, oh,—best of all thy graces—
  Give us thine own charity.

940   *Contribution.—Prov.* **3: 9.**   FRANCIS.

With my substance I will honor
  My Redeemer and my Lord;
Were ten thousand worlds my manor,
  All were nothing to his word.

2 While the heralds of salvation
  His abounding grace proclaim,
Let his friends, of every station,
  Gladly join to spread his fame.

3 Be his kingdom now promoted,
  Let the earth her Monarch know;
Be my all to him devoted;
  To my Lord my all I owe.

WESTMINSTER. 8, 7.

1. On - ward, Chris - tian, though the re - gion Where thou art be drear and lone;

God has set a guar - dian le - gion Ve - ry near thee; press thou on.

941   *"Leaving us an example."*   JOHNSON.

ONWARD, Christian, though the region
  Where thou art be drear and lone;
God has set a guardian legion
  Very near thee; press thou on.

2 By the thorn-road, and none other,
  Is the mount of vision won;
Tread it without shrinking, brother;
  Jesus trod it; press thou on.

3 Be this world the wiser, stronger,
  For thy life of pain and peace;
While it needs thee, oh, no longer
  Pray thou for thy quick release.

4 Pray thou, Christian, daily rather,
  That thou be a faithful son;
By the prayer of Jesus, "Father,
  Not my will, but thine, be done."

942   *Courage and Faith.*   ANON.

FATHER, hear the prayer we offer!
  Not for ease that prayer shall be,
But for strength that we may ever
  Live our lives courageously.

2 Not for ever by still waters
  Would we idly quiet stay;
But would smite the living fountains
  From the rocks along our way.

3 Be our strength in hours of weakness,
  In our wanderings, be our guide;
Through endeavor, failure, danger,
  Father, be thou at our side!

943   *Progress.—Isa.* 40 : 31.   BONAR.

LIKE the eagle, upward, onward,
  Let my soul in faith be borne:
Calmly gazing, skyward, sunward,
  Let my eye unshrinking turn!

2 Where the cross, God's love revealing,
  Sets the fettered spirit free,
Where it sheds its wondrous healing,
  There, my soul, thy rest shall be!

3 Oh, may I no longer dreaming,
  Idly waste my golden day,
But, each precious hour redeeming,
  Upward, onward press my way!

944   *Patience and Self-denial.*   HASTINGS.

PILGRIMS in this vale of sorrow,
  Pressing onward toward the prize,
Strength and comfort here we borrow
  From the Hand that rules the skies.

2 'Mid these scenes of self-denial,
  We are called the race to run;
We must meet full many a trial
  Ere the victor's crown is won.

3 Love shall every conflict lighten,
  Hope shall urge us swifter on,
Faith shall every prospect brighten,
  Till the morn of heaven shall dawn.

4 On the Eternal arm reclining,
  We at length shall win the day;
All the powers of earth combining,
  Shall not snatch our crown away.

351

CLARENDON. C. M.

1. Oh, still in ac-cents sweet and strong Sounds forth the an-cient word,—

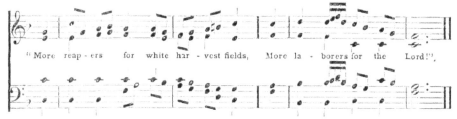

"More reap-ers for white har-vest fields, More la-borers for the Lord!",

945   *Zeal.—John 4: 35.*   S. LONGFELLOW.

Oh, still in accents sweet and strong
   Sounds forth the ancient word,—
" More reapers for white harvest fields,
   More laborers for the Lord!"

2 We hear the call; in dreams no more
   In selfish ease we lie,
But girded for our Father's work,
   Go forth beneath his sky.

3 Where prophets' word, and martyrs' blood,
   And prayers of saints were sown,
We, to their labors entering in,
   Would reap where they have strown.

946   *Beneficence.*   DODDRIDGE.

Jesus, our Lord, how rich thy grace!
   Thy bounties how complete!
How shall we count the matchless sum!
   How pay the mighty debt!

2 High on a throne of radiant light
   Dost thou exalted shine;
What can our poverty bestow
   When all the worlds are thine?

3 But thou hast brethren here below,
   The partners of thy grace;
And wilt confess their humble names,
   Before thy Father's face.

4 In them thou mayst be clothed and fed,
   And visited and cheered;
And in their accents of distress,
   Our Saviour's voice is heard.

947   *The Martyr-spirit.*   HEBER.

The Son of God goes forth to war,
   A kingly crown to gain;
His blood-red banner streams afar:
   Who follows in his train?

2 Who best can drink his cup of woe,
   And triumph over pain,
Who patient bear his cross below—
   He follows in his train.

3 A glorious band, the chosen few,
   On whom the Spirit came:
Twelve valiant saints, their hope they knew,
   And mocked the cross and flame.

4 They climbed the dizzy steep to heaven
   Through peril, toil, and pain:
O God! to us may grace be given
   To follow in their train!

948   *" Ye do it unto me."*   FODEN.

What shall we render, bounteous Lord
   For all the grace we see?
The goodness feeble worms can yield
   Extendeth not to thee.

2 To tents of woe, to beds of pain,
   We cheerfully repair,
And, with the gift thy hand bestows,
   Relieve the mourners there.

3 Thus passing through the vale of tears,
   Our useful light shall shine,
And others learn to glorify
   Our Father's name divine.

JEWETT. 6. D.

1. My Je - sus, as thou wilt! Oh, may thy will be mine; In - to thy hand of love

I would my all re - sign; Through sor - row, or through joy, Con - duct me

as thine own, And help me still to say, My Lord, thy will be done!

949   SCHMOLKE.   *" Not my will, but thine."*

My Jesus, as thou wilt!
　Oh, may thy will be mine;
Into thy hand of love
　I would my all resign;
Through sorrow, or through joy,
　Conduct me as thine own,
And help me still to say,
　My Lord, thy will be done!

2 My Jesus, as thou wilt!
　Though seen through many a tear,
Let not my star of hope
　Grow dim or disappear:
Since thou on earth hast wept,
　And sorrowed oft alone,
If I must weep with thee,
　My Lord, thy will be done!

3 My Jesus, as thou wilt!
　All shall be well for me;
Each changing future scene
　I gladly trust with thee:
Straight to my home above
　I travel calmly on,
And sing, in life or death,
　My Lord, thy will be done!

950   BONAR.   *" He knoweth the way."*—Job 23: 10.

Thy way, not mine, O Lord,
　However dark it be!
Lead me by thine own hand;
　Choose out the path for me.
I dare not choose my lot:
　I would not, if I might;
Choose thou for me, my God,
　So shall I walk aright.

2 The kingdom that I seek
　Is thine: so let the way
That leads to it be thine,
　Else I must surely stray.
Take thou my cup, and it
　With joy or sorrow fill,
As best to thee may seem;
　Choose thou my good and ill.

3 Choose thou for me my friends
　My sickness or my health;
Choose thou my cares for me,
　My poverty or wealth.
Not mine, not mine the choice,
　In things or great or small;
Be thou my Guide, my Strength,
　My Wisdom, and my All.

WOODWORTH. L. M.

1. My God, my Fa - ther, while I stray Far from my home, on life's rough way,

Oh, teach me from my heart to say, "Thy will be done, thy will be done."

951 C. ELLIOTT.
"Thy will be done."—Matt. **6:10.**

My God, my Father, while I stray
Far from my home, on life's rough way,
Oh, teach me from my heart to say,
"Thy will be done, thy will be done!"

2 What though in lonely grief I sigh
For friends beloved no longer nigh;
Submissive still would I reply,
"Thy will be done, thy will be done!"

3 If thou shouldst call me to resign
What most I prize,—it ne'er was mine;
I only yield thee what was thine:
"Thy will be done, thy will be done!"

4 If but my fainting heart be blest
With thy sweet Spirit for its guest,
My God, to thee I leave the rest;
"Thy will be done, thy will be done!"

5 Renew my will from day to day;
Blend it with thine, and take away
Whate'er now makes it hard to say,
"Thy will be done, thy will be done!"

6 Then when on earth I breathe no more,
The prayer oft mixed with tears before,
I'll sing upon a happier shore:
"Thy will be done, thy will be done!"

952 ANON.
"Nevertheless, afterward."—Heb. **12:11.**

I BLESS thee, Lord, for sorrows sent
To break the dream of human power,
For now my shallow cistern's spent,
I find thy fount and thirst no more.

2 I take thy hand and fears grow still:
Behold thy face, and doubts remove;
Who would not yield his wavering will
To perfect truth and boundless love!

3 That truth gives promise of a dawn,
Beneath whose light I am to see,
When all these blinding vails are drawn,
This was the wisest path for me.

4 That love this restless soul doth teach
The strength of thy eternal calm;
And tunes its sad and broken speech,
To sing ev'n now the angels' psalm.

953 ANON.
God loves and chastens.—Heb. **12:6.**

I CANNOT always trace the way
Where thou, almighty One, dost move;
But I can always, always say,
That God is love, that God is love.

2 When fear her chilling mantle flings
O'er earth, my soul to heaven above,
As to her native home, upsprings,
For God is love, for God is love.

3 When mystery clouds my darkened path,
I'll check my dread, my doubts reprove;
In this my soul sweet comfort hath,
That God is love, that God is love.

4 Yes, God is love;—a thought like this,
Can every gloomy thought remove,
And turn all tears, all woes, to bliss,
For God is love, for God is love.

HE LEADETH ME. L. M. D.

1. He lead-eth me! oh, blessed tho't, Oh, words with heavenly comfort fraught! Whate'er I do, where-

REFRAIN.

e'er I be, Still 'tis God's hand that leadeth me. He lead - eth me! he lead - eth me! By

his own hand he leadeth me; His faithful follower I would be, For by his hand he lead-eth me.

954   *"He leadeth me."*   ANON.

HE leadeth me! oh, blessed thought,
Oh, words with heavenly comfort fraught!
Whate'er I do, where'er I be,
Still 't is God's hand that leadeth me.—
           REF.

2 Sometimes 'mid scenes of deepest gloom,
Sometimes where Eden's bowers bloom,
By waters still, o'er troubled sea,—
Still 't is his hand that leadeth me!—REF.

3 Lord! I would clasp thy hand in mine,
Nor ever murmur nor repine,
Content, whatever lot I see,
Since 't is my God that leadeth me.—REF.

4 And when my task on earth is done,
When by thy grace the victory's won,
Ev'n death's cold wave I will not flee,
Since God through Jordan leadeth me.—
           REF.

955   *"I love thee, Lord!"*   ANON.

THOUGH sorrows rise and dangers roll,
In waves of darkness o'er my soul;

Though friends are false, and love decays,
And few and evil are my days;
Though conscience, fiercest of my foes,
Swells with remembered guilt my woes;
Yet ev'n in nature's utmost ill,
I love thee, Lord! I love thee still!

2 Though Sinai's curse, in thunder dread,
Peals o'er mine unprotected head,
And memory points, with busy pain,
To grace and mercy given in vain;
Till nature, shrinking in the strife,
Would fly to hell to 'scape from life;
Though every thought has power to kill,
I love thee, Lord! I love thee still!

3 Oh, by the pangs thyself hast borne,
The ruffian's blow, the tyrant's scorn,
By Sinai's curse, whose dreadful doom
Was buried in thy guiltless tomb;
By these my pangs, whose healing smart,
Thy grace hath planted in my heart—
I know, I feel thy bounteous will,
Thou lov'st me, Lord! thou lov'st me still!

HELENA. C. M.

1. When lan - guor and dis - ease in - vade This trem - bling house of clay,

'Tis sweet to look be - yond my pain, And long to fly a - way;

956   *"Sweet to lie passive."*   TOPLADY.

WHEN languor and disease invade
This trembling house of clay,
'Tis sweet to look beyond my pain,
And long to fly away;—

2 Sweet to look inward, and attend
The whispers of his love;
Sweet to look upward to the place
Where Jesus pleads above;—

3 Sweet on his faithfulness to rest,
Whose love can never end;
Sweet on his covenant of grace
For all things to depend;—

4 Sweet, in the confidence of faith,
To trust his firm decrees;
Sweet to lie passive in his hands,
And know no will but his.

5 If such the sweetness of the streams,
What must the fountain be,
Where saints and angels draw their bliss
Immediately from thee!

957   *"Blessed be the Lord."—Job 1 : 21.*   MONTGOMERY.

ONE prayer I have—all prayers in one—
When I am wholly thine;
Thy will, my God, thy will be done,
And let that will be mine.

2 All-wise, almighty, and all-good,
In thee I firmly trust;
Thy ways, unknown or understood,
Are merciful and just.

3 May I remember that to thee
Whate'er I have I owe;
And back, in gratitude, from me
May all thy bounties flow.

4 And though thy wisdom takes away,
Shall I arraign thy will?
No, let me bless thy name, and say,
"The Lord is gracious still."

5 A pilgrim through the earth I roam,
Of nothing long possessed;
And all must fail when I go home,
For this is not my rest.

958   *Light in Darkness.*   MOORE.

O THOU who driest the mourner's tear!
How dark this world would be,
If, when deceived and wounded here,
We could not fly to thee!

2 When joy no longer soothes or cheers,
And ev'n the hope that threw
A moment's sparkle o'er our tears,
Is dimmed and vanished too;—

3 Oh, who would bear life's stormy doom,
Did not thy wing of love
Come, brightly wafting through the gloom
Our peace-branch from above?

4 Then sorrow touched by thee grows bright,
With more than rapture's ray;
As darkness shows us worlds of light
We never saw by day.

SILOAM. C. M.

1. My times of sor-row and of joy, Great God! are in thy hand;
My choic-est com-forts come from thee, And go at thy com-mand.

959   *"My times."—Ps. 31:15.*   BEDDOME.

My times of sorrow and of joy,
  Great God! are in thy hand;
My choicest comforts come from thee,
  And go at thy command..

2 If thou shouldst take them all away,
  Yet would I not repine;
Before they were possessed by me,
  They were entirely thine.

3 Nor would I drop a murmuring word,
  Though the whole world were gone,
But seek enduring happiness,
  In thee, and thee alone.

960   *"To die is gain."—Phil. 1:21.*   NOEL.

When musing sorrow weeps the past,
  And mourns the present pain;
How sweet to think of peace at last,
  And feel that death is gain!

2 'Tis not that murmuring thoughts arise,
  And dread a Father's will;
'Tis not that meek submission flies,
  And would not suffer still.

3 It is that heaven-born faith surveys
  The path that leads to light,
And longs her eagle plumes to raise,
  And lose herself in sight.

4 Oh, let me wing my hallowed flight
  From earth-born woe and care,
And soar above these clouds of night,
  My Saviour's bliss to share.

961   *"It is I."—Matt. 14:27.*   C. ELLIOTT.

When waves of trouble round me swell,
  My soul is not dismayed;
I hear a voice I know full well,—
  "'Tis I; be not afraid."

2 When black the threatening skies appear,
  And storms my path invade,
Those accents tranquilize each fear,—
  "'Tis I; be not afraid."

3 There is a gulf that must be crossed;
  Saviour, be near to aid!
Whisper, when my frail bark is tossed,—
  "'Tis I; be not afraid."

4 There is a dark and fearful vale,
  Death hides within its shade;
Oh, say, when flesh and heart shall fail,—
  "'Tis I; be not afraid."

962   *Smitten with a pierced hand.*   EDMESTON.

O thou whose mercy guides my way,
  Though now it seems severe,
Forbid my unbelief to say
  There is no mercy here!

2 Oh, may I, Lord, desire the pain
  That comes in kindness down,
Far more than sweetest earthly gain,
  Succeeded by a frown.

3 Then though thou bend my spirit low,
  Love only shall I see;
The gracious hand that strikes the blow
  Was wounded once for me.

DENNIS. S. M.

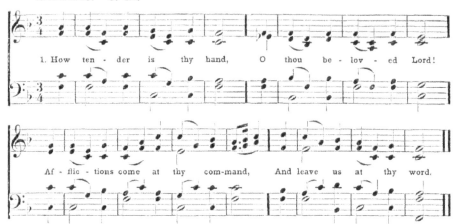

1. How ten - der is thy hand, O thou be - lov - ed Lord!

Af - flic - tions come at thy com-mand, And leave us at thy word.

963   *Kindness even in affliction.*   HASTINGS.

How tender is thy hand,
  O thou beloved Lord!
Afflictions come at thy command,
  And leave us at thy word.

2 How gentle was the rod
  That chastened us for sin!
How soon we found a smiling God,
  Where deep distress had been!

3 A Father's hand we felt,
  A Father's heart we knew;
With tears of penitence we knelt,
  And found his word was true.

4 We told him all our grief,
  We thought of Jesus' love;
A sense of pardon brought relief,
  And bade our pains remove.

5 Now we will bless the Lord,
  And in his strength confide;
For ever be his name adored;
  For there is none beside.

964   *"My times."—Psalm 31 : 15.*   LLOYD.

"My times are in thy hand:"
  My God! I wish them there;
My life, my friends, my soul, I leave
  Entirely to thy care.

2 "My times are in thy hand,"
  Whatever they may be;
Pleasing or painful, dark or bright,
  As best may seem to thee.

3 "My times are in thy hand;"—
  Why should I doubt or fear?
My Father's hand will never cause
  His child a needless tear.

4 "My times are in thy hand,"—
  Jesus, the crucified!
The hand my cruel sins had pierced,
  Is now my guard and guide.

965   *"Shall know hereafter."—John 13.7.*   EDMESTON.

Along my earthly way,
  How many clouds are spread!
Darkness, with scarce one cheerful ray,
  Seems gathering o'er my head.

2 Yet, Father, thou art Love;
  Oh, hide not from my view!
But when I look, in prayer, above,
  Appear in mercy through!

3 My pathway is not hid;
  Thou knowest all my need;
And I would do as Israel did,—
  Follow where thou wilt lead.

4 Lead me, and then my feet
  Shall never, never stray;
But safely I shall reach the seat
  Of happiness and day.

5 And, oh, from that bright throne
  I shall look back, and see,—
The path I went, and that alone
  Was the right path for me.

SELVIN. S. M.

1. If through unruffled seas, Tow'rd heaven we calmly sail, With grateful hearts, O God, to thee,

We'll own the fav'ring gale, With grateful hearts, O God, to thee, We'll own the favoring gale.

966   *"We walk by faith.—2 Cor. 5: 7.*   TOPLADY.

IF, through unruffled seas,
  Toward heaven we calmly sail,
With grateful hearts, O God, to thee,
  We'll own the favoring gale.

2 But should the surges rise,
  And rest delay to come,
Blest be the sorrow—kind the storm,
  Which drives us nearer home.

3 Soon shall our doubts and fears
  All yield to thy control:
Thy tender mercies shall illume
  The midnight of the soul.

4 Teach us, in every state,
  To make thy will our own;
And when the joys of sense depart,
  To live by faith alone.

967   *"Spare me!'—Ps. 39: 9.*   DECK.

IT is thy hand, my God;
  My sorrow comes from thee:
I bow beneath thy chastening rod,
  'Tis love that bruises me.

2 I would not murmur, Lord;
  Before thee I am dumb:
Lest I should breathe one murmuring word,
  To thee for help I come.

3 My God, thy name is Love;
  A Father's hand is thine;
With tearful eyes I look above,
  And cry, "Thy will be mine!"

4 I know thy will is right,
  Though it may seem severe;
Thy path is still unsullied light,
  Though dark it oft appear.

5 Jesus for me hath died;
  Thy Son thou didst not spare:
His piercèd hands, his bleeding side,
  Thy love for me declare.

6 Here my poor heart can rest;
  My God, it cleaves to thee:
Thy will is love, thine end is blest,
  All work for good to me.

968   *"Dealeth as with sons."—Heb. 12: 7.*   HASTINGS.

BE tranquil, O my soul,
  Be quiet every fear!
Thy Father hath supreme control,
  And he is ever near.

2 Ne'er of thy lot complain,
  Whatever may befall;
Sickness or sorrow, care or pain,
  'Tis well appointed all.

3 A Father's chastening hand
  Is leading thee along;
Nor distant is the promised land,
  Where swells the immortal song.

4 Oh, then, my soul, be still!
  Await heaven's high decree;
Seek but to do thy Father's will,
  It shall be well with thee.

COMFORT. 7. D.

1. When our heads are bowed with woe; When our bit-ter tears o'erflow; When we mourn the

lost, the dear, Je-sus, Son of Ma - ry, hear! Thou our fee - ble flesh hast worn;

Thou our mortal griefs hast borne; Thou hast shed the human tear: Jesus, Son of Ma-ry, hear!

969   *"Son of Mary."—Heb. 7:14.*   HEBER.

WHEN our heads are bowed with woe;
When our bitter tears o'erflow;
When we mourn the lost, the dear,
Jesus, Son of Mary, hear!
Thou our feeble flesh hast worn;
Thou our mortal griefs hast borne;
Thou hast shed the human tear:
Jesus, Son of Mary, hear!

2 When the heart is sad within,
With the thought of all its sin;
When the spirit shrinks with fear,
Jesus, Son of Mary, hear!
Thou the shame, the grief, hast known;
Though the sins were not thine own,
Thou hast deigned their load to bear:
Jesus, Son of Mary, hear!

3 When our eyes grow dim in death;
When we heave the parting breath;
When our solemn doom is near,
Jesus, Son of Mary, hear!
Thou hast bowed the dying head;
Thou the blood of life hast shed;
Thou hast filled a mortal bier:
Jesus, Son of Mary, hear!

970   *Looking to Jesus.*   ANON.

WHEN along life's thorny road,
Faints the soul beneath the load,
By its cares and sins oppressed,
Finds on earth no peace or rest;
When the wily tempter's near,
Filling us with doubt and fear:
Jesus, to thy feet we flee,
Jesus, we will look to thee.

2 Thou, our Saviour, from the throne
List'nest to thy people's moan;
Thou, the living Head, dost share
Every pang thy members bear:
Full of tenderness thou art,
Thou wilt heal the broken heart;
Full of power, thine arm shall quell
All the rage and might of hell.

3 Mighty to redeem and save,
Thou hast overcome the grave;
Thou the bars of death hast riven,
Opened wide the gates of heaven;
Soon in glory thou shalt come,
Taking thy poor pilgrims home;
Jesus, then we all shall be,
Ever—ever—Lord, with thee.

MERCY. 7.

1. In the dark and cloud-y day, When earth's rich-es flee a-way,

And the last hope will not stay, Sav-iour, com-fort—com-fort me!

971   *Comfort.—2 Cor. 1:5.*   HERRICK.

In the dark and cloudy day,
When earth's riches flee away,
And the last hope will not stay,
  Saviour, comfort me!

2 When the secret idol's gone
That my poor heart yearned upon,—
Desolate, bereft, alone,
  Saviour, comfort me!

3 Thou, who wast so sorely tried,
In the darkness crucified,
Bid me in thy love confide;
  Saviour, comfort me!

4 Comfort me; I am cast down:
'Tis my heavenly Father's frown;
I deserve it all, I own:
  Saviour, comfort me!

5 So it shall be good for me
Much afflicted now to be,
If thou wilt but tenderly,
  Saviour, comfort me!

972   *"For he careth."—1 Pet. 5:7.*   R. HILL.

Cast thy burden on the Lord,
Only lean upon his word;
Thou wilt soon have cause to bless
His unchanging faithfulness.

2 He sustains thee by his hand,
He enables thee to stand;
Those, whom Jesus once hath loved,
From his grace are never moved.

3 Heaven and earth may pass away,
God's free grace shall not decay;
He hath promised to fulfill
All the pleasure of his will.

4 Jesus! guardian of thy flock,
Be thyself our constant rock;
Make us by thy powerful hand,
Firm as Zion's mountain stand.

973   *Love seen in Trials.*   COWPER.

'T is my happiness below
Not to live without the cross,
But the Saviour's power to know,
Sanctifying every loss.

2 Trials must and will befall;
But with humble faith to see
Love inscribed upon them all,—
This is happiness to me.

3 God in Israel sows the seeds
Of affliction, pain and toil;
These spring up and choke the weeds
Which would else o'erspread the soil.

4 Did I meet no trials here,
No chastisement by the way,
Might I not with reason fear
I should prove a castaway?

5 Trials make the promise sweet;
Trials give new life to prayer;
Trials bring me to his feet,
Lay me low, and keep me there.

FLEMMING.   8, 6.

1. O Holy Saviour! Friend unseen, Since on thine arm thou bid'st me lean. Help me, throughout life's changing scene, By faith to cling to thee!

974   *Clinging to Christ.*   C. ELLIOTT.

O Holy Saviour! Friend unseen,
Since on thine arm thou bid'st me lean,
Help me, throughout life's changing scene,
    By faith to cling to thee!

2 What though the world deceitful prove,
And earthly friends and hopes remove;
With patient, uncomplaining love,
    Still would I cling to thee.

3 Though oft I seem to tread alone
Life's dreary waste, with thorns o'ergrown,
Thy voice of love, in gentlest tone,
    Still whispers, "Cling to me!"

4 Though faith and hope are often tried,
I ask not, need not, aught beside;
So safe, so calm, so satisfied,
    The soul that clings to thee!

975   *A will resigned.—Luke* 22: 42.   WHITTIER.

I ask not now for gold to gild,
    With mocking shine, an aching frame;
The yearning of the mind is stilled—
    I ask not now for fame.

2 But, bowed in lowliness of mind,
    I make my humble wishes known;
I only ask a will resigned,
    O Father, to thine own.

3 In vain I task my aching brain,
    In vain the sage's thoughts I scan;
I only feel how weak I am,
    How poor and blind is man.

4 And now my spirit sighs for home,
    And longs for light whereby to see;
And, like a weary child, would come,
    O Father, unto thee.

THY WILL BE DONE.   (CHANT.)

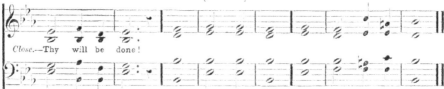

Close.—Thy will be done!

976   *Mark* 14: 36.   BOWRING.

"Thy will be | done!" || In devious way
The hurrying stream of | life may | run; ||
Yet still our grateful hearts shall say, |
    "Thy will be | done."

2 "Thy will be | done!" || If o'er us shine
A gladdening and a | prosperous, | sun, ||
This prayer will make it more divine— |
    "Thy will be | done."

3 "Thy will be | done!" || Tho' shrouded o'er
Our | path with | gloom, || one comfort—one
Is ours:—to breathe, while we adore, |
    "Thy will be | done."

LUX BENIGNA. 10, 4.

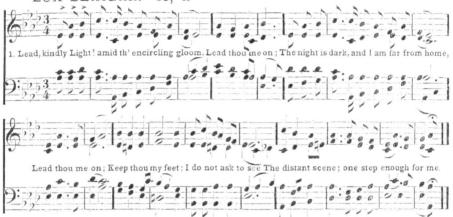

1. Lead, kindly Light! amid th' encircling gloom, Lead thou me on; The night is dark, and I am far from home,

Lead thou me on; Keep thou my feet; I do not ask to see The distant scene; one step enough for me.

NEWMAN.

977 *"Lead thou me on!"*

LEAD, kindly Light! amid the encircling
    Lead thou me on;   [gloom,
The night is dark, and I am far from home,
    Lead thou me on;
Keep thou my feet; I do not ask to see
The distant scene; one step enough for me.

2 I was not ever thus, nor prayed that thou
    Shouldst lead me on;
I loved to choose and see my path; but now
    Lead thou me on:

I loved the garish day, and, spite of fears,
Pride ruled my will. Remember not past
    years.

3 So long thy power has blessed me, sure it
    Will lead me on   [still
O'er moor and fen, o'er crag and torrent, till
    The night is gone;
And with the morn those angel faces smile
Which I have loved long since, and lost
    awhile!

GOD IS NEAR. P. M.

1. God is near thee, Therefore cheer thee, Sad soul! He'll de - fend thee,

When a - round thee Bil - lows roll, When a - round thee Bil - lows roll.

ANON.

978 *"Thou art near."*

GOD is near thee,
Therefore cheer thee,
    Sad soul!
He'll defend thee,
When around thee
    Billows roll.

2 Calm thy sadness,
Look in gladness
    On high!
Faint and weary,
Pilgrim, cheer thee!
    Help is nigh!

3 Hark the sea-bird,
Wildly wheeling
    Through the skies;
God defends him,
God attends him,
    When he cries!   363

PALESTINE.　L. M. 6l.

1. Peace, troubled soul, whose plaintive moan Hath taught each scene the notes of woe;

Cease thy complaint, suppress thy groan And let thy tears for-get to flow;

Be-hold, the pre-cious balm is found, To lull thy pain, to heal thy wound.

---

979   *"Balm in Gilead?"—Jer.* 8:22.   SHIRLEY.

Peace, troubled soul, whose plaintive moan
   Hath taught each scene the notes of woe;
Cease thy complaint, suppress thy groan,
   And let thy tears forget to flow;
Behold, the precious balm is found,
To lull thy pain, to heal thy wound.

2 Come, freely come, by sin oppressed;
   On Jesus cast thy weighty load;
In him thy refuge find, thy rest,
   Safe in the mercy of thy God;
Thy God's thy Saviour—glorious word!
For ever love and praise the Lord.

980   *"Eben-ezer."—1 Sam.* 7:12.   NEWTON.

Be still, my heart! these anxious cares
To thee are burdens, thorns, and snares:
They cast dishonor on thy Lord,
And contradict his gracious word;
Brought safely by his hand thus far,
Why wilt thou now give place to fear?

2 When first before his mercy-seat
Thou didst to him thy all commit,
364

He gave thee warrant from that hour
To trust his wisdom, love, and power:
Did ever trouble yet befall,
And he refuse to hear thy call?

3 He who has helped thee hitherto,
Will help thee all thy journey through;
Though rough and thorny be the road,
It leads thee home, apace, to God;
Then count thy present trials small,
For heaven will make amends for all.

981   *"As thy days."—Deut.* 33:25.   SIGOURNEY.

When adverse winds and waves arise,
And in my heart despondence sighs;
When life her throng of cares reveals,
And weakness o'er my spirit steals,
Grateful I hear the kind decree,
That "as my day, my strength shall be."

2 One trial more must yet be past,
One pang—the keenest and the last;
And when, with brow convulsed and pale,
My feeble, quivering heart-strings fail,
Redeemer! grant my soul to see
That "as her day, her strength shall be."

HANDY. L. M. 6l.

1. At eve-ning time let there be light; Life's lit-tle day draws near its close;

A - round me fall the shades of night, The night of death, the grave's re-pose;

To crown my joys, to end my woes, At eve-ning time let there be light.

982 *"At evening time."—Zech: 14:7.* ANON.

At evening time let there be light;
　Life's little day draws near its close;
Around me fall the shades of night,
　The night of death, the grave's repose;
　To crown my joys, to end my woes,
At evening time let there be light.

2 At evening time let there be light;
　Stormy and dark hath been my day;
Yet rose the morn divinely bright;
　Dews, birds, and blossoms cheered the
　　way;
　Oh, for one sweet, one parting ray!
At evening time let there be light.

3 At evening time there shall be light!
　For God hath spoken; it must be;
Fear, doubt, and anguish take their flight;
　His glory now is risen on me;
　Mine eyes shall his salvation see;
'Tis evening time, and there is light!

983 *"Jesus wept."—John 11:35.* GRANT.

When gathering clouds around I view,
And days are dark, and friends are few,
On him I lean, who, not in vain,
Experienced every human pain;
He sees my wants, allays my fears,
And counts and treasures up my tears.

2 If aught should tempt my soul to stray
From heavenly virtue's narrow way,—
To fly the good I would pursue,
Or do the sin I would not do,—
Still he, who felt temptation's power,
Shall guard me in that dangerous hour.

3 When sorrowing o'er some stone, I bend,
Which covers all that was a friend,
And from his voice, his hand, his smile,
Divides me, for a little while,
My Saviour sees the tears I shed,
For Jesus wept o'er Lazarus dead.

4 And oh, when I have safely passed
Through every conflict, but the last,—
Still, still unchanging, watch beside
My painful bed,—for thou hast died;
Then point to realms of cloudless day,
And wipe my latest tear away.

ROSE HILL. L. M.

1 How blest are those, how tru - ly wise, Who learn and keep the sa - cred road!

How hap - py they whom heaven em - ploys To turn re - bell - ious hearts to God:—

984   *The Ministry.—Dan.* 12 : 3.   STEELE.

How blest are those, how truly wise,
   Who learn and keep the sacred road!
How happy they whom heaven employs
   To turn rebellious hearts to God:—

2 To win them from the fatal way
   Where erring folly thoughtless roves,
And that blest righteousness display
   Which Jesus wrought and God approves.

3 The shining firmament shall fade,
   And sparkling stars resign their light;
But these shall know nor change nor shade,
   For ever fair, for ever bright.

985   *Welcoming a Pastor.*   MONTGOMERY.

We bid thee welcome in the name
   Of Jesus, our exalted Head;
Come as a servant; so he came,
   And we receive thee in his stead.

2 Come as a shepherd; guard and keep
   This fold from hell, and earth, and sin;
Nourish the lambs, and feed the sheep,
   The wounded heal, the lost bring in.

3 Come as a teacher, sent from God,
   Charged his whole counsel to declare;
Lift o'er our ranks the prophet's rod,
   While we uphold thy hands with prayer.

4 Come as a messenger of peace,
   Filled with the Spirit, fired with love!
Live to behold our large increase,
   And die to meet us all above.

986   *For Dedication.*   WILLIS.

The perfect world, by Adam trod,
Was the first temple,—built by God;
His fiat laid the corner-stone,
And heaved its pillars, one by one.

2 He hung its starry roof on high—
The broad, illimitable sky;
He spread its pavement, green and bright,
And curtained it with morning light.

3 The mountains in their places stood,
The sea—the sky—and "all was good."
And when its first pure praises rang,
The "morning stars together sang."

4 Lord, 'tis not ours to make the sea,
And earth, and sky, a house for thee;
But in thy sight our offering stands—
An humbler temple, "made with hands."

987   *The Ministry.*   BEDDOME.

Father of mercies, bow thine ear,
Attentive to our earnest prayer;
We plead for those who plead for thee;
Successful may they ever be.

2 Clothe thou with energy divine
Their words, and let those words be thine;
Teach them immortal souls to gain,
Nor let them labor, Lord in vain.

3 Let thronging multitudes around
Hear from their lips the joyful sound;
And light through distant realms bespread,
Till Zion rears her drooping head.

WARE. L. M.

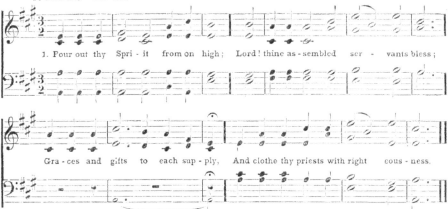

1. Pour out thy Spir - it from on high; Lord! thine as - sembled ser - vants bless;

Gra - ces and gifts to each sup - ply, And clothe thy priests with right cous - ness.

988   *Convocation.*   MONTGOMERY.

Pour out thy Spirit from on high;
  Lord! thine assembled servants bless;
Graces and gifts to each supply,
  And clothe thy priests with righteousness.

2 Wisdom, and zeal, and faith impart,
  Firmness with meekness from above,
To bear thy people on our heart,
  And love the souls whom thou dost love:

3 To watch and pray, and never faint;
  By day and night strict guard to keep;
To warn the sinner, cheer the saint,
  Nourish thy lambs, and feed thy sheep;

4 Then, when our work is finished here,
  In humble hope our charge resign:
When the chief Shepherd shall appear,
  O God! may they and we be thine!

989   *Seeking a Pastor.*   DODDRIDGE.

O Lord, thy pitying eye surveys
Our wandering paths, our trackless ways:
Send forth, in love, thy truth and light,
To guide our doubtful footsteps right.

2 In humble faith, behold we wait:
On thee we call at mercy's gate;
Our drooping hearts, O God, sustain,—
Shall Israel seek thy face in vain?

3 O Lord! in ways of peace return,
Nor let thy flock neglected mourn;
May our blest eyes a shepherd see,
Dear to our souls, and dear to thee.

990   *Prayer for Pastor.*   R. HILL.

With heavenly power, O Lord, defend
Him whom we now to thee commend;
Thy faithful messenger secure,
And make him to the end endure.

2 Gird him with all-sufficient grace;
Direct his feet in paths of peace;
Thy truth and faithfulness fulfill,
And arm him to obey thy will.

991   *Church Dedication.*   ANON.

On, bow thine ear, Eternal One!
  On thee our heart adoring calls;
To thee the followers of thy Son
  Have raised, and now devote these walls.

2 Here let thy holy days be kept;
  And be this place to worship given,
Like that bright spot where Jacob slept,
  The house of God, the gate of heaven.

3 Here may thine honor dwell; and here,
  As incense, let thy children's prayer,
From contrite hearts and lips sincere,
  Rise on the still and holy air.

4 Here be thy praise devoutly sung;
  Here let thy truth beam forth to save,
As when, of old, thy Spirit hung,
  On wings of light, o'er Jordan's wave.

5 And when the lips, that with thy name
  Are vocal now, to dust shall turn,
On others may devotion's flame
  Be kindled here, and purely burn!

BOND. C. M.

1. Oh, where are kings and em - pires now, Of old that went and came?

But, Lord, thy church is pray - ing yet, A thou - sand years the same.

992   *A growing kingdom.—Dan.* 2:44   COXE.

Oh, where are kings and empires now,
   Of old that went and came?
But, Lord, thy church is praying yet,
   A thousand years the same.

2 We mark her goodly battlements,
   And her foundations strong;
We hear within the solemn voice
   Of her unending song.

3 For not like kingdoms of the world
   Thy holy church, O God!   [ing her,
Though earthquake shocks are threaten-
   And tempests are abroad;—

4 Unshaken as eternal hills,
   Immovable she stands,
A mountain that shall fill the earth,
   A house not made by hands.

993   *"Little Flock."—Luke* 12:32.   BONAR.

Church of the ever-living God,
   The Father's gracious choice,
Amid the voices of this earth
   How feeble is thy voice!

2 A little flock!—so calls he thee
   Who bought thee with his blood;
A little flock, disowned of men,
   But owned and loved of God.

3 Not many rich or noble called,
   Not many great or wise;
They whom God makes his kings and priests
   Are poor in human eyes.

5 But the chief Shepherd comes at length;
   Their feeble days are o'er,
No more a handful in the earth,
   A little flock no more.

5 No more a lily among thorns,
   Weary and faint and few;
But countless as the stars of heaven,
   Or as the early dew.

6 Then entering the eternal halls,
   In robes of victory,
That mighty multitude shall keep
   The joyous jubilee.

994   *"Can a mother forget?"—Isa.* 49:14.   STEELE.

A mother may forgetful be,
   For human love is frail;
But thy Creator's love to thee,
   O Zion, cannot fail.

2 No, thy dear name engraven stands,
   In characters of love,
On thy almighty Father's hands;
   And never shall remove.

3 Before his ever-watchful eye
   Thy mournful state appears,
And every groan, and every sigh,
   Divine compassion hears.

4 O Zion, learn to doubt no more,
   Be every fear suppressed;
Unchanging truth, and love, and power,
   Dwell in thy Saviour's breast.

HOWARD. C. M.

1. O thou, whose own vast tem - ple stands, Built o - ver earth and sea,

Ac - cept the walls that hu - man hands Have raised to wor - ship thee.

995 *For Dedication.* BRYANT.

O thou, whose own vast temple stands,
Built over earth and sea,
Accept the walls that human hands
Have raised to worship thee.

2 Lord, from thine inmost glory send,
Within these courts to bide,
The peace that dwelleth without end,
Serenely by thy side!

3 May erring minds that worship here
Be taught the better way;
And they who mourn, and they who fear,
Be strengthened as they pray.

4 May faith grow firm, and love grow warm,
And pure devotion rise,
While round these hallowed walls the storm
Of earth-born passion dies.

996 *Church Dedication.* ANON.

God of the universe, to thee
This sacred fane we rear,
And now, with songs and bended knee,
Invoke thy presence here.

2 Long may this echoing dome resound
The praises of thy name;
These hallowed walls to all around
The triune God proclaim.

3 Here let thy love, thy presence dwell;
Thy glory here make known;
Thy people's home, oh, come and fill,
And seal it as thine own.

4 When sad with care, by sin oppressed,
Here may the burdened soul
Beneath thy sheltering wing find rest;
Here make the wounded whole.

5 And when the last long Sabbath morn
Upon the just shall rise,
May all who own thee here be borne
To mansions in the skies.

997 *"Who is sufficient?"* DODDRIDGE.

Let Zion's watchmen all awake
And take the alarm they give,
Now let them from the mouth of God
Their solemn charge receive.

2 'Tis not a cause of small import
The pastor's care demands,
But what might fill an angel's heart,
And filled a Saviour's hands.

3 They watch for souls for whom the Lord
Did heavenly bliss forego—
For souls that must for ever live
In rapture or in woe.

4 All to the great tribunal haste,
The account to render there;
And shouldst thou strictly mark our faults,
Lord! how should we appear?

5 May they that Jesus whom they preach,
Their own Redeemer, see,
And watch thou daily o'er their souls,
That they may watch for thee.

369

SALVATION. 8, 7. 6l.

1. { Christ is made the sure foundation, Christ the Head and Corner-stone, }
{ Chosen of the Lord, and precious, [*Omit* ....] } { Binding all the Church in one,

Ho-ly Zi - on help for ev - er, And her con - fi - dence a - lone, And her con-fidence a - lone.

998   *The Chief Corner-stone.*   NEALE. *Tr.*

CHRIST is made the sure foundation,
  Christ the Head and Corner-stone,
Chosen of the Lord, and precious,
  Binding all the Church in one,
Holy Zion's help for ever,
·   And her confidence alone.

2 To this temple, where we call thee,
  Come, O Lord of hosts, to-day:
With thy wonted loving-kindness,
  Hear thy servants as they pray;
And thy fullest benediction
  Shed within its wall alway.

3 Here vouchsafe to all thy servants
  What they ask of thee to gain,
What they gain from thee for ever
  With the blessèd to retain,
And hereafter in thy glory
  Evermore with thee to reign.

999   *"The Lamb's Wife."*   ANON.

BLESSED Salem, long expected,
  Vision bright of peace and dear!
Who of living stones erected,
  Moulded in the heavenly sphere,
And, by angel-guards protected,
  Dost in bridal-pomp appear.

2 From the heaven of heavens descending
  All prepared to meet thy Head,
In thy robes of light attending,
  Thou art to his presence led;
Golden glories, richly blending,
  Round thy streets and walls are shed.

3 Bright with pearls thy gates are beaming,
  Wide unfolded they remain:
Thither come, through grace redeeming,
  All who wear Christ's lowly chain:
And, his last award esteeming,
  Gladly share his cup of pain.

1000   *"They said, Alleluia."—Rev.* **19 : 3.**   BREVIARY.

HALLELUJAH! song of gladness,
  Song of everlasting joy;
Hallelujah! song the sweetest
  That can angel-hosts employ;
Hymning in God's holy presence
  Their high praise eternally.

2 Hallelujah! church victorious,
  Thou mayst lift this joyful strain:
Hallelujah! songs of triumph
  Well befit the ransomed train:
We our song must raise with sadness,
  While in exile we remain.

3 Hallelujah! strains of gladness
  Suit not souls with anguish torn;
Hallelujah! notes of sadness
  Best befit our state forlorn:
For, in this dark world of sorrow,
  We, with tears, our sin must mourn.

4 But our earnest supplication,
  Holy God, we raise to thee;
Bring us to thy blissful presence,
  Make us all thy joys to see;
Then we'll sing our Hallelujah,—
  Sing to all eternity.

AURELIA. 7, 6. D.

1. The Church's one foun-da-tion Is Je-sus Christ her Lord; She is his new cre-

a - tion By wa-ter and the word: From heaven he came and sought her To

be his ho - ly bride; With his own blood he bought her, And for her life he died.

1001 *The Church is Christ's.* STONE.

The Church's one foundation
　Is Jesus Christ her Lord;
She is his new creation
　By water and the word:
From heaven he came and sought her
　To be his holy bride;
With his own blood he bought her,
　And for her life he died.

2 Elect from every nation,
　Yet one o'er all the earth,
Her charter of salvation
　One Lord, one faith, one birth;
One holy name she blesses,
　Partakes one holy food,
And to one hope she presses,
　With every grace endued.

3 Though with a scornful wonder,
　Men see her sore oppressed,
By schisms rent asunder,
　By heresies distressed,
Yet saints their watch are keeping,
　Their cry goes up, "How long?"
And soon the night of weeping
　Shall be the morn of song.

4 Yet she on earth hath union
　With God the Three in One,
And mystic sweet communion
　With those whose rest is won;
With all her sons and daughters,
　Who by the Master's hand
Led through the deathly waters,
　Repose in Eden-land.

5 Oh, happy ones and holy!
　Lord, give us grace that we,
Like them, the meek and lowly,
　On high may dwell with thee:
There past the border mountains,
　Where in sweet vales the bride,
With thee by living fountains,
　For ever shall abide.

6 'Mid toil and tribulation
　And tumult of her war,
She waits the consummation
　Of peace for evermore;
Till with the vision glorious
　Her longing eyes are blest,
And the great Church victorious,
　Shall be the Church at rest.

WARSAW. H. M.

1. Christ is our Cor - ner-stone; On him a - lone we build; With his true saints a - lone

The courts of heaven are filled : On his great love Our hopes we place, Of present grace And joys above.

1002   *Laying a Corner-stone.*   CHANDLER.

CHRIST is our Corner-stone;
　On him alone we build;
With his true saints alone
　The courts of heaven are filled :
On his great love | Of present grace
Our hopes we place, | And joys above.

2 Oh, then with hymns of praise
　These hallowed courts shall ring!
Our voices we will raise,
　The Three in One to sing;
And thus proclaim | Both loud and long,
In joyful song, | That glorious Name.

3 Here may we gain from heaven
　The grace which we implore,
And may that grace, once given,
　Be with us evermore,—
Until that day | To endless rest
When all the blest | Are called away.

1003   *The Holy Spirit.—Luke* 11: 13.   BURTON.

O THOU that hearest prayer!
　Attend our humble cry;
And let thy servants share
　Thy blessing from on high;
We plead the promise of thy word,
Grant us thy Holy Spirit, Lord!

2 If earthly parents hear
　Their children when they cry;

If they, with love sincere,
　Their children's wants supply;
Much more wilt thou thy love display,
And answer when thy children pray.

3 Our heavenly Father thou,—
　We—children of thy grace,—
Oh, let thy Spirit now
　Descend and fill the place;
That all may feel the heavenly flame
And all unite to praise thy name.

1004   *The Church one.*   G. ROBINSON.

ONE sole baptismal sign,
　One Lord below, above,
One faith, one hope divine,
　One only watchword, love;
From different temples though it rise,
One song ascendeth to the skies.

2 Our sacrifice is one,
　One Priest before the throne,
The slain, the risen Son,
　Redeemer, Lord alone;
And sighs from contrite hearts that spring
Our chief, our choicest offering.

3 Head of thy church beneath,
　The catholic, the true,
On all her members breathe,
　Her broken frame renew;
Then shall thy perfect will be done
When Christians love and live as one.

APOLLOS. S. M. D.

1. How beauteous are their feet Who stand on Zi - on's hill! Who bring sal- va - tion

on their tongues, And words of peace re - veal. How charming is their voice! How

sweet their tidings are! "Zi - on, behold thy Saviour King; He reigns and triumphs here."

1005 *The Ministry.—Isa. 52: 7.*　　WATTS.

How beauteous are their feet
　Who stand on Zion's hill!
Who bring salvation on their tongues,
　And words of peace reveal.
2 How charming is their voice!
　How sweet their tidings are!
"Zion, behold thy Saviour King;
　He reigns and triumphs here."

3 How happy are our ears,
　That hear this joyful sound!
Which kings and prophets waited for,
　And sought, but never found.
4 How blessèd are our eyes,
　That see this heavenly light!
Prophets and kings desired it long,
　But died without the sight.

5 The watchmen join their voice,
　And tuneful notes employ;
Jerusalem breaks forth in songs,
　And deserts learn the joy.
6 The Lord makes bare his arm
　Through all the earth abroad;
Let every nation now behold
　Their Saviour and their God!

1006 *More laborers.—Matt. 9: 38.*　　C. WESLEY.

LORD of the harvest! hear
　Thy needy servants cry;
Answer our faith's effectual prayer,
　And all our wants supply.
On thee we humbly wait;
　Our wants are in thy view;
The harvest truly, Lord! is great,
　The laborers are few.

2 Convert and send forth more
　Into thy Church abroad;
And let them speak thy word of power,
　As workers with their God.
Give the pure Gospel-word,
　The word of general grace;
Thee let them preach, the common Lord,
　The Saviour of our race.

3 Oh, let them spread thy name;
　Their mission fully prove;
Thy universal grace proclaim,
　Thy all-redeeming love.
On all mankind, forgiven,
　Empower them still to call,
And tell each creature under heaven,
　That thou hast died for all.

SEASONS. L. M.

1. How blest the sa - cred tie that binds, In u - nion sweet, ac - cord - ing minds!

How swift the heavenly course they run, Whose hearts and faith and hopes are one!

1007   *"Of one heart."—Acts* **4:32.**   BARBAULD.

How blest the sacred tie that binds,
In union sweet, according minds!
How swift the heavenly course they run,
Whose hearts and faith and hopes are one!

2 To each the soul of each how dear!
What jealous care, what holy fear!
How doth the generous flame within,
Refine from earth and cleanse from sin!

3 Their streaming tears together flow,
For human guilt and human woe;
Their ardent prayers united rise,
Like mingling flames in sacrifice.

4 Nor shall the glowing flame expire
'Mid nature's drooping, sickening fire:
Soon shall they meet in realms above,
And heaven of joy, because of love.

1008   *"Members one of another."*   NEWTON.

KINDRED in Christ! for his dear sake,
A hearty welcome here receive;
May we together now partake
The joys which only he can give.

2 To you and us by grace 't is given
To know the Saviour's precious name;
And shortly we shall meet in heaven,
Our hope, our way, our end the same.

3 May he, by whose kind care we meet,
Send his good Spirit from above,
Make our communications sweet,
And cause our hearts to burn with love.

374

4 Forgotten be each worldy theme,
When Christians see each other thus;
We only wish to speak of him,
Who lived, and died, and reigns for us.

5 We'll talk of all he did and said,
And suffered for us here below;
The path he marked for us to tread;
And what he's doing for us now.

6 Thus, as the moments pass away,
We'll love, and wonder, and adore;
And hasten on the glorious day,
When we shall meet to part no more.

1009   *Matt.* **10: 40-42.**   KELLY.

COME in, thou blessed of the Lord,
Enter in Jesus' precious name;
We welcome thee with one accord,
And trust the Saviour does the same.

2 Those joys which earth cannot afford,
We'll seek in fellowship to prove;
Joined in one spirit to our Lord,
Together bound by mutual love.

3 And, while we pass this vale of tears,
We'll make our joys and sorrows known;
We'll share each others' hopes and fears,
And count a brother's cares our own.

4 Once more, our welcome we repeat;
Receive assurance of our love;
Oh, may we all together meet,
Around the throne of God above.

EVAN. C. M.

1. How sweet, how heavenly is the sight, When those who love the Lord

In one an - oth - er's peace de - light, And so ful - fill his word!

1010   1 *John* 4: 21.   SWAIN.

How sweet, how heavenly is the sight,
　When those who love the Lord
In one another's peace delight,
　And so fulfill his word!

2 When each can feel his brother's sigh,
　And with him bear a part!
When sorrow flows from eye to eye,
　And joy from heart to heart!

3 When, free from envy, scorn and pride,
　Our wishes all above,
Each can his brother's failings hide,
　And show a brother's love!

4 Let love, in one delightful stream,
　Through every bosom flow,
And union sweet, and dear esteem,
　In every action glow.

5 Love is the golden chain that binds
　The happy souls above;
And he's an heir of heaven who finds
　His bosom glow with love.

1011   1 *Corinthians* 12: 27.   C. WESLEY.

Happy the souls to Jesus joined,
　And saved by grace alone;
Walking in all his ways, they find
　Their heaven on earth begun.

2 The church triumphant in thy love,
　Their mighty joys we know:
They sing the Lamb in hymns above,
　And we in hymns below.

3 Thee in thy glorious realm they praise,
　And bow before thy throne;
We in the kingdom of thy grace:
　The kingdoms are but one.

4 The holy to the holiest leads,
　And thence our spirits rise;
For he that in thy statutes treads,
　Shall meet thee in the skies.

1012   " *One as we are one.*"—*John* 13: 1.   RAY PALMER.

Lord, thou on earth didst love thine own,
　Didst love them to the end;
Oh, still from thy celestial throne,
　Let gifts of love descend.

2 The love the Father bears to thee,
　His own eternal Son,
Fill all thy saints, till all shall be
　In pure affection one.

3 As thou for us didst stoop so low,
　Warmed by love's holy flame,
So let our deeds of kindness flow
　To all that bear thy name.

One blessèd fellowship of love,
　Thy living church should stand,
Till, faultless, she at last above
　Shall shine at thy right hand.

5 Oh, glorious day, when she, the Bride,
　With her dear Lord appears!
Then robed in beauty at his side,
　She shall forget her tears!

375

COLCHESTER. C. M.

1. Our God is love, and all his saints His im - age bear be - low;

The heart with love to God in - spired, With love to man will glow.

1013   *" God is love."*—1 John 4: 21.   ANON.

Our God is love, and all his saints
  His image bear below;
The heart with love to God inspired,
  With love to man will glow.

2 Our heavenly Father, Lord, art thou,
  Thy favored children we;
Oh, may we love each other here,
  As we are loved by thee.

3 Heirs of the same immortal bliss,
  Our hopes and fears the same;
With bonds of grace our hearts unite,
  With mutual love inflame.

4 So may the vain, contentious world
  See how true Christians love,
And glorify our Saviour's grace,
  And seek that grace to prove.

1014   *" One Family."*—Eph. 3: 15.   C. WESLEY.

Let saints below in concert sing
  With those to glory gone;
For all the servants of our King
  In earth and heaven are one.

2 One family—we dwell in him—
  One church above, beneath,
Though now divided by the stream,
  The narrow stream of death;—

3 One army of the living God,
  To his command we bow;
Part of the host have crossed the flood,
  And part are crossing now.

4 Ev'n now to their eternal home
  Some happy spirits fly;
And we are to the margin come,
  And soon expect to die.

5 Ev'n now, by faith, we join our hands
  With those that went before,
And greet the ransomed, blessèd bands
  Upon the eternal shore.

6 Lord Jesus! be our constant guide:
  And, when the word is given,
Bid death's cold flood its waves divide,
  And land us safe in heaven.

1015   *"Planted in Christ."*—Rom. 6: 5.   S. F. SMITH.

Planted in Christ, the living vine,
  This day, with one accord,
Ourselves, with humble faith and joy,
  We yield to thee, O Lord!

2 Joined in one body may we be:
  One inward life partake;
One be our heart, one heavenly hope
  In every bosom wake.

3 In prayer, in effort, tears, and toils,
  One wisdom be our guide;
Taught by one Spirit from above,
  In thee may we abide.

4 Then, when among the saints in light
  Our joyful spirits shine,
Shall anthems of immortal praise,
  O Lamb of God, be thine!

ARUNDEL. C. M.

1. Blest be the dear, u-nit-ing love, That will not let us part:

Our bod-ies may far off re-move; We still are one in heart.

1016 *"The Head, even Christ."—Eph.* 4:15.   C. WESLEY.

BLEST be the dear, uniting love,
   That will not let us part:
Our bodies may far off remove;
   We still are one in heart.

2 Joined in one spirit to our Head,
   Where he appoints we go;
We still in Jesus' footsteps tread,
   And show his praise below.

3 Oh, may we ever walk in him,
   And nothing know beside!
Nothing desire, nothing esteem,
   But Jesus crucified!

4 Partakers of the Saviour's grace,
   The same in mind and heart,
Not joy nor grief nor time nor place
   Nor life nor death can part.

1017 *Hebrews* 12:18-24.   WATTS.

Nor to the terrors of the Lord,
   The tempest, fire, and smoke;
Not to the thunder of that word
   Which God on Sinai spoke;—

2 But we are come to Zion's hill,
   The city of our God;
Where milder words declare his will,
   And speak his love abroad.

3 Behold the innumerable host
   Of angels clothed in light;
Behold the spirits of the just,
   Whose faith is turned to sight!

4 Behold the blest assembly there,
   Whose names are writ in heaven!
And God, the Judge of all, declare
   Their vilest sins forgiven.

5 The saints on earth, and all the dead
   But one communion make;
All join in Christ, their living Head,
   And of his grace partake.

6 In such society as this
   My weary soul would rest:
The man that dwells where Jesus is,
   Must be for ever blest.

1018 *"Two or Three."—Matt.* 18:20.   ANON.

OH, it is joy for those to meet
   Whom one communion blends,
Council to hold in converse sweet,
   And talk as Christian friends.

2 'Tis joy to think the angel train,
   Who 'mid heaven's temple shine,
To seek our earthly temples deign,
   And in our anthems join.

3 But chief 'tis joy to think that he
   To whom his church is dear,
Delights her gathered flock to see,
   Her joint devotions hear.

4 Then who would choose to walk abroad,
   While here such joys are given;
"This is indeed the house of God,
   And this the gate of heaven!"

BOYLSTON. S. M.

1. Blest be the tie that binds Our hearts in Chris - tian love:

The fel - low - ship of kin - dred minds Is like to that a - bove.

1019   *"One body in Christ."—Rom.* **12: 5.**   FAWCETT.

BLEST be the tie that binds
  Our hearts in Christian love :
The fellowship of kindred minds
  Is like to that above.

2 Before our Father's throne
  We pour our ardent prayers;
Our fears, our hopes, our aims are one,
  Our comforts and our cares.

3 We share our mutual woes,
  Our mutual burdens bear;
And often for each other flows
  The sympathizing tear.

4 When we asunder part,
  It gives us inward pain;
But we shall still be joined in heart,
  And hope to meet again.

5 This glorious hope revives
  Our courage by the way;
While each in expectation lives,
  And longs to see the day.

6 From sorrow, toil, and pain,
  And sin, we shall be free,
And perfect love and friendship reign
  Through all eternity.

1020   *"In the midst."—Matt.* **18 : 20.**   C. WESLEY.

JESUS, we look to thee,
  Thy promised presence claim;
Thou in the midst of us shall be,
  Assembled in thy name.

2 Not in the name of pride
  Or selfishness we meet;
From nature's paths we turn aside,
  And worldly thoughts forget.

3 We meet the grace to take,
  Which thou hast freely given;
We meet on earth for thy dear sake,
  That we may meet in heaven.

4 Present we know thou art,
  But oh, thyself reveal!
Now, Lord, let every bounding heart
  Thy mighty comfort feel.

5 Oh, may thy quickening voice
  The death of sin remove;
And bid our inmost souls rejoice,
  In hope of perfect love.

1021   *Party names.—1 Cor.* **12: 13.**   BEDDOME.

LET party names no more
  The Christian world o'erspread;
Gentile and Jew, and bond and free,
  Are one in Christ their head.

2 Among the saints on earth,
  Let mutual love be found;
Heirs of the same inheritance,
  With mutual blessings crowned.

3 Thus will the church below
  Resemble that above;
Where streams of pleasure ever flow,
  And every heart is love.

INVERNESS. S. M.

1. Our chil - dren thou dost claim, O Lord, our God, as thine:

Ten thousand blessings to thy name For good - ness so di - vine!

1022 *"And to your children."—Acts 2:39.* ANON.

Our children thou dost claim,
    O Lord, our God, as thine:
Ten thousand blessings to thy name
    For goodness so divine!

2 Thee let the fathers own,
    Thee let the sons adore;
Joined to the Lord in solemn vows,
    To be forgot no more.

3 How great thy mercies, Lord!
    How plenteous is thy grace!
Which, in the promise of thy love,
    Includes our rising race.

4 Our offspring, still thy care,
    Shall own their fathers' God!
To latest times thy blessings share,
    And sound thy praise abroad.

1023 *Suffer them to come.—Matt 19:14.* ONDERDONK.

The Saviour kindly calls
    Our children to his breast;
He folds them in his gracious arms,
    Himself declares them blest.

2 "Let them approach," he cries,
    "Nor scorn their humble claim;
The heirs of heaven are such as these,
    For such as these I came."

3 With joy we bring them, Lord,
    Devoting them to thee,
Imploring, that, as we are thine,
    Thine may our offspring be.

1024 *Our children.—Ps. 144:12.* FELLOWS.

Great God, now condescend
    To bless our rising race;
Soon may their willing spirits bend,
    The subjects of thy grace.

2 Oh, what a pure delight
    Their happiness to see;
Our warmest wishes all unite,
    To lead their souls to thee.

3 Now bless, thou God of love,
    This ordinance divine;
Send thy good Spirit from above,
    And make these children thine.

1025 *"Forbid them not."—Mark 10:14.* ANON.

Thou God of sovereign grace,
    In mercy now appear;
We long to see thy smiling face,
    And feel that thou art near.

2 Receive these lambs to-day,
    O Shepherd of the flock,
And wash the stains of guilt away
    Beside the smitten Rock.

3 To-day in love descend;
    Oh, come, this precious hour;
In mercy now their spirits bend
    By thy resistless power.

4 Low bending at thy feet,
    Our offspring we resign:
Thine arm is strong, thy love is great,
    And high thy glories shine.

HEBRON. L. M.

1. This child we ded - i - cate to thee, O God of grace and pu - ri - ty!

Shield it from sin and threatening wrong, And let thy love its life pro - long.

1026 *"This child we dedicate."* ANON.

This child we dedicate to thee,
O God of grace and purity!
Shield it from sin and threatening wrong,
And let thy love its life prolong.

2 Oh, may thy Spirit gently draw
Its willing soul to keep thy law;
May virtue, piety, and truth,
Dawn even with its dawning youth.

3 We too, before thy gracious sight,
Once shared the blest baptismal rite,
And would renew its solemn vow
With love, and thanks, and praises, now.

4 Grant that, with true and faithful heart,
We still may act the Christian's part,
Cheered by each promise thou hast given,
And laboring for the prize in heaven.

1027 *The promise—Acts 2: 39.* STEELE.

O Lord! encouraged by thy grace,
We bring our infant to thy throne;
Give it within thy heart a place,
Let it be thine, and thine alone.

2 Wash it from every stain of guilt,
And let this child be sanctified;
Lord! thou canst cleanse it, if thou wilt,
And all its native evils hide.

3 We ask not, for it, earthly bliss,
Or earthly honors, wealth or fame;
The sum of our request is this—
That it may love and fear thy name.

1028 *"Feed my Lambs."—John 21: 15.* BICKERSTETH

With thankful hearts our songs we raise,
To celebrate the Saviour's praise;
Yet who but saints in heaven above,
Can tell the riches of his love?

2 He, the good Shepherd, kindly leads
The wanderer, and the hungry feeds;
Deigns in his arms the lambs to bear,
And makes them his peculiar care.

3 Jesus, to thy protecting wing
Our helpless little ones we bring;　[they
Oh, grant them grace and strength, that
May find and keep the heavenward way.

1029 *"They are thine."—Isa. 40: 11.* HYDE.

Dear Saviour, if these lambs should stray
From thy secure enclosure's bound,
And, lured by worldly joys away,
Among the thoughtless crowd be found;—

2 Remember still that they are thine,
That thy dear sacred name they bear;
Think that the seal of love divine,
The sign of covenant grace they wear.

3 In all their erring, sinful years,
Oh, let them ne'er forgotten be;
Remember all the prayers and tears
Which made them consecrate to thee.

4 And when these lips no more can pray,
These eyes can weep for them no more,
Turn thou their feet from folly's way;
The wanderers to thy fold restore.

AZMON. C. M.

1. O God of Beth - el, by whose hand Thy peo - ple still are fed;
Who through this wea - ry pil - grim- age Hast all our fa - thers led!

1030   *Genesis* 28: 19-22.   DODDRIDGE.

O God of Bethel, by whose hand
Thy people still are fed;
Who through this weary pilgrimage
Hast all our fathers led!

2 Our vows, our prayers, we now present
Before thy throne of grace;
God of our fathers! be the God
Of their succeeding race.

3 Through each perplexing path of life
Our wandering footsteps guide;
Give us, each day, our daily bread,
And raiment fit provide.

4 Oh, spread thy covering wings around,
Till all our wanderings cease,
And at our Father's loved abode,
Our souls arrive in peace.

5 Such blessings from thy gracious hand
Our humble prayers implore;
And thou shalt be our chosen God,
Our portion evermore.

1031   *" Forbid them not."—Mark* 10: 14.   HASTINGS.

"Forbid them not," the Saviour cried,
" But suffer them to come;"
Ah, then maternal tears were dried,
And unbelief was dumb.

2 Lord, we believe, and we obey;
We bring them at thy word;
Be thou our children's strength and stay,
Their portion and reward.

1032   *The Covenant.—Gen.* 17: 7.   BICKERSTETH.

Our children, Lord, in faith and prayer,
We now devote to thee;
Let them thy covenant mercies share
And thy salvation see.

2 In early days their hearts secure
From worldly snares, we pray;
And let them to the end endure
In every righteous way.

3 Grant us before them, Lord, to live
In holy faith and fear;
And then to heaven our souls receive,
And bring our children there.

1033   *Sealing the Covenant.—Rom.* 6: 3.   WATTS.

The promise of my Father's love
Shall stand for ever good:—
He said, and gave his soul to death,
And sealed the grace with blood.

2 To this dear covenant of thy word,
I set my worthless name;
I seal the engagement of my Lord,
And make my humble claim.

3 I call that legacy my own,
Which Jesus did bequeath;
'Twas purchased with a dying groan,
And ratified in death.

4 Sweet is the memory of his name,
Who blessed us in his will,
And to his testament of love,
Made his own life the seal.

381

ORIOLA. C. M. D.

1. Dear Saviour, ev-er at my side, How loving thou must be, To leave thy home in heaven to guard
D. S.—The sweetness of thy soft, low voice

FINE.   D. S.

A lit-tle child like me! Thy beau-ti-ful and shin-ing face I see not, though so near;
I am too deaf to hear.

1034   *Child's Hymn.—Mark* 10:14.   FABER.

DEAR Saviour, ever at my side,
  How loving thou must be,
To leave thy home in heaven to guard
  A little child like me!
Thy beautiful and shining face
  I see not, though so near;
The sweetness of thy soft, low voice
  I am too deaf to hear.

2 I cannot feel thee touch my hand
  With pressure light and mild,
To check me, as my mother doth,
  While I am but a child;
But I have felt thee in my thoughts
  Fighting with sin for me;
And when my heart loves God, I know
  The sweetness is from thee.

3 And when, dear Saviour! I kneel down
  Morning and night to prayer,
Something there is within my heart
  Which tells me thou art there;
Yes! when I pray, thou prayest too—
  Thy prayer is all for me;
But when I sleep, thou sleepest not,
  But watchest patiently.

1035   *"Remember thy Creator."—Eccl.* 12:1.   ANON.

REMEMBER thy Creator now,
  In these thy youthful days;
He will accept thine early vow,
  And listen to thy praise.

2 Remember thy Creator now,
  Seek him while he is near;
For evil days will come, when thou
  Shalt find no comfort here.

3 Remember thy Creator now;
  His willing servant be:
Then, when thy head in death shall bow,
  He will remember thee.

4 Almighty God! our hearts incline
  Thy heavenly voice to hear;
Let all our future days be thine,
  Devoted to thy fear.

1036   *"God called the child."—1 Sam.* 3:10.   ANON.

DEAR Jesus, let thy pitying eye
  Look kindly down on me;
A sinful, weak, and helpless child,
  I come thy child to be.

2 O blessèd Saviour! take my heart,
  This sinful heart of mine,
And wash it clean in every part;
  Make me a child of thine.

3 My sins, though great, thou canst forgive,
  For thou hast died for me;
Amazing love! help me, O God,
  Thine own dear child to be.

4 For thou hast said, "Forbid them not:
  Let children come to me:"
I hear thy voice, and now, dear Lord,
  I come thy child to be.

SILOAM. C. M.

1. By cool Si - lo - am's sha - dy rill How fair the lil - y grows;

How sweet the breath be - neath the hill Of Sha - ron's dew - y rose!

1037 *A Christian Child.* HEBER.

By cool Siloam's shady rill
How fair the lily grows!
How sweet the breath beneath the hill
Of Sharon's dewy rose!

2 Lo! such the child whose early feet
The paths of peace have trod,
Whose secret heart, with influence sweet,
Is upward drawn to God.

3 By cool Siloam's shady rill
The lily must decay;
The rose that blooms beneath the hill
Must shortly fade away.

4 And soon, too soon, the wintry hour
Of man's maturer age
May shake the soul with sorrow's power
And stormy passion's rage.

5 O thou whose infant feet were found
Within thy Father's shrine, [crowned,
Whose years, with changeless virtue
Were all alike divine!

6 Dependent on thy bounteous breath,
We seek thy grace alone
In childhood, manhood, and in death,
To keep us still thine own.

1038 *The Covenant.—Gen. 17 : 7.* WATTS.

How large the promise! how divine
To Abr'ham and his seed:
"I'll be a God to thee and thine,
Supplying all their need."

2 The words of his extensive love
From age to age endure:
The Angel of the covenant proves,
And seals the blessings sure.

3 Jesus the ancient faith confirms,
To our great fathers given;
He takes young children to his arms,
And calls them heirs of heaven.

4 Our God!—how faithful are his ways!
His love endures the same;
Nor from the promise of his grace
Blots out the children's name.

1039 *Christ receiving children.* DODDRIDGE.

See Israel's gentle Shepherd stand,
With all-engaging charms!
Hark! how he calls the tender lambs,
And folds them in his arms!

2 "Permit them to approach," he cries,
"Nor scorn their humble name;
For 'twas to bless such souls as these,
The Lord of angels came."

3 We bring them, Lord! in thankful hands,
And yield them up to thee;
Joyful that we ourselves are thine,—
Thine let our offspring be.

4 Ye little flock! with pleasure hear,—
Ye children! seek his face;
And fly, with transport, to receive
The blessings of his grace.

BAVARIA. 8, 7. D.

FINE.

1. { Sav - iour, like a shepherd lead us: Much we need thy ten - der care; }
    { In thy pleas - ant pas - tures feed us, For our use thy fold pre - pare; }
D. C. Keep thy flock, from sin de - fend us, Seek us when we go a - stray.

We are thine: do thou be - friend us, Be the guardian of our way;

D. C.

1040   *Lambs of the Fold.—John* **21:15.**   MISS THRUPP.

Saviour, like a shepherd lead us:
   Much we need thy tender care;
In thy pleasant pastures feed us,
   For our use thy fold prepare:
We are thine: do thou befriend us,
   Be the guardian of our way;
Keep thy flock, from sin defend us,
   Seek us when we go astray.

2 Thou hast promised to receive us,
   Poor and sinful though we be;
Thou hast mercy to relieve us,
   Grace to cleanse, and power to free:
Early let us seek thy favor,
   Early help us do thy will;
Holy Lord, our only Saviour!
   With thy grace our bosom fill.

1041   *Sabbath School Meeting.*   ANON.

Saviour King, in hallowed union,
   At thy sacred feet we bow;
Heart with heart, in blest communion,
   Join to crave thy favor now!
Though celestial choirs adore thee,
   Let our prayer as incense rise;
And our praise be set before thee,
   Sweet as evening sacrifice.

2 Heavenly Fount, thy streams of blessing,
   Oft have cheered us on our way;
By thy power and grace unceasing,
   We continue to this day:

Raise we then with glad emotion
   Thankful lays: and while we sing,
Vow a pure, a full devotion
   To thy work, O Saviour King!

3 When we tell the wondrous story
   Of thy rich, exhaustless love,
Send thy Spirit, Lord of glory,
   On the youthful heart to move!
Oh, that he, the ever-living,
   May descend, as fruitful rain;
Till the wilderness, reviving,
   Blossoms as the rose again!

1042   *"These little ones."—Isa.* **40:11.**   MUHLENBERG.

Saviour! who thy flock art feeding
   With the Shepherd's kindest care,
All the feeble gently leading,
   While the lambs thy bosom share;
Now, these little ones receiving,
   Fold them in thy gracious arm;
There, we know, thy word believing,
   Only there, secure from harm.

2 Never, from thy pasture roving,
   Let them be the lion's prey;
Let thy tenderness, so loving,
   Keep them all life's dangerous way:
Then, within thy fold eternal,
   Let them find a resting-place,
Feed in pastures ever vernal,
   Drink the rivers of thy grace.

NETTLETON.   8, 7. D.

Come thou Fount of ev - er - y bless - ing, Tune my heart to sing thy grace;
Streams of mer - cy, nev - er ceas - ing, Call for songs of loud - est praise;
D. C.—Praise the mount—I'm fixed up - on it!— Mount of thy re - deem - ing love.

Teach me some me - lo - dious son - net, Sung by flam - ing tongues a - bove;

1043   *"Eben-ezer."*—1 *Sam.* **7 : 12.**   R. ROBINSON.

Come, thou Fount of every blessing,
Tune my heart to sing thy grace;
Streams of mercy, never ceasing,
Call for songs of loudest praise;
Teach me some melodious sonnet,
Sung by flaming tongues above;
Praise the mount—I'm fixed upon it!—
Mount of thy redeeming love.

2 Here I'll raise mine Eben-ezer;
Hither by thy help I'm come;
And I hope, by thy good pleasure,
Safely to arrive at home.
Jesus sought me when a stranger,
Wandering from the fold of God;
He, to rescue me from danger,
Interposed his precious blood.

3 Oh, to grace how great a debtor
Daily I'm constrained to be!
Let thy goodness, like a fetter,
Bind my wandering heart to thee;
Prone to wander, Lord, I feel it;
Prone to leave the God I love;
Here's my heart; oh, take and seal it;
Seal it for thy courts above.

1044   *Jesus in Glory.*—*Rev.* **19 : 12.**   BAKEWELL.

Hail, thou once despisèd Jesus!
Crowned in mockery a king!

Thou didst suffer to release us;
Thou didst free salvation bring.
Hail, thou agonizing Saviour,
Bearer of our sin and shame!
By thy merits we find favor;
Life is given through thy name.

2 Paschal Lamb, by God appointed,
All our sins on thee were laid;
By Almighty Love anointed,
Thou hast full atonement made:
All thy people are forgiven
Through the virtue of thy blood;
Opened is the gate of heaven,
Peace is made 'twixt man and God.

3 Jesus, hail! enthroned in glory!
There for ever to abide;
All the heavenly hosts adore thee,
Seated at thy Father's side:
There for sinners thou art pleading;
There thou dost our place prepare,
Ever for us interceding,
Till in glory we appear.

4 Worship, honor, power and blessing,
Thou art worthy to receive;
Loudest praises without ceasing,
Meet it is for us to give;
Help, ye bright angelic spirits.
Bring your sweetest, noblest lays;
Help to sing our Saviour's merits,
Help to chant Immanuel's praise!

385

WINDHAM. L. M.

1. 'Twas on that dark, that dole-ful night, When powers of earth and hell a-rose

A - gainst the Son of God's de - light, And friends betrayed him to his foes.

1045 *The Last Supper.—Luke 22: 19.* WATTS.

'Twas on that dark, that doleful night,
　When powers of earth and hell arose
Against the Son of God's delight,
　And friends betrayed him to his foes.

2 Before the mournful scene began,
　He took the bread, and blessed, and brake;
What love through all his actions ran!
　What wondrous words of grace he spake!

3 "This is my body, broke for sin;
　Receive and eat the living food:"
Then took the cup, and blessed the wine:
　"'Tis the new covenant in my blood."

4 "Do this," he cried, "till time shall end,
　In memory of your dying Friend;
Meet at my table, and record
　The love of your departed Lord."

5 Jesus, thy feast we celebrate;
　We show thy death, we sing thy name,
Till thou return, and we shall eat
　The marriage supper of the Lamb.

1046 *"Bread of heaven."—John 6: 55.* MRS. ALEXANDER.

O Jesus, bruised and wounded more
　Than bursted grape, or bread of wheat,
The Life of life within our souls,
　The cup of our salvation sweet!

2 We come to show thy dying hour,
　Thy streaming vein, thy broken flesh;
And still that blood is warm to save,
　And still thy fragrant wounds are fresh.

386

3 O Heart, that with a double tide
　Of blood and water, maketh pure!
O Flesh, once offered on the cross,
　The gift that makes our pardon sure!

4 Let nevermore our sinful souls
　The anguish of thy cross renew;
Nor forge again the cruel nails
　That pierced thy victim body through!

5 Come, Bread of heaven, to feed our souls,
　And with thee, Jesus, enter in!
Come, Wine of God! and as we drink,
　His precious blood wash out our sin!

1047 *The Institution.—1 Cor. 11: 24.* WATTS.

At thy command, our dearest Lord,
　Here we attend thy dying feast;
Thy blood, like wine, adorns the board,
　And thine own flesh feeds every guest.

2 Our faith adores thy bleeding love,
　And trusts for life in One that died;
We hope for heavenly crowns above
　From a Redeemer crucified.

3 Let the vain world pronounce it shame,
　And fling their scandals on the cause;
We come to boast our Saviour's name,
　And make our triumphs in his cross.

4 With joy we tell the scoffing age,
　He that was dead has left his tomb;
He lives above their utmost rage,
　And we are waiting till he come.

HAMBURG. L. M.

1. Oh, the sweet won-ders of that cross Where my Re-deem-er loved and died!
Her no-blest life my spir - it draws From his dear wounds, and bleed-ing side.

1048 *Parting Song.—Gal.* **6 : 14.** WATTS.

Oh, the sweet wonders of that cross
  Where my Redeemer loved and died!
Her noblest life my spirit draws
  From his dear wounds, and bleeding side.

2 I would for ever speak his name
  In sounds to mortal ears unknown;
With angels join to praise the Lamb,
  And worship at his Father's throne.

3 Praise God, from whom all blessings flow,
  Praise him, all creatures here below;
Praise him above, ye heavenly host;
  Praise Father, Son and Holy Ghost.

1049 *The Lord our Righteousness.* J. WESLEY. *Tr.*

Jesus, thy Blood and Righteousness
  My beauty are, my glorious dress;
'Midst flaming worlds, in these arrayed,
  With joy shall I lift up my head.

2 Lord, I believe thy precious blood,—
  Which, at the mercy-seat of God,
For ever doth for sinners plead,—
  For me, ev'n for my soul, was shed.

3 Bold shall I stand in thy great day,
  For who aught to my charge shall lay?
Fully absolved through these I am,
  From sin and fear, from guilt and shame.

4 When from the dust of death I rise
  To claim my mansion in the skies—
Ev'n then, this shall be all my plea:
  Jesus hath lived, hath died for me.

5 This spotless robe the same appears,
  When ruined nature sinks in years;
No age can change its glorious hue,
  The robe of Christ is ever new.

6 Oh, let the dead now hear thy voice:
  Bid, Lord, thy mourning ones rejoice;
Their beauty this, their glorious dress,
  Jesus, the Lord our Righteousness.

1050 *Living to Christ.—Phil.* **1 : 21.** DODDRIDGE.

My gracious Lord, I own thy right
  To every service I can pay,
And call it my supreme delight
  To hear thy dictates and obey.

2 What is my being, but for thee,
  Its sure support, its noblest end?
Thine ever-smiling face to see,
  And serve the cause of such a Friend.

3 I would not breathe for worldly joy,
  Or to increase my worldly good;
Nor future days nor powers employ
  To spread a sounding name abroad.

4 'Tis to my Saviour I would live,
  To him who for my ransom died;
Nor could the bowers of Eden give
  Such bliss as blossoms at his side.

5 His work my hoary age shall bless,
  When youthful vigor is no more;
And my last hour of life confess
  His dying love, his saving power.

387

FEDERAL STREET. L. M.

1. Je - sus! and shall it ev - er be, A mor-tal man a - shamed of thee?

A-shamed of thee, whom an - gels praise, Whose glo-ries shine through end-less days.

1051   *"Ashamed of me."—Mark 8. 38.*   GRIGG.

Jesus! and shall it ever be,
  A mortal man ashamed of thee?
Ashamed of thee, whom angels praise,
  Whose glories shine through endless days.

2 Ashamed of Jesus! sooner far
  Let evening blush to own a star;
He sheds the beams of light divine
  O'er this benighted soul of mine.

3 Ashamed of Jesus! that dear Friend
  On whom my hopes of heaven depend!
No; when I blush—be this my shame,
  That I no more revere his name.

4 Ashamed of Jesus! yes, I may,
  When I've no guilt to wash away;
No tear to wipe, no good to crave,
  No fears to quell, no soul to save.

5 Till then—nor is my boasting vain—
  Till then I boast a Saviour slain!
And oh, may this my glory be,
  That Christ is not ashamed of me!

1052   RAV. PALMER. *Tr.*
     Jesus all in all.

Jesus, thou joy of loving hearts,
  Thou fount of life! thou light of men!
From the best bliss that earth imparts,
  We turn unfilled to thee again.

2 Thy truth unchanged hath ever stood;
  Thou savest those that on thee call;
To them that seek thee, thou art good,
  To them that find thee All in All.

3 We taste thee, O thou Living Bread,
  And long to feast upon thee still;
We drink of thee, the Fountain Head,
  And thirst our souls from thee to fill!

4 Our restless spirits yearn for thee,
  Where'er our changeful lot is cast;
Glad, when thy gracious smile we see,
  Blest, when our faith can hold thee fast.

5 O Jesus, ever with us stay;
  Make all our moments calm and bright;
Chase the dark night of sin away,
  Shed o'er the world thy holy light!

1053   *"Not your own."—1 Cor. 6: 19.*   S. F. SMITH.

Oh, not my own these verdant hills,
  And fruits, and flowers, and stream, and
But his who all with glory fills,   [wood:
  Who bought me with his precious blood.

2 Oh, not my own this wondrous frame,
  Its curious work, its living soul;
But his who for my ransom came;
  Slain for my sake, he claims the whole.

3 Oh, not my own the grace that keeps
  My feet from fierce temptations free:
Oh, not my own the thought that leaps,
  Adoring, blessèd Lord, to thee.

4 Oh, not my own; I'll soar and sing,
  When life, with all its toils, is o'er,
And thou thy trembling lamb shalt bring
  Safe home, to wander nevermore.

SESSIONS. L. M.

1. Je - sus is gone a - bove the skies, Where our weak sen - ses reach him not;

And car - nal ob - jects court our eyes, To thrust our Sav - iour from our thought.

1054 *The Memorial of our Lord.* WATTS.

JESUS is gone above the skies,
　Where our weak senses reach him not;
And carnal objects court our eyes,
　To thrust our Saviour from our thought.

2 He knows what wandering hearts we have,
　Apt to forget his lovely face;
And, to refresh our minds, he gave
　These kind memorials of his grace.

3 Let sinful sweets be all forgot,
　And earth grow less in our esteem;
Christ and his love fill every thought,
　And faith and hope be fixed on him.

4 While he is absent from our sight,
　'Tis to prepare our souls a place,
That we may dwell in heavenly light,
　And live for ever near his face.

1055 *"We would see Jesus."—John 6.35.* ANON.

HERE let us see thy face, O Lord,
　And view salvation with our eyes,
And taste and feel the living Word,
　The Bread descending from the skies.

2 Thou hast prepared this dying Lamb,
　Hast set his blood before our face,
To teach the terrors of thy name,
　And show the wonders of thy grace.

3 Jesus, our Light! our Morning-star!
　Shine thou on nations yet unknown;
The glory of thy people here,
　And joy of spirits near thy throne.

1056 *"Our exalted Lord."* STEELE

To Jesus, our exalted Lord,
That name in heaven and earth adored,
Fain would our hearts and voices raise
A cheerful song of sacred praise.

2 But all the notes which mortals know,
Are weak, and languishing, and low;
Far, far above our humble songs,
The theme demands immortal tongues.

3 Yet whilst around his board we meet,
And worship at his sacred feet,
Oh, let our warm affections move,
In glad return of grateful love.

1057 *"Eat, O friends!"—Cant. 5:1.* WOLFE.

DRAW near, O Holy Dove, draw near,
　With peace and gladness on thy wing;
Reveal the Saviour's presence here,
　And light, and life, and comfort bring.

2 "Eat, O my friends—drink, O beloved!"
　We hear the Master's voice exclaim:
Our hearts with new desire are moved,
　And kindled with a heavenly flame.

3 No room for doubt, no room for dread,
　Nor tears, nor groans, nor anxious sighs;
We do not mourn a Saviour dead,
　But hail him living in the skies!

4 While this we do, remembering thee,
　Dear Saviour, let our graces prove
We have thy blessèd company,
　Thy banner over us is love.

389

EASTON. L. M.

1. My God, and is thy ta-ble spread, And doth thy cup with love o'er-flow?

Thith-er be all thy chil-dren led, And let them all thy sweetness know.

1058 *" Thou preparest a table."— Ps.* 23: 5. ANON.

My God, and is thy table spread,
　And doth thy cup with love o'erflow?
Thither be all thy children led,
　And let them all thy sweetness know.

2 Hail, sacred Feast, which Jesus makes,
　Rich banquet of his flesh and blood!
Thrice happy he, who here partakes
　That sacred stream, that heavenly food.

3 Oh, let thy table honored be,
　And furnished well with joyous guests;
And may each soul salvation see,
　That here its sacred pledges tastes.

4 To Father, Son, and Holy Ghost,
　One God whom heaven and earth adore,
From men, and from the angel-host,
　Be praise and glory evermore!

1059　　　*Feeding on Christ.* MONTGOMERY.

I FEED by faith on Christ; my bread,
　His body broken on the tree;
I live in him, my living Head,
　Who died, and rose again for me.

2 This be my joy and comfort here,
　This pledge of future glory mine:
Jesus, in spirit now appear,
　And break the bread, and pour the wine.

3 From thy dear hand, may I receive
　The tokens of thy dying love,
And, while I feast on earth, believe
　That I shall feast with thee above.

1060　　*At the Cross.— John* 19: 25. ANON.

DEAR Lord, amid the throng that pressed
　Around thee on the cursèd tree,
Some loyal, loving hearts were there,
　Some pitying eyes that wept for thee.

2 Like them may we rejoice to own
　Our dying Lord, tho' crowned with thorn;
Like thee, thy blessed self, endure
　The cross with all its cruel scorn.

3 Thy cross, thy lonely path below,
　Show what thy brethren all should be;
Pilgrims on earth, disowned by those
　Who see no beauty, Lord, in thee.

1061　　*The day of Espousals.* WATTS.

JESUS, thou everlasting King!
　Accept the tribute that we bring;
Accept the well-deserved renown,
　And wear our praises as thy crown.

2 Let every act of worship be,
　Like our espousals, Lord! to thee;
Like the dear hour, when, from above,
　We first received thy pledge of love.

3 The gladness of that happy day—
　Our hearts would wish it long to stay;
Nor let our faith forsake its hold,
　Nor comfort sink, nor love grow cold.

4 Each following minute, as it flies,
　Increase thy praise, improve our joys;
Till we are raised to sing thy name,
　At the great supper of the Lamb.

HAPPY DAY. L. M.

f. CHORUS.

1. Oh, happy day, that fixed my choice On thee, my Sav-iour, and my God!
Well may this glow-ing heart re-joice, And tell its rap-tures all a - broad. Hap - py

FINE.　　　　　　D. S.

day, hap-py day, When Je-sus wash'd my sins a-way! He taught me how to watch and pray,
And live re-joic - ing ev-ery day;

1062　　*"Happy Day!"—Ps.* 56:12.　DODDRIDGE.

Oh, happy day, that fixed my choice
　On thee, my Saviour, and my God!
Well may this glowing heart rejoice,
　And tell its raptures all abroad.
Cho.—Happy day, happy day,
　When Jesus washed my sins away!
He taught me how to watch and pray,
　And live rejoicing every day:
Happy day, happy day,
　When Jesus washed my sins away.

2 Oh, happy bond, that seals my vows
　To him who merits all my love!
Let cheerful anthems fill his house,
　While to that sacred shrine I move.—
　　　　　　　Cho.

3 'Tis done, the great transaction's done:
　I am my Lord's, and he is mine:
He drew me, and I followed on,
　Charmed to confess the voice divine.—
　　　　　　　Cho.

4 Now, rest, my long-divided heart!
　Fixed on this blissful centre rest;
With ashes who would grudge to part,
　When called on angel's bread to feast.
　　　　　　　—Cho.

5 High heaven, that heard the solemn vow,
　That vow renewed shall daily hear;
Till in life's latest hour I bow,
　And bless in death a bond so dear.—
　　　　　　　Cho.

1063　　*"Ye are bought with a price."*　DAVIES.

Lord, I am thine, entirely thine,
　Purchased and saved by blood divine,
With full consent thine I would be,
　And own thy sovereign right in me.
Cho.—Happy day, happy day,
　When Jesus washed my sins away!
He taught me how to watch and pray,
　And live rejoicing every day;
Happy day, happy day,
　When Jesus washed my sins away.

2 Grant one poor sinner more a place
　Among the children of thy grace;
A wretched sinner, lost to God,
　But ransomed by Immanuel's blood.—
　　　　　　　Cho.

3 Thine would I live, thine would I die,
　Be thine through all eternity;
The vow is passed beyond repeal;
　And now I set the solemn seal.—Cho.

4 Here at that cross where flows the blood
　That bought my guilty soul for God,
Thee, my new Master now I call,
　And consecrate to thee my all.—Cho.

5 Do thou assist a feeble worm
　The great engagement to perform;
Thy grace can full assistance lend,
　And on that grace I dare depend.—Cho.

DUNDEE. C. M.

1. How sweet and aw - ful is the place, With Christ with - in the doors,

While ev - er - last - ing love dis - plays The choic - est of her stores!

1064   *Persistent Love—Jer. 31: 3.*   WATTS.

How sweet and awful is the place,
    With Christ within the doors,
While everlasting love displays
    The choicest of her stores.

2 While all our hearts, and all our songs,
    Join to admire the feast,
Each of us cries, with thankful tongue,—
    "Lord, why was I a guest?"

3 "Why was I made to hear thy voice,
    And enter while there's room,
When thousands make a wretched choice,
    And rather starve than come?"

4 'T was the same love that spread the feast,
    That sweetly drew us in;
Else we had still refused to taste,
    And perished in our sin.

5 Pity the nations, O our God!
    Constrain the earth to come;
Send thy victorious word abroad,
    And bring the strangers home.

1065   *"Prepare us Lord."—2 Chron. 30: 18.*   ANON.

PREPARE us, Lord, to view thy cross,
    Who all our griefs hast borne;
To look on thee, whom we have pierced—
    To look on thee and mourn.

2 While thus we mourn, we would rejoice;
    And, as thy cross we see,
Let each exclaim, in faith and hope,
    "The Saviour died for me!"

1066   *Feeding on Christ.—John 6: 34.*   ANON.

TOGETHER with these symbols, Lord,
    Thy blesséd self impart;
And let thy holy flesh and blood
    Feed the believing heart.

2 Let us from all our sins be washed
    In thy atoning blood;
And let thy Spirit be the seal
    That we are born of God.

3 Come, Holy Ghost, with Jesus' love,
    Prepare us for this feast;
Oh, let us banquet with our Lord,
    And lean upon his breast.

1067   *"Greater love hath no man."*   NOEL.

IF human kindness meets return,
    And owns the grateful tie;
If tender thoughts within us burn,
    To feel a friend is nigh;—

2 Oh, shall not warmer accents tell
    The gratitude we owe
To him, who died our fears to quell—
    Who bore our guilt and woe!

3 While yet in anguish he surveyed
    Those pangs he would not flee,
What love his latest words displayed,—
    "Meet and remember me!"

4 Remember thee—thy death, thy shame,
    Our sinful hearts to share!—
O memory! leave no other name
    But his recorded there.

DEDHAM. C. M.

1. Ac - cord-ing to thy gra - cious word, In meek hu - mil - i - ty,

This will I do, my dy - ing Lord, I will re - mem - ber thee.

1068 *"I will remember thee."*   MONTGOMERY.

ACCORDING to thy gracious word,
  In meek humility,
This will I do, my dying Lord,
  I will remember thee.

2 Thy body, broken for my sake,
  My bread from heaven shall be;
Thy testamental cup I take,
  And thus remember thee.

3 Gethsemane can I forget?
  Or there thy conflict see,
Thine agony and bloody sweat,
  And not remember thee?

4 When to the cross I turn mine eyes,
  And rest on Calvary,
O Lamb of God, my sacrifice!
  I must remember thee:—

5 Remember thee, and all thy pains
  And all thy love to me;
Yea, while a breath, a pulse remains,
  Will I remember thee.

6 And when these failing lips grow dumb,
  And mind and memory flee,
When thou shalt in thy kingdom come,
  Then, Lord, remember me!

1069   *"The Cup of Blessing."*   C. WESLEY.

JESUS, at whose supreme command,
  We now approach to God,
Before us in thy vesture stand,
  Thy vesture dipped in blood.

2 Now, Saviour, now thyself reveal,
  And make thy nature known;
Affix thy blessèd Spirit's seal,
  And stamp us for thine own.

3 Obedient to thy gracious word,
  We break the hallowed bread,
Commemorate our dying Lord,
  And trust on thee to feed.

4 The cup of blessing, blest by thee,
  Let it thy blood impart;
The broken bread thy body be,
  To cheer each languid heart.

1070   *"Friend of Sinners."*   BURNHAM.

JESUS! thou art the sinner's Friend;
  As such I look to thee;
Now, in the fullness of thy love,
  O Lord! remember me.

2 Remember thy pure word of grace,—
  Remember Calvary;
Remember all thy dying groans,
  And then remember me.

3 Thou wondrous Advocate with God!
  I yield myself to thee;
While thou art sitting on thy throne,
  Dear Lord! remember me.

4 Lord! I am guilty—I am vile,
  But thy salvation's free;
Then, in thine all-abounding grace,
  Dear Lord! remember me.

HENLEY. 10.

1. Here, O my Lord, I   see thee face to face;   Here would I touch and handle things unseen;

Here grasp with firmer hand th' eter-nal grace   And   all my wea - ri - ness up-on thee lean.

1071   *Sweet Foretastes.*   BONAR.

HERE, O my Lord, I see thee face to face;
  Here would I touch and handle things
    unseen;
  Here grasp with firmer hand the eternal
    grace,
  And all my weariness upon thee lean.

2 Here would I feed upon the bread of God;
  Here drink with thee the royal wine of
    heaven;
  Here would I lay aside each earthly load,
  Here taste afresh the calm of sin for-
    given.

3 Too soon we rise; the symbols disappear:
  The feast, though not the love, is passed
    and gone;
  The bread and wine remove, but thou art
    here—
  Nearer than ever—still my Shield and
    Sun.

4 Feast after feast thus comes and passes by;
  Yet, passing, points to the glad feast
    above,—
  Giving sweet foretaste of the festal joy,
  The Lamb's great bridal feast of bliss
    and love.

1072   *Penitent Prayer.*   BICKERSTETH.

NOT worthy, Lord! to gather up the crumbs
  With trembling hand that from thy
    table fall,

A weary, heavy-laden sinner comes
  To plead thy promise and obey thy call.

2 I am not worthy to be thought thy child,
  Nor sit the last and lowest at thy board;
  Too long a wanderer and too oft beguiled,
  I only ask one reconciling word.

3 One word from thee, my Lord! one smile,
    one look,
  And I could face the cold, rough world
    again,
  And with that treasure in my heart could
    brook
  The wrath of devils and the scorn of men.

4 And is not mercy thy prerogative—
  Free mercy, boundless, fathomless, divine?
  Me, Lord! the chief of sinners, me forgive,
  And thine the greater glory, only thine.

5 I hear thy voice; thou bid'st me come and
    rest;
  I come, I kneel, I clasp thy piercéd feet;
  Thou bid'st me take my place, a welcome
    guest,
  Among thy saints, and of thy banquet eat.

6 My praise can only breathe itself in prayer,
  My prayer can only lose itself in thee;
  Dwell thou for ever in my heart, and there,
  Lord! let me sup with thee; sup thou
    with me.

RAYNOLDS.   11, 10.

1. We would see Jesus—for the shadows lengthen   A-cross this lit - tle landscape of our life;

We would see Je - sus our weak faith to strengthen,   For the last wea - riness—the fi - nal strife.

1073   *"We would see Jesus."*   ANON.

WE would see Jesus—for the shadows
   lengthen
   Across this little landscape of our life;
We would see Jesus our weak faith to
   strengthen,
   For the last weariness—the final strife.

2 We would see Jesus—the great Rock
   Foundation,
   Whereon our feet were set with sover-
   eign grace;
Not life, nor death, with all their agitation,
   Can thence remove us, if we see his face.

3 We would see Jesus—other lights are
   fading,
   Which for long years we have rejoiced
   to see;
The blessings of our pilgrimage are failing,
   We would not mourn them, for we go
   to thee.

4 We would see Jesus—this is all we're
   needing,
   Strength, joy and willingness come with
   the sight;
We would see Jesus, dying, risen, pleading,
   Then welcome day, and farewell mortal
   night!

1074   *"Trust, strength, calmness."*   JOHNSON.

SAVIOUR, in thy mysterious presence kneeling,
   Fain would our souls feel all thy kindling love;
For we are weak, and need some deep
   revealing
   Of trust, and strength, and calmness
   from above.

2 Lord, we have wandered forth through
   doubt and sorrow,
   And thou hast made each step an onward one;
And we will ever trust each unknown
   morrow,—
   Thou wilt sustain us till its work is done.

3 In the heart's depths a peace serene and
   holy
   Abides, and when pain seems to have
   its will,
Or we despair,—oh, may that peace rise
   slowly,
   Stronger than agony, and we be still!

4 Now, Saviour, now, in thy dear presence
   kneeling,
   Our spirits yearn to feel thy kindling
   love;
Now make us strong, we need thy deep
   revealing
   Of trust, and strength, and calmness
   from above.

GOLDEN HILL. S. M.

1. Dear Sav - iour! we are thine, By ev - er - last - ing bands;

Our hearts, our souls, we would as - sign En - tire - ly to thy hands.

1075   *"The Body of Christ —1 Cor. 12: 27.*   DODDRIDGE.

Dear Saviour! we are thine,
   By everlasting bands;
Our hearts, our souls, we would resign
   Entirely to thy hands.

2 To thee we still would cleave
   With ever-growing zeal;
If millions tempt us Christ to leave,
   Oh, let them ne'er prevail!

3 Thy Spirit shall unite
   Our souls to thee, our Head;
Shall form in us thine image bright,
   And teach thy paths to tread.

4 Death may our souls divide
   From these abodes of clay;
But love shall keep us near thy side,
   Through all the gloomy way.

5 Since Christ and we are one,
   Why should we doubt or fear?
If he in heaven has fixed his throne,
   He'll fix his members there.

1076   *"Christ and his members one."*   WATTS.

Jesus invites his saints
   To meet around his board;
Here pardoned rebels sit, and hold
   Communion with their Lord.

2 This holy bread and wine
   Maintain our fainting breath,
By union with our living Lord,
   And interest in his death.

3 Our heavenly Father calls
   Christ and his members one;
We, the young children of his love,
   And he, the first-born Son.

4 Let all our powers be joined,
   His glorious name to raise;
Pleasure and love fill every mind,
   And every voice be praise.

5 To God, the Father, Son,
   And Spirit, glory be,
As was, and is, and shall remain
   Through all eternity!

1077   *"When they had sung a hymn."*   WOLFE.

A parting hymn we sing,
   Around thy table, Lord;
Again our grateful tribute bring,
   Our solemn vows record.

2 Here have we seen thy face,
   And felt thy presence here,
So may the savor of thy grace
   In word and life appear.

3 The purchase of thy blood—
   By sin no longer led—
The path our dear Redeemer trod
   May we rejoicing tread.

4 In self-forgetting love
   Be our communion shown,
Until we join the church above,
   And know as we are known.

ADRIAN. S. M.

1. Like No - ah's wea - ry dove, That soared the earth a - round,

But not a rest - ing - place a - bove The cheer - less wa - ters found;—

1078 *The Ark of God.* MUHLENBERG.

Like Noah's weary dove,
  That soared the earth around,
But not a resting-place above
  The cheerless waters found;—

2 Oh, cease, my wandering soul,
  On restless wing to roam;
All this wide world, to either pole,
  Hath not for thee a home.

3 Behold the ark of God!
  Behold the open door!
Oh, haste to gain that dear abode,
  And rove, my soul, no more.

4 There safe thou shalt abide,
  There sweet shall be thy rest;
And every longing satisfied,
  With full salvation blest.

1079 *"This is my blood."* ANON.

Blest feast of love divine!
  'Tis grace that makes us free
To feed upon this bread and wine,
  In memory, Lord, of thee!

2 That blood which flowed for sin,
  In symbol here we see,
And feel the blessèd pledge within,
  That we are loved of thee.

3 Oh, if this glimpse of love
  Be so divinely sweet,
What will it be, O Lord, above,
  Thy gladdening smile to meet!

1080 *Christ, our Righteousness.* C. WESLEY.

For ever here my rest!
  Close to thy bleeding side;
This all my hope, and all my plea,—
  For me the Saviour died.

2 My Saviour, and my God!
  Fountain for guilt and sin!
Sprinkle me ever with thy blood!
  And cleanse and keep me clean.

1081 *"The banqueting house."* C. WESLEY

Jesus, we thus obey
  Thy last and kindest word,
And in thine own appointed way
  We come to meet thee, Lord!

2 Thus we remember thee,
  And take this bread and wine
As thine own dying legacy,
  And our redemption's sign.

3 Thy presence makes the feast;
  Now let our spirits feel
The glory not to be expressed,—
  The joy unspeakable!

4 With high and heavenly bliss
  Thou dost our spirits cheer;
Thy house of banqueting is this,
  And thou hast brought us here.

5 Now let our souls be fed
  With manna from above,
And over us thy banner spread
  Of everlasting love.

397

ALETTA. 7.

1. When on Si - nai's top I see God des - cend, in ma - jes - ty,

To pro-claim his ho - ly law, All my spir - it sinks with awe.

1082   *Three Mountains.*   MONTGOMERY.

WHEN on Sinai's top I see
God descend, in majesty,
To proclaim his holy law,
All my spirit sinks with awe.

2 When, in ecstacy sublime,
Tabor's glorious steep I climb,
At the too transporting light,
Darkness rushes o'er my sight.

3 When on Calvary I rest,
God, in flesh made manifest,
Shines in my Redeemer's face,
Full of beauty, truth, and grace.

4 Here I would for ever stay,
Weep and gaze my soul away;
Thou art heaven on earth to me,
Lovely, mournful Calvary!

1083   *" Lovest thou me?"*   COWPER.

HARK! my soul! it is the Lord;
'Tis thy Saviour—hear his word;
Jesus speaks, and speaks to thee,
"Say, poor sinner, lovest thou me?

2 "I delivered thee when bound,
And when bleeding, healed thy wound:
Sought thee wandering, set thee right,
Turned thy darkness into light.

3 "Can a woman's tender care
Cease toward the child she bare?
Yes, she may forgetful be,
Yet will I remember thee.

4 "Mine is an unchanging love,
Higher than the heights above;
Deeper than the depths beneath—
Free and faithful—strong as death.

5 "Thou shalt see my glory soon,
When the work of grace is done;
Partner of my throne shalt be!
Say, poor sinner! lovest thou me?"

6 Lord! it is my chief complaint,
That my love is weak and faint;
Yet I love thee, and adore;—
Oh, for grace to love thee more.

1084   *"Thy people shall be my people."*   MONTGOMERY.

PEOPLE of the living God,
I have sought the world around,
Paths of sin and sorrow trod,
Peace and comfort nowhere found.

2 Now to you my spirit turns—
Turns, a fugitive unblest;
Brethren, where your altar burns,
Oh, receive me into rest!

3 Lonely I no longer roam,
Like the cloud, the wind, the wave;
Where you dwell shall be my home,
Where you die shall be my grave;—

4 Mine the God whom you adore,
Your Redeemer shall be mine;
Earth can fill my soul no more,
Every idol I resign.

PLEYEL'S HYMN. 7.

1. Bread of heaven! on thee we feed, For thy flesh is meat in - deed:

Ev - er let our souls be fed With this true and liv - ing bread!

1085   *"This is my Body."*   CONDER.

BREAD of heaven! on thee we feed,
For thy flesh is meat indeed:
Ever let our souls be fed
With this true and living bread!

2 Vine of heaven! thy blood supplies
This blest cup of sacrifice:
Lord! thy wounds our healing give,
To thy cross we look and live.

3 Day by day with strength supplied,
Through the life of him who died:
Lord of life! oh, let us be,
Rooted, grafted, built on thee!

1086   *"Christ, our Passover."*   CAMPBELL

AT the Lamb's high feast we sing,
Praise to our victorious King,
Who hath washed us in the tide,
Flowing from his wounded side.

2 Where the Paschal blood is poured,
Death's dark angel sheathes his sword;
Israel's hosts triumphant go
Through the wave that drowns the foe.

3 Christ, our Paschal Lamb, is slain,
Holy victim, without stain;
Death and hell defeated lie,
Heaven unfolds its gates on high.

4 Hymns of glory and of praise,
Father, unto thee we raise;
Risen Lord, all praise to thee,
With the Spirit ever be.

1087   *"Thine for ever."—John* 17: 9.   M. F. MAUDE.

THINE for ever! God of love,
Hear us from thy throne above!
Thine for ever may we be,
Here, and in eternity!

2 Thine for ever! oh, how blest
They who find in thee their rest!
Saviour, Guardian, heavenly Friend,
Oh, defend us to the end!

3 Thine for ever! Saviour, keep
These thy frail and trembling sheep;
Safe alone beneath thy care,
Let us all thy goodness share.

4 Thine for ever! thou our Guide,—
All our wants by thee supplied,—
All our sins by thee forgiven,—
Lead us, Lord, from earth to heaven!

1088   *"Wounded for our transgressions."*   ANON.

JESUS, Master! hear me now,
While I would renew my vow,
And record thy dying love;
Hear, and help me from above.

2 Feed me, Saviour, with this bread,
Broken in thy body's stead;
Cheer my spirit with this wine,
Streaming like that blood of thine.

3 And as now I eat and drink,
Let me truly, sweetly think,
Thou didst hang upon the tree,
Broken, bleeding, there—for me!

DYKES. 7. 6l.

1. Rock of A - ges, cleft for me! Let me hide my - self in thee;

Let the wa - ter and the blood, From thy wound-ed side that flowed,

Be of sin the dou - ble cure; Cleanse me from its guilt and power.

TOPLADY.

1089   *(Original form.)*

Rock of Ages, cleft for me!
Let me hide myself in thee;
Let the water and the blood,
From thy wounded side that flowed,
Be of sin the double cure;
Cleanse me from its guilt and power.

2 Not the labor of my hands
Can fulfill the law's demands;
Could my zeal no respite know,
Could my tears for ever flow,
All for sin could not atone,
Thou must save, and thou alone.

3 Nothing in my hand I bring,
Simply to thy cross I cling;
Naked, come to thee for dress,
Helpless, look to thee for grace;
Vile, I to the fountain fly,
Wash me, Saviour, or I die!

4 While I draw this fleeting breath,
When my eyelids close in death,
When I soar to worlds unknown,
See thee on thy judgment-throne,
Rock of Ages, cleft for me!
Let me hide myself in thee.

400

C. WESLEY.

1090   *" I am thine ; save me."*

Now, O God, thine own I am!
Now I give thee back thine own:
Freedom, friends, and health, and fame,
Consecrate to thee alone:
Thine I live, thrice happy I!
Happier still if thine I die.

2 Take me, Lord, and all my powers;
Take my mind, and heart, and will;
All my goods, and all my hours,
All I know, and all I feel,
All I think, or speak, or do—
Take my soul and make it new!

R. HILL.

1091   *Christ lifted up.—John* **12 : 32.**

Ye who in these courts are found,
Listening to the joyful sound,—
Lost and helpless, as ye are,
Sons of sorrow, sin, and care,—
Glorify the King of kings,
Take the peace the gospel brings.

2 Turn to Christ your longing eyes,
View his bleeding sacrifice;
See in him your sins forgiven,
Pardon, holiness, and heaven:
Glorify the King of kings,
Take the peace the gospel brings.

ROCK OF AGES. 7. 6l.

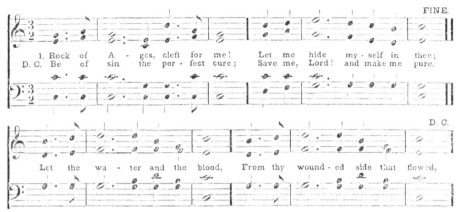

FINE.

1. Rock of A - ges, cleft for me! Let me hide my - self in thee;
D. C. Be of sin the per - fect cure; Save me, Lord! and make me pure.

D. C.

Let the wa - ter and the blood, From thy wound - ed side that flowed,

1092   *The Rock of Ages.*   TOPLADY.

Rock of ages, cleft for me!
Let me hide myself in thee;
Let the water and the blood,
From thy wounded side that flowed,
Be of sin the perfect cure;
Save me, Lord! and make me pure.

2 Should my tears for ever flow,
Should my zeal no languor know,
This for sin could not atone,
Thou must save and thou alone:
In my hand no price I bring;
Simply to thy cross I cling.

3 While I draw this fleeting breath,
When mine eye-lids close in death,
When I rise to worlds unknown,
And behold thee on thy throne,
Rock of ages, cleft for me!
Let me hide myself in thee.

1093   *"Son of God, to thee I cry."*   MANT.

Son of God, to thee I cry:
By the holy mystery
Of thy dwelling here on earth,
By thy pure and holy birth,
Lord, thy presence let me see,
Manifest thyself to me.

2 Lamb of God, to thee I cry:
By thy bitter agony,
By thy pangs to us unknown,
By thy Spirit's parting groan,
Lord, thy presence let me see,
Manifest thyself to me.

3 Prince of Life, to thee I cry:
By thy glorious majesty,
By thy triumph o'er the grave,
Meek to suffer, strong to save,
Lord, thy presence let me see,
Manifest thyself to me.

4 Lord of glory, God most High,
Man exalted to the sky,
With thy love my bosom fill,
Prompt me to perform thy will;
Then thy glory I shall see,
Thou wilt bring me home to thee.

1094   *Matthew* 26: 20.   HASTINGS.

Saviour of our ruined race,
Fountain of redeeming grace,
Let us now thy fullness see,
While we here converse with thee;
Hearken to our ardent prayer,—
Let us all thy blessing share.

2 While we thus, with glad accord
Meet around thy table, Lord,
Bid us feast with joy divine,
On the appointed bread and wine:
Emblems may they truly prove,
Of our Saviour's bleeding love.

3 Weak, unworthy, sinful, vile,
Yet we seek thy heavenly smile:
Canst thou all our sins forgive?
Dost thou bid us look and live?
Lord, we wonder and adore!
Oh, for grace to love thee more!

DORRNANCE. 8, 7.

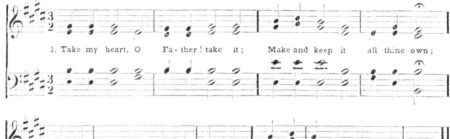

1. Take my heart, O Fa - ther! take it; Make and keep it all thine own;

Let thy Spir - it melt and break it— This proud heart of sin and stone.

1095 *"Create in me a clean heart."* ANON.

Take my heart, O Father! take it;
Make and keep it all thine own;
Let thy Spirit melt and break it—
This proud heart of sin and stone.

2 Father, make me pure and lowly,
Fond of peace and far from strife;
Turning from the paths unholy
Of this vain and sinful life.

3 Ever let thy grace surround me;
Strengthen me with power divine,
Till thy cords of love have bound me:
Make me to be wholly thine.

4 May the blood of Jesus heal me,
And my sins be all forgiven;
Holy Spirit, take and seal me,
Guide me in the path to heaven.

1096 *"His banner over me was love."* R. PARK.

Jesus spreads his banner o'er us,
Cheers our famished souls with food;
He the banquet spreads before us,
Of his mystic flesh and blood.

2 Precious banquet; bread of heaven;
Wine of gladness, flowing free;
May we taste it kindly given,
In remembrance, Lord, of thee!

3 In thy trial, and rejection;
In thy sufferings on the tree;
In thy glorious resurrection;
May we, Lord, remember thee.

1097 *"In remembrance."—Luke* 22:19. E. DENNY.

While in sweet communion feeding
On this earthly bread and wine,
Saviour, may we see thee bleeding
On the cross, to make us thine.

2 Though unseen, now be thou near us,
With the still small voice of love;
Whispering words of peace to cheer us—
Every doubt and fear remove.

3 Bring before us all the story,
Of thy life, and death of woe;
And, with hopes of endless glory,
Wean our hearts from all below.

1098 *"Follow me."—Matt.* 4:19. ANON.

Jesus calls us, o'er the tumult
Of our life's wild, restless sea;
Day by day his sweet voice soundeth,
Saying, Christian, follow me!

2 Jesus calls us—from the worship
Of the vain world's golden store;
From each idol that would keep us,—
Saying, Christian, love me more!

3 In our joys and in our sorrows,
Days of toil and hours of ease,
Still he calls, in cares and pleasures,
Christian, love me more than these!

4 Jesus calls us! by thy mercies,
Saviour, may we hear thy call;
Give our hearts to thy obedience,
Serve and love thee best of all!

NAOMI. (HASLAM.) 8, 7.

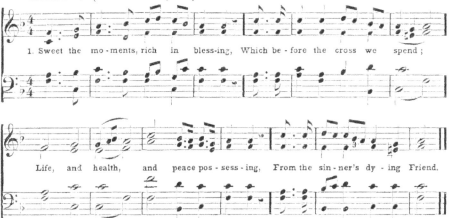

1. Sweet the mo-ments, rich in bless-ing, Which be-fore the cross we spend;

Life, and health, and peace pos-sess-ing, From the sin-ner's dy-ing Friend.

1099   *Standing by the cross.*   SHIRLEY.

SWEET the moments, rich in blessing,
  Which before the cross we spend;
Life, and health, and peace possessing,
  From the sinner's dying Friend.

2 Truly bless'd is this station,
  Low before his cross to lie,
While we see divine compassion,
  Beaming in his gracious eye.

3 Love and grief our hearts dividing,
  With our tears his feet we bathe;
Constant still, in faith abiding,
  Life deriving from his death.

4 For thy sorrows we adore thee,
  For the pains that wrought our peace,
Gracious Saviour! we implore thee
  In our souls thy love increase.

5 Here we feel our sins forgiven,
  While upon the Lamb we gaze;
And our thoughts are all of heaven,
  And our lips o'erflow with praise.

6 Still in ceaseless contemplation,
  Fix our hearts and eyes on thee,
Till we taste thy full salvation,
  And, unvailed, thy glories see.

1100   *"Fitly framed together, groweth."*   ANON.

FROM the table now retiring,
  Which for us the Lord hath spread,
May our souls, refreshment finding,
  Grow in all things like our Head!

2 His example while beholding,
  May our lives his image bear;
Him our Lord and Master calling,
  His commands may we revere.

3 Love to God and man displaying,
  Walking steadfast in his way,
Joy attend us in believing,
  Peace from God, through endless day.

4 Praise and honor to the Father,
  Praise and honor to the Son,
Praise and honor to the Spirit,
  Ever Three and ever One.

1101   *"Wash me."—Ps.* **51: 2.**   ANON.

JESUS, who on Calvary's mountain
  Poured thy precious blood for me,
Wash me in its flowing fountain,
  That my soul may spotless be.

2 I have sinned, but oh, restore me!
  For unless thou smile on me,
Dark is all the world before me,
  Darker yet eternity.

3 In thy word I hear thee saying,
  Come and I will give you rest;
Now the gracious call obeying,
  See, I hasten to thy breast.

4 Grant, oh, grant thy Spirit's teaching,
  That I may not go astray,
Till the gate of heaven reaching,
  Earth and sin are passed away.

CARTHAGE. 8, 7.

1. Christ, a - bove all glo - ry seat - ed! King e - ter - nal, strong to save!
To thee, Death, by death de - feat - ed,.... Tri - umph high and glo - ry gave.

1102   *"He ever liveth."—Heb. 7: 25.*   ANON.

CHRIST, above all glory seated!
    King eternal, strong to save!
To thee, Death, by death defeated,
    Triumph high and glory gave.

2 Thou art gone, where now is given,
    What no mortal might could gain;
On the eternal throne of heaven,
    In thy Father's power to reign.

3 There thy kingdoms all adore thee,
    Heaven above and earth below,
While the depths of hell before thee,
    Trembling and defeated bow.

4 We, O Lord! with hearts adoring,
    Follow thee above the sky:
Hear our prayers thy grace imploring,
    Lift our souls to thee on high.

5 So when thou again in glory
    On the clouds of heaven shalt shine,
We thy flock shall stand before thee,
    Owned for evermore as thine.

1103   *Glorying in the Cross.*   MORAVIAN.

CROSS, reproach, and tribulation!
    Ye to me are welcome guests,
When I have this consolation,
    That my soul in Jesus rests.

2 The reproach of Christ is glorious!
    Those who here his burden bear,
In the end shall prove victorious,
    And eternal gladness share.

3 Bonds and stripes, and evil story,
    Are our honorable crowns;
Pain is peace, and shame is glory,
    Gloomy dungeons are as thrones.

4 Bear, then, the reproach of Jesus,
    Ye who live a life of faith!
Lift triumphant songs and praises
    Ev'n in martyrdom and death.

1104   *"Keep me ever!"*   ANON.

HOLY Father, thou hast taught me
    I should live to thee alone;
Year by year thy hand hath brought me
    On through dangers oft unknown.

2 When I wandered, thou hast found me;
    When I doubted, sent me light,
Still thine arm has been around me,
    All my paths were in thy sight.

3 Therefore, Lord, I come, believing
    Thou canst give the power I need;
Through the prayer of faith receiving
    Strength—the Spirit's strength, indeed.

4 I would trust in thy protection,
    Wholly rest upon thine arm;
Follow wholly thy direction,
    Thou, mine only guard from harm!

5 Keep me from mine own undoing,
    Help me turn to thee when tried,
Still my footsteps, Father, viewing,
    Keep me ever at thy side!

RATHBUN. 8, 7.

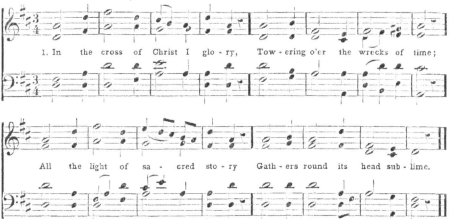

1. In the cross of Christ I glo-ry, Tow-ering o'er the wrecks of time;

All the light of sa-cred sto-ry Gath-ers round its head sub-lime.

1105　　*Glorying in the Cross.*　　BOWRING.

In the cross of Christ I glory,
　Towering o'er the wrecks of time;
All the light of sacred story
　Gathers round its head sublime.

2 When the woes of life o'ertake me,
　Hopes deceive, and fears annoy,
Never shall the cross forsake me:
　Lo! it glows with peace and joy.

3 When the sun of bliss is beaming
　Light and love upon my way,
From the cross the radiance, streaming,
　Adds more lustre to the day.

4 Bane and blessing, pain and pleasure,
　By the cross are sanctified;
Peace is there, that knows no measure,
　Joys that through all time abide.

5 In the cross of Christ I glory,
　Towering o'er the wrecks of time;
All the light of sacred story
　Gathers round its head sublime.

1106　　*Jesus on the Cross.*　　R. LEE.

When I view my Saviour bleeding,
　For my sins, upon the tree;
Oh, how wondrous!—how exceeding
　Great his love appears to me!

2 Floods of deep distress and anguish,
　To impede his labors, came;
Yet they all could not extinguish
　Love's eternal, burning flame.

3 Now redemption is completed,
　Full salvation is procured;
Death and Satan are defeated,
　By the sufferings he endured.

4 Now the gracious Mediator
　Risen to the courts of bliss,
Claims for me, a sinful creature,
　Pardon, righteousness, and peace!

5 Sure such infinite affection
　Lays the highest claims to mine;
All my powers, without exception,
　Should in fervent praises join.

6 Jesus, fit me for thy service;
　Form me for thyself alone;
I am thy most costly purchase,—
　Take possession of thine own.

1107　　*Praise for a Saviour.*　　ANON.

Let our songs of praise ascending,
　Rise to thee, O God most high;
While before thee, humbly bending,
　Glory to thy name we cry.

2 Age to age thy glory beareth
　On the stream of time abroad;
Race to race thy name declareth,
　Son of Mary! Son of God!

3 Heaven exults and earth rejoices
　In the work that thou hast wrought;
Lord, attune our trembling voices,
　Let us praise thee as we ought.

PATNAH. 7, 6. D.

1. { O Bread, to pilgrims giv - en,   O Food, that angels eat, }
{ O Man-na, sent from heaven, For heaven-born natures meet! } Give us, for thee long pin - ing,

To eat till rich-ly filled ; Till, earth's de-lights re - sign - ing, Our ev-ery wish is stilled.

1108   *Ancient Communion Song.*   RAY PALMER. *Tr.*

O BREAD, to pilgrims given,
  O Food that angels eat,
O manna, sent from heaven,
  For heaven-born natures meet!
Give us, for thee long pining,
  To eat till richly filled;
Till, earth's delights resigning,
  Our every wish is stilled.

2 O Water, life-bestowing,
  From out the Saviour's heart!
A fountain purely flowing,
  A fount of love thou art;
Oh, let us, freely tasting,
  Our burning thirst assuage!
Thy sweetness, never wasting,
  Avails from age to age.

3 Jesus! this feast receiving,
  We thee unseen adore;
Thy faithful word believing,
  We take, and doubt no more;
Give us, thou true and loving!
  On earth to live in thee;
Then, death the vail removing,
  Thy glorious face to see.

1109   *" Jesus and his blood."*   MASSIE. *Tr.*

I BUILD on this foundation,—
  That Jesus and his blood
Alone are my salvation,
  The true eternal good.

To mine his Spirit speaketh
  Sweet words of soothing power,
How God to him that seeketh
  For rest, hath rest in store.

2 My merry heart is springing,
  And knows not how to pine:
'T is full of joy and singing,
  And radiancy divine.
The sun whose smiles so cheer me
  Is Jesus Christ alone:
To have him always near me
  Is heaven itself begun.

1110   *Hope at the Cross.*   ANON.

WHEN human hopes all wither,
  And friends no aid supply,
Then whither, Lord, ah! whither
  Can turn my straining eye?
'Mid storms of grief still rougher,
  'Midst darker, deadlier shade,
That cross where thou didst suffer,
  On Calvary was displayed.

2 On that my gaze I fasten,
  My refuge that I make;
Though sorely thou mayst chasten,
  Thou never canst forsake:
Thou, on that cross did languish,
  Ere glory crowned thy head!
And I, through death and anguish,
  Must be to glory led.

MISSIONARY HYMN. 7, 6. D.

1 { From Greenland's icy mountains, From India's coral strand, }
  { Where Afric's sunny fountains [*Omit* .... } Roll down their golden sand; From [many an

ancient riv - er, From many a palmy plain, They call us to de-liv-er Their land from error's chain.

IIII   *"Come over, and help us."*   HEBER.

FROM Greenland's icy mountains,
  From India's coral strand,
Where Afric's sunny fountains
  Roll down their golden sand,—
From many an ancient river,
  From many a palmy plain,
They call us to deliver
  Their land from error's chain.

2 What though the spicy breezes
  Blow soft o'er Ceylon's isle;
Though every prospect pleases,
  And only man is vile;
In vain with lavish kindness
  The gifts of God are strown;
The heathen, in his blindness,
  Bows down to wood and stone!

3 Shall we, whose souls are lighted
  With wisdom from on high,—
Shall we, to men benighted,
  The lamp of life deny?
Salvation, oh, salvation!
  The joyful sound proclaim,
Till earth's remotest nation
  Has learned Messiah's name.

4 Waft, waft, ye winds his story,
  And you, ye waters, roll,
Till, like a sea of glory,
  It spreads from pole to pole;

Till o'er our ransomed nature
  The Lamb for sinners slain,
Redeemer, King, Creator,
  In bliss returns to reign!

1112   *The Day of Jubilee.*   GOUGH.

How beauteous, on the mountains,
  The feet of him that brings,
Like streams from living fountains,
  Good tidings of good things;
That publisheth salvation,
  And jubilee release,
To every tribe and nation,
  God's reign of joy and peace!

2 Lift up thy voice, O watchman!
  And shout, from Zion's towers,
Thy hallelujah chorus,—
  "The victory is ours!"
The Lord shall build up Zion
  In glory and renown,
And Jesus, Judah's lion,
  Shall wear his rightful crown.

3 Break forth in hymns of gladness;
  O waste Jerusalem!
Let songs, instead of sadness,
  Thy jubilee proclaim;
The Lord, in strength victorious,
  Upon thy foes hath trod;
Behold, O earth! the glorious
  Salvation of our God!

GROSTETTE. L. M.

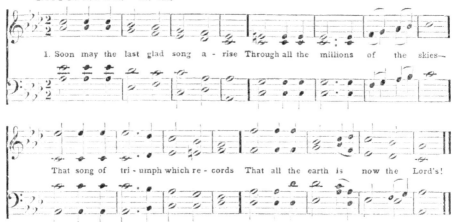

1. Soon may the last glad song a - rise Through all the millions of the skies—

That song of tri - umph which re - cords That all the earth is now the Lord's!

1113   *The last Song.—Rev.* **11: 15.**   ANON.

Soon may the last glad song arise
Through all the millions of the skies—
That song of triumph which records
That all the earth is now the Lord's!

2 Let thrones and powers and kingdoms be
Obedient, mighty God, to thee!
And, over land and stream and main,
Wave thou the sceptre of thy reign!

3 Oh, let that glorious anthem swell,
Let host to host the triumph tell,
That not one rebel heart remains,
But over all the Saviour reigns!

1114   *"Shall comfort Zion."—Isa.* **51: 3.**   MRS. VOKE.

Behold the expected time draw near,
The shades disperse, the dawn appear!
Behold the wilderness assume
The beauteous tints of Eden's bloom!

2 Events with prophecies conspire,
To raise our faith, our zeal to fire:
The ripening fields, already white,
Present a harvest to the sight.

3 The untaught heathen waits to know
The joy the gospel will bestow;
The exiled captive, to receive
The freedom Jesus has to give.

4 Come, let us, with a grateful heart,
In this blest labor share a part;
Our prayers and offerings gladly bring,
To aid the triumphs of our King.

1115   *Christ's coming to reign.*   BATHURST.

Jesus! thy church, with longing eyes,
For thine expected coming waits;
When will the promised light arise,
And glory beam from Zion's gates?

2 Ev'n now, when tempests round us fall,
And wintry clouds o'ercast the sky,
Thy words with pleasure we recall,
And deem that our redemption's nigh.

3 Oh, come and reign o'er every land;
Let Satan from his throne be hurled,
All nations bow to thy command,
And grace revive a dying world.

4 Teach us, in watchfulness and prayer,
To wait for the appointed hour;
And fit us, by thy grace, to share
The triumphs of thy conquering power.

1116   *"To thy tents, O Israel!"*   KELLY.

O Israel! to thy tents repair:
Why thus secure on hostile ground?
Thy King commands thee to beware,
For many foes thy camp surround.

2 A nobler lot is cast for thee,
A kingdom waits thee in the skies;
With such a hope, shall Israel flee,
Or yield, through weariness, the prize?

3 No; let a careless world repose
And slumber on through life's short day,
While Israel to the conflict goes,
And bears the glorious prize away.

LONG. L. M.

1. Arm of the Lord! a-wake, a-wake; Put on thy strength, the nations shake; And let the world, a-

dor - ing see Triumphs of mercy, wrought by thee, Triumphs of mercy, wrought by thee.

1117   *Awake, arm of the Lord!*   SHRUBSOLE.

ARM of the Lord! awake, awake;
Put on thy strength, the nations shake;
And let the world, adoring, see
Triumphs of mercy, wrought by thee.

2 Say to the heathen, from thy throne,
"I am Jehovah—God alone!"
Thy voice their idols shall confound,
And cast their altars to the ground.

3 No more let human blood be spilt,
Vain sacrifice for human guilt;
But to each conscience be applied
The blood that flowed from Jesus' side.

4 Almighty God! thy grace proclaim,
In every clime, of every name,
Till adverse powers before thee fall,
And crown the Saviour—Lord of all.

1118   *Zion's Glory.*   SHRUBSOLE.

ZION! awake, thy strength renew,
Put on thy robes of beauteous hue;
And let the admiring world behold
The King's fair daughter clothed in gold.

2 Church of our God! arise and shine,
Bright with the beams of truth divine;
Then shall thy radiance stream afar,
Wide as the heathen nations are.

3 Gentiles and kings thy light shall view,
And shall admire and love thee too;—
They come, like clouds across the sky
As doves that to their windows fly.

1119   *Conversion of the World.*   ANON.

SOVEREIGN of worlds! display thy power;
Be this thy Zion's favored hour;
Bid the bright morning Star arise,
And point the nations to the skies.

2 Set up thy throne where Satan reigns,—
On Afric's shore, on India's plains,
On wilds and continents unknown,—
And make the nations all thine own.

3 Speak! and the world shall hear thy voice;
Speak! and the desert shall rejoice;
Scatter the gloom of heathen night,
And bid all nations hail the light.

1120   *Missionaries.*   NOEL.

MARKED as the purpose of the skies,
This promise meets our anxious eyes,
That heathen lands the Lord shall know,
And warm with faith each bosom glow.

2 Ev'n now the hallowed scenes appear;
Ev'n now unfolds the promised year;
Lo! distant shores thy heralds trace,
And bear the tidings of thy grace.

3 'Mid burning climes and frozen plains,
Where pagan darkness brooding reigns,
Lord! mark their steps, their fears subdue
And nerve their arm, and clear their view.

4 When, worn by toil, their spirits fail,
Bid them the glorious future hail;
Bid them the crown of life survey,
And onward urge their conquering way.

MISSIONARY CHANT. L. M.

1. Ye Christian her-alds! go, pro-claim Sal - va-tion through Im - man-uel's name;

To dis-tant climes the ti - dings bear, And plant the Rose of Sha - ron there.

1121 *"Go ye into all the world."* ANON.

YE Christian heralds! go, proclaim
Salvation through Immanuel's name;
To distant climes the tidings bear,
And plant the Rose of Sharon there.

2 He'll shield you with a wall of fire,
With flaming zeal your breast inspire,
Bid raging winds their fury cease,
And hush the tempest into peace.

3 And when our labors all are o'er,
Then we shall meet to part no more,—
Meet with the blood-bought throng, to fall,
And crown our Jesus—Lord of all!

1122 *Missionary Convocation.* COLLYER.

ASSEMBLED at thy great command,
Before thy face, dread King, we stand;
The voice that marshaled every star,
Has called thy people from afar.

2 We meet, through distant lands to spread
The truth for which the martyrs bled;
Along the line, to either pole,
The thunder of thy praise to roll.

3 Our prayers assist, accept our praise,
Our hopes revive, our courage raise;
Our counsels aid, to each impart
The single eye, the faithful heart.

4 Forth with thy chosen heralds come,
Recall the wandering spirits home;
From Zion's mount send forth the sound,
To spread the spacious earth around.

410

1123 *"Sun of righteousness."—Mal.* 4:2. ANON.

O SUN of righteousness, arise,
With gentle beams on Zion shine;
Dispel the darkness from our eyes,
And souls awake to life divine.

2 On all around, let grace descend,
Like heavenly dew, or copious showers;
That we may call our God our friend;
That we may hail salvation ours.

1124 *Home Missions.* BRYANT.

LOOK from thy sphere of endless day,
O God of mercy and of might!
In pity look on those who stray,
Benighted, in this land of light.

2 In peopled vale, in lonely glen,
In crowded mart, by stream or sea,
How many of the sons of men
Hear not the message sent from thee!

3 Send forth thy heralds, Lord, to call
The thoughtless young, the hardened old,
A scattered, homeless flock, till all
Be gathered to thy peaceful fold.

4 Send them thy mighty word to speak,
Till faith shall dawn, and doubt depart,
To awe the bold, to stay the weak,
And bind and heal the broken heart.

5 Then all these wastes, a dreary scene,
That make us sadden as we gaze,
Shall grow with living waters green,
And lift to heaven the voice of praise.

MENDON. L. M.

1. Though now the na - tions sit be - neath The darkness of o'er - spread - ing death,

God will a - rise with light di - vine, On Zi - on's ho - ly tow'rs to shine.

1125 *"O Light of Zion!"* BACON.

Though now the nations sit beneath
The darkness of o'erspreading death,
God will arise with light divine,
On Zion's holy towers to shine.

2 That light shall shine on distant lands,
And wandering tribes, in joyful bands,
Shall come thy glory, Lord, to see,
And in thy courts to worship thee.

3 O light of Zion, now arise!
Let the glad morning bless our eyes!
Ye nations, catch the kindling ray,
And hail the splendor of the day.

1126 *The kingdom coming.* MONTGOMERY.

From day to day, before our eyes,
Grows and extends the work begun;
When shall the new creation rise
O'er every land beneath the sun?

2 When, in the sabbath of his love,
Shall God from all his labors rest;
And bending from his throne above,
Again pronounce his creatures blest?

3 As sang the morning stars of old,
Shouted the sons of God for joy;
His widening reign while we behold,
Let praise and prayer our tongues employ;

4 Till the redeemed in every clime,
Yea, all that breathe, and move, and live,
To Christ, through every age of time,
The kingdom, power, and glory give.

1127 *Prayer for a Revival.* KINGSBURY.

Great Lord of all thy churches! hear
Thy ministers' and people's prayer;
Perfumed by thee, oh, may it rise,
Like fragrant incense to the skies.

2 May every pastor, from above
Be new inspired with zeal and love,
To watch thy flock, thy flock to feed,
And sow with care the precious seed.

3 Revive thy churches with thy grace;
Heal all our breaches, grant us peace;
Rouse us from sloth, our hearts inflame
With ardent zeal for Jesus' name.

4 Thus we our suppliant voices raise,
And, weeping, sow the seed of praise;
In humble hope, that thou wilt hear
Thy ministers' and people's prayer.

1128 *"Ascend thy throne."* BEDDOME.

Ascend thy throne, almighty King,
And spread thy glories all abroad;
Let thine own arm salvation bring,
And be thou known the gracious God.

2 Let millions bow before thy seat,
Let humble mourners seek thy face,
Bring daring rebels to thy feet,
Subdued by thy victorious grace.

3 Oh, let the kingdoms of the world
Become the kingdoms of the Lord!
Let saints and angels praise thy name;
Be thou thro' heaven and earth adored.

411

ZION. 8, 7, 4.

{ On the mountain's top ap-pear-ing, / Welcome news to Zi-on bear-ing— Lo! the sa-cred her-ald stands. / Zi-on, long in hos-tile lands: } Mourning

cap-tive! God himself shall loose thy bands. Mourning captive! God himself shall loose thy bands.

1129   *The gospel herald.—Isa. 52 : 7.*   KELLY.

On the mountain's top appearing,
Lo! the sacred herald stands,
Welcome news to Zion bearing—
Zion long in hostile lands:
    Mourning captive!
God himself shall loose thy bands.

2 Has thy night been long and mournful?
Have thy friends unfaithful proved?
Have thy foes been proud and scornful,
By thy sighs and tears unmoved?
    Cease thy mourning;
Zion still is well beloved.

3 God, thy God, will now restore thee;
He himself appears thy Friend;
All thy foes shall flee before thee;
Here their boasts and triumphs end:
    Great deliverance
Zion's King will surely send.

4 Peace and joy shall now attend thee;
All thy warfare now is past;
God thy Saviour will defend thee;
Victory is thine at last:
    All thy conflicts
End in everlasting rest.

1130   *Psalm 125 : 2.*   KELLY.

Zion stands with hills surrounded—
Zion, kept by power divine;
All her foes shall be confounded,
Though the world in arms combine;
    Happy Zion,
What a favored lot is thine!

2 Every human tie may perish;
Friend to friend unfaithful prove;
Mothers cease their own to cherish;
Heaven and earth at last remove:
    But no changes
Can attend Jehovah's love.

3 In the furnace God may prove thee,
Thence to bring thee forth more bright,
But can never cease to love thee;
Thou art precious in his sight;
    God is with thee—
God, thine everlasting light.

1131   *Sun of Righteousness.*   WILLIAMS.

O'er the gloomy hills of darkness,
Cheered by no celestial ray,
Sun of righteousness! arising,
Bring the bright, the glorious day;
    Send the gospel
To the earth's remotest bound.

2 Kingdoms wide that sit in darkness,—
Grant them, Lord! the glorious light:
And, from eastern coast to western,
May the morning chase the night;
    And redemption,
Freely purchased, win the day.

3 Fly abroad, thou mighty gospel!
Win and conquer, never cease;
May thy lasting, wide dominion
Multiply and still increase;
    Sway thy sceptre,
Saviour! all the world around.

SICILY. 8, 7.

1. Sav - iour, vis - it thy plan - ta - tion! Grant us, Lord, a gra - cious rain:

All will come to des - o - la - tion, Un - less thou re - turn a - gain.

1132 *"Let my Beloved come into his garden."* NEWTON.

SAVIOUR, visit thy plantation!
Grant us, Lord, a gracious rain:
All will come to desolation,
Unless thou return again.

2 Keep no longer at a distance,
Shine upon us from on high,
Lest, for want of thine assistance,
Every plant should droop and die.

3 Once, O Lord, thy garden flourished;
Every part looked gay and green;
Then thy word our spirits nourished:
Happy seasons we have seen.

4 But a drought has since succeeded,
And a sad decline we see:
Lord, thy help is greatly needed:
Help can only come from thee.

5 Let our mutual love, be fervent:
Make us prevalent in prayer;
Let each one esteemed thy servant
Shun the world's bewitching snare.

6 Break the tempter's fatal power,
Turn the stony heart to flesh,
And begin from this good hour
To revive thy work afresh.

1133 *Home Missionary Hymn.* ANON.

HARK! the sound of angel-voices,
Over Bethlehem's star-lit plain;
Hark! the heavenly host rejoices,
Jesus comes on earth to reign.

2 See celestial radiance beaming,
Lighting up the midnight sky;
'Tis the promised day-star gleaming,
'Tis the day-spring from on high.

3 Westward, all along the ages,
Trace its pathway clear and bright;
Star of hope to Eastern sages,
Radiant now with gospel light.

4 Angels from the realms of glory,
Peace on earth delight to sing;
Christian, tell the wondrous story,
Go proclaim the Saviour King!

1134 *Home Missions.* ANON.

WHERE the woodman's axe is ringing,
Where the hunter roams alone,
Where the prairie-flowers are springing,
Make the great Redeemer known.

2 While, from California's mountains,
Pure and sweet the anthem swells;
Oregon's dark wilds and fountains
Hail the sound of Sabbath-bells.

3 Like an arméd host with banners,
Terrible in war array,
Zion comes with glad hosannas,
To prepare her Monarch's way.

4 Unto him all power is given,
All the world his sway shall own,
And on earth, as now in heaven,
Shall his will be done alone.

PERRY. 7. D.

1. Hark! the song of Ju-bi-lee, Loud as might-y thun-ders roar, Or the full-ness

of the sea, When it breaks up-on the shore! Hal-le-lu-jah! for the Lord

God om-nip-o-tent shall reign! Hal-le-lu-jah! let the word Ech-o round the earth and main.

1135 *"The Lord God reigneth."—Rev.* 11: 15. MONTGOMERY.

Hark! the song of Jubilee,
 Loud as mighty thunders roar,
Or the fullness of the sea,
 When it breaks upon the shore!
Hallelujah! for the Lord
 God omnipotent shall reign!
Hallelujah! let the word
 Echo round the earth and main.

2 Hallelujah! hark, the sound,
 From the depths unto the skies,
Wakes above, beneath, around,
 All creation's harmonies!
See Jehovah's banner furled,
 Sheathed his sword, he speaks—'tis done!
And the kingdoms of this world
 Are the kingdoms of his Son!

3 He shall reign from pole to pole,
 With illimitable sway;
He shall reign, when like a scroll
 Yonder heavens are passed away.
Then the end: beneath his rod
 Man's last enemy shall fall:
Hallelujah! Christ in God,
 God in Christ, is all in all!

1136 *2 Thessalonians* 2: 8. ANON.

Come, Desire of nations, come!
 Hasten, Lord, the general doom!
Hear the Spirit and the Bride;
 Come, and take us to thy side:
Thou, who hast our place prepared,
 Make us meet for our reward;
Then, with all thy saints descend:
 Then, our earthly trials end.

2 Mindful of thy chosen race,
 Shorten these vindictive days;
Hear us now, and save thine own,
 Who for full redemption groan!
Now destroy the Man of Sin,
 Now thine ancient flock bring in!
Filled with righteousness divine,
 Claim a ransomed world for thine.

3 Plant thy heavenly kingdom here;
 Glorious in thy saints appear:
Speak the sacred number sealed,
 Speak the mystery revealed;
Take to thee thy royal power;
 Reign! when sin shall be no more;
Reign! when death no more shall be;
 Reign to all eternity!

WATCHMAN, TELL US. 7. D.

1. Watchman! tell us of the night, What its signs of prom-ise are ;— Traveler! o'er yon mountain's height, See that glo - ry - beam-ing star !— Watchman! does its beauteous ray Aught of joy or hope foretell?—Traveler ! yes ; it brings the day, Promised day of Is - ra - el :—

1137   *"Tell us of the night."*   BOWRING.

WATCHMAN! tell us of the night,
  What its signs of promise are;—
Traveler! o'er yon mountain's height,
  See that glory-beaming star!—
Watchman! does its beauteous ray
  Aught of joy or hope foretell?—
Traveler! yes; it brings the day,
  Promised day of Israel:—

2 Watchman! tell us of the night;
  Higher yet that star ascends;—
Traveler! blessedness and light,
  Peace and truth, its course portends;—
Watchman! will its beams alone
  Gild the spot that gave them birth?—
Traveler! ages are its own;
  See, it bursts o'er all the earth!—

3 Watchman! tell us of the night,
  For the morning seems to dawn;—
Traveler! darkness takes its flight,
  Doubt and terror are withdrawn;—
Watchman! let thy wanderings cease;
  Hie thee to thy quiet home!—
Traveler! lo! the Prince of peace,
  Lo! the Son of God, is come!

1138   *Home Missions.*   HOW.

SOLDIERS of the cross! arise;
  Gird you with your armor bright;
Mighty are your enemies,
  Hard the battle ye must fight;
O'er a faithless fallen world,
  Raise your banner in the sky,
Let it float there, wide unfurled,
  Bear it onward, lift it high.

2 'Mid the homes of want and woe,
  Strangers to the living word,
Let the Saviour's herald go,
  Let the voice of hope be heard;
To the weary and the worn,
  Tell of realms where sorrows cease;
To the outcast and forlorn,
  Speak of mercy, grace, and peace.

3 Guard the helpless, seek the strayed,
  Comfort troubles, banish grief;
With the Spirit's sword arrayed,
  Scatter sin and unbelief:
Be the banner still unfurled,
  Bear it bravely still abroad,
Till the kingdoms of the world
  Are the kingdoms of the Lord.

WEBB. 7, 6. D.

1. The morning light is breaking; The darkness disap-pears; The sons of earth are wak-ing
D. S. Of na-tions in com-mo-tion,

FINE.

To pen-i-ten-tial tears; Each breeze that sweeps the o-cean Brings tidings from a-far,
Prepared for Zion's war.

1139   *The morning light.—Isa.* **65:8.**   S. F. SMITH.

The morning light is breaking;
The darkness disappears;
The sons of earth are waking
To penitential tears;
Each breeze that sweeps the ocean
Brings tidings from afar,
Of nations in commotion,
Prepared for Zion's war.

2 See heathen nations bending
Before the God we love,
And thousand hearts ascending
In gratitude above;
While sinners, now confessing,
The gospel call obey,
And seek the Saviour's blessing,—
A nation in a day.

3 Blest river of salvation!
Pursue thine onward way;
Flow thou to every nation,
Nor in thy richness stay:
Stay not till all the lowly
Triumphant reach their home:
Stay not till all the holy
Proclaim—"The Lord is come!"

1140   *Departure of Missionaries.*   EDMESTON.

Roll on, thou mighty ocean;
And, as thy billows flow,
Bear messengers of mercy
To every land below.

416

Arise, ye gales, and waft them
Safe to the destined shore;
That man may sit in darkness,
And death's black shade no more.

2 O thou eternal Ruler,
Who holdest in thine arm
The tempests of the ocean,
Protect them from all harm!
Thy presence, Lord, be with them,
Wherever they may be:
Though far from us, who love them,
Still let them be with thee.

1141   *The Gospel Banner.—Ps.* **60:4.**   HASTINGS.

Now be the gospel banner,
In every land, unfurled;
And be the shout,—"Hosanna!"
Re-echoed through the world;
Till every isle and nation,
Till every tribe and tongue,
Receive the great salvation,
And join the happy throng.

2 Yes,—thou shalt reign for ever,
O Jesus, King of kings!
Thy light, thy love, thy favor,
Each ransomed captive sings:
The isles for thee are waiting,
The deserts learn thy praise,
The hills and valleys greeting,
The song responsive raise.

MUNICH. 7, 6. D.

1 { Our country's voice is pleading, Ye men of God, a - rise! }
  { His pro-vi-dence is lead-ing, The land be - fore you lies; } Day-gleams are o'er it brightening,

And promise clothes the soil; Wide fields for harvest whitening, In - vite the reaper's toil.

1142 *Home Missions.* MRS. ANDERSON.

OUR country's voice is pleading,
    Ye men of God, arise!
His providence is leading,
    The land before you lies;
Day-gleams are o'er it brightening,
    And promise clothes the soil;
Wide fields for harvest whitening,
    Invite the reaper's toil.

2 Go where the waves are breaking
    On California's shore,
Christ's precious gospel taking,
    More rich than golden ore;
On Alleghany's mountains,
    Through all the western vale,
Beside Missouri's fountains,
    Rehearse the wondrous tale.

3 The love of Christ unfolding,
    Speed on from east to west,
Till all, his cross beholding,
    In him are fully blest.
Great Author of salvation,
    Haste, haste the glorious day,
When we, a ransomed nation,
    Thy sceptre shall obey.

1143 *Idols rejected.—Isa.* 2: 20. BORTHWICK.

AND is the time approaching,
    By prophets long foretold,
When all shall dwell together,
    One shepherd and one fold?
Shall every idol perish,
    To moles and bats be thrown,
And every prayer be offered
    To God in Christ alone?

2 Shall Jew and Gentile, meeting
    From many a distant shore,
Around one altar kneeling,
    One common Lord adore?
Shall all that now divides us
    Remove and pass away,
Like shadows of the morning
    Before the blaze of day?

3 Shall all that now unites us
    More sweet and lasting prove,
A closer bond of union,
    In a blest land of love?
Shall war be learned no longer,
    Shall strife and tumult cease,
All earth his blessèd kingdom,
    The Lord and Prince of Peace?

4 O long-expected dawning,
    Come with thy cheering ray!
When shall the morning brighten,
    The shadows flee away?
O sweet anticipation!
    It cheers the watchers on,
To pray, and hope, and labor,
    Till the dark night be gone.

MISSION SONG. 8, 7. D.

1. Hark ; the voice of Jesus calling,—Who will go and work to-day ? Fields are white, the harvest waiting,

D. S.—Who will answer, gladly saying,

FINE. D. S.

Who will bear the sheaves a-way ? Loud and long the Master calleth, Rich reward he of-fers free ;
"Here am I, O Lord, send me."

1144   *"The Laborers are few."*   CROSBY.

Hark! the voice of Jesus calling,—
  Who will go and work to-day ?
Fields are white, the harvest waiting,
  Who will bear the sheaves away ?
Loud and long the Master calleth,
  Rich reward he offers free ;
Who will answer, gladly saying,
  "Here am I, O Lord, send me."

2 If you cannot cross the ocean
  And the heathen lands explore,
You can find the heathen nearer,
  You can help them at your door ;
If you cannot speak like angels,
  If you cannot preach like Paul,
You can tell the love of Jesus,
  You can say he died for all.

3 While the souls of men are dying,
  And the Master calls for you,
Let none hear you idly saying,
  "There is nothing I can do!"
Gladly take the task he gives you,
  Let his work your pleasure be ;
Answer quickly when he calleth,
  "Here am I, O Lord, send me."

1145   *"What thy hand findeth to do."*   MRS. GATES.

If you cannot on the ocean
  Sail among the swiftest fleet,

418

Rocking on the highest billows,
  Laughing at the storms you meet,
You can stand among the sailors,
  Anchored yet within the bay,
You can lend a hand to help them,
  As they launch their boat away.

2 If you are too weak to journey
  Up the mountain, steep and high,
You can stand within the valley,
  While the multitude go by ;
You can chant in happy measure,
  As they slowly pass along ;
Though they may forget the singer,
  They will not forget the song.

3 If you have not gold and silver
  Ever ready to command ;
If you cannot toward the needy
  Reach an ever open hand,
You can visit the afflicted,
  O'er the erring you can weep ;
You can be a true disciple
  Sitting at the Saviour's feet.

4 If you cannot in the harvest
  Garner up the richest sheaf,
Many a grain both ripe and golden
  Will the careless reapers leave ;
Go and glean among the briers,
  Growing rank against the wall,
For it may be that the shadow
  Hides the heaviest wheat of all.

BEAUTEOUS DAY. P. M.

1 { We are watching, we are waiting. For the bright prophetic day:
{ When the shadows, weary shadows From the world shall roll [*Omit.*] a - way. We are waiting

for the morning, When the beauteous day is dawning; We are waiting for the morning,

For the golden spires of day. Lo! he comes! see the King draw near; Zion, shout! the Lord is here.

1146 *"We are watching."*—Luke **12: 37.** ANON.

WE are watching, we are waiting,
　For the bright prophetic day:
When the shadows, weary shadows,
　From the world shall roll away.—CHO.

2 We are watching, we are waiting,
　For the star that brings the day:

When the night of sin shall vanish,
　And the shadows melt away.—CHO.

3 We are watching, we are waiting,
　For the beauteous King of day:
For the Chiefest of ten-thousand,
　For the Light, the Truth, the Way.—
　　　　　　　　　　　　　　CHO.

1147 *The Baptism of the Spirit.* AVELING.

HAIL! thou God of grace and glory!
　Who thy name hast magnified,
By redemption's wondrous story,
　By the Saviour crucified;
Thanks to thee for every blessing,
　Flowing from the Fount of love;
Thanks for present good unceasing,
　And for hopes of bliss above.

2 Hear us, as thus bending lowly,
　Near thy bright and burning throne;
We invoke thee, God most holy!
　Through thy well-belovéd Son;

Send the baptism of thy Spirit,
　Shed the pentecostal fire;
Let us all thy grace inherit,
　Waken, crown each good desire.

3 Bind thy people, Lord! in union,
　With the sevenfold cord of love;
Breathe a spirit of communion
　With the glorious hosts above;
Let thy work be seen progressing;
　Bow each heart, and bend each knee;
Till the world, thy truth possessing,
　Celebrates its jubilee.

MIDDLETON. 8, 7. D.

Light of those whose dreary dwelling Borders on the shades of death!
Rise on us, thy love revealing, Dissipate the clouds beneath:
D. C. Scattering all the night of nature, Pouring day upon our eyes.

Thou of heaven and earth Creator, In our deepest darkness rise,—

1148   *"The true Light."—John* **1:9.**   C. WESLEY.

Light of those whose dreary dwelling
  Borders on the shades of death!
Rise on us, thy love revealing,
  Dissipate the clouds beneath:
Thou of heaven and earth Creator,
  In our deepest darkness rise,—
Scattering all the night of nature,
  Pouring day upon our eyes.

2 Still we wait for thine appearing;
  Life and joy thy beams impart,
Chasing all our fears, and cheering
  Every poor benighted heart:
Come and manifest thy favor
  To the ransomed, helpless race;
Come, thou glorious God and Saviour!
  Come, and bring the gospel grace.

3 Save us, in thy great compassion,
  O thou mild, pacific Prince!
Give the knowledge of salvation,
  Give the pardon of our sins;
By thine all-sufficient merit,
  Every burdened soul release;
Every weary, wandering spirit,
  Guide into thy perfect peace.

1149   *God's Promise.—Isa.* **54:10.**   HASTINGS.

Zion, dreary and in anguish,
  'Mid the desert hast thou strayed!
Oh, thou weary, cease to languish;
  Jesus shall lift up thy head.

Still lamenting and bemoaning,
  'Mid thy follies and thy woes!
Soon repenting and returning,
  All thy solitude shall close.

2 Though benighted and forsaken,
  Though afflicted and distressed;
His almighty arm shall waken;
  Zion's King shall give thee rest:
Cease thy sadness, unbelieving;
  Soon his glory shalt thou see!
Joy and gladness, and thanksgiving,
  And the voice of melody!

1150   *" Come quickly."—Rev.* **22:20.**   C. WESLEY.

Come, thou long-expected Jesus,
  Born to set thy people free;
From our fears and sins release us,
  Let us find our rest in thee:
Israel's Strength and Consolation,
  Hope of all the saints thou art;
Dear Desire of every nation,
  Joy of every longing heart.

2 Born, thy people to deliver;
  Born a child, and yet a King!
Born to reign in us for ever,
  Now thy precious kingdom bring:
By thine own eternal Spirit,
  Rule in all our hearts alone;
By thine all-sufficient merit,
  Raise us to thy glorious throne.

STOUGHTON. 8, 7. D.

1. Glorious things of thee are spoken, Zion, cit - y of our God! He, whose word cannot be broken,
D. S.—With salvation's walls surrounded,

Formed thee for his own a-bode: On the Rock of Ages founded, What can shake thy sure repose?
Thou may'st smile at all thy foes.

1151 *"Glorious things."—Ps. 87.* NEWTON.

1 Glorious things of thee are spoken,
  Zion, city of our God!
He, whose word cannot be broken,
  Formed thee for his own abode:
On the Rock of ages founded,
  What can shake thy sure repose?
With salvation's walls surrounded,
  Thou mayst smile at all thy foes.

2 See! the streams of living waters,
  Springing from eternal love,
Well supply thy sons and daughters,
  And all fear of want remove:
Who can faint, while such a river
  Ever flows their thirst to assuage?—
Grace, which, like the Lord, the Giver,
  Never fails from age to age.

3 Round each habitation hovering,
  See the cloud and fire appear,
For a glory and a covering,
  Showing that the Lord is near!
Thus deriving from their banner,
  Light by night, and shade by day,
Safe they feed upon the manna
  Which he gives them when they pray.

1152 *The Covenant.—Isa. 60: 18.* COWPER.

Hear what God, the Lord, hath spoken;
  O my people, faint and few,
Comfortless, afflicted, broken,
  Fair abodes I build for you;
Scenes of heartfelt tribulation
  Shall no more perplex your ways;
You shall name your walls "Salvation,"
  And your gates shall all be "Praise."

2 There, like streams that feed the garden,
  Pleasures without end shall flow;
For the Lord, your faith rewarding,
  All his bounty shall bestow.
Still in undisturbed possession
  Peace and righteousness shall reign;
Never shall you feel oppression,
  Hear the voice of war again.

3 Ye, no more your suns descending,
  Waning moons no more shall see,
But, your griefs for ever ending,
  Find eternal noon in me.
God shall rise, and shining o'er you,
  Change to-day the gloom of night;
He, the Lord, shall be your Glory,
  God your everlasting Light.

ST. BRIDE. S. M.

1. Come, Lord, and tar-ry not! Bring the long-looked-for day;

Oh, why these years of wait-ing here, These a-ges of de-lay?

1153 *"Come, Lord Jesus."—Rev.* **22: 20.**   BONAR.

Come, Lord, and tarry not!
Bring the long-looked-for day;
Oh, why these years of waiting here,
These ages of delay?

2 Come, for thy saints still wait;
Daily ascends their sigh;
The Spirit and the Bride say, Come!
Dost thou not hear the cry?

3 Come, for creation groans,
Impatient of thy stay,
Worn out with these long years of ill,
These ages of delay.

4 Come, and make all things new,
Build up this ruined earth,
Restore our faded paradise,—
Creation's second birth.

5 Come and begin thy reign
Of everlasting peace;
Come, take the kingdom to thyself,
Great King of Righteousness!

1154   *Declension.—Lam.* **1: 4.**   BETHUNE.

Oh, for the happy hour
When God will hear our cry,
And send, with a reviving power,
His Spirit from on high.

2 We meet, we sing, we pray,
We listen to the word,
In vain;—we see no cheering ray,
No cheering voice is heard.

3 While many crowd thy house,
How few, around thy board,
Meet to recount their solemn vows,
And bless thee as their Lord!

4 Thou, thou alone canst give
Thy gospel sure success;
Canst bid the dying sinner live
Anew in holiness.

5 Come, then, with power divine,
Spirit of life and love!
Then shall this people all be thine,
This church like that above.

1155   *"Revive thy work."—Hab.* **3: 2.**   MRS. BROWN.

O Lord, thy work revive,
In Zion's gloomy hour,
And make her dying graces live
By thy restoring power.

2 Awake thy chosen few
To fervent, earnest prayer;
Again may they their vows renew,
Thy blessèd presence share.

3 Thy Spirit then will speak
Through lips of feeble clay,
And hearts of adamant will break,
And rebels will obey.

4 Lord, lend thy gracious ear;
Oh, listen to our cry;
Oh, come and bring salvation here:
Our hopes on thee rely.

LUTHER. S. M.

1. O thou whom we a-dore! To bless our earth a-gain, As-sume thine own al-might-y power, And o'er the nations reign, And o'er the na-tions reign.

1156   *Philippians* 2:10, 11.   C. WESLEY.

O THOU whom we adore!
  To bless our earth again,
Assume thine own almighty power,
  And o'er the nations reign.

2 The world's Desire and Hope,
  All power to thee is given;
Now set the last great empire up,
  Eternal Lord of heaven!

3 A gracious Saviour, thou
  Wilt all thy creatures bless;
And every knee to thee shall bow,
  And every tongue confess.

4 According to thy word,
  Now be thy grace revealed;
And with the knowledge of the Lord,
  Let all the earth be filled.

1157   *"The Lord shall arise."*—*Isa.* 60:2.   WARDLAW.

O LORD our God! arise;
  The cause of truth maintain;
And wide o'er all the peopled world
  Extend her blessèd reign.

2 Thou Prince of life! arise,
  Nor let thy glory cease;
Far spread the conquests of thy grace,
  And bless the earth with peace.

3 Thou Holy Ghost! arise,
  Extend thy healing wing,
And, o'er a dark and ruined world,
  Let light and order spring.

4 All on the earth! arise,
  To God the Saviour sing;
From shore to shore, from earth to heaven,
  Let echoing anthems ring.

1158   *Psalm* 117.   WATTS.

THY name, almighty Lord,
  Shall sound through distant lands:
Great is thy grace, and sure thy word;
  Thy truth for ever stands.

2 Far be thine honor spread,
  And long thy praise endure,
Till morning light, and evening shade,
  Shall be exchanged no more.

1159   *"Thy kingdom come!"*   JOHNS.

COME, kingdom of our God,
  Sweet reign of light and love!
Shed peace, and hope, and joy abroad,
  And wisdom from above.

2 Over our spirits first
  Extend thy healing reign;
There raise and quench the sacred thirst,
  That never pains again.

3 Come, kingdom of our God!
  And make the broad earth thine;
Stretch o'er her lands and isles the rod
  That flowers with grace divine.

4 Soon may all tribes be blest
  With fruit from life's glad tree;
And in its shade like brothers rest,
  Sons of one family.

WESLEY.   11, 10.

1. Hail to the brightness of Zion's glad morning! Joy to the lands that in darkness have lain!

Hushed be the accents of sorrow and mourning; Zi-on in triumph begins her mild reign.

1160   *The Promise.—Isa.* **51: 3.**   HASTINGS.

HAIL to the brightness of Zion's glad
    morning!
   Joy to the lands that in darkness have
    lain!
   Hushed be the accents of sorrow and
    mourning;
   Zion in triumph begins her mild reign.

2 Hail to the brightness of Zion's glad
    morning,
   Long by the prophets of Israel foretold;
   Hail to the millions from bondage return-
    ing;
   Gentiles and Jews the blest vision behold.

3 Lo! in the desert rich flowers are springing,
   Streams ever copious are gliding along;
   Loud from the mountain-tops echoes are
    ringing,
   Wastes rise in verdure, and mingle in
    song.

4 See, from all lands—from the isles of the
    ocean,
   Praise to Jehovah ascending on high;
   Fallen are the engines of war and commo-
    tion,
   Shouts of salvation are rending the sky.

1161   *"Days of thy mourning."—Isa.* **60: 20.**   RAY PALMER.

WAKE thee, O Zion, thy mourning is ended,
   God, thine own God, hath regarded thy
    prayer:

Wake thee, and hail him, in glory de-
    scended,
   Thy darkness to scatter, thy wastes to
    repair.

2 Wake thee, O Zion, his Spirit of power
   To newness of life is awaking the dead;
   Array thee in beauty, and greet the glad
    hour
   That brings thee salvation through Jesus
    who bled.

3 Saviour! we gladly with voices resounding,
   Loud as the thunder, our chorus would
    swell;
   Till from rock, wood, and mountain its
    echoes rebounding,
   To all the wide world of salvation shall
    tell!

1162   *Isaiah* **42: 10-13.**   C. S. ROBINSON.

ISLES of the South! your redemption is
    nearing;
   Lift, with the waves, the glad song of
    the free!
   He that was promised, in triumph ap-
    pearing,
   Now wields his sway o'er the land and
    the sea.

3 Loud from the tops of the mountains sing
    praises;
   Valleys shall ring with the echoing strain;
   Mighty in war, be the standard upraises,
   Glorious in peace, he advances to reign!

HOMER. 7. D.

Fount of ev - er - last - ing love! Rich thy streams of mer - cy are,
Flow - ing pure - ly from a - bove; Beau - ty marks their course a - far.
D. C. Thou hast heard her sad com - plaint, Floods of grace are sweep - ing wide!

Lo! thy church, a - thirst and faint, Drinks the full re - fresh - ing tide;

1163   *A Revival.*   RAY PALMER.

Fount of everlasting love!
  Rich thy streams of mercy are,
Flowing purely from above;
  Beauty marks their course afar.

2 Lo! thy church, athirst and faint,
  Drinks the full, refreshing tide;
Thou hast heard her sad complaint,
  Floods of grace are sweeping wide!

3 God of mercy! to thy throne
  Now our fervent thanks we bring;
Thine the glory, thine alone,
  Joyous praise to thee we sing.

4 While we lift our grateful song,
  Let the Spirit still descend;
Roll the tide of grace along,
  Widening, deepening, to the end!

1164   *Gospel Increase.*   C. WESLEY.

See! how great a flame aspires,
  Kindled by a spark of grace!
Jesus' love the nations fires,—
  Sets the kingdoms on a blaze;
Fire to bring on earth he came;
  Kindled in some hearts it is;
Oh, that all might catch the flame,
  All partake the glorious bliss!

2 When he first the work begun,
  Small and feeble was his day:
Now the word doth swiftly run;
  Now it wins its widening way:

More and more it spreads and grows,
  Ever mighty to prevail;
Sin's strongholds it now o'erthrows,—
  Shakes the trembling gates of hell.

3 Sons of God! your Saviour praise;
  He the door hath opened wide;
He hath given the word of grace;
  Jesus' word is glorified;
Jesus, mighty to redeem—
  He alone the work hath wrought;
Worthy is the work of him,—
  Him who spake a world from naught.

1165   *The World's Conversion.—Ps. 72.*   AUBER.

Hasten, Lord! the glorious time
  When, beneath Messiah's sway,
Every nation, every clime,
  Shall the gospel's call obey.

2 Mightiest kings his power shall own,
  Heathen tribes his name adore;
Satan and his host, o'erthrown,
  Bound in chains, shall hurt no more.

3 Then shall wars and tumults cease,
  Then be banished grief and pain;
Righteousness and joy and peace
  Undisturbed shall ever reign.

4 Bless we, then, our gracious Lord;
  Ever praise his glorious name;
All his mighty acts record;
  All his wondrous love proclaim.

ANVERN. L. M.

1. Triumphant Zi - on, lift thy head From dust, and darkness, and the dead; Tho' humbled

long, awake at length, And gird thee with thy Saviour's strength, And gird thee with thy Saviour's strength.

1166   *"Triumphant Zion!"—Isa.* **52 : 1.**   DODDRIDGE.

TRIUMPHANT Zion, lift thy head
From dust, and darkness, and the dead;
Though humbled long, awake at length,
And gird thee with thy Saviour's strength.

2 Put all thy beauteous garments on,
And let thy various charms be known:
The world thy glories shall confess,
Decked in the robes of righteousness.

3 No more shall foes unclean invade,
And fill thy hallowed walls with dread;
No more shall hell's insulting host
Their victory and thy sorrows boast.

4 God, from on high, thy groans will hear;
His hand thy ruin shall repair;
Nor will thy watchful monarch cease
To guard thee in eternal peace.

1167   *"Thine own Messiah, reigns."*   ANON.

WHY on the bending willows hung,
Israel! still sleeps thy tuneful string?—
Still mute remains thy sullen tongue,
And Zion's song denies to sing?

2 Awake! thy sweetest raptures raise;
Let harp and voice unite their strains:
Thy promised King his sceptre sways:
Jesus, thine own Messiah, reigns!

3 No taunting foes the song require;
No strangers mock thy captive chain;
But friends provoke the silent lyre,
And brethren ask the holy strain.

426

4 Nor fear thy Salem's hills to wrong,
If other lands thy triumph share:
A heavenly city claims thy song;
A brighter Salem rises there.

5 By foreign streams no longer roam;
Nor, weeping, think of Jordan's flood:
In every clime behold a home,
In every temple see thy God.

6 Then why, on bending willows hung,
Israel, still sleeps the tuneful string?
Why mute remains the sullen tongue,
And Zion's song delays to sing?

1168   *God's ancient people.*   ANON.

DISOWNED of heaven, by man oppressed,
Outcasts from Zion's hallowed ground,
Oh, why should Israel's sons, once blessed,
Still roam the scorning world around?

2 Lord! visit thy forsaken race,
Back to thy fold the wanderers bring;
Teach them to seek thy slighted grace,
And hail in Christ their promised King.

3 The vail of darkness rend in twain
Which hides their Shiloh's glorious light,
The severed olive branch again
Firm to its parent stock unite.

4 Hail, glorious day, expected long, [pour,
When Jew and Greek one prayer shall
With eager feet one temple throng,
With grateful praise one God adore.

FREDERICK. 11.

1. I would not live alway : I ask not to stay Where storm after storm ris-es dark o'er the way;

The few lurid mornings that dawn on us here Are enough for life's woes, full enough for its cheer.

1169 *"I would not live alway."*—*Job* 7: 16. MUHLENBERG.

I would not live alway: I ask not to stay
Where storm after storm rises dark o'er
  the way;
The few lurid mornings that dawn on us here
Are enough for life's woes, full enough for
  its cheer.

2 I would not live alway, thus fettered by sin—
Temptation without and corruption within:
Ev'n the rapture of pardon is mingled with
  fears,
And the cup of thanksgiving with peni-
  tent tears.

3 I would not live alway; no, welcome the
  tomb;
Since Jesus hath lain there, I dread not
  its gloom;
There sweet be my rest till he bid me arise
To hail him in triumph descending the skies.

4 Who, who would live alway, away from
  his God,
Away from you heaven, that blissful abode,
Where the rivers of pleasure flow over
  the bright plains,
And the noontide of glory eternally reigns?

5 Where the saints of all ages in harmony meet,
Their Saviour and brethren transported
  to greet;
While the anthems of rapture unceasingly roll,
And the smile of the Lord is the feast of
  the soul.

1170 *(Sing also* SCOTLAND, *p.* 237.) HEBER.

Thou art gone to the grave! but we will
  not deplore thee,
Though sorrows and darkness encompass the tomb,
The Saviour hath passed through its
  portals before thee,
And the lamp of his love is thy guide
  through the gloom.

2 Thou art gone to the grave! we no longer
  behold thee,
Nor tread the rough paths of the world
  by thy side;
But the wide arms of mercy are spread
  to enfold thee,
And sinners may hope, for the Sinless
  hath died.

3 Thou art gone to the grave! and, its mansion forsaking,
Perchance thy weak spirit in doubt
  lingered long;
But the sunshine of glory beamed bright
  on thy waking,
And the sound thou didst hear was the
  seraphim's song.

4 Thou art gone to the grave! but we will
  not deplore thee,
Since God was thy ransom, thy guar-
  dian, and guide:
He gave thee, he took thee, and he will
  restore thee;
And death has no sting, since the
  Saviour hath died.

427

ZEPHYR. L. M.

1. Why should we start and fear to die! What timorous worms we mor-tals are!

Death is the gate of end-less joy, And yet we dread to en-ter there.

1171   *"His beloved sleep."—Ps. 127:2.*   WATTS.

WHY should we start, and fear to die?
  What timorous worms we mortals are!
Death is the gate of endless joy,
  And yet we dread to enter there.

2 The pains, the groans, the dying strife
  Fright our approaching souls away;
We still shrink back again to life,
  Fond of our prison and our clay.

3 Oh, if my Lord would come and meet,
  My soul should stretch her wings in haste,
Fly fearless through death's iron gate,
  Nor feel the terrors as she passed.

4 Jesus can make a dying bed
  Feel soft as downy pillows are,
While on his breast I lean my head,
  And breathe my life out sweetly there!

1172   *"He shall enter into peace."*   HILL.

GENTLY, my Saviour, let me down,
  To slumber in the arms of death;
I rest my soul on thee alone,
  Ev'n till my last, expiring breath.

2 Soon will the storm of life be o'er,
  And I shall enter endless rest;
There I shall live to sin no more,
  And bless thy name, for ever blest.

3 Bid me possess sweet peace within;
  Let child-like patience keep my heart;
Then shall I feel my heaven begin,
  Before my spirit hence depart.

428

4 Oh, speed thy chariot, God of love!
  And take me from this world of woe;
I long to reach those joys above,
  And bid farewell to all below.

5 There shall my raptured spirit raise
  Still louder notes than angels sing,—
High glories to Immanuel's grace,
  My God, my Saviour, and my King!

1173   *Death of the Righteous.*   BARBAULD.

How blest the righteous when he dies,—
  When sinks a weary soul to rest!
How mildly beam the closing eyes!
  How gently heaves the expiring breast!

2 So fades a summer-cloud away;
  So sinks the gale when storms are o'er;
So gently shuts the eye of day;
  So dies a wave along the shore.

3 A holy quiet reigns around,—
  A calm which life nor death destroys;
Nothing disturbs that peace profound,
  Which his unfettered soul enjoys.

4 Farewell, conflicting hopes and fears!
  Where lights and shades alternate dwell;
How bright the unchanging morn appears!
  Farewell, inconstant world! farewell!

5 Life's duty done, as sinks the clay,
  Light from its load the spirit flies;
While heaven and earth combine to say,—
  "How blest the righteous when he dies!"

REST. L. M.

1. A - sleep in Je - sus! bless-ed sleep! From which none ev - er wake to weep;

A calm and un - dis - turbed re - pose, Un - bro - ken by the last of foes.

1174 *"Asleep in Jesus."—*1 *Thess.* 4:14.   MRS MACKAY.

ASLEEP in Jesus! blessèd sleep!
From which none ever wake to weep;
A calm and undisturbed repose,
Unbroken by the last of foes.

2 Asleep in Jesus! oh, how sweet
To be for such a slumber meet!
With holy confidence to sing
That death hath lost its venomed sting!

3 Asleep in Jesus! peaceful rest!
Whose waking is supremely blest;
No fear—no woe, shall dim the hour
That manifests the Saviour's power.

4 Asleep in Jesus! oh, for me
May such a blissful refuge be:
Securely shall my ashes lie,
And wait the summons from on high.

5 Asleep in Jesus! far from thee
Thy kindred and their graves may be:
But thine is still a blessèd sleep
From which none ever wake to weep.

1175   *A dying believer.*   BRUCE.

THE hour of my departure's come;
I hear the voice that calls me home;
At last, O Lord! let trouble cease,
And let thy servant die in peace.

2 Not in mine innocence I trust;
I bow before thee in the dust;
And through my Saviour's blood alone
I look for mercy at thy throne.

3 I leave the world without a tear,
Save for the friends I held so dear;
To heal their sorrows, Lord! descend,
And to the friendless prove a Friend.

4 I come, I come, at thy command;
I give my spirit to thy hand;
Stretch forth thine everlasting arms,
And shield me in the last alarms.

5 The hour of my departure's come;
I hear the voice that calls me home;
Now, O my God! let trouble cease;
Now let thy servant die in peace.

1176   *Death of an Infant.*   STEELE.

So fades the lovely, blooming flower,—
Frail smiling solace of an hour!
So soon our transient comforts fly,
And pleasure only blooms to die.

2 Is there no kind, no lenient art,
To heal the anguish of the heart?
Spirit of grace! be ever nigh,
Thy comforts are not made to die.

3 Thy powerful aid supports the soul,
And nature owns thy kind control;
While we peruse the sacred page,
Our fiercest griefs resign their rage.

4 Then gentle patience smiles on pain,
And dying hope revives again;
Hope wipes the tear from sorrow's eye,
And faith points upward to the sky.

429

CHINA. C. M.

1. Why do we mourn de - part - ing friends, Or shake at death's a - larms?

'Tis but the voice that Je - sus sends, To call them to his arms.

1177   *"We are confident."—2 Cor. 5: 8.*   WATTS.

Why do we mourn departing friends,
  Or shake at death's alarms?
'Tis but the voice that Jesus sends,
  To call them to his arms.

2 Are we not tending upward, too,
  As fast as time can move?
Nor would we wish the hours more slow,
  To keep us from our love.

3 Why should we tremble to convey
  Their bodies to the tomb?
There the dear flesh of Jesus lay,
  And scattered all the gloom.

4 The graves of all the saints he blessed,
  And softened every bed;
Where should the dying members rest,
  But with the dying Head?

5 Thence he arose, ascending high,
  And showed our feet the way;
Up to the Lord we, too, shall fly,
  At the great rising day.

6 Then let the last loud trumpet sound,
  And bid our kindred rise;
Awake! ye nations under ground;
  Ye saints! ascend the skies.

1178   *"To die is gain."—Phil. 1: 21.*   PRATT.

Why should our tears in sorrow flow,
  When God recalls his own;
And bids them leave a world of woe
  For an immortal crown?

2 Is not ev'n death a gain to those
  Whose life to God was given?
Gladly to earth their eyes they close,
  To open them in heaven.

3 Their toils are past, their work is done,
  And they are fully blest:
They fought the fight, the victory won,
  And entered into rest.

4 Then let our sorrows cease to flow,—
  God has recalled his own;
And let our hearts in every woe,
  Still say,—"Thy will be done!"

1179   *Job 3: 17-20.*   ANON.

How still and peaceful is the grave!
  Where, life's vain tumults past,
The appointed house, by heaven's decree,
  Receives us all at last.

2 The wicked there from troubling cease;
  Their passions rage no more;
And there the weary pilgrim rests
  From all the toils he bore.

3 There servants, masters, small and great,
  Partake the same repose;
And there, in peace, the ashes mix
  Of those who once were foes.

4 All, leveled by the hand of death,
  Lie sleeping in the tomb,
Till God in judgment calls them forth,
  To meet their final doom.

BARBY. C. M.

1. Oh, for an o-ver-com-ing faith, To cheer my dy—ing hours';

To tri-umph o'er ap-proach-ing death, And all his fright-ful powers!

1180 *"Where is thy sting?"*—1 Cor. **15:55.** WATTS.

Oh, for an overcoming faith,
  To cheer my dying hours;
To triumph o'er approaching death,
  And all his frightful powers!

2 Joyful, with all the strength I have,
  My quivering lips should sing,—
"Where is thy boasted victory, grave;
  And where, O death, thy sting?"

3 Now to the God of victory
  Immortal thanks be paid;—
Who makes us conquerors, while we die,
  Through Christ, our living Head!

1181 *"I shall go to him."*—2 Sam. **12:23.** H. K. WHITE.

Thro' sorrow's night, and danger's path,
  Amid the deepening gloom,
We, followers of our suffering Lord,
  Are marching to the tomb.

2 There, when the turmoil is no more,
  And all our powers decay,
Our cold remains in solitude
  Shall sleep the years away.

3 Our labors done, securely laid
  In this our last retreat,
Unheeded o'er our silent dust
  The storms of earth shall beat.

4 Yet not thus buried or extinct,
  The vital spark shall lie:
For o'er life's wreck that spark shall rise
  To seek its kindred sky.

5 These ashes, too, this little dust,
  Our Father's care shall keep,
Till the last angel rise and break
  The long and dreary sleep.

6 Then love's soft dew o'er every eye
  Shall shed its mildest rays,
And the long-silent voice awake
  With shouts of endless praise.

1182 *Resurrection sure.*—2 Cor. **4:14.** RAY PALMER.

When downward to the darksome tomb
  I thoughtful turn my eyes,
Frail nature trembles at the gloom,
  And anxious fears arise.

2 Why shrinks my soul?—in death's embrace
  Once Jesus captive slept:
And angels, hovering o'er the place,
  His lowly pillow kept.

3 Thus shall they guard my sleeping dust,
  And, as the Saviour rose,
The grave again shall yield her trust,
  And end my deep repose.

4 My Lord, before to glory gone,
  Shall bid me come away;
And calm and bright shall break the dawn
  Of heaven's eternal day.

5 Then let my faith each fear dispel,
  And gild with light the grave;
To him my loftiest praises swell,
  Who died from death to save.

OLMUTZ. S. M.

1. "For ev-er with the Lord!" So, Je-sus! let it be;

Life from the dead is in that word; 'Tis im-mor-tal-i-ty.

1183   *"For ever."—1 Thess. 4: 17.*   MONTGOMERY.

"FOR ever with the Lord!"
  So, Jesus! let it be;
Life from the dead is in that word;
  'Tis immortality.

2 Here, in the body pent,
  Absent from thee I roam:
Yet nightly pitch my moving tent
  A day's march nearer home.

3 My Father's house on high,
  Home of my soul! how near,
At times, to faith's aspiring eye,
  Thy golden gates appear!

4 "For ever with the Lord!"
  Father, if 'tis thy will,
The promise of thy gracious word
  Ev'n here to me fulfill.

5 So, when my latest breath
  Shall rend the vail in twain,
By death I shall escape from death,
  And life eternal gain.

6 Knowing as I am known,
  How shall I love that word,
And oft repeat before the throne,
  "For ever with the Lord!"

1184   *"The death of the righteous."*   S. F. SMITH.

OH, for the death of those
  Who slumber in the Lord!
Oh, be like theirs my last repose,
  Like theirs my last reward!

2 Their bodies in the ground,
  In silent hope may lie,
Till the last trumpet's joyful sound
  Shall call them to the sky.

3 Their ransomed spirits soar
  On wings of faith and love,
To meet the Saviour they adore,
  And reign with him above.

4 With us their names shall live
  Through long succeeding years,
Embalmed with all our hearts can give,
  Our praises and our tears.

1185   *"Your fathers, where are they?"*   DODDRIDGE.

How swift the torrent rolls,
  That bears us to the sea!
The tide which hurries thoughtless souls
  To vast eternity!

2 Our fathers, where are they,
  With all they called their own?
Their joys and griefs, and hopes and cares,
  And wealth and honor gone!

3 God of our fathers, hear,
  Thou everlasting Friend!
While we, as on life's utmost verge,
  Our souls to thee commend.

4 Of all the pious dead
  May we the footsteps trace,
Till with them, in the land of light,
  We dwell before thy face.

DUNBAR. S. M.

1. One sweet - ly sol - emn thought Comes to me o'er and o'er.—
CHO.—There'll be no sor - row there, There'll be no sor - row there;

Near - er my home, to - day, am I Then e'er I've been be - fore.
In heaven a - bove, where all is love, There'll be no sor - row there.

1186 *"Nearer."—Rom.* 13:11. CARY.

ONE sweetly solemn thought
   Comes to me o'er and o'er,—
Nearer my home, to-day, am I
   Then e'er I've been before.

2 Nearer my Father's house,
   Where many mansions be;
Nearer to-day the great white throne;
   Nearer the crystal sea.

3 Nearer the bound of life,
   Where burdens are laid down;
Nearer to leave the heavy cross;
   Nearer to gain the crown.

4 But, lying dark between,
   Winding down through the night,
There rolls the deep and unknown stream
   That leads at last to light.

5 Ev'n now, perchance, my feet
   Are slipping on the brink,
And I, to-day, am nearer home,—
   Nearer than now I think.

6 Father, perfect my trust!
   Strengthen my power of faith!
Nor let me stand, at last, alone
   Upon the shore of death.

1187 *" I will wait '—Job* 14:14. BONAR.

A FEW more years shall roll,
   A few more seasons come;
And we shall be with those that rest,
   Asleep within the tomb;—

2 A few more storms shall beat
   On this wild rocky shore;
And we shall be where tempests cease,
   And surges swell no more:—

3 A few more struggles here,
   A few more partings o'er,
A few more toils, a few more tears,
   And we shall weep no more:—

4 Then, O my Lord, prepare
   My soul for that blest day;
Oh, wash me in thy precious blood,
   And take my sins away!

1188 *The Long Repose.* BONAR.

REST for the toiling hand,
   Rest for the anxious brow,
Rest for the weary way-worn feet,
   Rest from all labor now!

2 Soon shall the trump of God
   Give out the welcome sound,
That shakes thy silent chamber-walls,
   And breaks the turf-sealed ground.

3 Ye dwellers in the dust,
   Awake! come forth and sing!
Sharp has your frost of winter been,
   But bright shall be your spring.

5 'Twas sown in darkness here,
   'Twill then be raised in power;
That which was sown an earthly seed
   Shall rise a heavenly flower.

GREENWOOD. S. M.

1. It is not death to die—
To leave this wea - ry road,
And 'mid the bro - ther - hood on high, To be at home with God.

1189   *" Where is thy victory?"*   BETHUNE.

It is not death to die—
To leave this weary road,
And 'mid the brotherhood on high,
To be at home with God.

2 It is not death to close
The eye long dimmed by tears,
And wake, in glorious repose
To spend eternal years.

3 It is not death to bear
The wrench that sets us free
From dungeon chain,—to breathe the air
Of boundless liberty.

4 It is not death to fling
Aside this sinful dust,
And rise, on strong exulting wing,
To live among the just.

5 Jesus, thou Prince of life!
Thy chosen cannot die;
Like thee, they conquer in the strife,
To reign with thee on high.

1190   *Death of a Minister.*   MONTGOMERY.

Servant of God, well done!
Rest from thy loved employ;
The battle fought, the victory won,
Enter thy Master's joy!

2 The voice at midnight came;
He started up to hear;
A mortal arrow pierced his frame;
He fell, but felt no fear.

3 His spirit with a bound
Left its encumbering clay:
His tent, at sunrise, on the ground
A darkened ruin lay.

4 Soldier of Christ, well done!
Praise be thy new employ;
And, while eternal ages run,
Rest in thy Saviour's joy.

1191   *" A place for you."*—*John* 14: 2.   BENNETT.

I have a home above,
From sin and sorrow free;
A mansion which eternal love
Designed and formed for me.

2 My Father's gracious hand
Has built this sweet abode;
From everlasting it was planned—
My dwelling-place with God.

3 My Saviour's precious blood
Has made my title sure;
He passed thro' death's dark raging flood
To make my rest secure.

4 The Comforter is come,
The earnest has been given;
He leads me onward to the home
Reserved for me in heaven.

5 Loved ones are gone before,
Whose pilgrim days are done;
I soon shall greet them on that shore
Where partings are unknown.

434

DAWN. S. M.

1. And is there, Lord, a rest For wea - ry souls de - signed,

Where not a care shall stir the breast, Or sor - row en - trance find?

1192 *"A rest."—Heb. 4:9.*   RAY PALMER.

AND is there, Lord, a rest
  For weary souls designed,
Where not a care shall stir the breast,
  Or sorrow entrance find?

2 Is there a blissful home,
  Where kindred minds shall meet,
And live, and love, nor ever roam
  From that serene retreat?

3 For ever blessèd they,
  Whose joyful feet shall stand,
While endless ages waste away,
  Amid that glorious land!

4 My soul would thither tend,
  While toilsome years are given;
Then let me, gracious God, ascend
  To sweet repose in heaven!

1193 *"How long, O Lord!"*   DONAR.

THE church has waited long
  Her absent Lord to see;
And still in loneliness she waits,
  A friendless stranger she.

2 How long, O Lord our God,
  Holy and true and good.
Wilt thou not judge thy suffering church,
  Her sighs and tears and blood?

3 Saint after saint on earth
  Has lived and loved and died;
And as they left us one by one,
  We laid them side by side.

4 We laid them down to sleep,
  But not in hope forlorn;
We laid them but to ripen there,
  Till the last glorious morn.

5 We long to hear thy voice,
  To see thee face to face,
To share thy crown and glory then,
  As now we share thy grace.

6 Come, Lord, and wipe away
  The curse, the sin, the stain,
And make this blighted world of ours
  Thine own fair world again.

1194 *The Pious Dead.*   MANT.

FOR all thy saints, O God,
  Who strove in Christ to live,
Who followed him, obeyed, adored,
  Our grateful hymn receive.

2 For all thy saints, O God,
  Accept our thankful cry,
Who counted Christ their great reward,
  And yearned for him to die.

3 They all, in life and death,
  With him, their Lord, in view,
Learned from thy Holy Spirit's breath
  To suffer and to do.

4 For this thy name we bless,
  And humbly pray that we
May follow them in holiness,
  And live and die in thee.

ST. ASAPH.　C. M. D.

1. Be - hold the western evening light! It melts in deepening gloom: So calm - ly Christians

sink a - way, De - scending to the tomb. The winds breathe low, the withering leaf Scarce

whispers from the tree: So gently flows the part-ing breath, When good men cease to be.

1195 *"Precious in the sight of the Lord."* PEABODY.

BEHOLD the western evening light!
　　It melts in deepening gloom:
So calmly Christians sink away,
　　Descending to the tomb.

2 The winds breathe low, the withering leaf
　　Scarce whispers from the tree:
So gently flows the parting breath,
　　When good men cease to be.

3 How beautiful on all the hills
　　The crimson light is shed!
'Tis like the peace the Christian gives
　　To mourners round his bed.

4 How mildly on the wandering cloud
　　The sunset beam is cast!
'Tis like the memory left behind
　　When loved ones breathe their last.

5 And now above the dews of night
　　The rising star appears:
So faith springs in the heart of those
　　Whose eyes are bathed in tears.

6 But soon the morning's happier light
　　Its glory shall restore,
And eyelids that are sealed in death
　　Shall wake to close no more.

1196 *"Number our days."—Ps.* 90:12. HEBER.

BENEATH our feet and o'er our head
　　Is equal warning given;
Beneath us lie the countless dead,
　　Above us is the heaven!

2 Death rides on every passing breeze,
　　And lurks in every flower;
Each season hath its own disease,
　　Its peril every hour!

3 Our eyes have seen the rosy light
　　Of youth's soft cheek decay;
And fate descend in sudden night
　　On manhood's middle day.

4 Our eyes have seen the steps of age
　　Halt feebly to the tomb;
And yet shall earth our hearts engage,
　　And dreams of days to come?

5 Then, mortal, turn! thy danger know;
　　Where'er thy foot can tread,
The earth rings hollow from below,
　　And warns thee of her dead!

6 Turn, mortal, turn! thy soul apply
　　To truths divinely given:
The dead, who underneath thee lie,
　　Shall live for hell or heaven!

AMSTERDAM. 7, 6. D.

Rise, my soul and stretch thy wings, Thy better portion trace;
Rise from transi - tory things Toward heaven, thy native place ; Sun and moon and stars decay,

Time shall soon this earth remove ; Rise, my soul ! and haste away   To seats prepared a - bove.

1197   *Christian Outlook.*   SEAGRAVE.

2 Rivers to the ocean run,
    Nor stay in all their course;
Fire, ascending, seeks the sun;
    Both speed them to their source;
So a soul, that's born of God,
    Pants to view his glorious face,
Upward tends to his abode,
    To rest in his embrace.

3 Cease, ye pilgrims! cease to mourn,
    Press onward to the prize;
Soon our Saviour will return
    Triumphant in the skies!
Yet a season, and you know
    Happy entrance will be given;
All our sorrows left below,
    And earth exchanged for heaven.

1198   *"Our earthly house."*—2 Cor. 5: 1.   BURTON.

Time is winging us away
    To our eternal home;
Life is but a winter's day—
    A journey to the tomb;
Youth and vigor soon will flee,
    Blooming beauty lose its charms;
All that's mortal soon shall be
    Enclosed in death's cold arms.

2 Time is winging us away
    To our eternal home;
Life is but a winter's day—
    A journey to the tomb;
But the Christian shall enjoy
    Health and beauty, soon, above,
Far beyond the world's alloy,
    Secure in Jesus' love.

GENEVA. 7, 6. D.

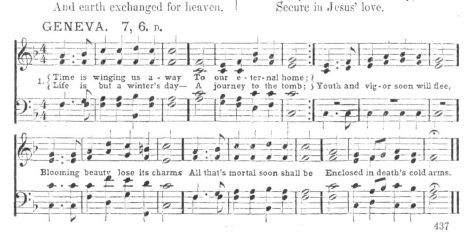

Time is winging us a - way   To   our   e - ter-nal home;
Life   is   but a   winter's day—   A   journey to the tomb; Youth and vig-or soon will flee,

Blooming beauty lose its charms All that's mortal soon shall be   Enclosed in death's cold arms.

MEINHOLD. P. M.

1. Je - sus lives! no long - er now Can thy ter - rors, Death, ap - pall me;

Je - sus lives! and well I know, From the dead he will re - call me;

Bet - ter life will then com - mence, This shall be my con - fi - dence.

1199 *"Ye shall live also."—John 14: 19.* GELLERT.

JESUS lives! no longer now
　Can thy terrors, Death, appall me;
Jesus lives! and well I know,
　From the dead he will recall me;
Better life will then commence,
This shall be my confidence.

2 Jesus lives! to him the throne
　Over all the world is given;
I shall go where he is gone,
　Live and reign with him in heaven:
God is pledged; weak doubtings, hence!
This shall be my confidence.

3 Jesus lives! I know full well,
　Naught from him my heart can sever;
Life nor death, nor powers of hell,
　Joy nor grief, henceforth, for ever:
God will power and grace dispense,
This shall be my confidence.

4 Jesus lives! henceforth is death
　Entrance into life immortal;
438

Calmly I can yield my breath,
　Fearless tread the frowning portal;
Lord, when faileth flesh and sense,
Thou wilt be my confidence!

1200 *Death of an infant.* WINKWORTH. *Tr.*

TENDER Shepherd, thou hast stilled
　Now thy little lamb's brief weeping;
Ah, how peaceful, pale, and mild
　In its narrow bed 'tis sleeping,
And no sigh of anguish sore
Heaves that little bosom more.

2 In this world of care and pain,
　Lord, thou wouldst no longer leave it;
To the sunny heavenly plain
　Thou dost now with joy receive it;
Clothed in robes of spotless white,
Now it dwells with thee in light.

3 Ah, Lord Jesus, grant that we
　Where it lives may soon be living,
And the lovely pastures see
　That its heavenly food are giving;
Then the gain of death we prove,
Though thou take what most we love.

BARTIMEUS.　8, 7.

1. Cease, ye mourners, cease to lan-guish O'er the grave of those you love:

Pain and death, and night and an-guish En-ter not the world a-bove.

1201　*Comfort.—Ps.* 116:15.　COLLYER.

CEASE, ye mourners, cease to languish
　O'er the grave of those you love;
Pain and death, and night and anguish
　Enter not the world above.

2 While our silent steps are straying
　Lonely thro' night's deepening shade,
Glory's brightest beams are playing
　Round the happy Christian's head.

3 Light and peace at once deriving
　From the hand of God most high,
In his glorious presence living,
　They shall never, never die.

4 Now, ye mourners, cease to languish
　O'er the grave of those you love;
Far removed from pain and anguish,
　They are chanting hymns above.

1202　*"Abide with us."—Luke* 24: 29.　MRS. CLARK.

TARRY with me, O my Saviour!
　For the day is passing by;
See! the shades of evening gather,
　And the night is drawing nigh.

2 Deeper, deeper grow the shadows,
　Paler now the glowing west,
Swift the night of death advances;
　Shall it be the night of rest?

3 Lonely seems the vale of shadow;
　Sinks my heart with troubled fear;
Give me faith for clearer vision,
　Speak thou, Lord, in words of cheer.

4 Let me hear thy voice behind me,
　Calming all these wild alarms;
Let me, underneath my weakness,
　Feel the everlasting arms.

5 Feeble, trembling, fainting, dying,
　Lord, I cast myself on thee;
Tarry with me through the darkness;
　While I sleep, still watch by me.

6 Tarry with me, O my Saviour!
　Lay my head upon thy breast
Till the morning; then awake me—
　Morning of eternal rest!

1203　*"Thy will be done."*　HASTINGS.

JESUS, while our hearts are bleeding
　O'er the spoils that death has won,
We would at this solemn meeting,
　Calmly say,—thy will be done.

2 Though cast down, we're not forsaken;
　Though afflicted, not alone;
Thou didst give, and thou hast taken;
　Blesséd Lord,—thy will be done.

3 Though to-day we're filled with mourning,
　Mercy still is on the throne;
With thy smiles of love returning,
　We can sing—thy will be done.

4 By thy hands the boon was given,
　Thou hast taken but thine own:
Lord of earth, and God of heaven,
　Evermore,—thy will be done!

NUNDA. L. M. D.

1
{ How vain is all be-neath the skies! How transient ev - ery earth-ly bliss! } 2. The evening-
{ How slender all the fond-est ties That bind us to a world like this! } The withering

cloud, the morning dew,
grass, the fading flower, Of earthly hopes are emblems true,—The glory of a pass-ing hour.

1204   *Heaven alone unfading.*   FORD.

How vain is all beneath the skies!
How transient every earthly bliss!
How slender all the fondest ties
That bind us to a world like this!

2 The evening-cloud, the morning-dew,
The withering grass, the fading flower,
Of earthly hopes are emblems true,—
The glory of a passing hour.

3 But, though earth's fairest blossoms die,
And all beneath the skies is vain,
There is a land whose confines lie
Beyond the reach of care and pain.

4 Then let the hope of joys to come
Dispel our cares, and chase our fears:
If God be ours, we're traveling home,
Though passing through a vale of tears.

1205   *Burial of Believers.*   WATTS.

Unvail thy bosom, faithful tomb!
Take this new treasure to thy trust,
And give these sacred relics room
To seek a slumber in the dust.

2 Nor pain, nor grief, nor anxious fear,
Invade thy bounds;—no mortal woes
Can reach the peaceful sleeper here,
While angels watch the soft repose.

3 So Jesus slept; God's dying Son   [bed!
Passed through the grave and blessed the
Rest here, blest saint!—till, from his throne,
The morning break, and pierce the shade.

4 Break from his throne, illustrious morn!
Attend, O earth! his sovereign word;
Restore thy trust;—a glorious form
Shall then arise to meet the Lord.

MERIBAH. C. P. M.

1. When thou, my righteous Judge, shalt come To bring thy ransomed peo - ple home, Shall

I a-mong them stand? Shall such a worthless worm as I,
Who sometimes am a-fraid to die, Be found at thy right hand?

MILLINGTON. 8, 7, 7.

1 { What is life? 'tis but a va-por, Soon it van-ish-es a - way. }
{ Life is but a dy - ing ta - per—O my soul, why wish to stay? } Why not spread thy wings and fly

Straight to yonder world of joy? Why not spread thy wings and fly Straight to yonder world of joy?

1206 *"What is your life?"—Jas. 4: 14.* KELLY.

WHAT is life? 'tis but a vapor,
　Soon it vanishes away.
Life is but a dying taper—
　O my soul, why wish to stay?
Why not spread thy wings and fly
Straight to yonder world of joy?

2 See that glory, how resplendent!
　Brighter far than fancy paints;
There, in majesty transcendent,
　Jesus reigns the King of saints.
　Why not spread, etc.

3 Joyful crowds his throne surrounding,
　Sing with rapture of his love;
Thro' the heavens his praise resounding,
　Filling all the courts above.
　Why not spread, etc.

4 Go, and share his people's glory,
　'Midst the ransomed crowd appear;
Thine a joyful wondrous story,
　One that angels love to hear.
　Why not spread, etc.

1207 *The Great Tribunal.* HUNTINGDON.

WHEN thou, my righteous Judge, shalt come
To take thy ransomed people home,
　Shall I among them stand?
Shall such a worthless worm as I,
Who sometimes am afraid to die,
　Be found at thy right hand?

2 I love to meet thy people now,
Before thy feet with them to bow,
　Though vilest of them all;
But, can I bear the piercing thought,
What if my name should be left out,
　When thou for them shalt call?

3 O Lord, prevent it by thy grace,
Be thou my only hiding-place,
　In this the accepted day;
Thy pardoning voice, oh, let me hear,
To still my unbelieving fear,
　Nor let me fall, I pray.

4 Among the saints let me be found,
Whene'er the archangel's trump shall
　　sound,
　To see thy smiling face;
Then loudest of the throng I 'll sing,
While heaven's resounding mansions ring
　With shouts of sovereign grace.

JUDGMENT HYMN. P. M.

1. The day of wrath! that dreadful day, When heaven and earth shall pass away! What power shall be the

sinner's stay? How shall he meet that dread-ful day? How shall he meet that dreadful day?—

Use slurs and repeat for Hymn 1210.

1208 *"The Day of the Lord."*—2 *Pet.* 3. 10.   W. SCOTT.

THE day of wrath! that dreadful day,
When heaven and earth shall pass away!
What power shall be the sinner's stay?
How shall he meet that dreadful day?—

2 When, shriveling like a parchéd scroll,
The flaming heavens together roll,
And louder yet, and yet more dread,
Swells the high trump that wakes the dead!

3 Oh, on that day, that wrathful day,
When man to judgment wakes from clay,
Be thou, O Christ, the sinner's stay,
Though heaven and earth shall pass away.

1209 *The Lord coming.*—2 *Thess.* 1: 7.   HEBER.

THE Lord shall come! the earth shall quake:
The mountains to their centre shake;
And withering from the vault of night,
The stars withdraw their feeble light.

2 The Lord shall come! but not the same
As once in lowly form he came,—
A silent Lamb before his foes,
A weary man, and full of woes.

3 The Lord shall come! a dreadful form,
With wreath of flame, and robe of storm,
On cherub-wings, and wings of wind,
Anointed Judge of human kind!

4 While sinners in despair shall call,
"Rocks, hide us! mountains, on us fall!"
The saints, ascending from the tomb,
Shall sing for joy, "The Lord is come!"

412

1210 *The judgment.*—*Rev.* 20: 6.   COLLYER.

GREAT God, what do I see and hear!
The end of things created!
The Judge of man I see appear,
On clouds of glory seated:
The trumpet sounds; the graves restore
The dead which they contained before;
Prepare, my soul, to meet him.

2 The dead in Christ shall first arise,
At the last trumpet's sounding,
Caught up to meet him in the skies,
With joy their Lord surrounding;
No gloomy fears their souls dismay,
His presence sheds eternal day
On those prepared to meet him.

3 But sinners, filled with guilty fears,
Behold his wrath prevailing;
For they shall rise, and find their tears
And sighs are unavailing:
The day of grace is past and gone;
Trembling they stand before the throne,
All unprepared to meet him.

4 Great God! what do I see and hear!
The end of things created!
The Judge of man I see appear,
On clouds of glory seated:
Beneath his cross I view the day
When heaven and earth shall pass away,
And thus prepare to meet him.

STETTIN. P. M.

1. { When my last hour is close at hand, My last sad journey tak - en, }
{ Do thou, Lord Je-sus! by me stand; Let me not be for-sak - en : } O Lord! my spir-it

I re-sign In - to thy lov-ing hands di-vine; 'Tis safe with-in thy keep-ing.

1211 *"Into thine hand."—Ps.* **31**: **5.** GERMAN.

WHEN my last hour is close at hand,
My last sad journey taken,
Do thou, Lord Jesus! by me stand;
Let me not be forsaken:
O Lord! my spirit I resign
Into thy loving hands divine;
'Tis safe within thy keeping.

2 Countless as sands upon the shore,
My sins may then appall me;
Yet, though my conscience vex me sore,
Despair shall not enthrall me;
For as I draw my latest breath,
I'll think, Lord Christ! upon thy death,
And there find consolation.

3 I shall not in the grave remain,
Since thou death's bonds hast severed:
By hope with thee to rise again
From fear of death delivered,
I'll come to thee, where'er thou art,
Live with thee, from thee never part;
Therefore I die in rapture.

4 And so to Jesus Christ I'll go,
My longing arms extending;
So fall asleep, in slumber deep,
Slumber that knows no ending;
Till Jesus Christ, God's only Son,
Opens the gates of bliss, leads on
To heaven, to life eternal.

1212 *Christ coming to Judgment.* MILLS. *Tr.*

THE trumpet sounds!—the day has come!
In glory Christ revealing;
To men the day of final doom—
Their state for ever sealing:
He comes!—the Son of man is here,
Borne on a cloud, see him appear
Arrayed in robes of judgment!

2 He speaks!—the listening skies are still;
All eyes on Jesus centre,
While awe and dread the bosom fill:—
"Come ye your kingdom enter!"—
He says to those who mercy sought:
And then,—to all who prized it not,—
"Depart from me, ye cursèd!"

3 The blissful saints ascend on high,
Clothed with the light of heaven;
Their Saviour leads them thro' the sky;—
What burst of joy is given!
For now they see, with raptured eyes,
That faith and love receive the prize,
Through grace rich, free, abounding.

4 And see!—they take the mansions bright,
Where God prepared their dwelling;
Like angels now;—and, to their sight,
Their joys are onward swelling;
They knew in part,—now, all is clear;
Nor doubt, nor sorrow enters here,
To break their bliss unceasing.

TAMWORTH. 8, 7, 4.

See th'e - ter - nal Judge de - scend-ing! View him seat - ed on his throne!
Now, poor sin - ner, now la - ment-ing, Stand and hear thine aw - ful doom;

Trum - pets call thee, Trumpets call thee, Stand and hear thine aw - ful doom.

1213 *"They shall look on him."—John* 19 :37. ANON.

See the eternal Judge descending!
View him seated on his throne!
Now, poor sinner, now lamenting,
Stand and hear thine awful doom;
Trumpets call thee,
Stand and hear thine awful doom!

2 Hear the cries he now is venting,
Filled with dread of fiercer pain;
While in anguish thus lamenting
That he ne'er was born again—
Greatly mourning
That he ne'er was born again.

3 "Yonder sits my slighted Saviour,
With the marks of dying love;
Oh, that I had sought his favor
When I felt his Spirit move—
Golden moments,
When I felt his Spirit move!"

1214 *The Judge coming.—Matt.* 25 : 34. CENNICK.

Lo! he cometh,—countless trumpets
Wake to life the slumbering dead;
'Mid ten thousand saints and angels,
See their great exalted Head:
Hallelujah—
Welcome, welcome, Son of God!

2 Full of joyful expectation,
Saints behold the Judge appear:
Truth and justice go before him—
Now the joyful sentence hear;
Hallelujah!—
Welcome, welcome, Judge divine!

3 "Come, ye blessèd of my Father!
Enter into life and joy;
Banish all your fears and sorrows;
Endless praise be your employ;
Hallelujah!—
Welcome, welcome to the skies!"

1215 *"Lo! he comes!"—Zech.* 12 : 10. C. WESLEY.

Lo! he comes with clouds descending,
Once for favored sinners slain!
Thousand thousand saints attending,
Swell the triumph of his train!
Hallelujah!
Jesus comes, and comes to reign.

2 Every eye shall now behold him,
Robed in dreadful majesty!
Those who set at naught and sold him,
Pierced and nailed him to the tree,
Deeply wailing,
Shall the true Messiah see!

3 Lo! the last long separation,
As the cleaving crowds divide,
And one dread adjudication
Sends each soul to either side!
Lord of mercy!
How shall I that day abide?

4 Yea, Amen! let all adore thee,
High on thine eternal throne!
Saviour, take the power and glory;
Make thy righteous sentence known!
Men and angels
Kneel and bow to thee alone!

BREST. 8, 7, 4.

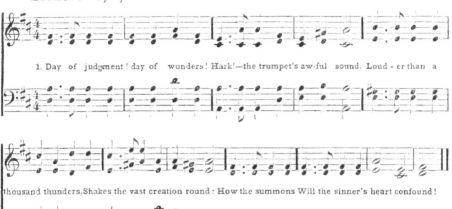

1. Day of judgment! day of wonders! Hark!—the trumpet's aw-ful sound, Loud-er than a thousand thunders, Shakes the vast creation round: How the summons Will the sinner's heart confound!

1216 *"Day of wonders."—Matt.* 25: 34. NEWTON.

Day of judgment! day of wonders!
Hark!—the trumpet's awful sound,
Louder than a thousand thunders,
Shakes the vast creation round:
How the summons
Will the sinner's heart confound!

2 See the Judge, our nature wearing,
Clothed in majesty divine!
You, who long for his appearing,
Then shall say, "This God is mine!"
Gracious Saviour!
Own me in that day for thine.

3 At his call, the dead awaken,
Rise to life from earth and sea;
All the powers of nature, shaken
By his looks, prepare to flee:
Careless sinner!
What will then become of thee?

4 But to those who have confessed,
Loved and served the Lord below,
He will say,—"Come near, ye blessed!
See the kingdom I bestow;
You for ever
Shall my love and glory know."

1217 *"The Mighty God."—Matt.* 24: 27. GOODE.

Lo! the mighty God appearing—
From on high Jehovah speaks!

Eastern lands the summons hearing,
O'er the west his thunder breaks:
Earth beholds him:
Universal nature shakes.

2 Zion all its light unfolding,
God in glory shall display:
Lo! he comes,—nor silence holding,
Fire and clouds prepare his way:
Tempests round him
Hasten on the dreadful day.

3 To the heavens his voice ascending,
To the earth beneath he cries—
"Souls immortal now descending,
Let the sleeping dust arise!
Rise to judgment;
Let my throne adorn the skies.

4 "Gather first my saints around me,
Those who to my covenant stood;
Those who humbly sought and found me,
Through the dying Saviour's blood:
Blest Redeemer!
Choicest sacrifice to God!"

5 Now the heavens on high adore him,
And his righteousness declare:
Sinners perish from before him,
But his saints his mercies share:
Just his judgment!
God, himself the Judge, is there.

NORTHFIELD.   C. M.

1. Lo, what a glorious sight appears To our be-liev-ing eyes!

The earth and seas are

earth and seas are passed away, And the old rolling skies.

The earth and seas are passed a - way, And the old roll-ing skies.
The earth and seas are passed away,

passed away, The earth and seas are passed a - way,

1218   *"Your descending King."—Rev.* 21 : 2.   WATTS.

Lo! what glorious sight appears,
   To our believing eyes!
The earth and seas are passed away,
   And the old rolling skies.

2 From the third heaven where God resides—
   That holy, happy place,—
The New Jerusalem comes down,
   Adorned with shining grace.

3 Attending angels shout for joy,
   And the bright armies sing,—
"Mortals! behold the sacred seat
   Of your descending King:—

4 "The God of glory, down to men,
   Removes his blest abode;
Men, the dear objects of his grace,
   And he their loving God:—

5 "His own soft hand shall wipe the tears
   From every weeping eye;
And pains, and groans, and griefs, and fears,
   And death itself shall die!"

6 How long, dear Saviour! oh, how long
   Shall this bright hour delay?
Fly swifter round, ye wheels of time!
   And bring the welcome day.

1219   *Messiah's Reign —Isa.* 2: 2.   LOGAN.

Behold, the mountain of the Lord
   In latter days shall rise
On mountain tops, above the hills,
   And draw the wondering eyes.

2 To this the joyful nations round,
   All tribes and tongues, shall flow;
Up to the hill of God, they'll say,
   And to his house we'll go.

3 The beam that shines from Zion's hill
   Shall lighten every land;
The King who reigns in Salem's towers
   Shall all the world command.

4 No strife shall vex Messiah's reign,
   Or mar the peaceful years;
To ploughshares men shall beat their swords,
   To pruning-hooks their spears.

1220   *"Come, Blessed Lord?"*   DENNY.

Light of the lonely pilgrim's heart!
   Star of the coming day!
Arise, and with thy morning beams
   Chase all our griefs away.

2 Come, blessed Lord! let every shore
   And answering island sing
The praises of thy royal name,
   And own thee as their King.

3 Jesus! thy fair creation groans,
   The air, the earth, the sea,
In unison with all our hearts,
   And calls aloud for thee.

4 Thine was the cross, with all its fruits
   Of grace and peace divine;
Be thine the crown of glory now,
   The palm of victory thine.

CANAAN. C. M. D.

1. { Bride of the Lamb, a-wake, a-wake! Why sleep for sorrow now? [*Omit* ....] }
   { The hope of glo - ry, Christ, is thine, [*Omit* ....] A child of glo - ry thou. }
   D. C.—Hath sighed for one that's far a-way,—[*Omit* ....] The Bridegroom of thy heart.

2. Thy spir - it, through the lone - ly night, From earth-ly joy a - part,

1221　　*"The Lamb's Wife."*　　DENNY.

BRIDE of the Lamb, awake, awake!
　Why sleep for sorrow now?
The hope of glory, Christ, is thine,
　A child of glory thou.

2 Thy spirit, through the lonely night,
　From earthly joy apart,
Hath sighed for one that's far away,—
　The Bridegroom of thy heart.

3 But see! the night is waning fast,
　The breaking morn is near;
And Jesus comes, with voice of love,
　Thy drooping heart to cheer.

4 Then weep no more; 'tis all thine own,
　His crown, his joy divine;
And, sweeter far than all beside,
　He, he himself is thine!

1222　*"Behold, I come quickly."—Rev.* 22: 4.　ANON.

SOON will the heavenly Bridegroom come:
　Ye wedding-guests draw near,
And slumber not in sin, when he,
　The Son of God, is here!

2 Come, let us haste to meet our Lord,
　And hail him with delight;
Who saved us by his precious blood,
　And sorrows infinite!

3 Beside him all the patriarchs old,
　And holy prophets stand;
The glorious apostolic choir,
　And noble martyr band.

4 As brethren dear they welcome us,
　And lead us to the throne,
Where angels bow their vailèd heads,
　Before the Three in One;—

5 Where we, with all the saints of God,
　A white-robed multitude,
Shall praise the ascended Lord, who deigns
　To bear our flesh and blood!

6 Our lot shall be for aye to share
　His reign of peace above:
And drink, with unexhausted joy,
　The river of his love.

1223　　*"Come, Lord Jesus!"*　　DENNY.

HOPE of our hearts, O Lord, appear,
　Thou glorious Star of day!
Shine forth, and chase the dreary night,
　With all our tears, away.

2 No resting-place we seek on earth,
　No loveliness we see;
Our eye is on the royal crown,
　Prepared for us and thee.

3 But, dearest Lord, however bright
　That crown of joy above,
What is it to the brighter hope
　Of dwelling in thy love?

4 What to the joy, the deeper joy,
　Unmingled, pure, and free,
Of union with our living Head,
　Of fellowship with thee?

447

AUGUSTUS.   C. M.

1. There is an hour when I must part With all I hold most dear;

And life, with its best hopes, will then As noth-ing-ness ap-pear.

1224   *"Be ye also ready."—Matt. 24. 44.*   REED.

THERE is an hour when I must part
  With all I hold most dear;
And life, with its best hopes, will then
  As nothingness appear.

2 There is an hour when I must sink
  Beneath the stroke of death;
And yield to him who gave it first,
  My struggling vital breath.

3 There is an hour when I must stand,
  Before the judgment-seat;
And all my sins, and all my foes,
  In awful vision meet.

4 There is an hour when I must look
  On one eternity;
And nameless woe, or blissful life,
  My endless portion be.

5 O Saviour, then, in all my need
  Be near, be near to me:
And let my soul, by steadfast faith,
  Find life and heaven in thee.

1225   *"That awful Day"*   WATTS.

THAT awful day will surely come,
  The appointed hour make haste,
When I must stand before my Judge
  And pass the solemn test.

2 Thou lovely Chief of all my joys,
  Thou Sovereign of my heart!
How could I bear to hear thy voice
  Pronounce the sound, "Depart!"

3 Oh, wretched state of deep despair!
  To see my God remove,—
And fix my doleful station where
  I must not taste his love!

4 Jesus, I throw my arms around,
  And hang upon thy breast:
Without a gracious smile from thee,
  My spirit cannot rest.

5 Oh, tell me that my worthless name
  Is graven on thy hands!
Show me some promise in thy book,
  Where my salvation stands.

6 Give me one kind, assuring word,
  To sink my fears again;
And cheerfully my soul shall wait
  Her three score years and ten.

1226   *The Solemn Test.*   ADDISON.

WHEN, rising from the bed of death,
  O'erwhelmed with guilt and fear,
I see my Maker face to face,—
  Oh, how shall I appear?

2 If yet, while pardon may be found,
  And mercy may be sought,
My heart with inward horror shrinks,
  And trembles at the thought;—

3 When thou, O Lord! shalt stand disclosed
  In majesty severe,
And sit in judgment on my soul,
  Oh, how shall I appear?

TAPPAN. C. M.

1. On Jordan's rug - ged banks I stand, And cast a wish - ful eye To Canaan's

fair and hap-py land, To Canaan's fair and hap-py land, Where my posses - sions lie.

STENNETT.
1227 *"Let me go over!"—Deut. 3: 25.*

ON Jordan's rugged banks I stand,
And cast a wishful eye
To Canaan's fair and happy land,
Where my possessions lie.

2 Oh, the transporting, rapturous scene,
That rises to my sight!
Sweet fields arrayed in living green,
And rivers of delight!

3 O'er all those wide extended plains
Shines one eternal day;
There God, the sun, for ever reigns,
And scatters night away.

4 No chilling winds, or poisonous breath,
Can reach that healthful shore;
Sickness and sorrow, pain and death,
Are felt and feared no more.

5 When shall I reach that happy place,
And be for ever blest?
When shall I see my Father's face,
And in his bosom rest?

6 Filled with delight, my raptured soul
Can here no longer stay;
Though Jordan's waves around me roll,
Fearless I'd launch away.

WATTS.
1228 *Jesus exalted.—Rev. 5: 6-10.*

BEHOLD the glories of the Lamb,
Amid his Father's throne;
Prepare new honors for his name,
And songs before unknown.

2 Let elders worship at his feet,
The church adore around,
With vials full of odors sweet,
And harps of sweeter sound.

3 Now to the Lamb that once was slain,
Be endless blessings paid!
Salvation, glory, joy remain
For ever on thy head!

4 Thou hast redeemed our souls with blood,
Hast set the prisoners free,
Hast made us kings and priests to God,
And we shall reign with thee.

WATTS.
1229 *"A building of God."—2 Cor. 5: 1.*

THERE is a house not made with hands,
Eternal, and on high;
And here my spirit waiting stands,
Till God shall bid it fly.

2 Shortly this prison of my clay
Must be dissolved and fall;
Then, O my soul, with joy obey
Thy heavenly Father's call.

3 We walk by faith of joys to come;
Faith lives upon his word;
But while the body is our home,
We're absent from the Lord.

4 'Tis pleasant to believe thy grace,
But we had rather see;
We would be absent from the flesh,
And present, Lord, with thee.

LOWRY. L. M.

1. Oh, for a sweet, in-spir-ing ray, To an-i-mate our fee-ble strains,

From the bright realms of end-less day— The bliss-ful realms where Je-sus reigns!

1230 *"The Lamb is the light."—Rev. 21:23.* STEELE.

Oh, for a sweet, inspiring ray,
To animate our feeble strains,
From the bright realms of endless day—
The blissful realms where Jesus reigns!

2 There, low before his glorious throne,
Adoring saints and angels fall;
And, with delightful worship, own
His smile their bliss, their heaven, their all.

3 Immortal glories crown his head,
While tuneful hallelujahs rise,
And love and joy, and triumph spread
Through all the assemblies of the skies.

4 He smiles,—and seraphs tune their songs
To boundless rapture, while they gaze:
Ten thousand thousand joyful tongues
Resound his everlasting praise.

5 There all the followers of the Lamb
Shall join at last the heavenly choir:
Oh, may the joy-inspiring theme
Awake our faith and warm desire!

1231 *"Eye hath not seen."—1 Cor. 2:9.* GIBBONS.

Now let our souls, on wings sublime,
Rise from the vanities of time,
Draw back the parting vail, and see
The glories of eternity.

2 Born by a new celestial birth,
Why should we grovel here on earth?
Why grasp at transitory toys,
So near to heaven's eternal joys?

3 Should aught beguile us on the road,
When we are walking back to God?
For strangers into life we come,
And dying is but going home.

4 Welcome, sweet hour of full discharge!
That sets our longing souls at large,
Unbinds our chains, breaks up our cell,
And gives us with our God to dwell.

5 To dwell with God—to feel his love,
Is the full heaven enjoyed above;
And the sweet expectation now
Is the young dawn of heaven below.

1232 *"They shall see his face."—Rev. 22:4.* ANON.

Lo! round the throne, a glorious band,
The saints in countless myriads stand:
Of every tongue redeemed of God,
Arrayed in garments washed in blood.

2 Through tribulation great they came;
They bore the cross, despised the shame;
But now from all their labors rest,
In God's eternal glory blest.

3 They see the Saviour face to face;
They sing the triumph of his grace;
And day and night, with ceaseless praise,
To him their loud hosannas raise.

4 Oh, may we tread the sacred road
That holy saints and martyrs trod;
Wage to the end the glorious strife,
And win, like them, a crown of life!

PARK STREET. L. M.

1. Hark! how the choral song of heaven Swells full of peace and joy a-bove; Hark! how they strike their golden harps, And raise the tuneful notes of love, And raise the tuneful notes of love.

1233 *The New Song.—Rev. 5: 9.* ANON.

HARK! how the choral song of heaven
  Swells full of peace and joy above;
Hark! how they strike their golden harps,
  And raise the tuneful notes of love.

2 No anxious care nor thrilling grief,
  No deep despair, nor gloomy woe
They feel, when high their lofty strains
  In noblest, sweetest concord flow.

3 When shall we join the heavenly host,
  Who sing Immanuel's praise on high,
And leave behind our doubts and fears,
  To swell the chorus of the sky?

4 Oh, come, thou rapture-bringing morn!
  And usher in the joyful day;
We long to see thy rising sun
  Drive all these clouds of grief away.

1234 *"A Rest."—Heb. 4: 9.* RAY PALMER.

LORD, thou wilt bring the joyful day!
  Beyond earth's weariness and pains,
Thou hast a mansion far away,
  Where for thine own a rest remains.

2 No sun there climbs the morning sky,
  There never falls the shade of night,
God and the Lamb, for ever nigh,
  O'er all shed everlasting light.

3 The bow of mercy spans the throne,
  Emblem of love and goodness there;
While notes to mortals all unknown,
  Float on the calm celestial air.

4 Around that throne bright legions stand,
  Redeemed by blood from sin and hell;
And shining forms, an angel band,
  The mighty chorus join to swell.

5 O Jesus, bring us to that rest,
  Where all the ransomed shall be found,
In thine eternal fullness blest,
  While ages roll their cycles round!

1235 *"Many mansions."—John 14: 2.* RAY PALMER.

THY Father's house!—thine own bright
    home!
  And thou hast there a place for me!
Though yet an exile here I roam,
  That distant home by faith I see.

2 I see its domes resplendent glow,
  Where beams of God's own glory fall;
And trees of life immortal grow,
  Whose fruits o'erhang the sapphire wall.

3 I know that thou, who on the tree
  Didst deign our mortal guilt to bear,
Wilt bring thine own to dwell with thee,
  And waitest to receive me there!

4 Thy love will there array my soul
  In thine own robe of spotless hue
And I shall gaze, while ages roll,
  On thee, with raptures ever new!

5 Oh, welcome day! when thou my feet
  Shalt bring the shining threshold o'er;
A Father's warm embrace to meet,
  And dwell at home for evermore!

WOODLAND. C. M.

1. There is an hour of peaceful rest, To mourning wanderers given; There is a joy for

souls distressed, A balm for ev - ery wounded breast: 'T is found a - bove—in heaven.

1236 *"No more death."—Rev.* 21 : 3, 4. TAPPAN.

THERE is an hour of peaceful rest,
　To mourning wanderers given;
There is a joy for souls distressed,
　A balm for every wounded breast:
　　'Tis found above—in heaven.

2 There is a home for weary souls,
　By sin and sorrow driven,—
When tossed on life's tempestuous shoals,
Where storms arise, and ocean rolls,
　And all is drear—but heaven.

3 There faith lifts up her cheerful eye
　To brighter prospects given;
And views the tempest passing by
The evening shadows quickly fly,
　And all serene—in heaven.

4 There fragrant flowers immortal bloom,
　And joys supreme are given;
There rays divine disperse the gloom;
Beyond the confines of the tomb
　Appears the dawn of heaven!

1237 *"A great multitude."—Rev.* 7:9. WATTS.

GIVE me the wings of faith, to rise
　Within the vail, and see
The saints above, how great their joys,
　How bright their glories be.

2 I ask them—whence their victory came?
　They, with united breath,
Ascribe their conquest to the Lamb,—
　Their triumph to his death.

3 They marked the footsteps he had trod;
　His zeal inspired their breast;
And following their incarnate God,
　Possess the promised rest.

4 Our glorious Leader claims our praise,
　For his own pattern given,—
While the long cloud of witnesses
　Show the same path to heaven.

1238 *"Far better."—Phil.* 1 : 23. WATTS.

FATHER! I long, I faint, to see
　The place of thine abode;
I'd leave thine earthly courts, and flee
　Up to thy seat, my God!

2 Here I behold thy distant face,
　And 't is a pleasing sight;
But, to abide in thine embrace
　Is infinite delight!

3 I'd part with all the joys of sense,
　To gaze upon thy throne;
Pleasure springs fresh for ever thence,
　Unspeakable, unknown.

4 There all the heavenly hosts are seen;
　In shining ranks they move;
And drink immortal vigor in,
　With wonder and with love.

5 Father! I long, I faint to see
　The place of thine abode;
I'd leave thine earthly courts to be
　For ever with my God!

NAUMANN. C. M.

1. There is an hour of hallowed peace, For those with cares oppressed, When sighs and sorrow-

ing shall cease, When sighs and sor - row-ing shall cease, And all be hushed to rest:—

1239   *"Sow in tears."—Ps.* 126: 5.   TAPPAN.

THERE is an hour of hallowed peace,
   For those with cares oppressed,
When sighs and sorrowing shall cease,
   And all be hushed to rest:—

2 'Tis then the soul is freed from fears
   And doubts, which here annoy;
Then they, who oft have sown in tears,
   Shall reap again in joy.

3 There is a home of sweet repose,
   Where storms assail no more;
The stream of endless pleasure flows,
   On that celestial shore.

4 There, purity with love appears,
   And bliss without alloy;
There, they, who oft have sown in tears,
   Shall reap again in joy.

1240   *"Things not seen."*—2 Cor. 4: 18.   STEELE.

OH, could our thoughts and wishes fly,
   Above these gloomy shades,
To those bright worlds, beyond the sky,
   Which sorrow ne'er invades!—

2 There, joys, unseen by mortal eyes
   Or reason's feeble ray,
In ever-blooming prospects rise,
   Unconscious of decay.

3 Lord! send a beam of light divine,
   To guide our upward aim;
With one reviving touch of thine,
   Our languid hearts inflame.

4 Oh, then, on faith's sublimest wing,
   Our ardent hope shall rise
To those bright scenes, where pleasures
   Immortal in the skies.   [spring

COVENTRY. C. M.

1. Oh, could our thoughts and wish - es fly, A - bove these gloom - y shades,

To those bright worlds be - yond the sky, Which sor - row ne'er in - vades!

RHINE. C. M.

1. O moth-er dear, Je-ru-sa-lem, When shall I come to thee? When shall my sor-rows have an end? Thy joys when shall I see? Thy joys when shall I see?

1241   *The New Jerusalem.—Rev. 21:10.*   DICKSON.

O MOTHER dear, Jerusalem,
  When shall I come to thee?
When shall my sorrows have an end?
  Thy joys when shall I see?

2 O happy harbor of God's saints!
  O sweet and pleasant soil!
In thee no sorrow can be found,
  Nor grief, nor care, nor toil.

3 No dimly cloud o'ershadows thee,
  Nor gloom, nor darksome night;
But every soul shines as the sun,
  For God himself gives light.

4 Thy walls are made of precious stone,
  Thy bulwarks diamond-square,
Thy gates are all of orient pearl—
  O God! if I were there!

1242   *Faith and the Future.*   BATHURST.

OH, for a faith that will not shrink
  Though pressed by every foe,
That will not tremble on the brink
  Of any earthly woe!—

2 That will not murmur nor complain
  Beneath the chastening rod,
But, in the hour of grief or pain,
  Will lean upon its God;—

3 A faith that shines more bright and clear
  When tempests rage without;
That, when in danger, knows no fear,
  In darkness, feels no doubt;—

4 Lord, give us such a faith as this,
  And then, whate'er may come,
We'll taste, ev'n here, the hallowed bliss
  Of an eternal home.

SHINING SHORE. P. M.

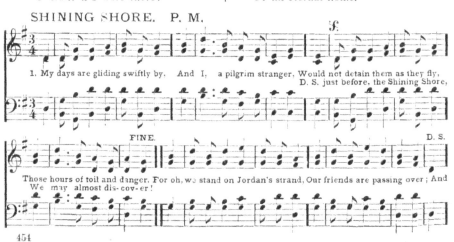

1. My days are gliding swiftly by. And I, a pilgrim stranger, Would not detain them as they fly,
D. S. just before, the Shining Shore,

FINE.   D. S.

Those hours of toil and danger. For oh, we stand on Jordan's strand, Our friends are passing over; And
We may almost dis-cov-er!

JOYFUL SOUND. C. M. D.

1 { Je - ru - sa - lem! my hap - py home! Name ev - er dear to me! }
  { When shall my la - bors have an end, [Omit.. } In

D. C. Where con - gre - ga - tions ne'er break up, [Omit..] And

FINE.   D. C.

joy, and peace, in thee? Oh, when, thou cit-y of my God, Shall I thy courts as - cend,
Sab - baths have no end.

1243   *The New Jerusalem.—Rev.* 7:15.   DICKSON.

JERUSALEM! my happy home!
  Name ever dear to me!
When shall my labors have an end,
  In joy, and peace, in thee?

2 Oh, when, thou city of my God,
  Shall I thy courts ascend,
Where congregations ne'er break up,
  And Sabbaths have no end?

3 There happier bowers than Eden's bloom,
  Nor sin nor sorrow know:
Blest seats! thro' rude and stormy scenes,
  I onward press to you.

4 Why should I shrink at pain and woe?
  Or feel, at death, dismay?
I've Canaan's goodly land in view,
  And realms of endless day.

5 Apostles, martyrs, prophets there,
  Around my Saviour stand;
And soon my friends in Christ below,
  Will join the glorious band.

6 Jerusalem! my happy home!
  My soul still pants for thee;
Then shall my labors have an end,
  When I thy joys shall see.

1244   *"Jordan's Strand."—Josh.* 1:11.   NELSON.

My days are gliding swiftly by,
  And I, a pilgrim stranger,
Would not detain them as they fly
  Those hours of toil and danger.
    For oh, we stand on Jordan's strand,
    Our friends are passing over;
  And just before, the Shining Shore
  We may almost discover!

2 We'll gird our loins, my brethren dear,
  Our heavenly home discerning;
Our absent Lord has left us word,
  Let every lamp be burning.—REF.

3 Should coming days be cold and dark,
  We need not cease our singing;
That perfect rest naught can molest,
  Where golden harps are ringing.—REF.

4 Let sorrow's rudest tempest blow,
  Each chord on earth to sever;
Our King says, Come, and there's our
    home,
  For ever, oh, for ever!
    For oh, we stand on Jordan's strand,
    Our friends are passing over;
  And just before, the Shining Shore
  We may almost discover!

VARINA. C. M. D.

While thro' this changing world we roam From in-fan-cy to age, Heaven is the Christian pilgrim's home, His rest at ev-ery stage. From earth his freed affections rise,

To fix on things a - bove, Where all his hope of glo - ry lies, Where all is perfect love.

1245   *"Our conversation."—Phil. 3: 20.*   MONTGOMERY.

WHILE thro' this changing world we roam
 From infancy to age,
Heaven is the Christian pilgrim's home,
 His rest at every stage.

2 From earth his freed affections rise,
 To fix on things above,
Where all his hope of glory lies,
 Where all is perfect love.

3 There, too, may we our treasure place—
 There let our hearts be found;
That still, where sin abounded, grace
 May more and more abound.

4 Henceforth, our conversation be
 With Christ before the throne;
Ere long we, eye to eye, shall see,
 And know as we are known.

1246   *The New Song.*   WATTS.

EARTH has engrossed my love too long;
 'Tis time I lift mine eyes
Upward, dear Father! to thy throne,
 And to my native skies.

2 There the blest man, my Saviour, sits;
 The God! how bright he shines!
And scatters infinite delights
 On all the happy minds.

3 Seraphs, with elevated strains,
 Circle the throne around;
And move, and charm the starry plains,
 With an immortal sound.

4 Jesus, the Lord, their harps employs;
 Jesus, my love, they sing;
Jesus, the life of both our joys,
 Sounds sweet from every string.

5 Now let me mount, and join their song,
 And be an angel too;
My heart! my hand! my ear! my tongue!
 Here's joyful work for you.

6 I would begin the music here,
 And so my soul should rise;—
Oh, for some heavenly notes to bear
 My spirit to the skies.

1247   *"Where is he?"—Job 14: 10.*   NEWTON.

IN vain our fancy strives to paint
 The moment after death,
The glories that surround a saint
 When yielding up his breath.

2 One gentle sigh the bondage breaks;
 We scarce can say—he's gone!
Before the willing spirit takes
 Its mansion near the throne.

3 Thus much, and 'tis enough to know,
 Saints are completely blest;
Have done with sin, and care, and woe,
 And with their Saviour rest.

4 On harps of gold they praise his name,
 And see him face to face;
Oh, let us catch the heavenly flame,
 And live in his embrace!

JORDAN. C. M. D.

1. {There is a land of pure de - light, Where saints im - mor - tal reign; } And
{In - fi - nite day ex - cludes the night, [*Omit* ....]}
pleasures ban - ish pain. 2. There ev - er - last - ing spring a - bides, And nev - er -
with'ring flowers; Death, like a nar - row sea, di - vides This heavenly land from ours.

1248 *"Go over this Jordan."—Josh.* 1: 2. WATTS.

THERE is a land of pure delight,
   Where saints immortal reign;
Infinite day excludes the night,
   And pleasures banish pain.

2 There everlasting spring abides,
   And never withering flowers;
Death, like a narrow sea, divides
   This heavenly land from ours.

3 Sweet fields beyond the swelling flood
   Stand dressed in living green;
So to the Jews old Canaan stood,
   While Jordan rolled between.

4 But timorous mortals start and shrink
   To cross this narrow sea;
And linger, shivering on the brink,
   And fear to launch away.

5 Oh, could we make our doubts remove,
   Those gloomy doubts that rise,
And see the Canaan that we love
   With unbeclouded eyes:—

6 Could we but climb where Moses stood,
   And view the landscape o'er,
Not Jordan's stream, nor death's cold flood,
   Should fright us from the shore.

1249 *"Hold fast."—Rev.* 3: 11. ALEXANDER.

THE roseate hues of early dawn,
   The brightness of the day,
The crimson of the sunset sky,
   How fast they fade away!

2 Oh, for the pearly gates of heaven!
   Oh, for the golden floor!
Oh, for the Sun of Righteousness,
   That setteth nevermore!

3 The highest hopes we cherish here,
   How soon they tire and faint!
How many a spot defiles the robe
   That wraps an earthly saint!

4 Oh, for a heart that never sins!
   Oh, for a soul washed white!
Oh, for a voice to praise our King,
   Nor weary day nor night!

5 Here faith is ours, and heavenly hope,
   And grace to lead us higher;
But there are perfectness and peace,
   Beyond our best desire.

6 Oh, by thy love and anguish, Lord,
   And by thy life laid down,
Grant that we fall not from thy grace,
   Nor fail to reach our crown!

BEULAH. 7. D.

1. Who are these in bright array, This in-nu-mer-a-ble throng, Round the al-tar night and day,
D. S. Wisdom, rich-es, to ob-tain,

FINE.　　　　　D.C.

Hymning one triumphant song?—"Worthy is the Lamb, once slain, Blessing, honor, glory, power,
New dominion ev-ery hour."

1250　　"*Who are these?*"—*Rev.* 7: 13.　　MONTGOMERY.

Who are these in bright array,
　This innumerable throng,
Round the altar night and day,
　Hymning one triumphant song?—
"Worthy is the Lamb, once slain,
　Blessing, honor, glory, power,
Wisdom, riches, to obtain,
　New dominion every hour."

2 These through fiery trials trod;
　These from great affliction came:
Now, before the throne of God,
　Sealed with his almighty name,

Clad in raiment pure and white,
　Victor-palms in every hand,
Through their dear Redeemer's might,
　More than conquerors they stand.

3 Hunger, thirst, disease unknown,
　On immortal fruits they feed;
Them the Lamb, amid the throne,
　Shall to living fountains lead:
Joy and gladness banish sighs;
　Perfect love dispel all fears;
And for ever from their eyes
　God shall wipe away the tears.

I'M A PILGRIM. P. M.

FINE.　　　　　D.C.

1. I'm a pilgrim, and I'm a stranger; I can tarry, I can tarry but a night! ⟩ Do not detain me, for I am going ⟩
D. C. I'm a pilgrim, &c.　　⟨ To where the fountains are ever flow- ⟩
(ing:

1251　　*A Pilgrim.*—*Heb.* 11: 13.　　ANON.

I'm a pilgrim, and I'm a stranger;
I can tarry, I can tarry but a night!
Do not detain me, for I am going
To where the fountains are ever flowing:
　I'm a pilgrim, etc.

2 There the glory is ever shining!　[there!
Oh, my longing heart, my longing heart is

Here in this country so dark and dreary,
I long have wandered forlorn and weary:
　I'm a pilgrim, etc.

3 There's the city to which I journey;
My Redeemer, my Redeemer is its light!
There is no sorrow, nor any sighing,
Nor any tears there, nor any dying!
　I'm a pilgrim, etc.

MT. BLANC. P. M.

1. We are on our journey home, Where Christ our Lord is gone; We shall meet around his throne,
When he makes his people one, In the new, In the new Je - ru - sa - lem.
In the new Je - ru - sa - lem.

1252 *"The holy city."—Rev.* **21 : 2.**

C. BEECHER.

2 We can see that distant home,
  Though clouds rise dark between;
Faith views the radiant dome,
And a lustre flashes keen
  From the new Jerusalem.

3 Oh, holy, heavenly home!
  Oh, rest eternal there!

When shall the exiles come,
Where they cease from earthly care,
  In the new Jerusalem!

4 Our hearts are breaking now
  Those mansions fair to see;
O Lord! thy heavens bow,
And raise us up with thee,
  To the new Jerusalem.

OAK. 6, 4.

1. I'm but a stranger here, Heaven is my home;
   Earth is a des - ert drear, Heaven is my home; Dan - ger and sor - row stand
Round me on ev - ery hand, Heaven is my Fa - ther-land, Heaven is my home.

1253 *Heaven is my Home.*

TAYLOR.

2 What though the tempests rage,
    Heaven is my home;
Short is my pilgrimage,
    Heaven is my home;
And time's wild, wintry blast,
Soon will be overpast,
I shall reach home at last,
    Heaven is my home.

3 Therefore I murmur not,
    Heaven is my home;
Whate'er my earthly lot,
    Heaven is my home;
And I shall surely stand,
There, at my Lord's right hand,
Heaven is my Father-land,
    Heaven is my home.

SHEBA. 6. D.

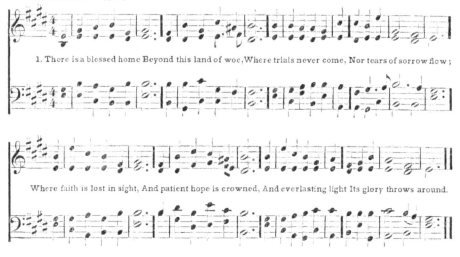

1. There is a blessed home Beyond this land of woe, Where trials never come, Nor tears of sorrow flow;

Where faith is lost in sight, And patient hope is crowned, And everlasting light Its glory throws around.

1254　　*"A blessed Home."*　　BAKER.

THERE is a blessèd home
　Beyond this land of woe,
Where trials never come,
　Nor tears of sorrow flow;
Where faith is lost in sight,
　And patient hope is crowned,
And everlasting light
　Its glory throws around.

2 There is a land of peace,
　Good angels know it well;
Glad songs that never cease
　Within its portals swell;
Around its glorious throne
　Ten thousand saints adore
Christ, with the Father, one,
　And Spirit, evermore.

3 Oh, joy all joys beyond,
　To see the Lamb who died,
And count each sacred wound
　In hands, and feet, and side;
To give to him the praise
　Of every triumph won,
And sing through endless days
　The great things he hath done.

4 Look up, ye saints of God,
　Nor fear to tread below
The path your Saviour trod
　Of daily toil and woe;

Wait but a little while
　In uncomplaining love;
His own most gracious smile
　Shall welcome you above.

1255　　Rev. **21: 23-27.**　　ANON.

THERE is no night in heaven;
　In that blest world above
Work brings no weariness,
　For work itself is love.
There is no grief in heaven;
　For life is one glad day,
And tears are of those things
　Which all have passed away.

2 There is no want in heaven;
　The Tree of Life supplies
Its twelve-fold fruitage still,
　Life's spring which never dries.
There is no sin in heaven;
　Behold that blessèd throng!
All holy is their robe,
　All holy is their song.

3 There is no death in heaven;
　For they who gain that shore
Win immortality,
　And they can die no more.
There is no death in heaven;
　But when the Christian dies,
The angels wait his soul,
　And waft it to the skies!

PARADISE. P. M.

1. O Par - a -dise, O Par - a -dise, Who doth not crave for rest. Who would not seek the

Where loy-al hearts and true

hap - py land, Where they that loved are blest? Where loy - - al hearts and true Stand

ev - er in the light, All rap-ture through and through, In God's most ho - ly sight.

1256   *"O Paradise."*   FABER.

O PARADISE, O Paradise,
Who doth not crave for rest,
Who would not seek the happy land
Where they that loved are blest?
Where loyal hearts and true
Stand ever in the light,
All rapture through and through,
In God's most holy sight.

2 O Paradise, O Paradise,
The world is growing old;
Who would not be at rest and free
Where love is never cold?
Where loyal hearts and true, etc.

3 O Paradise, O Paradise,
'Tis weary waiting here;
I long to be where Jesus is,
To feel, to see him near;
Where loyal hearts and true, etc.

4 O Paradise, O Paradise,
I want to sin no more,
I want to be as pure on earth
As on thy spotless shore;
Where loyal hearts and true, etc.

5 O Paradise, O Paradise,
I greatly long to see
The special place my dearest Lord
In love prepares for me;
Where loyal hearts and true, etc.

6 Lord Jesus, King of Paradise,
Oh, keep me in thy love,
And guide me to that happy land
Of perfect rest above;
Where loyal hearts and true,
Stand ever in the light,
All rapture through and through,
In God's most holy sight.

GUIDANCE. 8, 7. D.

Time, thou speedest on but slowly, Hours, how tardy is your pace! Ere with Him, the high and ho - ly, (Omit.................... I hold converse face to face.

Here is naught but care and mourning; Comes a joy, it will not stay; Fair-ly shines the

sun at dawn-ing, Night will soon o'er-cloud the day, Night will soon o'er-cloud the day.

1257 WINKWORTH. *Tr.*
"The King in his beauty."

TIME, thou speedest on but slowly,
  Hours, how tardy is your pace!
Ere with Him, the high and holy,
  I hold converse face to face.
Here is naught but care and mourning;
  Comes a joy, it will not stay;
Fairly shines the sun at dawning,
  Night will soon o'ercloud the day.

2 Onward then! not long I wander
  Ere my Saviour comes for me,
And with him abiding yonder,
  All his glory I shall see.
Oh, the music and the singing
  Of the host redeemed by love!
Oh, the hallelujahs ringing
  Through the halls of light above!

1258 CONDER.
The Consummation.—Rev. **7: 17.**

JESUS, blessed Mediator!
  Thou the airy path hast trod;
Thou the Judge, the Consummator!
  Shepherd of the fold of God!
Can I trust a fellow-being?
  Can I trust an angel's care?
O thou merciful All-seeing!
  Beam around my spirit there.

2 Blessèd fold! no foe can enter;
  And no friend departeth thence;
Jesus is their sun, their centre,
  And their shield Omnipotence!
Blessèd, for the Lamb shall feed them,
  All their tears shall wipe away,
To the living fountains lead them,
  Till fruition's perfect day.

3 Lo! it comes, that day of wonder!
  Louder chorals shake the skies:
Hades' gates are burst asunder;
  See! the new-clothed myriads rise!
Thought! repress thy weak endeavor;
  Here must reason prostrate fall;
Oh, the ineffable Forever!
  And the eternal All in All!

VESPER. 8, 7.

1. This is not my place of rest - ing,— Mine's a cit - y yet to come;

On - ward to it I am hast - ing— On to my e - ter - nal home.

1259 *"This is not your rest."* BONAR.

This is not my place of resting,—
  Mine's a city yet to come;
Onward to it I am hasting—
  On to my eternal home.

2 In it all is light and glory;
  O'er it shines a nightless day:
Every trace of sin's sad story,
  All the curse, hath passed away.

3 There the Lamb, our Shepherd, leads us
  By the streams of life along,—
On the freshest pastures feeds us,
  Turns our sighing into song.

4 Soon we pass this desert dreary,
  Soon we bid farewell to pain;
Never more are sad or weary,
  Never, never sin again!

1260 *"The sea of glass."—Rev.* 15: 2. WORDSWORTH.

Hark! the sound of holy voices
  Chanting at the crystal sea,
Hallelujah, hallelujah,
  Hallelujah, Lord, to thee!

2 Multitudes, which none can number,
  Like the stars in glory stand,
Clothed in white apparel, holding
  Palms of victory in their hands.

3 They have come from tribulation,
  And have washed their robes in blood,
Washed them in the blood of Jesus;
  Tried they were and firm they stood.

4 Mocked, imprisoned, stoned, tormented,
  Sawn asunder, slain with sword,
They have conquered death and Satan
  By the might of Christ the Lord.

5 Now they reign in heavenly glory,
  Now they walk in golden light,
Now they drink, as from a river,
  Holy bliss and infinite.

6 Love and peace they taste for ever,
  And all truth and knowledge see
In the Beatific Vision
  Of the blessèd Trinity!

1261 *Beyond the river.—Rev.* 22: 16. ANON.

Great Redeemer, Friend of sinners!
  Thou hast wondrous power to save;
Grant me grace, and still protect me,
  Over life's tempestuous wave.

2 May my soul, with sacred transport,
  View the dawn while yet afar;
And, until the sun arises,
  Lead me by the Morning Star.

3 See the happy spirits, waiting
  On the banks beyond the stream;
Sweet responses still repeating,—
  Jesus, Jesus is their theme.

4 Swiftly roll, ye lingering hours,
  Seraphs, lend your glittering wings;
Love absorbs my ransomed powers,
  Heavenly sounds around me ring!

EWING. 7, 6. D.

1. Je - ru - sa - lem, the gold - en, With milk and hon - ey blest! Be-neath thy con-tem-

pla - tion Sink heart and voice op - prest: I know not, oh, I know not What

so - cial joys are there, What ra - dian - cy of glo - ry, What light beyond com-pare.

1262 *The New Jerusalem.* NEALE. *Tr.*

JERUSALEM, the golden,
  With milk and honey blest!
Beneath thy contemplation
  Sink heart and voice oppressed:
I know not, oh, I know not
  What social joys are there,
What radiancy of glory,
  What light beyond compare.

2 They stand, those halls of Zion,
  All jubilant with song,
And bright with many an angel,
  And all the martyr throng;
The Prince is ever in them,
  The daylight is serene;
The pastures of the blessed
  Are decked in glorious sheen.

3 There is the throne of David;
  And there, from care released,
The song of them that triumph,
  The shout of them that feast:
And they who, with their Leader,
  Have conquered in the fight,
For ever and for ever
  Are clad in robes of white.

464

1263 *Short toil.*"—1 *John* 2: 17. NEALE. *Tr.*

BRIEF life is here our portion;
  Brief sorrow, short-lived care;
The life, that knows no ending,
  The tearless life, is there:
Oh, happy retribution!
  Short toil, eternal rest;
For mortals, and for sinners,
  A mansion with the blest!

2 And there is David's fountain,
  And life in fullest glow;
And there the light is golden,
  And milk and honey flow;
The light, that hath no evening,
  The health, that hath no sore,
The life, that hath no ending,
  But lasteth evermore.

3 There Jesus shall embrace us,
  There Jesus be embraced,—
That spirit's food and sunshine,
  Whence earthly love is chased:
Yes! God, my King and Portion,
  In fullness of his grace,
We then shall see for ever,
  And worship face to face.

MIRIAM. 7, 6. D.

1. Je - ru - sa - lem, the glorious! The glo - ry of th'e - lect,— O dear and future vis - ion

D. S. To thee my thoughts are kindled,

FINE.　　　　　　　　　　　　　　　D. S.

That ea - ger hearts ex - pect! Ev'n now by faith I see thee, Ev'n here thy walls discern ;
And strive, and pant, and yearn !

1264 *"A City."—Heb.* 11: 14.　NEALE. *Tr.*

JERUSALEM, the glorious!
　The glory of the elect,—
O dear and future vision
　That eager hearts expect!
Ev'n now by faith I see thee,
　Ev'n here thy walls discern;
To thee my thoughts are kindled,
　And strive, and pant, and yearn!

2 The Cross is all thy splendor,
　The Crucified, thy praise;
His laud and benediction
　Thy ransomed people raise;—
Jerusalem! exulting
　On that securest shore,
I hope thee, wish thee, sing thee,
　And love thee evermore!

3 O sweet and blessèd Country!
　Shall I e'er see thy face?
O sweet and blessèd Country!
　Shall I e'er win thy grace?—
Exult, O dust and ashes!
　The Lord shall be thy part;
His only, his for ever,
　Thou shalt be, and thou art!

1265 *"Lamps trimmed."—Matt.* 25: 6.　BORTHWICK.

REJOICE, rejoice, believers!
　And let your lights appear!

The shades of eve are thickening,
　And darker night is near;
The Bridegroom is advancing;
　Each hour he draws more nigh;
Up! watch and pray, nor slumber;
　At midnight comes the cry.

2 See that your lamps are burning,
　Your vessels filled with oil;
Wait calmly your deliverance
　From earthly pain and toil.
The watchers on the mountains
　Proclaim the Bridegroom near,
Go, meet him, as he cometh,
　With hallelujahs clear.

3 The saints, who here in patience
　Their cross and sufferings bore,
With him shall reign for ever,
　When sorrow is no more:
Around the throne of glory
　The Lamb shall they behold,
Adoring cast before him
　Their diadems of gold.

4 Our hope and expectation,
　O Jesus, now appear!
Arise, thou Sun so looked-for,
　O'er this benighted sphere!
With hearts and hands uplifted,
　We plead, O Lord, to see
The day of our redemption,
　And ever be with thee.

RUSSELL.   7, 6. D.

1. There is a land im - mor - tal, The beau-ti - ful of lands; Be - side its ancient por - tal A si - lent sen - try stands; He on - ly can un - do it, And o - pen wide the door; And mortals who pass through it, Are mortal nev - er - more.

MC KELLAR.

1266   *"They seek a country."—Heb. 2:14*

THERE is a land immortal,
  The beautiful of lands;
Beside its ancient portal
  A silent sentry stands;
He only can undo it,
  And open wide the door;
And mortals who pass through it,
  Are mortal nevermore.

2 Though dark and drear the passage
  That leadeth to the gate,
Yet grace comes with the message,
  To souls that watch and wait;
And at the time appointed
  A messenger comes down,
And leads the Lord's anointed
  From cross to glory's crown.

3 Their sighs are lost in singing,
  They're blessèd in their tears;
Their journey heavenward winging,
  They leave on earth their fears:
Death like an angel seemeth;
  "We welcome thee," they cry;
Their face with glory beameth—
  'Tis life for them to die!

MRS. BANCROFT.

1267   *Believers' outlook.*

OH, for the robes of whiteness!
  Oh, for the tearless eyes!
Oh, for the glorious brightness
  Of the unclouded skies!

2 Oh, for the no more weeping
  Within the land of love,
The endless joy of keeping
  The bridal feast above!

3 Oh, for the bliss of dying,
  My risen Lord to meet!
Oh, for the rest of lying
  For ever at his feet!

4 Oh, for the hour of seeing
  My Saviour face to face,
The hope of ever being
  In that sweet meeting-place!

5 Jesus, thou King of glory,
  I soon shall dwell with thee;
I soon shall sing the story
  Of thy great love to me.

6 Meanwhile my thoughts shall enter,
  Ev'n now, before thy throne,
That all my love may centre
  On thee, and thee alone.

BERNARD. 7, 6. D.

1. For thee, O dear, dear Coun-try! Mine eyes their vi - gils keep; For ve - ry love, be -

hold - ing Thy hap-py name, they weep: The men-tion of thy glo - ry Is

unc-tion to the breast, And med - i-cine in sick - ness, And love, and life, and rest.

1268   *"They seek a country."*   NEALE. *Tr.*

For thee, O dear, dear Country,
　Mine eyes their vigils keep;
For very love, beholding
　Thy happy name, they weep:
The mention of thy glory
　Is unction to the breast,
And medicine in sickness,
　And love, and life, and rest.

2 Thou hast no shore, fair ocean!
　Thou hast no time, bright day!
Dear fountain of refreshment
　To pilgrims far away!
Upon the Rock of Ages
　They raise thy holy tower;
Thine is the victor's laurel,
　And thine the golden dower.

3 With jasper glow thy bulwarks,
　Thy streets with emeralds blaze;
The sardius and the topaz
　Unite in thee their rays;
Thine ageless walls are bonded
　With amethyst unpriced;
The saints build up its fabric,
　The corner-stone is Christ.

4 O sweet and blessèd Country,
　The home of God's elect!
O sweet and blessèd Country,
　That eager hearts expect!
Jesus, in mercy bring us,
　To that dear land of rest;
Who art, with God the Father,
　And Spirit, ever blest.

1269   *"No more sea."*   BONAR.

No seas again shall sever,
　No desert intervene;
No deep sad-flowing river
　Shall roll its tide between:
Love and unsevered union
　Of soul with those we love,
Nearness and glad communion,
　Shall be our joy above.

2 No dread of wasting sickness,
　No thought of ache or pain,
No fretting hours of weakness,
　Shall mar our peace again:
No death our homes o'ershading,
　Shall e'er our harps unstring;
For all is life unfading
　In presence of our King!

TULLY. 7, 6. D.

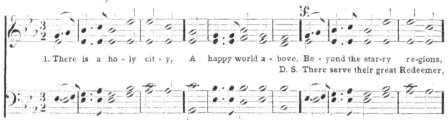

1. There is a ho - ly cit - y, A happy world a - bove, Be - yond the star-ry re - gions,
D. S. There serve their great Redeemer,

FINE.   D. S.

Built by the God of love; An ev - er-last - ing tem - ple— And saints arrayed in white,
And dwell with him in light.

1270 *"He hath prepared a city."* ANON.

THERE is a holy city,
A happy world above,
Beyond the starry regions,
Built by the God of love;
An everlasting temple—
And saints arrayed in white,
There serve their great Redeemer,
And dwell with him in light.

2 The meanest child of glory
Outshines the radiant sun;
But who can speak the splendor
Of that eternal throne
Where Jesus sits exalted,
In god-like majesty?
The elders fall before him,
The angels bend the knee.

3 The hosts of saints around him
Proclaim his work of grace;
The patriarchs and prophets,
And all the godly race,
Who speak of fiery trials
And tortures on their way—
They came from tribulation
To everlasting day.

4 And what shall be my journey,
How long my stay below,
Or what shall be my trials,
Are not for me to know;

In every day of trouble,
I'll raise my thoughts on high;
I'll think of the bright temple,
And crowns above the sky.

1271 *The New Paradise.* DAVIS.

O PARADISE eternal!
What bliss to enter thee,
And, once within thy portals,
Secure for ever be!
In thee no sin nor sorrow,
No pain nor death, is known;
But pure glad life, enduring
As heaven's benignant throne.

2 There all around shall love us,
And we return their love;
One band of happy spirits,
One family above:
There God shall be our portion,
And we his jewels be;
And, gracing his bright mansions,
His smile reflect and see.

3 So songs shall rise for ever,
While all creation fair,
Still more and more revealéd,
Shall wake fresh praises there:
O Paradise eternal!
What joys in thee are known!
O God of mercy! guide us,
Till all be felt our own.

IMMANUEL'S LAND. 7, 6. D.

1. The sands of time are sinking, The dawn of heaven breaks, The summer morn I've sighed for, The fair sweet morn awakes : Dark, dark hath been the midnight, But day-spring is at hand, And glory, glory dwelleth In Immanuel's land, And glory, glory dwelleth In Immanuel's land.

1272   *"Immanuel's Land."*   MRS. COUSIN.

THE sands of time are sinking,
  The dawn of heaven breaks,
The summer morn I've sighed for,
  The fair sweet morn awakes:
Dark, dark hath been the midnight,
  But day-spring is at hand,
And glory, glory dwelleth
  In Immanuel's land.

2 Oh, Christ, he is the fountain,
  The deep sweet well of love;
The streams of earth I've tasted,
  More deep I'll drink above.
There to an ocean fullness
  His mercy doth expand,
And glory, glory dwelleth
  In Immanuel's land.

3 With mercy and with judgment,
  My web of time he wove,
And aye the dews of sorrow
  Were lustered with his love.
I'll bless the hand that guided,
  I'll bless the heart that planned,
When throned where glory dwelleth,
  In Immanuel's land.

1273   *"He is mine, and I am his."*   MRS. COUSIN.

OH, I am my Belovéd's,
  And my Belovéd's mine;
He brings a poor vile sinner
  Into his "house of wine."
I stand upon his merit;
  I know no other stand,
Not ev'n where glory dwelleth,
  In Immanuel's land.

2 I've wrestled on towards heaven,
  'Gainst storm, and wind, and tide,
Now, like a weary traveler
  That leaneth on his guide,
Amid the shades of evening,
  While sinks life's lingering sand,
I hail the glory dawning
  From Immanuel's land.

3 The bride eyes not her garment,
  But her dear bridegroom's face;
I will not gaze at glory,
  But on my King of Grace—
Not at the crown he gifteth,
  But on his piercéd hand;—
The Lamb is all the glory
  Of Immanuel's land.

REST FOR THE WEARY. P. M.

1. In the Christian's home in glory There remains a land of rest, There my Saviour's gone be-fore me, To ful-fill my soul's re-quest.

CHORUS.

There is rest for the wea-ry, There is
On the oth-er side of Jor-dan, In the

rest for the wea-ry, There is rest for the wea-ry, There is rest for you!
sweet fields of E-den, Where the tree of life is blooming, There is rest for you!

1274   *"There remaineth a rest."*   HUNTER.

2 He is fitting up my mansion,
  Which eternally shall stand;
For my stay shall not be transient
  In that holy, happy land.—Cho.

3 Death itself shall then be vanquished,
  And his sting shall be withdrawn;

Shout for gladness, O ye ransomed!
  Hail with joy the rising morn.—Cho.

4 Sing, oh, sing, ye heirs of glory!
  Shout your triumphs as you go;
Zion's gates will open for you,
  You shall find an entrance through.—
                        Cho.

BEYOND. (Chant.) HYMN 1276.

Home

Home

CHRIST CHURCH. H. M.

1. Je - ru - sa - lem on high My song and cit - y is, My home when-e'er I die,

REFRAIN.

The centre of my bliss: Oh, happy place! When shall I be, My God, with thee, To see thy face?

1275   *The New Jerusalem.*   CROSSMAN.

JERUSALEM on high
 My song and city is,
 My home whene'er I die,
 The centre of my bliss:
  Oh, happy place!
  When shall I be,
  My God, with thee,
  To see thy face?

2 There dwells my Lord, my King,
 Judged here unfit to live!
 There angels to him sing,
 And lowly homage give:—REF.

3 The Patriarchs of old
 There from their travels cease;

The Prophets there behold
 Their longed-for Prince of Peace:—REF.

4 The Lamb's Apostles there
 I might with joy behold,
 The harpers I might hear
 Harping on harps of gold.—REF.

5 The bleeding Martyrs, they
 Within these courts are found,
 All clothed in pure array,
 Their scars with glory crowned:—REF.

6 Ah me! ah me! that I
 In Kedar's tents here stay:
 No place like that on high;
 Lord, thither guide my way:—REF.

1276   *"Lord, tarry not."*   BONAR.

BEYOND the smiling and the weeping |
 I shall be soon; ||
Beyond the waking and the sleeping, |
Beyond the sowing and the reaping, |
 I shall be soon. ||
Love, rest and home! Sweet home!
 Lord! tarry not, but come.

2 Beyond the blooming and the fading |
 I shall be soon; ||
Beyond the shining and the shading, |
Beyond the hoping and the dreading, |
 I shall be soon; ||
Love, rest and home! Sweet home!
 Lord! tarry not, but come.

3 Beyond the parting and the meeting |
 I shall be soon; ||
Beyond the farewell and the greeting, |
Beyond the pulse's fever beating, |
 I shall be soon; ||
Love, rest and home! Sweet home!
 Lord! tarry not, but come.

4 Beyond the frost-chain and the fever |
 I shall be soon; ||
Beyond the rock-waste and the river, |
Beyond the ever and the never, |
 I shall be soon. ||
Love, rest and home! Sweet home!
 Lord! tarry not, but come.

471

BENEVENTO. 7. D.

1. While, with cease-less course, the sun Hast-ed through the form-er year,

Man-y souls their race have run, Nev-er more to meet us here:
D. S. We a lit-tle long-er wait, But how lit-tle none can know.

Fixed in an e-ter-nal state, They have done with all be-low;

NEWTON.

1277   *New Year.*

WHILE, with ceaseless course, the sun
Hasted through the former year,
Many souls their race have run,
Nevermore to meet us here:
Fixed in an eternal state,
They have done with all below;
We a little longer wait;
But how little none can know.

2 As the wingèd arrow flies
Speedily the mark to find;
As the lightning from the skies
Darts, and leaves no trace behind,—
Swiftly thus our fleeting days
Bear us down life's rapid stream;
Upward, Lord, our spirits raise,
All below is but a dream.

3 Thanks for mercies past receive;
Pardon of our sins renew;
Teach us henceforth how to live,
With eternity in view:
Bless thy word to old and young;
Fill us with a Saviour's love;
When our life's short race is run,
May we dwell with thee above.

472

RAY PALMER.

1278   *Close of the Year.*

THOU who roll'st the year around,
Crowned with mercies large and free,
Rich thy gifts to us abound,
Warm our praise shall rise to thee.

2 Kindly to our worship bow,
While our grateful thanks we tell,
That, sustained by thee, we now
Bid the parting year—farewell!

3 All its numbered days are sped,
All its busy scenes are o'er,
All its joys for ever fled,
All its sorrows felt no more.

4 Mingled with the eternal past,
Its remembrance shall decay;
Yet to be revived at last
At the solemn judgment-day.

5 All our follies, Lord, forgive!
Cleanse us from each guilty stain;
Let thy grace within us live,
That we spend not years in vain.

6 Then, when life's last eve shall come,
Happy spirits, may we fly
To our everlasting home,
To our Father's house on high!

ST. GEORGE. 7. D.

1. Come, ye thankful peo-ple, come, Raise the song of Har-vest Home! All is safe-ly gath-ered in, Ere the win-ter storms be-gin: God our Mak-er doth pro-vide For our wants to be sup-plied: Come to God's own temple, come, Raise the song of Harvest Home!

1279 *Song for Harvest.* ALFORD.

COME, ye thankful people, come,
Raise the song of Harvest Home!
All is safely gathered in,
Ere the winter storms begin:
God our Maker doth provide
For our wants to be supplied:
Come to God's own temple, come,
Raise the song of Harvest Home!

2 We ourselves are God's own field,
Fruit unto his praise to yield:
Wheat and tares together sown,
Unto joy or sorrow grown:
First the blade, and then the ear,
Then the full corn shall appear:
Grant, O Harvest-Lord, that we
Wholesome grain and pure may be!

3 For the Lord our God shall come,
And shall take his harvest home:
From his field shall in that day
All offences purge away:
Give his angels charge at last
In the fire the tares to cast:
But the fruitful ears to store
In his garner evermore.

4 Then, thou Church Triumphant, come,
Raise the song of Harvest Home!
All are safely gathered in,
Free from sorrow, free from sin:
There, for ever purified,
In God's garner to abide:
Come, ten thousand angels, come,
Raise the glorious Harvest Home!

1280 *General Thanksgiving.* STRONG.

SWELL the anthem, raise the song;
Praises to our God belong;
Saints and angels join to sing
Praises to the heavenly King.

2 Blessings from his liberal hand
Flow around this happy land:
Kept by him, no foes annoy;
Peace and freedom we enjoy.

3 Here, beneath a virtuous sway
May we cheerfully obey;
Never feel oppression's rod,
Ever own and worship God.

4 Hark! the voice of nature sings
Praises to the King of kings;
Let us join the choral song,
And the grateful notes prolong.

473

GLASGOW. C. M.

1. Lord! while for all man-kind we pray, Of ev - ery clime and coast,

Oh, hear us for our na - tive land, The land we love the most.

1281   *National.*   WREFORD.

Lord! while for all mankind we pray,
  Of every clime and coast,
Oh, hear us for our native land,
  The land we love the most.

2 Oh, guard our shore from every foe,
  With peace our borders bless,
With prosperous times our cities crown,
  Our fields with plenteousness.

3 Unite us in the sacred love
  Of knowledge, truth, and thee:
And let our hills and valleys shout
  The songs of liberty.

4 Here may religion, pure and mild,
  Smile on our Sabbath hours;
And piety and virtue bless
  The home of us and ours.

5 Lord of the nations, thus to thee
  Our country we commend;
Be thou her refuge and her trust,
  Her everlasting friend.

1282   *A Marriage Hymn.*   BERRIDGE.

Since Jesus freely did appear
  To grace a marriage feast,
Dear Lord, we ask thy presence here,
  To make a wedding guest.

2 Upon the bridal pair look down,
  Who now have plighted hands;
Their union with thy favor crown,
  And bless the nuptial bands.

3 Oh, may each soul assembled here,
  Be married, Lord, to thee!
Clad in thy robes, made white and fair,
  To spend eternity!

1283   *National Fast.*   STEELE.

See, gracious God, before thy throne,
  Thy mourning people bend!
'Tis on thy sovereign grace alone,
  Our humble hopes depend.

2 Alarming judgments from thy hand,
  Thy dreadful power display;
Yet mercy spares this guilty land,
  And yet we live to pray.

3 Oh, bid us turn, almighty Lord,
  By thy resistless grace;
Then shall our hearts obey thy word,
  And humbly seek thy face.

1284   *Prayer for Seamen.*   BACON.

We come, O Lord, before thy throne,
  And, with united plea,
We meet and pray for those who roam
  Far off upon the sea.

2 Oh, may the Holy Spirit bow
  The sailor's heart to thee,
Till tears of deep repentance flow,
  Like rain-drops in the sea!

3 Then may a Saviour's dying love
  Pour peace into his breast,
And waft him to the port above
  Of everlasting rest.

NEW YORK TUNE. C. M.

1. Our Fa - ther! through the com - ing year We know not what shall be;

But we would leave with - out a fear Its or - dering all to thee.

1285 *New Year.* ANON.

Our Father! through the coming year
We know not what shall be;
But we would leave without a fear
Its ordering all to thee.

2 It may be we shall toil in vain
For what the world holds fair;
And all the good we thought to gain,
Deceive and prove but care.

3 It may be it shall darkly blend
Our love with anxious fears,
And snatch away the valued friend,
The tried of many years.

4 It may be it shall bring us days
And nights of lingering pain;
And bid us take a farewell gaze
Of these loved haunts of men.

5 But calmly, Lord, on thee we rest;
No fears our trust shall move;
Thou knowest what for each is best,
And thou art Perfect Love.

1286 *Close of the Year.* WATTS.

Thee we adore, eternal Name!
And humbly own to thee
How feeble is our mortal frame,
What dying worms are we!

2 The year rolls round, and steals away
The breath that first it gave;
Whate'er we do, whate'er we be,
We're traveling to the grave.

3 Great God! on what a slender thread
Hang everlasting things!
The eternal state of all the dead
Upon life's feeble strings!

4 Infinite joy, or endless woe,
Attends on every breath;
And yet, how unconcerned we go
Upon the brink of death!

5 Waken, O Lord, our drowsy sense,
To walk this dangerous road!
And if our souls are hurried hence,
May they be found with God.

1287 *Close of the Year.* DODDRIDGE.

Awake, ye saints! and raise your eyes,
And raise your voices high:
Awake, and praise that sovereign love,
That shows salvation nigh.

2 On all the wings of time it flies,
Each moment brings it near:
Then welcome each declining day,
Welcome each closing year.

3 Not many years their rounds shall run,
Nor many mornings rise,
Ere all its glories stand revealed
To our admiring eyes.

4 Ye wheels of nature! speed your course;
Ye mortal powers! decay;
Fast as ye bring the night of death,
Ye bring eternal day.

NEW YEAR'S HYMN. 11, 5.

1. Come, let us a-new our jour-ney pur-sue, Roll round with the year, And nev-er stand still till the Mas-ter ap-pear. 2. His a-dor-a-ble will let us glad-ly ful-fill, And our tal-ents im-prove, By the pa-tience of hope and the la-bor of love.

1288 *New Year's Hymn.* C. WESLEY.

3 Our life is a dream; our time as a stream
    Glides swiftly away,
And the fugitive moment refuses to stay.

4 The arrow is flown, the moment is gone;
    The millennial year
Rushes on to our view, and eternity's here.

5 Oh, that each in the day of his coming
    may say,

"I have fought my way through;
I have finished the work thou didst give
    me to do."

6 Oh, that each from his Lord may receive
    the glad word,
    "Well and faithfully done!
Enter into my joy, and sit down on my
    throne."

AMERICA. 6, 4.

1. My coun-try! 'tis of thee, Sweet land of lib-er-ty, Of thee I sing: Land where my fa-thers died! Land of the Pilgrims' pride! From ev-ery mountain side Let freedom ring!

AUSTRIA. 8, 7. D.

1 { Blest be thou, O God of Israel, Thou, our Father, and our Lord! }
  { Blest thy majes-ty for-ev-er! Ev-er be thy name a-dored. } 2. Thine, O Lord are power and great. [ness,

Glo-ry, victory, are thine own ; All is thine in earth and heaven, Over all thy boundless throne.

1289　　1 *Chron.* 29:10-13.　ONDERDONK.

Blest be thou, O God of Israel,
　Thou, our Father, and our Lord!
Blest thy majesty for ever!
　Ever be thy name adored.

2 Thine, O Lord, are power and greatness,
　Glory, victory, are thine own;
All is thine in earth and heaven,
　Over all thy boundless throne.

3 Riches come of thee, and honor,
　Power and might to thee belong;
Thine it is to make us prosper,
　Only thine to make us strong.

4 Lord, to thee, thou God of mercy,
　Hymns of gratitude we raise;
To thy name, for ever glorious,
　Ever we address our praise!

1290　　　*Public Fast.*　COTTERILL.

Dread Jehovah! God of nations!
　From thy temple in the skies,
Hear thy people's supplications,
　Now for their deliverance rise;—
Lo! with deep contrition turning,
　In thy holy place we bend;
Hear us, fasting, praying, mourning;
　Hear us, spare us, and defend.

2 Though our sins, our hearts confounding,
　Long and loud for vengeance call,
Thou hast mercy more abounding,
　Jesus' blood can cleanse them all;
Let that mercy vail transgression,
　Let that blood our guilt efface;
Save thy people from oppression,
　Save from spoil thy holy place.

1291　　*National Song.*　S. F. SMITH.

My country! 'tis of thee,
　Sweet land of liberty,
　　Of thee I sing;
Land where my fathers died!
Land of the Pilgrims' pride!
From every mountain side
　　Let freedom ring!

2 My native country, thee—
　Land of the noble free—
　　Thy name—I love;
I love thy rocks and rills,
Thy woods and templed hills:
My heart with rapture thrills
　　Like that above.

3 Let music swell the breeze,
　And ring from all the trees
　　Sweet freedom's song:
Let mortal tongues awake;
Let all that breathe partake;
Let rocks their silence break,—
　　The sound prolong.

4 Our fathers' God! to thee,
　Author of liberty,
　　To thee we sing:
Long may our land be bright
With freedom's holy light;
Protect us by thy might,
　　Great God, our King!

DUKE STREET. L. M.

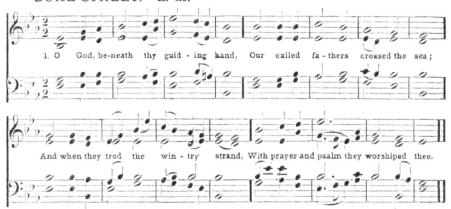

1. O God, be-neath thy guid-ing hand, Our exiled fa-thers crossed the sea;

And when they trod the win-try strand, With prayer and psalm they worshiped thee.

1292   *Forefathers' Day.*   BACON.

O God, beneath thy guiding hand,
  Our exiled fathers crossed the sea,
And when they trod the wintry strand,
  With prayer and psalm the worshiped
    thee.

2 Thou heardst, well pleased, the song, the
    prayer—
Thy blessing came; and still its power
Shall onward through all ages bear
  The memory of that holy hour.

3 What change! through pathless wilds no
    more
  The fierce and naked savage roams;
Sweet praise, along the cultured shore,
  Breaks from ten thousand happy homes.

4 Laws, freedom, truth, and faith in God
  Came with those exiles o'er the waves,
And where their pilgrim feet have trod,
  The God they trusted guards their graves.

5 And here thy name, O God of love,
  Their children's children shall adore,
Till these eternal hills remove,
  And spring adorns the earth no more.

1293   *The New Year.*   DODDRIDGE.

Great God! we sing that mighty hand
By which supported still we stand;
The opening year thy mercy shows;
Let mercy crown it till it close.

2 By day, by night, at home, abroad,
Still we are guarded by our God;
478

By his incessant bounty fed,
By his unerring counsel led.

3 With grateful hearts the past we own;
The future, all to us unknown,
We to thy guardian care commit,
And peaceful leave before thy feet.

4 In scenes exalted or depressed,
Be thou our joy, and thou our rest;
Thy goodness all our hopes shall raise,
Adored through all our changing days.

5 When death shall interrupt our songs,
And seal in silence mortal tongues,
Our Helper, God, in whom we trust,
In better worlds our souls shall boast.

1294   *The New Year.*   DODDRIDGE.

Our Helper, God! we bless thy name,
Whose love for ever is the same;
The tokens of thy gracious care
Open, and crown, and close the year.

2 Amid ten thousand snares we stand,
Supported by thy guardian hand;
And see, when we review our ways,
Ten thousand monuments of praise.

3 Thus far thine arm has led us on;
Thus far we make thy mercy known;
And while we tread this desert land,
New mercies shall new songs demand.

4 Our grateful souls, on Jordan's shore,
Shall raise one sacred pillar more;
Then bear in thy bright courts above,
Inscriptions of immortal love.

DOXOLOGIES.

1 L. M.

PRAISE God, from whom all blessings flow!
Praise him, all creatures here below!
Praise him above, ye heavenly host!
Praise Father, Son, and Holy Ghost!

2 L. M. 6l.

To God the Father, God the Son,
And God the Spirit, three in one,
Be honor, praise, and glory given,
By all on earth, and all in heaven.
As was through ages heretofore,
Is now, and shall be evermore.

3 L. M. D.

ETERNAL Father, throned above,
Thou fountain of redeeming love!
Eternal Word! who left thy throne
For man's rebellion to atone;
Eternal Spirit, who dost give
That grace whereby our spirits live:
Thou God of our salvation, be
Eternal praises paid to thee!

4 C. M.

To Father, Son, and Holy Ghost,
One God whom we adore,
Be glory as it was, is now,
And shall be evermore.

5 C. M.

LET God the Father, and the Son,
And Spirit, be adored,
Where there are works to make him known,
Or saints to love the Lord.

6 C. M. D.

THE God of mercy be adored,
Who calls our souls from death,
Who saves by his redeeming word
And new-creating breath;
To praise the Father and the Son
And Spirit all-divine,—
The one in three, and three in one—
Let saints and angels join.

7 S. M.

YE angels round the throne,
And saints that dwell below,
Worship the Father, praise the Son,
And bless the Spirit, too.

8 S. M.

THE Father and the Son
And Spirit we adore;
We praise, we bless, we worship thee,
Both now and evermore!

9 H. M.

To God the Father's throne
Your highest honors raise;
Glory to God the Son;
To God, the Spirit, praise;
With all our powers, Eternal King,
Thy name we sing, while faith adores.

10 7.

SING we to our God above
Praise eternal as his love;
Praise him, all ye heavenly host—
Father, Son, and Holy Ghost.

11 7. 6l.

PRAISE the name of God most high,
Praise him, all below the sky,
Praise him, all ye heavenly host,
Father, Son, and Holy Ghost;
As through countless ages past,
Evermore his praise shall last.

12 7. D.

PRAISE our glorious King and Lord,
Angels waiting on his word,
Saints that walk with him in white,
Pilgrims walking in his light:
Glory to the Eternal One,
Glory to his only Son,
Glory to the Spirit be
Now, and through eternity.

479

13   C. P. M.

To Father, Son, and Holy Ghost,
Be praise amid the heavenly host,
  And in the church below;
From whom all creatures draw their breath,
By whom redemption blessed the earth,
  From whom all comforts flow.

14   8, 7.

Praise the Father, earth and heaven,
  Praise the Son, the Spirit praise,
As it was, and is, be given
  Glory through eternal days.

15   8, 7. 6l.

Praise and honor to the Father,
  Praise and honor to the Son,
Praise and honor to the Spirit,
  Ever Three and ever One,
One in might, and one in glory,
  While eternal ages run.

16   8, 7. D.

Praise the God of all creation;
  Praise the Father's boundless love:
Praise the Lamb, our expiation,
  Priest and King enthroned above:
Praise the Fountain of salvation,
  Him by whom our spirits live:
Undivided adoration
  To the one Jehovah give.

17   8, 7, 4.

Glory be to God the Father,
  Glory be to God the Son,
Glory be to God the Spirit,
  Glory to the Three in One;
    Hallelujah!
God, the Lord is God alone.

18   8, 7, 4.

Great Jehovah! we adore thee,
  God the Father, God the Son,
God the Spirit, joined in glory
  On the same eternal throne;
    Endless praises
  To Jehovah, Three in One.

19   10.

To Father, Son, and Spirit, ever blest,
Eternal praise and worship be addressed;
From age to age, ye saints, his name adore,
And spread his fame, till time shall be no
  more.

20   6, D.

To Father and to Son,
  And, Holy Ghost! to thee,
Eternal Three in One!
  Eternal glory be;
As hath been, and is now,
  And shall be overmore:
Before thy throne we bow,
  And thee, our God, adore.

21   7, 6. Iambic.

To thee be praise for ever,
  Thou glorious King of kings!
Thy wondrous love and favor
  Each ransomed spirit sings:
We'll celebrate thy glory
  With all thy saints above,
And shout the joyful story
  Of thy redeeming love.

22   7, 6. Trochaic.

Father, Son, and Holy Ghost,
  One God, whom we adore,
Join we with the heavenly host
  To praise thee evermore:
Live, by heaven and earth adored,
  Three in One, and One in Three,
Holy, holy, holy Lord,
  All glory be to thee!

23   11, or 5, 6.

O Father Almighty, to thee be addressed,
With Christ and the Spirit, one God ever blest,
All glory and worship, from earth and from
  heaven,
As was, and is now, and shall ever be given.

24   6, 4.

To God—the Father, Son,
  And Spirit—Three in One,
    All praise be given!
Crown him in every song;
To him your hearts belong;
Let all his praise prolong—
  On earth, in heaven.

CHANTS AND OCCASIONAL PIECES.

TE DEUM LAUDAMUS.

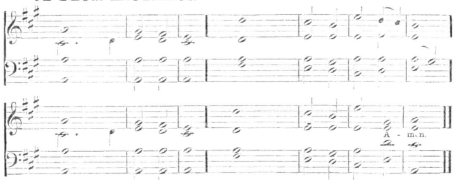

I

1 WE praise thee, | O — | God; ‖ we acknowledge | thee to | be the | Lord. ‖
 All the earth doth | worship | thee, ‖ the Father | ever- | last- — | ing. ‖

2 To thee all angels | cry a- | loud, ‖ the heavens, and | all the | powers there- | in.
 To thee cherubim and seraphim, con- | tinually · · do | cry, ‖ Holy, holy, holy, Lord |
 God of | Saba- | oth; ‖

3 Heaven and earth are full of the majesty | of thy | glory. ‖ The glorious company
 of the apostles praise thee. The goodly fellowship of the | prophets | praise — |
 thee. ‖
 The noble army of martyrs | praise — | thee. ‖ The holy church throughout all the |
 world · · doth ac- | knowledge | thee, ‖

4 The Father, of an | infi- · nite | majesty; ‖ thine adorable, | true and | only | Son; ‖
 Also the Holy | Ghost, the | Comforter. ‖ Thou art the King of glory, O Christ,
 thou art the everlasting | Son · · of the | Fa- — | ther. ‖

5 When thou tookest upon thee to de- | liver | man, ‖ thou didst humble thyself to
 be | born — | of a | virgin. ‖
 When thou hadst overcome the | sharpness · · of | death, ‖ thou didst open the king-
 dom of | heaven · · to | all be- | lievers. ‖

6 Thou sittest at the right hand of God, in the | glory · · of the | Father. ‖ We believe
 that thou shalt | come to | be our | judge.
 We therefore pray thee, | help thy | servants, ‖ whom thou hast redeemed | with
 thy | precious | blood. ‖

7 Make them to be numbered | with thy | saints, ‖ in | glory | ever- | lasting. ‖
 O Lord, save thy people, and | bless thine | heritage; ‖ govern them and | lift them |
 up for- | ever. ‖

8 Day by day we | magni- · · fy | thee; ‖ and we worship thy name ever, | world with- |
 out — | end. ‖
 Vouchsafe, O Lord, to keep us this | day with-out | sin; ‖ O Lord, have mercy
 upon us, have | mer-cy up- | on — | us. ‖

9 O Lord, let thy mercy | be up- | on us, ‖ as our | trust — | is in | thee. ‖
 O Lord, in | thee · · have I | trusted; ‖ let me | never | be con- | founded. ‖ A- |
 men. ‖

481

GLORIA IN EXCELSIS.

2 PART I.

GLORY be to | God on | high, || and on earth | peace, good- | will··towards | men. ||
We praise thee, we bless thee, we | worship | thee, || we glorify thee, we give thanks
to thee | for thy | great — | glory. ||

PART II.

O Lord God, | heavenly | King, || God the | Father | Al-—— | mighty! ||
O Lord, the only-begotten Son | Jesus | Christ, ||
O Lord God, Lamb of God, | Son··of the | Fa-—— | ther, ||

PART III.

That takest away the | sins··of the | world, || have mercy up- | on — | us. ||
Thou that takest away the | sins··of the | world, || have mercy up- | on — | us. ||
Thou that takest away the | sins··of the | world, || receive | our — | prayer.
Thou that sittest at the right hand of | God the | Father, || have mercy up- | on — | us.

PART I.

For thou only | art — | holy, || thou | only | art the | Lord. ||
Thou only, O Christ, with the | Holy | Ghost, || art most high in the | glory··of |
God the | Father. | A- men. ||

PSALM 23.

3

1 THE Lord is my shepherd; I | shall not | want. || He maketh me to lie down in
green pastures; he leadeth me beside the | still — | waters. ||

2 He restoreth my soul; he leadeth me in the paths of righteousness for his |
name's — | sake. || Yea, though I walk through the valley of the shadow of
death, I will fear no evil: for thou art with me; thy rod and thy staff | they — |
comfort me. ||

3 Thou preparest a table before me in the in the presence of mine enemies, thou anointest
my head with oil: my | cup··runneth | over. || Surely goodness and mercy shall
follow me all the days of my life; and I will dwell in the house of the | Lord, for |
482 ever. || A- | men. ||

MATTHEW 11.

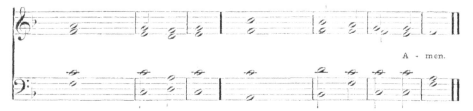

A - men.

4

Matthew 11.

1 COME unto me all ye that labor and are | heavy | laden, || and | I will | give you | rest.

2 Take my yoke upon you, and learn of me; for I am meek and | lowly · · in | heart: || and ye shall find | rest · · unto | your — | souls.

3 For my yoke is easy, and my | burden · · is | light, || for my yoke is easy, | and my | burden · · is | light.

4 And the Spirit and the bride say, come. And let him that | heareth · · say, | come. || And let him that is athirst come; and whosoever will, let him take the | wa- | ter · · of | life — | freely. A- | men.

5

PSALM 1.

1 BLESSED is the the man that walketh not in the counsel | of the · · un- | godly, || nor standeth in the way of sinners, nor sitteth in the | seat — | of the | scornful.

2 But his delight is in the | law · · of the | Lord; || and in his law doth he | medi- | tate | day and night.

3 And he shall be like a tree planted by the | rivers · · of | water, || that bringeth forth his | fruits — | in his | season;

4 His leaf also | shall not | wither: || and whatso- | ever he | doeth shall | prosper.

5 The ungodly | are not | so: || but are like the chaff which the | wind — | driveth · · a- | way.

6 Therefore the ungodly shall not | stand · · in the | judgment. || Nor sinners in the con-gre- | gation | of the | righteous:

7 For the Lord knoweth the | way · · of the | righteous: || but the way of the un- | godly | shall | perish.

Glory be to the Father, and | to the | Son, || and | to the | Holy | Ghost;

As it was in the beginning, is now, and | ever | shall be, || world | without | end. A- | men.

6

PSALM 8.

1 O LORD, our Lord! how excellent is thy name in | all the | earth, || who hast set thy | glory · · a- | bove the | heavens!

2 Out of the mouth of babes and sucklings hast thou ordained strength be- | cause of · · thine | enemies, || that thou mightest still the | ene-my | and · · the a- | venger.

3 When I consider thy heavens, the | work of · · thy | fingers, || the moon and the stars, | which thou | hast or- | dained;

4 What is man that thou art | mindful | of him? || and the son of man | that thou | visit-est | him?

5 For thou hast made him a little lower than the | angels, || and hast crowned him with | glory · · and | honor.

6 Thou madest him to have dominion over the | works · · of thy | hands; || thou hast put | all things | under · · his | feet:

7 All sheep and oxen, yea, and the beasts of the field; the fowl of the air, and the | fish · · of the | sea, || and whatsoever passeth | through the | paths · · of the | seas.

8 O | Lord, our | Lord! || how excellent is thy | name in | all the | earth!

Glory be to the Father, etc.

PSALMS 96, 100, 103.

7

PSALM 100.

1 MAKE a joyful noise unto the Lord, | all
ye | lands! || Serve the Lord with gladness:
come before his | presence | with— | singing!

2 Know ye that the Lord | he is | God: ||
It is he that hath made us, and not we
ourselves; we are his people, | and the ||
sheep·· of his | pasture.

3 Enter into his gates with thanksgiving, and
into his | courts with | praise: || Be thank-
ful unto him, and | bless— | his— | name.

4 For the Lord is good; his mercy is | ever-
lasting; || And his truth endureth to |
all— | generations.   Glory, etc.

8

PSALM 103: 1-8, 19-22.

1 BLESS the Lord, | O my | soul! || And, all
that is within me! | bless his | holy | name.

2 Bless the Lord, | O my soul! || And for-|
get not | all his | benefits:

3 Who forgiveth all | thine in-| iquities; ||
Who | healeth·· all | thy dis-| eases;

4 Who redeemeth thy life | from de | struc-
tion; || Who crowneth thee with loving ||
kindness·· and | tender | mercies;

5 Who satisfieth thy mouth with | good— |
things; || So that thy youth is re-| new-
ed | like the | eagle's.

6 The Lord executeth righteous-| ness and
judgment || For | all that | are op-| pressed:

7 He made known his ways | unto | Moses, ||
His acts unto the | children·· of | Isra-| el.

8 The Lord is merci— | ful and | gracious, ||
Slow to anger, and | plenteous | in—| mercy.

9 The Lord hath prepared his | throne·· in |
the | heavens; || And his kingdom | ruleth |
over | all.

10 Bless the Lord, ye his angels, that ex-||
cel in | strength, || That do his command-|
481

ments, hearkening unto the | voice of |
his— | word!

11 Bless ye the Lord, all | ye his | hosts! || Ye
ministers of | his, that | do his | plea-| sure!

12 Bless the Lord, all his works! in all places
of | his do-| minion: || Bless the | Lord, |
O— my | soul!   Glory, etc.

9

PSALM 96.

1 OH, sing unto the Lord a | new — |
song: || Sing unto the | Lord, — | all
the | earth.

2 Sing unto the Lord, | bless his | name; ||
Shew forth his sal-| vation··from | day
to | day.

3 Give unto the Lord, O ye kindreds | of |
the | people, || Give unto the | Lord — |
glory·· and | strength.

4 Give unto the Lord the glory due un-|
to his | name: || Bring an offering, and |
come in-| to his | courts.

5 Oh, worship the Lord in the | beauty··of |
holiness: || Fear be-| fore him, | all the |
earth.

6 Say among the heathen that the | Lord— |
reigneth: || The world also shall be estab-
lished that it shall not be moved: he
shall judge the | people | righteous-| ly.

7 Let the heavens rejoice, and let the |
earth be | glad; || Let the sea | roar,·· |
and the | fullness··there-| of.

8 Let the field be joyful, and all that | is
there-| in: || Then shall all the trees of
the wood re-| joice be-| fore the | Lord.

9 For | he — | cometh, || For he | cometh·· |
to | judge the | earth:

10 He shall judge the world with | right-
eous-| ness, || And the | people | with |
his truth.   Glory, etc.

PSALMS 95, 84.

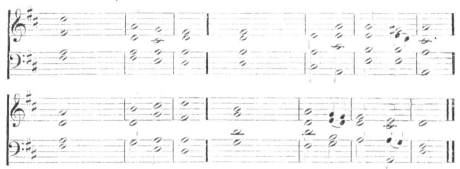

IO   PSALM 95.

1 On, come, let us sing un- | to the Lord; || Let us heartily rejoice in the | strength of our sal- | vation. ||

2 Let us come before his presence | with thanks- | giving; || And show ourselves | glad in | him with | psalms.

3 For the Lord is a | great — | God; || And a great | King a- | bove all | gods.

4 In his hands are all the corners | of the | earth; || And the strength of the | hills is | his — | also.

5 The sea is his, | and he | made it; || And his hands pre- | pared the | dry — | land.

6 Oh, come, let us worship, | and fall | down, || And kneel be- | fore the | Lord our | Maker:

7 For he is the | Lord our | God; || And we are the people of his pasture and the | sheep of | his — | hand.

8 Oh, worship the Lord in the | beauty of | holiness; || Let the whole earth | stand in | awe of | him:

9 For he cometh, for he cometh to | judge the | earth; || And with righteousness to judge the world, and the | peo-ple | with his | truth.   Glory be to the etc.

II   PSALM 84.

1 How amiable are thy | tab-er- | nacles, || O | Lord — | of — | hosts! ||

2 My soul longeth, yea even fainteth, for the | courts··of the | Lord; || my heart and my flesh crieth out | for··the | liv-ing God.

3 Yea, the sparrow hath found her an house, and the swallow a nest for herself, where she may | lay··her | young, || even thine altars, O Lord of hosts! my | King — | and··my | God. ||

4 Blessed are they that | dwell in··thy | house; || they will be | still — | prais-ing | thee.

5 Blessed is the man whose | strength··is in | thee, || in whose heart | are··the | ways··of | them, ||

6 Who passing through the valley of Baca | make··it a | well; || the rain | al-so | fil-leth··the | pools.

7 They go from | strength··to | strength; || every one of them in Zion ap- | peareth·· be- | fore — | God. ||

8 O Lord of hosts! | hear··my prayer; || give ear, | O — | God··of | Jacob!

9 Behold, O | God··our | shield! || and look upon the | face··of thine··an- | ointed. ||

10 For a day in thy courts is better | than·· a | thousand; || I had rather be a door-keeper in the house of God than to dwell in the | tents··of | wick-ed-ness.

11 For the Lord God is a | sun··and | shield; || the Lord will give grace and glory; no good thing will he withhold from | them·· that | walk··up- | rightly. ||

12 O | Lord··of | hosts! || blessed is the | man··that | trusteth··in | thee. Glory be to the Father, etc.

PSALM 90.

12
PSALM 90.

1 Lord, thou hast been our | dwelling- | place, || In | all — | gener- | ations.

2 Before the mountains were brought forth, or ever thou hadst formed the | earth·· and the | world, || Even from everlasting to ever- | lasting, | thou art | God.

3 Thou turnest man | to de -| struction; || And sayest, Re- | turn, ye | children ·· of | men.

4 For a thousand years in thy sight are but as yesterday, | when·· it is | past, | And as a | watch — | in the | night.

5 Thou carriest them away as with a flood; they are | as a | sleep: || In the morning they are like | grass which | groweth | up.

6 In the morning it flourisheth, and | groweth | up; || In the evening it is cut | down, and | wither- | eth.

7 For we are consumed | by thine | anger, || And by thy | wrath — | are we | troubled.

8 Thou hast set our iniquities | before | thee, || Our secret sins in the | light·· of thy | counte- | nance.

9 For all our days are passed away | in thy | wrath: || We spend our years as a | tale — | that is | told.

10 The days of our years are three-score years and ten; and if by reason of strength they be | four-score | years, || Yet is their strength labor and sorrow; for it is soon cut off, | and we | fly a- | way.

11 Who knoweth the power | of thine | anger? || Even according to thy fear, | so — | is thy | wrath.

12 So teach us to | number·· our | days, || That we may apply our | hearts — | unto | wisdom.

Glory be to the Father, etc.

PSALM 130.

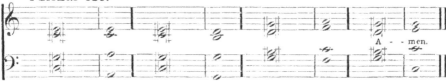

13
PSALM 130.

1 Out of the | depths || Have I cried unto thee, O | Lord. ||

2 Lord, hear my | voice: || Let thine ears be attentive to the voice of my suppli- | cations. ||

3 If thou, Lord, shouldst mark in- | iquities, || O Lord, who shall | stand? ||

4 But there is forgiveness with | thee, || That thou mayst be | feared. ||

5 I wait for the Lord, my soul doth | wait, || And in his word do I | hope. ||

6 My soul waiteth for the Lord more than they that watch for the | morning: || I say, more than they that watch for the | morning. ||

7 Let Israel hope in the | Lord: || For with the Lord there is mercy, and with him is plenteous re- | demption. ||

8 And he shall redeem | Israel || From all his in- | iquities. ||

REVELATION 4.

14

1 HOLY, holy, holy, | Lord·· God Al- | mighty! ‖ which was, and | is, and | is to | come.

2 Thou art worthy, O Lord, to receive glory, and | honor··and | power; ‖ for thou hast created all things, and for thy pleasure they | are and | were cre- | ated.

3 Worthy is the Lamb | that was | slain, ‖ to receive power, and riches, and wisdom, and strength, and | honor,··and | glory,··and | blessing.

4 Blessing, and honor, and | glory,··and | power, ‖ be unto him that sitteth upon the throne, and unto the | Lamb for- | ever··and | ever.

FUNEREAL.

15

1 BLESSED are the dead, who die in the | Lord from | henceforth: ‖ Yea, saith the Spirit, that they may rest from their labors; and their | works do | follow | them.

2 Blessed and holy is he that hath part in the first resurrection: on such the second death | hath no | power; ‖ but they shall be priests of God and of Christ, and shall reign with | him a | thousand | years.

3 Unto him that loved us, and washed us from our sins in | his own | blood, ‖ and hath made us kings and priests to God and his Father; to him be glory and do- | minion··for- | ever and | ever.

16
FUNEREAL.

1 BLESSED are the dead, who die in the | Lord from | henceforth; ‖ Yea, saith the Spirit, that they may rest from their labors, | and their | works do | follow them.

2 Our days on earth are as a shadow, and there is | none a- | biding; ‖ we are but of yesterday; there is but a | step··between | us and | death;

3 Man's days are as grass: as a flower of the field | so he | flourisheth; ‖ he appeareth for a little time, then | vanish-eth | a-—| way.

4 Watch! for ye know not what hour your | Lord doth | come; ‖ Be ye also ready; for in such an hour as ye think not, the | Son of | Man — | cometh.

5 It is the Lord; let him do what | seemeth··him | good; ‖ The Lord gave, and the Lord hath taken away, and blessed be the | name — | of the | Lord.

6 Blessed are the dead, who die in the | Lord from | henceforth; ‖ Yea, saith the Spirit, that they may rest from their labors, | and their | works do | follow them.

BAPTISMAL.

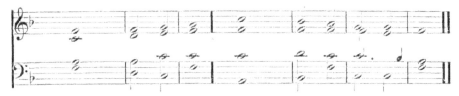

17

1 THUS saith the Lord that made thee, and formed thee, | who will | help thee, ||
Fear not, O Jacob my servant, and | Israel· ·whom | I have | chosen.

2 The mercy of the Lord is from everlasting to everlasting upon | them that | fear
him. ||
And his righteousness | unto | children's | children.

3 To such as | keep his | covenant: ||
And to them that remember his com- | mand-· ·ments to | do — | them.

4 One shall say, I am the Lord's; and another shall call himself by the | name of |
Jacob; ||
And another shall subscribe with his hand to the Lord, and surname himself | by
the | name of | Israel.

5 Doubtless thou art our Father, though Abraham be ignorant of us, and Israel ac- |
knowledge· ·us | not. ||
Thou, O Lord, art our Father, our Redeemer; from ever- | lasting | is thy | name.
Glory be to the Father, etc.

18   BAPTISMAL.

Before the Administration.

1 AND Jesus said, Suffer little children, and forbid them not to | come· ·unto | me; ||
For of such is the | kingdom· ·of | heaven.

2 He shall feed | his flock· ·like a | shepherd: ||
He shall gather the lambs with his arm and | carry· ·them | in his | bosom.

3 I will pour my Spirit upon thy seed, and my blessing up- | on thine | offspring; ||
And they shall spring up as among the grass, as | willows· ·by the | water — |
courses.

After the Administration.

1 THEN will I sprinkle clean | water· ·up- | on you, ||
And | ye shall | be — | clean:

2 A new heart also | will I | give you, ||
And a new spirit | will I | put with- | in you,

3 And I will | take away the stony heart | out of· ·your | flesh, ||
And I will | give· ·you a | heart of | flesh.
Glory be to the Father, etc.

19 STOWELL. L. M.

SOLO.—SOPRANO.

1. From ev-ery storm-y wind that blows, From ev-ery swell-ing tide of woes,

CHORUS.

2. There is a place where Je-sus sheds The oil of glad-ness on our heads,

There is a calm, a sure re-treat: 'T is found be-neath the mer-cy-seat.

A place than all be-sides more sweet; It is the blood-bought mer-cy-seat.

20 SANCTUS.

Ho-ly! Ho-ly! Ho-ly! Lord God of Sa-baoth! Heaven and earth are full, full of thy

glo-ry; Heaven and earth are full, are full of thy glo-ry

Glo-ry be to thee,

thee, Glo-ry be to thee, to thee, to thee O Lord most high.
Glo-ry be to thee, Glo-ry be, &c.

21 DOXOLOGY. L. M.

Praise God. from whom all blessings flow, Praise him, all creatures here below;
Praise God. from whom all bless - ings flow, Praise him, all creatures here be - low,—

Praise him a - bove, Praise him a -
Praise him, all creatures here be - low; Praise him a-bove. Praise him a - bove,

bove. Praise him a-bove, ye heavenly host;
Praise him a-bove, ye heaven - ly host; Praise him a-bove, Praise him a - bove,

Praise Father, Son, and Ho - ly
Praise him a - bove, ye heaven-ly host; Praise Fa - - ther, Son, and Ho - ly

Ghost,—Praise Fa - ther, Son,......and Ho - ly Ghost,—Praise Father, Son, and Ho - ly Ghost.

DOXOLOGY. L. M. (Concluded.)

CHORUS.—ad lib.

Hal-le-lu-jah, Hal-le-lu-jah, Hal-le-lu-jah, A-men, A-men,— Hal-le-lu-jah,

Hal-le-lu-jah,

DUET.　　　　　　　　　　　　　　　　　　　　TUTTI.

Hal-le-lu-jah, Hal-le-lu-jah, Hal-le-lu-jah, Hal-le-lu-jah, Hal-le-lu-jah, Hal-le-

lu-jah, Hal-le-lu-jah, A-men, A-men, Hal-le-lu-jah, A-men, Hal-le-lu-jah, A-men.

22 BRIDGEWATER. L. M.

1. To God the Fa-ther, God the Son, And God the Spir-it, Three in One,　　　Be

Be honor, praise, and

honor, praise, and glory given, Be hon-or, praise, and glory given, By all on earth, and all in heaven.

glo-ry given, Be honor, praise, and glory given, By all　　on earth,　　and all in heaven.

23 TURNER. C. M.

1. To Fa-ther, Son, and Ho-ly Ghost, One God, whom we a-dore, Be

Be glo-ry as it

glo-ry as it was, is now, Be glo-ry as it was, is now, And shall be ev-er-

Be glo-ry as it was, is now, and shall be ev - - er -

was,.... is now, And shall be ev-er-more, And shall be ev-er-

more; Be glo-ry as it was, is now, And shall be ev-er-more.

24 CONCORD. S. M.

Wor-

1. Ye an-gels round the throne, And saints that dwell be-low, Worship the Fa-ther,

ship the Father, praise the Son,

praise the Son,.... Worship the Father, praise the Son, And bless the Spir-it, too.

25 BRANNAN. 7, 6, 8.

1. Lamb of God! whose bleed-ing love We now re-call to mind,

Send the an - swer from a - bove, And let us mer - cy find:
D. S. Oh, re - mem - ber Cal - va - ry, And bid us go in peace!

Think on us, who think on thee, And ev-ery burdened soul re - lease;

2 By thine agonizing pain,
  And bloody sweat, we pray—
By thy dying love to man,
  Take all our sins away:
Burst our bonds, and set us free,
  From all iniquity release;
Oh, remember Calvary,
  And bid us go in peace!

3 Let thy blood, by faith applied,
  The sinner's pardon seal;
Own us freely justified,
  And all our sickness heal:
By thy passion on the tree,
  Let all our griefs and troubles cease;
Oh, remember Calvary,
  And bid us go in peace!

26 SOLITUDE. 7. (See Hymn 731.)

1. Je - sus, Je - sus! vis - it me; How my soul longs af - ter thee!
2. Lord! my long - ings nev - er cease; With-out thee I find no peace;

When, my best, my dear - est Friend! Shall our sep - a - ra - tion end?
'Tis my con - stant cry to thee, Je - sus, Je - sus! vis - it me.

INDEX OF SUBJECTS.

INDEX OF SUBJECTS.

INDEX OF AUTHORS OF HYMNS.

[Of some few hymns in this Collection it seems impossible to trace the authorship exactly. Yet it is thought best to print the names which are found floating around in connection with them, and wait for further search.]

INDEX OF AUTHORS OF HYMNS.

ALPHABETICAL INDEX OF TUNES.

It is to be understood that most of the Music, included in this Collection, is introduced "by permission," either purchased or given. It must, therefore, not be used in any other without the consent of the authors, or of those who hold the copyright of the Tunes.

[THE NUMBERS REFER TO HYMNS.]

ALPHABETICAL INDEX OF TUNES.

502

METRICAL INDEX OF TUNES.

Index of First Lines.

[THE NUMBERS REFER TO HYMNS.]

INDEX OF FIRST LINES.

INDEX OF FIRST LINES.

509

Milton Keynes UK
Ingram Content Group UK Ltd.
UKHW020912290324
440282UK00017B/21